THE BOY BRIGAND;

OR,

THE DARK KING OF THE MOUNTAINS.

A TALE OF ITALY.

Where the sun rides high in a cloudless sky,
  And the dulcet notes of the soft guitar
Saluteth the breeze as it passeth by,
  Laden with perfumes from near and afar.

The report of the carbine, loud and clear,
  From rock to hill and hill to rock resound;
Bold brigands mount the defiles, dark and drear,
  When night her sable mantle spreads around.—COATES.

BEAUTIFULLY ILLUSTRATED.

LONDON:
HENRY LEA, 112, FLEET STREET, E.C.
AND ALL BOOKSELLERS.

THE BOY BRIGAND;

OR,

THE DARK KING OF THE MOUNTAINS.

SATANIELLO MURDERS THE PRIEST.

CHAPTER I.

INTRODUCTORY—WHO GIOVANI SATANIELLO WAS—A
FEW WORDS ABOUT HIS FATHER AND MOTHER.

WE are in Rome.

In that ancient city of literature and the fine
arts—where some of the greatest Italian masters
that the world ever produced first saw the light of
day—where Michael Angelo lived—where Benuvento
Cellini flourished—began the events which we intend to describe in the course of this story.

In Rome Giovani Sataniello was born.

In Rome Giovani Sataniello, "The Boy Brigand" spent his youth—received his education, and
perpetrated his first deed of darkness and of sin.

In Rome Sataniello's father had lived—and in
Rome he had died. But not in his own house—

1

upon his own bed—surrounded by a family ready to deplore his loss—by a wife in tears—darling children clustering around his pillow, bidding him to remain among them—quietly and having made his peace with his Saviour previous to bidding his last farewell to this earth—previous to taking his sojourn " to that bourne from whence no traveller returns " — no, he had departed this world quickly and suddenly, and in the greatest agony.

His body tortured by the most intense sufferings—his heart a prey to the most excruciating remorse.

Yes, Sataniello s father had expiated a life of wickedness and of sin on the gallows.

Yes, he that would have called Giovani Sataniello his son, had he lived to know him, had been a murderer—a guilty sinner, and he had surrendered his body to the justice of man ere he appeared before the ever-seeing Almighty, to render Him an account of his stewardship here below.

Yes, Giovani Sataniello the elder, had been executed for a horrid and blood-thirsty murder—from which the minds of the whole world recoiled with dismay and horror, when they read the description of it in the public papers.

Giovani Sataniello, "the Boy Brigand," the son of the murderer, had inherited all his father's vices. But he had what his father had not—a good heart, a generous nature—albeit his inclinations were of a roving disposition—of a wayward nature.

In bye-gone days, many years before the beginning of the story, Giovani's father was not a man of fortune and of noble birth, he was a peasant, a poor man. He was wont to dwell in the neighbourhood of the Vatican.

Things were far from being prosperous with him, and he wanted bread—he wanted money.

One summer's evening that one of the rubicund cardinals was emerging from the place of worship, he followed him, spied him, and when the reverend gentleman had arrived to a solitary spot, in the outskirts of Rome, where it was surely not his prayers or his breviary that brought him there; he advanced towards him, and in a supplicating, imploring tone of voice, he had said—

" Oh, reverend, good father, help me in my distress—to the poor and the forlorn, oh, do give a few alms! He will pray for thee . . . and many a Pater Noster and an Ave Maria will he repeat for thy welfare."

" Go thy ways; interrupt me not in my devotions," had answered the cardinal, in an abrupt and a rough manner; and as he spoke, had hurried on away from him, as if a poor man was a reptile, a worthless being, from whom it is man's duty to keep distant.

But Giovani Sataniello was famished, and his rage was kindled by the hard words of the priest, and a secret vengeance sprung within his heart, and his craving for gold was great.

And when he had seen a big diamond ring shining upon the prelate's finger, and when he had seen the valuable jewellery that he carried about his person, his thirst for his blood became intense, and rage knew no bounds.

But he kept his feelings closeted within his breast, and sneaked away behind the cardinal, but his eye lost not sight of his future victim.

His eye was riveted upon him and followed him in the distance.

Giovani Sataniello's mind was now made up—he should murder and rob that man, who had said to him, " Begone, begone, and interrupt me not."

His manly pride had received a shock which maddened his brain.

He looked indeed the picture of crime, creeping noiselessly and stealthily behind the cardinal, with his features bent upwards, and his clenched fists in a threatening attitude.

The weather also seemed to be admirably suited to his purpose.

The clouds—dark, thick, heavy clouds—were fast gathering above; the atmosphere was close and sultry; every outward appearance proclaimed the approach of a storm.

The evening, that was at first bright and clear, began gradually to assume darker shades—the heavens, where but a few instants ago golden stars were seen shining, were now denuded of the slightest light, and everything around was quiet and still.

CHAPTER II.

GIOVANI SATANIELLO'S FATHER BECOMES A MURDERER—THE STRUGGLE—THE DEATH BLOW.

SILENCE now reigned supreme.

The cardinal had not noticed Sataniello, whom, however, he knew well, for passing to and fro before the place where he dwelt he could not but have recognised his features had his glance rested upon him.

But he had not bestowed even a glance upon the beggar.

He had looked upon him as a nuisance, from which one should get rid of as soon as possible, and he had accelerated his step.

There again the hand of Providence was to be witnessed in this trifling occurrence, for had the cardinal seen him who addressed him, a welcome suspicion might have flashed across his mind.

He might have thought, and wisely too, that to stray in the country alone, unguarded, and without any weapons to protect himself in case of assault, was by no means a prudent step to take.

Had he been charitable it would doubtless have saved his life.

Doubtless Giovani Sataniello would have never plotted the dark deed which he was about to accomplish, had his prayer been acceded to.

But it was not to be.

Fate had ordered that the things which will occur should come to pass—fate had ordered that the prelate should behave as we have seen he did.

But the prelate, although unconscious of being followed, seemed anxious and pre-occupied.

His gaze wandered afar before him, and he looked as if he expected the arrival of a new comer.

And yet no steps were heard.

Not a sound was audible.

" She will not come to-night, I am sure," the prelate now murmured in a subdued tone of voice. " This is the second night that Leonora has disappointed me. Perhaps something has occurred to the maiden . . . . Hark, methinks I hear the sound of footsteps . . . . "

And he listened.

And he stood still.

And he listened again, but with no avail.

The wind now began to blow with a fierce intensity. The clouds above grew darker and darker, and heavy drops of rain fell in heavy torrents from the dark vault of heaven.

The cardinal drew his broad-brimmed hat over his forehead, buttoned his coat, and in nowise undaunted by the fierceness of the weather, waited again and again.

He appeared restless, and endeavoured not to disguise the annoyance which he felt at the disappointment he experienced.

He had come out of Rome—there in the country to meet some one, and that some one had failed to be punctual. What could be the cause of the delay? He mused and pondered, and meanwhile the minutes drew on.

And the rain abated.

And the pale glare of the moon shone forth upon him.

And he suddenly turned round, and he beheld Sataniello.

And he grew nervous, and became frightened.

His pulse beat quicker and quicker—his heart throbbed with suspense, and still he spoke not.

Giovani Sataniello's patience, however, was now at an end, and he walked on.

The victim might escape—his glance had met that of the prelate, and yet neither had broken the stillness of the night.

The cardinal had made no attempt to fly from him. He on his side had given no outward sign of his hostile intentions.

Sataniello now looked around and around.

His cursory glance appeared to satisfy him—not a moving being was to be seen as far as the eye could reach.

But there were many a huge pile of stones—many an uncarved piece of carrara marble—many a remnant of once famous buildings about, and perhaps some one was concealed therein.

Sataniello, however, thought not of those things. There were diamonds and jewels to be had. He had asked a trifling pittance to alleviate his hunger—his intentions then were honest and pure—and what reception had he received at the hands of one whose duty it was not only to do, but to preach charity? Why, we have seen that it was anything but a favourable one. Now there was an opportunity which offered itself to him, by which he might earn many a glittering golden coin; and one thrust—but one single thrust of that common stiletto, which he ever carried in his belt, would place him in the possession of enough to keep him from starvation, at least for many months to come. Sataniello looked round again and again, took a second cursory glance of all that which surrounded him. No spy was there—no one to watch and be the witness of his dark and nefarious deed; no living being close at hand—no Papal carabineer in the vicinity.

Clear his path lay before him; and walking before him, in an unsteady step, was the prelate. One second he remained uncertain as to what he should do; but if blood was to be spilt, delay was dangerous.

"Now, or never!" he thought; and, as quick as lightning, he rushed behind the cardinal, and grasped his throat strongly and firmly.

"I am a poor man—you are abounding in wealth," he sullenly whispered into his victim's ears; "you refused me a scudi—die! die! you uncharitable apostle of God!"

The cardinal attempted to struggle, and to rid himself of the iron grasp which held him so tightly that the power of speech was entirely denied to him. His resistance, however, exasperated his antagonist, whose rage had attained its highest pitch. He threw down the prelate; with a firm and nervous hand he tore open the thin and costly shirt which the cardinal wore beneath his garments, and then—then—when the skin was bare, he plunged his poniard to the hilt in the bosom of the fallen man!

The sharp instrument had penetrated to the region of the heart, which at once ceased to beat, and the blood flowed copiously and freely. The knife was made of good steel, and it was, besides, of a metal that tells its tale. The hot blood spirted away and away, and covered Sataniello's hands and clothes with a crimson hue. But he heeded not so trifling a detail. The spoil was that which presented itself uppermost to his mind. The sight of the ghastly, pale features of his victim, who lay in a pool of blood on the cold ground—the sight of his sunken eyes, from which the last spark of life had for many minutes already fled—might have deterred many a murderer; but he was an Italian, and not easily to be frightened.

"I have murdered a man—aye, and a priest, too—in cold blood," he thought; "I must now reap the reward of my guilt."

And his sinewy hand made its way into the garments of the dead prelate, and the first thing that he discovered was a heavy leather purse full of golden coins.

The murderer now hastily rose up and hastened, believing that he heard the sounds of footsteps; but, finding that his ear had deceived him, he resumed his avaricious search.

So he knelt down again, and again his hand made its way to the breast-pocket of his victim.

And there he found a cross of our Saviour of the most costly description, most exquisitely carved, set in stones of the purest water.

But when he came to the ring—the big diamond ring—he experienced some trouble in getting it off the finger, as it fitted there rather tightly; but he soon did away with the difficulty — he broke it off with a nervous twist, and after having rid it of that which ornamented it, threw it far away in the field.

"I am rich now," he exclaimed, weighing in his palm the massive jewellery that he had taken from the cardinal, his eye fascinated by the sparks which glittered from the diamond.

His, alas, was wealth dearly purchased.

And when he had rifled the body of all that it possessed, he stood up and endeavoured to remain still; but he staggered, and would have fallen senseless to the ground, had not his throat been suddenly grasped by the hand of a young girl who happened at this moment to make her appearance upon the spot where the murder had been perpetrated.

The girl, however, soon relinquished her hold, and, as if she dreaded the contact of the man whom she had handled but an instant previously, she stepped backwards, and gazed fiercely upon him with her dark blue eyes.

CHAPTER III.

A TALE OF LOVE—ARRIVAL OF PAPAL CARABINEERS—THE ARREST.

SHE it was whom the priest had been expecting.

She was fair and beautiful to behold.

The muslin dress in which she was attired became her to a nicety. Her forehead was high and expansive, and she presented truly the appearance of one of those Roman virgins of olden times, with her wavy, fair hair hanging loosely in abundant clusters over her beautifully rounded, symmetrical, and pale shoulders.

"Why hast thou murdered my friend, dastardly

coward ?" she asked of the murderer, in a low and sinister tone of voice.

Giovani, however, answered her not.

A cold perspiration hung over his forehead, and his hand, which had been so firm and so true to its work, shook like an aspen leaf.

He was at length pondering over the immensity his guilt, and, a prey to his thoughts, he heeded not the strange voice that emanated from the lips of "the Girl in White."

"Knowest thou not," the fair girl continued, "that Monsignor Lottaringi was my lover! That he was the first and only one that ever whispered tales of love into my ear. That he promised me heaven if I listened to his entreaties. That I have yielded to him, and that I am no longer a spotless virgin?"

And the maiden laughed with a sarcastic, diabolical, ironical laugh, horrid to hear.

"There, yonder," the girl proceeded—and, as she spoke, she stretched forth her hand and pointed to the heap of stones a few yards removed from the spot where she stood—"there, a few evenings ago, when he sat upon that piece of marble, with his arm around my waist, and my lips close to his lips, Lottaringi—dear Lottaringi!—told me that I was a very lovely maiden, and that I was a remarkably well-made girl. You see I don't disguise his words—I speak as he spoke. And he kissed me on the lips, and he said, 'Leonora, why art thou so fantastic?'"

And the maiden laughed again.

Giovani Sataniello spoke not a word, but he stood and gazed upon the fair creature that was addressing him.

"What a pity it is, Miss Leonora," he began, after a moment's respite, "that you will keep wandering among the ruins in the darkness of night. Why do you not come down the town at noon, when the lovely Roman ladies drive in their elegant carriages? Handsome would that one be who could surpass you in elegance and beauty."

"Why should I show myself in public? Am I not mad? Am I not called the crazy Leonora? And did I not hear the Padre in the mountain whisper to a companion the other day, 'How sad it is that the poor thing should be out of her mind.'"

And Leonora, the youthful Roman maiden—the crazy Leonora, as she was called by all who knew her in the neighbourhood of the Holy City, remained motionless.

There was a pause, during which Giovani Sataniello thought that it would be, perhaps, best for him to return to town, sooner than to remain wandering about in the vicinity of Rome with his garments damped with the blood of his victim.

During that pause Leonora also had collected her mind, and although it was currently reported that she was not in her right senses, still she knew that she was addressing a man that had been guilty of a foul murder, and that the object of his murder had been one she loved deeply.

"Have I not a lovely short neck?" Leonora mused, in an infantine voice, placing her two hands under her glossy, luxuriant hair, "Have I not fine blue eyes?"

And she stopped short.

"Foolish girl that I am!" she shrieked in a loud voice, as if she had been bitten by some concealed adder, "I am only repeating what my dear Lottaringi was wont to tell me."

And then the corpse of the cardinal attracted her gaze.

"There thou art, poor Lottaringi," she said, in a half-audible voice. "No more quiet *tête-à-têtes*—no more solitary rambles among the ruins—no more will I see thee, and pray with thee !"

And she fell upon her knees, and she wept.

And she made an appeal to Providence. Was it to restore life to the senseless being that lay cold and lifeless before her? Was it to give or remit her sufficient strength to bear his loss? Whatever motives, however, Leonora had in so doing we know not. It is for us a mystery, and is likely, we should say, to remain so; for, unlike the magicians of Egypt, we are unable to read the minds of men or women.

Had a painter stood amidst the ruins in that particular spot on the outskirts of Rome where occurred the scene which we have just described, what a beautiful and melancholy picture he could have drawn.

Here stood Sataniello, with his gaze bent upon the ground, a prey to those bitter, excruciating thoughts which must ever haunt those who are guilty of any crime.

There Leonora reclined, upon an adjacent pile of stones, weeping, and her face buried in her tiny white hands.

To crown the tableau, fully stretched upon his back, with stiffened fists and ghastly eyes, bespeaking the horrid glare of death, lay Monsignor Lottaringi, the once popular preacher and elegant cardinal, whose return, doubtless, was anxiously expected at the Vatican.

But time flew on, and Sataniello's father was silent, and Leonora, the crazy Roman girl, spoke not.

The stars now shone forth, and the evening again grew bright and clear.

Everything around was quiet and still, and yet two beings stood before one another, and exchanged not one word.

Sataniello, however, soon broke up the silence that reigned.

"Didst thou love the man that I have murdered just now, fair Leonora?" he asked.

"Leonora!"

Leonora remained dumb.

"Who speaks !—who dares to call me by name?" she murmured, in a soft, low tone of voice.

"I do. I am the culprit!" Sataniello's father responded, in that submissive, respectful manner in which inferiors generally indulge when addressing those whom rank has placed above them.

"And why do you presume to speak to me—to address me? You belong no longer to society. It is to gaol you ought to be taken, to await your trial. Oh, I will go to see you executed, and I will laugh, and I will delight in your sufferings!"

And Leonora indulged in that sarcastic laugh inherent to mad people.

It was quite light now.

Before, Leonora had taken but a very imperfect glance of Sataniello; now she stared him full in the face.

And it struck the mad girl that the late prelate was a fat and a bloated man, rubicund and coarse-looking, and that the murderer who stood before her, although belonging by birth to a humble grade of society, was slim and pale—nay, aristocratic in his appearance.

And it struck her that the late prelate's physiognomy was far from being handsome. And she leaned forward and gazed upon the face of the corpse.

And she nearly staggered; and she shrank away

from those features which were now rendered repulsive by the agonies and sufferings of death.

And Leonora—the crazy Leonora—thought again that the murderer had, in every respect, the advantage over him whose dead body lay but a yard or two distant.

And such were the ravings of a mad girl's brain. And when she saw Sataniello advancing towards her, and kneeling before her, she believed herself in a dream!

And when he spoke, she endeavoured to fly away, and to hide herself in some of the dark spots that surrounded her.

And yet she wished to stay.

How strange!

The mad girl was beginning to feel an interest in the man who had slain him whom she thought had her heart.

He was now dead, and dead men tell no tales.

"Leonora — lovely Leonora! bewitching Leonora!" Sataniello began — "I have laid myself open to the justice of men, and I shall hereafter have to appear before a higher tribunal. But I regret it not. They say you are out of your senses!—they say you are crazy!—they say you are mad, Leonora! I believe it not. Many a time unheeded have I watched you yonder. Many a time have I slept in the orchard which adjoins your villa—my presence concealed by the shrubs and the big, dark trees. Many a time have I listened with rapture to those sweet Italian tunes which you sing so well. Thy voice then came to my heart—love even kindled within it. It sprang slowly but surely. And can I help my feelings—could I help my breast beating with love for you? But I kept that love secret: it has laid buried within me for many a long year.

"I watched you, ere now, and saw the priest meeting you—his lip adjoining thy lips—and a feeling of vengeance arose within me.

"Thou knowest not," the murderer continued, in an endearing, loving tone, what sensations I experienced. Whole nights have I spent with my eye rivetted upon the feeble light which thou keepest ever burning in thy abode.

"I knew I was a peasant—only a peasant. I knew that thou wast a lady by birth—a descendant of one of the proudest families of the land. Yet I hoped—yet something told me that a day would come when I should meet thee, when I should be enabled to discharge from my heart the heavy weight which hangs upon it.

"I have loved thee! oh, yes, with all the strength of the purest love! and had I seen thy pretty face ere my hand inflicted the fatal wound upon the reverend signor. This night would not have sealed my doom!"

These words were the last which the murderer pronounced—his breast was too full to enable him to articulate any new sentence.

So, in deep silence, he gazed upon the Roman girl, who had listened attentively to every syllable he had pronounced.

Her blue eyes, full of expression, and beaming with a strange light, were fixed upon the speaker.

No living soul could have interpreted the meaning of that look.

It was not the look of a mad girl, yet there was something unearthly in it.

"What is thy object, my friend?"

She called a murderer "my friend!"

The girl paused.

"What is thy object in speaking to me as thou hast done? If thou valuest thy liberty, why dost thou remain here with thy feet rooted to the ground? Shrink from man, for it will be man by whom thou wilt fall. Keep away from the noise and turmoil of large towns, where thy guilt must soon be discovered. To the mountains, to seek for shelter! There thou wilt meet with an innocent maiden. Thou art handsome, and thou seemest to me not a fool. She will not know that thy hands are stained with human blood, and will, I imagine, become thy bride. But thou art wasting thy time in addressing a mad girl, who understands not the meaning or pith of thy words."

"But I deny that," exclaimed Sataniello, with the frenzy of the lover, who has at last caught hold of the object of his desire, "Those wavy ringlets of yours, Leonora, bespeak love! Those eyes of yours, so limpid and so pure, bespeak love! That noble breast of thine, which heaves with emotion, betrays love! All that belongs to Leonora is love! Thy first love was guilty, thrice guilty. You need'st not fear, Leonora, to sin again."

"Is that thou, a murderer, that speaketh as thou hast done?" slowly inquired Leonora, as if some doubt was still hanging upon her mind, "Well may the Romans call me a mad girl, when sensible people talk as thou hast done. "Think, man," she continued, "of what thou asks. To bring an orphan in this world, without a home, without a family—the offspring of a mad girl and of a murderer!"

"Yes, let it be so. Oh, do not forsake me, I beseech thee, Leonora! I was poor, I am poor—I was brought up and educated by a priest—he taught me how to read and write; and they call this education; and I have brains, and I feel that had I been born in a different sphere of life, I might have been somebody. But Rome is rotten to the core. Her youth, her energies, her finest blood is polluted by ignorance and priestcraft; and those very priests that rule over it are the first ones to stop progress which must ultimately destroy their prestige, and from which one day will spring a new era of enlightment and of civilisation."

Thus spoke the murderer to the mad girl.

How beautiful Leonora appeared now!

How manly and handsome Sataniello was!

It was indeed a fine couple!

The soft blue eyes of Leonora formed a striking but still a handsome contrast with the fierce expression of Sataniello's gaze. Her slender and slight frame was greatly at variance with the robust and manly form of the Italian peasant, and yet these two beings felt a strange, unaccountable inclination towards each other.

And that such a thing should have been wrought in so short a period is wonderful indeed.

Still it was so.

And the murderer wandered among the ruins, in the vicinity of Rome, for weeks and weeks, and months and months, Leonora watched over him, and when the emissaries of the police were on the look out for him who had killed the Cardinal—the mad maiden placed them off their guard, and saved him from arrest.

And Leonora gradually recovered her senses, and the idea that she was the mistress of a murderer nigh drove her mad again; but she had advanced too far now to retreat.

She did love Sataniello, and she trembled for his apprehension.

He had wished her to go with him, and fly to the mountains, but there was a certain hesitation which ever hung upon her mind, and which on many an occasion prevented her to carry out the wishes of Sataniello.

But everything has an end.

The days were now numbered.

Ere long Sataniello would fall into the hands of justice.

God, ever watchful, had ordained that it should be so.

And yet Sataniello was getting fonder and fonder of Leonora—he could kiss the path upon which she walked, so great, so fervid, and so vigorous was the love he entertained for the crazy Leonora. He loved, he worshipped, he adored Leonora.

For what woman, he thought, except an angel, would have listened to lagnuage of love, emanating from one whose hands were stained with innocent blood.

But Leonora, they say, was mad.

The hour had now arrived.

Sataniello stood upon the cottage door of Leonora's residence.

It was midnight.

"Must we part again, dearest?" he exclaimed, clasping fondly against his manly breast her heaving bosom. "Oh, do fly with me, I beseech thee, far away, where, removed from the scene of my crime, I may pray God until he will forgive me."

"Good bye, good bye," Leonora replied, and the lips—the rosy and voluptuous lips of the beautiful Roman girl, met those of her lover—when, hark! a voice was heard.

"Oh, my God! oh, my God!" shrieked Leonora, "the Papal Carabineers are coming. Oh, I see their steel helmets shining by the moonlight."

"I am betrayed. I remember how closely Petro, the padre, watched and spied me to-day, when I crossed the field yonder—no doubt can remain upon my mind. For the sake of a paltry reward he has given that information which will lead to my discovery. It is all over now, I know it, I feel it. Oh, they are coming. Oh, I hear the horses' hoofs rattling in the distance. Where can I fly? Where can I go? Where will I be safe, oh, Leonora?"

And the murderer shook and trembled.

A guilty conscience has no peace, and since the day that he had felled the prelate to the ground he had endured what no mortal ever endured before.

Words would be powerless to express the amount of his mental sufferings.

Meanwhile Leonora stood still in breathless suspense.

She feared to see the object of her love snatched away from her for ever!

An invisible hand held her feet firmly rooted to the ground!

She wished to bid her lover to come within her abode, and yet her lips were sealed.

"Run across the high road, it may be time yet," she whispered at length into Sataniello's ears. "Lose not an instant."

And a second had scarcely elapsed ere she altered her mind, and said—

"Stay, oh stay—doubtless you have been watched—doubtless this house is already surrounded. Oh, Sataniello," she continued, hesitatingly, and in a low whisper, "Why not seek shelter behind that thick hedge?"

And she stretched forth her hand, and she was about to speak, when her words died away ere they had emanated from her well-shaped mouth.

And all in a moment she became speechless, and the sight of four muzzles of loaded guns pointed against her lover's breast, caused her blood to run cold in her veins.

And as the house became gradually and rapidly surrounded by a crowd of armed peasants and a detachment of papal carabineers—all brought together to apprehend one man—she gave a loud shriek, and ere it could have been prevented, she staggered and fell.

The scene which Leonora had witnessed was too much for her, and when she found that the whole of her conversation had been overheard by the men present, who had only remained concealed to watch a fit opportunity to show themselves forth—and when the thought flashed across her, that it would be known that she was, and had been the mistress of a murderer, she lost all control over herself—her knees gave way beneath her—and as if she was stricken by thunder, she had been stunned to the ground with a heavy, heartrending crush.

"Surrender at once, and allow thyself to be pinioned, if thou valuest thou head," were the first words that struck Sataniello's ears, and the heavy palmy hands of the stalwart, fierce-looking soldiers had been laid upon his shoulders, and his wrists secured in a pair of tight, screwy irons.

Sataniello at first had attempted to struggle against his antagonists to disengage himself from the powerful grasp that held him, but finding resistance useless he soon gave way, and he was cast in a prison—and he was tried and executed.

And by a singular coincidence the same morning that he died, Leonora was confined of a handsome dark-eyed boy, who is to be the hero of this tale.

And such were the father and mother of Giovani Sataniello.

CHAPTER IV.

THE BOY BRIGAND AND JOANITTA.

AND such was he! the son of a murderer and of a Roman mad girl.

And at the period that this tale begins he was seventeen years of age.

He had never known his father, as my readers can conclude by the perusal of the foregoing particulars, and his mother, the pretty Leonora, did not survive long the only man whom she really did love.

Hence she died when he was a child, and he had no recollection whatever of her.

What he knew was taught him in a charity school where he was placed, and where he was far from being well treated—the remembrance of his being the bastard offspring of a man who had slain a cardinal being uppermost in the minds of the clerical gentlemen who had control over his education.

The consequence was that young Sataniello was very glad when he left school, having scarcely learnt to read and write, and when he was enabled to do no work, and to stroll about the streets of the Holy City and its neighbourhood during the night, and to lay among the lazzaroni during the day, eating maccaroni and basking in the sun.

Some people have no ambition.

Some men would be satisfied to live all their lives upon a hundred a year.

Some boys care not what become of them if they have always enough to eat and drink, and a little money to spend.

But, "my boy," Sataniello, was not such.

He would have thousands.

He would have a castle to live in, fine horses to ride, plenty of money to give to those he loved, and to buy dashing, handsome clothes to sport in.

All these luxuries cannot be got without cash.

All these things must be purchased.

How was he to obtain a fortune ?

Surely it was not in basking in the sun, and eating maccaroni all day long.

Sataniello was no fool.

Sataniello knew that.

He knew that there was no opening for him in Rome.

He knew that if he went straightforward to work he would take years to put a few pounds together.

It was not one or two coppers that he would get thrown at him by some visitor struck with his manly demeanour—with the fiery expression of his dark eye—with his proud gait—that would enable him to buy a pair of gold ear-rings for little Joanitta, a girl of thirteen years old, with whom Sataniello had already formed a kind of friendship.

She was a beggar like him.

She was a child of love, like him.

He pitied her, he felt for her, although the same stigma rested upon his expansive and well-shaped forehead.

Sataniello had made up his mind—he would be a highwayman, he would be a brigand.

But he required funds to start upon "to make a beginning."

How he acquired them will be shortly related.

He was a wild Italian boy.

He was always up to mischief.

He had the courage of his father.

The warm blood and fantastic ideas of his mother.

And, above all, he possessed no uncommon powers of discernment, which placed him in a position to plot his plans ere he carried them out.

It would never do for him to be left in the "lurch."

It would never do for him to commit a robbery—to be detected, and to be taken into custody, and imprisoned for life.

He hated the sight of a prison.

Sataniello had an abhorrence of a dungeon.

He disliked large towns.

He preferred the wildness of the mountainous districts.

He had travelled on foot through the best part of the papal states, and he had visited a country which he thought was eminently well suited to be the scene of his daring exploits. Numberless caverns—endless woods—high cliffs abounded there, wherein he could seek a shelter if in distress, a spot wherein he might retire after a week's depredations.

He would attack boldly the rich and the strong.

He would be fearless as to results.

He would encounter death.

He would fight boldly.

He would have a band, and lead them on.

He would amass a fortune.

He would protect the poor at the expense of the rich.

His father had died by the hand of man.

By his hand would many a man die.

It seemed to him that he had a craving for blood.

As he valued his life, he would value that of others.

If he died, there was no one to regret him, to shed tears over his mournful fate.

If he lived, he would make those around him happy.

We have already said that the scene which we are about to describe did take place in Rome.

It was many, many years ago.

Now I do not fancy, my dear readers, that we are on the eve of relating stories which occurred when Adam delved and Eve spun.

Not so, indeed.

Half a century exactly has elapsed since the event which we are about to allude to.

On the Piazza del Popolo, clustering together like so many bees, were about thirty Italian boys and girls.

The eldest of the males might have reached, at the utmost, seventeen years of age.

It was He !

Sataniello, "the Boy Brigand."

The youngest of the females could not have mustered more than thirteen summers.

It was she !

Joannitta, Sataniello's future bride.

Sataniello was feeling his pockets—not a copper, not a scudi could he call his own.

With regard to his fair companion, she was as badly off.

They loved each other dearly and tenderly.

They were both poor.

They were both friendless if not homeless.

They had both to carve their way in this big world—in this wide, wide world, where many a good son, many a good husband may want, unless he places his energies together, and faces boldly starvation and misery.

But we must never say "die."

Many who read my book may think that there is not a good time coming.

Cheer up, my friends, and all will be right.

Sataniello was thoughtful. Although young, he had the mind of a man, far beyond his years.

Joannitta was thoughtless.

Like all those belonging to her "sex,"—that is to say, belonging to that wandering tribe called gipsies, in Italy denominated lazzaronis, she lived au jour le jour, heeding not the morrow.

Sataniello, however, had something in hand.

He had conceived a plot, which he was about to carry out.

Not many hours had he before him.

Up to the present period, he had confined himself to petty larcenies—but his hand had never yet dabbled in blood.

He would not kill, unless compelled to do so.

Where his own life and safety were concerned, it was only fair that he should look out for himself.

He intended to do that through life.

There is nobody that can blame him.

Who is your best friend but yourself ?

If he had had only himself to look after, Sataniello might not, perhaps, have appeared so thoughtful.

But there was Joannitta—and who was Joannitta, and what kind of girl was she ? the reader may ask.

Well—Joanitta was the Boy Brigand's favourite, Joannitta was his "sweetheart."

For he was a precocious boy.

And she also was a precocious girl.

But he was her protector, and he must needs find her pretty clothes and pretty jewellery to wear.

He did not like to do things by halves.

"The whole hog or none," was his motto.

Perhaps, as she is to fill rather a prominent part in the course of this story, it will be as well to give a minute description of those attractions which she possessed to an eminent degree.

She had beautiful hazel eyes, surmounted by lashes which one would have fancied were painted with a pencil, so symmetrical were they. Her head of hair was of the most luxuriant description. Her mouth was small. Her lips were like two cherries, and her teeth were as white as snow.

Her hands were beautifully made — and the shape of her tiny feet could not have been found fault with by the most critical observer.

It was, however, the *tout ensemble* which attracted notice. Aye, many a foreign distinguished visitor had asked Joanitta to come with him—that he would buy her some earrings.

But she had always declined all offers.

"I have a fine fellow to take care of me," she would answer. "If to-day I am badly off, it will not always be so. I have confidence in my Sataniello."

And she was right.

And she was a 'cute girl.

And time will tell whether she acted wrongly in remaining faithful to Sataniello.

No more can be said about Joanitta.

She was as childish and as innocent, to all outward appearance, as any English girl of the same age ; but the sun of the South is rather warm, and girls there become women when we are thinking of sending our children to school.

The conversation which was taking place among the lazzaroni was of too unimportant a character for us to dwell upon it. Suffice it to say that Sataniello joined not in the jokes freely circulating around, but kept his eyes rivetted upon the windows of a house in the distance.

CHAPTER V.

SAME SUBJECT CONTINUED.

In that house he meant to effect plunder.

He knew that but a few days ago a wealthy traveller had knocked and entered there, and had been welcomed by a pretty and loving young wife.

He knew that only two women, besides himself, resided in the abode.

One was the wife—the other the female servant.

He knew that he had only to attempt a robbery, and that he would meet with success, therefore he had not to fear any resistance—no strength was to be encountered.

No blood, he hoped was to be spilt.

He had robbed, it is true, but never yet had he taken human life away.

And he was anxious to carry out his guilty designs at once, for his conscience was not easy, and his safety hung upon a thread.

For that very morning the Boy Brigand, our friend, our daring friend, and undaunted future bandit, had committed a dreadful theft, and his mind was ill at rest.

Every instant he fancied that he saw the agents of police advancing towards him to take him into custody.

And naturally he was restless.

For in the morning of the day, when we first saw him, he had made his way through a large and motley crowd, and he had stealthily and secretly followed the pious parishioners that went to the place of worship, and when they were all engaged in their devotions, he had hid himself in a dark recess which stood behind the altar.

The boys that attend upon the priest while he says mass had not noticed him.

He had been watchful, and when he saw that he was safe he spoke not.

The melancholy and yet sonorous sounds of the organ had struck his ear, he had heard the pious congregation joining in the holy psalms—he had seen the priest (although he was himself in a spot from whence he could not be detected)—reading the book of prayer, and his evil inclinations had remained unchanged.

He had watched the holy ceremony, and when the church was empty and deserted, when the last man and woman had disappeared from his gaze, he had walked boldly up to the altar, and, fearless of consequences, had robbed the golden chalice, in which "the Bread of Life" was kept.

The evildoer must have been on his side — the evildoer must have protected his dark deed, for he was allowed to walk away with his boon, and no one had stopped him in his course.

He was enabled to go to a working jeweller, who cared not how he got precious metal in his way to melt, and he had sold to him for half its value what was worth many a pound.

With that money he had bought clothes.

With that money he had plotted his future plans.

What they were we will soon see.

"Joanitta," he said, rising from among the group that surrounded him, "Come here."

The girl obeyed.

She looked at him, and in her glance was an expression of the most intense curiosity.

He had spoken peremptorily and sharply, and she was at a loss to make out the meaning of his abrupt voice.

"Why do you speak to me so roughly, Giovani?" she asked. "What have I done to you to address me as if I were one of those common dogs that wander about the street at night?"

"Listen to me, and endeavour not to enter into a useless dialogue, Joanitta," the Boy Brigand replied.

"Be silent !"

Joanitta's lips were closed in an instant, and she stood before him like a marble statue.

She was all attention.

Sataniello, however, spoke not.

He mused for a while.

"Joanitta," he began, after a moment of silence, "let us stray away from this group of lazy, indolent Romans, who spend their days in gazing upon the shining towers of the Vatican—come, come along with me to some remote spot, where I can talk to you without my presence being heeded, or my conversation listened to."

And he walked on with Joanitta by his side.

When they had reached a lonely lane, where no one was nigh, he bid her to stay her course.

"Joanitta," he said, "to-night we leave Rome—to-night we must leave Rome."

"And my mother, what will she say?" Joanitta inquired in reply.

"The time has arrived, Joanitta, when you must choose between your mother and myself. You must take a resolution. If you like to come with me, and share my dangers and fortunes, you can. If you prefer a life of idleness and indolence, I will not endeavour to shake your wishes."

"Giovani," the girl replied, "I love thee. I have told thee so before, and you know it——But," and she clasped her lovely arms round the Boy Brigand's neck, and her breast heaved heavily, and she endeavoured to speak, but there was a something which hindered her from pursuing her dialogue.

"Hurry on with your speech, and delay me not here," Sataniello replied. "Of what earthly use is it for you, Joanitta, to speak of love to me now? My time is precious. My liberty is at stake!"

"What have you done, then?" Joanitta inquired.

"Have you acted so wrongly as to fear already the

UNEXPECTED MEETING.

Papal dragoons. Oh, do tell me! perhaps I may save thee from——"

"Enough—enough—enough, girl!" the Boy Brigand replied. You are surely a weak-minded, foolish maiden. Good bye, Joanitta—good bye! I must say a last farewell to thee, for this night will see me on my way to the mountains."

Joanitta, despite her youthful innocence, began to see what the ideas of the Boy Brigand were. She had, it is true, detected during the acquaintance which she had made with him, his inclinations for a roving and desperate kind of life; but she had never thought that he would have taken a decision at so short a period as he had done.

So she looked at him, and her lips quivered; and she seemed as if she were inclined to speak, and yet was afraid to do so.

"Joanitta, before I go," the Boy Brigand said, "I must leave you a little keepsake. You asked me to make you a present of a pair of earrings—here they are."

And our Boy Brigand presented the golden trinkets to the young maiden.

Now Joanitta knew that Sataniello got no money except that which he robbed, or had given to him out of charity by the passers-by; and, nevertheless, she guessed at once the value of the earrings which she held in her tiny hands, and placed them in her bosom without asking any questions.

"Oh, thank you—thank you, Giovani," she muttered.

And again she kissed the Boy Brigand.

They remained clasped in each other's arms, and tears were seen trickling down the young girl's lovely features.

"Once again, Joanitta," the Boy Brigand resumed, "will you come with me—will you fly away with me? Will you leave Rome this evening?"

"But my mother?" and still Joannitta's thoughts reverted to home.

The Boy Brigand allowed her to go on.

"And what, I wonder, will mother say if I leave her thus abruptly?"

And the maiden wept outright.

"I will have no 'but' in the matter," the Boy Brigand replied, whose attention was now directed in another channel, and who wished to break off an interview which he knew it was unwise to prolong.

"Joanitta, Joanitta, I will have no 'buts;' I repeat you must make up your mind at once, and that quickly, too!"

These last words were pronounced in a tone of voice which required an immediate reply.

"And if you like to share my destinies, Joanitta, you will swim in wealth, as I will give you plenty of money, and you will be able to send it to those you hold dear."

"Whereas, if on the other hand, you prefer to remain alone, I will not compel you to follow me; but I see nothing for you but poverty and wretchedness.

"And why should pretty Joanitta remain poor and wretched all her life long?"

The Boy Brigand pronounced this last sentence in a subdued and loving tone, which at once set the girl's mind at rest, and dispelled like a shadow whatever reluctance she might previously have had to part from those she loved.

"I will follow you wherever you go, Giovani," the maiden now said; "but do not ask me to do that which is wicked, because I know I will be powerless to accomplish it."

"Never mind about the future, Joanitta. The past belongs to no one; the present is ours, and we must make most of that. But if you come with me you will have companions. Paublas is coming with us."

The maiden said not a word. But when she heard that Paublas was to accompany them, she seemed anything but pleased; for Paublas, although a boy of sixteen, was one of the most consummate ruffians that the world ever produced; and Joanitta had always entertained the greatest hatred against him.

But she had been too wise to show it.

Hence Paublas knew not that he was disliked.

In this case we need not give a description of him, as we will see him ere long.

"And Paublas is coming with us, then?" the girl inquired.

"Yes."

"When?"

"Now."

"No."

"When, then?"

"When twelve o'clock will strike at the Cathedral of St. Peter's, we will take our flight towards the mountains on two vigourous steeds that he will keep in readiness for us. I will ride one, Paublas will ride the other, and you will stand behind my back; and when the horses will be tired and exhausted, we will buy others. I have seen about it already, and all our preparations are made; and if my last plan does not fail, why, Joanitta, you will be my little queen, and I will keep and worship you like a queen."

"And where is all the money to come from?" Joanitta inquired hesitatingly.

"From this purse!" and the Boy Brigand shook a leather bag full of pieces of gold before the bewildered maiden.

Joanitta knew not what to make of what she saw.

She had heard of miracles being accomplished by the hands of strange men—she had heard of wonderful changes having been wrought—but never in her life had she imagined that such things as she witnessed could be carried out.

In the morning Giovani Sataniello was poor,—penniless we may say; at noon—and it was scarcely twelve o'clock in the day—he was, to her mind, as rich as a Rothschild.

"It is time now that you should leave me, Joanitta," the Boy Brigand said. "Meet me at at eleven o'clock at this place. In the meantime, go home. Kiss affectionately those you love. But for heaven's sake do not betray by your demeanour the sudden departure which you contemplate."

Joanitta was about to speak, but the Boy Brigand allowed her not to open her lips; for he had scarcely concluded his sentence than he vanished from her sight in one of the adjoining windings of the lane.

The Boy Brigand, however, had not gone far when he was accosted by a youth of about the same age as himself, who tapped him gently upon the shoulder.

"Well, Paublas," the Boy Brigand inquired of the new-comer, "hast thou done what I bid thee to do?"

The individual who was thus addressed placed his finger upon his mouth, as if to enjoin silence.

"Not a word should be spoken here!" he whispered. "The walls even sometimes have ears; our conversation may be overheard, and our plans dashed to the ground."

"True, very true, friend," the Boy Brigand replied; "but time flies on; and we have many a thing to accomplish within a given period. What about the horses?"

And he pronounced these last words in a half-audible whisper.

"Fear not about that part of the business," Paublas answered sharply; "I have bribed the ostler of the White Horse Inn. To-night, when the inmates will all be at rest—when they will all be plunged in the deepest slumber, he will admit me into the stables by a back door, where the horses will await my arrival already saddled, and fit for their long journey. By the secret entrance will I lead them into the high road. You will meet me there. We will each seize hold of the reins of our steeds, and once in the saddle, we are our own masters once more; and with our freedom before us, we can dash onwards—and onwards—until we reach the wildness and safety of the mountains.

"'Tis well!" the Boy Brigand replied; "but what about the wealthy traveller that lives upon the Piazza."

"To that also I have given my most careful attention," Paublas replied; "but I fear that it will be tight work with him. All the money which he possesses now lies in a drawer in the room where he sleeps at night. But he has thousands there."

"And are you sure that the treasure is there."

"Yes."

"How do you know?"

"I'll tell you.

"While I was on the Piazza, lounging carelessly about, I chanced to hear him say to the maid to keep a watch over those who should enter the house, and not to allow any one to go up stairs. Since I have obtained upon reliable authority the details which I have given to thee."

"Paublas, thou art a precious companion," the Boy Brigand pursued. "But wilt thou not flinch when the hour comes."

"Flinch! Dost thou mean to insult me? Dost thou mean to brand me with the name of a coward?"

And when he uttered these words a sinister smile appeared upon Paublas' lips, which had assumed a snowy white.

No wonder now that Joanitta had a kind of antipathy against Paublas.

The Boy Brigand and his companion were two different boys indeed, both in character and outward appearance.

For Giovani Sataniello, the Boy Brigand, was an interesting youth of about eighteen years of age.

He was tall and handsome.

He had a fine head of hair.

His eye was limpid clear; and although it possessed at times a fierce and dark expression of cruelty, at others it was as soft, as mild, and as pure as that of a young maiden.

Upon his manly features were stamped the outward appearances of strength and resolution, which proclaimed him to be a being of no common cast—an individual endowed with that intrepidity and that undaunted courage which could not but carry him through many a critical position of life, with the most unaccountable and astonishing success.

The Boy Brigand was one of those brave and courageous natures that women admire—that men respect.

He was one of those to whom the weak and oppressed would apply for protection.

He was one of those whose sight cowardly men would dread; whose company strong and wealthy men even would fear.

Not so, indeed, with Paublas.

His appearance was far from being prepossessing.

His forehead was low and ill-shaped.

His eyes were hollow, sunken, and false.

And repulsive was his whole being.

And those were the two companions that were to begin life together — that were hand-in-hand to become the terrors of the mountains; and to whom the most desperate ruffians that the country ever produced were to enlist their gratuitous but bloodthirsty services.

CHAPTER VI.

THE ROBBERY—ASSAULT—MURDER.

The Boy Brigand was not blind to his own guilt.

He knew that to steal was wrong.

He knew that to kill was an offence condemned by God and punished by man; and yet before a few hours would have closed over his destiny, he would attempt another theft.

And as he made a rule ever to be punctual he reached the Piazza in good time.

He had said to Paublas that he would meet him at twelve o'clock, and he was true to his word, and he was at the spot appointed when the last sound of the bell had tolled from the high dome of St. Peter's Cathedral the hour of midnight.

No one appeared!

The Piazza remained deserted, and Paublas was late!!

The night was dark and sultry.

The rattle of carriages had long ago already subsided.

All was still.

The Boy Brigand's attention was, however, now drawn towards some object advancing towards him, and his fears were alleviated.

It was Paublas at last!

At first he had thought that it was some stranger —some spy—nay, some one sent to apprehend him, but as the form grew near and nearer, he had no difficulty in recognising the step of his young companion—of his young partner in his career of murder and of crime.

The two boys shook hands together.

"Now to work," Sataniello said; and they walked straight towards the house where they contemplated the robbery.

The door was closed.

By what means were they to effect their entrance? Had Paublas foreseen that?

No, he had not; but the Boy Brigand had—withdrawing a skeleton key out of his pocket he soon placed it in the lock, and as if by enchantment the door receded before him.

Flowers of a most costly description ornamented the staircase, and their delicious perfumes were spread throughout the whole house.

Thin and artistically-marked carpets covered the grounds, and prevented their steps from being heeded, or noticed by the inmates.

The Boy Brigand and his companion were now safely within the house But they had to pass through many a suite of apartments ere they reached the place where the treasure was kept.

Through one room, two rooms, three rooms they passed, and onward they went.

They had now reached the particular spot they sought.

The Boy Brigand whispered to his companion to remain outside, and steadily and stealthily he entered the chamber.

And then he saw what he did not expect.

There were two beings instead of one!

They seemed, however, sound asleep.

Upon a large and sumptuous couch he saw the traveller, whom he was about to rob of his goods and chattels—by his side was his wife. One of the arms of the young woman surrounded her husband's neck, his head reclined gently upon her snowy and voluptuous breast. Their lips were not, literally speaking, close together, but it was easy to perceive that they had not been long asleep, and that love had only exhausted for a while two beings who doted upon each other.

And the Boy Brigand thought of Joanitta!

And the Boy Brigand wondered whether she would keep true to her word—whether she would meet him and join him in his flight.

Whether she would consent to hurry on to the mountain with him—there to spend days, aye, nights—in the consummation of uninterrupted love of everlasting bliss?

For he adored Joanitta! For she was the being for whom he lived—for whom he entered heedlessly in a career of wickedness, of brigandage, of dissipation and murder.

It was for her that he was resolved to encounter the most horrid of deaths!

It was for her that he wished to accumulate opulence—to swim into the most extravagant wealth.

He cared not how he would come into the possession of the coin which he needed.

He cared not how he forced his way through a heap of bleeding corpses—through a stream of everlasting running blood—if Joanitta could be made happy by these means.

She was the "star" to which he looked.

She was the "star" which lighted his path, until now dreary and irksome.

Without Joanitta his life would be a burden to him—his existence a period of everlasting disappointment—of blighted hopes.

But he had no time to ponder over these things.

With a steady step he walked towards the drawer where the treasure was kept.

With fearless determination he turned the key into its lock, while his other hand was upon his poniard, and round his belt were two heavy pistols, already loaded.

Armed to the teeth also, and awaiting the word of command, stood Paublas, outside the apartment, watching every one of his steps—the slightest of his movements.

And he was about to see whether plunder was to be had—when, lo! Hark!—the stranger awoke, and as quick as lightning he rushed upon the Boy Brigand.

A struggle, short, but decisive, ensued.

The traveller was by far the bigger man. He was in the prime of life, and Sataniello was but a boy—a youth of eighteen summers at the utmost.

But if the limbs of the stranger were well set—if his muscle was strong and as hard as iron—he had to contend with an antagonist of unheard of strength and undaunted courage.

It would have been impossible to say how long the fight would have lasted, had not Paublas, who was on the watch, suddenly made his appearance, and plunged to the hilt in the stranger's neck the shining steel which he held threateningly.

Paublas' blow had been a severe, terrible blow.

At that instant the young wife arose from her slumbers.

"Oh Heavens! Heavens!" she exclaimed. "Blood! Blood!" as she hid her features within her tiny hands.

And the instinct of life was uppermost in her mind.

And remembering that she was exposed to the gaze of two strangers—that she had but a slight attire to cover her frail but beautifully-made form—she hid herself beneath the counterpane, and in a supplicating voice besought the Boy Brigand not to murder or to take away her life.

But he heard her not. Engrossed in his search the womanly voice reached not his ears.

But Paublas, the cruel Paublas, who took a delight in murder, had already seized hold of the powerless frail creature.

And he held his poniard, streaming with blood—horrid, frightful to contemplate, and he was gazing upon his victim with a ferocious, fiendish joy, and his eye darted fire, and he was about to launch her into eternity.

When the Boy Brigand turned round and frustrated him in his merciless attempt—

"Murder not a weak woman!" he said, "Man's blood is ours; but a woman's should never be taken, except under the most necessary occasion."

And he dragged him out of the room, whispering into his ear—

"We need not stay here any longer; I have the bank notes in my hand—they are all French ones; and if we delay not here we have time to convert them into money ere the news of the murder reaches the frontier."

And onward and onward they went, and they found the horses ready and already saddled, and they jumped on their backs, and away, away they dashed towards the mountains."

Without Joanitta!

Without his love!

Without his sweetheart had the Boy Brigand been compelled to leave Rome, for the cries of the murdered man had already kindled alarm in the neighbourhood, and they had scarcely time to effect their departure ere the carabineers were sent in their pursuit.

And as the two boys darted on their course, and with their spurs hurried on their vigorous and fresh steeds, many a time they were on the eve of being captured by the troop of soldiers following them. But their cattle was good—their breed was valuable, and they sped on with the rapidity that only Andalusian horses can attain.

And after days and days, changing their mounts at the inn where they halted, purchasing cattle for three times its value, and paying for their purchase with good sterling gold,—they soon reached the safety of the mountains, and three days after their departure they were free! !

Free again!

The carabineers had followed them as long as their chargers would carry them, but the time had come when they could go on no longer, and they had given up a pursuit which they knew was useless!

*   *   *   *   *

Twelve months have elapsed since the events which we have related.

The Boy Brigand troop was now increased.

When he left Rome he had only one companion.

Now he had ten followers.

They were all youths like himself.

The eldest of the secret band did not number more than twenty years of existence.

The Boy Brigand, Sataniello, was the captain.

Paublas, the merciless and cruel Paublas, was the lieutenant.

The other members of the troop held no rank, and were bound to obey implicitly and without grumbling whatever order was given to them.

The captain, Sataniello, the Boy Brigand, gave an order, and his order became law.

Paublas saw that it was duly executed.

Any deviation from the accomplishment of the order was punished "by death."

There were no court martials that sat over the culprit.

If he was found guilty by the captain, a bullet was at once sent through his heart.

The members of the troop were aware of the determination of character of their leader — they feared him, and obeyed him like slaves.

These were, indeed, a strange troop!

They lived in subterranean caverns, which, doubtless, had once been the den of wild beasts, but which had now been converted to their own use.

It was situated amidst the chain of mountains which cover the whole of the Italian territory.

The entrance of the cavern was always guarded by a sentry, who paced to and fro, and who would have given the alarm had any one been bold enough to venture to close to it.

But no countryman had ever to the memory of

man had sufficient courage to approach it for at least 800 yards around.

The shepherds even who grazed their flock in the green fields, which stretched themselves forth a mile or two distant, had always kept clear of the spot alluded to.

There was a beautiful slanting valley yonder.

There were vineyards in the neighbourhood.

And when one stood on the high cliffs which abounded, he could see in the distance the rippling blue waters of the sea shining in the horizon.

As you walked forth from the cavern, and emerged forth through edges, and clusters, and stumps of old trees—through which no one would have dared to go through except such men as the ones who belonged to the Boy Brigand's band—you reached the high road.

There, on both sides of the way, and where the path was clear, and a carriage could easily roll along, there were at nearly every step old wooden crosses erected, bearing inscriptions of a most extraordinary nature, which would have frightened any traveller who, unarmed, would stray there.

These crosses were those which surmounted the tombs of those unfortunate victims which had been assassinated by the numerous bandits that had always dwelt in those rough mountains.

These inscriptions, which were in the Italian language, could have been translated thus—

Here
has been murdered a traveller,
Pray God for his soul !

At other places the following could also have been read—

Here
Have been murdered together father and son,
They both lay in the same resting-place.
May God be merciful to them!

. . . .
. . . . . .
. . . .
. . .

But the inscriptions which most frequently met the gaze were simple and terrible in their meaning, and ran thus—

Here a man has been killed.

. . . . . .
. . . .
. .

All along the hedges which surrounded the two sides of the road, situated in the thickest part of the forest, the same signs of murder and robbery were everywhere to be witnessed.

And these tokens of nefarious deeds, committed in days gone by, and in the present time, lasted for a distance of upwards of three miles, and then you came to a little streamlet of limpid, clear water, running through pebbles of the most various colours, until it went down to the sea, where it mingled with the briny ocean.

There was also a path which lost itself in an immense forest of pine trees, and of which the opening led to a high rocky cliff, from which could be seen the dark, surging, and boiling depth of a terrific abyss, wherein, doubtless, many an unconscious victim had been hurled downwards by the brigands that infested the mountain.

At the time that we introduce our readers to this new scenery, the Boy Brigand was away from his troop.

Not many days ago one of the band had strayed away—had fallen among a troop of carabineers—been confined in a dungeon, and that very morning was he to be executed.

The Boy Brigand had said that he would see him on the scaffold, and he had kept his promise.

But it was not the execution only that brought him to Rome. He wished to see Joanitta, whom, ere long, will soon again be introduced to our readers.

And having attired himself in the costume of an Italian padre, he had wended his way towards the town, where the imposing and solemn scene was to be enacted, and, fearless of danger, he had seen his late companion go through the last penalty of the law.

He had stood in the motley crowd—his gaze had met the gaze of the culprit—and the presence of his late captain had given him strength in the hour of need.

The brigands were now in the cavern, where the clashing of tumblers circulating freely around, and the sounds of boisterous laughter were plainly discernible.

They were revelling in some drunken feast.

Meanwhile an individual had arrived at the spot, and he placed his ear against the door—a thick, heavy iron door, and listened.

By this time one of the band, who was known by the name of Bloodthirsty Dick, was saying—

"Our poor companion must have made rather an ugly grimace. I wonder how he felt when the executioner placed his hand upon his neck?"

"Now I am not sure of his being dead yet," a voice replied. "I would not at all be astonished if we were to see him back with our captain. Sataniello is a clever, astute chief; and he may have hit upon some plan to secure his liberty."

"Yes," replied another, "he was successful in changing his bank notes. How daringly he acted too! He went to the bank himself, and exchanged them for gold."

"They asked him a few questions, did they not?" inquired a hunchback, who acted as cook to the band, and whose duty it was to bury the dead bodies after having rifled them of all they possessed.

"Yes, they did ask him a question or two, I believe," Paublas now said. "But Sataniello has that kind of palpable off-hand way about him, and he was dressed in the uniform of that French officer that we waylaid and killed the evening after we fled from Rome, and they never suspected him. But silence now," he said, "our captain will certainly be back ere long."

"Now I think," said another voice, "that it was our captain's duty to deliver poor Jack from the hands of the police; and I consider that he has acted wrong in not ordering us to be all in arms, and to attempt to rescue him by strength."

"Sataniello had his reasons if he acted as he did," Paublas replied.

"And what were they, pray?" Bloodthirsty Dick inquired. "Was he not one good and hearty companion? Was he not always first to lay hold of those whom we wished to attack; and when we were thinking of it, had he not already done the job."

"Yes, we lost a valuable hand there!" some one pursued.

"Now do not be so fast," continued a bandit, and who was called 'The Monk,' "There is one thing which is as clear to me as the sun at noonday—if poor Jack is no more, the captain was justified in allowing him to remain a prisoner."

"There he goes again," replied a man in an ironical tone of voice. "There he goes again, the 'Monk' always finds reasons for everything. In an instant I do not doubt but what he will say that we are perfectly justified to kill a man, 'or to plunge pins in the woman's calves,' when they refuse to tell us where their money is."

These last words were followed with a loud laughter; and the Boy Brigand, who had listened and overheard the whole conversation, drew back, coughed loudly, as if to induce the inmates of the cavern to believe it was his first appearance, and with a firm step advanced towards the cavern, and with the handle of his pistol knocked heavily against the door.

"Here we are ! In an instant we will open the door."

"Do not," a voice replied, "Who knows but that it is a spy."

"Nonsense—nonsense!" a brigand replied. "The sentry outside would have given us the alarm."

They were yet uncertain how to act, when a shrill whistle was heard.

Their doubts were soon set at rest, for who could it be but Sataniello.

"It is all serene, I see," Paublas said, opening the heavy massive iron door. 'Tis the Captain."

And the Boy Brigand soon made his appearance.

"Well, my boys," he said, entering the cavern, "I have seen poor William fall by the hand of the executioner. When his last hour came, he looked towards me, and in my gaze he found that courage that he so much required in the hour of need. He died, like a brave Italian, fearlessly, and without exhibiting those outward signs of weakness which some of us, although strong-minded, could not but experience at so critical a moment.

"I once thought," Sataniello continued, in an excited tone of voice, "that it was a sin to let him die without an attempt on our part to rescue him from his perilous and lamentable position ; but our endeavours would have been useless."

And he paused, as if to collect his thoughts.

"We could never," he continued, "have been rewarded for the risk and danger which we must have encountered had we tried to free our late companion. It would have been madness to think of restoring him to that freedom which he so highly valued. The guard that surrounded him numbered, I am sure, over three hundred strong. Even the Papal caribineers were on the *qui vive*, eagerly watching the surrounding approaches of the Piazza, as if they dreaded an unexpected attack,—the sudden appearance of our gallant band."

"Hurrah ! hurrah ! hurrah ! for Sataniello, our fearless master and chief," one voice exclaimed—and the walls of the subterranean vault echoed with the sonorous and manly voices of the brigands, and for many a minute following the wooden solitude was disturbed by their hearty and continuous acclamations.

Sataniello watched with pleasure the ferocious countenances of his followers, usually so sullen and so fierce, light up with evident marks of satisfaction, and he felt happy—nay, delighted—to see that his behaviour had met with the approval of those over whom he had so great an ascendancy.

"What news—what news, boys, have you got for your Captain ?" Sataniello inquired. "Have you heard of any favourable tidings which might induce us to plan an expedition ?"

"Yes," the Hunchback replied· "not far off there is capital plunder to be had."

"And where is it, pray ?" the lieutenant Paublas inquired, who wished to know how the Hunchback could have become master of a discovery that he had been unable to make. "I was under the impression that I had as good information as any one, but I suppose I am mistaken."

The Hunchback listened attentively.

He seemed to swallow the words that had been pronounced.

He was in raptures.

He had at last got hold of that which nobody else knew, and he laughed and he giggled, and a fiendish smile appeared upon his pale and tightly compressed lips.

"Do not keep me in suspense, then," Paublas impatiently said, "and tell us where lays that great treasure which thou hast at last found."

And he pronounced the last words in that bantering tone which men will adopt when they hear a story related to them, the best part of which they totally disbelieve.

Sataniello had stood upright since the beginning of the conversation. Not a word had he said. There he listened, with his hand upon the guard of his sword, anxious to hear the Hunchback speak.

"You know," the Hunchback began, addressing the audience which surrounded him, "the cottage of old Rebecca, the Fortune-teller, the Gipsy of the Mountains—she who told our chief that he would marry a duchess of the land—she who told our lieutenant that he would die shot in the breast—she who told me that I would become the chief of the tribe—"

"Yes, yes," replied the Brigands in one unanimous voice, and what about Rebecca, the Gipsy ?"

"I'll tell you," the Hunchback replied. "Yesterday she went to the Bank of Viterbo, and then she drew out a hundred pounds, with which she intends to buy cattle. For Rebecca, although a gipsy, is a great farmer."

"Well—well—well."

"Well," the captain interrupted, "is it to tell us where there is a poor, weak, harmless old woman to be murdered, and a paltry one hundred pounds to be stolen, that you have kept us awaiting so long. Silence, man, for the future, unless thou hast something more important to communicate."

"£100 is not by any means so small a sum that we should turn up our noses at it," one of the brigands pursued. "By Santa Maria, I think that we ought to settle the old dame and pocket the coin."

"Who speaks—who dares to speak ?" Sataniello now inquired, and he drew his pistol from his girth, and he held it threateningly towards the last spokesman.

This behaviour on the captain's part gave rise to a universal murmur of dissatisfaction. It was the spiteful growl of mercenary brigands frustrated in their evil designs, and a fresh incident occurred which, for an instant, concentrated the whole of the brigands attention.

It was the voice of bloodthirsty Dick, who, regardless of the danger which he ran of the muzzle of a pistol which the Boy Brigand had suddenly turned against him, rose, and, in a clear bold voice, said—

"I hope, captain, that you will excuse me if I speak; but if I do so I am only expressing the sentiments of my fellow companions. We are far from being flush with money just now, and a hundred golden coins among us would be acceptable indeed, and, saving your respect, would be a very desirable improvement to such poor beggars as we."

" Since when, then," Sataniello pursued, " have I been the means of preventing you to enrich yourselves. Surely such are, or never were my intentions. If I say to you do not kill a weak and harmless creature, who is, has been, and doubtless again will be useful to us, I do not intend, my friends, to deprive you of those benefits which you have derived by her death. Here is double the amount that you would have gained by staining your hands with her blood."

Thus speaking, Sataniello threw upon the table around which the bandits were sitting, two hundred golden pieces bearing the effigy of the then reigning King of Naples.

And there was a general scramble ; and it would have been doubtful to say to whose lot the greater share of the yellow heap that lay before the brigands would have fallen, had not Sataniello given orders that an equal share should fall to every one.

Paublas, the lieutenant, however, partook not of the spoil, and he had his reasons for so doing ; for the captain, after having appropriated to himself the lion's share, always gave to the second in command ten times as much as to any other follower of the " secret band."

When silence had again been restored, and the brigands in their respective places remained dumb, Sataniello at length began.

" And has any other member of the band anything else to suggest besides what Mr. Hunchback has already said ?"

" I have, sir," a youth said, timidly.

That youth was one of the brigands, whom they called the Giant. But if his voice was weak, far his manners rather coy and reserved, they and were from being in accordance with his bodily strength.

The Giant—and the name was far from being misappropriated—was indeed a fine specimen of humanity. He was strong and bold-looking ; the muscles of his arms, the sinews of his hands, and the whole formation of his being, were such as to place you in mind of those marble statues that one sees exhibited in museums.

He was above six feet six inches high.

His features, although far from being of a classical regularity, were large and masculine, and might by some have been termed handsome.

His chest was broad and expansive, and as his only under garment was a loose red flannel shirt, which left the best part of his neck exposed to the winds, one could see long dark glossy hair growing all over his brow and sunburnt rough skin, which gave him more the appearance of a wild Indian than of a civilised human being.

His might, strange to say, was nigh incredible.

He had done things that no man had ever perpetrated before, and his feats of boldness and strength were such as to cause him to be looked upon as a demigod by his other companions.

In his sober moments he was as mild as a lamb. Then he would not injure, in his timid and onward course, even the hare, pursuing heedlessly his onward course through vine-clad hills, luxuriant green fields, and thick underwoods, which abounded in the forest.

But in his rage he would spare none.

Then he was implacable—his lips quivered—his eye darted fire, and his whole being shook and trembled.

In those fits he would be terrible. The tears of a woman, the cries of a child, would be powerless to soften the fiendish appetite which he would have for human flesh ; and it would take hours to restore quietness to his mind, once his hot blood was kindled within his passionate breast.

The plan which he had suggested as extremely feasible was received with renewed roars of laughter.

Born and bred in the country, his ideas were ever bent towards agricultural and farming pursuits, and he had proposed that three of the band should sally forth to the village of Tivoli, and therefrom steal from a wealthy farmer that dwelt there three hundred heads of horned cattle, and several flock of sheep, which he proposed to sell at a neighbouring market.

Sataniello had listened attentively to all that had been said. He had heard the weak—nay, ridiculous suggestions of his followers; many a time he had shown unmistakeable signs of his impatience ; still he had waited without interrupting them.

Now he thought it was his turn to address them.

" It strikes me, my friends," he said, peremptorily, " that if you were left to yourselves you would indeed be very shortly brought to ruin. Why you are suggesting petty larcenies—futile excursions, which would be more in accordance with the characters of low thieves—common gaol-birds—than with that of daring, brave highwaymen. Danger we fear not—death we are ready to encounter—but our expedition must not be fruitless, our endeavours doomed to come to no purpose. If we fight and spill our blood, we must have our reward with it —yet all the better if we become the owners of large spoil without any risk. And now to the point. Be all attention, as I have something important to communicate to you."

" Attention ! attention !" Paublas continued, repeating their captain's order.

And the brigands having had their names called out, and the muster being full, with the exception of the sentry outside, the captain began—

" You all know, I suppose, where the Villa Vecchia is ?"

The Brigands answered not, but shook their heads in the affirmative.

" To-night, then, at ten o'clock sharp it must be attacked. The owner and inhabitant of the place is an army contractor. Ten days only has he left Tuscany, after having equipped the whole of the Grand Duke's troops. He has within his desk many valuable bank-notes, and we will require, I think, to have a horse with us to carry that which would be too heavy for man's arm."

Sataniello, it should be remarked, never told his followers what sums he became possessed of. He gave them what he thought proper, and what he deemed was sufficient for them.

Generally they were satisfied ; but, if they were not, they ventured not to show openly their dissatisfaction.

Such outbursts would never have been tolerated by Sataniello.

He was fully aware that the day that he would allow insubordination to make its way to his troop, his reign was at an end.

He was fully aware that he was dreaded, but not loved by all.

He knew that Paublas would willingly have taken his life away to become the captain of the troop.

But Paublas would never have been able to lead on his men like Sataniello ; Paublas would never have been able to keep them in the same subjection as the Boy Brigand—now a dashing bold youth— kept them

Let not the reader imagine that the supreme rank which Sataniello held in the troop was the work of the day.

It is true he was always their chief, but his boldness, his courage, were such as to warrant him in aiming at the command of a troop ; and his determination had been such as to preserve for him the rank that many others would have lost, had they found themselves in so many awkward situations as he had.

On more than one occasion had the Italian authorities endeavoured to clear the country from the fearless bands of Brigands that infested it.

Often and often had detachments after detachments of soldiers been sent in the pursuit of them, and often had they been compelled to retreat with many a severe loss to deplore.

Officers and men alike had been aimed at, and had fallen out of the ranks. Their breasts pierced through with bullets, springing from guns shouldered by invisible riflemen.

Frequently had the search been given up as useless by the courageous but demoralised soldiers.

At one memorable epoch, however, a sergeant, bolder than his predecessors, had sworn to capture those men who did so much harm, whose terrible depredations could no longer be tolerated.

At the head of a guard of twenty men he had followed and tracked the pick of the band for many a consecutive day — during the sunny hours of noon—during the cool and dark hours of midnight.

His courage had not failed him, and he had pursued the brigands through rocky cliffs—through streamlets of muddy, deep waters—along tortuous roads—endless highways—down luxuriant valleys—up high mountains, and at the very moment that he was sure of his prey he was doomed to be disappointed.

He would be on the eve of seeing his hopes rewarded at last—he would believe the band to be surrounded on all sides, tracked like wild beasts into a den from which he would know of no exit—of no earthly escape—when they would all disappear as if by witchcraft behind a wall of rocks, along which would stretch far, far away untrodden paths, of which the sinuosities, until now unknown to the sergeant, would be as familiar to the brigands as the road which led from Rome to Naples.

And the sergeant in no ways deterred, or disappointed by the ill success of his campaign, had renewed his excursion over and over again, until one fine morning, while rising from a hearty breakfast, artistically laid beneath the shadow of an oak tree, he had received his death blow from the hands of the chief of the band.

And when it was known what reward the sergeant had received for his praiseworthy exertions, the bandit's rest no longer was disturbed. The police received the order of keeping a stricter watch, and extra sentries stationed to the parts in the immediate vicinity of the brigands' place of resort.

But that was all, and no more had been done to check the immense power that the brigands were daily acquiring.

These dangers the Boy Brigand had gone through, to say nothing of those which still awaited him.

The reader may easily fancy what energy was required of the Boy Brigand to face many a critical position.

Although there did exist among the "Secret Band" a rigid discipline, still to confine ourselves to that exact truth, to which we intend to adhere through the course of this tale, it is only fair to state that instances had occurred when the Boy Brigand's authority had been disputed.

One or two bloody executions had followed, and the brigands, awe stricken, had retired to their respective abodes, and they had remained dark and sullen.

And time had pursued its slow but steady course, and the old proverb, "Out of sight out of mind," had been strikingly illustrated by the entire forgetfulness which the brigands had displayed at the loss of their doomed companions.

For, albeit, these men lived together, it was plunder and their love of blood that had brought them together, and they formed not with each other those sterling friendships that are contracted and kept up by those who move in the honest path of life.

Sataniello, however, loved and liked "The Monk," and his love was reciprocated by the latter, who had a kind of devoted admiration for his gallant and fearless chief and leader.

The "Giant's" mind was not amenable to such high feelings.

Like all herculean-built men, what he possessed in strength he was deficient of in other respects.

Thus nature has ordered that it should be so.

Those who have a powerful mind sometimes have a weak and frail body, and *vice versa*.

But the brigands were awaiting the captain's further orders, when Sataniello began—

"Let no time be lost. It is now five o'clock, we have a long distance to go. Let every man arm himself to the teeth and await my return."

And followed by the "Hunchback," he left the tavern to retire to his abode to attend to those details of dress which he should carry out, previous to sallying forth on the expedition which he contemplated.

CHAPTER VII.

THE ATTACK.

THE brigands, headed by Sataniello, walked separately, divided into groups of twos and threes.

They soon arrived in sight of the Villa Vecchia, the surrounding neighbourhood of which was plunged into the deepest silence.

Yonder stood a village, and now and then could be perceived the sudden glare of a light looming in the distance—now appearing as if it were close at hand, now disappearing altogether from their gaze.

"It seems to me," said the Giant, to break the monotony which reigned, "that if we wished to capture the village which stands at the bottom of the hill we could easily do so.

"Yes," replied the Monk, in a laughing tone, "I think that we had better send the Hunchback to the mayor of the town, whoever he may be, to inform him that Sataniello and his troop are about to pay him a visit. That he need not fear for his life if he takes the early precaution of taxing every inhabitant with so much a head. But unless the request is complied with, his brains will be quietly blown in, and fire set to the houses adjoining his own."

This joke—if it can be called a joke—was received with a hearty laugh by the other members of the troop, and, had an unconscious individual been behind the men hurrying on to a destination known only to themselves, wherein they might meet their doom, he would certainly have taken them for a

THE SCRAMBLE FOR THE SPOIL.

group of inoffensive peasants on their homeward journey, but never would have guessed what their terrible errand was, so mirthful and so thoroughly happy did they appear.

The brigands walked on, and soon were in the immediate vicinity of the Villa Vecchia.

It was a most beautiful country residence.

It stood upon a declivity, and was surrounded by a dark ditch, which, however, stopped its winding on both sides of the entrance, where a handsome carved flight of steps led to the door.

Growing over the ditch, in all the wildness and beauty of nature uncontrolled, were big oak trees, some of which, bent by the ravages of time, or shook by the tempestuous winds that raged in the

vicinity, very nigh reached the windows of the drawing-room, situated on the left side on the ground floor.

The Villa Vecchia was a two storey house, and above were the sleeping apartments.

Sataniello, hid among the trees, took a rapid survey of the ditch, of the house, and, for a time, mused silently, ere he made up his mind through what particular spot he would effect his sudden entrance in the drawing-room, where light was to be seen peeping through the damask curtains.

Beyond doubt there was company there.

But he expected that, and yet he lost no time.

"Hunchback!" he whispered, in an under tone, "stand here. If you see any one coming, aim

3

steady and well, and fire, and that will be our signal for retreat. But mind and keep your eyes
open."

The Hunchback, as quick as lightning, had answered Sataniello's command—and we need not
say that he promised faithfully to obey.

"With regard to you, Bloodthirsty Jack," he
continued, always in a scarcely audible voice, "you
will also have to remain outside to keep a look-out.
Behind the large statue that ornaments the flight of
steps will your post be. You must see, and not be
seen. And if any one happens to emerge from the
villa, whether it be man, woman, child, master, or
servant, it matters not,—delay not, and strike them
at once to the ground with your naked blade! For
no tidings of our attack must reach the village ere
our plot is fully carried out.

Having given one or two sundry other orders,
and having placed two other sentries around the
villa for fear of escape on the part of any of its inmates, the Boy Brigand turned round.

"Where are you, my brave fellows?" he asked,
in an under tone.

"Here, awaiting the word of command," was the
reply.

And Paublas, the Giant, the Monk, and the remaining members of the troop clustered around
their leader in breathless suspense.

The Boy Brigand listened.

"Hark!" he said; "I hear more than one man's
voice. Doubtless there will be a struggle. But
never mind, boys. Keep your weather eye open—
use the steel—like Italian brigands only can!—

"And forward now!"

* * * * * *

Sataniello pronounced these last words boldly and
loudly, and, ere an instant had elapsed, he was on
level of the drawing-room, closely followed by
Paublas.

The ditch had been no barrier to his onward
course—to his dashing attempt.

In one bold jump he had cleared it with the
swiftness and rapidity of the doe.

His noble example had soon been followed.

Less than a minute brought all the brigands together.

"Now, to work, my boys, and in earnest! Not a
minute to lose!"

And such was the peremptory order that first
broke the stillness of the night.

And no sooner spoken than done.

And up the hatchet went, and down it came, and
the shutters were broken open.

And up the hatchet went again, and down it came,
and the windows were smashed to atoms.

And up the hatchet went, and down it came, at last,
with a heavy, frightful crash, and a huge entrance
was at last effected to the drawing-room.

Those obstacles had yielded—but what would
have resisted the heavy muscular and oft-repeated
blows of the terrible Giant, whose passions were now
kindled by the approach of danger, and who rushed
rather than walked in the drawing-room, closely
followed by the Boy Brigand, Sataniello, the Monk,
and Paublas—the cruel and merciless Paublas, who
gloated beforehand over the scene which he was
about to witness—of which he was to be one of the
silent, but active actors.

The Boy Brigand and his band are now in the
drawing-room, where four persons have arisen from
a table where the pile of cards proclaims them to
have been indulging in a rubber of whist.

Three of them are men—the other is a woman of
about forty years of age.

A shriek—a piercing, frightful shriek is heard.

It is the woman, who, frightened to death, falls
upon the ground in a fainting-fit.

There is one already *hors de combat.*

But three male personages remain, and one seems
bent to fight.

No wonder, too! His red uniform proclaims
him to be one of Her Majesty's officers, and a
British soldier seldom or never surrenders.

An attempt—a bold attempt—is made by him to
rush towards the bell-strings, to pull them, and to
cause an alarm. He has no weapon about him,
but if he had he would resist—he would try to save
the house where he is a visitor, from pillage.

But this day he must submit.

The Giant has him already on the waxen floor.

He tries to struggle—his mouth foams—his eye
darts fire; but his Herculean antagonist only
laughs at him, and his smile shows to the Britisher
in what contempt he holds his *dwarfy* exertion to
get rid of his powerful and iron grasp.

The two other individuals are old, and their fore-
heads, furrowed by many a wrinkle, bespeak their
long residence in the world. And yet they wish to
stay in it still. And they fall upon their bended
knees, and in a supplicating voice beseech mercy at
the hands of the ruffianly intruders.

The oldest of the two is dragged to a seat by
Paublas, where he stands motionless. He ventures
not even to lift his forehead—for above it a glittering poniard hangs unceasingly and threateningly
like the sword of Damocles.

The last one of all is the master of the house.

He is the wealthy army contractor.

He had a watch and a chain—rings!

The Boy Brigand has already relieved him of
these superfluous ornaments, and he allows him to
walk free.

But he would prefer anything but a freedom
which he knows will have to be dearly purchased.

He knows that one loud word, one attempt to escape, would be purchased by instantaneous death.

But the army contractor is the one whom Sataniello wanted—to whom he had to speak to afterwards
"on particular business."

"My good man," Sataniello began, addressing
the army contractor, "you seem restless and pre-
occupied, but you need not fear for your life if
you remain still. Its only your money I want, and I
am aware that there is a good deal of it within these
walls, and not so far distant as one should imagine."

And the Boy Brigand pointed to an adjacent
room, which was used by the army contractor as
his study, and a low derisive laugh escaped the lips
of the Boy Brigand.

"You see," he continued, "that I am well acquainted with all that concerns you my noble and
wealthy friend. Sataniello generally gets very reliable information, and as a general rule he has
always his own way wherever he goes. The servants are all in bed, and, doubtless, sound asleep;
and if you make a movement to awake them you
are a dead man. I hope that you hear me, and
that the guests here will see the wisdom of my
words, and not make more noise than they can
possibly help. Sometimes I set fire to the house
I have ransacked, but if you behave 'like a good
boy' I will dispense with it in your case."

"Who speaks of fire? Oh, heaven above!"
a voice exclaimed, and the elderly Senorita, who
but a few minutes ago had sunk upon the ground,
opened her eyes, and gazed upon the brigands that
surrounded her.

"Yes, Senorita," Sataniello replied, "I am

telling your good husband that if he makes a noise I will set fire to his villa; and if you do not be very careful yourself I will soon carry out my threats."

These words had the necessary effect—she looked at the speaker for a moment, and then, as weak as a child, she fell upon an adjacent easy chair, and buried her face in her hands.

"Now, sir," Sataniello said, addressing the army contractor, "let us make haste, and the sooner we conclude our little affair together the better for you and the safer for me."

And thus speaking Sataniello took the army contractor by the collar and led him to his study, while the Giant and the Monk were fastening the young officer to a heavy chair, in such a manner as he was rendered totally powerless to do any mischief whatever.

When the Boy Brigand had retired the Giant now thought that his opportunity had come.

"My fair lady," he said, addressing the senorita, "give me as a keepsake that enamelled necklace of yours; it looks right well, and I would not like to part without a remembrance of you."

The senorita, doubtless, would have preferred to have been allowed to faint away, and to remain undisturbed, and so, in reply to the bandit's request, she gasped one or two sighs, and displayed all the outward signs of insensibility so as to induce him to believe that she was unconscious of the words which had been addressed to her.

The necklace was, however, soon surrendered to the Giant.

"Now it is my turn," the Monk pursued, "I want the earrings, my dear madam!"

The senorita again made no reply.

"Now give them up, and look sharp about it, if you do not wish to lose your ears also," he pursued, and the army contractor's wife was once more compelled to yield.

The Giant in the meantime was turning around the good lady, and it was evident to perceive from the close way in which he surveyed her, from head to foot, that there was something about her which still he strongly coveted.

"What do you fancy about our landlady?" the Monk inquired.

The Giant spoke not for awhile, but in an instant he opened his huge mouth, and in a slow and sonorous voice he said—

"I am admiring the dress of 'the old gal'—I think it is a very pretty one—a very tasty one. She is about the same size 'as my woman,' and I think that she would look remarkably well with it. So off with it, ma'am, and you'd better undress yourself at once, if you do not wish, for once in your life, to go through the hands of rather a queer lady's maid!"

"Oh gracious goodness me!" the dame replied.

There was no alternative but to obey, and she obeyed—keeping up at the same time a volley of words—beseeching the brigands not to injure her, or to harm her in any way.

"We will see about that, ma'am—it will all depend upon the manner with which your husband will act."

"Oh, he will do anything readily, I feel convinced," the woman replied, "sooner than risk our precious lives."

And as if these words seemed to have exhausted the good lady, who, in her shift, presented a droll appearance, indeed—she being on the darker side of forty—she fancied herself ill-treated, and to become interesting she fell into another swoon.

While these things were occurring in the drawing-room, the following conversation was taking place between Sataniello and the army contractor.

"You ought to be extremely obliged to me," Sataniello was saying, "for the civility which I displayed towards you and your family. Not a hair of any one's head have I touched yet, and willingly will I abstain from any violence."

"Oh, thank you, thank you," the contractor replied.

"Keep your congratulation for another day, and let us come to the point. In this safe you have, I understand, over 300,000 francs—the greater part of which is in notes. Where is the key? I will take the paper myself—my followers will carry off the specie."

"What, do you wish to ruin me? To take all I possess?"

An ironical, sarcastic laugh was Sataniello's only reply. And as the contractor seemed reluctant to bring forth his bunch of keys, he pursued—

"Now do not be foolish, and act like a man."

"Oh, I beseech you!"

"Beseech me not, but open the safe, if you do not fear for your life, unless I will soon settle your mind at rest altogether."

And Sataniello pronounced these words with such a determination, and with such readiness did he cock his pistol, that the army contractor soon prepared himself to open the iron safe.

"But hark!" the army contractor whispered, "I hear my wife's voice. The poor thing is sighing dreadfully. Oh, I am sure they are ill-treating her. Heaven knows to what extremities such followers as yours will go. Perhaps they are assaulting her—perhaps they are attempting to . . . "

And a sudden blush overspread the features of the army contractor.

Sataniello was not long ere he guessed its meaning.

"Oh, no! oh, no!" Sataniello began, "you may rest satisfied upon that point—they are only amusing themselves with your wife, just for a bit of fun—they will never attempt that which has naturally entered your mind, and which in several instances has already occurred. No, my followers are not such gallant fellows as you imagine them to be; and even if they were, I think that your wife's respectable and elderly appearance would soon damp whatever idea of that kind they might entertain. But 'tis no time for such discussion."

While Sataniello spoke the contractor had opened his iron box, and with his hand had presented to the brigand the sum which he required, and he was about to close the lid and to look it up again, when Sataniello said—

"Friend, do not be in so great a haste; my followers must come within, and take a survey of what there's to be had."

The contractor now saw that it would be useless to endeavour to shake his terrible companion's determination, so he bent his features downwards, and sighed heavily, fully prepared to face the worst that could be done.

When Sataniello reappeared in the drawing-room, he soon made a sign to his followers, and the Monk and the Giant searched the study to and fro, and they carried off the bags, and they passed them on to the Hunchback, who placed them as quickly as he got them in a large basket, which was fastened on the back of a swift horse, already in attendance.

The whole scene which we have described did not last above a quarter of an hour, so well and so systematically had Sataniello laid beforehand his plans of attack.

He seemed to be in every respect the identical person eminently suited for the difficult job which he had performed, for during the whole time he and his troop had been engaged in plundering the army contractor's house, not for an instant had he lost his self-possession—his natural coolness and extraordinary courage.

He had been the same throughout; and although at one time resistance appeared imminent, Sataniello had not had recourse to any bloody means—had not even thought it necessary to raise once the tenor of his voice.

More like the hero of a drama—more like a stage bandit, had he behaved than like a real brigand. His ideas were fantastic—his imagination was that of a wild boy, and he loved to produce effect in all things. Thus, when a quick survey had shown to him the safety of his position, he still remained in the drawing-room.

Many people, ourselves for instance, would have condemned such procrastination as an extremely imprudent step to take. Sataniello, however, would have received with the highest contempt any suggestion from his followers, tending to induce him to hurry to the mountains in an abrupt manner. He wished to make those around him believe that he feared not man, and that God, and God only, was the supreme Judge, whose power he acknowledged, before whose verdict he would willingly bow down his head.

Meanwhile the Boy Brigand was walking around the apartment, lifting now and then every piece of furniture that came within his hand, and inspecting closely every nook and corner, to convince himself that he left not behind him anything of such value and importance as would warrant him in his taking it away.

Thus he whiled away a few minutes.

And when the preparations for his safe departure were all present to his mind, he gradually assumed a carelessness and an off-hand sort of way, which very few could have mastered at so short a period, had they been in the critical situation in which he was placed. He advanced towards the British officer —whom we have already seen—and in a jocular tone of voice, he said—

"I am very sorry, captain, that I should have been compelled to act as I did, but the fortunes of war are such, you know, as to make us sometimes forget the code of polite society. I will not, however prolong your sufferings longer than I can help, so here is a knife with which your friends can cut the tight knots which bind you."

No sooner had Sataniello concluded his sentence than the army contractor bounded rather than walked towards the weapon which the Boy Brigand had placed upon the table—thinking that once the owner of the sharp instrument he would feel safer.

Sataniello, however, was not asleep.

"What are you about, you old fool?" he asked suddenly and peremptorily of the army contractor; "You put me in mind of the Neapolitan soldiers, who think

'That he that fights and runs away
Lives to fight another day.'

You act accordingly. Scarcely half an hour ago, when there was a very fair chance of your head being snatched off your shoulders, you were as quiet as a lamb, and now that you fancy that you see me already outside the windows you begin to show your teeth. I thought at first that you wanted

a lesson—your present behaviour confirms my anticipations. If you are too fast you must be reasoned with," Sataniello pursued, "and you could not have fallen in better hands than mine, for I will soon stop your little game, my boy. Here, Paublas."

Sataniello had pronounced these last words in a half ironical, half jocular tone. But the army contractor, who feared to look the Boy Brigand in the face, perceived not the smile that played upon his features.

He had made his own conjectures from what he heard, and what meaning an imagination under the influence of the greatest terror, such as the army contractor certainly was, would give to the most inoffensive speech, the reader can easily fancy.

To add to the effect of his master's words, Paublas, who had answered the captain's call, cocked his two pistols, and the whole troop followed his example.

The army contractor now thought that his doom was sealed.

"Oh, mercy, mercy!" he exclaimed, "I meant no harm, Mr. Robber! Oh, I beg your pardon," he continued, after a moment's respite, "I did not intend to give offence."

Sataniello, however, extremely enjoyed the fun, and was resolved to pursue it.

"Prepare yourself to die," he continued, sternly; "in five minutes you will have ceased to exist."

"Oh, heavens, heavens above!" the army contractor ejaculated, "what on earth have I done? You judge me too harshly, my friends. I am not so bad as you think!"

Another smile appeared on the lips of Sataniello; his gaze had just met that of the officer, and neither had sufficient control to be able to refrain themselves from indulging in a subdued and faint laughter.

"Oh, I know you too well," the Monk now said, addressing the contractor. "If we allow you to live you will never rest until you have pursued us, and discovered our place of retreat. I know you are of a bold and fearless disposition, although you do endeavour to disguise your real nature."

This was too much for the army contractor. He looked imploringly around the room. At last his eye caught a glimpse of his wife—who, fast asleep in an easy arm chair, seemed to have her imagination visited by dreams of the most pleasant description, if one could judge from her features, beaming now and then with the marks of the utmost satisfaction.

"Gussy, Gussy, dearest Gussy!" he exclaimed, "oh, do implore mercy for me! Do implore my pardon at the hands of those who keep me in a suspense worse than death itself—thy womanly tears may soften their hearts of . . ."

And he was about to accomplish his sentence, when the army contractor thought that it would be anything but wisdom to expect any leniency from those who, from his own account, possessed hearts of stone.

A heavy snore, however, was the only answer that awaited the unfortunate man's earnest supplications.

Gussy—for such was the endearing term with which the army contractor called his wife—did not reply. Once or twice she did open her eyes, but, like a great many married women, we are, alas! sorry to say, she, perhaps, did wish to see Sataniello keep true to his threats.

The situation was anything but a pleasant one, and the army contractor began to think that it was rather a matter of fact way of departing from this earth

At this moment Sataniello called Paublas close to his side, and whispered a few words into his ear.

"Oh, do not kill me, do not stab me in the dark!" the army contractor began anew, believing that the dialogue that was held in an under tone over his head related to the preparations that the brigands were making ere they despatched him in the next world.

"Oh, do spare me, and never again will I be so rash as I know I have been to-day!"

And as his fears were gradually creeping over him, the unfortunate man continued—

"Will you listen to me—will you believe me when I tell you that I love such daring characters as you—that I admire such deeds and courage as you daily accomplish. Indeed, I so fully appreciate high minds, brave and valiant hearts. Whatever position in life such individuals as you may fill, they are brave men still, and entitled, I maintain, to every honest and well-thinking man's respect."

Danger had half maddened the army contractor's brain, and he was heedlessly indulging in a rhetoric which it was rather surprising to see advocated by a person who had been ridden but a short time since of a very considerable sum of money. He was standing up—yes, truly and curiously indeed—and fighting the cause of men who had robbed him of all the cash he had within doors, who had even compelled his wife to undress herself to give her wearing garments to one man of the troop, who had fancied it.

And such is the craving that man has for life, that he would undergo any trial sooner than to willingly forfeit it.

But the army contractor was not at the end of his troubles yet.

"Now, Paublas," the captain began, "settle this fellow; and once dead, take his body, and bury it in the field yonder. The Hunchback will dig his grave."

Sataniello had said the last words in a cold, determined manner, and so much bent upon his resolve did he appear, that even the captain thought for an instant that the brigand was earnest in his design, and wished to see his sentence fully and immediately carried out.

When he had spoken, an indescribable terror had seized hold of the miserable army contractor—his teeth gnashed one against the other, his whole frame shook and trembled, as if he were a prey to a most delirious fever—his legs gave way, and he was indeed a pitiable object to look at.

"Mercy—mercy! forgiveness—forgiveness! Oh, do tell, what can I do for you! My friends, make your own terms—I will abide by them. Do you want any money? I have no more in the house. Do you want the whole of the furniture? Take it away—I will not heed you. But, for God's sake, hurt me not!"

"It is too late!—it is too late! You must die!" was the quick response of the band.

It would be useless to prolong this scene by describing it more fully, and by expatiating on every incident that did occur. So let it be said that Sataniello called his men around him, and for a short period they remained close together.

At one given signal, however, they all turned right about, and pointed the muzzles of their pistols against the contractor, whose eyes seemed to be ready to fall out of their orbits.

This last trial was the last blow. The army contractor fell upon his forehead, and remained in that position until a boisterous burst of laughter called him back to his senses.

He looked at them.

No words in the English language would be adequate to convey to the reader the exact expression that his features assumed for the first ten or twelve seconds.

His gaze met that of Sataniello, and once more called forth Sataniello's attention.

"Now, my friend," he said, "if you are let free, and allowed to go unmolested, will you promise us one thing?"

"Yes, certainly," the army contractor replied, readily.

"Will you swear, upon your oath, that never will you mention to any one what has occurred here to-night, and that you will endeavour to impress upon those that are here the necessity of their also holding their tongues about it, as you are the injured party, and not they. Further, will you swear that not by deed or by word will you ever be the means of giving or of showing such information as may lead the authorities to get upon the track of Sataniello's whereabouts; and that at any future period, were you to get informed of the apprehension of Sataniello, the Dark King of the Mountains—if such thing did occur, you would use your best efforts to enable him to regain his freedom?"

"These are rather hard terms," the contractor replied. "I am connected with the government of this country in more ways than one, and I don't see how I can."

"You need not say any more," Paublas interrupted, and he took out a pistol from his belt.

"Stay,—you will not let me pursue my phrase," the contractor went on; "and I do not see," he continued, "how I can refuse to do that which you ask me—moreover, after the leniency shown towards me."

"Do you swear it, then?" the whole band inquired, in a unanimous voice.

"I do!" was the reply.

"You are free, then, and one of us," the Boy Brigand quickly followed. "But before we go—before we wish you good bye, we must have a song. Although you reside at present in Italy—where business has brought you—we know that you are an Irishman. Now for a gallant tune."

"What, gentlemen!—what, my friends! Think of the request—think of the state of my audience! Surely you cannot be serious in asking me to do that which is nigh impossible?"

It was in vain that the army contractor urged on all that he had to say—it was in vain that he besought them not to press him—he had, however, to yield in the end.

And well he did so, and well it was for the safety of the brigands; for when the army contractor was just beginning the second verse of a song then in renown, a patrol that was beating the country espied the Hunchback, and called out to him—

"Hallo! what are you doing here at this hour of night—armed to the teeth—ready to discharge your pistol upon the first individual that you may see?"

"Sure," replied the Hunchback, "you are right there, governor, I am always on the watch. When you live in a country like this, where you are as likely as not to be attacked at any time by the Boy Brigand—by that cruel and merciless Dark King of the Mountains—I do not think that any one has a right to blame you. My master has been asked on a visit to this house. The dinner was splendid!

I had some of it down stairs, you may rest assured. Since the cloth has been removed they have been playing cards—have been at one thing or another—and they are now at something else. I hear some one singing, but what song it is I really can't tell, for I never heard such language before."

The corporal of the patrol was an Irishman, and a Roman Catholic. While a boy of fourteen years of age he had been sent by an uncle of his—the parish priest of Killurickickgarry—to Rome. The boy had idled away his time while at the university there, and had enlisted in the Papal troop, satisfied to await his uncle's death by spending his life in a small army, where he had plenty to eat, nothing to do, and no prospect, however remote, of any war, except with fellow companions and brothers in arms.

He looked at the Giant —and after having satisfied his mind that he was right enough—and even if it were the contrary, it would be perhaps as well not to inquire, as he had the advantage of him, and the hedge was close at hand, he whispered into his ears—

"Have you got anything in the bottle?"

"A drop," replied the Giant.

And the soldier and the bandit drank hastily one after the other.

The stuff was no weak one—it was no bad liquor—it came straight from Cognac, where it was manufactured, and a case a few days ago had fallen into the hands of the brigands.

The effect upon the corporal was instantaneous.

This time he had taken rather a long draught, and its effects showed itself in the way, for instead of giving the word of command to the patrol, which had stood at ease, while he was questioning the Giant, he returned towards the soldiers, and in a stentorian voice he had continued the last verse of the song that he heard the army contractor giving forth while he was partaking of the brigand's hospitality.

"Egad," the army contractor exclaimed, forgetting all at once the terrible trances through which he had passed, "Mr. Sataniello, have you got any Irishmen in your band? I'll take my oath it is only a Pat that could sing like the fellow that I have just heard."

At that moment the Giant entered the drawing-room to communicate to Sataniello what had just taken place, and his rencontre with the corporal of the patrol.

"Let us not tempt Providence," he replied in a whisper. "We have been lucky once to-night—we may not be so twice, so let us take our furlough for the present."

"Good bye, madam," he said, addressing the army contractor's wife, who had been awoke by her husband's voice. "Good bye, signor; good bye, captain. Perhaps one day you may require my services ; and for the future let me express a hope that you will be able to play your next rubber of whist without being so much disturbed as you have been this evening. Farewell again, madam, and may you have all trumps!"

With these words the Boy Brigand bowed to the company—wound his steps towards the window—bounded like a chamois across the ditch—close upon his heels following the other members of the troop.

While the sounds of their voices were still heard dying in the distance, the army contractor had seized hold of the knife, and was freeing the captain from the rope which had him fastened to the chair, in which he had remained for the best part of the evening.

"And what is that man's name?" the captain inquired, when with limbs cramped and stiffened by the cords which had held him a prisoner, he rose once more upon his feet.

"They call him Sataniello, the Dark King of the Mountains," replied the army contractor mournfully ; "and he has a right to the last name, for many a sovereign would be glad to have in his pocket the sum which he took away from my desk to-night. Oh," he pursued, "the result of five years hard toil and labour."

"Surely, you can prosecute him," the captain replied ; "if you have the numbers of the notes you can trace them."

"All very true, but I have pledged my word to a certain thing, and I will say nothing more about it. You are my guest, and may I ask of you the same secrecy that I intend to keep upon this matter."

"Oh no, oh no; we will have him locked up," exclaimed Gussy, who was becoming brave, like her husband, once the danger was over.

"My darling, keep quiet, and do not excite yourself," the army contractor pursued ; "and may I reckon upon Captain Wogan?" he added, looking earnestly at the British officer.

"I will do whatever you request me to do," the officer replied ; "only I sincerely wish that Captain Wogan and Mr. Sataniello may meet one day upon the same ground, and with the same weapon."

And thus speaking the officer went to the cupboard and filled a wineglass of a certain golden liquor, which appeared from its hue to be either sherry or brandy, but more likely the latter, considering that punch was always drank at the Villa Vocchia, after the cards had been set aside on the green baize.

Meanwhile the army contractor was indulging in the most pitiful lamentations on his lost treasures, and over the clever and ingenious way in which the brigands had deported themselves.

Thoughts of a very different nature were crowding themselves in rapid succession before the brains of his good Mrs.

She was still under the impression of the rough and impudent manner in which the brigands had acted, and she could not forget the treatment she had experienced at their hands and the loss of her earrings. Thus pondering she was endeavouring to settle in her mind to what particular shop she would sally forth the next day to replace these little things which she had been compelled to give up to those bloodthirsty and merciless brigands.

CHAPTER VIII.

SATANIELLO IN A NEW CHARACTER.

It must be confessed that the most remarkable success had attended all the excursions of the Boy Brigand since the day when we saw him in the Piazza del Popolo, following his new line of life. Whatever he had attempted he had carried out without meeting with those severe disappointments which attend most of man's enterprises.

Luck seemed decidedly to be on his side—his star on the ascendant.

There is a common saying to this effect, " That some men are born with a silver spoon in their mouths," thereby implying that wealth is to be their lot. Such, however, could not be said to Sataniello.

He was truly the architect of his own fortunes.

Had he remained in Rome—had he spent his days in idleness and following no profitable employment, he would still be the penniless and thoughtful youth that he was many months ago.

The times are changed—the days are not such as those in which the Boy Brigand lived.

Over half a century has elapsed, and by no means a small period in the history of mankind.

True, Italy is the land of rapine and brigandage.

True it was centuries ago—it is, and will be so again for years, until the rotten system that prevails at the Vatican is altered. Still, for all that, it would not be wisdom to imitate the Boy Brigand's career. Besides, many—nine hundred and ninety-nine out of a thousand—would feel inferior to the paramount situation which he had inwardly resolved to fill.

Whether he was the boy in the right place has already been shown.

Sataniello was truly a genius of his kind.

Men are born for certain things—they are brought in the world by the hand of destiny, for specific purposes.

Some are born to be slaves—others are born to be masters.

But how many live and die and leave no name behind them.

Better, we say—better a thousand times, that death should hurry you on to an early grave, which you can face with a bold heart, a clear conscience, sooner than to allow you to live—to drag on a life of sin—of wickedness, and leave behind you such reminiscences of your bygone days, as would cause the world to curse and loathe the spot where you first saw the light of day.

The Boy Brigand's thoughts now reverted to Joanitta.

He had seen her, it is true, on many an occasion since the day when she and he had that long conversation on the Piazza, which we gave in full for the benefit of our readers; but it had always been for short periods, and he had always been so closely watched, that not with any safety could he have reached the abode where the girl lived with her mother.

After his excursion to the army contractor's house, he and his followers had lost no time in regaining the subterranean cavern, and once the division of such boon as he had thought proper to allot to the brigands, had been made, the picture of Joanitta had presented itself uppermost to his mind.

A thing which caused his heart to beat with a happy throb, was the consolation which he felt at being able to supply his sweatheart with all that wealth can procure.

We will soon see Joanitta—we will soon wind our way towards her abode—still, for all that, it is only right that we should acquaint beforehand our readers with all the details which it is necessary they should know, in order that they should clearly understand all the points and intellects of our tale.

It was towards three o'clock in the afternoon, and two days after the events which we have related in the previous chapter, when Sataniello, who had at last watched his opportunity, wended his course towards the city of Rome.

His costume had nothing conspicuous—he was dressed alike the remainder of the Roman citizens

that he encountered at every step, and no one would have ever ventured to think that he was an outcast —a Boy Brigand—so firm and erect did he keep his head—so proud and straight were his shoulders —so quick and determined was his step—his whole gait—his outward appearance.

When he went anywhere, Sataniello always assumed a fictitious name.

Hence he was known as Signor Trancheschi.

He had walked for many a mile already—had left the Piazza del Popolo far behind him, where the wealthy portion of the Roman people were wont to dwell, and he had engaged into a labyrinth of small lanes.

Once or twice he stopped his course and looked up at the end corner of the street, and having satisfied his mind that he was going the right way, he had proceeded onwards.

Now he crossed a piazza and another piazza, and a small street offered itself to his gaze.

With one hand you could have touched both sides of the row, and from one house on the left, you could easily have effected an entrance to a house on the right, so close were the buildings to each other.

It was currently rumoured that such habitations could not have been healthy for its inmates, but the scarcity of diseases that attacked the inhabitants of the abode referred to, and the blooming countenances of the children that dwelt there, was a sufficient guarantee that the spot was far from being so unhealthy as people wished to make it.

Sataniello, or at least Signor Trancherchi, soon looked up at the door of a house which was wide open, and having satisfied his mind that it was the place he sought, he boldly entered and ascended the steps.

During his rapid journey across the town, many a pretty Roman girl had noticed the gallant Sataniello.

These charming Italian maidens—some of them so lovely and so loving, had wondered who this handsome citizen was. They remembered having seen his face before, but, like the angel's visit, his appearances to town were few and far between.

But let us quit the pretty maidens—let us allow them to make their own reflections upon the mysterious stranger—to revert our attention to the Boy Brigand, and to she whom he had come to town to visit and see.

He was not long in ascending the staircase which led to the rooms which were occupied by Joanitta's mother.

The senorita was sitting close by an ebony work-table, when she heard the sound of footsteps, which caused her to lift up her head to see from whence the sound proceeded.

Ere we go on any further we must inform our readers that Joanitta's mother was a receiver of stolen goods. It was she that was wont to receive the jewellery that the Boy Brigand and his band were successful enough in becoming masters of. It was she that had once recommended to the Boy Brigand the working jeweller to whom he brought the golden chalice that he had robbed from the altar. As long as Sataniello was beating the pavement of Rome, doing nothing, and always up to mischief, Joanitta's mother had strictly forbidden her daughter to have any conversation or intercourse with a common lazzaroni.

She would say to Joanitta, "Now, look here, my girl, I have got a little money—very little, indeed— and Sataniello had not a scudo to bless himself with—you will be but very ill-attending your future welfare if you allow him to engage your affections. He does no work, he has no means, and he can do no good, hence some day or another he must get in a scrape, and you will be compromised with him if you are seen frequently in his company.

That was a sound, substantial advice, that would have been very much to the purpose had it been given to a girl three or four years older than Joanitta; but she was really very young, and one might have fancied that she could not understand half of what was said to her.

But we have said somewhere that Joanitta was a precocious girl, and the Boy Brigand remarkably advanced for his age. And this was strictly correct.

And when this is told to the reader again easily will he be convinced that Joanitta listened attentively to her mother's caution, and "took it all in."

But she was resolved to use her own discretion about sundry matters, which it is not necessary for us to inquire deeply into at the present.

When the Boy Brigand was in Rome, occasionally haunted by the police, Senorita Lani (such was Joanitta's family's name) was perfectly right in ever keeping before her daughter's mind the necessity of her avoiding the society of a young wild boy, who might one day become a dangerous person to know.

And one knows not where bad acquaintances may carry us to. It may lead us in more troubles than the human mind can fancy, and be the means of preventing many a willing heart to bear as strongly as he would otherwise the hard toil of life; and a bad acquaintance made in early life may be the awkward stone which causes you to fall at the very moment when life, beginning to smile upon you, had hitherto showed you the road to rank and fortune.

Besides, the receiver of stolen goods had quite enough to do to keep her daughter, Joanitta, without being encumbered by a boy visitor, who would surely hang about the house at dining time, and get from Joanitta the dainty morsel that, perhaps, the charitable mother would deny to him.

The worthy lady was up to all these things. She had what is vulgarly called an eye to business, and a cuter blade did not exist in the whole of the Papal territory, nay, even from Rome to Naples, from Naples to Sardinia.

But as the earth turns round upon its axis so had things considerably altered within the short space of a few months.

Now the tables were turned.

Sataniello was no longer a common lazzaroni—he was a daring highwayman—a fearless bandit; and so great was his reputation all over Italy that he had already earned the epithet of the Dark King of the Mountains.

Scarcely a day elapsed but what the Senorita received some valuable jewellery to dispose of over which she had her per centage.

That even would have been a splendid remuneration in itself for her troubles and the risks she ran, but she had also made her own arrangements.

With that estimable prudence and praiseworthy foresight which is, we believe, one of the main characteristic points of persons who look after their own selves, Joanitta's mother always levied a certain secret tax upon everything she parted with, however trifling its value.

It will not, then, be very difficult to see that these little transactions answered remarkably well the widow's book.

Now we say widow because Joanitta had lost her father at an early age; in fact, we do not think she ever knew the author of her days, and it is a query whether Mrs. Lani herself would have been able to swear positively to the paternity of her child, so many admirers had she had at one time.

The good lady had never made much money.

Receivers of stolen goods, whether male or female—men that live by their wits—women that reckon for their bread upon the caprices and lusts of wealthy sinners—seldom or never thrive.

They may for a while, for a short-lived period have a glorious triumph—an ephemeral reign—but they soon fall again on the dunghill of vice, from which the greater number sprung from in the first instance.

The party by whom she had made the most money was the Boy Brigand, Sataniello, the Dark King of the Mountains.

And, as a matter of course, her feeling against him was far from being that bitter feeling, akin to hatred, that she had against him not many months ago.

Joanitta had noticed the change.

She had noticed an increase of wealth.

The tables were garnished with luxuriant viands, the bottles filled with delicious wines, the rooms decorated with neat and clean, if not sumptuous and elegant, furniture—all due to the Boy Brigand.

No wonder, then, that he was liked by the mother—beloved by the daughter—and a visit of his anxiously looked forward to, always carried with it some good news—some addition to their ill-gotten riches.

"How is the dear senorita to-day?" the Boy Brigand inquired, addressing Joanitta's mother. "What a delicious perfume arises from the cook-house. How are you getting on? well, I hope. How is the health? satisfactory, I should imagine, from the rubicund and blooming appearance of your cheeks. By-the-bye, if it is not an unpleasant question, may I ask whether you have any visitor for dining to-day; and if not, allow me to invite myself?

"To be sure—to be sure," the senorita replied, "you will have pot-luck with us to-day. I cannot answer for its being a very sumptuous repast; but what there is you are welcome to; and it is freely and heartily given, with the serenest wish that you will enjoy yourself."

Sataniello had not yet asked any news about Joanitta.

This incident may seem strange, perhaps, to some of my readers.

Not at all—it is just as it should be.

Now, my boys, the day that you will fall in love—the later in life the better for you—you will not care to let any one know that you have been such a foolish fellow as to let some big girl make an impression upon your mind, and keep you ever thinking about her, you will say—if I have been a fool let me keep it to myself, and say no more than I can help about it. And yet, you will not dislike the idea of being in love, and you would feel quite ready to administer a sound thrashing to the busibody who, unmindful of his own business, would try to persuade you to think about somebody else.

Now, knowing ones—we ask you, is not that true?

This being said *en passant*, let us return to the Boy Brigand.

No, he had not inquired about Joanitta.

But the old senorita did not leave him much time to think about love, for she soon drew his attention towards some more substantial pleasures—those of the tables.

"And I hope, my boy," she asked in a soft voice, "that you will have a good appetite to-day?"

THE BOY BRIGAND MEETS AN OLD ACQUAINTANCE.

"My boy," was the term by which Joanitta's mother ever addressed the Boy Brigand.

I wonder whether his reception at her hands would have been similar some two years ago, had Sataniello dropped hungry-famished upon the good lady.

It would seem that there are certain natures in this world, who, having but a very few qualities to boast of—if any at all—have to compensate them for the loss, a very fair average of pleasant vices, which enter under the denomination of mortal sins, and for the indulgence of which they will be duly and carefully punished at a stated day.

Mrs. Lani—let us call her by the English appellation, to prevent any mistake or any misunderstanding—was one of them.

She was an avaricious, a dissipated, and a greedy woman.

In Italy people are not so fond of getting inebriated as they are in this good old country, otherwise it is probable that Mrs. Lani would have, in addition to her other little piccadilloes, indulged now and then in copious libations.

When she was sitting down for dinner—at dinner—or rising from dinner, she was intrinsically happy and contented.

She did not eat to live—she lived to eat.

She was over fifty, and had she harboured any intention of disguising her age, she could not have succeeded in her purpose, for she looked considerably older.

4

Her hair, which was quite grey, had already in many places a strong tendency to a snowy white; and her cheeks which Sataniello had called blooming (was it out of derision?) were covered with a multitude of red, swollen pimples—unmistakable sign of her indulging rather too freely in the pleasures of the table.

Her forehead was furrowed by many a deep wrinkle, and yellow and decayed were her badly-set teeth.

Her chin, too, the chin of the good old dame, slightly protruded forward, and threatened in good time to join the upper part of her physiognomy, which, let it be confessed, would be no new improvement to her countenance.

Her nose had, it is true, preserved its original shape in all its purity—it was sharp and thin—and her nostrils, constantly damped by a dark, dirty hue, plainly showed how very fond of her pinch of snuff Joanitta's mother was.

She could never have been what you would call a good-looking woman.

But there was a kind of mocking, exciting, bold, lewd expression, which lurked in her grey eyes, that we dare say was not without its charms in days gone by.

And there she was now, the receiver of stolen goods, the harbourer of wealth dishonestly acquired.

What would have struck a close observer as exceedingly odd, as a striking illustration of Nature's wayward freaks, was the great disparity which existed between the mother and the daughter.

The former might once have been roguishly pleasing; now, beyond doubt, she was repulsive.

The latter was certainly pretty now; never could she become ugly.

Joanitta was one of those whose charms may lessen with the age, but whose beauty could never be entirely destroyed.

Report tells us that Ninon de Lenclos, a celebrated French woman, whose mind ever preserved its brilliancy, whose attractions were not weakened by years, when over eighty, had still many an anxious lover.

With regard to Joanitta we cannot go so far, but we can assert that she would, up to her last hour, remain pleasing.

Sataniello, we presume, thought as much; for we need not mince the matter, he was very fond of her; he loved her dearly, perhaps too fondly.

But why blame him? the poor fellow had faults, like everybody else; and is it a fault to love a pretty creature? My readers, I think not.

If it were we should all be guilty sinners.

For we all fancy some one.

If we do not, we ought.

We should all have sweethearts; woman's company elevates the mind and the character of man; but do not jump to conclusions—the object of our affection should be worthy of it.

You could read in Mrs. Lani's face the whole of her character.

There was no uprightness, no candour in her look.

There was a constant mockery ever hanging upon her compressed lips.

No generous heart ever throbbed within her faded and worn-out breast.

"Would you like, my boy," she said, addressing Sataniello, "to know the bill of fare? Generally I dine at two o'clock; but that confounded business of yours (alluding to some previous transaction she had with the Boy Brigand) kept me occupied all the blessed morning; and when I came in I was too tired to attend to anything. I am sorry I could not dine early, for there is a long interval between two in the afternoon and ten o'clock at night; and in the meantime one has time to regain an appetite, and prepare himself for supper. But I need not complain; I feed well when I do feed. To-day we have a jugged hare with rum, a slight taste of Madeira, and an idea of lemon; a brace of roast birds, a filet of soles with truffles, and one or two made dishes, which I hope you will enjoy. But this is all?"

Now a great many English boys, on hearing such a list of delicious things, would have been delighted.

They would have opened their eyes, oh! cracky, oh! it would have been a pleasure to see them engulphing when sitting down at the repast table.

But the Boy Brigand heeded not the words he heard.

"Confound her dinner, and herself too," was the thought which uppermost seized hold of his mind. "Where's Joanitta? What the deuce keeps her out so long?"

There he was musing, when the girl rushed into the apartment, her face all flurried, and holding a large bunch of flowers in her tiny, soft, silky, voluptuous, white hand.

"Och, och, och!" she ejaculated slowly, as if she were overcome with fatigue; "I am tired, awfully tired; and by the holy St. Peter I am famished."

And when she saw Sataniello a crimson hue overspread her pretty features.

And as her gaze met his, her roguish eye spoke volumes.

And she passed her fingers through her luxuriant, glossy hair, and she sat down upon a seat not far from him.

"How do you do to-day, Giovani?" she asked in a careless manner.

Her mother was there, and as she was a deep one —oh, awfully so—she did not wish to let anyone become acquainted with what she felt.

Lucky dog, the Boy Brigand was.

Sataniello at once answered her not.

He kept contemplating Joanitta, and he felt happy.

"There is a god for lovers," an old proverb says, and it must be true; for, had it not been so, Mrs. Lani would certainly have noticed the Boy Brigand's earnest gaze—the strange meaning of his look—and she would have been justified in asking him why he looked so steadfastly at Joanitta.

And she would have been perfectly justified; for we would, I am sure, be very reluctant to allow any individual to stare in that queer fashion upon any one that we hold dear.

It is no use to deny it.

The boy and the girl were enamoured of each other.

She was budding into youth—he had just sprung into manhood.

Glorious periods of life! when our minds are fresh, our hearts open to that sweet feeling—love!

A time comes when we think no more of these things; with them, however, it was quite the contrary.

Sataniello, after a while, spoke—

"It is a long time since I saw you last, Joanitta," he said.

"Over a fortnight, I am sure," the girl replied; and in her words could have been detected the following meaning: "and why have you remained so long away from those you adore?"

"I could not come sooner, Joanitta," he pursued, "I had a little game on hand which it took some time to play."

THE BOY BRIGAND; OR, THE DARK KING OF THE MOUNTAINS.

"And have you been successful?" Mrs. Lani now inquired, whose attention had been attracted by the last sentence.

"Yes, I have," the Boy Brigand replied; "and here is the result."

And while Mrs. Lani looked towards him, and while Joanitta listened, he withdrew from his pocket a small portfolio.

"Oh, what have you got in there?" Joanitta curiously inquired.

"Look, look!" This was Sataniello's only reply; and, ere the words had died away upon his lips, he spread upon the table the contents of the book, which were all the notes which he had so cleverly robbed from the army contractor.

Mrs. Lani was Sataniello's banker, so her joy was too great to be adequately described.

"Why, there are thousands there!" she ejaculated; "why, you are a wonderful boy! By Santa Maria, where have you found all that treasure? I never saw such lots of money before!"

"Yes, Joanitta," Sataniello replied, "It is all mine. 'Possession,' they say, 'is nine points of the law,' and I wonder who will take this away from me."

"Any fresh murder perpetrated?" Joanitta anxiously inquired.

"No; not a drop of blood spilt!" Sataniello replied.

And he related to the two women the daring adventure which we have described in our previous chapter.

"Well, well, that's the style that licks me," Joanitta pursued, and, unable to contain herself, she burst forth in a loud fit of laughter, and ran about the room in the greatest ecstasy.

She was young, foolish, and careless.

She only saw the money—heeded not the way it was got by.

"And what do you want me to do with all the tin, my boy?" Mrs. Lani inquired.

"Place it to the best use you can; send some of it over to England, to the old lady. It is safe there; and do not grudge anything to Miss Joanitta."

The mother's eye fell upon the Boy Brigand. "Why the lad is getting rich," she thought, and she allowed her mind to think no further.

When the Boy Brigand had made his last request she had smiled pleasantly.

She was quite proud to find some one who had implicit trust in her, and God knows that Sataniello had, for, we must tell the reader, that for the sake of Joanitta, he never called for any accounts.

He knew that he was rich, that he had plenty for himself and for others besides; that Mrs. Lani had no one to bequeath her money to except to her daughter, and he felt sure of Joanitta.

"Spend that," he continued, "as soon as you like. There is plenty to come from the same shop where I got that. I am fearless of danger, and love spoil, and I do get it, too, and no mistake."

Our readers ere now have seen that in these last words there was no exaggeration.

Meanwhile Mrs. Lani's thoughts reverted to Sataniello and to her daughter.

"By Jove!" she was pondering, "it would be a great thing for me if that bold boy would take care of Joanitta. He has already a nice fortune, and I know he would like the girl, for she is pretty, and she must command love. She will, it is true, have to associate with a brigand, a highwayman, but that is not to be pitied. She will only have to do what I have done before her, for, after all, who was the late Mr. Lani? Not much better, indeed, than Sataniello. He robs fearlessly on the high road while poor Lani sneaked about the streets; and he had to pay dearly for his want of pluck, poor fellow!"

And the good lady remembered that her late consort had been clothed, fed, and maintained at the expense of the Government for the last ten years of his vicious existence, and that when they had lived together they always quarrelled; and similar reminiscences of a rather unpleasant nature floating rapidly across her mind, she became drowsy, and she indulged rather freely in a crystal decanter that stood before her, and induced Sataniello to join her in her libations, and Joanitta followed her mother's example.

Mrs. Lani offered a shelter to Sataniello; and, as it was rather late to regain his cavern, he accepted her kind offer, and by rights in an hour the three beings ought to have been plunged in the deepest slumber.

Mrs. Lani was not long ere her lid closed. She was old, she had made a hearty meal, her digestion was good, and she was soon fast asleep.

Not so with Sataniello. Luxuriously lying upon a comfortable feather bed, between white, soft, clean sheets, he was enjoying a rest which he got not every day, and which contrasted agreeably with the rough couch which was his lot when he was in his retreat in the mountains.

He was pondering on what he had seen—he was thinking of Joanitta.

Joanitta was, indeed, very pretty. What a small creature she was!

And there would be no immense difficulty besetting his path if he told her again how ardent, how passionate was the love which he felt for her!

He believed in his own mind that she only wished for an occasion to love him as she ought.

With Joanitta he would not require to enter into a long discourse of his affection, which in many an instance means nothing; few words would convince her of the strength of his feelings.

She was also the girl that would suit him.

There was no nonsense about the maiden.

She would accompany him in his daring exploits. Watchful sentry, she would ever keep her eyes opened, and acquaint him with such dangers as would loom in the distance.

Under assumed garments she would wind her steps to neighbourhoods where she was unknown.

Who would suspect a weak, innocent woman—nay, a girl of scarcely fourteen?

She would stroll in the town and make appointments with dashing cavaliers, wealthy gents, and bankers' sons, and, unawares, such men would be pounced upon, and their bodies would be kept as ransoms until large sums were paid to the Boy Brigand for their recovery.

She would be the syren that would lead men to their doom.

And Joanitta would do anything for Sataniello.

Their acquaintance was not that of a day—it had already lasted for a considerable time.

Hitherto love had not yet spoken in all its maddening and voluptuous fury.

Yet they craved for each other's embraces.

Their ages had already told each other a tale, if their lips had remained closed.

What would the mother say? Sataniello thought at last.

But he soon dismissed from his gaze the picture of a woman whom he loathed, and whose company he only kept occasionally, because of Joanitta!

And such was the pith of his idea, that he could find no rest in slumber.

Besides, he had partook of a deliciously made vine, and his brain was heated, and his senses were keaner than ever.

And thus he was pondering—the slightest noise—the slightest rustle of the curtains against the windows of the room causing him to become restless and agitated.

Now a slight sound—an indescribable sound attracted his attention.

He rose upon his elbow, and his eye wandered swiftly around the apartment. In every nook and corner did it find its way. He was not afraid of any robbers—of any sly, untoward intruder, for who could the Boy Brigand fear? Surely, the Dark King of the Mountains was not to be cowed by living man. No, his feelings were actuated by a deep curiosity.

Did he think of the band of justice ever hanging over his head—not he! He had numerous spies in his pay—they would have given him a warning.

Not a soul, he felt confident, knew that Sataniello was in Rome.

The police is not so well kept in Rome as to cause brigands to fear.

But perhaps some of his troop might have followed him. They knew he had a treasure about him, and what had tempted him might have tempted others.

He got up, and went [towards the window and looked without.

Not a sign of any disturbance.

The lane was deserted, and the bright moon which peeped forth its rays showed him that all the inmates for yards around, were deeply sleeping.

He was now satisfied; and he had scarcely regained his couch, well bent upon trying to find some repose, when a slight sound again was discernible, followed by the light of a small lamp, and ere he had time to make a move the door of his apartment ran upon its hinges, and he saw Joanitta!

Joanitta, who was secretly and stealthily entering his bedroom.

She was but very scantily attired.

Her glossy, luxuriant, wavy hair, fell loosely upon her bare shoulders.

With one hand she kept her lovely breast concealed by a beautifully embroidered night-gown—with the other she held a bull's-eye, which cast forth the weak and uncertain glare that had kindled the Boy Brigand's attention.

Her lovely feet now appeared in all their perfection.

Such faultless extremities the Boy Brigand had never seen before, and their whiteness contrasted well indeed with the dark shade which the lamp produced upon the ground.

Her eyes kindled with a loving expression, which made them glitter like two diamonds; and had Sataniello read Shakespeare he certainly would have thought of Lady Macbeth wandering in the dark apartments of her palace during the stillness of night.

She was, indeed, as beautiful as a queen!

"Are you astonished to see me, Giovani?" she asked in a subdued tone of voice.

Sataniello gazed with undescribable delight upon the well-made form of that pretty girl.

"I have been thinking of thee ever since I left you. I could not sleep—I was restless—my mind was ill at rest—my heart palpitated, and I felt as if something was to occur."

"You have been thinking of me?" Joanitta replied; "and how is it that you never sought me? I was under the impression that when brigands craved for a treasure they had it at once or never."

And Joanitta pronounced the word "never" in a strange tone and voice.

Did she think that she was not the object of Sataniello's whole thoughts?

Did she think that her love remained unrequited? And was her behaviour an indiscreet way assumed by her to clear whatever doubts might be hanging upon her mind?

Sataniello smiled in reply to the young girl's genuine query.

Something inwardly told him that there was too much truth in Joanitta's words to expatiate upon them, and that he deserved but too fully the reproach of which she had cast upon him.

"Oh come, come Joanitta," Sataniello said, "come and let me whisper sweet tales of love in thine ears. Oh, come and let me tell you the strength of my love! How fondly I dote upon you! Thou art right Joanitta when thou sayest, that when I want one thing I do take it. But I did not wish to snatch love from you—to snatch a reluctant consent from those pretty pouting lips. Love is not like a miser's purse that you should take away by sheer strength."

Joanitta heard this sentence, and she made no immediate reply.

But those pretty pouting lips became suddenly enlivened with a radient, killing smile.

Who could have resisted the Italian maiden's blandishments?

No human being—not even a deity—could have said No, when Joanitta said Yes.

Meanwhile Sataniello indulged in a contemplation, which he, alas! feared would not last for ever.

He kept on admiring that striking dash that youth ever gives to beauty, so truly pourtrayed in the girl who stood before him.

And he thought of angels! and that superb look—that the fire of youthful passions kindled in a maiden's breast imparts to a naturally bright eye, made his thoughts, for once, in his life revert to heaven, and to all that's true, good, sublime, and beautiful.

And he still kept on gazing upon Joanitta's lovely form, which now and then trembled with that feverish agitation, inherent to those who are to forsake for ever the pure innocence of spotless girlhood.

And his glance was earnestly bent towards Joanitta's well-shaped figure; and he thought again that he could love that child—about to become a woman—like no man ever loved woman before.

For she was hitherto unstained by man's vicious and pernicious contact, and had fate permitted that such a creature should reciprocate the burning ardour of such a man as he!

Although a brigand—an highwayman—an outcast—the wandering offspring of a murderer and a Roman mad girl—could he hope for one who could sympathise with him—wipe away those tears that a youth must shed sometimes when at daggers drawn with God and mankind! Could he hope for one to console him in those moments of dreariness and of solitude. When we look anxiously for the hand of friendship, and are maddened to despair, aye, driven to curse the powers above, if our voice is unheeded—our supplications so many hollow sobs destined to die away unheard in the bleak paths around us!

Joanitta was Sataniello's first love!

He was proud of her! and he looked forward to the day—when dashing forward at the head of his troop—she would show that woman can sometimes teach man a lesson.

Joanitta would be his confidant.

Together they would plot deeds of heroism and of blood, by which wealth was to be amassed.

Thus wandering afar, he placed his feverish pulse round Joanitta's waist.

She replied mutely to his entreaties, and sat by his bed-side, and her soft hands played lovingly through the dark forest of hair that surrounded his proud forehead.

"And dost thou love me, Joanitta?"

A faint "yes" followed, and the girl's gaze was now bent downwards.

And Sataniello brought her lips close to his.

And they spoke not for awhile.

"How come you, then, to love such a one as I?" Sataniello inquired.

Joanitta looked at the Brigand.

"Listen!" she said, after a pause, "Thrown together in the same lonely path — both without friends—both without those kind parents who ever watch and guide their children's first footsteps in life, how could we prevent the smothering embers of fire kindled within our hearts to burst forth one day in all its ardent and uncontrolled warmth? For, what is mother to me? She is so selfish and reserved sometimes, that 'home,' a word sweet for others, is dreary, indeed, for me. I contrasted the buoyancy of your youth with the cold and stern reception which awaited me. Meeting you on the Piazza we soon grew accustomed to each other's society, and even when compelled to part we looked forward to the morrow. You took care of me as if I belonged to you, and I feel convinced that had I been your sister many brothers could have taken a pattern from you. Out of the few pieces of silver you managed to save you always found way to buy me some tasty presents. Whether I was ill-humoured or not, your behaviour was unchanged—you never were cross with me; and of my sulky and capricious moods you seldom took any heed. Can you wonder, then, Giovani, that I became so fond of you, that I am really ashamed to confess it?"

Sataniello, meanwhile was in raptures. Not a syllable did he utter, for fear of interrupting the young girl whose speech sounded like sweet music to his ear.

"And then, one morning," Joanitta continued, in a silvery voice, "you coolly informed me at a moment's notice that you were about to leave Rome —you asked in a rough, abrupt manner, assumed, I suppose, for the occasion, to share your destiny. I assented. To the spot where you bid me to await your arrival I punctually wound my step at the hour named, and in useless suspense I spent the whole night long, hoping to see you coming. The morning followed, and I was doomed to the bitterest disappointment. Off you had gone, and left not a word behind you; and it was only after hours of the greatest anxiety—after days, which seemed years to me—that I at length received tidings from you, to acquaint me with your sudden departure—with the untoward reasons which prevented you to keep your rendez-vous; and when you return to town, and when you come to Rome, braving fearlessly all dangers—what's for? To see Joanitta, to bring wealth and comfort within her poor abode. For if we are comparatively rich now, to whom do we owe the best part of our wealth? Oh, I need not answer, Sataniello, I see by your look that you have heard enough—that you well understand that if I have forgotten for once a woman's delicacy, the strength and ardour of my love is my only excuse, and will be deemed amply sufficient by you to palliate the bold step I have taken—acting as I have done."

"Oh, Joanitta, you speak like a being from above!" Sataniello exclaimed in the deepest ecstasy. "Oh! how delighted, how glad, how happy I feel. Thy words, Joanitta, have maddened my brain with a fever of volupty, and which causes my whole frame to tremble with a hitherto unknown delight—I experience sensations which I never felt before. Oh, the power of love is great! To love and to be loved; and to receive an avowal of the latter from the girl's lips is more than I can bear! Oh, what bliss! What sweet and soft language. Joanitta, dear Joanitta, dearest Joanitta repeat to me again what thou hadst said! Repeat to me those loving words again, whilst thy pouting lips—so innocent and yet so bold—seem to have been moulded to pronounce. Oh, now I begin to know what joy is! Oh, how I do delight in my roving life, for this is my reward. And what need I care for the world, if I have a darling one to love me?"

Having thus spoken, the Boy Brigand stopped short, and, after having reflected for a while, he pursued:

"And what will you do without me, when once I am gone, Joanitta?"

"Gone?" the maiden inquired, as quick as thought; "gone where? Surely you do not intend to resume that wicked life which you have been leading. Sataniello, you are rich now! Do not tempt Providence; but do reform your ways while it is time yet. You know there is an old proverb which says 'it is never too late to mend,' Why not abide by it? If you only knew how uneasy I am when you are away, never again would you dream of returning to your old avocations."

"Joanitta, you talk like all women. I am only beginning, and you tell me to stop. Why I want about a hundred times as much as I have already, and then I will settle down, and not before. But as I must return to the mountains I do not wish to go alone. A girl, Joanitta, may be made just as happy within my rocky abode, as within the polished drawing-rooms of a busy town. Still, will that girl follow me this time wherever and whenever I go?"

"Yes, she will," the maiden replied; and the subdued tone of her voice was drowned by the sounds of a beautiful clock on the chimney-piece, of which the hand marked the hour of midnight.

And the Boy Brigand clapsed Joanitta closer and closer to his breast, and their youthful and loving lips met in a mutual avowal of love.

And the clock struck one, and repeatedly did Giovani embrace the beautiful maiden, and lovingly did his feverish pulse encircle her slim and slender waist; and it struck two, and a bashful blush o'erspread her features; and it struck three, and unable to withstand her lover's lustrous gaze, she closed her expressive eyes beaming with the marks of the most intense enjoyment; and it struck four, and the sweet perfume of her breath covered Sataniello's forehead with its genial warmth; and it struck five and six, and ere the last stroke of the pendulum had died away two beings were plunged into pleasures new to them, into the supreme ecstasy of a mutual love.

CHAPTER VIII.

TIVOLI GARDENS.—THE BOY BRIGAND AND JOANITTA CREATE A SENSATION.

HAD an invisible being whispered into Joanitta's

ears the words " How long do you wish your happiness to last ?

What would she have answered ?

What would we all have answered ?

For ever, and ever !

Would it have been any use to do so ? Would it have stopped time in its steady and onward course ? No, everything has a conclusion. Hours of bliss, hours of sorrow, have their end.

The only difference is this: the first ones glide on quicker than we would wish them, while the others hang wearily upon us, and make us long for their termination. And so it was with the two lovers.

The morning came, and its bright light dawned upon Joanitta, and caused her to awake.

She arose from her slumbers, and her first gaze reverted to Sataniello.

There he was, apparently lifeless, and sleeping deeply.

A thought, a bitter, excruciating thought flashed across her mind—if he was to awake no more. And she remembered that there was such a thing as death; and she remembered that at a moment's notice a supreme power might plunge her and her lover into everlasting eternity.

And was she, and was he prepared to die ?

If Sataniello awoke no more, what would become of her ? Had she ever realised to her mind before this dreadful, heartrending idea ? Before she had not, now she did ; and she began to repent.

The step which she had taken was a guilty one. She had heedlessly given way to the burning fever of her brutal passion, without the accomplishment of her love being sanctioned by the holy ceremony of marriage.

Why did she not think of these things before ? This is the question which we would have asked of Joanitta, had we been able to speak to her; and, as a matter of course, she would have blushed—she would have been ashamed to answer, and may have wept an apology.

And would this have been sufficient to palliate her conduct ? We leave the reader to form his own opinion.

We only say this, *en passant*, as we hope it may act as a warning for those who, like Joanitta, would feel inclined to behave as foolishly as she did.

But we are reluctant to proceed, fearing that our words will have but very little effect, and that ere we can prevent it, many will follow her footsteps.

Human nature is human nature, and the world will not mend.

Having thus wisely settled this difficult point, let us proceed.

Joanitta became fretful, and her rosy fingers rested upon Sataniello's forehead.

The pressure of the strange hand drew him from his sleep, and he looked around him.

At first he forgot where he was ; He fancied himself in prison, but his mind was soon at rest. There were no iron bars ; and, smiling upon him, he beheld Joanitta.

He was about to speak when Joanitta's mother entered the room.

" Oh! what do I see ? Oh, Sataniello! Oh you wicked, sinful boy!"

And the good old lady lifted up her hands to the ceiling of the room to call heaven to her assistance.

The Boy Brigand, in no way undaunted, watched her going through her pantomime ; and when apparently she had done, he coolly said—

" Good morning to you, Madam!"

" Good morning, sir! And are you not ashamed of yourself, sir ?" and Mrs. Lani pronounced the words in a stern, inquisitive tone of voice, of which the Boy Brigand took no more heed of than if she had been a total stranger to him and Joanitta.

The maiden, meanwhile, spoke not, and her gaze bent downwards, feared to encounter that of her mother.

" And you are a nice child, Miss Joanitta! Oh! who would ever have supposed that a mother would have been called to witness such things! Oh dear, oh dear !"

And Mrs. Lani was about to dwell upon the impropriety of what she saw, when she thought it wiser to regain her room.

She had offered hospitality to Sataniello, and what could she expect from a Boy Brigand ? She ought to have kept the entrance of her house closed against such a character if she did not wish to witness what she had seen.

Gradually, however, Mrs. Lani reasoned with herself, and after all she came to the conclusion that there was not so much harm done as it would at first sight appear.

Sataniello had acted precisely in the same manner as her late husband had acted towards her, and they were not the less happy for it afterwards.

The same blood that ran in her veins ran within Joanitta's frame, and if she had not been able to resist the evil temptations of the serpent, how could she, in common fairness, expect her daughter to do so ?

To be sure Mother Eve had been as bad as she, and she was not the only woman that had acted like she and Joanitta had.

So, when the mother and daughter met, no more was said about the matter.

Mrs. Lani had her code of morals, and she looked upon the behaviour of the Boy Brigand as a sufficient guarantee for his love for her child.

Hence he would take care of her and her turbulent daughter.

" Giovani," the girl began, " asked me to go back with him to the mountain ; will you allow me to do so, mother?"

" I like your boldness, indeed !" Mrs. Lani replied. " You wish my sanction ; oh, what a pity ! you think a good deal of it, I dare say ; at least, as far as I can judge, I should imagine that you are perfectly careless of what conclusion I may arrive at. But, if you wish to go, you may go, and a good riddance it will be to me."

And Mrs. Lani spoke in a half-serious, half-jocular tone of voice, which did not remain unheeded by the two lovers. But having attained their object, they made no observation thereupon.

" Go, by all means, go ; and the sooner the better," Mrs. Lani still mused, as if answering her own thoughts.

The breakfast followed, the hours passed on, and the first day of the lover's honeymoon soon glided on, and night succeeded.

" What shall we do now?" Joanitta inquired ; " I should so like to have a dance. Will you come to the Tivoli Gardens, Sataniello?"

" I will; but if I were to be recognised?" and he uttered this sentence in an anxious tone.

" Oh, there is no fear of that ; the place is so public, that the police will never dream of looking for you there," the girl quickly pursued.

" Joanitta, I am reluctant," the Boy Brigand began anew.

" Remain here, then," the girl pursued, sullenly.

" No I won't," the Boy Brigand replied ; " I will do what you want. Is it likely, that when a pretty little wife like you desires something, it would be denied to her? Joanitta, I love you too much for that!—a wish of yours is an order for me. The shades of night are falling fast, so if you purpose to make a start, come on."

"I am ready," Joanitta replied; "but ere we go, we must wish good-bye to mother."

The Boy Brigand had already forgotten Mrs. Lani, who was away on some errand of her own. She soon returned however.

"Good-bye, my children," she said; "may luck be with you!"

"Where are you off to like this?" she went on after a while.

"Oh, not very far," Sataniello replied.

"Shall I see you again this evening?" Mrs. Lani followed.

"You may, and you may not," the Boy Brigand answered.

And then mother and daughter parted for the first time in their life.

And how can you account for the carelessness displayed by Joanitta? Easily enough: a child is like a dog—like an animal—in the way in which it is trained will it grow up.

Mrs. Lani was no specimen of a parent.

We have already described to our readers her character as a woman.

They see now what kind of mother she was.

Not only in Italy do such women—such mothers—exist.

There are a great many women like her in London, more so even than in Rome.

Sataniello and Joanitta were not long ere they had cleared the doorstep, and an instant found them in the streets.

They walked arm-and-arm, and as lively and happy as a newly married couple generally is.

They also had been united, but in their own fashion, and they were perfectly satisfied.

The Boy Brigand was with Joanitta, we have already seen, had had her forebodings.

Tivoli Gardens, where the two lovers were sallying forth, were situated a few miles from the city.

As they neared the spot the sounds of sweet music warned them that within gaiety was at its height.

These were gardens of that kind as are to be found in every town.

In London we have Cremorne Gardens and Highbury Barn—in Paris there are Mabille and the Chateau des Fleurs—places meant for youth, and for the myriad of pleasure-seekers that abound in all cities.

The spot where Tivoli Gardens were situated was standing at the bottom of the high-road which led to the mountains. It was a convenient place for the brigands of Sataniello's troop, and they had hitherto managed so well to preserve their incognito that up to the present time they had never been discovered, and their real avocation had never been looked into, however doubtful their appearance might have been.

To reach the interior of the gardens you had to go through a small path surrounded by high, luxuriant green trees, and then you came to the platform where people indulged in dancing.

This place of entertainment had not been got up in a very expensive style. It placed you more in mind of a country garden at the back of a wayside inn than of anything else.

However, it was the only one of its kind, and whether they liked it or not, people had to go there or remain at home, for they had no choice.

Consequently they paid in their entrance-fee, which, in English currency, would have made about the value of a shilling, and they went in.

Around them Joanitta and Sataniello saw a great many women and men apparently happy.

Among the visitors the Boy Brigand recognised some of his old "pals"—boys that, like him, had grown to man's estate, and that he was wont to meet on the piazza, while, alike them, he was an idle fellow—a careless lazzaroni—trusting to public charity for his bread.

They knew not that he was Sataniello, the Dark King of the Mountains, because it never occurred to their minds that the bold boy, Giovani—that gallant bandit—relating whom the most daring and dangerous deeds were freely circulated, and seeing him no more among them on the Piazza, they had forgotten him.

He was gone, doubtless, to some remote climate to improve his condition; perhaps to obtain a lucrative situation, and he was too proud to write to them.

Such were the conjectures his former companions were making, and they did not puzzle their imagination much more about him.

On a wooden bench, meanwhile, did Joanitta take a seat.

The Boy Brigand reclined by her side, and the weather being oppressive they called for some refreshment.

Meanwhile, let us take a glance at those who composed the gay assemblage of beings who congregated before us.

Far away there was the Giant.

He, too, had ventured to come to town.

Wearied with the solitude of the cavern he had strayed towards Rome, seeking a change of scenes—enactments which his feverish brain needed.

Close to him, and leaning against a heavy oak tree, was a tall, fine, handsomely-made woman.

She was called "The Lamb" by the frequenters of Tivoli Gardens.

From the description which will follow, our readers will soon perceive what irony was conveyed in the nickname by which the big woman was known, and to which, let us confess, she really did not object.

Her real name was Pamela.

At the moment when we introduce her to our readers she was in an attitude which bespoke truly the waywardness of her nature—the utter recklessness which she possessed to an eminent degree.

Upon her hip rested her left hand, while with her right she held a tumbler full of a reddish wine, which, from its mocky and sloppy hue, proclaimed it to belong to that class of made-up beverages which are sold in all places of resort, where drunkenness and dissipation are the order of the day.

"The Lamb" was not a woman, who, to dispense with any useless phraseology, would have kindled every one's fancy, still, for all that, there was a coarse beauty, a natural freshness about her which was worth its price.

And Pamela got it, too!

Her look could not have been mistaken—it told what she really was—a brazen-faced, dissipated, gay woman.

And she was not ashamed of her calling; nay, she gloried in it. She was proud of it.

She was fully aware that creatures of her kind generally die of a violent death, or quietly at the hospital, and she rather liked the idea of it.

"For once in my life," she would say, in a jocular manner, "I will be well taken care of, and secure a berth," as she expressed it — she had already sold her body to an eminent Italian surgeon, who had purchased it, having come to the conclusion that never had he seen a woman whose outward appearance, even to the naked eye, proclaimed so strongly the sensual passions, which Pamela could not disguise to the most careless observer.

Pamela's lips would have been in themselves a very fit study for a physiognomist.

Her lips were thick, pouting, and rosy; and they betrayed what her glance betrayed—a strong craving for the nervous, feverish, and gratifying pleasures of love.

Her skin was transparently white, and her hair of a golden hue, was still plentiful, albeit the glossy forest which surmounted her forehead had, to a certain extent, been already thinned by a continual life of debauch.

She was dressed in a costume which made her look more like a male than a female; and had she kept her attire closely fastened, one might have fancied that nature had made a mistake. She had on a pair of blue velvet trousers, a vest and jacket to match, but the latter being opened exhibited to the gaze of the stranger that which she might as well have kept hidden beneath the soft folds of the cloth.

For it was no sight! and yet Pamela knew that her bust was exposed, and she attempted not to conceal it; and she seemed anxious to allow her powerfully-made charms to be catechised by every passer-by, who could not but gaze with admiration upon the queenly breast that she was endowed with.

This was the Giant's fancy.

What a difference between she and Joanitta!

The first one was tall and strongly built—the second was small, and her whole make was frail and womanlike.

The music now poured forth its beautiful strains, and Sataniello and Joanitta being tired of sitting still, rose from the wooden bench and strolled on the platform.

And the orchestra, striking a lively tune, Sataniello encircled Joanitta's frame, and he and she went through the figures of an Italian dance with so much gracefulness and precision, that the young couple soon became the observed of all observers.

With her waist so slim and so slender, with her wavy fair hair hanging so softly upon her symmetrical shoulders, with her pretty feet so tiny, and yet so well-shaped, Joanitta was a fit subject to attract notice.

She was a girl among many, that one could not but admire.

On the other hand, Sataniello was also handsome, and manly looking.

There was an original expression about him, which would have induced many to say "although that man is humbly dressed, he keeps an incognito to suit reasons of his own."

We know that this was precisely the case; but Sataniello thought that he would have passed in a crowd, and although Joanitta's remarks had greatly tended to make him conceited—a defect in a man's character which he hitherto possessed not—still he knew not that he was so dashing, so accomplished, and so distinguished a looking cavalier, as to produce an undescribable impression upon those whom he saw for the first time.

"Who are they?" one of the spectators inquired.

"Who is she? A pretty girl and no mistake!" another followed.

"I do not know her, do you?" a young fellow pursued, questioning a friend on his right, meanwhile cocking up his eye-glass and looking impertinently at the girl through it.

"She is fresh to this place, apparently," a sober, grey-haired individual went on with far-fetched wisdom, accenting deeply every word he uttered, as if he wished to convince the lookers-on of his knowledge of things.

"And who is he? What a rakish customer he looks!" a girl ejaculated.

"No he don't! Now do not be afeared, he won't take any notice of you, Pol. He has got something better in hands than a lushy beauty of your stamp," was the quick reply.

And an earnest quarrel took place between the beings that had just spoken—two girls that cordially hated each other, and only looked for an opportunity to tell each other their own mind.

"And you cannot tell me who that is, governor?" a curious visitor again was inquired from the Giant, who, attracted by the crowd, had also wound his footsteps towards the knot of people, among whom he saw Sataniello, his captain.

One can easily fancy his astonishment.

"How am I to know?" he sullenly replied to the questioner. "I am a stranger here, like yourself; do you think that I keep a list of all those that come here? I have quite enough to do without that, God knows!"

The party who had questioned the Giant, looked at him, and willingly would he have dealt him a good poke in the ribs had he seen his way of departure clear before him; but fearing that he would have fallen into a trap, in which he would have got a beating that he would not forget in a hurry, he went away like a dog with his tail within his hind legs, growling as he went along. "Why if you won't answer a fellow, you might, at least, be civil!"

The Giant, meanwhile, had joined Pamela, and they were busily puzzling their brain to know what brought Sataniello to the gardens.

"He got a good deal of money, Pamela!" the Giant was whispering into the girl's ears, "from that ere army contractor, as I spoke to you about, and, as the Hunchback said, he bagged it all, and he has not given us a rap yet."

"And why do you stand it? Why do you not make him stump up," Pamela retorted. "You risk your life, and you are entitled to the blunt just as well as he is."

"Yes, to be sure we are! But it is not everybody that can or dares to speak to Sataniello as he likes? Why he would think as little of blowing up a man's brains, as he would of smoking the cigar which he holds in his hand!"

"And who would think so?" Pamela continued. "Does he not look as mild as a child, gazing upon that little fair girl that he has with him. But he lies!"

"I will put you up to a thing or two," Pamela continued, "when you return to the cavern, you may say to the others that you have seen the captain enjoying himself at Tivoli Gardens, with a smart damsel, that, doubtless, takes all his money from him, and hence deprives the band of it. You will then kindle an hostile feeling against Sataniello; and when he will see that the whole band is against him, for the future he will be more generous."

"Pamela, I'll try my best, but I can't answer for success, there is a sly coon among us that is called "The Monk," and by jove that fellow would die for the captain. I do not know what's the reason

THE BOY BRIGAND AND JOANITTA CREATE A SENSATION.

of that friendship which has sprung up among them two, but still it is so; and I do not doubt that if he heard of anything prejudicial to Sataniello, he would be the first one to carry the news."

"Never mind him! Do your duty, and fear no one!"

"I will, Pamela, as soon as I am back; I ain't no fool, and I know devilishly well that the captain has no right to keep all the money, and to give us what he thinks proper. I have been very dissatisfied for a long time past; but, as you know, my tongue is tied; at some other time I shall speak more freely; but I for one object to his little game, and I will soon stop it if I can."

CHAPTER IX.

THE SUDDEN RECOGNITION—THE ESCAPE.

WHETHER the Giant acted in accordance with the bad advice of Pamela, his mistress, will be seen by our readers as the story proceeds.

Meanwhile the dancing had subsided; and when the excitement inherent to those who engaged in the whirling movements of the dizzy waltz, or of any other Terpsichorean exertions, had given place to those moments of reflection which mostly follow all bodily exercises, Sataniello and Joanitta were very much astonished to find that their movements had been closely watched.

To dispel the attention of the lookers-on from them, they strolled towards some of the less-frequented parts of the garden, hoping that within a few minutes their presence would no more be noticed than that of any other visitors.

And in coming to this last conclusion they were perfectly justified; that is, as far as it related to the casual observers, which composed the greater part of those who were present at Tivoli that night.

But there was one being among the motley crowd—among that gay and thoughtless multitude—whose eye followed Sataniello wherever he went, and who, in company with another person, spied him as he left the neighbourhood of the orchestra, and followed closely in his track.

"Egad!" the mysterious being was muttering to himself, "I have seen that face before now. Those features are familiar to me; but who can he be?"

And he was walking slowly behind Joanitta and Sataniello, he and his friends keeping at a respectful distance, for fear that the Boy Brigand should notice that he was followed by any one.

"I say, do you know who that man is, my lord?" the mysterious stranger inquired of his companion.

"No," was the immediate reply of he who had been addressed by the name of My Lord.

"Would you like to know?" the mysterious stranger continued.

"Yes, that I would; his appearance struck me at first as being peculiar in the extreme; and although up to this moment I am kept in the dark, I feel convinced that he is some extraordinary Italian."

"And you are right, my lord; that man who is walking apparently so palpably before us—mixing so freely among us—is an outcast, a felon!"

"By jingo! do you speak true?" his lordship pursued. "This place is very badly lighted up, and for a valuable attaché of Her Majesty's Neapolitan embassy to be so close to a character of that kind is endangering, without much use, his valuable freedom."

And who was this mysterious stranger?

Who was that man, reader, who, one out of many, had detected Sataniello's presence?

Was it any of the Boy Brigand's former companions?

We should say not; for we are reluctant to think that any one who would ever have been on a footing of intimacy with Sataniello, could have been seen walking on friendly terms with a proud English nobleman.

Was it any of the Boy Brigand's numerous victims, who, at length, had recognised his features, and who, with that courage inherent to a creature born on English soil, was resolved to lay hold of him, and take a striking revenge?

This would have been a more wise conclusion to come to.

For it would have been the true one.

The man who, in company with Lord Charlestown, was following Sataniello, was a gentleman, every inch of him, in his demeanour; but he possessed that military appearance which at once showed, to any connoisseur in those matters, that he was once, if not now, in some branch of her Majesty's service.

And had anyone taken him to be an officer, he would not have been mistaken, for the steady and undaunted watchman now before us was Captain Wogan, whom we have seen but a very short time ago, and who, after the memorable night that the Boy Brigand had effected an entrance into the Villa Vecchia, had wended his way to town for a little recreation, never suspecting, however, that he was on the eve of meeting Sataniello, the Dark King of the Mountains, at so frequented a place as the Tivoli Gardens.

To Captain Wogan's mind there now remained not the slightest particle of doubt about his having recognised Sataniello, and he was pondering on the best and surest means to make the Boy Brigand his prisoner, and to place him in the hands of justice.

This daring deed, beautifully coloured, and often related with a spice of exaggeration in the saloons of the Neapolitan embassy, would obtain for Captain Wogan a name of courage and intrepidity for which he longed anxiously.

He already fancied hearing himself congratulated by the male portion of mankind upon his undaunted *sangfroid*, and the beautiful ladies would ask him many questions of the following description:—

"Oh, do tell us, Captain, how he looked. Do relate to us how the whole thing occurred—we are so anxious to know! And do you mean to say that Lord Charlestown was with you? How did he behave in so terrible a crisis? Did he act bravely? Of course he did; a nobleman with £10,000 yearly could not do otherwise!"

These thoughts were crowding themselves in the Captain's mind while he was following the Boy Brigand, and although his lordship was reluctant to get mixed up in a quarrel, Captain Wogan was there, and he should show no signs of cowardice if he wished not to be covered with ridicule by his equals—when back in the aristocratic "saloons" of his lordship's head quarters.

Joanitta, meanwhile, on her own side was not idle.

"Sataniello," she said, suddenly, in a subdued whisper, "you are watched."

It was long after dusk, thus the girl's features could not have been noticed; but had the dim starry radiance fell upon her countenance at the moment she spoke, Sataniello would have been struck with the whiteness of her face.

Quick as lightning had the thoughts of the morning reverted to her mind.

Sad, and bitter, and excruciating, indeed, would have been the winding up of the first day of their newly-began honeymoon, were Sataniello to fall in the clutches of his pursuers.

The Boy Brigand was not cowed by the information just given.

"Take no heed of them who follow us," Sataniello pursued. "If we betray any sign of anxiety, any movement which may lead them to think that we are guilty of any crime, and long for flight, we are doomed; otherwise, we are as safe here as we would be within my rocky and inaccessible abode in the mountains."

The two individuals were closely following Sataniello and Joanitta, but they were yet too far away from the Boy Brigand to hear the pith of their conversation.

"I am on the alert," Sataniello replied to one of Joanitta's queries. "They may come as soon as they like—I will fight until I die—never will I surrender. Oh, Joanitta, why did you ask me to come here! This garden will be the witness of my doom. Something told me as I walked along that my visit would be productive of no good."

"Cheer up, Sataniello," Joanitta pursued, "I will fight for you if necessary."

Had the Boy Brigand been unwatched the probabilities would have been that he would have rewarded Joanitta's renewed marks of affection with a fervid, affectionate kiss, but as he was situated he contented himself by squeezing the girl's arm close to his chest.

Joanitta turned round, and so carelessly did she do so, that the captain thought that it was only a casual movement of the girl, and he never dreamt that she turned round to look by whom she was followed.

"Sataniello," she said, "do you know who is behind you? why, it is Lord Charlestown, the English attaché of the Neapolitan embassy. I have seen him many times before, and he is very wealthy."

"All the better for us, Joanitta," Sataniello answered, "Why it is Providence that sends these two men after us. Leave all, then, to me; you will soon see what the Boy Brigand can do. I have in my pocket a muffler which can stop any cries, however loud, emanating from the most powerful lungs. Wait only for an instant, and you will confess with me that you never saw a thing clever done. This night, Joanitta! I will make at least a couple of thousands pounds.

The girl's anxiety for the Boy Brigand was now to its culminating point, and when she heard Sataniello speaking as he had done, she immediately believed that her lover's brain was wandering under some momentaneous lunacy,—that the danger at hand was so great that his imagination was seized by some unaccountable hallucination; but that he was still in his right senses was the last thing which occurred to the pretty Joanitta.

"You see that hedge yonder, don't you, Joanitta?" The Boy Brigand inquired.

"What about it?" the maiden answered.

"Well, not ten yards behind there is a chaise awaiting me, with two of the swiftest horses that ever drew vehicle. If all is lost our means of escape are close at hand. Two men are only against us. One is tall enough, it is true. I know him well. I have seen him before. He is a bold, courageous fellow; I dare say I will have tight-work with him. But the other, who do you say he is, a nobleman? Why I will carry him away on my shoulders, and I will amuse my band for days to come with a live lord, until I can command a high ransom for him. Oh how inconsiderate some people are to be sure," the Boy Brigand continued. "Now if Lord Charlestown only minded his own business, he would not get into the pickle that awaits him to night."

"Speak lower," Joanitta pursued, "they are coming closer upon us."

This last sentence died upon Joanitta's lips.

Captain Wogan, accompained by Lord Charlestown, had surrounded Sataniello and Joanitta in a spot, behind which was a thick bough, a cluster of branches and trees, and which hid the deep edge of which we have already spoken.

"I am speaking to Sataniello, the Dark King of the Mountains, am I not?" Captain Wogan inquired.

"You are, sir," the Boy Brigand replied. "What do you require of me? I will be most happy to serve you in any way I can; moreover, finding that you have acted more bravely than prudently by coming only two to capture a man that never surrenders. If you are willing to let me take my departure unmolested, gentlemen, not a hair of your head will I touch; whereas, if on the other hand you show any determination which I may consider detrimental to me, or likely to hinder me in taking to a safe flight—if I consider such a measure necessary, I only say these words in reply:—Beware of the Boy Brigand's wrath justly kindled. Beware of his terrible vengeance!"

"We are not at the theatre of San Carlos, witnessing a representation of the gentleman highwayman, Lord Charlestown continued with more coolness than was advisable under the circumstances. Reply, at once; will you surrender to two English gentlemen who will do you no harm? I, for one, promise you that I will use my utmost influence to preserve you from capital punishment, for I like your manners, and, further, I promise to take care for the future of that pretty little Italian maiden that clings to you so tightly now."

No endeavour had yet been made on either side to have recourse to violence.

"Go your way, and molest me not, gentlemen," the Boy Brigand pursued, stretching forth his finger in an opposite direction from which he was standing.

The flippant impertinence of Lord Charlestown had not yet been noticed, although the passionate and vindictive nature of Joanitta, which was kindled as soon as her lover's fate was called into question, was already wasting her fervent and trembling frame.

"Our position is getting a serious one," Joanitta swiftly whispered into Sataniello's ear, "let us extricate ourselves as soon as possible."

These words produced a startling effect upon Sataniello.

"Out of my path you besotted, fit-for-nothing, aristocrats! I despise you, and I fear you not. Yes, the Boy Brigand defies you! Assistance may arrive unexpectedly to you, and I may then be doomed to be a prisoner, but I will not wait, so, come what may, let me pass!" And Sataniello now endeavoured to make a move from the spot where he stood.

"Oh, quietly, my friend," Captain Wogan pursued. "Surrender at once, I repeat, or you are a dead man!"

And as he spoke he aimed a pocket pistol to the Boy Brigand's forehead. The trigger was already cocked up, and the slightest movement on the part of Captain Wogan would lay Sataniello senseless to the ground.

The Boy Brigand gnashed his teeth!

For once in his life he had been baffled—frustrated in his designs; for once in his life he had found his master in the person of a brave, daring, English officer.

He had been too late!

It is he who should have acted like Captain Wogan had.

He had allowed the grass to grow under his feet, as a common saying expresses it; and he had been the victim of his procrastination. But his delay should be explained.

With a careless forgetfulness, rendered terrible by what was occurring now, the Boy Brigand had forgotten his pistols at Joanitta's abode, and it was only when he required their immediate use that he discovered his absence of mind.

Between life and death did the Boy Brigand now stand.

All the events which we have related, had taken place quicker than any human pen can describe them. The dialogue which had been exchanged, had been rapidly spoken, and the whole intercourse between the Boy Brigand and his pursuer had not lasted above twenty minutes at the utmost.

Joanitta herself was at her wit's end.

She was in an uncertainty, which, without exaggeration, was in her imagination worse to her than death.

She thought at one time of rescuing her lover; but she was closely held a prisoner by Lord Charlestown, who seemed to take a delight in pressing close to his breast the heaving chest of the lovely maiden.

The Boy Brigand saw the eyes of his lordship glistening with those sparks of brightness which are to be witnessed in those who are exceedingly pleased with occurrences of this life, provided it satisfy their minds—gratifies their wishes; and, notwithstanding his rage he was unable to help himself,—and yet he could not dash to the ground that effeminate nobleman, from whose grasp Joanitta could easily have freed herself, did she not by her struggle fear to endanger her lover's life. For she knew from the determination which overspread Captain Wogan's features, that he would have discharged his pistol as freely as he would have given her a kiss.

Things, meanwhile, were in this state, when the sound of footsteps were heard close at hand.

"Here! here!" Lord Charlestown exclaimed, "Whoever you are, give us whatever assistance you can to help us to become masters of Sataniello, the Dark King of the Mountains!"

The Boy Brigand gasped for breath at this particular moment.

The moonlight streamed full upon his features, and seeing the frightful expression of Sataniello's countenance, Joanitta uttered a piercing cry of undescribable terror.

It was all over with them!

To escape was nigh impossible; the Boy Brigand thought again and again; and thus pondering, the cold steel of the muzzle of the pistol which rested upon his forehead kept ever present before his mind the horrible and sudden death which awaited him, were he to make the slightest attempt to fly away. And he stood still, his feet rooted to the ground, and his body shaking nervously; his heart, subject to throbbing palpitations; his mind a prey to the most excruciating thoughts; his cheeks as pale as death! But his anxiety of mind was too great to last, and ere long he would succumb were no change to take place.

Fortunately the footsteps were now plainly discernible, and the crushing of the boot against the various pebbles which covered the ground struck the ear as becoming every second more distinct.

And, after a mute and breathless suspense, Pamela's features appeared.

And the Giant's huge frame followed.

At first the latter was uncertain to which side he would range himself, as Pamela's advice had, in a great measure, tended to alienate whatever good feeling the Giant might have had for his chief.

However, quick and instantaneous reflection told him that they both swam in the same boat, that if Sataniello perished, ere long a similar doom would be his lot; after all, Sataniello was his captain and chief. He was in trouble, it was his duty to come to his rescue, and to protect him in the hour of need.

Pamela whispered a syllable in the Giant's ear.

Curious to say, after the sentiments which we have heard her express, she was bidding her lover to rid the handsome Sataniello from Captain Wogan's custody.

"Who have you got there?" the Giant inquired, in a rough voice, trying to assume the manner of an ignorant peasant.

"Sataniello, the Boy Brigand!"

"Oh, it aint he," the Giant pursued; "you may as well let that man be free. Sataniello is an ugly, carrotty, red-haired fellow! I saw him once; and I would not forget him in a hurry."

"Will you lay hold of him, I demand of you, in the name of outraged justice?" Captain Wogan inquired from the Giant, in a feverish tone, rendered the more excitable by the fear of losing his prey, relating to whose identity he had no doubt. "Will you, or will you not, do what I bid you?"

"Now be cool, my friend, and do not excite yourself," the Giant pursued. "Of course I will make him a prisoner; there is rather a handsome reward offered for his apprehension, and a poor farmer like me may have it as well as anybody else; for I am sure such gentlefolks as you would never dream of laying claim to it."

It would have been impossible for anyone, had that one been the most experienced detective that Scotland Yard ever produced, to have been able to tell how the Giant intended to act.

The Boy Brigand's curiosity was intense.

Joanitta's impatience also was such as to cause her heart to heave heavily, and once she thought her last hour had arrived, so strong, and so piercing was the sudden sensation which she experienced in the region of the heart.

"All right, my friends," the Giant began, "Sataniello will be safely located to night within the walls of the city prison. Let me seize him, and once within my grasp, I answer for him. Only remove this pistol; for, although I am not a coward, I hate the sight of fire-arms."

"Moreover, when placed in the hands that do not know how to use them at the proper time," Sataniello coldly and fearlessly and quickly pursued.

As soon as the weapon had been withdrawn, with the swiftness of a tiger, he rushed upon Captain Wogan—who, believing himself surrounded by friends, was too thunderstruck with the treason of the Giant to realise at once the real nature of his critical position. And Sataniello, having become possessed of the Captain's pistol, exclaimed—

"As you did not take away my life," the Boy Brigand observed, in his fiendish rage, his eyes darting fire, his lips quivering with heavenly joy at his unexpected escape, "I will only leave you a little keepsake: I will break you this arm off, and make you insensible for a while, otherwise you will be in our way."

And, ere the captain could make a movement, Sataniello discharged his pistol through his late pursuer's right shoulder.

By a wayward turn of destiny the roles had been altered once more.

The arm of the captain fell pendant by his side, his face became gradually whiter and whiter, and he would have fallen senseless to the ground, had not the Giant seized hold of the helpless body, and with his two strong arms carried it to the brink of a ditch, where he allowed it to fall stiffly, caring little whether the shock which the captain would experience would convert a necessary wound into a cool-blooded murder.

Lord Charlestown, who had witnessed the deed, uttered a cry of surprise; but he soon recovered his self-composure.

"My boys, do not go to the same extremities with me as you have done with poor Wogan," he coolly pursued; "I have got a little cash in my pocket, and a splendid repeater, that I got at Dent's three days before I left London; you are welcome to it—it keeps very good time. But do not have recourse to any unnecessary violence."

Lord Charlestown pronounced these words, as far as appearances went, as quietly as he would have asked the waiter of an hotel to bring up a glass of sherry and bitters. A great many men—for instance, the army contractor—become cowards all in a moment; but Lord Charlestown belonged to a family which had won its title and crests in the days when courage and manliness led to honour and fortune, and he was a true representative of his fearless and valiant ancestors.

"And what are you going to do with me?" his lordship inquired.

"Take you away to the mountains, so as to obtain a good ransom for your gentle blood; and if the money is not forthcoming within a given period, you will be put to death, as a matter of course!"

"As a matter of course!" Lord Charlestown pursued. "Why, you Italian bandits are the most extraordinary individuals I ever saw. However, if I must go with you, I shall. I came to Italy for pleasure, but I had no idea that, alike Monte Christo, the hero of a French novel, I would make a personal acquaintance with brigands. However, let us sally forth,—it is no use for me to shriek, it would be useless. But as you only want my money, and not my blood, I will go with you with pleasure, however reluctant I may be to part with the coin when the time comes."

And surrounded by Sataniello, the Giant, and Joanitta, Lord Charlestown walked on; and they soon found a path which led to a gateway, through which they went, and in a few steps they stood by the side of an elegant travelling post-chaise.

"Pray step in, my lord! Allow me to introduce you to Mrs. Joanitta Sataniello, my wife, my lord. There is also a friend of mine, whom we call the Giant. I am sorry that Miss Pamela, another lady, is not able to come with us—it would have made the journey more pleasant, as, according to my opinion, female society always tends to enliven the weary hours of man's existence. And what do you think yourself, my lord?"

The Boy Brigand uttered these words in so mild a tone—the bow which he made to his lordship as he spoke was so graceful, the unaffected ease which attended the whole of his movements was indeed so natural—that it would have been scarcely possible to imagine how Sataniello could have attained, in so short a period, the refined and polished manners that many a gentleman of the land would have envied.

Although the night was pretty dark, still there was light enough for the personages who composed the group before us to have a full view of each other; and Lord Charlestown was not slow in perceiving the slight incident to which we have alluded, and it struck him that the Boy Brigand was one of those extraordinary highwaymen, about whom we read in books, and who nevertheless are frequently to be met with in Italy.

For there to be a bandit is an occupation to which many indeed do resort—and moreover, at the time when the events which we describe occurred, the police was anything but well kept—and there was then, as there is still now, a great scope for the display of the bold adventurous talents that Sataniello possessed to a high degree.

As the story proceeds, the lives and adventures of the strange men that formed Sataniello's band will be fully related; and it will be seen that a few of the Boy Brigand's followers were individuals who had been born in the higher classes of life, and who, by an unaccountable succession of unexpected events, had been compelled to fly to the mountains to obtain a living, which they were unable to obtain in a more honourable, but, certainly, less profitable manner.

Lord Charlestown, we have seen, had not replied at once to Sataniello, so he repeated his query,

and after having again alluded to the subject of the ladies—to whom the Boy Brigand, as we have already witnessed ourselves, was perhaps a trifle too partial for his age—he concluded a long-winded sentence, by saying—

"And do you not agree with me, my lord, when I say that, without womanly society, life would be irksome to many?"

Strange as the question was, his lordship could not help exclaiming, with that carelessness that Irishmen will display in the most critical circumstances—

"Egad! I consider you a most original highwayman—and, above all, one of the most gallant fellows that I have ever met!

"I am glad to hear, my lord, that you have formed so high an opinion of me," Sataniello quickly retorted. "It sounds well in my ears, for it at least leads me to hope that you will have no occasion to regret the little trip which you are making with us. The only thing which I am afraid you will dislike is the monetary part of the transaction. But live and let live is a saying which I thoroughly appreciate. You are a nobleman—I am an outcast; you are rich—I am poor; and to establish an equilibrium between our social positions, divide our means for once in the way is what I always intend to carry out, where I will, with you or anybody else, have a chance to do so."

"How much do you want? For God's sake, speak! You are making a great mistake in fancying that I am a wealthy man. I am as needy as yourself. Be reasonable, and do not extort too much from me."

Thus speaking, Lord Charlestown pricked up his ears—like we all do—when our finances are threatened to be taxed in some sense or another.

"I will let you know that in good time, my lord," Sataniello replied. "But everything in its place; meanwhile, make your mind easy. You will acquaint me with the real state of your affairs, and if, from what I hear, I consider that I should be lenient, I will act accordingly. At present, however, I could give you no decisive answer, as I have not yet made up my mind with regard to the ransom—at least, so far as the amount is concerned."

The Boy Brigand accentuated the word "amount" in a manner which was anything but pleasant to his lordship.

"Why not conclude the matter at once?" Lord Charlestown began anew. "I would give you a cheque as readily now as I would to-morrow, as I see no other way of parting with you. I have my note-book by me, and a speedy determination on your part might save a good deal of delay."

"I dare say that would suit you very well, my lord," the Boy Brigand replied. "Do you see any green in the corner of my eye?"

"I am at a loss to understand," replied his lordship, who detected not the meaning of the Boy Brigand's vulgar phrase, although the look—the sly look—with which he accompanied his speech required no explanation.

"I will soon explain myself."

"How so?"

"Easily enough."

"Go on, go on," Lord Charlestown pursued; "come to the point at once; I am in dreadful suspense."

"I will not keep you so long, then," Sataniello concluded. "If I were to let you go free, you might give me—what do you call it, a cheque?"

"Yes, a cheque!" his lordship echoed; "and, candidly, do you mean to tell me that you do not

THE BOY BRIGAND; OR, THE DARK KING OF THE MOUNTAINS.

know what I mean by a cheque?" Lord Charlestown inquired.

"That I certainly do not," Sataniello replied; "I must plead the utmost ignorance on this head, notwithstanding the flattering compliment which you have just paid me."

"Look here, then, sir," Lord Charlestown began, "here is my book; if I sign my name at the bottom of this paper, and tear out one of the fly leaves, you can take it to my banker; and, as it says pay to bearer or to my order, the whatever sum is mentioned you are bound to get—no questions would be asked, as in your hands this slip would be as good as gold."

"That's all very fine," Sataniello pursued; "but I will have no paper, my lord—I will have the ransom in gold, and nothing but gold."

"You may please yourself about that," his lordship replied; "but you are losing your valuable time—once rid of me you might try the same thing with somebody else."

"That is very palpable, certainly," Sataniello pursued; "but what guarantee have I that if I set you at liberty you will pay me at once? Why, you would go to your banker, and say to him. 'The Dark King of the Mountains made me his prisoner—compelled me to give him an order for such an amount. Having a due regard for my head, and labouring under a natural fear, I did what he requested me at the time; but do not pay him a penny piece.' Further, my lord, you would let the detective know all about the little business, and doubtless I would be pinned as dead as mutton, when I would go down to draw the 'yellow boys.' No fear! I know a trick worth two of that; and mind this—you do not leave my presence until I get for your valuable skin that price which I think I am fairly entitled to receive for it."

Sataniello uttered this last sentence in such a determined manner that Lord Charlestown adopted the same plan that any other wise man would have adopted under similar circumstances, and he remained silent.

In the first onslaught his lordship had looked upon his meeting with the Boy Brigand as a very good joke, which would make a capital story for an after-dinner chat at the club; but he was beginning to get tired of the Boy Brigand's confounded twaddle, and, to be candid, and express ourselves as he would have done, he was at length getting literally disgusted with the cool way with which Sataniello was treating a man of his high rank.

"And are you ready to take your departure, my lord?" Joanitta now inquired, in a sarcastical tone of voice—at which his lordship, despite his awkward position, could not help smiling, considering the pretty lips which pronounced the words alluded to. "Perhaps you may have some message to send to your hotel before leaving town so abruptly; if so, we can easily get some one who will punctually attend to any wish of yours. There is a dashing girl of the name of Pamela standing outside, who is all attention."

At that moment the post-boy appeared at the carriage door. He was not in the secret of what had taken place; he had been hired by the Boy Brigand, and he was anxious to sally forth on his journey, for the sooner he would reach the end the sooner would he return to his home.

He was one of those wide-awake customers who see at a glance what is going on, and although a youth he was no exception to the rule, and No. 1 was paramount with him. Thus he had wisely kept his eyes closed. There are none so blind as those who will not see, and not for an instant had he dreamt of attempting to call any assistance to rescue his lordship, whose rank he was far from knowing. He was, moreover, aware of this—that brigands are a generous class of men, and as easily as they get their money do they squander it; and he had come to the determination that it would be much more in accordance with his own interest to help Sataniello, whose band he would willingly have joined, than it would have been to try to free his prisoner, who was a stranger to him, and whose gratitude was too problematical, in his opinion, to be safely relied upon.

Besides, the last step was one which he could not have carried out successfully, even had he been willing or anxious to do so; and if he failed, he was sure of losing his head—a perspective which would cool the mind of many a more enterprising and courageous being than an Italian post-boy.

It was getting late, and Sataniello, growing gradually impatient, placed his head outside the window, and in a commanding and peremptory tone of voice bid the driver, who had already regained his seat, to start onwards, as there was nothing to detain him any longer.

Some of my readers, perhaps, may ask how it was that in such a public place as Tivoli Gardens, the sounds of the pistol which had shot Captain Wogan to the ground had kindled no alarm; and how it was also that the Boy Brigand had been allowed to act as he had done, and to accomplish his dark deeds, without his behaviour being noticed or heeded by any unexpected visitor.

To this again we think it our duty to give an answer—

At eleven o'clock at night there were always fireworks taking place at Tivoli Gardens—an incident which Sataniello had been made aware of by Joanitta—and had endeavoured to effect his escape precisely at the moment when the visitor's attention was too much engrossed by the entertainment provided for them to allow them to stray along the footpaths, where they must have become the witnesses of that which we have spared no trouble in minutely describing for our perusers' enlightenment. The Boy Brigand had acted as we have seen he had done.

Meanwhile the chaise rolled on, and his lordship, reclining upon the soft cushions which lined the inside of the vehicle, was sleeping deeply.

He had tried as long as he could to keep opened his weary eyelids, but although he was a man whose nerves were not easily shook, still, for all that, he had witnessed that evening too many new scenes, not to be, to a certain extent, awestruck by them. He had tried to think, but reflection hanging heavily upon his mind, he had sought in repose this quietness which he indeed greatly required after the excitement which he had undergone.

The Giant, who had remained silent also during the whole time which had elapsed since his lordship had entered the chaise, indulged also in a half doze, and the only person who, properly speaking, was on the watch was Sataniello.

The chaise had now reached the summit of a hill, when the sounds of several horses' hoof were heard dashing along upon the causeway far behind.

At the back of the vehicle there was a small aperture, covered with a piece of glass, in truth the whole size and dimension was not above half a foot long and of about the same width.

Sataniello rose up, and looked through it.

In the movement which he made to stand upright he awoke his lordship from his drowsy slumbers.

"Confound you, William!" the nobleman said, fancying himself in his chamber speaking to his footman, he having not regained yet his consciousness. "Why the dence do you awake me so early?" and the distinguished scion of an old house reclined again upon the cushion, and having seemingly made himself comfortable, snored again, and more deeply this time than he had hitherto done.

"Joanitta," the Boy Brigand whispered into the girl's ear, "we are pursued; I think that we are followed by mounted soldiers."

The girl answered not for a while.

"I hope you are mistaken," she muttered after awhile, and she placed her arm around Sataniello, as if she wished to make sure of her lover's presence.

Her hand had reached the region of Sataniello's heart, and she felt his breast heaving heavily, and her own heart too began to beat with quick, rapid pulsations.

The Boy Brigand sat down again.

The noise seemed to have diminished.

And he breathed like guilty men only can breathe when pursued by the hands of justice. And when again he was master of himself he leant over the Giant's shoulders.

The Giant at first heard not Sataniello.

He shook him violently.

"There are soldiers following us, I fear," the Boy Brigand began. "Have you got your pistols loaded? Let us be ready to defend ourselves in case of an attack. Oh, God! Oh, God!" Sataniello muttered, "Joanitta, it was the worst day's luck that ever occurred to me. I have only one pistol, and that is the one which I wrung from Captain Wogan's grasp; and of what avail, I ask, would one single instrument like that be were to be surrounded by five or six men with their double barrelled carbines?"

Sataniello's words were not long ere they found a reply in the Giant's mouth.

"Let them come, Captain," he sullenly whispered, "let them come, and I will take a steady aim; if I miss them with my pistol, there is a knife, which is not made for children to wield. I will teach them a lesson or two."

As long as the chaise could keep on the pace which it had hitherto assumed—as long as the horses which were drawing the vehicle would dash on at the rate at which they had since they had left Tivoli Gardens—the Boy Brigand's mind was not ill at rest, for he knew that ere long the windings of the road would bring him within the vicinity of a neighbourhood which he knew well, among sinuosities in the mountains familiar only to himself and the band, where he might find a safe refuge from his pursuers, and from which he could command such a position as to enable him to shoot at the soldiers sent after him without his presence being heeded by any one, being all the time as safe as if he had been within the rocky walls of his abode.

And onward the chaise flew, and nothing was heard beyond the rattle of the wheels over the rough pebbles; and onward it dashed, kindling sparks of fire from the stoning as it rolled along; and still Lord Charlestown slept, and still Sataniello kept a steady, constant, and breathless watch.

The noise behind had subsided—only for awhile, however, for ere five minutes had elapsed again it was audible.

Carefully this time, for fear of awaking Lord Charlestown, did the Boy Brigand look through the little opening in the back part of the chaise.

taken.

Sad reality stared him full in the face.

His pursuers could not see him—could not hear him, for they were too far distant from him; so outside did he place his features, and in a low, hoarse whisper, he exclaimed to the post-boy—

"Drive on, drive on, my boy! I am Sataniello, the Boy Brigand, the King of the Mountains! A guinea for every hundred yards will you get! Fear my vengeance if I am caught!"

This sentence produced an instantaneous effect upon the youth to whom it was addressed, and click, clack, went the whip—and the vehicle bounded upwards, and it shook as if the springs were about to be dashed to a thousand pieces.

And now for a frightful check, and Lord Charlestown was thrown right off from his seat into the arms of the Giant, who, being of no very amiable disposition, sent his lordship back to his place with one of those blows peculiarly his own, which, for a minute at least, deprived him of the power of speech.

My lord, thus abruptly shook, rubbed his eyes, and fancying himself in a madhouse, spoke not.

The noise was getting every instant more distinct. The sound of the horses' hoofs was every minute becoming plainer, and the radiant brightness of the moon shone upon the breastplates and steel helmets of the pursuers, whom Sataniello had no difficulty in recognising for a detachment of Papal dragoons.

However swift and gamely horses may be on leaving the stable by a fine summer's night, the cooling breeze of a genial atmosphere favouring the start, when dashed along in their onward course by a bold equestrian with a sharp-cutting whip, a shining pair of good steel spurs; however anxious and ready the cattle to clear the distance, while league after league, mile after mile, it hurries on towards its destination, there is a certain time in every journey when the metal must lose its original brilliancy, when, with limbs stiffened by too great exertions in stepping over the ground—now dashing along the soft bank, then over the hard stoning of the high road—the best blood that ever was put in harness must slacken its staying powers, reduce for a moment its pace, ere, with foaming mouth and breathing nostrils, it assumes once again its rapid trot—its swift, bounding canter.

Thus the critical hour in every traveller's journey, which we have endeavoured to reproduce as graphically as it laid in our power, had sounded for Sataniello.

Heartrending but true, it was unfortunately the case with him. Very nigh exhausted by the last gamely effort which the horses which drew the post-chaise had made to answer the well-known call of their rider, they could no longer run with that rapidity which Sataniello wished them, and which he would have considered slow had they gone on as quick as lightning, so feverish and over-exerted was his imagination — upon so high a pedestal did he place his freedom, the forfeiture of which led to prison—to an infamous death on the gallows.

And he raved, and his eyes kindled with a fiendish rage; and he would murder Joanitta; he would murder Lord Charlestown ; aye, and the Giant too! if he could; and destroy himself afterwards, if a weapon was at hand, sooner than to surrender alive! sooner than to lose his liberty! sooner than to allow himself to be captured.

The vehicle had now reached the bottom of a hill, and it arrived to a spot from which three roads branched off in different directions.

A huge piece of stone stood in the middle, and

upon it was erected a large wooden cross, beneath which an altar, devoted to the worship of some known saint, figured prominently.

These signs are to be witnessed in nearly every country where Roman Catholicism is the religion of the state; and the world knows that no place on the Continent is more given to superstition than Italy.

It was so at the period when we write; but since the events which we have endeavoured to describe great changes have been wrought.

The gallant Garibaldi — the greatest hero of modern times, the true friend of liberty, the disinterested patriot—had opened the eyes of his countrymen, and plainly shown them that the time has come for a great nation to awake from its lethargy, and, like the phœnix that rises out of its ashes, to fulminate brilliantly and prominently in the bloom of a new era.

CHAPTER X.

THE BOY BRIGAND IS NEARLY CAPTURED — PRESENCE OF MIND OF JOANITTA — SATANIELLO'S HOME IN THE MOUNTAINS.

"HERE they come!" Joanitta exclaimed. "I hear the horses' hoofs plainly! In an instant they will be down upon us!"

"Fear not, Joanitta," Sataniello replied. "While I am with you, you are safe! If I must shed the last drop of my blood, I will; but never will I give myself up!"

The sounds of the horses' hoofs were every instant becoming plainer and plainer. In a second or two they would be within a few arms' lengths.

Their pursuers would be close to them.

Lord Charlestown now attempted to look out of the chaise.

"Be still, will you, my good friend!" the Giant said. "If you say a word you will be sent to a place where I should think you do not care to go just now."

And he placed his huge palm upon the nobleman's shoulder as he spoke.

"Do not handle me!" Lord Charlestown exclaimed. "Do not touch me, otherwise I will scream as loud as I can!"

"Will you?"

"Yes!"

"Try it, my friend! and if your lips are opened to seek assistance, let me, beforehand, inform you, that you will never open them again—in this world, at least!"

Lord Charlestown looked at the Giant. There was too much earnestness in the phrase which he uttered to trifle any longer with a brigand—with a man who evidently meant what he said.

The chaise darted on; and it had to slacken its course, as it was now within a small park, where there was scarcely room for the vehicle to move.

"Oh, heaven protect us!" Joanitta muttered.

Ere she had concluded the sentence in a half-audible voice, the chaise was surrounded by a brigadier and four mounted troopers; they belonged to the Papal dragoons. They were fine-looking men; and, from their appearance, it was no difficult matter to perceive that they would fight—they would struggle with any antagonist, however powerful, sooner than to allow those they sought to escape from them after a weary pursuit.

In no way undaunted, the post-boy smacked his whip, and went on.

"Stop, will you?" the brigadier now said.

He was a tall, handsome Italian, mounted on a grey charger; and the tone of his voice was anything but reassuring to such beings as those who, alike the Boy Brigand, the Giant, and Joanitta, were placed in such a critical position.

The post-boy went on still, and took no heed of what he heard.

"I say! Halloa, there! Will you stop?"

And the brigadier, followed by his four men, was close behind the vehicle.

The post-boy still kept going on as fast as the narrowness of the road would allow him.

Will you stop your course, I ask," the brigadier again inquired, but this time in an impatient, excited manner.

"Stop, yes—what do you want? Why do you wish us to stay? I have got some miles to go from the house, and my time is my money."

"I know that; still, will you yield, I have a few words to say."

"All right, governor."

There was a silence.

"What is it?" the post-boy continued.

"Who have you got within."

"Three gentlemen and a lady."

"Who are they?"

"How am I to know? I was hired this morning by a sober, respectable party—he told my master that I should wait for him at the hotel of San Carlo, on the piazza. I never asked him any question—post-boys seldom do; but he seemed to me to 'be all there.'"

"And do you come from the hotel of San Carlo?" the brigadier inquired again, endeavouring to scan the features of the driver over the carriage.

"Of course I do—ain't I telling you so for the last hour."

"No nonsense, if you please. What are you talking about?"

"I am talking the truth. You wish me to tell you who I have got within my chaise—I tell you over again—three gentlemen and a lady. You further ask who they are? I tell you again—I do not know."

"Be civil."

"I am."

"You are not."

"Why, look here, governor," the post-boy continued, "it is no use my remaining at a stand still here; if you have got anything else to inquire from me do so at once, as I am in a hurry."

"I do not care about that."

"You must, though."

"Indeed!"

"Yes, I am the agent of higher authorities that ever had to control you, and I am now doing my duty, and endeavouring to serve the ends of justice."

"Oh, that is another thing altogether; I did not know that. Of course, if you are looking out after any one it is right that you should do so. I am sure I will give you every information I possibly can."

"That's better."

"I am glad to hear you say so. My friend, I will do all I can, but you cannot expect me to give any details, which sounds as Greek to me."

And the post-boy thus speaking turned round upon his saddle, and his glance betrayed the keenest attention."

"And you come from the hôtel San Carlo?"

THE GIANT SHOWING HIS STRENGTH.

"Yes."

"When did you leave Rome?"

"At eight o'clock to-night."

"You have been a long time stepping over the ground."

"I think not, brigadier; I have whipped my horses as often as I deemed it fair to the poor brutes. They cantered as fast as they could; but poor old Bess has been a long time upon the road, and she is not a two-year-old; you cannot expect a horse of ten years of age to run as fast as a younger one. Now, if you wish me to talk to you about cattle I will."

The post-boy felt quite happy—he was brought upon a subject which he thoroughly understood, and

my readers are fully aware (if they are not let me acquaint them with the fact) that all those who have to deal with horse-flesh are thoroughly at home when the breed is called into question, and there is no topic upon which they delight more to indulge in than that one which a long experience has enabled them to become masters of.

Thus he was about to enter into a long desserta-tion of all the merits and demerits of the mounts that he ever had since the age of thirteen when the brigadier reverted his attention to things which, let it be confessed, were more to the point.

"And you do not know who your travellers are?"

"Well, sir, what is all this about?" a womanly

voice inquired. And Joanitta placed her soft figure outside the window.

The brigadier contemplated the pretty countenance of the young girl, which was considerably set to advantage by the rays of the moon, which now shone forth. He was rather taken aback; he was sent in the pursuit of a bold, merciless, cruel, Brigand, so he thought; and, instead of an ugly-looking customer, he detected the lovely visage of Joanitta.

Lord Charlestown in the meantime knew not how to act. If he said a word, he might be freed from the custody of the Boy Brigand, and save himself a large sum of money; while, on the other hand, if he remained silent, he would be doomed to undergo a long captivity which he by no means relished.

"Madam," the brigadier continued, "I am discharging my duty. I have been informed that Sataniello, the Dark King of the Mountains, was on this road, and, as a matter of course, I stopped you to inquire whether he is within your vehicle."

"Strange proceeding on your part," Joanitta continued, carelessly, "to hinder a travelling party from reaching its destination. We know nothing of Sataniello, the Dark King of the Mountains, as you call him. I believe——"

"I must satisfy my mind about that," the brigadier replied.

"You are at leisure to do so."

Joanitta had scarcely pronounced this last sentence than her arm was smartly pinched, and in turning round she saw the Boy Brigand, who was looking daggers at her.

"Why do you speak as you have done?" he whispered, suddenly.

The Giant in the meantime kept Lord Charlestown's mouth closely muffled, although he felt confident that his lordship would not endanger his life by calling out for assistance, which would be fatal to him; still he wished to be on the safe side.

"What do you wish me to do?" Joanitta inquired.

"Just to let me have a peep within. If I saw Sataniello, the Dark King of the Mountains, I would know him in a hundred."

"Would you?"

"I think so."

"What kind of an individual is he? I have heard a good deal about him; and if you say that he is close at hand, I would request of you to keep company with us; for, if he perceived so good a detachment escorting our little party he would not feel inclined to rifle us of what we possess."

"I will do this if you like," the brigadier replied; "but I must first know whom I am escorting."

"My husband, Sir."

Joanitta pronounced these words as if any farther question would be nothing short of impertinence.

"And who is your husband, pray, if it is a fair question to ask?"

"Lord Charlestown."

The brigadier was already in the act of dismounting to carry out his threat, when the girl's answer induced him to alter his line of conduct.

"I beg your pardon," he said, "for intruding upon your company, still, as I have my doubts, I must clear my mind ere I leave you."

"Very well, Sir."

"Is Lord Charlestown inside?"

"Yes."

"Can I speak to him?"

"He is asleep. I will awake him."

The Giant now shook Lord Charlestown by the arm.

"My lord," he said, "if you betray us, you can, but do not expect to be taken alive," "I will stab you as true as I am here, for there is no humbug about me. If I am to be executed for what I have done, it matters but little how many murders I add to my list."

Lord Charlestown heard these words whispered into his ears—his teeth began to rattle, and although he was unwilling to show that he was cowed by the determined speech of his terrible companion, he could not refrain his whole body from shaking nervously.

The brigadier and his men were close behind—he could hear their voices as plainly as if they were beside him, and it was hard, indeed, it must be admitted, that he should be compelled to lose the only chance of escape he might meet with for many days to come, without saying a word in his own defence.

When Joanitt ahad spoken, the brigadier had scanned her pretty features, and as it was currently rumoured (the tongue of gossip always exaggerating and falsifying the real state of things) that Sataniello had an abhorrence of women, and that he took no uncommon delight in placing females through the most awful tortures, he began to think that he had acted rather rashly in stopping a chaise wherein were conveyed so illustrious a personage as a nobleman and his wife.

How the brigadier and his men had been sent by the police after Sataniello, and how it occurred that he had been followed, requires explanation.

Scarcely had the vehicle in which the Boy Brigand Joanitta, and Lord Charlestown entered, taken departure from Rome than some visitors who had been to Tivoli Gardens had strayed towards the spot where the events which we have related had taken place.

The body of Captain Wogan had attracted the attention of one of the party; and a bold young fellow had found his way to the ditch, and brought upon his shoulders the senseless body of the gallant officer.

For some time he had been unable to answer their queries; finally he recovered for a while his consciousness—but it was short and brief, and the only words which he uttered were—

"Sataniello, the Boy Brigand . . . the Dark King of the Mountains, is my assassin."

With his finger he had pointed towards the direction where he had last seen the Boy Brigand. He had been pressed for further information, but the pain which he felt being too acute, he had again fainted away, without being for the time able to throw any further light upon the matter. The alarm had been given, and the soldiers had been ordered to beat the high road, and thus they had come upon the track of the Boy Brigand. Had the mounted party been informed that Lord Charlestown had been made a prisoner, and his precious person taken away to obtain a ransom at some future day, it would have been very probable that he would have acted more cautiously and more prudently than we have seen him doing up to the present period.

He had expected to find the Boy Brigand surrounded by his band, and he had accordingly brought along with him a heavy detachment, expecting that he would have a serious battle to go through ere he would become the master of a brigand, whose body, whether dead or alive, would have been paid for by the Roman authorities with its weight of gold.

To find him in a vehicle—in a post-chaise—was the last thought which came to his mind, although he knew the strange ways such men as those belonging

THE BOY BRIGAND ; OR, THE DARK KING OF THE MOUNTAINS.

to Sataniello's stamp, will have recourse to seek safety in a hasty flight.

The brigadier, therefore, resolved that he should leave no stone unturned ere he satisfied his mind that Sataniello was not within his reach, for nothing would have afforded him more disappointment than to be told afterwards—

"Why, you came upon Sataniello, the Boy Brigand, and you allowed him to escape. You are a fine one, indeed, to be a brigadier in the Papal dragoons !"

It may be as well here to inform our readers that the Papal dragoons are about the only corps of soldiers which are kept up in a state of real efficiency and of good drill by the Roman minister of war. The foot regiments are an indolent set of individuals, officered by men who hold the priestcraft in too high a respect ever to be able to make a good soldier; and the manner, indeed, in which they behaved during the Italian campaign—the hasty and cowardly way in which they surrendered to Victor Emanuel's troops, although commanded by De Lamoriciere, a brave general, who had led the French flag to victory more than once in the sunny regions of Algeria (a French possession abroad), has long ago shown us that they were fitter, indeed, to be constantly bending upon their marrow bones in churches than to discharge a soldier's duty, which is to fight and conquer—never to say die—to be fearless of dangers, and to shed his last drop of blood for his country's glory, sooner than to allow himself to become a prisoner of war.

To hold the same brave and courageous ideas that prompted every action of the Boy Brigand, and to turn them to good account, and not to the pursuit of the wayward and dangerous life that Sataniello had chosen since the day when he left the city of Rome.

"Do you say, madam," the brigadier resumed, apparently addressing Joanitta, "that your husband, Lord Charlestown, is within."

"I am," exclaimed Lord Charlestown, unable to resist any longer the temptation of proclaiming his identity, and endeavouring to place his face outside to confront the brigadier.

It would have been much more to his advantage had Lord Charlestown adhered to the strictest silence. Finding no one to answer him, the brigadier might have guessed that there was something wrong; but finding so quick a reply to his query he took it for granted that he had hindered a respectable travelling party from proceeding onwards.

However, he had still his doubts, and he still kept on questioning the travellers.

"My husband, Lord Charlestown," Joanitta replied, in answer to some of the brigadier's questions, "is a special queen's messenger, entrusted with a very particular message from the English Government to the Court of Naples. If all the details which I give you are not sufficient to satisfy you, it would be better for you to keep on following our vehicle until we come to the British Embassy, when you can make all the necessary inquiries relating to Lord Charlestown's respectability."

There was a sneering tone plainly discernible in Joanitta's voice. One or two questions more would he ask, and then he would retire, and return to Rome, from whence he had come.

"I would like to see your passport," he said.

"You may see it, if you like," Joanitta replied boldly, "but it will place us to a good deal of trouble, as it is in one of the boxes beneath the carriage."

"I dare say it is all fair and square," the brigadier

pursued. "Can I do anything for you, my Lord Charlestown ?"

The brigadier pronounced these words with an evident intention of endeavouring to make his peace with a nobleman whose vehicle he had kept at a stand still for at least half-an-hour.

"No, no," his lordship replied, in a voice so faint that it was scarcely heard,

The brigadier, however, caught the sound of it.

"I am very sorry," he continued, "that I should have been compelled to hinder you, my lady; but my duty is my excuse. Go on, driver, go on."

And thus speaking the brigadier gave orders to his troop to retrace their steps, and in one minute the horses' hoofs were heard dying in the distance.

His lordship felt sadly crest-fallen indeed, when he saw that he was still Sataniello's prisoner.

He had had, moreover, no other alternative than to act as we have seen he had done, for unless he gave at once a definite answer to the brigadier the Giant's words would have come to pass.

Lord Charlestown's waistcoat had been unfastened by Sataniello. He felt the cold steel of the Giant's poignard touching his skin ; he had chosen the region of the heart, and he knew that a thrust there always tells its tale, so one may easily fancy Lord Charlestown's predicament.

He had no doubt but that if he endeavoured to acquaint the brigadier with the real state of things, his mouth would have been gagged to suffocation ere he could have concluded his story, and the knife plunged into his chest.

Sataniello and the Giant were fearless, resolute characters. What they threatened to do they generally carried out, and Lord Charlestown was as confident as if he had known them for so many years instead of so many hours, that had his two captors been captured through him, never would he leave alive the carriage in which he was seated, and which in its style was a very commodious vehicle.

When silence had again been restored, the Boy Brigand began anew the conversation which had dropped as soon as the brigadier and his troop had retraced their steps.

The respective feelings of all those who composed the company inside the vehicle were too different not to cause them to indulge in the strangest reflections, which it would be too difficult for us to analyse in their minutest accuracy.

Suffice it to say that a human being does not lose a liberty which endangers his life without his mind being a prey to the most extraordinary musings, while another, so placed as the Boy Brigand, does not regain a freedom, and issue from the uncertain trance in which he had been kept without a joy of the highest description—without that inward satisfaction which no pen, however experienced, could adequately describe.

"I think " Sataniello said, as soon as the chaise had reached the end of the narrow passage where it had been journeying, "that we had better go down here and dismiss the post-boy. Yonder I see a path which will lead us to our cavern—to our home, and we might as well do so now as to keep on here. We are now safe, and were we to remain longer within this vehicle the brigadier and his men might become acquainted with some fresh tidings which would induce them to return on our pursuit, and if they have been baffled this time by Joanitta's presence of mind, which I really believed she was far from possessing, on another occasion they might be less easily persuaded. What think you, my Lord Charlestown ?"

My Lord Charlestown thought that there was a

good deal of bold impertinence in his new host's query, but he abstained from mentioning his opinion relating to the same.

"I have always thought," he replied, "that it is always well in this life to make the most of a bad job. I have nothing to say either one way or the other I should imagine, but if I am to go with you, the sooner I am safely located within your roof the better, for I can take the necessary steps then to obtain my delivery."

"Could not have spoken more to the point; you are a gentleman, my lord."

And with this high appreciation of my lord's character, Sataniello bid the post-boy to stay his course.

In an instant his order was obeyed.

"We are agoing to alight here, my boy," Sataniello began. "How much?"

"What you like to give me. I do not have every day such a gallant customer as Sataniello, the Dark King of the Mountains. I have done my best. I have whipped the poor brutes as hard as it laid in my power; and if we were caught it was not their fault; it was owing to this confounded road, which, indeed, seems to have been made in the onslaught to ruin the horses that trot along it."

"Here you are, then; only you must remain dumb about what you know."

And Sataniello placed his hand in his pocket, and gave a few pieces of gold to the post-boy.

The latter never looked at them; the weight was sufficient enough to tell him that he would have no occasion to regret having driven a man who paid him like if he were truly as rich as the name which they had given him, namely, the King of the Mountains.

"I am all right enough, governor," he said; "you need not fear about me. I know that them that hold their tongue never get into trouble; whereas the others that's always a jawing are always connected with some bit of mischief or another. This is how I'll be."

And the post-boy placed significantly his finger across his lips, so as to show Sataniello that he meant what he said.

"Good-bye, Sir!" the post-boy said.

And he stood by the horse's head, as if he seemed reluctant to part from Sataniello.

The Giant, Sataniello, Joanitta, and Lord Charlestown, were now all outside the vehicle, and a picturesque group, indeed, they formed with the different aspects of their attire and their respective appearances.

It was evident that the post-boy wished to speak to Sataniello, and yet was afraid to do so.

"Sir," said he, "I do not like to go away from you; I would prefer a roving, independent sort of life; I am tired of riding along the high road from Rome to Naples, and I long for a change of some kind."

He pronounced these words in a significative manner, that Sataniello, however, detected not at first.

"What do you mean?" he asked. "How can I interfere with you? Your calling is entirely out of my line, and I cannot help you."

"You can, Sir, if you like."

Sataniello felt quite puzzled. He was far from foreseeing in the lad's request the wish which, ere a few minutes would have elapsed, he would express.

"I am standing here, my boy," he continued, "If you have anything to communicate, do so at once, as I have no time to lose. I have paid you handsomely, I should say, for your journey; what more can you want of me?"

"You misunderstand me," the post-boy replied. "God knows, I do not grumble; but I have taken quite a liking to you, Sir, and I would like to remain with you altogether."

The driver pronounced this sentence in an affectionate tone of voice, which Sataniello noticed at once, so he quickly responded—

"Do you want to join my band, then?"

"That's exactly what I should like to do, Sir; you have hit my wish upon the nail. Will you take me?"

"Stand upright, and let us look at you!" Sataniello said.

Joanitta was looking at the post-boy. He noticed the girl's look, and he at once complied with the request.

He was not at all a bad-looking boy—we may say a youth—for the being who had asked Sataniello to allow him to join his band was strong and healthy; and although he was not above five feet six or seven inches high, he was of a strong, healthy build, and looked considerably older than he actually was.

"What's your age?" Sataniello inquired.

"Sixteen years come September," he replied.

"Do you know what you will have to do?"

"No, Sir, I do not; but I am sure it cannot be so very difficult as, perhaps, I may imagine."

"How do you know? you never tried."

"I am aware of that."

"How can you tell that you would be suited for the life such men as we do lead?"

"Because I think I have a taste for it."

"Do you only think so?"

"Oh, no, I am sure of it," the post-boy replied, fearing that Sataniello might refuse to have him were he to prevaricate in anything he gave utterance to.

"Will you take my advice?"

"I will, Sir."

"Will I tell you what that advice is?"

"I wish you would."

"Remain a post-boy, then: you earn an honest living when you return to town; your conscience is clear and your mind easy; whereas if you come with me you will have to perpetrate all kinds of wicked deeds; you will have doubtless to dabble your hands into innocent blood. How would you like that?"

"Would not object to it."

"You would not?"

"No."

"And why do you wish to become a brigand?"

"Because I got no money."

"And do you think that if you were a bandit you would make a fortune?"

"I do."

"Upon what grounds do you back your opinion?"

"Upon what I saw to-day. I have been driving this here pair of horses for this last four years, and the devil an 'aporth can I put by. I have had lots of travellers in my chaise—some were princes, others were soldiers, others were lawyers, others were priests, others were bri——."

"Spout it out, man; do not be afraid to speak," Sataniello pursued, seeing that the post-boy was doubtful as to whether he should call the individual who stood before him by his real name. "Others were brigands, then?" Sataniello inquired.

"Right you are, Sir."

"And who paid you best?"

"The priests and the brigands."

"Why do you not become a priest, then, instead of a brigand?"

"I would not like to be a friar, I would be anything but a priest. But says I to myself, if these two callings can afford to throw money away, it must be a paying game."

"What do you call throwing money away?" Sataniello again interrogated.

"To give a man anything over what he is entitled to."

"Are you of a saving nature, then?"

"No; but although I find fault with others, it would be the very thing I would do myself."

"Are you really anxious to join me?"

"That I am, Sir, and no mistake."

"When will you be at liberty, then?"

"At once," the post-boy replied resolutely.

"What will you do with the chaise?"

"Stick to it."

"What will become of the horses."

"I'll keep them too."

"What will your master say when he finds the hours passing away, the days following each other, and no post-boy returning?"

"Devil a bit would he care about the post-boy, if he got the vehicle and the mounts returned to him."

"You must have been a bad servant to him," Sataniello continued.

"You are mistaken, Sir; I was not."

"Yet you want to leave him?"

"I do."

"Give me your reasons."

"Listen, Sir, and I'll give them to you. My master is a very rich chap, so they say, but as I never reckoned with him, I cannot say whether it is right or not; however, he could afford to give me more than he does."

"What does he give you?"

Then the post-boy replied to the Boy Brigand, and gave him the amount he earned daily in the Italian money currency; but as our readers might not understand it, we may as well calculate the amount ourselves; so we will infer that the post-boy earned that amount of Roman money which would be equivalent to a shilling in this country.

"Do you only get a shilling a day?" the Boy Brigand resumed.

"That's all."

"Does not that keep you?"

"It would if I was by myself."

"Surely you are not married yet?"

"I am not."

"Surely you do not keep a woman, either?"

"I do not."

"Where does the money go, then?"

"You forget, sir, that one sometimes has a family."

"I must admit I did; but I can explain to you the reason of that, having never had a father or a mother, or if I had I never knew them. It is very improbable that my mind should revert to the last thing about which I should think of. And what family have you got?"

"A mother and sister."

"Do they work?"

"At times they do."

"Not always then?"

"No, it is all very well to say why don't you work—but you cannot always get work to do. Now to-morrow, if I left my master, what would become of me; I got no money, no friends, and the paltry pittance that I get goes towards keeping three people alive."

"But you have not told me yet the reasons why you wish to leave your master."

"He has behaved bad to me.'

"Explain yourself."

"Now, look here; he took me when I was a lad, he gave me sixpence a day then. I have grown up. I have become a man now."

And the post-boy stood up and maintained himself as stiff as a piece of iron.

"And he won't give you any more now?"

"He did one year ago increase me to a shilling a day. A fortnight since I spoke to him quietly. 'Master,' says I to him, I 'got no money to bring home, my salary will not keep me and my family comfortable; can you increase my remuneration?'"

"What did he say?"

"'Saddle the brown mare—a gentleman is waiting outside; and do not talk to me again of your family trouble, for if you do I'll give such a remembrance of my fist as you seldom got.'"

"Did you speak to him again?"

"I was not such a fool—I knowed right well that if he turned me out there is lots that'll do my work, so I kept my feelings within me; and I says to myself, I will remember that; as soon as I see a favourable opportunity that offers, I eagerly seize it."

"Will you not flinch when danger is at hand?"

"That I won't, I can assure you. Try me first, and if I do not suit you may give me, as we call it among ourselves, the dirty kick-out."

Sataniello had listened to the post-boy's story, and to abide by that exact truth by which we intend to adhere to during the course of this tale, let us inform our readers that he felt greatly interested by it. He liked the appearance of that Italian youth; and although he wished to join Sataniello's band through motives of revenge, the Boy Brigand never took any heed of the cause which prompted him to come to the determination which we have seen he had taken.

"What's your name?" he asked.

"Pedro, Sir."

"Any other?"

"Yes, Sir; but I would like to keep my family name dark."

"That's sufficient."

"What will you do now?" the post-boy inquired.

"Go home."

"Shall I go with you?"

"Of course."

"What shall I do with the chaise and pair?"

"I'll tell you. Do you see that pathway there yonder?"

"I see it."

"By the side of that path do you see the road?"

"Which one do you mean—the one to the right or to the left?"

"To the left."

The post-boy gazed forward, and after a second he replied quickly—

"The one slanting downwards by the river-side, ain't it?"

"The very one."

"Am I to drive there?"

"Yes, you will see a shed behind a rock—it is hidden by the beauties of the mountain—there is just enough place for a carriage to pass through."

"I will be able to do that, Sir—what about the cattle?"

"Once you have placed the carriage in a safe place you can walk straight on. Leave the horses harnessed to the chaise until you have found out the place which I tell you—it is about twenty yards behind the rock; it is as pretty a spot as you could wish to see—a small stream of water runs through the middle of it, and the rock forms now and then natural caverns, wherein you can place the horses until we find a more suitable place for them.

"You will find oats and fodder there, as not long ago we kept a horse that has since died. Once that you will have seen the poor animals well attended to you may come back here. But this path," and the Boy Brigand pointed to a road made for foot travellers, which was close by his side.

"When you reach the top of it, you will find one of my men in readiness awaiting your return—he will then conduct you to the cavern, where you will, doubtless, find all the company assembled.",

"Thanks, Sir."

"Do you understand all I said?"

"Every word, Sir."

"Have you got anything else to ask?"

The post-boy shook his head in the negative.

"Farewell, then," Sataniello concluded; "attend to what I bid you to; and farewell again until this evening." And Sataniello waved his hand and he walked on, followed by Joanitta and Lord Charlestown.

The Giant was in the rear, watching everything around, and keeping an attentive look-out after every one of Lord Charlestown's movements.

CHAPTER XII.

THE END OF A JOURNEY—SATANIELLO FALLS IN WITH A RECRUIT—WHERE AN ENGLISH NOBLE-MAN BEGINS TO THINK THAT ITALIAN BRIGANDS MANAGE TO DO THINGS PRETTY WELL.

WHEN Pedro, the post-boy, bent upon carrying out his captain's orders, had disappeared behind the sinuosities of the road, the little party, composed of the individuals whom we have already described, and who are by this time perfectly familiar to us, walked on.

They had now attained the summit of a height, from which one could command a splendid view indeed.

Sataniello called Lord Charlestown's attention to the beautiful scenery that surrounded them.

As far as the eye could reach the sight was agreeably seduced by white, ivy-surrounded cottages, strewn at rare intervals here and there in the country beneath.

On one side sweeping valleys, enlivened by the river winding its capricious ways through a most imposing landscape, a sunny land stretching away in bright meadows and luxuriant vineyards; on the other, nothing but high mountains, steep and huge rocks, where vegetation seemed to be unknown.

Far, far away, as if to complete the scenery—higher and higher than anything else which caught the eye—stood the cross of some neighbouring church or monastery, proclaiming, in its mute but thrilling eloquence, the story of man's redemption.

Lord Charlestown gazed upon the beautiful landscape which unfolded itself before him.

"Mr. Sataniello," he said, addressing the Boy Brigand, "I have a favour to ask you—will you grant it to me?"

"I must first know what it is."

"How long am I likely to remain your prisoner?"

"That will depend entirely upon yourself. As soon as we have fixed the price of your ransom,

I will send some of my men to town to get it, or go myself, and the sooner you do it the better for you."

"I am fully aware of that. In the meantime, how will I manage to spend my time? I will be allowed to go free, and take walks around?"

"Accompanied by one of my band, you will; not otherwise."

"I would not expect it."

"What favour did you wish, my lord?"

"I need not ask you, now, as you have cleared my mind of the doubts which hung upon it."

"You might as well tell me what it was about."

"I will, if you wish. Noticing the beauty of this scenery, I thought at once that a sketch of it would look very well. I am a pretty good drawer. You would sign your name at the corner, saying, 'This was sketched by Lord Charlestown while my prisoner,' and I could show it to my friends when back to England."

"I have no objection to that," Sataniello replied. "I will do whatever you require of me; and if I can act fairly towards you, without injuring my own interests, you will not find me wanting. You will have no reason to complain, I am sure, of the treatment which you will receive at my hands; but I do not lead the dangerous life which it has been my destiny to follow without being compelled to make some one suffer; and I am sorry that circumstances have made you the party which I should hit upon."

While he concluded the last words of this sentence Sataniello bowed like a man of the world. Indeed, had his lordship been addressed by one of his equals, he could not have found more civility than that displayed by the Boy Brigand.

The four beings that composed the party that had just alighted from the post-chaise had already been walking for some time, and they were, at the moment at which we write, in the immediate vicinity of the cavern.

We have already said, in the previous chapter of this romance, that the spot where Sataniello's band dwelt was hidden from the gaze of man by the sinuosities of the numerous paths which surrounded it—by the mountains which were also close at hand.

Concealed as it was by impenetrable boughs and thick clustering high trees, it made of Sataniello's home a fit place indeed for the resort of such a man as he was.

Although fear never entered his courageous mind, still, for all that, he had more reasons than one to be cautious.

He knew that the authorities were ever watchful, and they would have paid any amount of money to become acquainted with the real whereabouts of his abode.

To reach the main entrance of the cavern one had to force his way through a subterranean strait, which was known only to the Boy Brigand and his troop.

From the spot where Lord Charlestown stood he could not yet see the aperture of the subterranean passage; and to prevent his being placed in a position at a future period to give any clue to justice by which they might discover Sataniello's home, he acted in a manner which was deserving of the highest praise, and which could not but tend to preserve for him that perfect safety that he had so long enjoyed.

Herein he asked Joanitta for the loan of a very tasty little handkerchief which she carried in her pocket, and with it he bandaged his lordship's eyes

Thus, unable to see whither he was going, Lord Charlestown, in the Boy Brigand's company, proceeded onward. At the end of the strait which we have described there was a large cavern, which led to three smaller ones. Had they been built by the brigands themselves for their own use they could not have answered their purpose better. The walls possessed a picturesque and extraordinary appearance, well in accordance with the wayward nature of those which they sheltered during the bright hours of the day—during the long hours of the night, when outside would be heard the high blasts of the hurricane sweeping everything before it.

There hung threateningly from the roof heavy pieces of rock, which one would fancy were about to fall from the roof, when least expected, destroying everything beneath which they might encounter. There the hand of time had carved whole statues in the rough stone.

On the left-hand side of the main entrance, and when you had proceeded a few yards along the underground passage, there was a bench of granite, which projected from the rocks; immediately beyond it a flight of steps was perceivable, which conducted you to a small vault, where the ammunition of Sataniello's troops was wont to be kept. Emerging from it, through an aperture which was scarcely large enough to allow a single being to pass through, there was an excavation which stretched forth on one side towards a spot where a natural shelter against the pursuits of the Papal dragoons and the fierceness of the weather could be found. The rays of light peeped forth from an opening many feet above; and had it been possible for anyone to climb up the steep sides of that little square of ground, you would have reached the top, from which you could see the valley beneath, your shadow all the while being hidden by the natural projection of the stone.

The dampness of the atmosphere very shortly convinced Lord Charlestown that he was underground, and it was with feelings of the greatest enjoyment that he was ridden of the piece of cambric which had been fastened at the back of his head for the last few minutes.

His curiosity was great, and he longed for the moment when his eyes would again see light, and when he could cast his glance around him, upon the spot where he was, upon the objects which formed the principal furniture of the brigand's home.

"How very unpleasant it must be to be blind," Lord Charlestown said, as soon as the handkerchief had been withdrawn from him. "I pity those poor fellows who are doomed to everlasting darkness."

"The force of habit, my lord, is second nature," replied the Boy Brigand. "I have known blind men that were decidedly more contented than those who are endowed with a good sight. There is an old chap that stands just outside the Vatican—if you have been in Rome you must have noticed him—why he is as happy as the day. He sells prayer-books, and lots of stuff of the same kind, and makes a good living by it. Those who pass to and fro pity him, and buy from him that which, if he was not afflicted with the infirmity to which you allude, they would, in all probability, leave alone. Now that man walks from the Vatican to his house, that stands upon the hill within three miles of Rome, morning and evening, and the devil a steadier stepper is there to be found for a hundred miles around. He knows every winding of the road, could tell how many miles you have walked were you to accompany him; and, although one would

think it strange, he can pick upon the first league stone that you like to mention. I have also heard that he can thread cotton through a needle much quicker than myself or yourself could, my lord."

Lord Charlestown listened attentively to the Boy Brigand, and never said a word in reply. He was beginning to think that Sataniello was a strange individual indeed, with the extraordinary notions which some men entertain, and which induces them to think that what God does is always for the best, and who never lose an opportunity of endeavouring to persuade that right is wrong, and that wrong is right.

"What is your opinion of my crib, my lord?" the Boy Brigand inquired from Lord Charlestown, as soon as he perceived the strictness with which the nobleman was scanning his abode.

"First-class lodging. I had no idea that so much style and comfort could be realised in a place of this kind."

Thus speaking, Lord Charlestown looked around him, and shook his head to persuade his listeners that he was by no means indulging in a joke at Sataniello's expense.

The opinion, however, which the nobleman had just given expression to was far from being exaggerated. The particular locality (if we can thus call it) where we introduced our readers being indeed furnished in a manner which one would have certainly expected from a Brigand like the Dark King of the Mountains.

Sataniello in the meantime took a chair which stood by his side, and in a most inviting and engaging way asked his lordship to make himself at home.

"Thank you, I will," Lord Charlestown replied. "Although I may be said to have slept all night, I am very tired, and a rest may do me good."

And his lordship acted by his words, for in an instant he was sitting as comfortable and as calmly as if he was in any other place than in those of a brigand's resort—anything but a prisoner whose life depended upon an amount of money of which the non-payment might place him in a very awkward position.

The Giant had followed the Boy Brigand, but he had soon disappeared, leaving Joanitta, Lord Charlestown, and his guest together. The Giant knew that the post-boy would shortly return from his errand, and unless he met some one to guide him and show him his way, he would have run great risk of losing himself among the rocks amidst which the home of the bandits was situated.

We have said that we should bestow a little attention upon the furniture of Sataniello's abode. Let us do so at once, for fear of neglecting a comparatively trilling detail which might be obliterated from our minds while led on to describe the interesting events which will occur in the course of this tale.

There was in one corner an iron bedstead, surmounted by linen of a snowy-white, and it was a wonder to Lord Charlestown how Sataniello had managed to get this important addition to one household so snugly settled in his rooms, and how, also, he had firstly become possessed by it.

The ground, which, in the brigands' cavern, was only covered by rough wooden planks, was in that of the captain hidden by a wapper floor, which was kept in a state of perfect cleanliness by the Hunchback, whose particular duty it was to attend to all things relating to a menial capacity.

A fire was constantly kept alight in the early

part of the day, to do away with whatever dampness might exist, and a splendid tiger's skin by the couch side struck one as being rather an expensive luxury to be used for as a carpet.

Sataniello had also a taste for reading, for there was on a shelf devoted to books a great many volumes written in Italian, which belonged to the past and present literature of the country in which he lived. The works of Tasso, of Dante, of the Decamerone, and of Boccacio, were to be seen standing promiscuously on the front row; the remainder were stories and novels written by the authors of the day.

The Boy Brigand took a great delight in perusing any tale connected with daring highwaymen, fearless bandits; and, doubtless, many a scheme which he plotted was derived from those interesting romances, to the perusal of which he always devoted the greater portion of his leisure hours.

Three daggers, made of the best steel, and which at some time or another had been used by Sataniello in his nightly expeditions, were artistically arrayed along the wall, covered with a variety of cheap pictures—penny illustrations—which he had bought in his trips to town.

A pair of the best make of English pistols lay in a box, of which the upper part was opened at the time, and it was easy to perceive that he prized them very much, as they were kept in very good order.

A short carbine hung along the wall, and, strange to relate, an ivory cross of a pretty good dimension, representing a carved picture of our Saviour dying for our salvation upon it, stood immediately beneath it upon a mahogany drawers, wherein Sataniello's wardrobe was stored up.

Different emblems, indeed, of virtue and of sin—of religion and of wickedness—striking examples of life and death!

One would have fancied that to be religious in the true meaning of the word would have been the last thing to which the Boy Brigand would have turned his attention; yet his mind, let us admit it, was amenable to occasional impulses—he sometimes thought of a world to come, and while under the weight of harrowing reflection, he would look in a true light upon his sinful career—the evil which he was daily committing would appear prominently before his gaze, and at last repentance would dawn upon him.

Then he would rove in the country alone, unarmed, and he would walk for miles and miles without stopping—would bound from rocks to rocks, and seek danger in clearing the numerous chasms which he encountered in his course. Finally exhausted, with limbs stiffened, he would retire to his abode, and endeavour to obtain, by indulging in heavy libation, a forgetfulness which he needed to appease the wild and furious storm kindled within his overheated brain. He would go to sleep, and next morning he would awake to resume once more the life which he had been leading, and which one day or another might, if ill-success attended his expeditions placed him in the hands of a justice from which he hoped for no leniency, as his own heart told him that he had no right to expect any mercy from a society against which he had waged a cruel and bitter war.

The Boy Brigand, unlike many unprivileged natures, was endowed with a little education, and with a deep and clear-thinking mind.

Thus, when he would retrograde upon his past conduct, and think over that which he had done, his imagination would be ill at rest.

He would give a thought to Joanitta.

The girl had, it seemed, sought him, and he not her; he had watched his opportunity, and when he had met it he eagerly seized it.

He had not been worse than any other Italian; he had met a girl whom he loved, and he had told her so plainly. The result of their mutual confessions we have already described, and we need not again expatiate upon it.

In short, he felt himself justified, and did not blame his conduct; and from the lonely and paramount situation of his rank he would not find any one to blame him.

For had any one with good and right ideas called Sataniello's conduct to account, it is very probable that the reception which he would have given him would have deterred him from returning to the subject again.

Meanwhile, a very tasty supper had been served up by Joanitta, who was already *au fait* of her new position, and who could not have made herself more useful than she had done without being asked or shown to do so, had she been Sataniello's companion for as many years as she really had known him for months.

The table upon which the repast was served shone with a bright cleanliness which was really pleasant to witness; and decanters, which were filled by a golden wine, seemingly pleased his lordship, who, being accustomed to pay and find neatness everywhere he went, delighted to find it in a place where he the least expected it.

The Boy Brigand had always some game within the larder, whether it was in the shooting season or not, and while enjoying it his lordship began to think that, doubtless, the Boy Brigand would revert to the amount of money he expected from him, in exchange of which he would obtain his freedom. He hoped that the sum he would name would not be too heavy to place him to an inconvenience which might not be desirable; moreover, at the very particular moment that he had fallen in Sataniello's hands.

While musing he drank the sherry, and after awhile he lights up a cigar, and presenting his cigar case to Sataniello he asked whether he would have one.

The two weeds were now blazing forth and the atmospheae filled with the puffing of the two smokers, very nigh suffocating, when Lord Charlestown suggested the propriety of opening the door to enable the fresh air to come in.

———

CHAPTER XIII.

THE BOY BRIGAND MAKE HIS OWN TERMS—HE TAKES A TRIP TO NAPLES, WHEREIN HE HEARS ONE THING OR TWO WHICH MAY LEAD TO SOMETHING ELSE.

WHEN the nobleman and the bandit were comfortably sitting together, the Boy Brigand began to think that it was high time that he should have an eye to business.

He had within his abode a smart looking man—a nobleman besides—who could command, without much trouble, as many hundreds as he wished them. He knew that the latter had only to speak—to say "I want a hundred," and he believed that the wish would have been as easily granted as it was spoken.

But the Boy Brigand was not aware of this, namely, that the nobility and gentry of old En-

THE POST BOY'S ASTONISHMENT.

gland are sometimes " hard up," and that the proud descendant of an ancient family is, at times, just as badly off as the journeyman printer, who looks forward to the " pay-day," to bring either home and comfort to his family; or if he be a bachelor, awaits the time when he can have his little lark like everybody else, and amuse himself in his own fashion.

The Boy Brigand, although of a low origin, so far as we have seen, although comparatively an uneducated man, was aware of the frivolity of women, and he could not but come to the conclusion that if he left Joanitta alone with Lord Charlestown, the nobleman might find out, as well as himself, that Joanitta was a pretty little Italian maiden—that

she had good eyes, good hair, a nice-shaped bust, nicely modelled feet and hands, and that it was a great mistake to allow so bewitching a girl to remain hidden in the mountain district of an Italian home, when she would have been much better suited to ornament the monotony of a bachelor's quarters.

Sataniello knew all that—he was further aware of the old saying, quoted somewhere, we believe, in a good book, which ladies are very fond of praising to refractory children, who will have nothing to do with it—he was aware of this, "that the mind is strong, but the flesh rather weak."

That Book is the Bible.

We do not read it when we are young and careless, but an hour comes, when, within its sublime contents,

7

we find ease to our mind, renewed freshness to our imagination—when, from the relief which it affords to all who may peruse it, we are led on to think that our time has not been lost.

"Now, my lord," the Boy Brigand began, "you are my prisoner—you value your life, I know."

"I do," Lord Charlestown replied.

"And what price do you put upon your head?" the Boy Brigand continued.

"A very small one," Lord Charlestown pursued. "I am of no use to any one while alive, and my death only would benefit others."

"And would you like to benefit others?" Sataniello inquired.

"Yes, I would," the nobleman replied, with a smile.

"You are rather of a philanthropic nature," Sataniello resumed; "and I was far from thinking that you could entertain the feelings which you just gave way to."

"Errare humanum est," Lord Charlestown replied, with a pedantic knowledge, very much out of place indeed in the present circumstances.

"I don't understand what you mean by that," the Boy Brigand continued; "that's Greek to me!"

"If you had said it was Latin to you, it might have been a more appropriate remark," the nobleman pursued; "'Errare humanum est' is a Latin phrase, which conveys the following meaning, namely, that man is likely to commit errors."

"Damn the Latin, and you too," Sataniello pursued; "I want to attend to the main point. I have brought you here, and if you like the place you are welcome to remain in it. I will give four days to think about your own ransom; at the end of that time I will send you back to your ancestors, if you have not made up your mind."

At that moment the post-boy came in, accompanied by the Giant.

"You have found your way all right, I see," the Boy Brigand began; "how do you fancy your new home?"

"I do not object to it. There is, however, an ugly customer whom I just saw, and I do not quite relish his countenance."

"Who is that?" the Boy Brigand inquired.

"The Hunchback," the new recruit replied; "he seemed to grin at me when I spoke to him. I will have none of his 'kid' while I am here; and if he is under the impression that he will walk on me, I will soon show him his mistake."

"Right you are, my boy!" Sataniello continued; "I like to see your pluck; you are just the kind of chap we want; and I am sure you will do. But have you had your supper yet?"

"I have not."

"You must be hungry?"

"I am, Sir. The devil a bit of grub have I had since this morning, and I am beginning to get quite hungry."

"I am going to bring comfort to your soul," Sataniello pursued; "you will not be starved while you are here. There is always a large quantity of provisions on hand; there they are, and you are at liberty to help yourself when you want—only, let me caution you, do not get boozy; for, except on certain nights of the week, when we rest after an expedition—that is to say, on Wednesday and Thursday—there is very severe punishment inflicted upon any delinquent who indulges in more lushing than he can stand."

"Leave that to me, Sir," the post-boy continued; "I will not lie myself open to your censure. I do like a drop of beer, or a drop of spirits occasionally; but I ain't a 'swiper.'"

"That is sufficient," Sataniello pursued; "good night; the Giant will take you to your new berth, and see that you are properly attended to—and for the future you must attend to yourself."

"Thank you, Sir," the post-boy pursued; and as he spoke he left the Captain's abode, accompanied by the Giant, with whom he seemed already to be on terms of close intimacy.

When the two men had disappeared from Sataniello's presence, and he and the nobleman and Joanitta, who had just returned from an errand, were all together, Lord Charlestown reverted to the subject of the ransom.

"My friend," he said, "I was only joking just now.—What of the sum which you have fixed upon to grant me my liberty? Speak—it is your duty to do so—and if I think that I can comply with your request, I will give you an immediate answer."

Sataniello mused for awhile, during which the nobleman kept on scanning his guest from head to foot.

He was in the greatest anxiety to hear what Sataniello was about to say.

We cannot be astonished at it, as he knew that the amount which would be named by the Dark King of the Mountains would be such as to place him to a good deal of inconvenience.

"I must have £2000, my lord, paid in gold to me; and then you are no longer my prisoner."

"£2000!" his lordship ejaculated. "No, no! you must be joking; surely you cannot be in earnest?"

"I am, my lord."

"Where am I to get £2000 at a moment's notice?"

"That's no affair of mine. I have got you; I will hold you until I get it."

"Pray alter your mind."

"I will not."

"Do, I beseech you!"

"My lord," Sataniello pursued, "you do not know my character. I am of a jovial, friendly disposition sometimes; but I never alter my mind. £2000 is nothing to you; an English nobleman like you ought to be able to give twice or thrice the amount without any inconvenience."

"I dare say; but I am 'hard up.'"

"So am I."

"You cannot be."

"How do you make that out?"

"Rightly enough. If you want money you waylay the first wealthy traveller who passes by. Bang goes an ounce of your lead in his nut, and it is all up with him; and the only thing you have got to do is to send one of your men to rifle the body, and you pocket the coin."

"I do not deny that, my lord," the Boy Brigand pursued; "but when I see a clear way of increasing my little stock, I do not let it escape."

"But £2000!" the nobleman ejaculated; "that is a fabulous sum, and I will never be able to raise it in twenty-four hours."

"Nonsense, nonsense, my lord! Surely you hold your skin in too great a respect I am sure to compel me to bury it in such damp vaults as the ones which run beneath the place where you are now sitting."

Although the nobleman was far from thinking that his host would put him to the extremities which he was just alluding to, his lordship was anything but satisfied with his safety, considering the place where he stood, and the character of the individual who was addressing him.

"Now, come," he said, "let me off a thousand."

Sataniello made no immediate reply, but indulged in a laugh, which willingly would have been indulged in too by the nobleman, were he not beginning to think at length that his position offered no great scope for ludicrousness of any kind.

"I will manage to give £1100," the nobleman began.

"No, you won't." Sataniello replied.

"Look here, I'll do my best; I will make it £1200!"

"I dare say you would."

"What, won't you take £1300?"

The Boy Brigand shook his head in the negative.

"I will act fair—I will make it £1400."

"You may do so, if you like, but I will detain you here until I get the remaining £600."

"Come, come," said Lord Charlestown, tapping the Boy Brigand on the shoulder, "let us say it £1500."

"I know you will go up, my lord."

"Well, come, I will write you a cheque for £1600, and pay you the £400 when I come your way again."

"You will not be so green as that, I should think," the Boy Brigand pursued; "for if I manage to get £2000 from you this time, and got a fresh opportunity of capturing you again, I would certainly take you again, and bid higher the next time."

"I am astonished at you," Lord Charlestown continued; "you are as nearly as bad as my lawyer in Lincoln's-inn—you rob me illegally, and you risk your life and your freedom, whereas he pilfers me without risking anything at all; but what will become of me between two sharks like you—an Italian brigand and an English solicitor, who can only be beaten in roguery by one class of men, namely, the Irish attorneys."

The Boy Brigand could not refrain a smile when he heard his lordship giving utterance to the sentences which he had just spoken.

"Be generous, Mr. Sataniello, and let me say that I will give you £1700."

"I am tired of answering you, my lord."

"£1800," his lordship ejaculated quickly, hoping yet that he might induce his host to alter his mind. Sataniello remained mute.

"£1900," the nobleman still kept on.

"You will say that you will give £2000, my lord," the Boy Brigand pursued, "for if you do not I will increase it to another thousand."

This was an alternative which was left to Sataniello, and upon which Lord Charlestown had never thought.

"I will make it £2000," he pursued; "but how will you get the money?"

"I will go to town myself and fetch it."

"You will!"

"Of course; do you think that I am chicken-hearted? Not I! I will walk in the place where you keep your money as boldly as a king, or as you would yourself, my lord, and then cash whatever order you may give me; but beforehand I'll take good care to see that it is all square, and that there is no shuffling in this little transaction."

"Would you doubt my word?" Lord Charlestown inquired. "There is a motto by which I abide, and which I should like to see followed by every one of the class to which I belong to, namely, these words, 'My word is as good as my bond;' these should always find a true illustration in noblemen's actions; and as they are the aristocracy of the land, and as by birth, education, and wealth, they are generally acknowledged to be superior to other mortals, they should lead all that is great and praiseworthy, and be the last ones to drag their proud names in the gutter, to barter their respectability and their rank for the sake of patronage or pecuniary motives, which, I am sorry to say, is getting too much the case now-a-days."

Sataniello listened to his flash words with great attention; and although he would feel contented and pleased enough to get hold of the glittering gold, still, he would have liked a little delay on the nobleman's part, by which he might be enabled to enjoy a few hours longer a companionship which his intellectual mind told him could not but make a considerable improvement upon his manners, already refined—upon a brain that longed for the infusion of a worldly knowledge, which the Boy Brigand possessed not, having never been in a position to acquire it.

"I do not doubt, my lord," he replied, "that you would fulfil any promise which you might make; but as in the eyes of the world you might be excused for the non-fulfilment of a word, that, in the fear of death, you might have been compelled to give expression to—it would be questionable, indeed, to conclude what step you would take in such a peculiar and extraordinary matter like the present one."

"I do not wish to leave you before you are paid your ransom," the nobleman began; "I will await the result in all quietude here, but I asked and pressed you to such an extent to reduce the amount of the price asked, because, as true as I am standing here, I have only £1600 laying at my banker's, and I feel convinced that ere another letter of credit can come from England, where I will have to write to, it will entail a good deal of delay; and as I am not a common personage, it might lead to fresh pursuit on the part of the police, as Captain Wogan is sure, when he recovers his consciousness, to go to the Roman authorities, and ask them to grant him a detachment of soldiers, with which he will beat the country, I am sure, if allowed to do so, in the hope of revenging himself for the harsh treatment which on two occasions he has met at your hands. He told me on the evening when you disposed of him in the peremptory manner in which you did, that he had met you once before at an army contractor's, where he got severely handled by one of your troop, and when he experienced so great an insult that he has sworn never to leave this country until he has taken a striking revenge against you, if he can."

"Whatever may loom in the future, my lord," the Boy Brigand replied, "I cannot tell, but, up to this date, I seem to have got the best of him, and as I am always on the watch, I do not think that he is likely to pounce upon me without I will be fully prepared to receive him. Now, although I said just now that I would not reduce your ransom, I will do so—you have spoken to me like a gentleman, I will endeavour to act in the same way towards you—I will be satisfied with £1500, thereby allowing you a few pounds to yourself, as not to send you off this place in a plight which I would not like to find myself placed in, and which I would be the last one to inflict upon one whose high sentiments and high feelings I greatly respect, and whose servant I humbly beg to call myself."

Lord Charlestown had been listening attentively to the Boy Brigand, and when he had concluded his sentence he held out his hand to Sataniello, who shook it nervously.

"I am a man of the world," Lord Charlestown pursued, quite moved by Sataniello, who with his head buried in his shoulders, seemed to have been induced to ponder on his fate as he had withdrawn his palm from the nobleman's grasp. "Yes, I am generally acknowledged to be what is called a man of the world, and I can make excuses for the course which you lead, Mr. Sataniello, although, understand me, I do not intend to palliate it. Born in a country where superstition and priestcraft sways society — born in a country where education is only freely given to those who are called upon to impose upon the credulity of the uneducated, and who live upon the 'fat of the land,' careless of whatever misery might exist abroad—you thought that the roving, adventurous life of a brigand, of a daring highwayman, would be more in accordance with your ideas than that of a drone, whose career is devoid of the smallest particle of ambition, and whose narrow-minded brain suggests to him no wish for any deviation from a stupid every-day kind of life, which I know would be irksome to such a man as you. Had you lived three centuries ago, and with the bold and enterprising spirit which you possess, you must have stepped to fame and glory. In days gone by, when courage, and boldness, and adventurous natures were sure to be employed by the lords of the manors, to serve whatever purpose they had in view, you would have become a dashing cavalier, commanding a gay troop, of which you would be proud; and to lead them on to the fight, to bloody contests, to merciless encounters, would have been the ambition which you would have possessed. From a private soldier you would have risen to the grade of an officer—you would have got your troop in a smart cavalry regiment, and, doubtless, there would have been no opportunity wanting for you when you could have won your spurs on the field of battle. But, my friend," Lord Charlestown continued, "the times are no more when a gallant knight in his castle, with his sentry pacing to and fro during the hour of night, to walk the vicinity of the deep ditches to see if no attack from a neighbouring foe was not contemplated, and his own lord and master reigned over his kindred and his clan, with the supreme power of a king. These days would have suited you, but they are gone, never to return again, and that which was accomplished by my proud and wealthy ancestors is now deemed a crime by the authorities, enlightened, as they call it, by the march of civilisation; and that which a century or two ago would have obtained its striking reward, only leads now to the gallows, to a shameful scaffold!"

Had some unknown individual stood within the Boy Brigand's abode while the sentiments above expressed were flowing from Lord Charlestown's lips—had he gazed upon the lovely features of Joanitta, Sataniello's young mistress—had he also contemplated the deep gloom which overhung the Boy Brigand's forehead, which he now held upwards, as if the nobleman's words had brought a momentary relief to his soul, blistered at times by excruciating memory—that individual indeed would have been amply repaid for the attention which he might have bestowed upon the present scene.

"My Lord Charlestown," the Boy Brigand replied, "willingly would I reform now if I could; but I am gone too far to retrace my steps; and I would not feel obliged to you were you to endeavour to make me shake a resolution which I have taken against society—to wage a bitter, constant war against a world that denies to me. If I had been brought up like many other children—if I had had a mother and father to nurse my youthful days—if I had had a religious, good education instilled into my brain—if I had been taught that which is good, that which is bad—if I had found some one to take me by the hand, and to give me a profession anything but that of a priest—if I had had what many others had, namely, a fair field and no favour: and if then, through too great an inclination to sin, too great a craving for the guilty satiation of guilty pleasures—if, in one word, I had brought myself within the pale of the laws—within an act by which my head can be screwed in, until it is smashed to pieces, and tortured to death by the most frightful pain—I would not complain. But such was not my case.

"Do you know, my lord, who I am? I fear not to speak the truth to you, as within a short acquaintance with you I have already judged the generosity of your character. Joanitta is there; she can listen to my story. It will not be a long one, and she knows the best part of it; therefore she will not learn anything more than what she knows already. Do you know, my lord, who I am?"

And Sataniello repeated his question with a feverish, wild excitement, which very much frightened his lordship, who withdrew his seat with evident alarm.

"Well, then, I may as well tell you," he shrieked, leaving no time to his lordship to speak; "I am the bastard offspring of a Roman mad girl and of a murderer. My mother was called the crazy Leonora, so the people told me; so the boys threw that to my face when I used to show them a ruffled temper, and my father—"

Here the Boy Brigand took out a pocket-handkerchief, and wiped his forehead, which was covered with a damp moisture, showing the high pitch of excitement to which he had worked himself.

"My father! Search the registry of the prison—ask the walls within the prison churchyard where the bones of the murderer of Cardinal Lottaringi lay—ask the Judas who brought up his bastard offspring whether they acted towards an inoffensive child like they ought to have done? Ask public opinion whether it will cast away from a child's forehead the stigma which rests upon the bastard of a murderer and of a Roman mad girl? Ask heaven above how it can permit such things to occur? Ask an omnipotent God why He will allow woman to bear a child who is doomed to have a blighted career?—who comes into this world for no purpose except to doubt, when he attains the age of reflection, that Supreme Power which no one can doubt; which is perceptible at every step we take, in whatever land we may roam, beneath whatever sky the hand of destiny has decided that we should wander. Now, my lord, that I have spoken to you like I would not have done to any other man, in conclusion I say—Does my conduct deserve an excuse which many would deny me?"

Thus speaking, Sataniello fell upon a seat, from the rising position which, in his intense excitement, he had assumed.

Joanitta leant on his shoulders, and her warm, womanly tears brought to the Brigand's heart a relief that nothing else in this world could have afforded him.

Lord Charlestown made no answer. "It is late," he muttered, after awhile; "I would like to retire to the sleeping apartment which you would have assigned me."

"Here it is," the Boy Brigand replied; "I hope you will be comfortable to-night, and get up in the morning with a hearty appetite for your breakfast."

THE BOY BRIGAND ; OR, THE DARK KING OF THE MOUNTAINS.

His lordship wished to retaliate—to say that he would not deprive Sataniello of his own room, and be accommodated at his expense.

"Never mind about me, my lord," he replied ; "I have seen that a few yards distant a nice crib should be prepared for me. I have slept ere now upon the hard stoneing of the high road, awaiting the hour when the sentry, or the watch, would awake me to assure me that the rattle of a carriage brought forth plunder, may-be involving a blood-thirsty murder ; and I have not found myself worse off for all that. Good night, my lord ; and if you have any forebodings as to accepting my hospitality, may you be brought to think that £1500 is not earned in one day, and that in common justice it deserves extra civility."

With these words the Boy Brigand and Joanitta withdrew from the nobleman's presence, leaving him to ponder on the extraordinary revelation which he had heard that evening—to dream upon the way-wardness of destiny, which, from what he had seen, accomplished sometimes freaks of such a peculiar turn, that it would sound preposterous and impossible when related in the most fantastic tale that the human brain could produce.

. . . . . .

The next morning Sataniello entered the noble-man's abode.

"How have you slept, my lord ?" he asked.

"Very comfortably indeed," he replied.

"I suppose you can guess the reason of my being up so early, my lord ?"

His lordship, with his eyes half closed, was at a loss to understand at first Sataniello's meaning.

"No, I do not," he replied, suddenly.

"Have you forgotten all about the £1500 ? " the Boy Brigand asked.

"I have not ; what can I do?"

It was evident now that the nobleman was brought back to a subject which he evidently understood, he would place no difficulty in the accomplishment of it.

"Give me that pocket-book — there, in the corner," he said, pointing to a small Russian leather-case, which lay carelessly upon the chimney-piece. I'll attend to it."

The Boy Brigand was not slow in carrying his lordship's request into effect.

The nobleman took out his cheque-book ; and out of it he drew a leaf, upon which he signed his name.

"What did you make the amount, my lord ?"

"£1500 you told me yesterday."

"That's right."

"I knew you would not alter your words."

"You have had no reasons to think that I would, have you ?"

"On the contrary," the nobleman pursued, "I think that you would be the last one in the world to break a promise. Upon my signature you will obtain the amount claimed."

"Thank you, my lord," the Boy Brigand continued ; " but I want something else besides that."

Although Lord Charlestown the previous evening had had a long conversation with the Boy Brigand ; and although he was beginning to think that he was an individual upon whom one could rely, still, for all that, he was anxious to hear what he was about to say.

Lord Charlestown was in a critical position, indeed.

He was the prisoner of a man upon whose generosity he entirely relied.

It is true that he had acted well towards him up to the time we see him, but he might alter his mind at a moment's notice.

Thus Lord Charlestown was anxious to know what the Boy Brigand required from him besides the order for the £1500.

He was not long in speaking.

"I wish you, my Lord Charlestown, " to write out to me a letter."

"A letter !"

"Yes."

"What for?"

"I will soon tell you."

It never occurred to Lord Charlestown that it had reference to the money which had been set upon his head.

"What do you want a letter for ?" he asked.

"Just a few lines from you to corroborate the genuineness of the cheque just given."

"Oh, I see," Lord Charlestown continued, "you would wish me to write a word or two to the effect that you should get paid the amount above named."

"Exactly, my lord."

"What would you have me write ?"

"I'll leave that to you—you are an educated man, I am not."

"All right, my friend," the nobleman pursued : "I will comply at once with your wish," and thus speaking filled half a note-paper page with a few sentences.

"I would like to hear, my lord, what you say."

"Of course you shall, my friend."

Lord Charlestown glanced over what he had written, and read as follows:—

"To the manager of the Royal Bank of Naples.
    "Dear Sir,—
            "The bearer, Mr. Sataniello, is provided with an order from me for £1500. Please to pay it to him in whatever way he may require it. I mention this because I think he would like the whole amount paid in gold. I hope you have been well since I last saw you—will. step in and look you up shortly.
                "Yours truly,
                    "CHARLESTOWN."

"What do you think of that, Mr. Sataniello ?" the nobleman inquired.

"It will do very well with a few alterations."

"Please let me know what they are, to enable me to alter them."

"You can say then, my lord, for it is only the substitution of one name for another."

"Is not your name Sataniello?" the nobleman inquired.

"It is while I am here in this cavern in the mountain, free from arrest, free from all those who might wish to lay hold of my body ; but when I go anywhere—take a trip to Naples for instance," and the Boy Brigand winked slyly his expressive eye, "I call myself Mr. Francherchi, for it would not do for me if I went and told every one that I was Sataniello, the Dark King of the Mountains !"

"I quite understand your motives, and approve them," Lord Charlestown replied ; "you could not be too cautious."

And as he uttered those last phrases he ran his pen through Sataniello, and substituted it with the Boy Brigand's new adopted name ; but afterwards he found that the writing looked careless, tore up the paper and wrote a fresh one, which completely met with the Boy Brigand's approval this time.

"You see," Lord Charlestown pursued, " that I do all I can to serve you ; I do not place any obstacles in your path ; and I, indeed, exert myself to the best of my ability to place you in a position to have all fair and square, and from meeting with more difficulties than one can reasonably help."

The Boy Brigand took up the letter and the cheque upon the Royal Bank of Naples.

"That's right enough, I dare say, my lord! What would be my best time to go to that place? Naples is a good way from here."

"Will you go on foot, or will you ride there?" Lord Charlestown inquired.

"No, I will take the coach that runs between Rome and Naples, it is a very good convenience; and, besides, I want to see what kind of people travel by it—whether the luggage is of any value at all as a rule, as it may give me a wrinkle if I wish to attack it at some future period."

"Attack the coach?" Lord Charlestown inquired; "surely you would not dare to do that, would you?"

A smile appeared upon Sataniello's lips.

"I have often thought of it," he replied; "but it also struck me it would be spoiling 'the ship for a pennyworth of tar,' as I might very likely lose two or three of my men, and once deprived of them find out that it was not worth while to murder about half-a-dozen people. I might, for instance, hit upon a bundle of old clothes—an old lady with an antiquated dog upon her knees; a dragoon travelling inside, who would fight like a brigand himself, to show to his companions that he is fearless and brave; two or three students going to study the beauties of our old Italian schools, and nothing else to repay me for the risks I would have ran. Thus you can easily perceive that I do not heedlessly rush at things without due consideration. I like to see what I am about first; 'Am I right, or any other man?'"

Lord Charlestown could not help smiling when he heard the Boy Brigand making use of an expression which he thought was rather a funny one at the time; and which half a century after the events which we describe was to have become quite a common, ludicrous saying in the good old city of London.

"Why," the nobleman replied, "you are a cute fellow, and no mistake; but I should advise you to set upon your journey as soon as you like, as the earlier you arrive at Naples the better chance you will have of getting my cheque honoured, although I do not think for a single instant that the manager would make any objection in paying you; still, for all that, you had better be on the safe side, and call at the bank during business hours, which is between nine and four for the public, and much longer for the poor clerks, whose noses are bent all day over a lot of intricate accounts, in which the greater part take no interest, as they are, generally speaking, very inadequately remunerated."

The Boy Brigand was listening carefully to the nobleman's speech; every instant he was becoming acquainted with details which he had never heard before.

"So," the nobleman pursued, "if the chief cashier, who is always a much greater man in his own opinion, and thinks that he is a better man than the board of directors, managers, and all the staff together, was to see you entering the bank late, moreover to call for such an amount as my note gives you credit for, it might lead to your being questioned, and perhaps catechised in a manner that I feel convinced you would not like much."

"I am very much obliged to you, my lord," the Boy Brigand replied; "I will not lose an instant, and now I am off. I have given necessary orders to Paublas, my lieutenant, to see that every wish of yours is attended. There are dice, cards, backgammon, and chess, in the drawers; and if you fancy a game, I dare say that you will find plenty to accommodate you; besides, there is Joanitta, whom I leave behind me, and I am sure that she will keep you alive while I am away."

With these words Sataniello walked along the subterranean passages which led from the abode where he stood to the entrance of the cavern, and he soon found himself in the open air.

CHAPTER XIV.

WHEREIN THE BOY BRIGAND STILL JOURNEYS TOWARDS NAPLES—WHICH FURTHER TELLS OF HIS ARRIVAL THERE.

As the light slowly descended from the orient sky, dispelling before it, in its steady course, the dark shadows from the land, the clouds melted away, the dawning sun emerged from apparently unknown regions, and proclaimed in its radiant rising the wake of nature, and, to all outward appearance, the break of a fine day.

Gradually the morning light revealed the surrounding scenery, and as Sataniello proceeded onwards he was enabled to perceive the smoke beginning to peep through the solitary thatched-roof cottages scattered here and there.

Yonder the fields were gilded with golden hue—the birds warbled forth their tuneful songs—on the moors the hare and the rabbit were running their mirthful race, and everything around seemed by their sprightly concerts to bid the sleeping world to arouse from its usual slumbers.

Nature was filled with harmony—the grass glittered with morning dew, and as the morning drew on, and the sun began to shine brighter and brighter, darting its warm rays on the country, a sweet music was to be heard from every branch and tree.

It was on such a morning that Sataniello, having taken a hasty leave from his mountainous home, wound his steps towards that of Naples.

Within his pockets he had all the documents which were necessary to him to obtain the ransom upon which he had fixed Lord Charlestown's head.

He had spoken to none ere he left—not even to Joanitta—who knew not that he was already so far away from her.

With Lord Charlestown only had he had an interview, which we have already described.

In a few minutes he had accomplished whatever he had to do.

Sataniello was a clever man, and he was fully aware that no success can ever attend those who hold procrastination in too high an opinion.

There is an old saying to the following effect, namely, that you should never delay until the morrow what you can do at the time of which you think of it, when you have an opportunity of immediately carrying it out.

Sataniello always made it a rule to attend to things at once.

He would never postpone that which ought to have a hasty fulfilment.

Thus he had spoken at once to the nobleman, and his was rather sharp work.

Now he was hurrying towards Naples.

He would have preferred a long walk along the country road—occasionally mingling among the people at the wayside inn—sooner than to go and bury himself within or without an uncomfortable old stage-coach, which would rattle along with so shaky a move as to give you quite a headache.

Sataniello liked to speak to the countrymen, and to treat them to a glass of whatever they would fancy to drink; and he would be delighted to hear the blessings of the poor people freely bestowed upon his head.

He would then give them a piece of silver, equivalent in this country to a five-shilling piece, and they would look at him with astonishment; and as he would get away from them he would hear them say—

"I do not doubt but what that is Sataniello, the Dark King of the Mountains—he seemed a poor man, and yet he acted like a wealthy man." None but a brigand could, in those poor people's opinion, realise the type of the being above described, and they placed him down for what he really was—they would suppose him to follow a calling which he loved.

As the Boy Brigand stepped on the ground towards the village of V——, where he knew that he would find the coach in attendance, and where he knew that he could secure a good place on the top seats of the vehicle, his mind reverted to the daring enterprise which he was carrying out all by himself.

It is true he was a complete stranger in Naples—he was a Roman, not a Neapolitan.

They were different towns—different people lived in their respective places—they were governed by different people, and he had nothing to fear. The letter which he had in his pocket was quite sufficient to back his word in saying that he became possessed of the cheque by fair means; but seeing his appearance, which was that of the common class to which he belonged, the banker might have his forebodings and refuse to honour the bill of Lord Charlestown for £1500, unless he had the honour of calling upon him personally.

Sataniello could not but know that the money which he was about to draw was considerable, indeed.

It is a very good round sum in this country, but in Italy, where the value of money, in the days we write, was much greater than in England, where living was much cheaper, £1500 was looked upon as a fortune in itself. He, therefore, was very anxious to know the result of his trip to Naples; he wished also to return as soon as he could to Joanitta, whom he still loved deeply, and whom he did not like to leave behind him.

Necessity has no law, and he had been compelled to act as he had. Besides, his band was numerous, and of late he had often thought that Paublas, his lieutenant, only sought an opportunity to turn against him—to betray him, if he could fairly do so.

Whether Sataniello was right in coming to such a conclusion we really do not know, nor can we tell up to the present period.

There were many men in this world whom Sataniello would have feared; but although Lord Charlestown was not a coward, the Boy Brigand had no dread of the nobleman.

He would have done anything to serve him if he could.

We have our likings and our dislikings, and why, we can scarcely account for it ourselves, we will take a fancy for one character that our neighbour would, perhaps, hate at first sight.

Thus it was with Sataniello.

He had listened to the nobleman's upright ideas—to his *exposé* of a nobleman's duty, and he had produced so great and so favourable an impression upon Sataniello, that more than once, as he strolled onwards, he was on the point of returning to his mountainous home, and of giving the nobleman his freedom.

If he had only followed the promptings of his heart, such would have been the step which Sataniello would have taken.

To give to Lord Charlestown his liberty, without attaching any condition to his obtaining the same, would have pleased the Boy Brigand in the extreme.

To be generous before others, and to act in a manner as to give him no cause ever to repent for his determination, was Sataniello's constant dream.

It was a praiseworthy ambition it must be confessed.

But Sataniello had many other things besides that to study.

The monetary part of the business was a chapter of his book to which he should devote just as much, if not more, attention than to the others.

Money, that cursed money—without which we would not be enabled to go on—does more harm than good, is productive of more crime than it is of virtue, and it is likely to remain so as long as the world will indulge in its present evil ways.

The Boy Brigand had now reached a wayside inn. He entered the house, and he asked whether the coach, which was just standing outside, would be long ere it would start.

He had not done speaking when the driver rushed in, and in a bold, hasty voice informed all those present that he would be off in a few minutes.

Sataniello was not long to take the hint, and he soon found himself on the top of the coach.

Ere five minutes had elapsed the horses were dashing along, carrying the Boy Brigand to the city of Naples.

Doubtless they would have liked to know who he was, for such a knowledge would have placed them in the receipt of a good sum of money, which was everywhere offered for his apprehension.

But the travellers were not likely to find out from the Boy Brigand who he was, and where he came from.

Although Sataniello could be exceedingly communicative when he was among friends, when surrounded by strangers not a syllable would flow from his lips.

He had been travelling for some time when the vehicle stopped.

He alighted, and he walked along a footpath which ran parallel to the road.

He was tired of sitting, and he wished for a little bodily exercise.

As he was strolling he came upon a height, from which he gazed upon the Bay of Naples, which was immediately before him.

The day was remarkably fine; and the waters, upon which a few boats were to be seen, were as smooth as a sheet of ice.

In the distance he saw the city.

Naples, until now, was unknown to him; but he would soon become acquainted with the metropolis.

He hailed a boat, and he jumped into it.

And from the country, a few miles from the town, he sailed to the town of Naples, and in a quarter of an hour he found himself safely landed upon the shore.

In a few quick, rapid strides he soon brought himself in the heart of the city, and he looked around him.

Then he stood upon the Piazza-Francesca, and

immediately before him he saw the offices of the Royal Neapolitan Bank.

He took his portfolio, and he opened it.

He was not slow in perceiving that his papers were all in order.

Firstly he took up Lord Charlestown's letter, which he placed in his breast pocket. Secondly, he attended to the cheque.

"My name," says he, "is Signor Francherchi. I must mind that."

With these words he crossed the Piazza, and he opened a big, heavy, massive door, which ran upon its hinges, creaking all the while—like as if it wanted some reparations—and he entered the offices.

He saw a desk before him, and towards it he walked.

A young clerk stood immediately behind it.

"What can I do for you, Sir?" he asked, with that obsequious yet bold and justified attention which is bestowed by those who earn their living honestly upon those who do nothing, and who manage to subsist anyhow.

Sataniello thanked him for his attention.

"I want this cheque of Lord Charlestown's cashed, Sir."

"What is the amount?" the clerk asked quickly.

"One thousand five hundred pounds, Sir," Sataniello replied, in the coolest manner possible, as if he had been accustomed all his life to draw heavy cheques at the very bank where we see him paying a visit for the first time.

The clerk was evidently a fresh hand. His part of the business ended with examining the cheque; so he referred him to another "employé," who, having catechised the piece of paper produced, in his turn also entered into communication with Sataniello.

"Do you want the whole amount now, Sir?" he inquired.

"I do."

"How will you have it?"

"In gold, if you please."

The Boy Brigand pronounced these words sharply and peremptorily, which struck the clerk as being rather strange.

It was rather an odd request to require one thousand five hundred pounds in gold, of which the weight could not but inconvenience anyone. He could, perhaps, have made some remarks to Sataniello about it, when he thought it right that, previous to parting with his coin, he should see that everything was in proper condition.

"Will you wait half a minute here, Sir?" he querulously said to Sataniello. "I will be back with you in an instant."

"Let me have all gold, I repeat," Sataniello replied. "I will have none of your flimsy paper."

While he was still speaking he found himself accosted by a messenger, who told him to follow him.

At first the Boy Brigand was at a loss to know what all the things he was undergoing really meant; and now he felt still more surprised at his being spoken to by a man whom the Boy Brigand thought must have occupied some very important position in the bank, if he could judge from his uniform, which was superior to some of the shabby garments—called office-coats — worn by the weazel-eyed intelligent-looking clerks, selling their brains to a public company for a yearly pittance which would be despised by a well-behaved, honest mechanic.

Sataniello followed the individual with the uniform through a succession of numerous "employés," all doing very little, and apparently endeavouring to make people believe that they were working very hard; and after having ascended a staircase, he found himself in the presence of a gentleman who came to greet him, and who held out to him a hand, which Sataniello shook very cordially indeed, although unable at first to make out how he could have kindled such feelings of friendship—in a complete stranger to him—in a man whom he had never seen before.

CHAPTER XV.

THE BRIGAND AND THE FINANCIAL MAN—WHEREIN SATANIELLO'S INTRODUCTION TO THE MANAGER OF THE ROYAL NEAPOLITAN BANK PLACES HIM IN A POSITION TO LISTEN TO THE BEST PART OF A CONVERSATION, WHICH IS MEANT FOR ANYONE BUT HIMSELF.

IT may perhaps seem strange to my readers that Sataniello could have received such a welcome as we described in the last portion of the previous chapter. Still it was so.

Furthermore, it is not difficult to explain the reasons which led the manager of the Royal Neapolitan Bank to display all of a sudden the extraordinary outburst which we have witnessed in the shape of a person shaking hands with another, a complete stranger to him.

When a client enters a bank with an order upon them, or whatever mercantile or monetary concern any persons like to fancy, he is certain to be well received by the officials.

On the other hand, if he enters the same place with different feelings, being rather short, for instance, and wishing to borrow, cold, indeed, will be the reception awaiting him.

It is true that the manager expected to find a gentleman in the stead of a rough countryman like the Boy Brigand was to all first outward appearances.

Sataniello was one of those who gain by being known, while with others it is quite the contrary.

It is wonderful how altered one's opinion of the Boy Brigand could be in the short space of a few days.

Having sufficiently explained, we hope, the reasons of the manager's way of acting, let us resume our narrative.

When Sataniello had answered the request of the manager, who insisted upon his making use of a comfortable easy-chair which was close at hand, he remained silent, fully prepared to answer every question which might be placed to him in a manner as to dispel whatever shadow of suspicion might exist in any one's mind relating to his respectability.

"Mr. Francherchi," the manager said, "I hope that you will excuse me for having taken the liberty of detaining you here; but the amount of your cheque, although not considerable, deserves to have all the attention bestowed upon it to prevent any future mistake."

"Certainly, certainly, Sir!" the Boy Brigand replied; "I am very happy that you are so particular as you are. It must tend greatly to facilitate the dispatch of the business. With regard to the delay to which you place me, do not mention it; my time is my own, and an hour here or there does not much matter."

"Thank you; very much obliged!" the manager pursued; and he scraped and he bowed to the Boy Brigand as if he was one of the lords of the land—one of the Neapolitan potentates.

SATANIELLO CONFRONTS THE POST BOY.

Sataniello now did what he had not been enabled to do before, namely, to contemplate the features of the manager.

They struck him as being very ugly, and yet he possessed an acute, keen, grey eye, which denoted the man of business. He was a fat, short, dwarfy little man; and, as he sat in a big chair, before a bigger desk still, he looked like a man who meant indeed to be in earnest about whatever he might take in hand.

"I have given orders," the manager said to Sataniello—or, to be more accurate, Mr. Francherchi—'to have the £1500 placed in a big leather bag for you. By-the-bye," he continued, "how is Lord Charlestown—living in Naples still?"

"Yes," the Boy Brigand said; "he is living close by."

"I know," the manager continued, "that he is an attaché to the English embassy here; but not having seen him lately, I thought that perhaps he had left Naples temporarily; and do you tell me that you were speaking to him this morning?"

"I was," Sataniello replied; "and he gave me this note in case of my meeting with any difficulties regarding the trifle which I am about to draw."

The manager did not make any remarks upon what he heard; but he bowed respectfully to his visitor.

Although he could not but think that he was

some humble Italian, as far as his garb was concerned, he might perhaps be the owner of some princely fortune.

The financial man thought on these things, and he said to the Boy Brigand—

"If you do not want the whole of the bullion to-day, we will take care of it, Sir, and open a separate account with you."

The Boy Brigand shook his head in the negative.

The manager soon saw that it would be no use to push the matter.

He went to a corresponding-whistle which stood by him, and blew in it.

A kind of half-servant, half-secretary—doubtless receiving the pay of the former and having the education of the latter—answered the call.

"Just prepare a receipt for Mr. Francherchi," the manager said, solemnly.

A minute had not elapsed ere the amanuensis returned.

The manager took up the paper and read it.

"Will you be kind enough to sign this," the manager began.

"I will, as soon as I get the gold. I take with one hand and give with the other. Do you understand, Sir?"

"Extraordinary man, that!" the manager muttered, who had never had occasion before to come across so knotty and so particular a client—although to stick to the letter, to the etiquette, and to the ceremonious part of anything connected with business, is certainly the right thing to adhere to.

The gold was quickly brought up in a heavy leather bag, and, when once it was by his side, the Boy Brigand proceeded to see that the whole amount was fairly contained in it.

He was thus reckoning the golden coins, when a gentleman entered.

The Boy Brigand turned round and looked at him.

The new comer was a stylish young gentleman indeed!

There was a great difference between him and that individual who had just stepped into the manager's office.

The financial man had his head closely bent down upon his desk, so he did not notice the intrusion of a fresh personage in his room.

Sataniello, on his side only, had witnessed him; having, by a casual occurrence, turned his head around him to see from whence the noise proceeded.

Sataniello could not but think that the new comer was some Italian lord—some man who had estates which could scarcely be reckoned, so numerous were they!

He was not wrong in coming to that conclusion.

The man who remained so quietly in the manager's office, glancing on the paper of the day, and awaiting the moment when the pressure of business would enable the manager to relinquish his pursuits for awhile, was the Marquis of Piatelli.

"To what causes," said the manager, heedless of the Boy Brigand's presence, "am I to assign the honour of the Marquis of Piatelli's visit?"

"I want some money!"

The manager made a most respectful bow, and shortly afterwards he smiled complacently.

He had reason to do so; and this latter pantomime was part of his business.

The Marquis of Piatelli, however, noticed it not.

"Will you be kind enough to let me know the amount you require, Marquis Piatelli? and you will have it at once; or I will send it on, if you are in too great a hurry to wait."

The Marquis of Piatelli stated the amount.

Nothing more was said about it.

It would be paid on request, and there was an end to it.

"I am heartily sick of Naples!" the foreign nobleman began; "and I am going down the country with my sister."

"I hope you will enjoy it, Sir!"

Common-place remark enough, which soon provokes a common-place answer to the effect that one feels very grateful for your kind wishes.

"I suppose you will not go away for a few days my lord!"

"I am off to-morrow!"

"Indeed, my lord!"

These few words of the manager meant a good deal. They meant this—You carry out a thing in as much time as you would take to make up my mind.

"I tell you whither I am going," the marquis pursued—"on a visit to the old Duke of Don Saltara; he is a client of yours, is he not?"

"He was, marquis!" the manager replied; "he is not now."

This having concluded the amount of information which the manager thought it right or wise to give, he again resumed his conversation with the nobleman.

"I wish, Signor Marquis," he said, "that I was like you, my own master—independent of every one, and a long fortune to my back."

"I dare say you do," the nobleman replied; "if you were in my place to-morrow, you would wish to be in somebody else's; the plain fact of the matter is, the people are never satisfied!"

"That is very true, Signor," the manager replied; "can I do anything for you?"

"No, I am thankful to you all the same! Good-bye! To-morrow I will be wafted to the castle of the Duke of Don Saltara; and I hope that in that old residence, surrounded by endless woods, where game abounds, I will find a little distraction."

"At what o'clock will you leave town, my lord? I take the liberty of asking you this question, as I would make it my duty to see that you have a clerk from my office in case of your missing anything which at the last moment you may find wanting."

"I will leave this place to-morrow evening at ten o'clock. I have given orders to have my vehicle ready by 9·30, and surely there will be nothing to stop us; for once my mind is made up, I seldom alter it—and my sister is the same."

Sataniello had just now finished counting his gold.

"I find this all right, Sir," he said, addressing the manager. "I will tell Lord Charlestown, this evening, that I was very pleased with the quick manner in which you do business here."

Thus speaking, the Boy Brigand descended the staircases, which he had ascended to penetrate the manager's room.

His eye seemed to follow the street before him as soon as he was out of the building, but not so much with his mind wandering to things far off indeed.

"The Marquis of Piatelli," the Boy Brigand was saying to himself, "will leave Naples to-morrow at 10 p.m., he will be two miles from Velerbo at two o'clock in the morning. He must follow the high road; I cannot miss him. By Jove, it is some use to come to town, at all events! Heaven knows what jewellery the sister may have! Those proud ladies of the land always do carry their things with them when going on a visit anywhere."

And while he mused in the following strain, the Boy Brigand hastened his step, and disappeared in one of the many streets which branched off from the particular spot where he stood at the time we last saw him.

CHAPTER XVI.

THE BOY BRIGAND PICKS UP WITH A "MOUNT" ON THE OUTSKIRTS OF NAPLES — HE RETURNS TO HIS CAVERN.

As the Boy Brigand walked along, he could not help thinking of the good occasion which he had met in hearing that the Marquis Piatelli was about to fall within his way.

He had heard him say plainly that he was about to travel along a road which he knew well, and he was not long ere he made up his mind.

He should attack the chaise as it dashed along; he should stop its rapid course; he should take his precautions in such a manner as to ensure success.

While he strolled along, his quick steps brought him into the country, and there he saw a lad standing by his horse's head.

"What do you want for that hack of yours ?" he says, accosting him.

"It is my master's, not my own," the lad replied.

"Would you not part with it ?"

"No, Sir ; that I would not."

"Are you certain of it ?"

"Of course I am."

"What, you would not give me your horse ?"

"Give it to you?—No !"

"Why, you are a queer customer!"

"I am not."

"I tell you you are."

"How do you make that out?"

"Simply enough—you are a bumpkin."

"Who are you talking to like that ?" the lad questioned ; holding fast in his hands his horses reins,—"Why do you call me a bumpkin ?"

"Because you are one."

"What did I say or do to you to insult me ?" the lad asked. "You ask me to give you my horse, and I say I shall not give it to you. Do you understand me now ?"

The Boy Brigand, the gallant Sataniello gazed upon his new acquaintance.

"You are a deuced impertinent and cheeky chap!" he said.

"I do not care for that!"

"Neither do I !"

"Now, what is your little game ?" the lad inquired, looking earnestly at Sataniello.

"I say I want your horse."

"I will not give it you."

"If I pay you for it, will you let me jump upon his back ?" and spurs him away.

"Why should I do so ?"

"Because I want it."

"And who are you, pray ?"

"That is no business of yours."

"I say it is."

"All right."

"To whom does that hack belong to ?"

"To my father."

"Who is your father ?"

"A better man than you."

"Have you done ?"

"Not yet."

"I have seen a great many people in my day "—Sataniello paused—astonished with the pluck and the cool and determined manner of his new acquaintance, but I have never yet met a fellow like you."

"Who do you call a fellow ?"

"You, of course."

The Boy Brigand now turned round, and looked about him, to see whether he was watched.

A cursory glance soon showed him that as far as his eye could reach the country was clear.

The night was starry and radiant ; the hours had flown since his departure, and the Boy Brigand longed to return to his home.

Although not many hours had elapsed since his departure from his mountain cavern, yet he longed to embrace once more his darling, "his pet," his beautiful Joanitta !

To walk did not suit his book; to wander in the country on foot was anything but satisfactory to the Boy Brigand's mind.

He had seen a nice frisky horse before him. He was a judge of cattle, and he knew that if he could only become the owner of the little grey mare which stood before him, ere long he would be within the company of Joanitta.

Besides, he was anxious again to see Lord Charlestown, to show him that he had had the audacity, the self-possession, and the coolness to draw his cheque ; further to demonstrate to him, by the result of his errand, that he could do things well.

"My friend," he said, after a moment of silence, during which the lad who had the horse by his side was gazing upon him with astonishment, "I do not wish to take an unfair advantage of anybody."

While speaking, he tapped him on the shoulder.

"Explain yourself," the lad said. "What do you mean !"

"I mean this, my friend," Sataniello pursued, in a slow and peremptory tone. "I mean this : that you have got a nice little mare, and that I want it."

"You want it !"

"Yes, I do."

"But I could not part with it."

"I know that ; I would not rob you of your horse."

"You might wish to do so," the lad replied; "I do not doubt but what you would—but the next thing would be to master me."

"Do you think, then, that I could not lick you ?"

"Lick me !" I am sure you could not !"

"Will I try ?"

"You may if you like." The lad began, and he stood in a fighting attitude, which many would have feared to see ; for he was a strong-built lad, and he could take his part, if he wished to do so.

Sataniello, however, had had before now to deal with men more powerful in every respect than he who was addressing him.

He would not be cowed by a lad of about fifteen or sixteen, and he would soon show him, if necessary, that Sataniello was one who stood no impertinence from any one.

"Look here, my boy !" he said, addressing the lad; "how much did your father give for that nag of yours ?"

"I do not know; he never bought it."

"Did he get it as a present ?"

"I think not."

"Do you only think so ?"

"No, I know it."

"Did he steal it then?"

"No—he reared it up himself."

"Do you think he would like to sell it?"

"He would."

"And can't you find a purchaser?"

"Up to this time we have not; he wants too much for it, I guess."

"What is the price he has set upon it?"

"Twenty pounds."

"Would he take twenty pounds for it?"

"I know he would."

"And would you give it to him if I paid you twenty pounds."

"If you gave me the cash on the nail. I would, not otherwise."

Thus speaking, the lad looked at Sataniello just as if he thought that an individual like him could not boast of twenty pounds, nay, twenty pence.

"You have not all that money about you, I am sure," he said.

"I have," Sataniello replied.

"Let us look at it?"

"Do not be too fast, I tell you I will give you twenty pounds."

"I do not believe you."

"You are a broth of a boy to talk as you do. I tell you I will give you what you want for it."

"Will you though, the lad inquired.

"Did I not tell you so?"

"You did."

"Do you think I would break my word?"

"I do not know,"

"What for do you want that horse from me Surely you have no business with it."

"One knows his own affairs best, I should say"— Sataniello paused—

"Right you are! Give us the coin?"

"I will."

"Where is it."

"How would you like it?"

"Any way you like."

"In gold or silver?"

"Any way you like to give it to me, I say!

"Will you give me your horse, then?"

"Yes; but you would not take it away?"

The lad had been scanning the Boy Brigand, and he was beginning to come to the conclusion that the party who was speaking to him was only joking with him, and did not mean a word of what he said.

Sataniello now approached the horse, and tapped him on the neck.

"That's a good beast, I know," he muttered. "I am a judge of cattle, and I think he can crack along."

"Like a doe."

"How many miles would he clear in an hour?"

"I've never reckoned his speed," the lad pursued; "but it is a deuced good animal; if he was not, my father would never have reared him, and refused fifteen pounds for it but a few days ago."

The Boy Brigand was now feeling his pockets, out of which he drew a big leather purse.

The jingling of the gold attracted at once the lad's notice.

"You have got a good deal inside that!" he said.

"A little."

"Only a little?"

"Quite enough to purchase this nag of yours."

"And are you really going to give me twenty pounds for it?"

"I am."

"But what will father say?"

"He will say what he likes." Sataniello continued, "Here are twenty pieces of gold, take them to him; should he ask what has become of the horse, tell him."

The lad was now earnestly contemplating the Boy Brigand. He was at a loss to make anything out of him.

Yet he thought in his own mind that he must be a generous man; for he carried a good deal of gold about him, and that is a guarantee of respectability in every part of the world.

Whether we are in England or in Italy, when a man or a woman has always a good supply of the needful about them, they are sure to make way at some time or another.

He had been indulging in those ideas, when he remembered that he had not yet got the coin which had been promised to him.

"And what shall I tell my father?" the lad inquired.

"That you found a generous purchaser, and that he gave you the money; and when you will bring it home to your father, he will say no more about it. Now mind what I tell you."

The lad at first was rather astonished with the manner of Sataniello; but like any one else, he soon yielded to the ascendancy which the Boy Brigand possessed on every one.

"And what is your name, Sir?" he asked. "I never saw you in these here parts."

"I am fully aware of that."

"Will you not tell me, Sir?"

"Just shorten those stirrup straps a little bit for me, you are taller than I am; unless you did so I could not ride with ease."

"Are you a good horseman?"

"You will soon see."

The lad remained silent.

"You would have fought me a minute ago. know you are rather a plucky chap."

"I won't now, though."

"Why not?"

"I don't know. My feelings are quite altered now."

"Indeed?"

"Yes."

"How do you account for that?"

"By your manner, Sir."

"Do you think you would have mastered me," the Boy Brigand inquired, "had we come to fists together?"

"I would not like to give an opinion."

"You are perhaps wise?"

"I dare say I am."

"You want your money now?"

"If you please."

"How much is it?"

"Twenty pounds."

"Will you not take less?"

"I could not myself. But if you like to step along this road, I will take you to my father's house, and when in his company, you might come to easier terms with him than you would with me. But if you give me what you said you would, I know that you will have no occasion to repent: this is a game horse, and it will carry you for many a mile without slackening its original speed."

"You are a good boy, after all," Sataniello pursued—"Here, my boy, is the price of your father's horse."

Thus speaking, he held out his hand in which was the amount stated.

The lad took the coin, and reckoned it up.

"Sir," says he, "this is one pound too much !"

"I know that."

"Take it back, Sir ?"

"No, thank you, keep it for yourself."

"You do not mean it !"

"I do."

The Boy Brigand had scarcely pronounced the last words when he jumped in the saddle.

He sat on his horse for awhile ere he wished good bye to his new acquaintance.

"And what is your name, Sir ?" he asked.

"What do you want to know for ?"

"I do not know, but I am curious; and I am sure you will excuse me."

"I will, [although you behaved rather roughly towards me at first ; still I do not hold any bad feelings against you."

"I can easily tell that, Sir," the lad said ; and while he spoke, he kept on gazing upon the money which he held in his hand.

"Good bye, my boy !" Sataniello pursued, "I must be off. When you go back to your home, you may say to your father, I have sold your horse ! You may relate to him the interview you had with me ; and if he asks you who I was, you may tell him that you met Sataniello, the Dark King of the Mountains."

"And I will add that he behaved right well towards me."

It is impossible to state whether the Boy Brigand heard the reply which followed his speech, for he had scarcely spoken when he dashed his heels into the horse's sides, and ere a second had elapsed, he was far away.

Indeed, had any one seen the Boy Brigand cantering away towards his home upon his new purchase, with the radiant rays of the moon lighting up his noble and manly countenance, he would have fancied that he was gazing upon some gallant knight in the days of yore, hurrying towards the tower and battlements of the castle where lived his lady fair.

The little mare answered the Boy Brigand's calls far beyond his expectations, and as she dashed along the causeway with unremitting speed, he could not but rejoice inwardly at the choice which he had made.

At the rate at which he was going, he was not long ere he reached the vicinity of the cavern which he inhabited.

He was too tired to take the animal down to the place where the pair which had drawn the chaise from Rome had already been safely fastened by our young friend the postilion, Sataniello's new recruit, so he took off the saddle and the bridle, and having slung them upon his shoulder, he allowed his "mount" to graze freely in a green field enclosure which was close at hand. The animal neighed, and gambolled, and jumped about as soon as she was let free, and having satisfied himself that she was all right for the night, Sataniello wound his steps towards his home.

He went up along a rugged path, and in a few instants he reached the spot where the sentry was keeping watch.

The Monk that night happened to be on duty.

"Hilloa ! who goes there !" he inquired, not recognising at first Sataniello's appearance.

"A friend !" the Boy Brigand replied.

"Good night, Captain," the Monk exclaimed, detecting in a moment his master's voice ; "Welcome home, Captain !"

"Good night !" Sataniello replied ; and as he neared the Monk, he whispered into his ear the following words :—

"Everything been quiet since I left this morning, I hope."

"Perfectly so, Captain."

"Is the whole band within ?"

"Yes, Captain."

"All right ! I will send the Hunchback to relieve you, as you must be present at what I am about to say in a few moments. I have planned a great expedition."

The Monk listened attentively to his master, but said not a word in reply.

He, however, bowed respectfully, and he had scarcely resumed his steady up-and-down walk, than Sataniello was already within his abode.

―――

CHAPTER XVII.

WHICH TELLS OF THE BOY BRIGAND'S SUCCESS, AND WHICH SHOWS THE WHOLE BAND IN FULL STRENGTH.

"OH ! dearest, dearest Sataniello !" Joanitta exclaimed, as soon as she saw the manly form of the Boy Brigand standing before her, " Oh, how happy I am to see you safely back again !"

While thus speaking, Joanitta's arms clung affectionately round the Boy Brigand's broad neck, and his lips, close to her lips, mingled together in a voluptuous, amorous, feverish embrace.

'Tis sweet for those who love each other like Joanitta and the Boy Brigand did, to meet again after an absence, however short it may be.

While in town, Sataniello's thoughts had often reverted to his darling Joanitta, and it was only fair to state that the maiden's heart beat anxiously at the idea that Sataniello might fall in the hands of his merciless pursuers.

Now they were again together.

Joanitta would have liked never to part with Sataniello if she could. She dreaded the moment when he would sally forth upon the dangerous expeditions which he was constantly planning.

But a brigand's life is full of dangers ; his existence ever hangs upon a thread ; and so fully aware of this fact was Joanitta, that she loved her handsome Sataniello with a feeling which no one, except a bandit's bride, can experience.

Her rosy, voluptuous lips were clasped over those of her lover, and she pressed her voluptuous breast against his manly and fearless heart.

There were two beings, different indeed in their outward appearances, but who, nevertheless, would have died for each other.

Repeatedly did Sataniello kiss the loving maiden, and as repeatedly did she return his embraces.

It is very extraordinary indeed, but it has been ere now noticed, that few beings are greater slaves to Cupid than love children that are born out of reciprocated embraces ; and it seems that by a wayward and unaccountable whim of Nature, they should be more inclined than others to bow constantly to Love's power, and to indulge freely in its short-lived but enslaving pleasures.

With all the youthful exuberance of a young heart did Joanitta worship her gallant Sataniello. With all the ardour of the forlorn outcast, who longs for somebody's caresses, did Sataniello adore Joanitta.

They were truly made for each other !

As the glossy wavy hair of the young girl rested upon Sataniello's forehead, as some stray curls hung upon the fair part of her face, he snatched them with his lips, and he bit them as if it was sweet honey to his loving desires.

How long the young people would have remained pressed against each other's bosoms, speaking not, but their mutual silence interrupted only by the occasional subdued noise of a warm kiss, proclaiming volumes of reciprocated love, we are unable to say, had not Lord Charlestown entered the cavern, and surprised Joanitta and Sataniello in the amorous position in which we have described them.

When Lord Charlestown made his appearance, Joanitta relinquished her hold.

Unless she is irretrievably gone, unless she has already lost all sense of womanly purity, no girl o Joanitta's age will allow her feelings to give way before a perfect stranger.

For what else was Lord Charlestown to her.

A natural bashfulness overspread her features, and her enamelled countenance was soon tinged with a rosy hue.

"Back again to my old quarters, you see, my Lord!"

"Did you get the cheque cashed?" his Lordship inquired.

Sataniello made no reply at first, but took his purse from his breast, and displayed it to the nobleman. "My Lord," he said, "you are free."

"And what did you think of the manager of the Royal Neapolitan Bank?"

"A deuced civil fellow, I thought."

"Did he ask you any questions?"

"He did, of course."

"What did you say?"

"I really forget, but I palmed him off in first-class style; I dare say he was rather puzzled at my queer ways: but when he saw your letter that I showed him, he became quite attentive. I do not think that he could have believed that I was a bandit, for if he did, I fear that he would not have permitted me to take my departure from him with the flying colours which I did."

"And you got £1,500 then?"

"I did—all in gold too; and I assure you that it is no joke to carry such an amount upon one's self; and as I was cantering down the solitary road, I must confess, that although I am not much given to fear, the appearance of three or four stalwart men, inclined to rob me, would not have enhanced my spirits much, knowing that I was only by myself to protect a sum, which many would envy, and perpetrate any amount of dark deeds to obtain."

Lord Charlestown listened attentively to Sataniello's speech. "I am happy," he began, "that you met with no difficulties in the execution of your plans, sir, amidst your rough crew. I thought at every moment, that for the sake of the watch and chain I have about me, they would have slain me."

"Had any touched one single hair of your head, my Lord, on my return it would have been punished by instantaneous death. My men know too well the determination of my character, and they are too fully aware of the little leniency which I show, when my orders are not faithfully carried out, ever to interfere with my guests."

Sataniello concluded his phrase in a short, peremptory tone, which conveyed to Lord Charlestown a truthful idea of the Boy Brigand's resolute character.

"Nothing detains me, then?" he asked.

"My Lord," the Boy Brigand repeated, "you are at liberty to go. There is no coach to-day—it is too late; but if you like to start from this place to-morrow morning, I will see that you are guided to the proper place unmolested."

Lord Charlestown replied in the affirmative.

The reader can easily perceive that Sataniello always acted wisely. He contemplated attacking the chaise of the Marquis of Piatelli, and yet not a word did he say of his intention to Lord Charlestown.

There are certain things which ought always to be left in the back-ground, and the Boy Brigand knew how to use a certain discretion in the multifarious matters with which he was constantly busying his brain.

"I will go to-morrow morning," Lord Charlestown began, "and I can assure Mr. Sataniello that I will never forget my sojourn with you."

Lord Charlestown had evidently no more to say; so Sataniello wound his way towards the cavern where his band was.

Through one cavern—two caverns—along a short subterranean strait he walked, and in a few instants he found himself amidst his men.

The band was just finishing its supper, and the brigands, sitting peaceably round a rough wooden table, were engaged in a general conversation.

When he appeared they all closed their lips.

A fly could have been heard flying about, so complete was the silence which heralded the few minutes which followed his stepping in the cavern.

"To-morrow night," Sataniello began, "we will have light work. I intend to attack a postchaise which will come from Naples."

The bandits were eagerly devouring the words which flowed from their master's lips.

"Keep your carbines and your peignards in good order; and Paublas," he continued, addressing his Lieutenant, who had stood by him since his entrance, "you must see that everything is in good order previous to our sallying forth."

Paublas shook his head in the affirmative.

"Very little preparation is necessary, Captain," he continued. "The boys have been rather idle for these last few weeks, and they have everything prepared for the day of action."

"I need not say," Sataniello pursued, "that I shall expect every man to do his duty; but if any among them should fall below that which I consider to be the standard of behaviour, beware of my wrath, and fear my verdict—that's all."

Thus speaking, Sataniello left the brigands' cavern, and he soon disappeared from them, enjoining Paublas to send a relief-man to the Monk who was the standing sentry outside, and to acquaint him with all the particulars which he should require to know, to place him in a position to face without awe one of the most critical circumstances of a man's life.

Soldiers say that it would be impossible to describe accurately the nature of the sentiments which agitate their brain—the various emotions to which they are subject, when they assist for the first time in a battle.

What must it be, then, for such men as Sataniello and his band—for they who, even if they are successful enough to escape a sudden death—are doomed to drag on an existence which, if it does not lead them to the scaffold, is in most cases likely to end badly!

Meanwhile the resting hour had arrived, all the lights in the cavern had disappeared, and all was plunged in the deepest silence, and nought was heard beyond the monotonous step of the sentry pacing the ground above, while engaged in his dreary and solitary watch.

CHAPTER XVIII.

WHICH TELLS OF SATANIELLO'S EXPEDITION, AND
DISPLAYS THE APPEARANCE OF HIS FEARLESS
FOLLOWERS.

IN the morning Lord Charlestown had taken his
departure from Sataniello's home.

He reached Naples safely; and it was lucky
indeed for the Boy Brigand's sake that he did not
acquaint Lord Charlestown with his intention—with
the plan which he had plotted of waylaying the
carriage which would contain the Marquis Piatelli
and his fair sister.

Had he done so, it is very likely that Lord
Charlestown would have informed the Marquis Piatelli with the Boy Brigand's design.

Lord Charlestown met him on the piazza just
as he was entering Naples, after having alighted
from a conveyance which had brought him slowly,
but safely, it is true, to the capital of the Neapolitan
States.

Strange to say, however, when he shook hands
with the Marquis Piatelli, the thought never struck
him that he too might be attacked by this same
Sataniello.

The mind of man is so fanciful, and so likely to
wander from one thing to another, that often that
which we should like to remember at a certain time
escapes our memory precisely at the period when we
should wish to have it flashing across our thoughts.

Thus it was with Lord Charlestown; and it was
only when he saw the chaise conveying the Marquis
Piatelli and his fair sister towards the mountains—
when the last sounds of the wheels rattling over the
pavement had struck his ear—that he blamed himself for not having given to the Marquis a warning
which might have been the means of frustrating
Sataniello's plans, and of preventing plunder and
perhaps bloodshed.

Over sixteen hours had elapsed since Lord Charlestown's departure from Sataniello's abode.

The darkness of night had succeeded the light of
day.

The weather threatened to become tempestuous,
and the thick clouds which were rapidly gathering
above proclaimed the approach of a storm.

The moon, which was hidden in the dark bluish
vault of heaven, only shone from time to time; and
when its lurid, uncertain glimmer lit up the wild
solitude of the forest, the scene that offered itself to
the gaze was imposing indeed.

Deserted roads, endless footpaths branching off in
every direction, sinuous ascents, steep descents,
where scarcely the appearance of man could have
been detected, so bleak and so solitary did the country appear, when now and then it was brightened
up by the lurid flashes of the lightning.

And such was the night during which Sataniello
and his troop watched from an eminence standing
close to the high road the moment when the Marquis Piatelli's carriage would rattle along the causeway.

There he was, the terrible and undaunted Sataniello—the eye wide open—the ear listening to the
slightest noise—his whole attention concentrated
before him.

He looked indeed the picture of what he really
was.

Standing motionless and still, his hair cooled by
the heavy gusts of the sweeping blasts of the winds,
he would have frightened any solitary wayfarer.

With his carbine by his side, the softest sound,
however slight, would be for him the signal of renewed exertions.

Behind him Paublas, the Monk, the Giant, and
the Postboy, and the remaining members of the
band, with the exception of the Hunchback and the
sentry on duty, were assembled.

Paublas and the Monk could have been seen from
the road; the other brigands' bodies were hidden by
the rocks scattered before them.

The fall of a leaf—the rustling of the wind through
the adjacent foliage, caused the Postboy to prick up
his ear, as if danger was near at hand.

But upon Sataniello, Paublas, the Giant, and the
Monk, these trifling sounds produced no effect. So
accustomed to nightly watches, they conveyed to
their minds a meaning they knew well.

Yet Sataniello liked the suspense in which he
was. Death might be his doom—and he feared it
not.

Whether the night was like the present one,
boisterous and dreary, or whether the atmosphere
was mild, and the surrounding fields, damped by
the evening's dew, exhaled the sweet perfumes inherent to the country, it was all the same to him.

Whenever plunder was to be had, he was to be
found at his post. To be at the head of his troop,
ready to give the word of command, was the highest
ambition which Sataniello possessed.

Lamentable ambition indeed for one so young as
he was!

There he stood beneath the stately trees which
lined the particular spot of the road where he was,
awaiting the arrival of one more of his victims.

He who should have dreamt of youthful happiness—he who was yet in that golden period of life,
during which the mind, ever cheerful, seldom gives
way to despondency, resembled those incorrigible
criminals whom a long apprenticeship in the career
of vice has hardened for the execution of the most
nefarious purposes.

For many a weary, long hour, had the watch
already lasted.

The time was rapidly approaching when the
Marquis of Piatelli's carriage should loom in the distance—should reach the place where the troop was
stationed.

The suspense of the Boy Brigand was great, and
his anxiety was such as to cause him to keep his
eyes towards the west, from whence the travellers
would emerge.

The rattle of the carriage was now perceptible.

To enhance the terror of the scene, the rain began
to fall in heavy torrents, and the lightning flashed
now and then its lurid glare, casting its fitful light
on the countenances of the men who formed Sataniello's band.

The carriage had just attained the summit of a
hill, and the hoofs of the horses, hurrying towards
the direction where the band was on the watch, resounded upon the causeway.

When these unmistakeable signs of a close conflict were first discernible by the Postboy—Sataniello's new recruit—his heart beat and throbbed
within his breast with quick palpitations; yet he
said not a word, and his eye, rivetted upon Sataniello, taught him how to imitate his gallant and new
chief and leader.

The ambuscade being placed in a winding, the
presence of Sataniello and his men was not discernible.

As the road formed a sort of curb around the hill,
they could at different intervals see the chaise,
which, fearless of the storm, was dashing quickly
along.

The wind howled — at times with renewed strength and vigour, at others the sky was bright, and the glare of the stars enabled the silent witnesses of the scene which we are about to relate to prepare themselves for action.

"Attention, now, my boys," Sataniello whispered in an undertone as soon as the vehicle was getting nearer to his whereabouts. "Attention!"

All was excitement.

In one second the whole band were at their posts. Up to the present they had been standing at their ease.

Some, laying upon the ground, were indulging in a sleep, others were engaged in a conversation, of which the pith might be resumed in the following words :—

"I say," Paublas was saying to the Monk, 'what kind of a customer will the new chap be, I wonder ?"

"I heard great accounts of him," the Monk replied. "The Captain was telling me that he seemed a rather dangerous cove to interfere or meddle with."

"He is a Marquis, is he not ?" the Postboy inquired.

At first he had taken no notice of what he had heard ; but now that the subject, referring to a matter which would be productive of the greatest consequences to himself was brought into question, he pricked up his ears and listened in the most attentive manner.

It is extraordinary how acute the sense of hearing becomes on awaking from sleep, and how soon we learn to distinguish between sounds.

We should not forget that the Postboy was a new recruit—that but a few days ago he could have walked proudly and firmly in the city of Naples without his having occasion to fear the powers that be.

Now the case was quite different.

From an honest, hardworking postboy, or whatever his previous occupation might have been—and we have seen that that of postboy was the one—he had brought himself to the rank of a bandit, of an Italian brigand.

Up to the present period, and supposing that the bold troop commanded by Sataniello were to fall into the hands of the Papal dragoons, and every one of its members dragged into town to the Neapolitan gaol, he would have nothing to fear.

His joining the troop could not have told against him, because he was still innocent of any bad deed. He had not yet made himself an accomplice of the terrible companions whom he was destined to live with for the future.

It is not extraordinary, then, that he felt rather awkwardly situated, and that he looked anxiously forward to the moment when he would be compelled to join in the terrible plot about to be carried out.

The sentiments which he entertained were genuine enough, and the reader, we imagine, will not be slow in picturing them to himself.

"A Marquis ! Yes, he is a Marquis, and alive too," Paublas pursued, answering the Postboy's question.

"And he has lots of money ?" one of the band pursued.

"Of which, please God, we will take the liberty of ridding him as soon as we will get a chance."

"I know that Marquis well. He is rather a dashing nobleman in Naples," the Giant pursued. "He knows no end of his wealth ; and he is a determined chap after the ladies."

The Boy Brigand's attention was kindled as soon as the last word struck his ears.

He could not forget that if the character of the nobleman was a true one, it would be dangerous indeed to allow such a man to come within his roof if not killed to satisfy the ends of his meditated plunder, for when there he might try his little game with Joanitta.

The Boy Brigand, strange to say, always thought of her.

Whether she was such a girl as one seldom forgets—whether she was of such a loving disposition as to cause any male ever to long for her company, we know not.

Suffice it to say that Sataniello ever had her soft features present before his mind.

On more than one occasion he had had reason to judge of her womanly worth, so if she were the means of engrossing the whole of his thoughts, we are inclined to believe that there were strong reasons for it.

The warm reception which he had met on his return from Naples had been a hearty one, and he—not being yet fully impressed of Shakspeare's true words, namely, "Frailty, thy name is Woman"—never dreamt of the possibility of Joanitta turning unfaithful to him.

Whether she did so we are not in a position to state yet. Perhaps she might be ; but we cannot be too hasty in giving an opinion upon which we have no grounds to lay our foundation.

"By Jingo ! he's fond of the ladies, and no mistake about it," the Giant resumed. "He was wont to run after all the girls ; and I am sure that if the laws of this country were the same as in England—where I understand they manage these things better than we do—many a half-crown a week would he have to pay."

This conversation was taking place in an undertone ; and it would have been impossible for anyone, except that one was close to the speaker, to detect its meaning.

"My boys," Sataniello began, "leave all your twaddle for another day. The present time should be spent in a more profitable manner. Remember that ere long you will be called upon to do your duty."

Paublas fearlessly approached Sataniello, and spoke to him.

"Do not fear, Captain," he said ; "our men are anxious for a little excitement ; and even where they not so, your presence here would give them renewed pluck were they to be deficient of it—a thing I know they are not deficient of."

This mark of flattery, emanating from Paublas' lips, caused him to smile ; although we are far from believing that he thought for a single moment that Paublas words were genuine.

"The time will soon come," he said ; "and it will show me whether my troop is worthy of the trust which I repose in it—of the high opinions which I hold of every one of its respective members."

The vehicle was fast approaching, and the brigands, all bent upon their dark deed, were standing motionless behind the rocks.

Had any unknown being closely watched the vicinity where Sataniello's troop was stationed, he could have seen the muzzles of ten guns pointing through the apertures of the stone, behind which the men were hidden all in readiness, and anxiously awaiting to obey the commands of their courageous captain.

———

THE BOY BRIGAND ON HIS WAY TO NAPLES.

CHAPTER XIX.

WHICH BRINGS SEVERAL PEOPLE TOGETHER, AND
WHICH INTRODUCES FRESH PERSONAGES TO THE
READER—THE CHAISE OF THE MARQUIS PIATELLI
IS ATTACKED—RESULT.

THE sound of the carriage wheeling round was
becoming every instant plainer and plainer, and not
a syllable was uttered by the brigands.

Their eyes were fixed on the openings through
which they could see, and their gaze was directed
upon the high road.

Their fingers meanwhile were bent upon the locks
of their respective guns.

Awaiting their captain's orders, they stood like so
many marble statues.

We have omitted to say, that close by there was
a slanting path, about five yards the utmost in
length, by which the troop could easily in an instant
reach the high road.

Closer than anyone of his followers to the issue,
we could have noticed Sataniello.

Ever ready to brave the numerous dangers which
beset his path—ever ready to be the first to attack—
it could not be said that he could not be found at
his post.

9

The vehicle which conveyed the Marquis Piatelli and his fair sister to the castle of the Duke of Don Saltara was now running exactly at the spot behind which Sataniello and his men were keeping a faithful watch.

The hour had arrived.

If success was to be ensured, delay was dangerous.

With that foresight which Sataniello possessed to an eminent degree, he was not slow in coming to the above conclusion.

"Fire !" he exclaimed, in a bold voice.

Twelve shots answered the call.

"Well hit, my lads !" Paublas pursued ; "now to the rescue !"

The words of the lieutenant had scarcely been pronounced, when the whole band could have been seen following Paublas on the Boy Brigand's close track.

"Whoever you are, surrender to Sataniello, the Dark King of the Mountains !" the Boy Brigand ejaculated, as he came by the side of the carriage.

But the last sentence of his speech was not concluded, ere a man with a pistol in each hand appeared upon the footsteps of the carriage, from which Sataniello's words had withdrawn him.

Sataniello had been so much taken aback, and so little expected the determination which the Marquis Piatelli was showing, that for an instant he remained mute.

"Away, away from me, cowards ! scoundrels !" the Marquis exclaimed, "and let me pursue my journey."

A shot immediately followed this request.

The light had been momentaneous, and the bullet located itself within the sides of the carriage.

The target for which it had been meant had been missed.

The Marquis of Piatelli was therefore safe.

"Will you surrender, I repeat," Sataniello began anew.

To this question the Marquis discharged his two pistols.

Inexplicable, indeed, may be the following.

Although close to the Boy Brigand, and surrounded by the troop, the aim of the Marquis had been unproductive of any result.

He would doubtless have allowed himself to be captured had not his determination been kindled by an accident, which, in his rage, he had totally forgotten, and which was in a moment brought back to his mind.

The scene seemed to be changed.

Screams were now heard from within the carriage. They emanated, doubtless, from a woman's lips. Soft, although piercing, were the sounds which now rent the air.

"I challenge you all—yes, I challenge you ! never will I surrender ! never will I allow my sister to fall into the hands of such brigands—of such scoundrels as you ! No, never, never ! sooner than to do so, I will shed my last drop of blood !"

"Quietly, quietly ! my friend. Be cool," Sataniello replied, "what do you propose to do against my band ?"

"Shall I settle him, Captain ?" Paublas inquired, immediately following his master's words.

"Silence !" Sataniello replied.

The sight which offered itself now was imposing indeed.

The shaft-horse had been pierced by at least half-a-dozen shots, and his body was laying in a pool of blood, which ran profusely from his numerous wounds. In his fall he had so strained the neck of his fellow-companion horse, that the latter's neck seemed to be in a noose, and could not move.

In the saddle of the fallen horse was the postilion.

But a few minutes ago he had been alive— thoughtless of the imminent danger—of the sudden fate which awaited him. Now he was rapidly hurrying towards eternity.

As the moon shed now and then its lurid glare upon the causeway, his livid face could easily be seen, and his ghastly features would have been sufficient to frighten any passer by—anyone in fact who would have found himself suddenly by the spot where had occurred the events which we have related.

Hindered, therefore, by the bodies of the horse and postilion, the chaise was at a stand-still.

The Marquis Piatelli, up to this time, was not aware of the causes which had brought on the delay in his journey.

It is true that he had heard the several detonations, but he could not realize to his mind the possibility that the shaft-horse and postilion had been already done away with in so quick a time as that which had elapsed.

The screams inside the vehicle had now subsided. A conversation between the brother and her and Sataniello was now taking place—the female traveller having been wise enough to stay her exclamation.

The Marquis of Piatelli breathed heavily. It was evident that in the present case he realised the extent of his position.

"What do you want of me, Sir ?" he asked of Sataniello.

"Oh, very little !" the Boy Brigand replied; "we only require your luggage."

"Oh, thank you, you are welcome to that," the Marquis replied, as if a weight had been taken off his breast. "You may take the coat off my back if you allow us to remain free."

"Oh, do not misunderstand me, my friend," Sataniello replied ; "you and your companion, whoever she is, will have to come with us."

"I am going on a visit to the Duke of Don Saltara's," the Marquis replied, "and what shall I do ?"

"I am fully aware of that," Sataniello replied ; "I go, and will see him instead of you."

The Marquis of Piatelli looked at the Boy Brigand.

"I have seen you before. I saw you yesterday," he began, in an anxious tone of voice, thinking that the very fact of having been in the same room as the Boy Brigand a few days previously might have the effect of inducing him to act more leniently towards him.

"I dare say you have, my friend," he replied ; "a great many people see me ; but I am sorry to say that I never keep up any acquaintance with anyone."

So peremptorily had Sataniello replied to the Marquis, that he soon saw the uselesness of prolonging the subject further. He still, however, kept on contemplating Sataniello's features, and he could have no doubt upon his mind as to his having become the prisoner of the man who, but a few days ago, we may say, he had met in the manager's room of the Royal Neapolitan Bank.

During the time, and while the dialogue which we have related had taken place, no steps had been urged on Sataniello's part to make sure of his prisoners.

"I will beg of you, Sir," Sataniello began, "to step out of the carriage, as our time is precious, and we have no time to lose."

At first the Marquis showed a certain reluctance.

Sataniello soon perceived the *"mauvaise grace"* with which the person to whom he was speaking seemed to display on hearing him make his request.

"Do not make more delay than you possibly can," the Boy Brigand began. "I am extra civil with you, Marquis, you see ; because if you do, it would compel me to have recourse to the only extremity which remains to me, namely, to put you out of the way."

Sataniello pronounced this phrase in a cool and determined manner, which was anything but reassuring to the listener.

In one instant he was by the hedge of the road, gazing around him ; but the darkness again had set in, and he could see no one, only he could feel the shoulders of the brigands, who were watching him.

When Sataniello placed his head within the carriage, the perfume which agreeably surprised him was pleasing in the extreme.

A bouquet of flowers stood immediately before the female companion of the Marquis of Piatelli.

The shades of night were so thick that he could not see whether the traveller was fair or not—whether she was young or old—and his curiosity, one can easily guess, was great indeed.

He could, however, perceive two diamonds which sparkled before him. The diamonds were, we need not say, the eyes of the lady.

When he had sufficiently satisfied himself as to there being a lady in the vehicle, Sataniello opened his lips.

"Madam," he said, "you are my prisoner."

Not a syllable re-echoed the Boy Brigand's words.

He repeated his words.

The same silence on the lady's part.

Sataniello was at a loss to make out from whence such a determination to remain dumb could spring from.

"Paublas," he exclaimed, "bring me the bull's-eye."

In an instant it was brought to Sataniello, and with it he lighted up the vehicle.

Therein he saw the sister of the Marquis of Piatelli.

She was reclining backwards upon the soft cushion of the chaise, and her features, although remarkably pale, were so handsome that we think it right to give here a minute description of them.

She was dressed in a travelling costume, which, for costliness and elegance, rivalled anything which could be made by the most fashionable French dressmaker ; and her pretty, handsome hands, were covered with a pair of travelling kid gloves, which fitted to a nicety.

She had on a woollen cloak, lined inside with a rosy description of silk, and the upper part of it covering her bonnet, nought but her pale features could be seen.

Hidden by the folds of the glossy head-dress, her hair was shut from man's gaze.

Thus charmingly attired, she appeared like a female monk.

Her face was remarkably white, we have already said, but that gave to it a certain *je ne sais quoi*, which rendered her far more interesting.

Her mouth was small, indeed ; and although it was evident that the Marquis of Piatelli's sister had been frightened, that as soon as her eyes had met those of Sataniello, she had lost for awhile her consciousness ; still her fright had been powerless to deprive her lips of that rosy hue, which contrasted agreeably indeed with the paleness of her countenance.

Her nose was aquiline, and small to a degree ; and her soft, silky eyelashes, surmounted a pair of eyes, which, from her *tout ensemble*, must have been expressive and loving, did they accord themselves with the remainder of her attractions.

It took the time which we have taken to describe the fair companion of the Marquis of Piatelli to induce the Boy Brigand to come to a determination relating to that pretty creature whom he had been contemplating for the last few instants.

Although nothing would have created more dissatisfaction among his troop than to incur unnecessary delay on account of a woman—although the Boy Brigand was aware of that fact—still he would have to blame himself had he acted in a rough manner towards the lady whom fate had thrown within his path.

He therefore used all the courtesy which he thought it lay in his power to display, and he lost no time in awaking the lady, or at least in endeavouring to get her to become herself again.

In the front of the vehicle, and where the bouquet was to which we have already alluded, there was a closed pocket similar to those which doubtless many of our readers have noticed in the English vehicles.

These are made to enable the travellers to place within arm's length whatever they may require during the journey.

Sataniello took away the flowers and flung them outside. He knew that such a perfume would vitiate the close atmosphere of the vehicle, and having heard that the odour of flowers was prejudicial to people in their slumbers, he acted upon what he remembered.

In the meantime, he was closely inspecting the inside of the pocket.

At length he withdrew his hand, within which he had a salts perfume-bottle. He opened it, and placed it beneath the lady's nostrils.

She inhaled the strong odour, and she regained her consciousness.

"Senorita, sua prisoniera mia" (Miss, you are my prisoner), the Boy Brigand began, in good Italian.

Senorita, in that language, means "Lady."

Now that our readers are made fully acquainted with the meaning of the word, we will always adhere to it throughout the tale.

When speaking of certain countries, and the customs peculiar to the same, we think that one should always be as accurate as possible in relation to that which appertains to it.

Although the Senorita had opened her eyes, she soon closed them again.

"Senorita," he said, "I would wish you to come out of the carriage, as it will not go any further this evening."

"Where is my brother ? oh! where is he ? Do, pray, tell me. I hope he is safe?"

"Your brother, the Marquis Piatelli, is outside ; and if you please to comply with my request you will see him yourself."

At that moment the blast of the wind made its way through the open carriage, and the Senorita trembled and shivered with the cold night air.

This *denouement* to their journey was anything but that which she expected.

Once more it illustrates the old proverb, "Man proposes and God disposes."

Here but a few hours ago, we may say, the Senorita was leaving her palace in Naples, looking forward to the pleasant days which she thought she would pass at the castle of the Duke of Don Saltara; and, instead of that which her mind delighted in picturing to herself, she had become the prisoner of a cruel, fearless bandit.

"How do you know my brother's name?" the Senorita inquired.

"I have met him before," the Boy Brigand replied, in a cool tone of voice; and, thus speaking, he withdrew his head from the vehicle to allow the lady to act in accordance with the last wish which he had given utterance to.

The Marquis of Piatelli's sister knew that but one thing remained to be done, namely, to obey.

So, with the same manner as that which she would have displayed in alighting from her carriage had she been in any other place besides the present one, she rose from her seat.

At first rising she settled her toilet, fastened her cloak close to her chin, buttoned on one of her gloves which had become loose, and, so far equipped, she was received on the steps of the vehicle by Sataniello, who, taking her by the waist, placed her on the high-road.

This rough mark of courtesy had been accomplished quicker than we could have described it. So thunderstruck was Senorita by a proceeding which she was far from expecting, that she found not a word of reply.

Her heart, however, beat with feelings of satisfaction when throughout the darkness of night she heard the voice of her brother—unmistakable token to her that he was still in the land of the living.

"Ransack the vehicle and clear the road," the Boy Brigand began, "and I will keep watch."

Six of Sataniello's troop, among whom there was the Giant, proceeded to carry out the order just given.

In one instant the harness which attached the body of the dead horse to the vehicle was unfastened, and the Giant, helped by the Monk and two others, dragged the senseless animal by the side of a deep edge, where it was hurled downwards.

Once the horse had been disposed of, the postilion was next attended to.

Ghastly sight it would have been indeed for any one who for the first time would have assisted in that which we are about to describe.

In a pool of blood, and with his head resting between the hoofs of the fellow horse of the one which had been killed, lay the driver, who but a few hours ago smacked his whip with all the exuberance and thoughtlessness of a youth of eighteen or nineteen years of age.

The Monk and another one carried the body by the roadside.

There was a big heavy stone close by them—upon it they placed him.

The Giant took his pulse and he felt it; and the Monk, looking to find whether life was totally extinct in his frame, opened his garments and placed his hand upon his heart.

Paublas soon came with another bull's-eye, and, as each brigand carried one about him—when their hands were disengaged—this renewal of light was of much use under the present circumstances.

"That man is dead," Paublas exclaimed, as soon as the light of the lamp shone upon the postilion's features. "Any one could see that in a twinkling."

"The Lieutenant is right," the Monk pursued. "The heart has ceased to beat, his hands are as cold as ice, his eyelids have long ago closed, and it it useless to waste our time about him."

"He must have suffered a good deal," the Giant said. "Look how distorted his mouth is, to be sure."

"How could it be otherwise?" the Monk replied. "Look at his coat."

His garment was next inspected, and it was found that it was pierced in places by several bullets.

The Captain at that instant came up. "What are you doing here?" he asked.

"We are trying to bring this man to life."

"Talk not of humanity," Sataniello began, "He is dead. The next thing which we must do is to remove him from this place, for it would not answer our purpose to leave a corpse on the high road. Where's the Hunchback?"

"Here he is," a voice replied, and the latter approached Sataniello.

"Have you got your pick and shovel here?" the Boy Brigand inquired.

"Not about me, Captain," the Hunchback replied; "but they are not far off. I always carry them with me in case of need, and they are both laying in a heap beneath the rock yonder," and his hand pointed mechanically towards a direction which was not discernible by any of the troop, as the moon was now hidden by heavy clouds gathering in the sky, and as the night was intensely dark.

"Go and fetch them, and return here at once," the Captain pursued, in a peremptory tone of voice.

The Hunchback made no reply to his Captian, but the sounds of his heavy boots cracking over the road were immediately afterwards heard dying in the distance.

CHAPTER XX.

WHERE THE LUGGAGE OF THE MARQUIS OF PIATELLI IS RANSACKED — WHICH SHOWS THE MANNER IN WHICH THE POSTILION'S DEAD BODY IS MADE AWAY WITH — AND WHICH FURTHER TELLS OF THE SHORT-LIVED CAREER OF ONE OF SATANIELLO'S BAND.

WHEN the Hunchback, faithful in carrying out his Captain's orders, returned with the instruments which he had been bid to go in search of, the night was gradually drawing to a close.

As long as the darkness which reigned had kept on it was nearly impossible for Sataniello's troop to attend to the instructions which he had given, and it was a wonder also that the Marquis of Piatelli had not had recourse to flight, to escape from the brigands among whom he had fallen.

It was only the fear of a sudden death—which he knew would have been his lot—and, further, the reluctance which he also felt at leaving his sister in the hands of such ruffians as had attacked him, that induced him to remain where he was.

It is, however, exceedingly probable that, had he not allowed his mind to be prevailed upon by the last conclusion, he could have escaped during the row and turmoil which followed his alighting from the carriage.

But he knew not the spot where he was; and, even had he been successful enough to baffle the brigand's pursuit, he saw a very good chance of losing himself among the many roads which branched off in every direction.

When the Hunchback was once more upon the spot where the chaise stood, he saw three or four trunks scattered upon the high road, and the brigands in the act of examining carefully their contents.

"Are they worth while carrying with us?" Sataniello inquired.

"That they are, Sir," the voice of the Monk replied. "The whole of the Marquis's wardrobe is here. All her ladyship's dresses also, and such fine clothes I never saw. There is, besides, a little basket which I cannot open, and it weighs heavy, too."

"Oh, my diamonds!" the Senorita ejaculated in an underwhisper, which she thought no one heard.

There, however, she had been mistaken, for, at the very time that the above exclamation—uttered against her will, we may say, and prompted by the natural fear of losing that which a continental woman holds in so great a veneration and worship—had escaped her lips, Sataniello happened to pass close to her.

Sataniello was too prudent, and knew too well what he was about to allow the Senorita to think for one moment that her exclamation had been heeded by her new captor.

"Close all those boxes," Sataniello resumed, "and place them in a heap by my side. Let us, in the meantime, send the horse to the stable. By jove," he continued, "before long I will have quite a stud of my own.—Pedro, Pedro," Sataniello exclaimed.

The sounds of his voice died away in the distance, and the echo repeated the name.

"Pedro, Pedro," the Boy Brigand began again.

And only the echo answered his call.

"Where can that boy have gone to?" Sataniello whispered to himself. "Surely he has not shown the white feather. Have you seen our new recruit anywhere?" the Boy Brigand inquired again.

"Doubtless he took to his heels as soon as the first shot was fired," Paublas replied.

"Do not form too hasty an opinion," the Giant ejaculated, "he will be back again I should say."

"Yes, when there's no man to fear he will show forth again," the Hunchback continued.

"Pedro! Pedro!" Sataniello began again; and he was about to wend his steps towards the vehicle, when he nearly staggered.

The morning light was now at its culminating point, and everything around could be plainly perceptible.

He looked downwards.

A subdued groan escaped his lips.

"Oh! oh! friend Pedro," he exclaimed in a saddened tone. "Look here."

The eyes of the whole band were now directed towards the spot to which Sataniello pointed.

The post boy had not dreaded danger, as some of our readers might have been inclined to think.

He had not had recourse to a hasty flight, for there he was at the Giant's feet—

At least, not Pedro full of life, but Pedro's corpse.

"Postilions evidently are not a lucky class of men," Paublas began; "Pedro has been shot through the head."

"I thought some one fell down when I unloaded my pistol," the Marquis of Piatelli pursued, "but I was not certain of it, otherwise I should have spoken ere now."

"Poor fellow," the Giant began, "his career has not been a long one."

A deep silence followed these words.

"It would have been better for him," Sataniello ejaculated, "had Pedro returned to Naples to look after his mother and sister, sooner than to join my band; but as I am the indirect cause of his death those people will have no occasion to regret his downfall, for I will make it up to them if we can find them."

Repeated endeavours were made to restore life to Pedro's inanimate frame, but all their exertions failed to bring him to life again.

"It is no use to think any more about the calamity," Sataniello pursued. "Hunchback dig the grave; and as you will have two bodies to bury make it deeper, that's all, and look sharp about it."

The Hunchback had no occasion to be told twice, for he was by the roadside, and in an instant he was busily occupied in carrying out his task.

An hour had scarcely elapsed when the two youths rested side by side in a solitary grave, and once all solemn and imposing ceremony of burying their new companion and the unfortunate postilion had been gone through, Sataniello gave the necessary orders to carry away the Marquis of Piatelli's luggage to the cavern.

They were four boxes altogether. A kind of stretcher was made with the branches of a tree, and the luggage having been placed upon it, the bandits retraced their steps homewards.

The carriage had previously been dragged to a spot on the high-road, which offered of itself a safe shelter for anything of the kind, and the horse, led on by the bridle, was conducted to the field where Sataniello's previous mount had already been cast loose.

In the manner above described did the whole troop of Sataniello's walk across the country, and gloomy indeed was the return which the whole band effected to their mountainous home.

CHAPTER XXI.

WHERE THE BOY BRIGAND MAKES UP HIS MIND TO ACT IN A WAY WHICH MANY WOULD HAVE DREADED.

A FEW days had elapsed since the events which we have described, and the life which Sataniello led had not been disturbed by any incidents worthy our notice.

The Marquis of Piatelli had soon grown accustomed to the existence which he had, and although it was one which was anything but in accordance with his taste he had to keep his mouth dumb, and to wait the result of an adventure so strangely began.

The Marquis of Piatelli had been located in a cavern which had been fitted on purpose for him, and the Senorita had been introduced to Joanitta, against whom she had taken a decided dislike from the first moment which she had seen her.

On more than one occasion had the Marquis of Piatelli asked the Boy Brigand to tell him what was his intention relating to himself; but up to the present period he had refused to give him any answer.

Sataniello, however, had learnt from the Marquis all the details which he wished to become acquainted with.

What he could not learn from the Marquis he had easily found out from the Senorita.

The latter told him what Sataniello knew already, namely, that he had been asked on a visit to the castle of the Duke of Don Saltara, and that in company with his brother, they were going there when the vehicle had been attacked in the manner in which we have seen it had been.

Sataniello had further been acquainted with information which the Senorita, with a guilty thoughtlessness, had given him, although unasked for it, and which went to show that the noble Duke of Don Saltara was a very wealthy man, rather of a peculiar turn of mind.

Now, for instance, he had a great objection to send any of his rents to a banker, and he kept the whole of his property stored within some part of the castle, thereby losing all the interest which would accrue from the large capital which he possessed.

It was only when reflection followed the words which she uttered, that the Senorita blamed herself for what she had said, for she could not but think that, although there was no great meaning in her words, it might give to Sataniello an idea of besieging the castle of the Duke to search within for the gold which was treasured within it.

Unfortunately this was exactly the plan which at once entered Sataniello's brain; but he was not of that rash disposition which impels one to seek unnecessary danger, and who had come to the determination himself to pay a visit to the Duke.

As he had within his possession the whole wardrobe of the Italian nobleman—as he was of the same height as himself, he saw no reason why he should not personify the character of the Marquis Piatelli, and go and see the Duke himself.

Faith he had learnt a detail which would have induced him to resolve upon that bold step even had he had no thought of it.

The Marquis of Piatelli's father had recently died, and as he had been a great friend of the late Duke of Don Saltara, on his death-bed he had made him give him his promise that he should spend a few weeks with his old college friend, and be the bearer of a note which he wrote but a few days previous to his departing this world.

Never had the young Marquis seen the Duke of Don Saltara.

The letter of which we have spoken was in the Boy Brigand's possession—and to be the bearer of it—and to lie for a few days beneath the roof of the proudest Italian noblemen of the land, was a perspective which flattered Sataniello in the extreme.

Besides he had always some idea in his head, and common sense told him that out of such a visit something must spring out which would give him no reason to repent of his enterprise.

Sataniello had kept his design all to himself, and to none except to the Monk had he opened his mouth.

The latter highly approved of it.

It would, however, have been impossible for Sataniello not to have divulged the whole plan to his followers at some time or other.

That he had resolved to do; and he knew that nothing would have been more welcomed by the whole band than to see a fair prospect of new spoil.

It may seem strange to our readers that a bandit's life, so full of dangers, should be ambitioned by so many; but there are so many excitements always following each other that it answers well indeed the expectations of such men as Sataniello's troop, who craved for emotions, and to whom a honest existence would have been irksome.

It should not be imagined that the type of Sataniello and his followers can be enacted only within the bounds of a romance.

It is not so, for a perusal of the newspapers of the day will show to my readers that bands like that of Sataniello's exist at the present moment in Italy and Greece, and that the deeds which are performed by them fall below those which are narrated in the course of this narrative.

Yes, the Boy Brigand had made up his mind to pay a visit to the Duke of Don Saltara.

At first he had thought of bringing Joanitta along with him; but, knowing how awkward one is when incumbered with a lady in such a case as the one in point, he had finally decided that he should leave her behind him.

One thing, which was greatly in the Boy Brigand's favour, was the following:—

The castle of the Duke of Don Saltara was remote, it is true, from the brigand's cavern, but it was not so far distant as to make it impossible for his followers to be daily visited.

It was the intention of Sataniello to take the Monk with him.

He felt very much disappointed, nay, he could but mourn the death of Pedro, the Post-boy—for doubtless the latter, being known by the servants of the castle, it would have given to his journey and enterprise a character of truth, which a complete stranger would fail to do.

The Boy Brigand's appearance had greatly altered since the day when he left Rome in company with Paublas.

The hard life—the life of adventure which he had been leading—had hardened his features; and, although he had not yet seen twenty-five summers, he looked at least ten years older.

His moustachios and whiskers had grown with astonishing rapidity, and it was to his manly features no inconsiderable improvement.

At the moment at which we now see him, he had just been paying a visit to the Marquis of Piatelli, and, the information which he had required from him having been freely given, he was walking along the subterranean strait which led to what he called his head-quarters. Paublas, who of late had been unable to fathom the strange ways of his master, was following him: behind Paublas came the Hunchback.

We have already said that the Hunchback acted as valet to the Captain, and did all the dirty work of the troop.

His nature was degraded, and he liked all menial employments.

It is peculiar, but nevertheless true, that all those whom Nature, in her wayward freaks, has allowed to be brought into this world as cripples, should, as a rule, be deprived of those noble ideas which actuate the minds of handsomely-made men.

Now, for certain, if an individual is endowed with fine features, if his eyes sparkle with intelligence, his expansive forehead betrays deep ideas, it will generally be found that such a man possesses great powers of thought—in some cases extraordinary genius.

This is a peculiarity which has been noticed before, and as we can illustrate it in the instance of Sataniello and of the Hunchback, we here take the opportunity of referring to it.

The Hunchback, besides, was cruel by nature. He took a delight in torturing animals when he could do so; and they related a story of him which pourtrayed the low and degraded inclinations which actuated every one of his acts.

He had once been laid a wager that he would eat the ear of a traveller who had been waylaid by the troop. Although the amount had been, comparatively-speaking, a trifling one, he had nevertheless won the bet.

For this act Sataniello hated him; but he was handy to him, otherwise he should have made away with him long ago.

He was useful to the band in more ways than

one—a better cook could not have been got anywhere—and, as he was also besides a good servant, and a very few of Sataniello's followers would have condescended to undertake menial employments, he was allowed to live.

"Hunchback," the Captain said, "I wish to dress."

The Hunchback bowed.

"Be quick, and leave your bowings and scrapings for another day," the Captain began, impatiently.

The Hunchback did not wait much longer, but he made his exit. An instant afterwards he re-appeared, bearing in his hand a trunk of no small dimensions. He opened it, and out of it he drew a cambric pocket handkerchief most beautifully embroidered, with a Marquis's crest in the corner, and a small bottle of perfume, and a suit of velvet clothes of a most expensive description, a pair of patent leather Wellington boots with golden spurs, and a splendid dark beaver hat with an ostrich-feather proudly surmounting it.

The Boy Brigand now proceeded to his toilet.

The whole attire fitted him as if it had been made for him—and yet it had been cut for the Marquis of Piatelli, who was going on a visit to the Duke of Don Saltara, when he had been waylaid and captured by Sataniello's band as we have seen.

The Hunchback had retired.

"What do you think of me now?" the Boy Brigand said, turning round to Paublas; "will I do?"

The lieutenant spoke not, but nodded his head in the affirmative.

"Bye-the-bye," the Boy Brigand continued, "what did you do with the carriage which belonged to the Marquis, of whom I am now so gallantly sporting the uniform?"

"Captain," Paublas replied, "I have seen to it as you bid me. It is close at hand; and the horse, in company with the others, grazing as leisurely and as happily as if he were in the stables of his noble owner.

"Daring deed that of ours, Paublas," the Captain pursued, "I never thought that we would have mastered the Marquis as easily as we did. How he fought. How he bled. A gallant fellow was he! But let us speak no more about what is past. This night must see me within the walls of the castle. I will take the Monk with me. You must remain here to keep my troop in order, and, if there is any sign of mutiny, you know how to act."

Paublas answered not, but he held firmly in his grasp the handle of his pistol, and his threatening, resolute, and fearless look was a sufficient guarantee for the Boy Brigand that in his absence he had no reason to fear.

"And is the Monk aware that he is to accompany you, Captain?" Paublas inquired.

"Not yet," the Boy Brigand replied.

"Will I tell him?" the lieutenant interrogated.

"Yes, do;" was the reply; "and do not forget to impress upon his mind the fact that in an hour hence I will be ready."

And Paublas departed to execute his master's orders.

Now the reader might, perhaps, like to know who "The Monk" was. We will not keep him long in suspense. A few evenings after the Boy Brigand and Paublas had left Rome, they were walking in the high road in the neighbourhood of a village where stood a seminary where young men were brought up to become priests. They saw a youth heedlessly rushing towards them. They stopped him and asked him the object of his errand. He informed them that he was the son of a wealthy jeweller that lived in Florence, that he had forged his father's name to a bill for a rather heavy sum; that he was educated to become a priest, and that when the deed had been discovered, he had met with such hard treatment from the Senior Friar of the school, that life was now made unbearable to him, and that sooner than remain where he was he had fled away from them.

The Boy Brigand told him what kind of life he led, and he said to him that if he wished to join him, he would be too happy to accept him as a companion; and he had accepted their offer, and he became one of them, and they surnamed him the "Monk."

This is only but a cursory sketch of the Monk's life. As the story proceeds, the whole of his youth will be narrated for the benefit of our readers.

Had any stranger, unacquainted with the real character of the Boy Brigand, entered the grotto where Sataniello was, he would have been astonished indeed to see so dandified a youth in so rough and extraordinary a place.

He would have fancied that his mind was the object of some unearthly hallucination. He would have believed that his eyes saw not what they really did see. He would not have believed that he was deceived!

Sataniello looked indeed a fine Boy Brigand.

With his sword dangling by his side—with his tight-fitting uniform fastened by silvery buttons of a most exquisite pattern—with his close-fitting wrists with beautiful ornamental frill—with his fine boots—with his dark "sombrero" hat jauntily cast on one side.

He waited.

He pulled out of his pocket a splendid gold hunting-watch, upon the back case of which was designed a most artistical picture, and looked at it.

"By Jove!" he said, "the Monk does not seem to have taken much heed of my orders—he is late."

"No, he is not," a voice replied from the outside, and the Monk made his appearance.

"Here I am, Captain," he exclaimed, "awaiting your orders."

"That's right," the Boy Brigand replied, "I like to see punctuality;" and he looked steadfastly at the new comer.

"You are just the kind of companion I wanted," he pursued. You have every outward appearance of what you really are,—a devil-may-care kind of look that will surely attract the attention of the Duke's pretty abigails—blue eyes, fair sandy hair, and a white complexion, and not yet nineteen! surely it is not every day that the Duke's servants will meet such a handsome fellow as thou truly art."

"Captain," the Monk replied, "I would not care much about looks, if I could only have those fine whiskers of yours—that intrepid look——"

"Silence, silence, and be still," the Boy Brigand replied, "and listen to me. We are now going to the castle of the Duke of Don Saltara; you will see there a pretty chambermaid—her name is Maria. Now mind what I tell you: firstly, you must take her hands into yours; you must tell her that you never saw such a bewitching creature as she is; and secondly, when she will ask you who your master is, tell her that I am the Marquis Piatelli—that my wealth is immense—that I have three big castles in my country, two villas, and that no less than twenty horses feed daily in my stables—that you have been my servant for two years, and that my generosity knows no bounds. Not a word more will you say. You may, of course, make an appointment with her, and ask her to meet you by the moonlight, and so on. But of course that is your own look-out, not mine."

It is very probable that had the Monk been left to himself, he would have acted in a way exactly similar to that which he was bid to ; and as he had his master's interest at heart, we do not doubt that he would have lost an opportunity in praising him in the eyes of any stranger.

The first part of the Captain's injunctions would doubtless have been carried out ; but what is beyond doubt is this, that he required not to be spurred on to make love to any pretty girl.

For all boys—all youths we ought to say—whether they follow a profession, a honest trade, or are engaged in a life of reckless adventures like that of a brigand, are, as a rule, not slow in detecting a loving, handsome maiden from an ugly one, and when they meet the former, there are ninety chances to a hundred that they will endeavour to meet her again.

Thus the Monk was determined to make the most of his time while staying at the Castle of the Duke of Don Saltara's ; and if this Maria, whose name he had heard Sataniello mentioning, kindled his fancy, he would, like a true Italian, show her that his feelings were in the right place.

"Have you got everything that you require?" the Boy Brigand inquired of the youth before him.

"Yes ;" was the determined reply.

"Is the carriage ready outside?" Sataniello pursued.

"All ready," the Monk responded.

"Well, then, no more remains to do," Sataniello continued ; " so jump up on your seat, and drive as fast as you can."

While Sataniello spoke, he stood by the road's side ; and having ascertained himself that the two horses were safely harnessed to the vehicle, he entered the conveyance.

The Monk was already in the saddle ; he smacked his whip once, twice, thrice, and away—and away dashed the two horses, and up hill, down hill they went, never slackening their pace until they reached the end of their destination.

Ere long they did so ; for but a few hours after his departure from Sataniello's cavern, the Monk saw a huge building looming in the distance ; and as he grew nearer and nearer, the towers and battlements of the Duke of Don Saltara's castle struck his gaze.

CHAPTER XXII.

WHICH TELLS OF SATANIELLO'S WELCOME IN A DUCAL HOME—AND WHICH DESCRIBES THE MANNER WITH WHICH HE COMPORTED HIMSELF IN HIS NEW GUISE.

THE Boy Brigand was fast asleep in the coupe of the vehicle, when the halting of the carriage withdrew him from his slumbers.

He awoke and looked outside.

He was at a standstill before a sumptuous portico to which one had to ascend by the help of a handsomely carved flight of steps.

The Monk was soon out of the saddle, and he was about to ring the bell of the hall door, when some servants in a splendid livery attracted by the rolling of the vehicle showed their rubicund countenances to the two new-comers.

Sataniello alighted in an instant, and having given orders to unstrap his valuable luggage, which

let it be confessed was composed of the whole of the wardrobe of the Marquis of Piatelli.

The Boy Brigand was asked his name and he replied at once, The Marquis of Piatelli.

The menials bowed in reply, and conducted him through a marble staircase to the drawing-room where the old Duke was wont to receive his visitors

When Sataniello entered the gorgeously furnished apartment, he felt an awkward feeling gradually creeping over the whole of his frame.

He was thinking on the rashness of his enterprise.

But he was not one of those faint-hearted nature who would allow a treasure to escape from them for a want of determination.

So he coolly awaited the arrival of his host.

The drawing-room door now opened, and steps were heard outside.

Sataniello turned his head round to see from whence the noise proceeded.

He was, however, doomed to be disappointed.

It was only a servant who came to place his head within the apartment, where he had apparently no business.

Previous to his departing he addressed Sataniello.

"If you like to take a seat, Signor Marquis," he said, " The Duke, my master, will soon be with you."

Sataniello made no answer to the menial, but thought inwardly that it was a great fallacy indeed, for wealthy families to keep a pack of idle fellows like those he saw before him, to be constantly about the house, without, it appeared to him, their being either useful or ornamental.

Sataniello was thus thinking, when the sounds of footsteps again attracted his attention.

Naturally he looked around.

Before him he saw advancing, in a steady, slow step, an old gentleman, who, as far as he could judge, was at least sixty years of age.

"Welcome here, Marquis Piatelli," the Duke said ; for the new personage was the old duke, Don Saltara ; "your father and myself have been old friends ; and when I learnt the news of his death, I felt grieved to the very utmost."

Sataniello listened to the old nobleman with the deepest attention.

He personated the character of a marquis, whose father had lately been snatched from this world, and, as a matter of course, he endeavoured to look as sorrowful as he possibly could ; although, to tell the exact truth, instead of the stern countenance which he assumed at once like a clever actor, he would have been much more inclined to give way to such a smile as would be brought on by the critical position in which he found himself placed.

"Yes," Sataniello replied, " he was taken away rather abruptly."

"A disease of the heart, was it not?" the old Duke of Don Saltara inquired.

Now the Boy Brigand had not the remotest idea of the kind of disease which had seized hold of his supposed father, and he remained silent.

The old duke did not press the information.

"I fully understand, Marquis," he said, " your emotion, and I must apologize for having brought back to your mind a subject which, doubtless, must be sore to you."

Sataniello sighed.

"A good son, that," the Duke thought inwardly ; " how the poor fellow seems to feel the loss."

"He was a kind father to me," the Boy Brigand pursued, lamentably, " and I will never forget the blow which I have just received. No one knows what a good father is to one, unless he loses him

THE MONK CAUGHT KISSING MARIA.

New demonstrations of sympathy on the part of the old Duke.

He took Sataniello's hands in his, and shook it warmly.

"Pray take a seat, Marquis," the Duke began. 'You must be tired after your long journey."

"Well, I am," Sataniello replied. "This confounded vehicle rattles so unceasingly over the ground, that it makes one quite uncomfortable."

"Our roads want to be looked about, I am aware," the Duke of Don Soltara pursued. But you found t more easy going within a mile or two of the place?

I did, I must confess," Sataniello continued,

although as far as he was aware he did not notice any change for the better.

"This is all my own property about here," the Duke went on; "my father had a great taste for territorial aggrandisement; and he was never satisfied unless he was engaged in some kind of purchase or another. When he died, I found that he had left a great many broad-acres; but half of the rent goes towards paying interest for money which was advanced by lawyers, to defend lawsuits; for I must tell you, that my father was an awful man for quarelling with his neighbours, and he never felt at home unless at loggerheads with all the gentry of the neighbourhood."

Sataniello lent an attentive ear to his new host.

Like every one else, he had his ways about him, and he liked to indulge in telling every one else about his own affairs.

"Yes!" the Duke ejaculated after awhile. "I am very glad you came here Marquis Piatelli, you will find it dull enough, I dare say; but there is plenty of sport in my forests, and what between shooting in the day, riding in the vicinity, which presents a very beautiful landscape in certain parts, and listening to my daughter's music, you will manage to kill the time."

Sataniello bowed—

He rose, and half carelessly, half consciously he walked towards one of the looking-glasses, and he gazed at himself in it.

A smile appeared upon his lips.

He felt quite satisfied with himself.

The clothes which he wore, well-shaped, and of the finest material; the shirt he had on was of the most refined linen; and the sword which dangled by his side suited him more than anything else.

In his new guise, he felt contented and happy.

"You would like to have a little supper before you retire, I daresay," the old Duke said, "I will not long detain you here—I know how anxious for rest you must be now. So I will just ring the bell to give my orders."

Sataniello did now what he had been able to do before—to scrutinise the appearance of the Duke of Don Saltara.

He was a man whose features were aristocratic and expressive.

His black eye was sharp and piercing, and betrayed a good deal of intelligence, although he had seen many a summer pass over his head; his hair, of a snowy white, was still plentiful and glossy; and his teeth, which were seen to advantage when he smiled, were white and well set.

He was one of those whose appearance could not have been mistaken; and had any one, unaware of his rank, met him casually in a place of public resort, he could not but have come to the conclusion that the old Duke of Don Saltara was the type of an Italian gentleman.

The servant, whose particular duty it was to answer the bell, appeared.

The Duke of Don Saltara gave him his instructions.

The menial curtsied in reply to the Duke—and disappeared.

When the Boy Brigand and the Duke found themselves together again, Sataniello resumed the conversation which had been interrupted for awhile by the details which we have hitherto fully described.

"A fine, handsome, residence this, my Lord Duke," he said. "I wish I had so fine a castle to dwell in."

"But Villa Turentino is a very nice little spot," the Duke paused. "I remember I was a guest of your father some ten years ago; and I extremely liked it."

This remark brought Sataniello to his senses.

He had no idea of ever having possessed such a villa as that to which the old Duke referred.

In fact, he had entirely forgotten the role which he had assumed; and, but for a lucky presence of mind, he might have compromised himself.

"The villa is a nice little country home," Sataniello pursued; "but it is too close to Florence. I like either all country, or all town. I hate a half-and-half kind of thing."

"I quite agree with you," the old Duke ejaculated; and he was about to speak to further length when he was interrupted in his discourse by the appearance of a bewitching female, who happened to step into the drawing-room at the very moment at which we are writing.

"My daughter, Marquis," the old Duke began. "Bianca, allow me to introduce you to my young friend, the Marquis Piatelli, who has favoured us by coming to pay us a little visit."

The Signora was pretty—indeed, she realised the type of those Italian maidens whom we see reproduced in the Roman pictures of our great foreign artists!

The blue eye—the wavy dark hair—the bronzed, soft skin—the well-shaped hand—the exquisitely modelled foot—the slender waist—were to be witnessed in the Signora Bianca in their minutest perfection.

Sataniello gazed silently upon his new acquaintance; he thought her an extremely pretty woman; and inwardly compared her to Joanitta.

The young lady, Senorita Bianca, who had just been introduced to the Boy Brigand, was handsome indeed.

Yet his heart still leant towards Joanitta.

He compared the delicate and well-shaped features of the Senorita standing before him with those of his own sweetheart, and the poor girl occupied the foremost place in his mind.

He thought inwardly he preferred the girl whom he had left behind him to his new acquaintance.

He still mused, and his eye was fixed upon the duke's daughter.

Doubtless he could but notice the difference of the attire which was worn by the two women.

He could not help coming to the conclusion that the well-made dress which was worn by the patrician lady was far superior to the cheap stuff which Joanitta delighted to wear.

And notwithstanding all Bianca's advantages, he still would think that Joanitta had the superiority over Senorita Bianca.

So great is the power of love.

Beyond a shadow of doubt the gait, the demeanour of Senorita Bianca was more queenly than the careless appearance of that little girl who was wont to run about the piazza in her youthful innocence; and Sataniello swore to himself that he would never worship anyone so much as he did the Italian maiden.

But Joanitta was poor!

But Joanitta was of a humble birth!

The duke's daughter was wealthy, and could trace her ancestors upon many a dirty sheet of parchment lying in a confused heap in some of the iron safes where the family deeds were kept.

The Boy Brigand, however, cared not about these things.

He knew that the Duke was a miser—at least, what he had heard ere now had induced him to come to the last opinion—and he was also aware that the duke kept the whole of his treasures in some of the damp, dark vaults situated in some of the subterranean straits which ran beneath the old towers and battlements of Don Saltara Castle.

Now that the Boy Brigand, the Duke, and the Senorita Bianca were all together, he withdrew from his pocket a big envelope, which could not but contain a lengthy epistle.

This was the letter which the Marquis of Piatelli had received at the hands of his father, and which Sataniello had become possessed of when he had so cleverly made himself the master of all the luggage, wardrobe, and family papers belonging to the nobleman whose carriage he had waylaid.

Sataniello had already taken cognizance of the contents of the epistle and with a very subtle and clever hand he had closed the sealing-wax again in such an ingenious manner that the cleverest, even had they been told, could never have detected what he had been guilty of.

"This is a letter which my father gave me for you, Duke Don Saltara," said the Boy Brigand, with that courtesy and the refined manners which belong solely to the higher classes, and which a few only are successful in obtaining.

The Duke returned the bow which had been made to him by Sataniello.

For as he had spoken, Sataniello had made a most respectful salutation.

He feared to give way to a smile, and as he could easily perceive that the beautiful eyes of the Senorita Bianca were rested upon him in a mute manner, he had recourse to every means in his power to preserve his incognito, and to make every one believe that he was indeed the Marquis of Piatelli.

That he was an imposter would never have entered the minds of his host and his daughter; but still too much prudence could not be displayed.

Sataniello was very happy to hear the old duke informing him that he was a widower, and that he had but one child.

That child was the Senorita Bianca, whom we have already seen.

There was, therefore, but the glance of one woman to fear.

The Boy Brigand knew that women sometimes are much more observant than men; and he would not have been so much at home as he found himself after a few moments' reflection if he had had to deal with a large number of females.

The Duke Don Saltara took up the letter, and with a trembling, shaking hand, he opened it.

It was a long letter; and four sides of a foolscap paper there were, closely-written lines.

He was a long time before he had perused the whole of the contents.

His sight, besides, was beginning to grow dim; and more than once he had occasion to refer to Sataniello, and ask him what such-and-such a phrase meant.

The Boy Brigand, noways concerned, had always an answer ready.

It would never do for him not to have known his father's writing. So when he was asked what this and that word was, he invariably was provided with a reply, which from the beginning of the sentence was just the one which was necessary to complete the sense of the phrase.

"I am very sorry—very sorry indeed!"

The old Duke repeated that "the pressure of previous matters prevented me of late years paying a visit to your father. Nothing, I assure you, would have afforded me more pleasure than to have shaken hands with him, poor man, ere he departed this world!"

Sataniello made no reply, but assumed once more a sorrowful expression of countenance.

The Senorita Bianca, in the meantime, remained silent.

She felt that the moment was awkward to allow her to put in her spoke; so she kept turning the leaves of a book she had in her hands.

Nothing in our opinion is more annoying than to see people looking at us rather stedfastly; and although it is very probable that very few of us have

any reason to fear the glance of others, nevertheless we do not like to be stared at.

The Senorita Bianca was a young lady of the world, and despite the total seclusion to which she had been doomed since she had left the Italian convent, where she had been sent to complete her education; she was a woman of good breeding, and she was not unacquainted with the refined manners which proclaim one to be a lady in all countries of the world, when she turns those manners to the best account.

"This communication of your late father," the Duke began, "contains a good many important communications!"

Sataniello was uncertain how to act.

He did not know whether he should say that he was ignorant of the contents, or whether he should admit having a knowledge of that which was contained in the note which the old duke had been reading.

"Did your father read you this letter?" the Duke inquired.

The Boy Brigand took a while to consider.

The old Duke repeated his question.

During the short time which the Boy Brigand had to collect his thoughts, he had come to a determination, which was by far the wisest, considering the uncertainty and the critical position in which he found himself placed.

"No, my Lord Duke; my father did not read the letter to me!" he replied: "I remember that I asked him what he was writing, and he replied to me, 'My boy, it is better that the Duke Don Saltara should broach the subject to you himself; if he does not think proper to do so, why, the very fact of my telling you what the letter contains would be useless information if it leads to no satisfactory result. I never pressed my father upon any subject," Sataniello pursued, in a slow, determined manner, which had all the appearance of being genuine; "his manner was very strange of late, and he hated anything like contrariety."

"And like a good son," the Duke pursued, "you always took good care not to annoy him or to thwart him in his ways."

At one time Sataniello thought that he should take up his pocket-handkerchief, and seemingly wipe his tears; but after consideration, he came to the determination not to have recourse to a pantomime which he did not consider necessary.

Besides, he could not have wept had he wished so to do.

He tried hard to cry, but his eyes would remain dry; and he could not, like some natures can, force the tears to flow.

We have met individuals who could either weep or laugh at a moment's notice. Strange individuals these, who had so great a command on the system, that they could carry out anything they wished.

Sataniello would willingly have acted in a similar manner, but he found it impossible.

"More about this communication to-morrow," the Duke Don Saltara began—"you must be tired; and, as I make allowance for a long journey, I dare say you feel tired, and would like to seek in sleep a necessary repose."

The Boy Brigand was about to reply, when the sound of bells downstairs informed him that supper was ready.

The old Duke rose and said to Sataniello—

"Allow me, Marquis Piatelli, to introduce you to my dining-room!"

The Senorita Bianca was close at hand, and

standing by Sataniello, with her beautiful eyes bent downward.

Many individuals who would have found themselves placed in the same situation as the Boy Brigand would have been rather puzzled.

But Sataniello had read a large number of novels and books of all descriptions.

Therein he had learnt the manners and customs of the higher classes.

He remembered having read a tale where a gallant visitor at some French château took the liberty of asking the lady of the house to accept his arm and be escorted down stairs.

The thought, flashing back to his mind at so appropriate a moment, induced him to act in a similar manner as did the hero in whose daring deeds he had taken a deal of interest, so, in a bold step, he advanced towards the Senorita Bianca, and in a courteous manner offered her his arm.

The Senorita accepted it.

And thus side by side with a proud duke's daughter—with one of the noblest ladies of the land—the Boy Brigand, made a marquis by his own daring enterprise, descended the marble staircases, preceded by the old Duke of Don Saltara, who, with a trembling step, led the way.

The supper passed off in a quiet style. The old Duke, wrapt up in thought, never said a word of interest, beyond inviting Sataniello now and then to help himself to the delicious wine which was on the table in shining crystal decanters.

Sataniello was rather famished after his long journey, so he drank and he ate like a regular Italian monk, and soon found time to pay many flattering compliments to the Senorita Bianca.

Thus the evening passed on; and ere twelve o'clock had struck from the clock of the castle, the whole of the inmates residing within the walls of the princely residence of the Duke of Don Saltara were plunged into the deepest slumbers.

Sataniello's eyelids were not long ere they closed, and he never awoke until the following morning, when he was called by the footman, who informed him that in an hour's time the breakfast would be ready.

Sataniello rose to his feet, soon achieved his toilet, and in a few moments was taking a long walk in the beautifully-laid grounds which formed part of the gardens of the orchards which surrounded Don Saltara's castle, awaiting patiently the signal to wend his steps towards the drawing-room, where he remembered with delight the splendid supper of which he had partaken the previous evening.

CHAPTER XXIII.

WHERE SATANIELLO BEGINS TO THINK THAT HE IS IN FOR A GOOD THING—AND WHERE HE FINDS THAT "THE MONK" IS, PERHAPS, CARRYING OUT TOO STRICTLY THE INSTRUCTIONS WHICH HE GAVE HIM PREVIOUS TO THEIR MUTUAL DEPARTURE FROM THEIR HOME IN THE MOUNTAINS.

SATANIELLO was far from blaming himself for having acted in the bold manner in which he had done.

It is true that he had rested a good deal, but he went upon the principle, "faint heart never won fair lady," and he was wise enough to know that he would never have met the splendid occasion which he came across had he remained quietly in his cavern smoking his pipe and making love to Joanitta.

This would have been pleasant enough, we must admit, and this might have suited some slow, lazy sort of individuals, but this would never have come within the idea of an ever-plotting mind like that of the Boy Brigand.

Although he had said to the Duke of Don Saltara that he was unacquainted with the contents of the letter of his supposed father, we know better.

The Boy Brigand had read the whole of it.

As the mystery which hangs upon this letter will be explained by the old Duke himself, we may as well throw some light upon the matter, not to leave our readers in suspense.

Within it the Marquis of Piatelli's father was entering at great length upon the distant connection which existed between the Don Saltara and the Piatelli families ; and after many allusions to the respective ancestors of these two branches of old Italian houses, the Marquis of Piatelli concluded by saying that nothing would give more satisfaction than to see his son, the Marquis of Piatelli, united to the Duke's daughter, the proud Senorita Bianca of Don Saltara.

Sataniello, therefore, expected that when the Duke would speak to him on the subject, he would ask him whether he would like to marry the pretty Senorita Bianca.

The Boy Brigand was fully prepared for this request as the son of the Duke of Don Saltara.

Sataniello had a good deal of tact, and he had been very careful in the presence of the Senorita to plead ignorance upon a subject which it would have been awkward indeed to bring forward before a person, who, but a few hours ago, was a total stranger.

The reader may, perhaps, think the following information rather peculiar, but we do not doubt that he will place implicit reliance on it when he is told that the writer has travelled over all the countries which he describes, and is fully conversant with the habits, manners, and customs of Continental nations.

In England—except among the upper ten thousand, and such is the name given to the higher classes—marriages are contracted mostly from love, from mutual affection, reciprocated by two beings towards each other.

As a rule marriages in England are productive of very satisfactory results.

In most cases, a large family generally follows a few years' union ; and as the wife, generally speaking, is proverbially known to remain faithful to her husband, a couple live in great joy, and in supreme happiness.

Abroad the cases are quite different.

There are such unions there as marriages of convenience, and a girl is betrothed in some cases to a man she had never seen, to suit the wishes of their parents who think for their children, and who consider unions planned by them to be in every respect calculated to win the happy welfare of the two beings whom it may concern.

Thus it happened that a marriage between the Marquis of Piatelli and the Senorita Bianca was contemplated by the father of the former.

We are unable to say up to the present whether it will meet with the approbation of the Duke Don Saltara.

It is neither our business nor our duty to give way to supposition.

The characters of this story speak in their turns, and as we are only the reporters of scenes which are daily enacted, and of which we have often been the witnesses, we must content ourselves by awaiting quietly, and without undue impatience, the march of events.

Sataniello now could not but look on such a thing being likely to occur as a most ludicrous proceeding, and he fancied himself already leading to the altar the Senorita, and making of a good conscientious girl—at least he thought her to be so—a sham Marchioness of Piatelli.

He wondered what would have been the feelings of the respective actors of the Italian drama, had they been made acquainted by unknown ways with the real manner in which he had become possessed of the title which he bore!

He felt himself, however, quite satisfied, and like certain actors fancy themselves to be really the illustrious personages which they personate on the stage, when moving in everyday life, Sataniello was beginning to think that Nature had made a mistake, and that he should be the bonâ fide Marquis of Piatelli, and that the real owner of the title should take his place.

He would have willingly exchanged his position with that of the present Marquis of Piatelli.

At one time the following idea suggested itself to his mind—why should he not give orders to murder the man whose wardrobe he had robbed, whose social standing in society he had usurped, and by poisoning the sister, remove from himself all chances of his identity being found out.

Sataniello would not have objected to this latter means, however bloody the steps which he would be compelled to take to attain his aim, had he been certain of immediate success.

But he knew too little of the Marquis of Piatelli's family or antecedents to enable him to undertake a rôle which it would have required more knowledge than he possessed to keep up in a manner which would not cause him to be detected.

In short, Sataniello was perfectly contented, and, if it led to nothing, the time which he was spending at the Castle of the Duke of Don Saltara flew so rapidly that for the first time in his life he regretted being a bandit.

Nothing would have afforded him more satisfaction than to become the husband of Senorita Bianca had his heart been free, and his affection disengaged.

But we cannot believe that he would have forgotten pretty Joanitta for an utter stranger.

It would be impossible to say anything with a perfect chance of certainty relating to Sataniello's intention, for human nature is bad and corrupt in the extreme; and if he thought that he would have benefited himself by casting aside an Italian maiden whose innocence he had taken, whose mind was ever busy with her own being, it is probable that he might have done so.

For when a man's interest is called into question, which his own wishes are likely to be gratified, his selfish nature often comes out in its true light.

From our previous knowledge of Sataniello we should feel shy in condemning him.

We have no just cause to think that he would have forgotten Joanetta; in fact, we are inclined to believe that he would not have forsaken her for the noblest and handsomest Italian woman of the land in which he lived.

He was musing as he strolled along the foot-paths, lined with odoriferous perfuming flowers, when he was accosted by our old friend, the Monk.

"Is that you," he said, recognising at once his companion, "how do you like this scene?"

"First-rate, Captain;" he said, "the little chambermaid Maria is an extremely nice girl."

While he spoke, the Monk gave a wink—oh, such a wink!—to Sataniello that he considered it quite useless to put any further questions to his fellow-companion after the expressive marks which he had just given way to.

"I did everything you told me to do, Captain," the Monk pursued.

"What do you mean by that?"

"Why, what did you tell me?"

"I am sure, I do not remember."

To adhere exactly to the truth we may as well here inform our readers that the Boy Brigand was far from having forgotten his instructions to the Monk; but he wished to plead ignorance—to get the latter to make a full confession of the manner in which he had acted.

Sataniello was listening attentively, and was anxious to hear from the Monk whether he acted or not in accordance with his wishes.

"Well, Captain," the Monk began, "you told me to praise you to the ninety-nines."

"You did so, I hope?"

"Leave me alone. I know a trick worth two of any other—I knew perfectly well, that if I said that you were a great chap—of course, some of your polish would fall in for your servant, and so I lost no opportunity to tell a good lot of striking lies."

"Right! that's right," Sataniello replied; "but speak low, my friend—you may not know who may be in the vicinity."

The Monk saw the justice of his Captain's remark, and he abided by it.

He refrained from the high tone, and spoke in a lower intonation.

"You are a 'cute fellow in your way—" Sataniello pursued; "and you ought to be able to tell a good one, when you want to do so, for you come from the right quarter for that."

This allusion of the Boy Brigand, which referred to the seminary or school for priests, from which place the Monk had fled to join the band of Sataniello, caused the would-have-been Friar to laugh heartily.

"Do not laugh like that," Sataniello pursued. "Why cannot you smile like a gentleman. It is only a lot of pothouse boys and of uneducated individuals who know no better who will indulge in a coarse laughter. A gentleman's valet, and a marquis, too, should be more particular."

The Monk looked at his master.

The remarks of the Captain contained a good hint, and he saw the wisdom of it, and he believed it to be to the point; and he meant, if he could, never to lay himself open again to a similar charge on the part of the Boy Brigand, whose authority he respected perhaps more than any of the members of the troop.

CHAPTER XXIV.

WHERE THE MONK ENTERS INTO CLOSE CONVERSATION WITH SATANIELLO, AND WHERE HE TELLS HIM WHAT HE THINKS RELATING TO ITALIAN CHAMBERMAIDS, AND HOW FAR HE ACTED IN PRAISING HIM IN THE EYES OF THE HOUSEHOLD OF THE DUKE OF DON SALTARA.

"MARIA is a pretty girl, Captain," the Monk began—"a deuced nice girl, too, that she is and no mistake. . . . I took an inkling for the lass as soon as I clapped my eyes upon her. Such wicked, roguish eyes; such loving looks I never saw; such wavy hair, and there are such lots of it, too; such a waist, and such small feet and hands. I never met the like of her before, and I am now brewing it over in my mind whether it would not be right for me to carry her away with me when we leave this here place. It is really shocking that so pretty a girl should go to service. Why, she would be an ornament in any drawing-room, and her smile, and her manners. . . . Quite a lady. You never would take her for a servant-girl."

The Boy Brigand was smiling all the time, during which the Monk was giving way to his enthusiasm in the short overflowing sentence which he was uttering with that rapidity and buoyancy which belong to those who, like the Monk, are young and careless.

"I made rapid love to Maria—took her very little nails into my hand—did everything you told me to do, Captain. See, I am a good servant. I carry out your wishes to the letter. She did not seem to dislike me. Somehow or another I rather think she liked it."

The Monk pronounced these last words with the intonation of one who feels confident of what he says—"I asked her where the sleeping apartments were ; but she would not tell me where her crib lay. Do you know that I would not be astonished if the old Duke of Don Saltara——"

"Silence—silence !"—Sataniello began—"you forget yourself, Sir, I think ! Do you know that you are forgetting the respect which you owe to your chief and master ?"

The Monk was cowed. He remained silent and subdued, and for a while he spoke not a word ; but he had something else to say, and he soon opened his lips again—

"I know, Captain, all about it," he said ; "there is a lot of virtue among them Catholic girls ! Protestant maidens ain't half so particular, and I am sure not so shy. But I can explain it all to you. There's no smoke without there's a fire somewhere ; these confounded priests have all the papists beneath their own thumb—what between their spiritual conversations and their confessions, and such like, they ruin the minds of innocent girls."

We do not know whether the abuse which the Monk was bestowing upon the priests was deserved. There is no doubt that there was a good deal of truth in his plain, sensible way of speaking ; but, as far as we can judge, the reverend gentleman's influence seemed not totally lost, as it prevented Maria, the chambermaid, yielding to the loving proposals of such a gay Lothario as the Monk, from his own account, proved himself to be.

"And did she ask you any questions about me?" the Boy Brigand began—

"That she did ; and when I spoke it was a query if all the menials were not looking at me in amazement—'What !' I said, 'do you think that the Duke of Don Saltara, your master, is a wealthy man— why, he could not hold a candle to my master !'"

"Good—good !" Sataniello mused, encouraging by his manner the Monk to keep on speaking.

"'How many horses,' says I, 'do you keep in your stable ?' I asks the coachman, with the awkward ways which I suppose post-boys have.

"The coachman looked at me.

"He is a big, fat, carrotty kind of chap ; he is married to the cook. It is not generally known, but I have already found out all about the mysteries of the parlour below."

"How so ?" the Boy Brigand inquired.

"Bless my soul, I tried to make love to the cook too ! Nothing like having lots of them upon your list ; if you fail with the first you may have more luck with the second. Ever keep a faithful watch, and one is sure to have lots of fun.

"You would never have done for a priest, I fear!" the Boy Brigand went on.

"I am not so sure of that ; only I would have been compelled to have my little flirtations on the sly instead of doing it openly—that's all."

"I really begin to think that I would like to have been the Post-boy, and you the Marquis, if you tell me true ; why, there must be no end of sport downstairs !"

"There is, Captain ! But I am vexed, you know ; Maria is a very stylish little bit of stuff, and yet she won't listen to me. I snatched a kiss from her but last evening. I go to work at once, you see, and never lose any time. ' O, fie, fie !' she says, blushing all the while—' you are a nice stranger, to be sure.' "

"Never mind about your loving exploits ; never mind about Maria and all the kit of them. Let us attend to business ! You were speaking to me about the stable just now ; what about it?"

"Of course—of course ; ' I suppose you got a lot of cattle within the stables,' I inquired of the coachman, in a jeering tone."

" ' Deuced sight more than ever you saw, and you will see with your master,' he replied, surlily."

" He has taken quite a dislike to me, that fellow has. He is an old chap, you see, the coachman is ; and he knows right well—at least, if he does not know it he feels it, and that's about the same ; six of one and half a dozen of the other—that youth goes a long way with the female species. They like someone who can kiss well, and kiss and kiss again, and never grow tired of that little kind of entertainment."

" ' You need not be so sure of what you say, my friend,' I replied to the coachman ; ' how many horses has your master got ?

"The whole of the household was all attention."

It is astonishing how curious servants are as a rule. I will be bound to say that there is not a more inquisitive class of people upon the face of the earth.

CHAPTER XXV.

WHERE THE MONK STILL KEEPS ON TALKING, AND WHERE SATANIELLO STILL KEEPS ON LISTENING TO HIM — AND FROM WHAT HE HEARS COMES TO THE CONCLUSION THAT THE MONK WAS AS GOOD A COMPANION AS HE COULD HAVE CHOSEN TO ACCOMPANY HIM UPON HIS CRITICAL ERRAND.

"WELL, well, go on ! I am listening to you !" Sataniello began, hurrying on the Monk to make any further disclosures, and to acquaint him with all the information which he had obtained at the hands of the menials.

The Monk knew that Sataniello never asked, or made a request, twice ; so he immediately complied with his wishes.

" It is astonishing," he pursued, " what a curious class of people flunkeys are, as a rule ; why, they want to pick everything out of you. Talk about their masters ! why, they are angels, comparatively speaking, when compared to those who live by them !"

Sataniello was listening attentively to the Monk, and could not help thinking that there was a good deal of wisdom and of practical knowledge of the world in the youth before him.

"And you never told me yet what you said to the coachman!" Sataniello pursued, replying after awhile to the sedate remark which had been made by his follower.

"What I told him?"

"Yes."

"Oh, I made it out strong for him, and 'no kid' about it. I made him believe that you had the first horses in Italy, and he took it all in! He swallowed all my talk as if it were gospel."

"Do you think," Sataniello continued, "that he suspects anything?"

"Who?"

"The coachman."

"Not he!"

"Perhaps the other servants may!"

"No fear about them—I can vouch for that. I could tell in a twinkling whether there was anything going wrong; and if there was, Captain, I would let you know, and we would give them the slip."

"Like a shot!" the Boy Brigand pursued, in a wise, slow, sedate tone of voice.

"You have nothing more to say to me, I suppose?" Sataniello inquired.

"No, Captain, beyond what I have already told you."

"That's quite sufficient, too!" Sataniello pursued, placing the palm of his hand in a friendly manner upon the shoulder of his companion; "keep on at the same rate at which you seem to have been going. Puff me up; never lose an opportunity to do so, mind! Do not quarrel with any one downstairs; and if you will take my advice, do not be too fast with Maria."

"What, the chambermaid?"

"Yes! Girls do not like too much freedom all at once; they like a little courting, a good deal of kissing, and all that kind of thing, you know!"

The Monk, in answer, gave one of those knowing winks which would have made a whole audience laugh, had he been performing the rôle of some wide-awake customer upon the stage of the theatre of San Carlo.

"You will remember all my instructions, wont you?"

The Boy Brigand needed no answer.

He got one, however.

"I will, Captain; and I will act by them. I will be as talkative as a parrot when wanted; as silent as the grave when wisdom will show me to adopt the latter course."

Sataniello nodded his head, wishing to convey his approbation of what he heard by these silent marks; which could leave no doubt to the Monk as to his having realised in his master's mind all the latter's expectations beyond his most sanguine anticipations.

"It is early yet!" Sataniello said; "we have been conversing for some time already, and it would be as well to part now."

"Perhaps we have been watched!" The Monk pronounced the words in an under whisper.

The sound of footsteps dying away upon the pebbles upon the ground was now heard.

Sataniello turned round.

Had the two brigands been spied?

The Senorita Bianca was wont to take morning strolls in her garden. Lately her mind was uneasy, and she could not rest. Could she have been the being whose footsteps had just caught Sataniello's attention?

If so, the Boy Brigand's secret was no longer his own.

But perhaps the Senorita Bianca was also in his power.

Perhaps he had noticed something about her—some unmistakable signs, proclaiming a guilt—that a father only would be blind enough not to see.

What were those signs?

We will tell the reader about the suspicions which had entered Sataniello's brain.

Were they right ones or not?

That is the question!

Had he been watched, and had his conversation with the Monk been overheard; and if so, what was to be the result?

Meanwhile Sataniello sneaked swiftly and softly away from the spot where he stood, and very stealthedly regained the inner apartments of the Castle of Don Saltara.

On his side, the Monk was also wending his way towards the same direction.

His head was bent downwards, and he was pondering over the words of his master and captain.

He could not find out whether the assertion which had been ventured by Sataniello was likely to turn out a true one; and he knew inwardly that it would be useless to attempt to question the servants about the Senorita Bianca's ways.

However, he made up his mind to one thing.

He was not slow in detecting any sly talk—any undertone conversation; and ere long he would know whether there was any ground for him to remain plunged in deep anxiety.

So thinking, he also walked towards the Castle of Don Saltara; and at the moment his master was entering the dining-room the Monk was just thinking how he would encounter the numerous servants which composed the household of menials which was kept in the princely residence where he happened to be staying.

How long was his sojourn there to last?

Would he leave Don Saltara Castle safe and, with his gallant captain, both overladen with treasures, or would he be compelled to have recourse to a hasty flight to preserve his freedom?

No one knew it at the time—no one could have unravelled in a few instants the conclusion which the wayward hands of time, or the freaks of fortune, would bring forward.

The Monk was thus musing, when he reached the outskirts of Don Saltara Castle.

Maria, the chambermaid, was the first one whom he saw.

"How is my darling pet?" he asked.

The maiden made no reply.

She was one of those girls who listen attentively and make their own conclusions.

She liked the Monk.

She thought him a very nice young man.

Yet she did not wish to "let the cat out of the bag."

Had she told him that she loved him, the Monk was one of those individuals who would take the girl at her word, and leave her no time to think.

Maria, the chambermaid, knew that.

Had she had at all her own will, she would have have rushed into the Monk's arms and allowed him to kiss her freely.

She, however, felt that such a proceeding would be an ill-advised one.

"Now I am awfully fond of you, Maria," the Monk said; "for I am sure that you are the nicest girl in the whole of Italy!"

The girl blushed.

The Monk saw that his remark had produced an impression.

"Surely," the maiden said, "you do not mean what you say? You men are such flatterers! If you met another girl to-morrow it is exactly the same story which you would tell her."

The Monk grew bold.

He approached Maria.

He encircled her waist, and he gave a warm, loving kiss.

He felt her palpitating, heaving little breast against his own, and he evidently knew that she was not indifferent to his caresses.

"Where are you coming from like this!" she asked. "Do you like to walk about in the morning?"

"I do," said the Monk. "I delight in hearing the birds warbling forth their tuneful songs from every branch and tree. I love nature, and when contemplating God's great work I feel happy."

Maria concluded from what she heard that the Monk must be a very religious, steady, well-behaved youth.

Of course she was not aware of his being called the Monk. He went under an assumed name at the Castle of the Duke of Don Saltara.

Had she known who he was, what would she have said?

Meanwhile he kept Maria closely encircled within his arms.

"Will you let me go?" she inquired. "What would the other people say if they saw me as I am now?"

"What matters what they would say?" the Monk replied. "Why, they have done the thing before themselves."

He tried hard to lead Maria in a secluded spot, where, hid from the gaze of man, he could whisper into her ears sweet tales of love which need no spectator.

Maria was too much for him. She held her ground.

He gave her another kiss. The girl this time did not return it.

"I never in all my life—no, never," she muttered, fell across such a daring Lothario as you are. "Why you are a regular Turk."

The Monk smiled.

"Give me a kiss," he said, "and I will let you go."

"No I won't."

"You will."

"No I won't."

"I will make you."

"No I won't give you a kiss," the girl replied.

"You won't?"

"No."

"Why not?"

"Because I do not wish to do so."

"Then I will take one." And as he spoke he held the girl's beautiful head in his hands, and upon her rosy lips he impressed a voluptuous, loving kiss.

"Oh, shame upon you!" the girl said.

"I repeat it," the Monk replied, "you must give me a kiss."

At that instant a rustle was heard close by.

"Hush, hush!" Maria whispered, "there is some one coming. . . Oh, you will ruin me for life. . . . Oh, don't. Do not treat me as you do."

Did she comply with his wishes? Did Maria yield to the Monk's proposals? Did she act as he wished her to?

Reader, you want to know too much. We have no right to say anything more.

Be it sufficient to state that Maria and the Monk remained together a long while.

What they did during the whole time is a mystery for us.

We can but form our own conclusions, and leave the reader to do the same; and thus conclude the present chapter to begin another.

———

CHAPTER XXVI.

WHERE SATANIELLO HAS A LONG CONVERSATION WITH THE OLD DUKE OF DON SALTARA, DURING WHICH HE HEARS A GOOD DEAL.

IT is strange, nevertheless true, that the hours pass away very fast, when we find ourselves occupied in some task which meets with our tastes, and which beguile the time away.

Thus the days succeeded rapidly each other, and ere the Boy Brigand had been staying a week at the Castle of the Duke, he could scarcely realize to himself the possibility that he had already been the guest of a noble Duke for the period which had elapsed since his departure from his cavern.

The Senorita Bianca and Sataniello were always pleased to see each other; but the same feeling which existed between the Monk and Maria could not be said to be entertained by the two personages above alluded to.

It was on a fine evening that the following conversation which we will minutely reproduce, occurred between the Boy Brigand and the Duke of Don Saltara, quietly sitting together in the drawing-room of the ancestral demesne of the Don Saltara family.

"Marquis Piatelli," the Duke began, "what is your opinion relating my daughter?"

The Boy Brigand knew not what answer to make.

He thought it rather a strange question to come from a father's lips.

He mused for awhile ere he replied.

"I think her a very lady-like accomplished person," he replied.

"Do you think she would make a good wife?"

"Stranger question still," Sataniello again muttered to himself.

"I cannot speak relating to so very ticklish a subject," he pursued—"She seems to have a deal of education, and a good deal of refinement in her manners.

Now it may be as well to state, ere we proceed much further, that Sataniello had come within the possession of a secret which he treasured deeply within his heart.

What that secret is, we will acquaint our readers with—all in due course.

"But education and manners only are not the only requirements necessary for a mother of a family;" the Duke pursued. "A woman must have something else besides that."

"Well, you will excuse me, I am sure." The Boy Brigand pursued; "if I do not give you an definite answer, my Lord Duke. I could not come to any conclusion satisfactory to myself, and I feel confident that you will excuse me for not giving a hasty opinion."

"Would it be one favourable to Bianca?" the Duke of Don Saltara inquired.

"How could it be otherwise?" the Boy Brigand replied gallantly; "the daughter of a father like you must needs answer every expectation of her, however sanguine the expectation may be!"

The Boy Brigand pronounced these last words in as

SKETCH OF DON SALTARA CASTLE.

steady collected manner, which at once took up the Duke's fancy.

"Do you know, Marquis Piatelli," he asked, "why I spoke to you in the manner in which I have done ?"

"I am at a loss to guess, my Lord Duke," Sataniello replied.

"Do you remember a certain letter, which you brought me?"

"I do," the Boy Brigand replied.

"Did I not allude to it before?"

"You did, but without acquainting me with its contents, my Lord Duke."

"And shall I tell you what the letter contained ?"

Sataniello bowed. Had any one been close by,

he could have noticed a satirical smile upon his countenance.

"I do, my Lord Duke," he replied, "take a great interest in all that which you speak, and as moreover the communication which you are about to make to me is connected with the last moments of my poor father, you can easily understand the interest which I feel."

"Shall I read the letter to you now that the Senorita Bianca, closeted in her room, is not likely to disturb us ?"

"I would like to hear it."

Sataniello uttered this last sentence in so cool a manner, his appearance was so prepossessing, the anxiety which was depicted upon his countenance appeared so genuine that the Duke rose at once from the seat which he had taken.

He walked towards the large desk, which stood in the corner of the apartment.

He opened it.

Out of it he drew the letter.

The Boy Brigand recognised the writing, which he had seen before.

The old Duke of Saltara put on his spectacles.

Steadily and quietly he unfolded the paper.

Sataniello was meanwhile looking attentively at his host.

"Listen now," the old Duke began.

Sataniello nodded his head in acknowledgment.

The Duke began.

"MY DEAR DUKE OF DON SALTARA.

"We have known each other for years; we were college companions. Owing to circumstances over which we both had no control, we soon separated for many years. Now I feel my last hour rapidly coming on. I know that I will not live long. Willingly would I have accepted your kind invitation of spending a few months with you ; but now my hair is getting white, my limbs getting stiff; and to move away from my home is too great a labour for me With you the case is similar—we will therefore part from each other in this world without grasping each others' hands. But let me ask you a favour—I know your affairs well. My fortune is great, and I would feel so happy if from heaven I could see my handsome son, the heir to my estates, the worthy scion of an old house, allying his crest to that of the Don Saltara, to blend in one name the proud stock, of two of the oldest families in Italy. May my wish be realised—and may I trust that you will view my proposal with that encouragement which I expect to find at the hands of a man whose high character is too well known for me to expatiate upon it in my epistle. Farewell, farewell, my worthy, my faithful friend—farewell!
                                        "DON SALTARA."

At the bottom of this letter was appended the seal of the old Marquis of Piatelli.

"Do you understand now?" the old Duke began, "the reason which prompted me to make the questions ; which, Marquis Piatelli, I dare say you looked upon as rather odd at the time being."

No answer was given by the Boy Brigand, and a natural silence followed the words which had just been spoken.

"Would you like to become my son-in-law, Marquis?" the Duke began. "I have not, it is true, a very large fortune, but although my wealth is not great it is safely located. I have it all in gold, stored within the walls of my castle. Here, beneath me, lay a treasure."

The eyes of Sataniello sparkled like two diamonds; his gaze was rivetted towards the Duke.

The old Duke had at length spoken.

The Boy Brigand had heard it said in the country that the old Duke was something of a miser ; and that owing to the failure of several banks, he had converted the whole of his property in hard coin—golden pieces—which he kept stored within the walls of Don Saltara Castle.

Up to the present period he could only make his own conjectures; now he had at least the prospects of certainty.

"The honour would be too great for me, my Lord Duke," he said.

"Nonsense ! nonsense ! my friend," he replied. "Among noblemen the honour is on both sides."

"The Senorita Bianca might object to such a marriage."

"She !" the Duke pursued.

"She might," said the Boy Brigand. "Girls have strange ways, and freaks about them, and to wish her to marry me would perhaps be a reason for her to hate me."

"Do you think she would dare to question or to stand against the wishes of a loving and affectionate father ?"

"Her affections are perhaps already engaged. She may love some other."

"That could never be," the old Duke pursued; "the girl is as innocent as a child, and she could not unknown to me have entered into promises without consulting me. We have very seldom any visitors here, and when they are gentlemen they remain here so short a period that I feel convinced never yet has Bianca had an opportunity of losing her heart."

The old Duke spoke in all the consciousness of blissful ignorance. But from what the Boy Brigand had heard during his stay, he had learnt many a thing that the subtle observer would never have dreamt of.

"I would not have a girl to unite her destiny to me against her will," the Boy Brigand pursued—"give me time, and I will soon tell you whether Senorita Bianca's mind can be brought to anything like sound reasoning."

"Have you got any reason to think the contrary ?" the Duke inquired ; "if so, speak out, you will—I can pledge you my word—confer a great favour upon me by so doing."

"I have not," Sataniello replied; "but I thought it my duty to raise the objections which I have made. I hope you do not blame me for having acted as I have done."

"Blame you," the Duke replied quietly ; "certainly not, nothing is further from my mind. It only confirms the opinion which I hold of you, and which proves you to me what I have taken you to be, —a straightforward, honest, gallant heart, just the kind of man to make my daughter happy."

CHAPTER XXVII.

WHERE THE BOY BRIGAND AND THE DUKE OF DON SALTARA STILL KEEP ON TALKING— AND WHERE A MOST UNEXPECTED INCIDENT OCCURS.

SATANIELLO had now been staying for over a fortnight at the Castle of the Duke of Don Saltara.

On more occasions than one he had tried to speak of love to Senorita Bianca, but up to the present period she had answered by a deaf ear to his entreaties.

He saw it was no use to broach the subject over again.

The evening came, when the old Duke reverted to the proposal which we have seen he had made to the Marquis of Piatelli.

"Marquis Piatelli," he said to him, "have you made up your mind with regard to my daughter?"

"I fear to speak, Signor Duke," he replied.

"What sense do you wish to convey in your words?" the Duke replied.

"Nought more than what I wish to say, my Lord Duke," the Boy Brigand replied. "I have spoken to the Senorita Bianca over and over again. I have endeavoured to make her believe that I could not resist the languid charm of her beautiful eyes. But,

THE BOY BRIGAND; OR, THE DARK KING OF THE MOUNTAINS.

whenever I have spoken, she has answered me with the coolest disdain."

"What!" the Duke of Don Saltara inquired, "has my daughter acted in such a way towards you as to induce you to believe that your attentions were irksome?"

"She has, my Lord Duke of Don Saltara," the Boy Brigand replied; "and not later than yesterday evening she said to me, 'Marquis, you are a guest at my father's. As such I like and respect you. But do not attempt again to speak to me of love, for I cannot listen to you.'"

The Duke of Don Saltara's eyes sunk in their sockets.

He stood up, and his glance fell upon the speaker.

"Do you speak true, my friend?" he asked. "Do you tell me that your language is that of truth?"

"It is, my Lord Duke," the Boy Brigand replied.

The Duke of Saltara's features assumed a strange expression.

His eyes, which usually possessed a mild and soft gaze, were now furious, and his look was sufficient to cause any one to fear his presence.

His ire evidently had been kindled by the words which he had heard.

He walked up and down the room with a quick, sharp step.

Occasionally his hands trembled like aspen-leaves.

What he had heard was a terrible revelation to him.

"Has Bianca," he questioned, "acted towards you, Marquis, in the manner in which you say she has?"

The Boy Brigand nodded his head in the affirmative.

"You do not wish to ally your proud coat of arms with that of the Don Saltara," he said. "You think that, although reputed wealthy, I am poor."

Sataniello endeavoured to speak.

The Duke of Don Saltara left him no time to do so.

"I ought to have known," he said, "when I first broached the subject of matrimony to you, that from your reluctance you wished not to marry my daughter. Now you come forward with your excuses."

"Accuse me not, my Lord," Sataniello pursued. "What I have told you is truth. I would delight to be united to your daughter. Nothing would afford me greater satisfaction than to see my father's dream realised. But, of course, when a girl says No, where is the man who would compel her to act against her feelings?"

This remark seemed to relieve the mind of the Duke of Don Saltara.

"You judge my daughter too harshly," he began. "She loves you, I know."

There was a pause, which followed the Duke's words.

Meanwhile Sataniello had prepared his answer.

He felt that, under circumstances like the present, he could not be too circumspect in giving way to any expression, and so he quietly reflected over the sentences which he should utter previous to allowing them to spring from his lips.

"She does not love, my Lord Duke," he began. "I know that it is hard for one whom you have chosen as your future son-in-law to be compelled to reveal to you what is really the case. Still, as I know that what I say is based upon more than casual observation, I think I am bound to speak."

"From what cause, I wonder," the Duke of Don Saltara inquired, "could a dislike towards you spring from my daughter? I can state to this—that

since you have been my guest, Marquis Piatelli, your manners have been prepossessing and attentive in the extreme; and, if Bianca is resolved to remain an old maid, why she is very differently constituted from the girls who lived in my day."

It never occurred to the Duke's mind that his daughter—the proud, haughty, and lovely Bianca—could have engaged her affections to some being unknown, or perhaps familiar to him, upon whom he would have rested his choice.

"I do not believe," the Boy Brigand pursued, "that the Senorita looks upon me with any feelings bordering upon hatred; but that she will not have me as her husband is plain enough to me. There are many ways about a maiden by which a suitor knows how he should make up his mind; and, to be candid, my Lord Duke, I think that if I was to bend my knees before the Senorita Bianca for a century, and in the most endearing terms ask her to wed me, she would not consent."

"But she must," the Duke of Don Saltara replied. "I have made up my mind to a certain thing, and I will carry it out."

The Boy Brigand now began to think that he had placed himself in rather a critical position for having spoken in the bold manner which he had assumed.

It would not have suited his book at the present moment had he been compelled to marry the Senorita Bianca.

Whatever, however, might have been his future plans, he was resolved to hear the Duke of Don Saltara speaking his mind throughout.

That the old Duke had taken a decided fancy to him was a matter of great wonder to the Boy Brigand, for he forgot at times the character which he so well personified.

But we should remember that the Duke of Don Saltara believed him to be the son of a college friend of his.

The Piatelli family were reputed to be exceedingly wealthy.

Their lands stretched far and far away in the Neapolitan territory, and the Duke of Don Saltara, who knew the state of the Marquis of Piatelli's affairs better than the Boy Brigand himself did, was loth to allow so good a prospect to escape him.

Besides, when men get old they become tenacious to a degree which may appear to us extraordinary, but which nevertheless exists.

Was the Marquis of Piatelli to remain dumb to his offers? Was he to return to the Neapolitan capital? There, doubtless, he would meet some enticing Italian maiden with her loving eyes, and those blandishments which a worldling mixing with the world render so attractive, and he would lose his heart at the court of the reigning King of Naples, and forget the Senorita Bianca.

The Duke of Don Saltara was a peculiar old man.

We have already said that he was a miser, and that he longed for gold.

He kept hidden treasures beneath the castle walls—and it would only be when compelled by the direst necessity that he would divulge a secret which he held dear.

Sataniello knew but one thing—that he wished the old Duke to speak out.

Although forgetful of his present condition, he could not forget that he pourtrayed the character of an Italian Marquis, and as such he intended to act.

"But she must," were the last words which rung in Sataniello's ears.

That the old Duke was plainly and positively and earnestly decided on his becoming his son-in-law could be assigned to his last sentence.

The Duke of Don Saltara walked up and down the room in the greatest excitement.

"I have brought up my daughter Bianca," the Duke said, "with all the affection of a devoted father. All that wealth can procure I have freely given her. She has had resident governesses and tutors to reside at the castle for weeks at the time. Her music-master was rather an expensive toy to keep—yet I paid all for what I think she required. Now she is as accomplished as any girl in the land. With regard to her beauty, it is not my province here to speak. She is the remarkable image of her poor mother; and you may easily fancy, Marquis, by her, that I was not a bad judge of female attractions."

Notwithstanding the solemnity of the occasion, the Boy Brigand could not repress a smile, which was brought to his lips by his host's late remarks.

He bowed his head in acknowledgment of what he heard.

"And am I," the Duke continued, "to be frustrated in my wishes? Am I to permit a young girl to rebuke against my will because she has taken it into her head to do so? No, it shall not be. If you are willing to accept Bianca as your wife she will be the Marchioness Piatelli."

There was such an amount of earnestness and of anxious suspense depicted in the Duke's countenance when he spoke, that the Boy Brigand at one moment that he would have been powerless to give an answer.

From several little incidents which had come within his knowledge he had found out that the Senorita Bianca had not the power to bestow her hand.

She was already secretly married.

The marriage had been performed by one of the priests who lived in the neighbourhood.

The individual to whom the Senorita Bianca had united her destiny was a Protestant — hence a great mystery had been allowed to hang on the occurrence.

People in Italy are very bigoted, and the Senorita, knowing how attached her father was to the Church of Rome, had never divulged to him the real incidents of a narrative which we will describe shortly to our readers.

But the Boy Brigand had soon found out everything about the girl.

To reveal such a conclusion would not have answered his purpose, and so he remained silent.

"She will become the Marchioness of Piatelli," Sataniello began, after awhile, "if I am allowed to wed the Senorita Bianca—whom, let it be confessed, I love deeply. When you first spoke to me about your daughter such feeling did not exist in my breast; but since my stay here I have not been able to resist her numerous attractions—and, as the old saying expresses it, 'As the course of true love never ran smooth,' I am doomed also, I suppose, to meet with many disappointments on her part."

Sataniello pronounced these last last words in a manner which he had taken some time to study, and so well did he perform his part that the Duke of Don Saltara looked towards him with a steady gaze, and never supposed that he was acting a part, which he required to go through in no mean way to get acquainted with that which he wished anxiously to know.

"Oh, I am a happy man, then," the Duke replied, in answer to Sataniello's last phrase; "if you love my daughter she will be yours. No tears on her part will shake the resolve which I have taken. Your late father's missive is ever present before my eyes, and I think I ought to abide by it. But I wish you to know," he continued, "that if you marry my daughter I will not give her away penniless."

Here the Boy Brigand ejaculated a few sentences, which went to show that little indeed did he value the treasures of this earth if he could find one who, by her Christian behaviour and her womanly duties, could bestow happiness upon a home which his late father's death had rendered bleak and dreary.

"My sister wants a companion," he began. "She is an orphan now; and, if you will permit me, we would all live beneath your roof for half of the year, and if, with good care, you could be prevailed upon to come to Naples, we would all try to make you happy and comfortable."

"Your speech, my worthy young friend," the Duke of Don Saltara replied, "only leads me to think that I will have no occasion to repent for having made a choice which two fathers have sanctioned."

Sataniello would doubtless again have indulged in a new pantomime, tending to show to the Duke that he was grieving still over his late father's loss; but as he had of late indulged in a good deal of those outward expressions of his sorrow, he thought it wise to keep his eyes dry.

Had he, however, burst into a flood of tears, the old Duke would not have been more enlightened upon the real character of his guest, and would have admired and respected him all the more for it.

We do not wish to bring any ridicule upon any sons, or any members of any family mourning for the loss of a relative which they held dear. This is a natural feeling, which will always meet with respect at the hands of those who know how to judge well, and who possess the heart in the right place.

We have only alluded to the marks of sorrow displayed by Sataniello because there was something ludicrous contained in it, and because he was weeping on the behalf of an individual whom he had never known, and whose actual *bona fide* son he would willingly have murdered had it suited his purpose.

"Now, Marquis Piatelli," the Duke of Don Saltara began, "I will speak to you about business. My daughter's portion will not be a very large one : it is only £10,000, but there is a great comfort in what I am about to say to you—it is all in gold."

Sataniello listened attentively.

"I will not give you any paper; I will give you all in sound sterling metal. I keep it all here."

We remember, doubtless, the visit which the Boy Brigand paid to the manager of the Royal Metropolitan Bank, and we remember also the tenacity with which he insisted upon having the cheque which he held from Lord Charlestown paid in the same specie as the £10,000 just alluded to by the Duke of Saltara.

"Yes," the Duke of Don Saltara pursued, "as I collect my rents I place them in my vaults. People would tell me, I dare say, that I am doing wrong in acting thus, as I lose the interest upon my capital. But they are not aware of what I do, and I go upon this principle—' a bird in the hand is worth two in the bush ;' and if placed in a bank, which may fail, my money may be robbed from me; whereas if I have it beneath me, I am sure that no one can take away from me."

There was a good deal of logic in the Duke's words.

It was one, besides, which met greatly with the

Boy Brigand's approval, as he had a certain interest in getting acquainted with the particulars which he held.

"And do you tell me," he asked, in a slow, subdued tone of voice, "that the whole of your fortune lies hidden beneath the Castle vaults?"

"Not the whole of my fortune," the Duke pursued; "for I own a good deal of land about here; but the best part of my daughter's dowry, and all that I possess in ready cash is close at hand."

"Where do you keep it, do you say?" Sataniello inquired anew, assuming as careless a tone as it was wise to do under the circumstances.

"Exactly beneath the spot where I stand. The family vaults are there; and in a recess which stands immediately beneath the place where my great-grandfather was buried in the year of Our Lord 1699 are buried all my worldly goods."

The Boy Brigand did not question the old Duke any more.

He was on the eve of suggesting to him the propriety of keeping such a knowledge strictly confined to himself, but the fear of suspicion flashing across his host's mind prevented him from doing so.

"Am I to understand, then," the Duke of Saltara again inquired, "that you are anxious to wed my daughter Bianca? I will speak to her on the subject, and she must obey—yes, she must, I repeat."

The old man uttered the last sentence more peremptorily than he had done before.

"If she refuses to yield to my wishes, I will disinherit her—I will cast her loose upon the world!"

And the Duke shook and trembled at the idea of any resistance being offered to him.

"She would not, my Lord Duke, I feel convinced," Sataniello began, "act in such a manner as would thwart the wishes of one that should be orders to her. She holds, I am persuaded, your words in too great a respect not to heed them; but where should the ceremony take place?"

This was a suggestion which occurred to the Boy Brigand's mind.

On the onslaught of the moment he ventured to give way to it.

A few instants after he regretted having done so.

"Where?—where?" the Duke of Saltara exclaimed; "why, within my own palace, of course! It is here that you will marry my daughter."

"I would prefer taking her away to Naples. The king might honour me with his presence," the Boy Brigand pursued; "and it would give a dazzling éclat to our union. It would be a fitting way, indeed, for our families to be wedded—for the two remaining branches of two noble families to be blended together."

The old Duke seemed to consider the suggestion.

"I admire your ideas, my young friend," he pursued; "like youthful minds you delight in that display and in that pageantry which suits so well hearts that are not accustomed to the ways of the world. But must you be surrounded by princes, nobles, and by numerous guests to witness your ascent to the altar to be happy? Now, my boy! within these walls will you be united. I will send for my chaplain, who is now on leave, and within these walls will Bianca become the Marchioness of Piatelli."

"Never!—never! father," a voice exclaimed; and Senorita Bianca entered the apartment with the marks of the utmost bitterness depicted upon her features.

"Oh, father!" she said, "this is too much for me. You will only compel me to marry the man of my choice, and not a casual stranger—one that I cannot love."

Thus speaking the Senorita Bianca placed her hand to her head, and afterwards it made its way to her heart.

The Boy Brigand advanced towards her.

"Away—away from me!" she shrieked; "bitterly have I wept since you came within this roof! Sorely, indeed, has my heart bled since your features first met mine!"

These were the last words which the Senorita uttered for the time being. She tried to rush towards a chair to sustain herself, but ere she could do so, she fell heavily upon the floor, leaving the two witnesses of this extraordinary scene to form their own conclusions upon that which she had been so unexpectedly called upon to behold.

CHAPTER XXVIII.

WHERE THE BOY BRIGAND IS CALLED UPON TO RIDE TO THE NEAREST VILLAGE IN SEARCH OF A PHYSICIAN, AND WHERE HE DOES A LITTLE BUSINESS ON HIS WAY HOME WHICH REDOUNDS VERY MUCH TO HIS CREDIT.

So unexpected had been the scene which we have just related that the old Duke of Don Saltara was thunderstruck for awhile.

Sataniello approached the Senorita, and he felt her pulse.

Her whole body was getting gradually cold, and her eyes were closed.

He rushed towards the bell, and shook it violently.

"My Lord Duke," he said, "your daughter, the Senorita, is taken very unwell—call for immediate assistance."

"She must have been listening to our previous conversation about her," the old Duke replied; "what can be the matter with the girl? Oh! how pale she looks!"

The father's heart now began to be subdued.

Whilst he could quietly plot Bianca's marriage to satisfy his own wish, he could not contemplate her pale features without sorrow.

He ran out upon the landing, and sung out for help.

The distance between the top of the staircase and the hall where the servants were wont to eat was great, and his voice remained unheeded.

The Duke of Don Saltara was now in the greatest distress.

All his plans were dashed to the ground by this unexpected incident.

He regretted within his own heart the steps which he had taken, and he began to curse himself inwardly for the career which he had pleased himself to trace for his daughter.

"Bianca! Bianca! my dearest Bianca!" he softly whispered into her ears, "reply to me!"

Not a sound answered his call.

Bianca's form remained motionless.

He leaned upon her, and he took up her hand, and he kissed it affectionately.

He suddenly allowed it to escape from his grasp.

It fell heavily upon the carpetted floor.

"Bianca, dearest Bianca!" he muttered, still without avail.

"What a time those servants are taking in coming up," the Boy Brigand pursued, rushing about the room with quick strides, and assuming the greatest agony. "Do those fits ever take her? Have you noticed them before, my Lord Duke?"

The Duke of Don Saltara was too much absorbed to reply at once.

The Boy Brigand repeated his question.

This time the old Duke answered him.

"No, never have I noticed such a change in Bianca; why, I fear she is dying!"

Thus speaking, the Duke of Don Saltara's eyes filled with tears.

Had the Brigand Boy's heart been less hardened, he could not but have been softened by what he saw.

It was a sad spectacle, indeed, to contemplate the old Duke, leaning over the inanimate form of Bianca.

Her wavey, glossy hair hung in stray curls upon the velvety pile; her features were as pale as a shroud, and her lips were as white as those of a corpse.

"Bianca! Bianca! oh, say to me that you are still my own daughter!"

The Duke pronounced these words in such a shrieking, piercing tone of voice, that they reached his daughter's power of hearing.

She opened her beautiful eyes, and in an instant closed them again.

It was at that instant that one of the servants of the household, awakened by the sounds of the bell, entered the apartment where the Duke of Don Saltara, leaning upon his daughter's body, wrung his hands in the deepest agony.

He blamed himself for having wrought the terrible conclusion which had taken place.

"Call in medical assistance," the Boy Brigand began, addressing the menial. "Tell her Ladyship's chambermaid to attend upon her at once, and see her placed at once upon her couch."

It would have been the duty of the Duke to speak thus; but the Boy Brigand assumed an authority which the Duke was powerless to display.

We need not say that the message was not long ere it was carried abroad.

The Boy Brigand, descending the staircase, met the Monk coming towards him.

He addressed him peremptorily and sharply.

Other servants were standing by, and he should speak like a master to his inferior.

"Saddle the horse I rode yesterday," he said, in a clear voice, "and be yourself ready in five minutes, as I must go to the closest village about here to seek medical aid for the Senorita Bianca."

"Is she very ill, my Lord Marquis?" the Monk inquired, like one who would be deeply concerned by what had occurred.

"I will tell you more anon," he replied. "In the meantime, see about carrying out what I bid you—and do not delay, for an instant's procrastination may prove fatal."

While thus speaking, the Boy Brigand shook mournfully his head.

And when the sounds of the two horses emerging from the castle-yard were heard dying in the distance, many were the comments which were freely circulated in the servant's hall, and anxiously indeed was the doctor's arrived expected by the old Duke and by all the inmates of the Castle of Don Saltara, who respected too much an old and faithful master not to feel deeply interested in the Senorita Bianca's recovery.

While the two cavaliers rode along the road which led from the abode which they had left to the neighbouring village, the following conversation took place:—

"Captain," the Monk was saying, "what is all this about?"

"I am sure I cannot tell you," the Captain replied. "The Duke of Don Saltara was just insisting upon my becoming his son-in-law; and I, as a matter of course, did not object to a little winding-up which could have been feasible enough had not the Senorita Bianca taken it into her head to rush into the drawing-room where we were sitting—and, to render the whole affair romantic, fainted in a most unexpected manner."

"She must have been eavesdropping, then," the Monk replied.

"It is very probable that she did. Women sometimes will do anything. I dare say she did, for how could she have found out the Duke's intentions unless she became acquainted with them by foul means? It does not much matter however," the Boy Brigand pursued, "for sooner or later she must have heard the whole thing; and the very fact of her listening to a conversation which was meant for her will save to my future father-in-law the trouble of going over it again."

"Would you marry the Senorita Bianca?" the Monk inquired.

A loud laugh on the Boy Brigand's part answered this genuine query.

"Not if I know it! Where would it lead me to? With the real Marquis of Piatelli and sister alive such a proceeding would be madness. Once those two out of the way I may think about what it is wisdom to do. In the meantime let us hurry on."

The Monk was not slow in taking his Captain's hint.

Against his steed's side he pressed his spurs, and the steed cantered along.

Close by his side Sataniello kept at a similar pace.

The two cavaliers were thus trotting along the road, when the Boy Brigand suggested the propriety of slackening the pace.

"Do you know, Monk," the Captain inquired, "where we are bound to?"

"No more than the child unborn," his companion replied; "but I always follow you, Captain. I think that if I remain with you I must be right."

"Are you acquainted with the village yonder?"

"I think it is Viterbo," the Monk replied.

"Are there any doctors residing there?"

"I should say so," the Monk answered. "There used to be an old practitioner, who lived there some two years ago; he was a healthy, well-to-do man. He killed half his patients, so the busy tongues said; but as he was the only one in the village, he did a rattling business."

"Could you find his house?"

"I think I could."

"Is it far from here?"

"Not very."

"Many miles?"

"No, not above a quarter of a mile."

"Will he attend to our order at once?"

"Sure to."

"How do you make that out?"

"Why, if he knows that he is required at the Castle of the Duke of Don Saltara, he will give immediate orders to have his vehicle brought out; whereas, if some needy farmer was dying close by him, the devil a bit would he move; and I am sure the moribund would give up the ghost ere he would show."

"A bad character that——'"

"Nevertheless a true one."

"But is he clever?"

"Captain, I have already told what the people said about him; but we may as well hook him."

"All right, then, spur your steed on."

Again the two horses galloped onward.

The village of Viterbo was soon reached.

There was a large-sized residence, which stood prominently upon the principal piazza of the locality, which it was the two men's lot to visit.

Upon the door there was a large brass plate.

The name of the doctor shone forth in large letters.

There were two steps before the door, so the horses could come close to it.

With the handle of his pistol Sataniello knocked.

A face peeped out of the window above.

"Hallo!" the face inquired, "what want you at this time of night? Who are you?" the voice inquired.

"Two gentlemen!" the Monk replied.

"I see that as well as yourself; but what is your business?"

"'Tis the doctor, and no mistake!" the Monk exclaimed; "see how he dislikes turning out of his warm bed!"

The doctor, for it was him, was about to close his window. "My friends," he said, "speak out; it is deucedly cold."

"We want your valuable services!" the Boy Brigand began; "the Senorita Bianca Don Saltara is taken very unwell——"

"Who do you say?" the doctor inquired, still plunged in a half slumber.

"The Senorita Bianca!" the two voices answered.

"All right; I'll be down in a minute," the doctor replied.

It was many minutes, however, ere the surgeon made his appearance.

What between rubbing his eyes and pulling on his garments the time passed on quickly.

The Boy Brigand was beginning to get tired of waiting.

His horse's hoof was beating the pavement in its impatience to dart onward.

He was about to leave the piazza and to try some other house, when the hall door opened.

"My friends," the doctor said, "I hope you will excuse——"

"Certainly," the Monk replied.

"I have just been called out to rather a dangerous case of brain-fever, and I was fast relapsing into a quiet sleep when you awoke me—hence the delay which you experience."

"Never mind about the past, attend to the present," peremptorily began Sataniello. "Are you ready to start at once for the Castle of the Duke of Don Saltara?"

"Is the old gentleman taken ill?"

"No."

"Any of the servants?"

"No."

"Who can it be then, pray?" continued the talkative surgeon.

"The Senorita Bianca—I left her senseless!" the Boy Brigand pursued.

"You can go back at once, my worthy gentlemen," the surgeon continued; "when a lady is in the case everything must give place, and I will be there in a few moments. I will give immediate orders to harness my bay mare, and I will be at the Castle before you."

"You know your shortest road, don't you?" the Monk inquired.

"I should say so! If I had as many pounds as I went there, I would not be compelled to turn out at this time of night to earn a paltry living—here!

Santiago, Santiago, where the deuce are you?—why, you sleep like a top!"

The Boy Brigand and the Monk had now accomplished the errand for which they had set forth, and having nothing more to detain them, they turned away from the piazza, while the doctor was using all his endeavours to rouse his servant, who evidently had the same idea as his master concerning being disturbed in the middle of night.

"The old fellow," the Boy Brigand began, as soon as he was without reach of his voice being heard—"will be the best part of the night in getting himself ready. We must make the most of our time: do you think we could conveniently pay a visit to the cavern and return home to the Castle?"

"I fear not," the Monk replied; "but to-morrow I might find means of doing that which you wish to accomplish to-night."

"Right you are!"

"But what of it, Captain?"

"Just merely this—I wish the whole of the band to be in attendance to-morrow or the day after. I have heard a good deal this evening; and the old Duke of Don Saltara keeps treasures of unknown value within his vaults."

"Does he?"—and the Monk's glance sparkled with curiosity.

"Yes; and we must not lose an opportunity of becoming masters of them."

"True; but we want the whole band for that."

"We might, perhaps, manage singly."

"It might be dangerous!"

"We had better be on the safe side."

"You are as wise as King Solomon, Captain."

"And could you manage to see the band to-morrow?"

"I will try it."

"Can I rely upon you?"

"You have had no occasion to find fault with me as yet, Captain."

"I had better tell you what you must do."

"The more explicit the instructions the better for me."

"You know the White Bear Inn?"

"What, the half-way house?"

"Yes."

"Will you manage to see Paublas to-morrow?"

"That I will, Captain."

"Will you tell him, then, that he and the band must meet the evening after next at the White Bear. Inform him of the nature of the expedition. But, previous to going, you must do one thing."

"What is that, Captain?"

"How shall we manage about entering the vault?"

"Take an impression of the lock!"

"Have you got any wax for that effect?"

"I have not."

"I have, though."

"Once that done, you know how to act."

"I do."

"And how will you work your way to the vault?"

"Ask Maria, the chambermaid, to show it to me."

"Will she do so?"

"I do not know—I can only try. I will tell her that I am very fond of visiting subterranean passages, and all that kind of stuff; and she will, I dare say, take me to visit them. Then I will take a good survey of the place."

"But she cannot tell where the gold is."

"We will find that out ourselves."

"I need not say any more to you."

"I think not, Captain.   Leave it all to me, and you will find that you have a good servant."

These words were the last words which the two men pronounced, when they heard the rattle of a vehicle close behind them.

It was "Old Pill-box" plodding along in his old-fashioned gig.

"What say you about my way of waiting upon patients?" he inquired.

"A very laudable one indeed," the Boy Brigand replied.

Thus speaking, the two cavaliers and the vehicle entered the Castle yard, which had witnessed the departure of the former but an hour previously, and in a few instants afterwards the surgeon was shown to the chamber where the Senorita Bianca, apparently lifeless, lay upon a couch, surrounded by her loving father and the chambermaid, Maria, who, in anxious suspense, was awaiting, not so much the recovery of her young mistress, as the return of the Monk, about whose welfare she was rather anxious, considering the cruel band of robbers, commanded by a man of the name of Sataniello, who infested the surrounding neighbourhood of Don Saltara Castle.

––––

CHAPTER XXIX.

WHERE THE NEAPOLITAN DOCTOR IS INTRODUCED TO THE SENORITA BIANCA—WHERE HE WITNESSES A FATHER'S SORROW—AND WHERE THE BOY BRIGAND AGAIN APPEARS.

WHEN the doctor entered the room where the Senorita Bianca was lying upon her couch, he was welcomed by the Duke of Don Saltara.

"My daughter has been taken very ill," the Duke said. "I wonder what can be the matter with her? Please will you see?"

The physician nodded his head in the affirmative. With a slow, steady step he walked towards the spot where the Senorita Bianca happened to be lying.

Her head was reclining upon her pillow, and her pale features betrayed the most acute suffering.

It seemed as if the hand of death was about to snatch her away from this world for ever.

The physician approached the bed.

The Duke was leaning over his shoulder.

He took the girl's hand into his, and there he kept it for a few minutes.

"Your child is very bad, my Lord Duke," the physician said. "It is a sudden attack which has seized upon her; and, unless the greatest care be taken, I fear——"

He pronounced these words in a low voice.

Intently bent upon what he said, the Duke of Don Saltara kept his lips closed.

"You fear what?" he exclaimed.

"I fear that your daughter may not live."

"My daughter may not live! Oh! man, remember what you say. Think before you speak. Remember that you are addressing a father!"

"I know that, my Lord Duke," the doctor replied; "but I am also aware that your mind is strong as iron, if your heart be good——"

"What!" the Duke exclaimed. "Do you mean to tell me that all hope is gone?"

"Not of her recovery," the doctor replied, "but it will take time. She has been taken with a fever which is common enough in these parts, and which should be taken in time to avert the worst of consequences. I have been called, perhaps, too late."

The old Duke wrung his hands in despair. He strolled up and down the room as if he felt that the incident which we are just relating was his own work.

Maria, the chambermaid, now entered the apartment.

Upon her lovely countenance could be perceived the marks of the deepest sorrow.

At first she had thought that the Duke's daughter had only gone into a swoon; but now that she did not recover her consciousness she was beginning to dread that ere long her dear mistress would be taken away from this world.

The young girl felt for what she saw.

She mixed a calming potion.

She brought it to the bedside.

She endeavoured to make the Senorita Bianca drink some.

But she would not open her eyes.

All the doctor's skill had to be brought into requisition, but without avail.

The doctor now shook his head.

"Speak! speak! speak! my friend," the old Duke exclaimed, clasping strongly the physician's arm, and holding it in his powerful and nervous grasp ; but do not let me remain in an anxiety worse than death ! Oh, Bianca ! oh, Bianca!"

The doctor could not but feel his heart bleed at the sight which he witnessed.

He, too, had children ; and the idea that his young family might at no distant period be taken away from him caused him to groan inwardly.

"My Lord Duke," he said, "I have already spoken to you. Your daughter requires the greatest attention. Leave me alone with her."

"I will not quit this room. I will not move from my daughter if this is to be her death-bed! No, I will not! But I cannot conceive that you can be speaking true. Why, it was so sudden."

"She must have been suffering a long time," the physician said. "The crisis has come, and only at the last moment I am called in."

"Is it too late? Is it too late? Oh, do tell me!" the Duke inquired.

"My Lord Duke," the physician replied, "your daughter requires to be left alone. Will you allow me to attend her by myself. Here is Maria, her chambermaid, and she will wait upon her young mistress like no one else would, I know."

The Duke of Don Saltara seemed to be dumb to all the doctor's entreaties.

He remained sullen and silent.

"This is all my work," he muttered bitterly. "I wished to wed her to a man whom she did not love. Through some way or another she heard me, and as soon as the intelligence reached her she became distracted. Yes, this is the result."

The physician knew not what answer to make.

"I grieve deeply, my Lord Duke," he said, all the time holding the Senorita's hand within his own, "that poor Bianca should have been struck so suddenly with the dangerous fever which has chosen her as a victim ; but with time and with care all yet may not be lost."

These words seemed to give renewed strength to the heart of the Duke of Don Saltara.

"I had better leave you alone," he said. "Doctor, watch and remain by her bedside as long as you think it necessary, and you will not find me an ungrateful parent."

"My Lord Duke," the doctor replied, "I will do my best. Science sometimes may fail. In this

A CAPTIVE MAIDEN.

case, however, I trust and hope sincerely that it may not prove so."

While he was speaking the Duke listened attentively to him.

He had swallowed every word.

Have any of us ever been by the bedside of any dear relative?

There we have had occasion to judge the feelings of men and women.

We have seen the mother in tears—we have grieved for the father about to lose a dutiful and affectionate son—we have watched the human heart in all its phases.

The old Duke now walked out.

12

Ere, however, he did so he turned round.

He could not help gazing once more upon the lovely features of his sickly child, yet beautiful and interesting notwithstanding the changes a few hours' suffering had operated with her.

It is wonderful what extraordinary changes illness will effect in our frames.

He that looks healthy and blooming in the morning presents the appearance of a corpse in the evening if he is taken suddenly unwell.

The brightness of the eye gives way—the bloom that sits on the cheek disappears—the lip becomes white—the whole countenance assumes an appearance which betrays more than we can describe.

The Duke leaned by his daughter's side as soon as he was close to her.

He subsequently knelt down.

His mouth seemed to be muttering a prayer.

"Dearest Bianca," he said, "good-bye," and he gave her a loving, fatherly kiss.

Her forehead was cold.

The whole body motionless.

Sad forebodings induced him to think that he would never again see his daughter alive—that he was doomed never again to hear the sweet sounds of her melodious voice. Nay, the idea of death caused the Duke of Don Saltara to allow his eyes to be damped by those tears which betray a father's sorrow.

He felt that his presence was not required, and he abided by the doctor's advice.

It was, however, with a heart which was too full to enable him to speak that he retired.

Maria, the chambermaid, gazed after her master as he wended his steps towards the door.

The Senorita Bianca, in the meantime, gave no signs of a speedy recovery.

From the appearances now before the doctor, it was to be feared that she would not recover.

He had already spoken plainly to the father concerning his forebodings, and his duty as a medical man was now at an end.

When the doctor and Maria remained alone in the room where the Senorita Bianca was lying, the former began to question the chambermaid.

"At what o'clock was your mistress taken unwell?" he inquired.

"At what o'clock?" the girl inquired.

"Yes," replied the doctor, in that slow, steady manner which is adopted by certain people who wish to make you believe that what they say is really worth listening to.

"Yes, my girl," he continued, "at what o'clock was the Senorita Bianca taken unwell—will you answer me?"

The chambermaid collected her thoughts for a moment ere she replied.

"I do not exactly recollect, for I was down stairs; but I think I can, without deviating from the truth, tell you about the time."

"That will do; a few minutes does not matter."

"Well, Sir," Maria began, "it was at about ten o'clock at night, as well as I can recollect; of course you must not place too great reliance in what I say, for I am, like everybody else, liable to make a mistake."

"About ten o'clock, eh? and has she been in this senseless state since?"

The doctor pronounced these words in a quiet, cool, and collected manner, which showed that he was by no means taking a great interest in the girl whose sufferings he had been called upon to relieve.

Maria shook her head in the affirmative.

"Thank you," he said, "for your information; I do not want to know any more."

Thus speaking, the doctor sat down upon a chair which was close to the Senorita Bianca's couch.

He mused, and he gazed upon his patient.

She was like a corpse to all outward appearances.

About her frail and soft frame there was no signs of life.

Suddenly the body of the Senorita shook violently.

It seemed as if there was an unexpected reaction operating within her.

"She may get better," the doctor began; "she may recover."

The Senorita Bianca now recovered her senses.

"I wish to see father," she said, in a faint voice, which was scarcely audible by the doctor, but whose meaning was caught in an instant by the chambermaid.

As swift as a doe she darted outside the apartment.

Her absence was not of very long duration.

She soon re-appeared, accompanied by the Duke of Don Saltara.

The numerous servants who composed the household of the Duke were awaiting in the hall outside the result of their young mistress's illness.

They formed, indeed, an imposing and silent group.

There was the female cook, the coachman, the butler, and all the menials who for years had been receiving their wages and their livelihood from the old Duke; at first they did not believe that the report which they had heard was true, and they wanted to see their young mistress themselves, the Senorita Bianca, who was loved and respected by all.

Although the Duke's daughter was of a proud and haughty disposition with her equals, towards her inferiors she was distant and affectionate.

She would see that every one had his rights; and under no consideration whatever would she have allowed any injustice to be done towards any of them.

She was wont to regulate the servants' wages, and she was wont to see that all their wants were attended to, and that they should have no reason to complain.

Thus she was loved and respected by one and all.

The old Duke of Don Saltara was quite moved by the sympathy of these people.

He thanked them kindly for what they asked him; but he informed them that however anxious he might be to grant them their request, in common fairness he could not do it.

He showed them the wisdom of leaving his daughter undisturbed; and when he finally informed them that he, the father, had been forbidden to remain by his daughter's bed-side, the servants shook mournfully their heads and walked off.

They would not, however, quit the landing which stood close to the Senorita Bianca's bed-room before having heard satisfactory news relating to her, and in hopes of being informed with a change for the better, they remained outside.

As their behaviour was beyond reproach, and their presence without perfectly harmless, the Duke of Don Saltara saw no grounds why he should bid them to retire downstairs.

He had to force his way through them when Maria went in search of him.

As he walked along, his step was anything but firm and erect; and although there was a certain stiffness about his tread, one could easily perceive that the blow which he had just received was too much for him to bear.

Had he been unknown by those who surrounded him, he would have been taken for an inebriated man, for he looked not the collected individual whom we saw talking so quietly and so wisely to his guest, the supposed Marquis of Piatelli.

It has been said that sorrow renders a man mad at times; and it has also been asserted that the results of unexpected sufferings are very similar in their appearance to those produced upon one by too great an indulgence in the pleasures of Bacchus.

As he passed through the retinue of his servants, they ranged themselves on each side, so as to give their master a clear passage before him.

When the Duke of Don Saltara, accompanied by Maria, entered the room where his daughter lay on a bed of sickness, his gaze met that of Bianca.

In her look there was no reproachful feeling.

It seemed to say, " I do not accuse you, father—Good-bye!"

We understand fully what those words mean. Silence in some cases is worse to bear than the most rapid overflows imaginable.

The physician rose when he saw the sorrowing father appear.

What we describe had occurred within the space of a very short time.

Quicker than we could write it had these events occurred.

When his eye had met that of his daughter, the Duke had felt his heart beating with unknown pulsation—his brain had raved in a delirium of joy.

There was Bianca—there she was, apparently not dead yet.

Like a frenzied lunatic he rushed towards his daughter.

" Oh, Bianca !" he exclaimed, in the most endearing terms. " Oh, Bianca ! will you forgive me ? Recover—recover! Never again will I compel you to marry anyone! The man of your choice you will have ! Oh, forgive me !"

As she uttered these words, the Duke of Don Saltara clasped his daughter to his breast.

" Stay—stay ! What are you doing, my Lord Duke ?" the physician inquired. " Such excitement is too much for one in your daughter's state. Leave her alone, if you do not wish to hurry on the crisis, and thereby giving a worse turn than it otherwise might assume."

But the Duke was dumb.

The only creature whom he saw before him was the Senorita Bianca.

Again and again he clasped her to his breast.

Fervently he kissed her lips with a father's devoted affection.

" Farewell—farewell, father," the Senorita Bianca muttered ; " leave me—I feel I am dying."

These were the last words which the girl uttered. She had risen upon her couch.

The endeavour which she had made had exhausted her strength.

And then there was a horrid sight to witness.

Her lips rattled as if she was shivering on a cold winter's night. Her bosom heaved two or three times, and she opened her hands and closed them again.

Again she rose upon her pillow.

There was something vague in her looks.

She seized the sheets of the bed and tore them asunder.

It was, the doctor thought, the agony of death. It might have been the inward sufferings of a woman in labour.

The physician could not yet have seen what was really the case.

Never had he suspected that the Senorita Bianca was about to become a mother.

Never doubting such a thing as likely to take place, the thought had not entered his brain.

Oh, oh, oh !" she muttered, " oh, I suffer !"

Although she uttered these words in an undertone, the Duke of Don Saltara heard them.

It was, however, useless ; what could he do but be a silent witness to such a heartrending scene.

" Save my daughter, doctor," he exclaimed, " and I will give you my whole fortune !"

He was delirious—he was like one who was under some terrible nightmare.

Up and down the room he walked in the greatest state of excitement.

The crisis had now at length arrived.

The girl's head was propped up, and a potion was administered to her.

She would not drink it—she was too weak to do so.

The beverage was forced down her throat.

The physician took out his watch.

" In five minutes, my Lord Duke, we will see the result of this."

What anxiety was felt by a loving father we leave our readers to form an opinion.

Upon those words rested the whole of his future happiness.

For without his daughter life would be unbearable to the Duke of Don Saltara.

The time elapsed.

The whole frame of the Senorita Bianca shook violently—a gurgle followed. She opened her lips, as if about to speak, and she closed them again.

With a wild, superhuman stare, she looked around.

It was easy to perceive that she wished to speak.

She stretched forth her arms, and she held them towards her father, as if to receive an embrace from him.

He darted towards her.

But he had been too slow.

Ere he cleared the two yards which separated him from his child, she reclined stiffly upon her bed.

" The pulse has ceased to beat, my Lord Duke," the physician began. " Your daughter is no more : she is in Heaven now. Among the angels she has at length found a place upon a throne of happiness and glory. Let us all say, ere I depart, a prayer for the repose of her soul."

And the medical man fell upon his knees.

The old Duke followed his example.

Hence the chambermaid acted as he did.

Outside, the servants, who had silently watched the progress of the sickness, were now engaged in the deepest devotions.

At that moment the Boy Brigand, followed by the Monk, appeared.

He would have walked on, but the scene he witnessed stayed his course.

Like a statue he stood still ; immediately behind was his servant.

Sataniello knew that he had no business among all those who surrounded him.

He descended the staircase, and as he did so, he heard the mourning voices of the whole inhabitants of the Castle repeating a litany.

He heard a voice singing out—" Dead !—dead ! —dead !"

It was that of the Duke of Don Saltara, who, in his sorrow, could not but give way to loud expressions of his despair and of bitter disappointment.

CHAPTER XXX.

WHICH TELLS OF THE EVENTS WHICH OCCURRED AFTER THE SENORITA BIANCA'S SUPPOSED DEATH, AND WHICH BRINGS THE BOY BRIGAND AND THE MONK TOGETHER.

Two days had passed since the heartrending scene which we have described.

Dreary and sad was the life which the Boy Brigand led at the Castle.

He had not yet had an opportunity of paying a visit to the vaults beneath.

The countenance of his host was sullen and morose.

He was literally brokenhearted, and not a word did he speak.

The Marquis of Piatelli and the Duke used to have their meals together; but the conversation which passed between them was too unimportant to be dwelt upon.

The Duke of Don Saltara had but one thought.

Ever and anon his mind would revert to his daughter.

She had been buried in the family vault.

Owing to a few preparations which required to be made previously to her being interred, she was lying upon a catafalco, exposed to the open air.

The burial service had been performed in a quick and a hasty manner.

It had been carried out expeditiously to abide by the doctor's orders.

He had said that if the Duke's mind was allowed to ponder too much over the loss which he had sustained, he might at any time become distracted.

The Boy Brigand longed, then, for an opportunity to wish his host farewell.

The Duke of Don Saltara had taken quite a dislike to Sataniello.

Perhaps he looked upon him as the cause of his daughter's death.

For if he had not been on a visit to the Castle, what had taken place might not have occurred.

From the broken sentences of the Duke, it was easy to perceive that such was his feeling.

Sataniello, however, was not an individual to leave the field ere he had won the battle upon it.

We are speaking figuratively—our readers, doubtless, understand us.

We remember the object of Sataniello's visit at the castle of the Duke.

He had gone there for the sake of plunder.

From what he had heard, he knew that before him there was a very fair chance of turning his stay to some profitable account.

It would be a very bad policy on his part were he to remain the guest of the Duke of Don Saltara longer than he could help.

One thing—only one thing retained him.

He wanted to pay a visit to the vaults where the treasures were supposed to be hidden.

Except for those reasons, he had no wish to remain where he was.

He had given strict injunctions to the Monk to go and arrange with the other members of the troop.

In the early part of the day, when we again introduce Sataniello to our readers, had the Monk gone on the errand for which he had been sent.

Anxiously his return was looked forward to by the Boy Brigand.

Once back with him he would know how matters really stood.

Within his own heart Sataniello was beginning to think that delay was dangerous.

It is impossible for the mind of man to prophesy the future; many accidents might occur which would render his immediate departure from the Castle necessary.

It was late at night when we again see the Boy Brigand.

Two candles were burning on the chimney-piece.

Setting by the fire-side, plunged in his own thoughts, he was inwardly considering what steps he should take.

He was at a loss to account for the prolonged absence of the Monk.

More than ten hours had already elapsed since he had left the Castle.

Sataniello had strictly told him to report him the result of his interview with Paublas in the mountainous home of the Boy Brigand.

Often and often the Boy Brigand had thought of going out himself, stealthily and quietly, to effect his departure from the Castle, and to go himself to the cavern and inquire about the Monk.

Our readers can, doubtless, understand the anxiety of Sataniello.

Behind him he had left the Marquis of Piatelli and his sister.

It was impossible to form any idea of what Paublas might not do.

Sataniello knew thoroughly well the character of his lieutenant, and he had often thought that one day he would induce the brigands to mutiny, and then assume the command of his gallant troop.

His stay at the Castle had now extended for several weeks.

Never yet had he called upon his fearless followers. They might become amazed at his absence and fancying that they were deserted by their chief, lend a willing ear to any suggestions coming from their lieutenant, and which would have a tendency to lessen the supreme power of Sataniello, and to destroy the ascendancy which he had obtained over his band.

What rendered the supposition which the Boy Brigand was making more creditable was the slowness with which the Monk was carrying out his message.

We know perfectly well this, that when we have not a clear conscience, and when dangers are surrounding us, we fancy that there is every reason to fear.

The Marquis of Piatelli, besides, had proved himself to be no coward.

It was not to be presumed that he would attempt to escape; but still, finding his captivity irksome, he perhaps had bribed Paublas to his interests.

For instance, he might have said to him that he would speak to the reigning King of Naples to grant him a free pardon if he would set him free.

In his suspense, Sataniello was puzzled how to act.

If he had followed the promptings of his brain, ere now he would have set off.

But at every moment the Monk might appear.

Under these circumstances what was he to do?

Had we been situated as he was, we would have felt exactly the same as he did.

Sataniello was thus musing, when he felt a hand laid upon his shoulder.

A feeling of fright seized hold of him.

Who could it be?

Quickly he rose, and looked at the new comer.

It was the Monk.

With his finger upon his lips he enjoined silence.

"I have succeeded, Captain," he said, in an under-whisper.

"What tidings have you got?" he inquired, also in a low tone of voice.

"Captain, it is all right."

"Have you seen Paublas?"

"I have."

"It was time somebody went there, Captain; a great many things have occurred since we left."

"What do you mean?"

"The Marquis of Piatelli made a desperate attempt to obtain his freedom."

"How so? tell."

"I will tell you all by-and-bye, Captain ; "at present there is something more important on hand."

"Speak, I will not disturb you. But, in the first instance, explain yourself."

"I will do so, Captain."

"You have seen Paublas, you say?"

"I have."

"Is he coming?"

"In an hour's time."

"Where will he be ?"

"Upon that hill yonder."

"Which hill?"

"You can see it from yon window."

"But how will I know whether he is there or not?"

"We have plotted a signal."

"What for ?"

"To be altogether."

"The whole band?"

"Yes."

"Did you tell me that you were intending to pay a visit to the subterranean vault ?"

"I did."

"We can carry your idea out to-night."

"To-night ?"

"Certainly, Captain."

"How about the lock?"

"I have got the key to fit it."

"You have ?"

"Yes, look here."

"How did you manage that?"

"I took the impression with the wax you gave me."

"You did?"

"Yes, Captain."

"And where is the key ?"

"Here it is."

"Will it open the door ?"

"I think it ought."

"Are you sure ?"

"Positive."

"Have you already tried it ?"

"I have."

"When?"

"Yesterday morning."

"Anybody seen you ?"

"I think not."

"And is the whole band awaiting my commands ?"

"Yes, with the exception of two members."

"Why have they remained away ?"

"Paublas ordered it."

"He was right," the Boy Brigand pursued.

"I think we shall effect an entrance to the vault easily enough ; but the main point is to evade suspicion, and not to awake any of the inmates."

"We must be careful."

"We will be so ; but sometimes one is baffled."

"Listen, Captain."

"I am all attention."

"Shall I tell you what I did ?"

"Yes, I have asked you to do so for the last hour."

"You know when I left the Castle?"

"This morning. What about it ?"

"I went straight to the cavern. There I found Paublas and the whole of the troop. They were engaged in a long conversation about us, and they did not know what to make out of our long absence."

"'The Captain said he would not be long,' the Giant said."

"'And he has been away for two weeks,' Paublas replied."

"Did they grumble about it ?"

"Not precisely, but they seemed to feel your absence."

"You explained the whole thing to them, did you not ?"

"Of course I did, Captain."

"And what did they say when you spoke to them about this night's dark work ?"

"They were very satisfied with the tidings."

"Did they seem anxious for some excitement ?"

"Leave them alone for that. You do not want audiences Captain, I know."

The Monk pronounced these words in a sly tone of voice, which was fully understood by the Boy Brigand, who contented himself with smiling."

Am I to understand, then, that we have a clear field before us !" the Boy Brigand inquired, not rasing his tone.

"As far as I see, we have."

"There is one thing to be feared."

"What is that?"

"The Duke of Don Saltara himself."

"The Duke ?"

"Yes."

"Why he is in bed now, I should say."

"I hope so, for our sake."

"What makes you think otherwise ?"

"The servants were saying last night that he seldom sleeps since his daughter's death. They say that he occasionally pays a visit to the vaults, and remains hours and hours buried in prayer."

"That's rather awkward."

"Very much so, indeed."

"What should we do, then, if he was to surprise us !"

"Don't you know?"

"Why, settle him."

"Kill him ?"

"No."

"What, then ?"

"Just hold him until we have concluded what we want to do, and prevent him singing out so as to raise an alarm."

"And what's the signal ?"

"A very simple one indeed."

"Well, what is it ?"

"As soon as the hour is up."

"It must be close upon it now."

"Already ?"

"We have been talking for some time, you must remember."

"True."

"How long do you think I have been here?"

"At least three-quarters of an hour."

"The time approaches."

"Come, Captain, I will tell you now."

The Boy Brigand allowed himself to be led by the Monk.

In a few strides he was by the window's side.

With a gentle pressure of the hand the Monk opened.

A chilly breeze entered the apartment ; and but for the fortuitous forethought of the Boy Brigand the candles would have been blown out.

"I am glad we have still got a light," the Monk said.

"Why so?"

"It is part of the signal."

"The candles are ?"

"Most decidedly."

The Boy Brigand and the Monk were now looking, outside the window, on the country which, stretching itself as far as the eye could reach, presented one broad landscape of surpassing beauty.

It was a dark evening, yet the shades were not so thick as to prevent the sight distinguishing the curiosities of the numerous roads which branch in every direction.

The Monk pointed to the right with his forefinger.

The eye of the Boy Brigand followed the direction.

"You see that hill yonder?" he inquired.

"I do," the Boy Brigand replied.

"The hour is very nearly up, is it not?"

"It wants five minutes."

"Do you mind waiting?"

"Not at all."

Thus speaking, the two men stood side by side, without exchanging a syllable.

They remained thus for a few instants.

"The hour is up now," the Boy Brigand said, as soon as the five minutes had elapsed.

"And as sure as I am standing, they are true to their word. They are giving us the signal," the Monk replied quickly.

"I do not understand you."

"Look!"

"Oh, I see."

In the distance could be perceived the glare of a flickering light.

"But it has disappeared," the Boy Brigand pursued.

"I know that," the Monk replied.

"Paublas is to show the light three times."

"What then?"

"Wait until the light appears again."

"There it goes again," the Boy Brigand pursued, his eye rivetted towards the spot where the signs of his companions' presence were discernible.

"This is twice."

Another silence followed.

"What are we to do when we have satisfied our minds about them?" Sataniello inquired, quietly.

"Show them them that we are also ready and at our post."

"And to do so, how must we act?"

"You must put your candles out, leave a lapse of thirty seconds between each time, and light them twice, and then blow them out altogether."

For the third time a flickering light struck the Boy Brigand's gaze.

"Now, Captain, it is your turn to begin."

"While you do so, I will go downstairs to prepare the way for their entrance within the Castle walls."

"Will you come back again?" Sataniello inquired, as the Monk was receding towards the door.

"Not unless you think it necessary, Captain?"

"I do not."

"Well, I will go downstairs, then."

"You may."

"Captain," the Monk began, ere he went, "be careful as to what I bid you to do, and then you may join me; you know where the vault is?"

"I rather think I do," the Boy Brigand pursued; it is there that the body of the Senorita Bianca lay previous to being lowered into the family vault.

"You do not want me any more?"

"Not for the present."

"Steady, then, steady," the Monk replied, and he disappeared from the room.

So softly and so gently did he descend the steps, that no sounds were heeded; and by the time the Monk was reaching the lower part of the Castle, the Boy Brigand had concluded his work, and was also preparing himself to join his followers.

CHAPTER XXXI.

WHERE THE BOY BRIGAND, ACCOMPANIED BY HIS TROOP, PAY A NIGHTLY VISIT TO THE SUBTERRANEAN VAULTS OF DON SALTARA'S CASTLE, AND WHERE THE FIRST PART OF HIS DOINGS IS THERE RELATED, AND A THRILLING, UNEXPECTED INCIDENT IS CAREFULLY DESCRIBED.

IN less than twenty minutes after that which we have related in the previous chapter, Sataniello, surrounded by his troop, was standing at the entrance of the dark vault, wherein he purposed to pay a visit in company with all his fearless followers.

With an ingenuity which very few would have possessed, the Monk had received everyone of Sataniello's band.

He had kept a close watch, and as each respectively came in, he warned the others, so as not to destroy the success of the expedition by ill-timed hurry.

Thus, over eight members of the band, among whom we find our old acquaintances, Paublas, the Hunchback, and the Giant; the others, whose names we have refrained giving to our readers in full length owing to their insignificance, but which they will be called upon to perform in the course of this tale, effected a safe entrance to within the walls of Don Saltara's castle.

It was a bold undertaking, for at any time the alarm might be raised; and among the Duke's servants there were many a stalwart individual who would offer a rather sharp resistance to anything calculated to interfere with their master's interest.

Holding a bull's-eye in his hand, the Boy Brigand led the way.

Followed by his men, he threaded a narrow passage, and after a few strides, found himself by the side of a heavy, massive iron door.

With breathless suspense he examined the lock.

He had no occasion to ask for the key, for the Monk was already close to his Captain with it.

It was a shining, steel key, and it looked as if it had just been bought at a locksmith's shop.

The greatest care had been taken by him to make it look as neat as possible.

In a forge, which had been made by the Boy Brigand's troop to suit their various requirements, he had melted the metal, and having the impression of the lock in his possession which he had taken but a few days ago with a piece of sealing-wax which he had procured, he had felt no difficulty in accomplishing his task.

At first Sataniello experienced some difficulty.

The key fitted the lock, but it would not turn round.

He tried again; the second time he was more successful.

The door at length receded before him.

As the only impediment which existed before his entrance now ran upon its hinges, it produced a creaking noise, which many feared would attract the attention of the inmates abovestairs.

The vault, however, was situated many feet below the sleeping apartments, and the sound was not powerful enough to awaken the deep repose of the servants of the Duke.

There was a moment of suspense.

The whole band listened attentively to hear whether they heard any sounds of footsteps cautioning them of the approach of any living soul hostile to their bold undertaking.

Not a sound disturbed the silence of the damp subterranean passage.

Ashamed of his irresolution, Sataniello walked swiftly on.

Noiselessly and carefully did his steps clear the distance before him.

The lights of the bull's-eye which the brigands held was dim and flickering, and faintly only could they perceive that which surrounded them.

The ground was damp, and numerous cobwebs which hung from the top of the rocky ceilings bespoke the rare and scarce appearance of man within the spot where Sataniello and his troop had so cleverly entered.

The whole band now halted.

They stood before a short wooden spiral staircase which led downward.

Fearless of danger, Sataniello descended the steps.

The gloom of the place did not produce any effect upon him.

His glance ran around him, and he found himself in an arched cell of a few feet in width and corresponding height.

This place was a little more lively than the other places which he had visited.

A slight light was admitted from an aperture which doubtless led to the fields above him.

Sataniello began to think that he was doomed to disappointment.

Wherein he stood did not answer the description which the old Duke had given him relative to the spot where the treasures were kept.

Nothing but the smooth surface of the stone now met his touch.

It was a cell of a very peculiar form, and it induced him to think that it was used in former days to confine prisoners within, when the ancestors of the old Duke of Don Saltara were wont to indulge in those bold expeditions which occurred in the glorious days of knight-errantry.

Two yards before him he saw a slight aperture.

There was another door before him.

They had no ways of getting rid of this unexpected obstacle.

The Giant had a crowbar in his hand.

After a firm hold of it had been taken in the ground by digging the earth beneath, the whole strength of the troop was brought to bear upon it.

Thus, having a kind of purchase upon the iron instrument, the heavy door rose to the height of one or two inches.

The lock was wrenched off, and the door could easily be opened.

There was a larger cell than that which had previously met the gaze of Sataniello, and it appeared to him to be part of a series of dreadful receptacles combined in the thickness of this dungeon wall, but it extended far and far away before them.

In one corner lay scattered the remains of some human being.

It was a horrible skeleton, whose fate had doubtless been a terrible one.

Perhaps the place where he was had been appropriated to those prisoners who were doomed to confinement for life.

Some dark mystery, doubtless, clouded the unexpected sight which he met, for not a word relating to it had been spoken of by the Duke of Don Saltara.

Horrible recollections then flashed upon the mind of the Brigand Boy of the dreadful sufferings he had read of in books—that the miserable wretches immured in the dungeons underwent when thrown to the mercy of a cruel lord and master.

He fancied how some were tortured—some destroyed by expeditious and secret means—others by the more lingering process of starvation.

The idea now came to him—if he was to be captured and imprisoned by the Italian authorities.

Instinctively he thought that this was a sad warning to him.

The blood froze in his veins as he thought of dying thus.

His hair stiffened upon his head, and he felt a strange feeling creeping slowly and gradually over the whole of his frame.

He had work to undergo, and the transient sensation which he experienced was soon succeeded by calm and more consolatory reflections.

Whilst in this frame of mind he bid his men to follow close upon his track.

They all glided forward with a step so noiseless and swift, that Sataniello was not aware of the movements of his troop, so cautious were they in carrying out his orders, without making more noise than they possibly could.

The Boy Brigand now shaped his course differently.

He endeavoured to recall the exact road which had been described to him by the Duke of Don Saltara in the drawing-room where he was wont to have long conversations with him, but his memory failed him in the hour of need.

Still followed by his men, he proceeded for a short time along an onward passage, and presently he reached a spot where two avenues branched off, one to the right and one to the left.

He chose the latter, and found a second range of dungeons.

In one of these he knew that the treasures were kept.

The exact spot he could not recollect, however strongly he taxed his mind.

To see that he should not be baffled in his errand, he opened the door of several, to ascertain whether they were empty or not.

The passage which he had now taken, like all those he had previously traversed, was arched and flagged with stone, and brought him to a low square chamber, from which another flight of steps ascended.

Mounting them, he came to the other passages, and without pausing to consider, he hurried swiftly along the first.

Greatly surprised at the extent of the passage he had tracked, he could not help admiring the extraordinary solidity of the masonry, and owing to the light which he had, he gazed upon the freshness of the stone, which looked as if it had just come from the chisel.

Wondering whether this was the place where the money was kept, he stopped a few minutes to consider whether he should return, and fearful of losing his way in the labyrinth he had quitted, he determined to make a careful search of what surrounded him if he should return to the entrance.

Whilst so doing, he espied a heavy iron chest in the corner beneath an arched, small vault.

Ere, however, he opened it, he still walked on, when he came by the side of a deep stone building.

He was not long before he guessed the use of it.

Inscriptions upon it soon showed him that it was the place wherein were deposited all the defunct members of the Don Saltara family.

They stood and read the inscription upon it.

It was deeply engraved ; and, although many

years had elapsed since it was used for the gloomy purposes for which it was meant, the meaning could easily be made out.

In a few minutes the Boy Brigand became acquainted with the whole of the Don Saltara family genealogy.

They learnt how the first duke was buried there, a few days after a memorable battle wherein he had been killed at the head of a gallant and brave army.

Surmounting the upper part of the vault there was a terrible and ghastly sight.

We may as well devote a little of our space to describe it.

There lay, in full state upon a catapulco, the body of the Senorita Bianca.

Those who saw the remains of the late Duke of Wellington exposed to the gaze of the public at Chelsea Hospital, a few days after his death, will be able to form some idea of the solemn exhibition which the Boy Brigand and his followers contemplated.

At least a dozen candles were burning round the girl's corpse.

The rays of light were casting their bright shade upon her once lovely form.

The cluster of hair—which but two days ago the Boy Brigand had so much admired—appeared now to be hanging stiffly downwards, partly encircling her hollow cheek. Her hands, which were no longer brightened by that rosy hue produced by the circulation of the blood, were crossed upon her breast, as if she had died while praying.

Sataniello did not remain long contemplating the ghastly sight.

He pursued his course, followed by the brigands, in search of the treasure.

The Hunchback and the Giant, however, remained behind.

"I say," the Hunchback whispered into the Giant's ear, "the girl has got splendid earrings. See," he said, taking up the Senorita's hand, "she has beautiful rings upon her fingers. What say you? If we took them, it would be so much to the good."

"The Captain might object to it."

"What if he does?"

"He would not like it."

"I daresay not—he would like to have them for himself. I am going to do it if you are."

The Hunchback now placed his bull's-eye upon the girl's features.

"You may do what you like," the Giant replied; "I will not stay here."

"Why not?"

"I do not like, somehow or another, to interfere with dead people."

"Are you frightened, then?" the Hunchback inquired, sneeringly.

"That is my business, not yours, I suppose."

"Do not be offended,' the Hunchback pursued. I will soon take these little trinkets away. There is no one to miss them."

"The father might."

"What if he does? We will not wait until he comes."

"I am going ; so good-bye," the Giant said.

"Here the cripple said, "Why wont you stop?"

"I have already told you."

"You may go away, then," he replied ; and in an under-whisper he pursued, "We want no cowards among us."

Evidently this last sentence was not heard by the person to whom it was addressed—for we feel convinced that, had it reached the Giant's ears, he would have taken a terrible revenge for the expression now cast upon him.

Instead of moving on, however, he remained a yard or two in the distance, to watch the Hunchback —to see the result of his nefarious undertaking.

The earrings were soon unhooked from the Senorita's ears.

"What a simpleton that old Duke is," the Hunchback muttered, in contemplating the jewellery which he had become possessed of. "It would have been a great mistake, indeed, to bury such precious little trinkets."

So musing, he smiled sardonically.

"Here they go," he pursued. "This is number one," and he placed the earrings in his breast pocket, "and now for the rings."

The same success which had attended his previous endeavours failed now to reward him for the object which he had in view.

The Hunchback shook his head.

"What is to be done now?" he muttered. "Oh, I soon see! If I cannot take the rings off the finger, owing to their fitting too tightly, I will not be deceived all the same for that."

Out of his girdle he took a shining cutlass.

He felt the edge of it.

"That will do its work to my satisfaction, I should think," and he turned round to see whether he was watched by any one close at hand.

"No one to speak to the Captain about it," he muttered ; "so I better had look sharp about it, and the quicker I have done the better for me."

He held the cutlass in one hand, the white finger of the Senorita Bianca in the other.

The steel had scarcely touched the soft skin when he heard a groan.

Then he was deterred in his avaricious design.

The cut which he had made was but a slight one.

Ere he proceeded to make a deeper incision in the Senorita's finger he stopped short.

Another groan, more perceptible than the last one, now ejaculated from the supposed corpse's lips, and the Senorita Bianca's eyes opened.

She stared at him with a look which could only pertain to one who was alive.

This unexpected incident cowed the Hunchback.

He retreated three steps backward—his hand shook nervously—his body trembled with a puerile fear—his eye was sunk within his head—and his

THE DUKE AND HIS DAUGHTER.

his lamp dropped upon the ground. The heavy sound which it made could not but kindle Sataniello's attention, and cause him to appear on the spot where the Hunchback stood as if thunderstruck.

As we anticipated, Sataniello returned to the place where the strange scene which we have described had occurred.

The slightest of his movements being signals for his followers, the Boy Brigand was accompanied by the whole of his troop.

He seemed greatly astonished when he gazed upon the Hunchback's whole gait, and notwithstanding the injunctions which he had given on entering the vault, namely, that the strictest silence should be kept, he was the first to break it.

"What is the matter with you now, you stupid cripple?" the Boy Brigand asked. "What on earth are you about now?"

Instead of replying at once to his Captain, the Hunchback stared at him with a vacant look

"Have you lost your tongue to-night? What ails you? Are you mad or drunk?"

These were rather strong questions, and yet, not-

withstanding the Boy Brigand's palpable discontent the Hunchback still gave him no reply.

Again and again he stared wildly and stupidly at the Boy Brigand, and his finger pointed mechanically at the Senorita Bianca's body.

"There must be something strange in all this," Sataniello now thought, and, following the Hunchback's direction, he walked boldly towards the family vault.

CHAPTER XXXII.

WHICH TELLS OF A CORPSE COMING TO LIFE AGAIN — WHEN THE REAL NATURE OF THE SENORITA BIANCA'S DISEASE IS SOMEWHAT EXPLAINED, AND AN INCIDENT OR TWO RELATED AS THE STORY PROCEEDS.

HAD the old Duke of Don Saltara suddenly appeared in the vault—where his daughter had been exposed to the damp air for many hours past—and had he expected to find himself alone, his astonishment would have been great in contemplating the different countenances which were directed towards his daughter's body, eagerly looking at her features, as if she was destined to come to life again.

The Boy Brigand was wont to take the lead in all matters whree a good deal of discretion and no small amount of courage were required; hence, with a firm step, which no sight, however terrible, could have shaken, he walked closer than anyone else by the Senorita's side.

A subdued groan, which would not have been perceptible by any one far distant, was the first sign of life which Sataniello perceived.

Subsequently he placed his ear against the Senorita's lips, and he fancied that he could hear the regular breathings of some sensible being.

"That woman is alive, I am sure!" he ejaculated.

While so speaking his glance met that of the body.

Instinctively he retraced his steps.

There was something in that glance which had frightened him.

Can any one explain the strange feeling which creeps over the frame of any human being when placed in contact with the picture of death?

Then or never thoughts of a better world than the one in which we live ought to enter a Christian's mind.

Striking picture of mankind's forced submission to a superior Power—terrible illustration of a great God's final verdict—does a corpse offer to us!

Were those the ideas which presented themselves to Sataniello's imagination, as he stood motionless and silent ere he spoke?

Another groan, more audible than the former one, now escaped the Senorita's lips, and her lips moved, and her chest heaved, and it appeared to the beholders that her small mouth slightly opened apart, and that a rosy hue illuminated for awhile the pale features, upon which the Roman candles which were still burning cast their uncertain and fitful glare.

"Heavens above!" Sataniello exclaimed, as soon as he was close to the body. "There is something mysterious in that woman's sudden removal to this vault?"

And he gazed anew upon the Senorita's form.

No longer could he be mistaken. The Senorita Bianca was not dead yet; and, more curious still, she was about to give birth to a child, the legitimate offspring of her secret marriage.

But, as this requires some explanation, we may as well proceed to acquaint our readers with a few details which they should know to be better enabled to understand rightly the plot of this tale.

Hence, to be candid, we must inform those who peruse us that the Senorita Bianca was about to be confined.

Her offspring was the son of an English gentleman—whom we have already seen, and whom, doubtless, we shall meet again—to whom she had been duly married—the marriage having been kept secret on account of his belonging to the Church of England, the acknowledged faith of the country in which he lived.

The Senorita Bianca knew how bigotted her father was, and, fearing to kindle his wrath, she had not dared to make known to him the real state of things.

This being told, we can easily understand how bitterly any knowledge of her being betrothed by her father to a man whom she did not love would sting her heart, and how the fainting feat which she gave way to in a previous chapter was but the result of very natural consequences.

Thus, when the Senorita Bianca had been carried upon a bed of sickness, from which she was taken away apparently dead, the acute sufferings which a woman in labour must experience had been so keen and torturing that she had had no opportunity of communicating with her medical man.

Besides, the Italian doctor was by no means a very clever Esculapius; and the idea that the Senorita could ever have been married not having flashed across his mind, he never endeavoured to ascertain the causes of a fever whose symptoms he evidently mistook in his ignorance—so he allowed the poor creature to die, as he thought; and doubtless she would have carried her secret to the grave, had not an incident which was about to occur revealed to the Boy Brigand the startling truth.

Sataniello having therefore ascertained that that we have stated was the case, and that before him he beheld one about to become a mother, he undertook a task which was rather indelicate for one of the male sex to perform, and, in a few instants, he became possessed of a rosy, blooming child.

"Carry him away," he said, "at once," transferring his precious burthen to the Hunchback. "Take him to Joanitta, and enjoin her to take the greatest care of a male heir to the Don Saltara property. This is a valuable increase to our stock. We will bring him up among us, and never will he want as long as he lives. 'Tis a fine opportunity opportunity offered to us, for which we did not bargain; and here we have great scope to work on another's feelings and to draw from her a fortune if we need it."

The Hunchback looked at the infant which had just been entrusted to his care.

"A fine boy that," he said; and, thus speaking, he wrapped him carefully beneath his warm cloak, and, having received one or two more instructions from his Captain, he sallied forth on his onward journey.

When the Hunchback had disappeared, Sataniello and his band returned to the spot from which the Hunchback's loud astonishment had withdrawn them, and quietly proceeded to take away the treasure for which the expedition had been contemplated.

The place where the gold was had nothing peculiar about it, and, beyond thousands of pieces of the precious coin heaped together in glittering array, nothing worth describing was to be seen.

Stooping upon the cold damp ground, the brigands were too busily engaged in scraping together the wealth which was in store before them to heed anything else; and, as they were fulfilling their avaricious task, they presented truly the picture of so many worshippers to the god Mammon.

They placed the golden pieces in their pockets as fast as they could, and were filling heavy leather bags, which had been brought with them for the purpose.

A sigh now disturbed them in their avaricious and greedy performance.

It was that of a woman—that of Bianca.

It emanated from the place where the body was.

With the bull's-eye in his hand, the Boy Brigand rushed towards the spot.

He arrived just in time to be seized by the Senorita Bianca.

She clung around his neck, and, in a delirious voice, besought him to listen to her prayers.

"You have taken him away, I know. Oh, give me my child back, and you are welcome to all that which surrounds you. Plunder—plunder; every-thing away, but restore to me my beloved child."

Sataniello endeavoured to rid himself of the woman.

She looked more like a corpse than a living soul.

Surrounded by a big white shroud, she appeared truly like a ghost.

Mechanically the Boy Brigand stepped backwards.

At first the Senorita Bianca did not recognise Sataniello, who had taken the precaution of covering his face with a mask in case of his being detected; but, when her eye rested again upon him, she gave way to an exclamation which sounded like a shriek.

"Marquis Piatelli!" she ejaculated, "is that you? Oh, what have you been doing here? Oh, tell me—do tell me."

The Boy Brigand was by no means disconcerted.

"Remain silent," he said. "I will carry you upstairs to your room; and, if you keep this night's dark work as quiet as I most certainly shall, your father has no need to become acquainted with what has taken place here."

"But my child," she muttered, "where is he? Take it away if you choose, but let me gaze upon it for once, at least."

The Boy Brigand made no reply for awhile.

He will be returned to you in all in due time," he replied; but for the present, silence."

"Is it a boy" the Senorita inquired. "Oh, do let me have a look at him.

There was an earnestness, a motherly anxiety, in the words which would have softened the heart of a stone.

Sataniello, however, looked upon the whole thing as likely to become useful to him at some future period, and he contented himself by shaking his head in the negative.

"It is not in my power," he began, after awhile, "to comply with your request, Senorita. He has been taken away, and by this time, doubtless, he is far off."

"But he will die if exposed to the night air."

"Fear not. He will be in womanly hands before an hour has elapsed, and I can faithfully promise you that he will live."

The young woman lifted her hands towards the heavens, as if to call an omnipotent Power to her assistance.

"Who are you?" she muttered, in a feeble voice, glaring at the supposed Marquis. "Who can you be? What brought you hither? Who are these men that surround me on all sides?"

"This is my troop," Sataniello replied. "When I am gone I will acquaint you with my real charac-ter. And now, if you will allow me, I will carry you upstairs to your own apartments. This night I will not take my departure from the castle walls. To-morrow you will meet me at breakfast. I have saved your life. Will you promise me not to reveal what you have seen until I am out of sight?"

"What can I refuse to you?" she muttered in reply. "If you promise me not to hurt or destroy my child I will do what you bid me."

"That's enough," Sataniello replied. "And now for another part of my business."

The Senorita was now reclining upon the damp stone upon which she had been lying but a few hours previously.

"Here, my boys," the Boy Brigand began. "Have you concluded all that which you require here?"

A unanimous reply in the affirmative greeted his words.

"Very good," he said. "Now, effect your depar-ture, and, as soon as you are safely in the country, blow a sharp whistle. To-morrow I will be again among you."

This was the last adieu which Sataniello gave.

One by one the brigands disappeared.

The sound of their footsteps was heard in the distance.

The time which the Senorita spent in the vaults appeared to her to have been a century.

Face to face with the robber of her flesh and blood she stood mute and silent.

Not a word did either of the two beings utter.

Sataniello had nothing to say. The Senorita feared to speak.

The minutes passed away, and no sound struck Sataniello's ears.

"What can have occurred?" he muttered to him-self. "Have they been detected?"

In breathless suspense he listened.

"Senorita," he began, "you remember what you promised me? If through you I am detected your child will be immediately smothered by my hand."

"Oh, speak not thus!" the Senorita replied. "Do not lacerate a mother's heart. I give you my word—you may truly rely upon it."

A hum of voices was now heard above-stairs.

It sounded as if there was a discussion in the hall.

"I hear the coachman speaking," the Senorita began. "What is taking place upstairs? How I wonder. Oh, come up!"

The Boy Brigand required no such bidding.

Rapidly and swiftly he ascended the flight of steps, and in a minute he found himself in the hall with the Senorita Bianca.

As she appeared, she saw two figures gliding along in the darkness.

It was the coachman and another of the male servants.

So frightened had they been by the sight of their mistress, whom they believed in her grave, that they receded before her.

They looked upon her as an apparition.

The Boy Brigand heard the coachman muttering a prayer.

Meanwhile, and taking advantage of the obscurity which reigned, he ascended another flight of steps which led to her apartment.

At that moment a shrill whistle was heard.

"Your companions are safe," the Senorita mut-tered. "There is the signal."

The Boy Brigand heeded not his companion's voice.

He proceeded onwards, and when he had reached the apartment where the Senorita Bianca was wont to dwell, he entered the room with her, and, when he was within, he closed the door behind him to prevent any one entering.

"Senorita Bianca," he said, "we are now alone."

Astonished, bewildered, surprised by Sataniello's strange proceeding, the Senorita could find no strength to ask what he meant by so doing.

"Sit down here," the Boy Brigand began; "you must be weak, indeed, after all that which you have undergone. Do not fear. Not a hair of your head will I touch while I am with you."

These words seemed to relieve the Senorita's mind

Exhausted by all the sufferings which had lace-rated her frame within the last twenty-four hours, she reclined gently upon an easy chair which stood close to her.

While she did so the Boy Brigand went and closed the shutters.

Subsequently, he pulled together the curtains, so as to prevent any light being seen from the outside.

Having thus satisfied his mind that everything was as he wished it, he placed his bull's-eye on the ground,

"You wonder, I dare say, Senorita," he said, "what my object is in coming hither; but I will not keep you long in suspense."

It would be difficult, indeed, to describe the strange feelings which successively actuated the breast of the Duke's daughter.

She was at a loss to conceive what the Boy Brigand was about to accomplish.

She felt convinced that he did not intend to take away her life, for, had he wished to do so, there had been full opportunity for him before.

Her mind wandered from one thing to another, and anxiously did she await the moment when he would acquaint her with his intentions.

At one time her womanly innocence had received a severe shock.

What could have induced Sataniello to act as he was doing?

Was it to take an unfair advantage of her?

If such was the case, she was now entirely at his mercy.

To call for assistance would have been useless, and now she felt that she was entirely within the hands of her father's guest.

Up to the present period she had fancied him to be the Marquis of Piatelli. Now she was puzzled to know who he really was—and to have guessed him to be Sataniello, the Dark King of the Mountains, was a supposition which was not likely to enter her mind.

She was thus musing, when the Boy Brigand's voice drew her from her reveries.

"What is your husband's name, Madam?" he asked, abruptly.

This was the last question in the world which the Senorita expected.

She reluctantly opened her lips, as if to give an answer.

"I see," Sataniello said, perceiving the Senorita's awkward manner, "that you do not wish to divulge him to me."

"I have always kept it a secret," she replied; "and I would like to do so now."

"Are you ashamed to own him as a husband, then?" the Boy Brigand said, accentuating deeply every word he spoke.

This was too much for the Senorita Bianca.

Before such a remark silence, she thought, was an insult to him she loved.

"No, Marquis Piatelli," she replied; "I must call you by the name under which you were first introduced to me—I am not ashamed of my husband. He is a Protestant—"

"And an Englishman," the Boy Brigand quickly retorted.

"How, Sir, do you know it?" the Senorita inquired, her eyes sparkling with the marks of the most intense curiosity.

"I am a strange man," the Boy Brigand replied; "you perceive I am acquainted with everything in due course; further, I will tell you that he is a British officer, and that he is called Captain Wogan!"

"You have spoken the truth, Sir," the Senorita replied. "The man to whom I have united my destiny is all that which you state; I am proud of him, and I love him tenderly."

"Captain Wogan is my bitterest enemy, Senorita Bianca," the Boy Brigand replied; "and if he had it all his own way, long ago I should have been cast into a dungeon."

"You!" the Senorita muttered; "you!—the Marquis of Piatelli!"

"I am not a nobleman," Sataniello replied, coolly. "My present title has been assumed, and I am a brigand. They call me Sataniello; and the people in the country have been unanimous in bowing before the sway which I wield, for one and all have denominated me the Dark King of the Mountains!"

There was a bitter smile upon Sataniello's lips as he spoke.

The Senorita Bianca was too amazed to make any reply.

"Yes," Sataniello continued, "I am a brigand and an outcast, and I act as such. Captain Wogan once attempted to make me his prisoner, and I wounded him in return; but we Italians are spiteful, you know, and, ere I leave this room, I intend to take a striking revenge upon Captain Wogan's legitimate wife."

There are some natures which would have been cowed by such a speech—which would have rendered them powerless—and to whom the words which had been uttered would have been worse than a death-blow.

It seemed, however, that in the present instance, that which she had endured for the last few days had given renewed strength to the Senorita's constitution.

The Senorita caught not at first the fiendish meaning contained in Sataniello's sentence, and, after consideration, soon acquainted herself with its terrible signification.

"Surely, Sir," she said, falling upon her knees, 'you would not have recourse to that which you threaten; I am only a poor, weak, harmless woman, who has never injured you."

"Do you think, then," Sataniello replied, in an under-whisper, "that I have forgotten your scornful looks—the disdain with which you treated me while I was under your father's roof. I was a marquis then, and therefore worth your friendship, if not your love. Now I am a brigand—"

As he spoke, Sataniello rose and advanced towards the Senorita.

"Forgive me," she said, "for whatever I might have done to you. I heartily regret it; but do not carry out your threat."

"You are truly handsome!—beautiful!" Sataniello pursued; "it would be losing a fine occasion indeed were I to allow so well-modelled and so splendid a form to escape my grasp. I do not love you, I do not care for you; still you will be my own this night."

"Oh, do listen to a woman who beseeches you," Bianca replied; "oh, for heaven's sake do not cover me with shame! Oh, Sir, spare me!"

The Senorita uttered these words in a heart-rending tone of voice, and imploringly did she raise her hands towards Sataniella, clasped as if in prayer.

"To endeavour to alter my resolution is useless," Sataniello replied, his eye glistening with all the fire of man's brutal passions; "to-night I will cover the proud coat of arms of your family with a stigma that nothing will wipe off."

Thus speaking, he approached close to the Senorita Bianca.

His lip quivered, his heart beat, and he was bent upon his purpose.

"If you shriek," he said; "this knife will do its bloody work."

"Death, Sir, before dishonour," the Senorita replied. "Away—away from me, felon!—outcast! coward!—scoundrel!"

And as she uttered these last epithets she stood upright, and with the majesty of a queen, before Sataniello.

For an instant he was uncertain how to act.

But his passion was now kindled, and he rushed madly towards the Senorita, whom he fervently clasped in a feverish embrace.

"Help—help—help!" the Senorita exclaimed, with a shriek which resounded throughout the whole house; "help—help—help!"

———

CHAPTER XXXIII.

WHERE A SHORT INCIDENT IS RELATED, AND WHERE CAPTAIN WOGAN AND THE BOY BRIGAND MEET AGAIN UNEXPECTEDLY.

THE words of the Senorita had found an echo, which had been heard by the inhabitants of Don Saltara Castle.

The door of the room was now violently thrown open, and a figure appeared, holding a pistol in each hand.

The Boy Brigand quickly turned round.

Before him he saw Captain Wogan.

One instant enabled him to perceive the fiendish plan which Sataniello would have carried out had he not so suddenly appeared.

It would be impossible to attempt to convey to our readers an exact description of the bitter rage which was depicted upon Captain Wogan's countenance.

With the swiftness of lightning he wound his steps towards Sataniello. "I have found you at last, you cowardly hound!" he exclaimed, pointing his pistols to Sataniello's forehead—"on your knees before me, Sir, or you are a dead man!"

Sataniello had no firearms, so he thought it wise to act in compliance with Captain Wogan's request.

Quickly he did so, and he looked upwards.

The two men's gaze met, and there was an indefinable amount of hatred glistening in that look which passed between the soldier and the brigand.

"I will not shoot you like a dog," Captain Wogan began; "but I will place you in irons, and hand you over to the authorities, who will, I doubt not, sentence you to a death which you so richly deserve."

Sataniello never lost sight of his captor, but he feared him not; some strange voice bid him still to hope.

"Bianca," Captain Wogan now whispered, "run downstairs as fast as you possibly can, and bring here the whole of the household; we will then secure this bold and merciless bandit, and to-morrow we will entrust him to the safeguard of the Papal dragoons."

As the last word escaped his lips, the Captain happened to turn round to see whether his wish was quickly carried out.

The movement of his head did not last above a second at the utmost, but it had been enough for Sataniello.

In that short space of time he had seen a chance of escape.

Quickly he took hold of Captain Wogan's knees in his iron grasp, and by a quick sleight of hand laid him prostrate on the ground.

The sound of the pistol-shots immediately followed.

"I am safe again!" Sataniello exclaimed, and, quicker than we could depict it, he ran towards the window of the room.

Footsteps in the hall warned him that not a minute was to be lost.

"Come—come!" he heard the Senorita Bianca's voice saying; "come, we hold him safe!"

"Not yet, my good people—not yet!" the Boy Brigand replied; and so saying, he cleared the window, and jumped into a field beyond.

At the time that he was clearing the distance, the household entered the apartment, where Captain Wogan had just risen.

"Once more he has escaped me," he ejaculated sadly, as the strange faces showed themselves on the threshold; "he cannot be far away, though."

"Where is he?" the old Duke of Don Saltara inquired, entering the apartment, and too much frightened to ask Captain Wogan the reason which brought him within his roof.

The Captain gave all the information which he thought necessary; and, followed by a numerous escort, beat all the grounds without any avail, and an hour afterwards returned to the Castle to relate to the Duke the ill-success of his expedition and to confess to him all the circumstances which had led to his secret marriage with the Senorita Bianca.

We need not say that the old Duke never grumbled—never found the slightest fault with Bianca for having chosen herself a consort without his authority or sanction.

There she was before him, if not full of health and blooming, yet in a fair way of being restored to all the realities of life; and he was too contented to see that the hand of providence had allowed him to have his daughter restored to him, through the most extraordinary means which we have related, to be able to utter a word.

After an hour's time, however, and when he had heard from the Senorita Bianca's own lips the whole details of the Boy Brigand's visit to the vault with his troop and the loss of his grand-child, he breathed heavily, and like one whose heart is sadly embittered.

He called his daughter and Captain Wogan close to him.

"Here, my children," he said, putting his daughter's right hand in that of the military man, "may you live happy and contented together. Doubtless I would not have acted as I do now a few weeks ago; but what I have witnessed shows me that a daughter's affection should be consulted, and not any other motives; and it is my most sincere wish that everything which has taken place should be forgotten."

"I think, my Lord Duke, that you have forgotten to enjoin us to do a thing which we must carry out. It is a duty before which I will not flinch, and which I must carry out successfully."

"The recovery of one's lost child needs no bidding," the old Duke replied. "Fervently will I offer my prayers to heaven; and I feel certain that a merciful God will listen to them."

"Amen!" replied Captain Wogan and the Senorita Bianca.

Thus concluded the evening during which so many things had occurred, and shortly afterwards the whole of the inmates of Don Saltara Castle retired to their respective apartments to seek, in a refreshing slumber, a repose which they needed after what they had witnessed.

CHAPTER XXXIV.

WHICH REVERTS TO THE BOY BRIGAND—WHICH
DESCRIBES HIS ARRIVAL AT HIS CAVERN—AND
WHICH TELLS TO THE READER WHAT HE SAW
THERE.

It may be necessary ere we proceed any further
to explain how Sataniello managed to escape from
the vigilance and the search which had been made
after him by Captain Wogan and the numerous servants of the Duke of Don Saltara.

Some old proverb says that there is a god for
lovers and for thieves. We are not in a position to
state whether the remark alluding to the first one
is true; but what we can boldly and fearlessly assert
is this, there must be a god somewhere for thieves
and robbers.

Were it not so, Sataniello in the first instance
would certainly have found instantaneous death in
falling from the height from which he had sprung;
in the next, having safely reached a safe spot, he
would not have made the most of it—as we will
show he did—had he not been guided by some mysterious ascendancy.

When, owing to his quick perception, he had rid
himself of Captain Wogan's custody, he stepped to
the window.

To open it had been for him the work of an
instant.

He was accustomed to all that which had occurred to him, and to act as he did was no novelty
to him.

Sataniello, however, saw the distance which separated him from the apartment where he was, and
the spot beneath him.

It was a kind of yard with pavement in it; and in
one corner of it there was a large and deep excavation filled with straw.

He calculated the distance which separated him
from it.

He had no time to consider and ponder over what
he should do, for he knew that ere a few seconds
should have elapsed, no trouble would have been
spared to insure safely his valuable body.

Hence, when he perceived Captain Wogan approaching towards, and quickly loading his pistols
to have another trial at his life, he felt that delay
would be dangerous, and madly and heedlessly he
committed himself to the open air.

Although he had had no space to take a start,
yet so well had he measured the spot where he
wished to land, that six seconds only had elapsed
after his disappearance from the window before he
found himself upon the straw above alluded to.

That he was not hurt was at once patent to him;
he knew that from the elasticity of his limbs and
total absence of pain.

The first part of his scheme had been successfully
carried out; but it would never have done for him
to rest upon his laurels.

Being fully aware of this himself, he removed the
straw from beneath him; and when he had done so, and,
he remained hidden under half a dozen trusses, and,
in no way inconvenienced by the weight, he listened
in breathless suspense to hear whether he had been
detected.

To look in the particular place where Sataniello
had taken a momentary refuge, was never dreamt
of by Captain Wogan and his followers, and he heard
their conversation, and he heard the coachman
inting at the slyness of the Monk, who had taken

to his heels, as he described it, long before his
master's game was found out.

The steps came closer and closer to him during
the minute inspection which Captain Wogan was
making, and more than once did Sataniello lose all
hopes of ever returning to his mountainous home.

Heavy drops of heat wetted his brow, and he was
in a warm perspiration during the whole time which
followed his bold escape from Don Saltara Castle.

It was only when he had heard the last sounds of
footsteps dying in the distance, and long after that
the servants' door had been closed for the night,
that he thought of moving from the place where he
had now remained for upwards of an hour and
a half.

Carefully he removed the straw from above his
head, and looked up.

Everything around him was silent, and only one
light was to be seen issuing from the drawing-room
window, where the Duke, his daughter, and Captain
Wogan remained assembled for some time after the
meeting which they had had with Sataniello.

Having ascertained that no one was watching
him, Sataniello emerged from his hiding-place, and
looked around him to see where he was.

It served him but little to do so, for he found, to
his great annoyance, that he was standing at the
back of the Castle, and that he would have to be
most careful in forcing his way without, if he wished
unheeded to gain the open country.

After a great deal of watching on Sataniello's
part, and gliding swiftly along in a crouching posture, he at length reached a small path which
conducted him to a road which was familiar to
him.

" Freedom! blessed freedom!" he exclaimed, as
soon as he was distant enough from the castle not
to fear the sound of his voice being heeded, " Oh,
how I love thee! what is life to man without his
liberty? I have had a narrow escape of it to-night,
'tis true, still I do not despair; and if fortune
favours me as much as it has hitherto done, ere
many years will have elapsed, I will become the
owner of some princely fortune. What shall I do
then? Sataniello mused, as he strolled on. Shall I
go away from Italy, and settle down in some remote
part where my previous history will be unknown—
my antecedents a mystery to all—or shall I remain
in my own country?"

Thus soliloquising, he walked quickly onward.

He had been stepping over the ground for some
time now, when he came to the side of a large
wooden cross, at the bottom of which he saw a boy
sleeping.

The rays of the moon alighting upon the lad's
countenance bespoke him to be quite a youth, and
in the distance could be seen a few buildings, a
church, and a few cottages, scattered here and there
—a village, so called.

He advanced towards the boy, and shook him
gently.

The lad opened his eyes, and looked at the new
comer.

" What are you doing here, my boy? Do you
not find it cold?" Sataniello inquired, as soon as his
new acquaintance had sufficiently recovered from
his slumber to understand fully the meaning of the
words which were uttered.

" You are the first one who has spoken a kind
word to me since I left my home," the lad replied,
and I will not deny the truth to you. You must
be good and kind-hearted, otherwise you would
never have addressed me."

" Have you acted wrong, then?" Sataniello pur-

"that you find yourself all alone in the
y?"

lad stood upright.

countenance betrayed the annoyance which
in having been accused by Sataniello in the
r in which he had.

o, Sir," he said, proudly, "I have not. I
t I could have earned my bread if I sought it,
rmers would not employ me ; they said I was
all, and a good day's work could not be got
me."

re was a manliness and a certain amount of
ardihood in the words which the boy pro-
ed, which Sataniello noticed, and he inwardly
to feel a certain slight interest in the little
er's ways.

o not mistake my words," Sataniello resumed ;
uestion as I do, it is to find out whether you
rth helping or not; if you fancy that I am
htly actuated, I will walk on."

h, do not leave me thus," the boy continued ;
n to me, Sir !"

will do so," Sataniello pursued, "and I should
hear your story very much, as I think that
s something strange in your being here at this
y spot. Boys at your time of life have gene-
riends or parents to look after them, and I
lly wonder at your being all by yourself."

you only knew the truth," the lad pursued,
would not blame me for what I have done.
I left Rome have I met no success, and I am
ed to return home with my hands empty. I
t that I could support my family as well as
ther did, but I find that to do so is impos-
o me; nobody will give me a chance."

ho is your brother?" the Boy Brigand began.
had one once," the lad replied, "but he left
denly."

hat, do you mean to tell me, that he ran away
ome?"

e did, Sir," the lad continued, "and we never
why. Mother and sister were very fond of
nd we all feel deeply his absence."

hat was he—had he any trade?" Sataniello
d.

had no trade, Sir," the boy replied, "but he
drive along the high road, and a better whip
e was could not be found for many miles
."

hat was he, do you say?"

postilion, Sir. His master never could
t for the abrupt manner in which he left him;
though he set the police after him, he never
ind any trace of him."

d why did he set the police after him?" the
rigand pursued; "had he committed any

a thought seemed to flash across Sataniello's

nat is your brother's name, my boy?" he
affectionately.

ro,"—so we called him at home," the lad
, and he wept outright. "When mother and
ad been tired of waiting for his return, one
rning I took it into my head to go in search
. I am sure I have walked a good many
, and no tidings of his whereabouts have yet
me."

nat has become of your mother and sister?"
llo pursued.

ey are at home, waiting anxiously my return."
w have they managed to live since your
's absence?" the Boy Brigand pursued; "did
help them?"

"Yes, Sir," the boy replied, "Pedro's former
master gave us a trifle or two, but that's all, and we
have been entirely dependent upon charity since."

Sataniello mused, and seemed to think deeply
over what he had heard.

It was a strange coincidence that he should meet
the brother of Pedro the Postboy—his recruit, whose
short-lived career was brought to such an untimely
end, as our readers doubtless remember.

He looked upon this meeting as a warning from
providence that he should make some atonement to
the family for the loss which they had sustained,
owing entirely to his having taken Pedro into his
troop.

Sataniello was an individual whose character
could scarcely be defined. His mind was occasionally subject to be guided by impulses of generosity,
whilst at other times he delighted in all kinds of
cruelty.

It would have been difficult to conceive that one
who could not have been softened by womanly
tears—by womanly supplication, such as that of the
Senorita Bianca—should have been interested in a
small boy's welfare.

Had he not however, been the means of Pedro's
death, it is likely that he would have allowed the
boy to go away unheeded ; but as the case stood, he
was fully desirous of making the family some
reparation.

"And your journey has been productive of no
satisfactory result up to the present, I suppose?"
Sataniello pursued.

The lad, brought thus back to contemplate in the
face his forlorn position, shook his head in the
negative.

"It has not, Sir," he muttered slowly.

"And what would you say," Sataniello pursued,
"if I gave you enough to ensure comfort to your
mother and sister for the remainder of their lives?"

The boy shook his head, and rubbed his eyes,
like we sometimes do when we are suddenly awaken-
ing from some dream.

"I should sooner know where Pedro is," the lad
replied ; "and mother and sister would, too, I am
sure. It was not his money which we wanted—we
love him too much for that."

"And if I were to tell you, that you would never
see Pedro again."

"I would not believe you, Sir," the lad replied
"but perhaps you can tell me where I can find my
brother? if you can, oh! tell me! and I will go to
him; I do not care how far it is, I will walk it."

"Do you know the colour of gold?" Sataniello
pursued.

"I do well," the boy replied.

"If I give you some, what will you do with it?"

"Take it back to mother."

"You are a good-hearted lad, and, moreover, a
good son," the Boy Brigand replied ; "so here, take
this."

Thus speaking, he gave to his new acquaintance
a few golden coins, which, in the days that we are
writing of, especially in Italy, would have been considered a fortune by such humble people as the
parents of Pedro the Postboy must have been.

"What will you do now?" the Boy Brigand
asked.

"Keep my money hidden beneath my garments,
and trace my way towards the house where we
dwell ; although it is far enough, I will walk there,
and when I get at my journey's end, I will take a
good rest."

"That is a sensible fellow," the Boy Brigand
mused, as he glanced upon the lad before him, who

was busily occupied in fastening his jacket to conceal safely beneath it the present which the Boy Brigand had made him.

"When you return home," the Boy Brigand pursued, "give the money to your mother, and tell her that she will never see her son any more, and that he who gives you the information knows what he says to be true."

"Is he dead, Sir?—is he?" the lad inquired.

He had pronounced these words in an anxious tone of voice, which would have been sufficient to convince Sataniello that his loss would have been too severely felt by the boy did he begin to reveal at once the truth; so he remained silent, and shook hands with his young friend.

"May be, my lad," he said, "I shall have occasion to see you again. I must now say farewell, as I have important business to attend. Hurry on towards your journey. May Heaven speed you on your errand, and give to your parents sufficient strength to bear the sad tidings which you will convey to them!"

Thus speaking, Sataniello ascended a hill which led towards the mountain, leaving behind him the lad, who, in astonishment, remained rooted to the same spot as that where he had been standing when spoken to by the Boy Brigand.

His eye followed Sataniello's form in the distance, but when he could see him no longer, he returned by the side of the cross where he had been sleeping, and knelt down upon the ground to say a prayer previous to sallying forth.

By a singular coincidence, at the very moment that he was rising from his stooping position, and that he was concluding a fervent appeal to heaven to bless the path of the unknown stranger who had so kindly helped him in the hour of need, the Boy Brigand was witnessing another scene, to describe which we must begin another chapter.

—

CHAPTER XXXV.

THE CAPTIVE MAIDEN—SCENES OF BRIGAND LIFE—THE MUTINY.

SCARCELY had Sataniello reached the neighbourhood of his cavern than he heard the sound of voices, and he shortly afterwards saw two men advancing rapidly towards him.

They held a maiden captive between them, and it was impossible to say what their object was in dragging the girl away from the cavern.

Owing to the distance which separated him from the cavern, upon the outskirts of which the two men were seen, he could not yet distinguish the features of the girl.

However, as he approached nearer and nearer, no doubt remained upon his mind, and he soon ascertained who she really was.

Our readers may, perhaps, feel inclined to think that it was Joanitta, the Boy Brigand's sweetheart—the Boy Brigand's love; but we are happy to be in a position to deceive those who would have been tempted to come to such a conclusion.

It was the sister of the Marquis of Piatelli, and doubtless she was about to be outraged by the two followers of Sataniello, whom he soon encountered.

As soon as he appeared within sight of the Senorita, who for a few days already had been his prisoner, she beckoned him to come to her rescue —to save her from those who held her so firmly as to place her in the utter impossibility of making the slightest movement.

As quick as lightning the Boy Brigand answered her call.

The two brigands who held the girl were men belonging to Sataniello's band, whose names we have abstained from giving before; but now that they are placed before our notice, we deem it our duty to state that one went by the name of "Breeze," and the other was called "Tattoo."

The first had been so designated owing to the swiftness with which he could run over the ground; the other had been surnamed Tattoo, because, having been a seafaring man previous to joining Sataniello's band, he had various inscriptions and designs worked into the skin, which are to be frequently found on the breasts and arms of those who have made the sea their profession.

Sataniello was still dressed in the costume of an Italian marquis, and at first the maiden had been deceived.

Not being able to recognise in the individual who was advancing towards her the manly features of Sataniello, she had fancied that it was her own brother who had been successful enough to effect his escape from the cavern, where the Boy Brigand had left him to the care of Paublas.

Great was her disappointment when, instead of a friend, she discovered that the person whose aid she had implored was none other than Sataniello, who had waylaid her carriage, and who again appeared before her gaze.

"Tattoo!" the Boy Brigand began, accosting his two followers—"Breeze!—what is the meaning of all this?—and where are you taking this unfortunate woman to? Your designs, I fear, are far from being such as will meet with my approval."

"Blame us not," the brigands replied; "we are not acting in the cowardly way which appearances would lead you to think we are. We have taken this maiden away to extricate her from the brutal attempts of your Lieutenant. We felt sure that in acting as we have done no blame would be attached to us for our behaviour."

"Captain," Breeze began, "you have not a moment to lose; the whole band is in open rebellion. For the second time has the Marquis of Piatelli attempted to have recourse to flight, and when we left the cavern it was a scene of murder and bloodshed."

"What has become of the Monk?—of the Hunchback?"

"They have returned safely enough," Tattoo replied; "but Paublas has been exciting your men to mutiny; and it is plain enough that he wishes to have the command of the troop—but, Captain, we have always found you true to us, and to him we will not submit."

"These men speak the truth," the Marquis of Piatelli's sister pursued; "but for them I know not what would have been my fate. They have acted towards me in a honourable manner, which deserves the highest praise, and which I will not forget."

The maiden spoke with a genuineness which at once convinced the Boy Brigand that he had acted wrongly in fancying for one moment that Tattoo and Breeze were open to his blame; and he accordingly apologised to them for what he had said.

"Come back with me, my boys," Sataniello pursued, in a quick tone of voice; "if there is a rebellion, I must quiet it at once. May I rely upon you for assistance?"

THE BOY BRIGAND IN A PICKLE.

Tattoo and Breeze nodded their heads in the affirmative.

"Relinquish your hold of the lady," the Boy Brigand exclaimed at last; " she may have recourse to flight if she wishes to do so; but if she escapes, her brother's life will be taken in exchange for her liberty."

"Wherever you may go, I'll follow you," the maiden answered, timidly. "You have now my word that I will make no attempt to flee; hence, fear not to let me walk unmolested."

The Boy Brigand walked on.

Rapidly did he shape his course towards the cavern.

As he approached he heard a loud noise.

There was detonations of firearms, and shriekings and screams.

No sentry pacing to and fro before the entrance of the cavern was there to welcome his arrival.

Tattoo and Breeze feared to address Sataniello.

The Marchioness Piatelli's heart beat high. She dreaded to see her brother swooning in a pool of blood; for when she had been taken away from the cavern, she had heard her brother's voice defying any one who might venture to approach him.

It was under these circumstances that Sataniello appeared.

Joanitta was lying prostrate upon the ground; upon her couch close at hand slept soundly the infant which had been carried away from Don Saltara Castle.

He ascertained that they were not in any way hurt; and, accompanied by Breeze and Tattoo, he proceeded onward.

Now a sight offered itself to his gaze.

The Marquis of Piatelli had been hanged to a large iron hook which stood in one of the dungeons of the cavern.

He gnashed his teeth.

The first thing that greeted him was a corpse.

He sung out as loud as he possibly could, "Paublas!—Paublas!—Paublas!"

Not a sound answered his call.

As if by magic the noise had ceased as soon as he had entered the subterranean strait! Could he have been seen?

Doubtless this must have been the case.

The alarm, then, had been given, and everything was now silent and still.

Still followed by the two brigands and the maiden, he darted towards that part of the cavern where the whole band was wont to dwell.

There he found them all.

The left hand of Paublas was bleeding profusely.

14

Upon it there was a ghastly wound, inflicted by some sharp instrument.

"What has taken place during my absence?" Sataniello inquired, sternly.

No one ventured to give an answer.

"Are you deaf and dumb?" he ejaculated in a fierce voice; "I wish to know the truth—where is the Monk?"

The Giant went out to see whether he could find him; but he returned an instant afterwards to acquaint the Boy Brigand with the ill-success of his errand.

"Who has murdered the Marquis of Piatelli?" Sataniello again inquired.

Paublas stepped forward.

"Now, in the first instance," Sataniello said, addressing his lieutenant, "how came you to have that wound, Sir?"

"I beg to decline answering that question," Paublas replied. "You have just asked who gave orders to hang the Marquis."

"I did," the Boy Brigand replied, peremptorily; "and I want a quick answer."

"Well, I am the culprit," Paublas said.

"Who gave you leave to assume superior authority while I am away?"

"I used my own discretion."

"You will be punished for that."

"You will not have it always your own way here," Paublas now began, giving vent to a deep hatred which he entertained against Sataniello ever since he had joined his band. "Who is the man who will lay hands upon me?"

"It is not going to be a struggle between you and me, Mr. Paublas," Sataniello replied. "You have shown insubordination; and you know that a breach of our code of discipline is a thing which I never overlook."

A fiendish smile appeared upon Paublas' countenance.

His glance seemed to defy Sataniello.

"You are the man," the Boy Brigand said, "in whom I have hitherto vested my confidence. You were the first to join me; and, although there are many who would have forgotten an old friendship, I did not. Ever remembering that we began together our reckless and adventurous career, I appointed you my lieutenant.

These words were spoken by Sataniello in a cool and collected manner, and it required no very great discernment to perceive that he was coming to some determination.

Paublas attempted once or twice to stay his captain's speech; but, finding no loop open to him by which he might fairly contradict him, he remained silent.

"I would have had no occasion," the Boy Brigand pursued, "to alter my choice had you not this day given me an opportunity to do so. Paublas, you have betrayed me—you have proved false."

Paublas became white with revenge.

For many a month past he had entertained a strong dislike against his master,. and, if we must confess the truth, he also entertained for Joanitta a feeling akin to love.

When, years ago, they had played together on the Piazza, he had made her an avowal of the sentiments which had actuated him within, but she had rejected him with a profound disdain.

If our readers' memory does not fail them, they will remember that in the first chapters of this tale, when the Boy Brigand informed Joanitta of his intention of bringing Paublas with him, she had not endeavoured to conceal the contrariety which such information afforded to her mind.

Sataniello and Paublas were very different characters indeed; and, as we have already seen in the course of this story, the former was the nobler being of the two, if nobleness could be said to belong to either.

In point of looks, Sataniello was Paublas' superior—in point of education he had no rival, namely, among the beings of his own class and rank in the world.

Up to the time we see him, Sataniello had managed to carry out his plans with a success which could scarcely be credited were it not true, and the numerous treasures which he successively became possessed of had been of such a value as to satisfy him far beyond his most sanguine expectations.

Sataniello occasionally thought that Paublas was wont to contemplate Joanitta in a manner which was far from being respectful, and that he sometimes sought occasion to speak to the girl he loved when he ought to have been away with the remainder of the troop.

Nevertheless, he had said nothing, hoping inwardly that the ideas which had occurred to him were naturally prompted by that amount of jealousy which any being, however indifferent he may be, possesses when his sweetheart happens to be called into question.

He had always found Paublas apparently dutiful, and willing to carry out his orders to the letter; and, as a clever politician, he had not thought it wise to disturb the harmony of the subterranean existence which he and his followers led by bringing forward an accusation which he would not be in a position to substantiate.

Although the following saying is rather a vulgar one, we will take the liberty of quoting it here, namely, that you should not bark if you cannot bite—and upon the wisdom of that sentiment the Boy Brigand had taken good care to act.

Now, however, that the time had arrived, he was firmly bent upon ascertaining the whole truth; and no supplications, however heartrending and cringing, could have deterred Sataniello from acting in accordance with any plan which he had previously laid.

A good deal depended upon what he was about to hear. Thus, when he found that all his followers were listening to him, with the exception of the Monk and of the Hunchback, he resumed his speech.

Tattoo and Breeze stood immediately behind Sataniello, and anxiously were they awaiting the instant when he should act in such a manner as to give satisfaction to all.

The Boy Brigand was about to speak, when the huge frame of the Giant was seen crossing the threshold of the cavern where he now stood.

This was an incident which did not escape the close scrutiny of the Boy Brigand; but, as he had always through life made it a rule to deal with each case respectively one after the other, to address the Giant was the last thing of which he dreamed.

When the latter had appeared he had kept his features bent downwards, as if he feared to encounter the Boy Brigand's inquisitive and scrutinising gaze.

Sataniello was not wrong in thinking at the time that the Giant was in some manner mixed up with the mutiny which had taken place. How far he was justified in coming to such a conclusion will be shortly told as we proceed.

"Paublas," the Boy Brigand now began, "I cannot doubt that you have turned my absence to the worst account. I never condemn a man without first listening to what he has to say. If you can exculpate yourself you will find no alteration in me—if you do not, you know what you have to expect. And now, to come to the point, how did all the events which have taken place come to pass?"

Instead of boldly facing Sataniello, and standing upon his own ground, Paublas endeavoured to throw upon other shoulders the blame which was his main work. It was the Hunchback who induced the men to rebellion."

"It was the Hunchback, do you say? That is sufficient. He will die. Paublas, you are still my lieutenant, and I retract whatever I might have said."

The Boy Brigand was about to hold out his hand to Paublas, when he was prevented from so doing by our old acquaintance the Hunchback.

"He lies!—he lies, Captain!" the cripple exclaimed, with an outburst of voice which would have made any other walls besides those of the rocky cavern tremble with the echo of its piercing sound. "He is a traitor! That man has deceived us. But for his false story we would never have acted in the way in which we did. He told us that you were not coming back any more—that, gloating on the wealth which you had robbed from us, you were going to leave the country within a few hours. He induced the Giant to side with him; and he proclaimed himself the captain of the band. And he further said, 'Who will wrest the command from my hands when once I hold it?' Those were his identical words, Captain—may I never utter another syllable if they aint."

"Before such conflicting statements," Sataniello replied, "I know not how to act. Some one must be punished; there must be an example made, and heavily will the blow fall upon the head of the delinquent!"

A nearly imperceptible smile lighted up Paublas' countenance as he listened to the Cripple.

"I must have the truth. I do not question the accuracy of any of the remarks which any of you may make. I want to hear the testimony of some unbiassed individual who has not already listened to the previous conversation. Where is the Monk, I repeat?"

"The Monk!" Paublas exclaimed.

"The Monk!" the Cripple re-echoed. "He is not here; by this man's orders he has been cast into one of the cells with a pair of tight irons around his wrists. I just happened to have been with him as you came in; this accounts for my not being present here to receive you."

And the Hunchback pointed towards Paublas.

The Boy Brigand's forehead frowned deeply, and then deep wrinkles bespoke in a moment the astonishment and anger which the information he had received gave him.

So great was his rage, that for a moment he was unable to speak.

But like the fury of the storm, which is but transient, similarly also did Sataniello's discontent melt away before the curiosity which he felt at getting a clue to the mystery which surrounded the events that had occurred during his absence.

"The Monk in irons!" he exclaimed. "By whose verdict, I ask, was his freedom snatched from him?"

For the second time the Hunchback held his finger towards the direction where the Lieutenant was standing.

"Who holds the key of his cavern?" Sataniello inquired.

Not a voice answered the query.

"Have I been heard?" Sataniello exclaimed. "And what is the meaning of all this?"

"It means this, Captain, that I hold the keys, and that I will not give them up."

"You will not?"

"No," Paublas replied, sternly.

"Why?"

"The Monk has offended me."

"In what way?"

"Would not acknowledge me—"

"As Captain of the band. No, that he would not," Tattoo now put in, continuing the Lieutenant's unconcluded phrase, "and it will shortly be seen whether he was in the wrong or in the right box."

"Silence—silence!" Sataniello pursued. "Paublas, I order you to remit me at once the key of the place where the Monk is confined."

Thus speaking, he cocked his pistol, and aimed it at Paublas.

The sudden determination of the Captain soon did away with Paublas' stubbornness; reluctantly had he to comply with the request.

"Your hour has not come yet, Paublas," Sataniello said; and turning round he called the Hunchback to his side.

"Here," he ejaculated quickly, "look alive! bring the prisoner here. Everybody to-night seems to have his own tale. Let us now let the Monk speak for himself.

CHAPTER XXXVI.

WHERE THE MONK TALKS—WHERE SATANIELLO SHOWS HIS AUTHORITY, AND WHERE THE WHOLE BAND IS CALLED INTO REQUISITION TO CARRY OUT ONE OF THE CAPTAIN'S ORDERS, WHICH MEETS WITH THE APPROBATION OF EVERYONE EXCEPT PAUBLAS.

THE Hunchback was too well aware of the frame of mind in which he left Sataniello, when he had been despatched by him on his errand, to lose any time in bringing the Monk from the place of confinement where he had been cast by the unwarrantable command of the would-be captain.

Hence the cripple put his wits and his feet together, and notwithstanding the darkness which reigned, with the swiftness of a doe he opened the door of the cell where the Monk had thought of spending many a weary night, and brought him in a quicker time than we could describe it into the presence of Sataniello, whose cross-examination he contemplated, but whose wrath he had no cause to fear.

A great change had taken place in the Monk.

His features were not now the handsome ones which we knew him to possess—his expressive countenance being sadly disfigured by a ghastly wound on his left cheek, from which blood was flowing copiously.

The brightness of his eyes, however, had lost nothing of their former intelligence, and they sparkled with evident joy when he confronted Sataniello.

"How long have you been confined?" Sataniello inquired, affectionately from his follower, as soon as he was within a yard's distance from him.

"I do not know exactly," the Monk replied "if spoke according to the length and dreariness which the time seemed to me, I should say over a century; but to be accurate, I think that I had made at least two hours stay in that cold place, where it has been the Lieutenant's pleasure, unjustly, to send me."

"With regard to the justice or the injustice of your arrest," the Boy Brigand replied firmly, wishing to show his authority even towards one man whom he preferred to any other of his band. "I am the best judge. I have brought you here to listen to what you have to say for yourself—do not accuse any one—I know right from wrong; and if you have been sent to the dungeon without deserving it, the party who has been the means of it will take your place before one hour is over my head."

As he concluded his sentence, Sataniello allowed his glance to fall casually upon Paublas, whose mouth appeared to utter an oath when the meaning of the Boy Brigand's words reached his ears.

The Hunchback seemed to enjoy extremely the fun. In one corner he sat in a crouching attitude, grinning like a monkey, and anxious to ascertain what steps the Captain would take in a matter with which he did not interfere.

Every one had a kind of dislike against Paublas, and to witness him in a crest-fallen state would have afforded satisfaction to many.

"Relate to me the rebellion from beginning to end ; fear not to displease any one—you have now known me for some time to be too well cognisant of this fact, namely, that the happiness and welfare of my troop is my sole aim, and that I will punish severely any one who dares to disturb it."

"That is right enough, Captain," the Monk replied. "So help me God! Now I will tell you what I know."

There was a momentary pause, which did not, however, last long, for the Boy Brigand was impatient ; and as he did not endeavour to disguise the anxiety which he felt, the Monk soon began in the following terms :—

"Well, Captain, when we returned from Don Saltara Castle, we came here to the cavern, as you may suppose. When we were all together, the Lieutenant ordered us to attend in this very spot, and he said that he was about to make to us some communication, to which we should attentively listen. 'My friends,' he began, 'the ways of the Captain of late have been anything but calculated to forward the interests and welfare of our troop. Now he is at the Castle, where, doubtless, he is having it all as he wished, and he will not come back any more among us. He intends to forsake us, and to go to another country, where, upon the money which he has so urgently done us out of, he will luxuriate and enjoy himself, regardless of the gale which may await us. I will not stand it, my boys—I will not put up with his tyrannical, domineering spirit any more ; and I beg to inform you that I will take the command of the troop.'

"'You won't ; no, you won't,' I said, addressing Paublas ; 'as long as Sataniello, our brave and gallant Captain, is our master and chief, I will acknowledge no other—'

"You stepped forward, then, and stood by me?" the Boy Brigand inquired, interrupting the Monk's speech.

"I did, Captain ; and if the whole band had been against me I should have acted as I tell you I did. But it was not so, I am happy to say. The Hunchback kept aloof. Tattoo and Breeze endeavoured to take my part, and the Monk got severely punished for his boldness in thwarting Paublas' wishes."

"Well, well," the Boy Brigand went on, "continue your narrative."

Paublas, in the meantime, never attempted to say a word.

His false and ugly countenance bespoke the fear which he inwardly felt at the results which could not but follow the Monk's revelation.

Occasionally a mocking smile curled his lips.

The Giant, in the distance, was listening attentively.

Tattoo and Breeze, standing behind the Boy Brigand, remained motionless.

A good deal was to be enacted out of the scene which we are relating.

After awhile, during which the Monk seemed to collect his thoughts, he resumed the thread of his narrative.

"And what did the whole band do when Paublas spoke as he did?" the Boy Brigand pursued. "Was there any reluctance shown on their part to abide by the Lieutenant's orders ?"

"The step, Captain, which Paublas had taken was so unexpected, that I may fairly say they were all taken by surprise ; and they were too much overwhelmed by their astonishment to know how to act."

"That will do!" Sataniello pursued ; "go on, now."

The Monk had no occasion to be told twice to hurry his story.

"Captain," the Monk continued, "Paublas told us, when we were all around him, 'the Captain is not coming back among us !' "

"Is this statement true?" Sataniello inquired.

Thus speaking, he turned round, with a glance which betrayed his anxiety to hear the truth, and looked gradually and successively upon each respective member of the band.

"It is, Captain," the brigands replied, in an unanimous voice.

"And what have you got to say in your defence, Paublas?" Sataniello inquired, addressing his Lieutenant.

The Lieutenant's crest-fallen look was a sufficient answer.

It was easy to perceive that he felt that his doom was sealed.

"What have you got to say in your defence?" Sataniello inquired again.

This time, however, the words which he pronounced were uttered in a tone of voice which was peremptory and to the point, and which needed an instantaneous reply.

"Nothing as yet," Paublas replied.

"You have deceived me, Paublas," Sataniello pursued, with an avengeful look. "My revenge will be terrible !"

As he spoke the Boy Brigand placed his hand upon his poniard.

A sudden fear creeped on Paublas' countenance, and he became as white as a sheet.

He soon, however, recovered his usual composure, and he looked anxiously towards the Monk, who was about to speak.

"When Paublas' statement was made to us there was an universal manifestation of the troop's disapproval—all you brave followers seemed to be thunderstruck at the intelligence given. I did not for a moment believe what Paublas said ; and in my own heart I knew that you would not leave us, were you inclined to do so, without wishing us farewell."

The Boy Brigand shook his head in an approving manner.

"Will you acknowledge me as your captain, my boys," Paublas inquired ; "I will grant you everything that you require. When an expedition will contemplated I will apprise you of it, and when successfully carried out a fair division will be made. I will not take the lion's share, alike our late captain was wont to do."

The Boy Brigand's eye now became bright and fierce.

His whole frame was shaking with feelings of revenge.

Had he followed the promptings of his own mind —had he acted in accordance with the idea which he would have liked to carry out at once, he would have rushed upon Paublas and plunged his dagger to the hilt in the breast of the man against whom the charges were brought.

The sight which was offered to the other brigands was imposing in the extreme.

It showed how very tenacious of his rights Sataniello meant to be.

The whole band was now within the walls of the tavern.

The Giant, sitting in a corner, was listening to every word in deep suspense.

The Hunchback, in a crouching attitude, as we have already said, seemed to gloat over the whole scene which we are describing.

He owed a grudge to Paublas, and he was delighted to see him in a plight.

Terrible plight it was too, for the Boy Brigand's verdict would be a harsh one.

Seldom did Sataniello hold court martial against his men.

Seldom did he condemn any man to death.

Seldom did he pronounce any final sentence.

But when he did so, he was inexorable in seeing it carried out.

What punishment Paublas was to receive we will soon see.

The brigands were now awaiting Paublas' narrative.

They were anxious to hear whether he would speak the truth.

The fate of Paublas depended upon the Monk's words.

Not a sentence did the former lieutenant of the gallant band utter to screen himself from the accusation laid against him.

"Ah! ah!" the Boy Brigand exclaimed in a sinister tone of voice, "Mr. Paublas, you and I will have a word together."

Paublas looked at Sataniello.

He did not endeavour to screen himself—he knew too well that it was useless to have recourse to any apology—which the Boy Brigand would not accept.

That the guilt of Paublas was beyond doubt Sataniello had soon settled in his own mind, and he only wanted now to hear what had really taken place, so as to be able to shape his plans for the future.

He found out too late that his long absence from the cavern was productive of the sad conclusion which he so unexpectedly had been called upon to witness.

Willingly would he have wished to be able to overlook the matter.

But however anxious he was to do so, things had gone too far to be recalled.

Besides, Sataniello was about to become acquainted with a knowledge which he was anything but prepared to receive.

The Marquis of Piatelli had been hung in the first cell, whilst the Senora Joanitta was lying senseless upon the cold ground of his private abode.

Tattoo and Breeze had been seen by him hurrying on towards the country with a captive maiden.

Surely, all these events had been brought at the instance of some one.

He wished, then, to know how they came to pass.

The Monk resumed.

The promises of Paublas were alluring enough, and as soon as he spoke great many of them wavered as to what they should do.

"What if the Captain comes back?" the Giant inquired.

"'The Captain!' Paublas ejaculated, 'he will never come back here; he has made quite enough by us, and he will never return into this crib. Will you be on my side?' he continued, addressing the Giant."

"Well, what did the Giant say?" Sataniello exclaimed.

"He sided with Paublas, Captain, and he said to him, 'I am your man.'"

"Did you act as this man says?" Sataniello inquired, walking in a sharp, brisk, quick step towards the Giant.

"I am sorry I did, Captain; I am easily influenced; I knew that I was doing wrong when I helped Paublas. But it was not my fault, it was his and that of Pamela."

"What has Pamela to do with this?" Sataniello asked.

"Pamela," the Giant replied, "told me before now that you were not acting right towards us, and she advised me to turn against you, Captain, but I did not. Now, to-night, when Paublas said that you were not coming back, I sided with him, and helped him to carry out what he wished; I repent for what I did, and if you will forgive me I will never do it again."

Our readers may remember, doubtless, the incident which had occurred at Tivoli Gardens a few weeks ago, which was fully described to our readers at the time.

They will, perhaps, recollect her advice to the Giant, which she herself was far from following, for we saw her whispering a few words into the Giant's ears, which were to the effect of causing him to come to Sataniello's rescue.

Had he not done so, we cannot forget that he would have been taken in custody by Captain Wogan and Lord Charlestown, and dragged to a dungeon from which he would never escape, only to ascend the shameful steps of the scaffold.

When the name of Pamela was mentioned to him, the Boy Brigand passed no observation thereupon; but it was evident that he felt greatly annoyed at what he had heard.

"I hope you will not be hard upon me," the Giant said, as he glanced upon his captain, who stood before him in a wavering, uncertain attitude.

"I forgive you from the bottom of my heart," the Boy Brigand replied; "I know that you are easily led away. As far as I hear you have done no harm yourself—you have only been a tool into other hands; and as I understand your nature better than, perhaps, you do yourself, there is an end of the matter. You are sorry, you say, for what you did; openly do you confess the mistake you have made, and I am not one to forget that you have always acted respectfully and dutifully towards me, and now I show you that I remember it."

The Giant rose and thanked the Boy Brigand.

"When the Giant," the Monk pursued, "promised to lend his assistance to Paublas, he said in a trembling tone of voice, 'Now, my boys, I am your master.' No one objected to it, and I was the only one who stepped forward, and accordingly brought myself into trouble; for had you not returned, Captain, what would have become of me? I would have been left in the dungeon where I was cast, and died of hunger and starvation after a few days's terrible and excruciating sufferings."

"A better fate awaits you now, my friend," the Boy Brigand replied; "you have been sadly used—for the imprisoment which you suffered you will receive at my hands such compensation as will fill your heart with delight."

The Monk's features beamed with indescribable pleasure.

The words which he had heard truly, indeed, satisfied him.

The Monk had always liked the Boy Brigand.

The word "like" is, perhaps, too weak to use.

He loved him, we may safely say, like men can love each other.

He had, we remember, taken rather a prominent part in the expedition which Sataniello had taken to Don Saltara Castle, and he had occasion to judge his master's true character since he came into close contact with him; and he could not but acknowledge that, although Sataniello was rather of an extraordinary turn of mind, still at times, for all that, he knew that he was one who could be a friend in the hour of need: and what is more, that Sataniello would do anything he could—go through fire and water to serve any one for whom he had a liking.

Thus the Monk liked and loved Sataniello.

"You have now been talking for some time," the Boy Brigand continued, addressing the Monk, "and you have not told me anything yet. I want to know," he continued, "how the Marquis of Piatelli happened to be hung? I want to know how my dearest Joanitta happened to have been found by me senseless in my abode? how you came to be confined? and how all these terrible things came to pass?"

"Ain't I trying to do so, Captain?"

"You are, certainly."

"What do you find fault with me then, Sir?"

"I am not finding fault with you, my good friend," Sataniello replied, in an affectionate voice; "I wish you to come to the point, and at the rate at which you are going, we shall be here all night and all day. My revenge will be great—I long to punish the culprit. My head reels—my heart beats—my frame shakes—my imagination wanders, and I should—if I could be justified in doing so now—give to those who deserve it the punishment which they so richly deserve!"

Sataniello was like a tiger—anxious for blood, craving for the life of his lieutenant; and he longed for a struggle—a deadly struggle—when he could try his strength with that of Paublas.

Master him if he could—give in to him if he was beaten.

"While Paublas," the Monk resumed, "was telling us all that which I have previously related to you, Captain, we heard screams and a loud sound of voices issuing from the cavern where the Marquis of Piatelli was confined. Headed by Paublas, we rushed to the spot where the nobleman was, and we saw that he had freed himself from the irons which held him prisoner, and that he was determined to fight for his freedom.

"'I will give a thousand pounds,' the Marquis of Piatelli said, 'if I am allowed to leave this place.'

"'You are my prisoner,' Paublas replied, 'and I will keep you here.'

"The Marquis had in his hand a poiniard. Where he could have got the missile I know not.

"Suffice it to say that he was armed.

"That he was bent upon fighting hard was palpable to the whole band.

"Now that he is gone to another world," the Monk pursued, "I regret deeply that we acted towards him as we did I regret, Captain, that Paublas' orders should have been carried out so cruelly and promptly and mercilessly as they were. He was a brave and courageous man, and he died like a true heart."

"How was it that he happened to be hung?" Sataniello pursued.

"I am coming to it, Captain, in a minute.

"Paublas," the Monk pursued, "approached close to the Marquis of Piatelli, and asked him to surrender.

"'I will not give way to you,' the nobleman replied, his eye kindling fire—his whole frame shaking with ire.

"He knew that it was a case of life or death with him.

"Either he would obtain his freedom, or his doom was sealed.

"Our lieutenant, Paublas, placed his hand upon the Marquis.

"'Do not handle me,' he replied, 'do not touch me.'

"The whole of the band was present.

"There was, however, something so manly and so bold in the Marquis's manner, that many of us remained awe-struck by his determination.

"That he was bent upon resistance was plain to all of us.

"No one dared to approach him.

"Now that we felt confident that it would have been impossible for the Marquis to escape had he possessed five times the strength and determination which he had, still there is something so manly about a man who is ready to die, that the sublimity of his conduct was not thrown away upon us.

"The Marquis remained silent before us.

"Awaiting his doom, he spoke not a word.

"'Will you allow yourself to be pinioned?' Paublas inquired.

"'I will never surrender,' the Marquis replied.

"'I can make you go through the most abject sufferings, if I like,' Paublas pursued; 'therefore, if you value your life, be calm, and permit me to place the irons upon your hands. I am now the captain of this troop, and my orders are law.'

"At the moment when Paublas uttered these words," the Monk proceeded, "I must not forget to mention this, Captain, that there was a murmur of disapproval all round the cavern.

"He had taken us by storm; and although none ventured to doubt Paublas' statement, they seemed to think that you would come back among us again and set everything to rights. However, in the uncertainty in which we all were, we did not contradict him.

"The Giant was next called in.

"He came in without any weapon whatever.

"He was the one upon whom Paublas had fixed upon to do his dirty work.

"You have already spoken to the Giant, Captain," the Monk pursued, "and with that leniency which you possess, you have been merciful enough to grant him his pardon; therefore it is no use for me to expatiate upon his conduct.

"Of all of us he was the first one who submitted to Paublas, and who tried to induce us to acknowledge him as our captain. I believe, within my own mind, that he promised to the Giant to make him his lieutenant. There is always something at the bottom of every occurrence of a similar kind, and I am sure that he had some interest in seeing Paublas become our chief and master.

"'Here, my boys,' Paublas said, 'we are likely to have some tight work with this man; sieze hold of him.'

"The order was carried out instantaneously.

"The Giant advanced towards the Marquis.

"While he was attracting his attention in front, Paublas went at the back of the nobleman, and when he was about to defend himself, he found himself rudely seized by the hind shoulders.

"He tried to struggle hard before he should give up.

"But it was of no avail.

"A struggle ensued—it was a terrible struggle; four men were against one man, and they soon became masters of him. During the conflict which ensued, one of the band received a severe blow on the head, and when the Marquis of Piatelli was falling senseless upon the ground, screams were now heard close at hand, and the Marquis's sister rushed into the cavern. She came just in time to see her brother pierced by Paublas' poniard.

"He was, however, not mortally wounded.

"'Oh, my brother!—oh, my brother!' the maid exclaimed; 'oh, my dear brother!' and she seized hold of his forehead as she stooped down to imprint upon it a sister's kiss.

"The sight which we saw was too heart-rending to be described.

"'Remove that girl away!' Paublas pursued, with a fiendish smile. 'Remove her away from this place, and let the Marquis of Piatelli be hung in the dark vault close at hand.'

"'We are not executioners,' Tattoo and Breeze replied; 'we are not going to undertake a hangman's duty. We will not do as we are bid.'

"I stepped forward—what I had seen was too much for me, and I told my mind to Paublas, and I truthfully expressed to him the disgust which I felt for his conduct.

"I was then taken away by the Giant, and cast into the cell from which you gave orders to have me withdrawn; and as I was being led to it by the Giant, against whom I uselessly endeavoured to struggle, I saw Tattoo and Breeze hurrying towards the country with the Marchioness of Piatelli. The girl's mind was nearly distracted, and they were taking her away to the fields, where the change of scene might do her some good. More, Captain, I know not; and how the Marquis came to his death is a mystery which I cannot solve, as I was no longer a witness to what subsequently took place."

"That will do," Sataniello replied; "I want to hear no more. I will now cross-examine Paublas. I know that he's guilty, but I must satisfy my own mind."

Paublas kept on looking at the Captain as if he wished to say a word or two previous to being questioned.

However, he never opened his lips.

"In the meantime, my friends," the Boy Brigand pursued, "until my doubts are set at nought, pinion this man."

As he spoke, the Boy Brigand pointed to Paublas. The Lieutenant retrograded three steps backwards.

"Sataniello wishes to speak. Our brave and gallant chief is about to do justice. Silence! silence!"

These words were uttered by Tattoo and Breeze.

The Hunchback was getting more and more delighted.

The Monk's countenance beamed with extreme pleasure.

How sweet revenge is to be sure.

"Pinion this man," the Boy Brigand went on, "and let him at once be placed in a position not to do any harm."

This order had no sooner been given, than Paublas bounded towards the Captain.

He lifted his poniard, and with a feverish, cruel hand, he would have inflicted a blow upon Sataniello, had not the Monk perceived just in time the designs which Paublas was about to carry out.

He struggled hard, but he was soon cowed.

He attempted to get away, but he did not succeed.

He screamed and he howled, and besought mercy.

In one instant he was rendered totally powerless.

The irons were soon placed upon his wrists, and he stood before Sataniello like a prisoner in the dock. There was not one man who felt for him— not one soul who would have wished him to be released from the critical position in which he had placed himself.

CHAPTER XXXVII.

WHERE A COURT-MARTIAL IS HELD, WHERE PAUBLAS IS SENTENCED TO A SLOW DEATH.

WHEN the Boy Brigand had satisfied his mind that Paublas before him was secured, and unable to be any further cause of annoyance to him, he began thus:—

"Paublas, you are now my prisoner."

"I know that, and I want no idle remarks."

"You stand arraigned before me on two grave charges—that of having caused the death of the Marquis of Piatelli, and that of having made the Monk suffer a false imprisonment."

Paublas shook his head sullenly.

There was another charge which the Boy Brigand would have brought against Paublas had he been of a less political and less deep turn of mind than that which we know him to be.

How came Joanitta to be found in a senseless state?

Had she been ill-used and ill-treated by Paublas?

At the very time that Sataniello was at the castle of the Duke of Don Saltara, did the same cruel, base, and vile object which he had endeavoured to carry out upon the Duke's daughter, been enacted in the brigand's cavern with more success?

Had his pure sweetheart been allowed to fall within Paublas' embrace?

This was a conclusion which we looked upon as extremely probable, although we will not say anything about it in the present instance.

By-and-bye, and as the story proceeds, the truth will be told.

We therefore beg of our readers not to wish us to unravel in one instant that which they, doubtless, would like to know at once, but to follow quietly and steadily the march and the events which are about to occur.

"Do you plead guilty, Paublas?"

"To one charge I do, not to the other."

"What charge do you plead guilty to?"

"To having imprisoned the Monk."

"Oh, you will admit that?"

"I will."

"And you do not acknowledge that I am justified in bringing the other accusation against you?"

"I do not."

"Why?"

"Because I acted in self-defence."

"What do you mean?"

"What I say!"

"Very well, all in due course will I attend to you."

"I fear you not, Captain!"

"Do you say that you are innocent?"

"Of one charge I am."

"Not of the other?"

"No."

"My friends," Sataniello pursued, "I wish your attention. I am about to hold a court-martial upon Paublas, our former Lieutenant. I do not wish to act peremptorily. The sentence which I am about to pass must be unanimously carried out."

"Hear, hear!" several voices replied.

"The Monk—come here," Sataniello said.

"I am awaiting your commands, Captain."

"Take a sheet of note-paper, pen and ink, and write down everything which will take place here— it will be placed among the records of the band's proceedings."

It really must seem astonishing to our readers that Sataniello should be so particular in going through all the routine of a court-martial, especially when his orders would have been immediately carried out did he wish to do so on his own account.

But he wished to make his followers concur in what he should say.

The Monk shook his head in the affirmative when his Captain spoke.

Gliding with the silent swiftness of a shadow along the cavern, he vanished in an instant.

In a very short time he returned into the cavern.

With his right hand he held pen and ink, and with his left he held also paper.

Thus provided with the necessary materials for writing, he went and took a seat in a corner of the cavern.

He looked like the clerk, who, at an English police-court, takes down the names of the accused —or the policeman's statement, more properly speaking — the charges pronounced against the culprit.

Standing in an attentive attitude were all the brigands.

When Sataniello had satisfied his mind that everything was right, he thus began :—

"My friends, are you all ready, and listening?"

"We are," was the unanimous reply.

"At what o'clock did you return here?" Sataniello began.

"It was ten o'clock exactly when we entered the cavern."

"What did you then?"

"We had a bit of supper."

"What occurred afterwards?"

"Why, we all had a pipe."

"I do not wish," Sataniello replied sternly, "to hear all your nonsense. I am fully aware that you took care of No. 1, Paublas, and let alone anyone else. I am fully aware that you will attend to yourself."

"Do you blame me, Captain?"

"Certainly not."

There was a smile which curled the lips of the Captain, and which soon appeared upon the countenances of all his followers.

Notwithstanding the earnestness of the scene, still it was rather astonishing that he could not stay

a certain amount of good humour on hearing such an answer as the one which Paublas had given him.

"Well, after you had your supper and a pipe, what did you do then?"

"I said to the troop that you were not coming back."

"What right had you to do so?"

"It was only my idea."

"Upon what ground did you found it?"

"Because I thought you would not return among ourselves."

"What induced you to come to such a conclusion?"

"Having been away so long, I thought you would remain a little longer."

"You were mistaken, however."

"You need not tell me that, I see it as well as you."

"When you proclaimed yourself captain, was there any dissenting voice?"

"I beg to decline answering that question."

"You do. I will repeat it again, "was there a dissenting voice?"

"You have already had my reply."

"My friends," Sataniello pursued, turning round to the troop, "will you answer the query which I have just made?"

"Why, we never said yes or no. There was a moment of grumbling when we heard that you were not coming back," Tattoo said ; "but of course, as Paublas had been our lieutenant, we thought that it was only fair that he should assume the command."

"If he had behaved like he ought to have done, nobody should have objected to it. But you must remember that he had no right to take the command so long as I was alive.

"What was the time when you proclaimed yourself captain?" Sataniello inquired.

"Why, I should say it was eleven o'clock."

"What followed?"

"We heard sounds of voices issuing from the Marquis of Piatelli's place of confinement."

"You went to see what was the cause of it?"

"Yes, we found that he had freed himself from his irons, and that he was beating the door with his foot, and in the greatest state of excitement."

"What did you do then?"

"We got a light."

"You went inside?"

"I did."

"Did the Marquis try to escape?"

"Has not the Monk told you so already?"

"He has."

"Why do you want to know the same thing over again?"

"To see whether his story corresponds with your answers."

"You did your best to hold him your prisoner?"

"I did."

"This is so far right. Was there a struggle?"

"There was."

"What was the result of it?"

"We mastered the Marquis."

"You succeeded in placing him in irons again?"

"Yes."

"And why did you order him to be hung?"

"To prevent a recurrence of what had taken place."

"You have done what I should have done myself in the first place, namely, by putting the Marquis in a safe place, but why did you hang him?"

"I have already told you."

"This ends the great charge—now I hold you guilty of unwarrantable murder."

"What else have you got to say? What excuse

PEDRO'S BROTHER AT THE FOOT OF THE CROSS.

have you got to bring forward to palliate your conduct?"

The Lieutenant made no reply.

"And now about the Monk?" the Boy Brigand pursued. "Why did you send him to prison?"

"Because he refused to acknowledge my authority."

"Was he right or wrong in so doing?"

"The result has shown me that I made a mistake."

"Are you sorry for it?"

"No."

"Would you act again as you did?"

"If I knew that you would come back I would not—otherwise I most decidedly should."

"I find you then guilty of the charge of false imprisonment—you have assumed the justice in your hands, after been guilty of two things, which I cannot forget. What have you got to say why sentence of death should not be passed upon you?"

"Nothing."

"Is the sentence a right one, my friends?"

"Yes," the band replied.

"I condemn you to be taken and cast into the dungeon from whence the Monk came, and to be kept there until you die of starvation."

A heavy sigh escaped Paublas's lips.

"And now for action and your next lieutenant."

"Who is the senior member of the troop after Paublas?"

"I am," the Monk quickly replied.

"Do you object to the Monk being your lieutenant my friends?" the Boy Brigand pursued in a loud tone of voice.

"No, we do not."

"Do you all like the Monk?"

"We do."

"Are you satisfied with my choice?"

"We are."

"The court martial is now over—away with Paublas—away with him to the dungeon," the Boy Brigand pursued in a stern tone of voice."

15

"Away with him," repeated all Sataniello's followers.

And they all rose like one, and surrounded Paublas.

Paublas attempted to struggle.

With the sudden strength which his offended pride and indignation lent him, he rid himself of the iron which in the hurry of the moment had been carelessly fastened to his hands.

Then free he burst from their united hold.

The brigands followed him.

Paublas had just reached the door of the cavern.

But he was doomed to undergo his sentence.

Enraged at his resistance the brigands became merciless.

Sataniello remained looking on.

The time had now come.

The Giant's assistance was called, and ere five minutes had elapsed Paublas was cast into the dungeon; and while he pondered on his fate, he heard rejoicing around him.

Thus ended the mutiny.

Thus ended Paublas's career, for the present, as a Brigand.

Thus was the Monk elected to the rank of lieutenant, and the brigands resumed the existence which they had been leading—inwardly acknowledging the justice of the Captain's final verdict.

Meanwhile Sataniello had returned to his cavern.

Joanitta soon recovered her consciousness.

The first thing which Sataniello asked her was how she came to be found in that state in which she was.

Her answer gave balm and relief to Sataniello's heart.

Paublas had, it is true, endeavoured to make her listen to his entreaties, and he would have carried out his purpose had not the Marquis of Piatella's struggles and endeavours to obtain his freedom attracted his attention, and avert from her the blow which he would have inflicted upon her womanly honour, had not that accidental incident to which we have alluded occurred and which we have described.

CHAPTER XXXVIII.

WHICH TELLS OF PAUBLAS' IMPRISONMENT — AND WHICH BRINGS THE BOY BRIGAND INTO A VERY CRITICAL POSITION.

Two dreary long days had occurred since the events which we have related in the previous chapter.

The monotony of the brigand's life had not been disturbed by any unforeseen incident worth describing.

The hours which Paublas spent in his confinement seemed to be so many days to him.

Bitterly did he weep in his dungeon.

He had been so severely handled by the brigands that he was thrown in a state of unconsciousness into the cell.

When he recovered he found himself stretched on the ground of a gloomy vault.

At first he thought he must be dreaming.

He endeavoured to persuade himself that he was only under the influence of some terrible nightmare.

But when he rose he found that also his was real captivity.

He walked in his cell, and exhausted by his anxiety of mind, he went and laid down upon a bench which stood in one corner.

The most profound darkness reigned.

As he was lying upon his back, he found something which hurt his toe.

He seized hold of it, and he discovered that it was a knife.

It was so dark that he could not see—he could only feel.

It seemed to him to be a large knife with rather a sharp blade.

Feelings of hope mingled with joy entered his imagination.

He reflected deeply.

Starting to his feet he endeavoured to explore the cell.

A heavy chain which bound his leg, and which at least was two yards in length, prevented him from moving a certain distance.

To escape, alas! he thought was impossible.

He was doomed to die of starvation.

He placed his hands towards heaven, and prayed fervently.

The brigand's mind reverted to the Power above.

No help came to him.

He had always forgotten Providence; and now that he was forlorn and in a prison he made an appeal to it.

He was not relieved by the prayer which he made.

It is only them who constantly trust unto God who do not forget Him in the hour of their opulence and their happiness, that will find a friend in Him in adversity.

Paublas sank upon the ground again in despair.

He remembered the cause of his imprisonment.

That he richly deserved he could not but acknowledge.

He further knew that it would be useless to cry for help.

He was too well acquainted with Sataniello's character not to be convinced of the uselessness of seeking mercy at his hands.

The pangs of hunger began to make themselves felt.

His heart filled with anguish—his mind with sorrow.

He did not, however, repent of his conduct.

It was a bold game that which he had played.

Had Sataniello remained away a day more instead of a few hours he would have been the troop's captain.

Again Paublas sprung to his feet, and he strove with all his force to burst his bondage.

But the effort was fruitless.

And by lacerating his hands and straining his limbs, he only added bodily torture to his mental sufferings.

Exhausted, at length, he sank once more upon the stone-bench.

He slept for two or three hours.

Suddenly he awoke.

He thought he saw a ghost before him.

He fancied he felt the nose of some animal in a nook of the cavern.

He placed his hand to his features.

The smell which stuck to his fingers induced him to think that the cell was filled with rats.

Doubtless, in his sleep, he should be eaten alive.

Frightful position for one to be placed in.

Now he was beginning to become habituated to the gloom which reigned around him.

He remembered stories which had been related

to him by some of the brigands, and which told of unfortunate individuals being starved to death.

As the latter idea crossed his mind, he stretched out his hand to ascertain whether any provisions had been left him.

But he could find none.

There was a pewter jug in one corner.

Eagerly did he seize it.

He brought it to his lips.

But he soon threw it away to one corner, for it was absolutely empty.

The blood froze in his veins, and he thought of death—the terrible, bitter, sad death which awaited him.

He tried to sleep again.

He could not do so.

With his knife he digged the earth.

It was a long, dreary task.

He, however, kept on at his work.

Perhaps he might effect his escape.

The instrument was a sharp one.

He remained for hours digging away and away.

Occasionally he would hear sounds of footsteps.

It was some of the brigands walking along the cavern.

Then he would stop and listen attentively.

He would pause and stay his laborious task.

He had been digging the earth for at least four hours.

The time had flew quicker than before.

He was busily occupied, and the hours did not hang so heavily upon his imagination as they previously had; at least he found that there was a ray of light dawning upon him.

He was very faint, it is true.

Still there was a light.

In noways discouraged, he kept at the task, as the hole which he made continued to grow bigger and bigger.

Brighter and brighter become the light.

He had now made an aperture large enough for his body.

He could escape now was it not for the chain.

His hands were tied together—yet he did not despair.

He tried to free the chain from his legs.

Would success attend his endeavours?

Would he be free once more?

Would he ever see the light of day again?

The freshness of the atmosphere could have inclined him to think that the winds was passing through the aperture.

He tried over and over again to undo the chain.

He screwed it and screwed it around his limbs, tighter and tighter, and instead of freeing himself he made his captivity still more certain.

He prayed once more.

He made a last appeal to heaven.

Was he to succeed in escaping, he would mend his ways.

Again he attempted to break the chain which held him captive; after a good deal of repeated endeavours he found that his hand rested upon a screw.

To undo it was useless.

Now his knife made its way into the earth once more.

A large stone gave way.

He lifted it up.

Around it his chain was fastened to a hook.

He was now free!

But he should carry the stone with him.

It was not a very large one, and he had no difficulty in pushing it before him.

He laid upon his breast.

In a crouching attitude he groped his way along.

He now reached the end of the aperture.

He found himself upon a small plot of grass.

Above his head he saw a wall.

It was not above five feet in height.

He climbed up to the top of it.

He looked around him.

Close by his side he heard Sataniello's voice.

He had now reached the outside of the place where Sataniello had fixed his abode.

He heard the Boy Brigand mentioning the name of Paublas.

In breathless suspense he placed his ears against a small hole which stood in it.

The Boy Brigand was saying that he would go and see that morning whether Paublas was yet alive.

If Sataniello was to do so now what would become of him.

The knowledge which he became possessed of gave him renewed strength.

From the top of the wall he could see the country.

There was a kind of sinuous path which led into the fields.

Steadily and slowly he walked along it.

He soon found himself in the high road.

Dragging his chain behind him, holding his stone in his hand, he proceeded onwards.

For at least five hours he walked on.

He was now exhausted, and he felt that ere long he would succumb to the excruciating pain of hunger.

He saw a house in the distance.

He had at length come within a village.

There was a small cottage standing by the roadside, he walked towards it, and knocked gently at the door.

CHAPTER XXXIX.

WHERE PAUBLAS TELLS A GOOD MANY LIES— WHERE HE MEETS WITH A KIND-HEARTED ITALIAN—WHO GETS HIM INTO TROUBLE WITHOUT KNOWING IT.

A WOMAN answered Paublas' repeated calls.

"What do you want, my friend?" she asked.

"I am a poor wayfarer," Paublas replied, "who had fallen into the hands of Sataniello's troops; they robbed me of all the money which I had, and threw me into a dungeon, thus to let me die of hunger."

The woman looked at Paublas.

An inward fear seized hold of her frame.

She could not believe Paublas' statement.

His features were so repulsive that she became quite frightened.

The person to whom Paublas was speaking was a pretty country Italian woman, and she seemed to be good-natured.

"What do you say, my friend?" she asked.

"I have been made a prisoner by Sataniello."

"What! the Boy Brigand, the Dark King of the Mountains?"

"Yes."

"I thought," the woman pursued, "that he never hunted poor people?"

"So did I," Paublas replied.

There was a tone of sorrow in Paublas' way of

speaking which went to the heart of the Italian woman.

"You see," said Paublas, "that I am scarcely able to move ;" and he pointed to the chain which was fastened around his limbs.

"How did you manage to escape, then?" the woman asked.

Paublas related what we have already described to our readers.

"Oh!" said she, "you ought to be very grateful to Providence !"

"And so I am," Paublas replied, with a pitiful accent, which would have deceived a much more suspicious being than this woman; "and the first thing I did, when I found myself free, was to thank heaven."

"He is a good man, after all," the woman thought inwardly; "one must not, and should not, judge by appearances; still, for all that, there is something about that man's look which I didn't like at first. But we must not give away to foolish ideas like these, and I will help him if I can."

"Take a seat, my friend," the woman said ; "my husband will be in shortly, and you may speak to him then."

Paublas did as he was asked, and fell upon a chair.

He was literally tired, and to rest was a great relief to him.

"I suppose you are hungry, ain't you?" the woman pursued.

"I have not had a morsel of food for the last two days, and you must fancy how I feel after all that."

"What would you like?"

"Oh, anything you wish to give me."

The woman went to a cupboard and opened it.

Out of it she drew a brown household loaf of bread.

Paublas' eyes glistened when he perceived his hostess placing what is truly denominated "the staff of life" on a plate before him.

"Will you have a nice piece of bacon?" said the woman.

"Thank you," Paublas said, "how shall I ac-knowledge so much kindness ?"

"Do not mention it," the woman pursued, "you are welcome to it, as it is. Will you have a cup of milk ? That is all I have got in the house."

Paublas shook his head in the affirmative, and proceeded to dispatch the bread which had been given to him.

He began to eat like a hungry man only can.

Without exaggeration, he devoured the whole of the loaf.

Subsequently he drank the milk which had been offered to him.

While he was so doing, a new personage appeared.

He was a tall, stalwart, handsome, strongly-built countryman.

He seemed rather astonished to find a stranger in his house.

He was about to question him, when his wife whispered a few words in his ear.

"Is that true, mate, that you have been two days without food?"

Paublas replied that it was really the case, but that he would not have minded that had he not endured an imprisonment for a like period without any just cause.

"What are you going to do now?" the country-man inquired, as soon as he had ascertained that the stranger's appetite was in a fair way of being satisfied.

"I would like to get rid of my chain."

"What chain?" asked the countryman, who had not yet perceived the impediment which Paublas had about him.

Paublas rose up and showed the countryman how he was tied, and lifting the heavy stone which was fastened to the chain, he begged of him to take it away from his crippled limbs.

"I will soon set that to-rights; come along with me."

Paublas followed the countryman.

At the back of the cottage there was a large yard, such as is to be met at farmers' houses in the country.

He walked across it, and entered a small forge.

Therein was all the necessary materials to cut the chain.

It was not long ere Paublas found himself free again.

"Thank you ! oh, thank you !" Paublas pursued, "thank you !"

Although the same antipathy which the woman had felt for Paublas was in a great measure felt by the countryman, there was in Paublas' way of talk-ing such a seeming appearance of truth, that he allowed not his dislike to prevail.

"Would you know the Boy Brigand's place. I am told it is situated somewhere in the mountain."

"It is."

"Is it far from here ?"

"About five miles."

"Would you know it again

"I think so."

"Do you only think so

"No, I am sure of it."

"Why ?"

"I will tell you."

"I think it is your duty to apprise the Papal dragoons as to what has taken place."

"I intend to do so."

"When ?"

"As soon as I can.'

"Will you be able to do so to-day ?" the coun-tryman asked.

"What is about the time ?'

"Ten o'clock in the morning."

"We have plenty of time before us."

"Come on then."

"Where ?"

"To the barracks."

"Is it far from here ?'

"No, not very."

"How many brigands are there ?"

"Ten altogether."

"Were they at home when you left them ?"

"Yes."

"Do you think they have any idea you have escaped ?"

"I should say not."

"Are they likely to go and pay a visit to the cavern where you were ?"

"They consider that I am safe, and they will not trouble their minds about it."

"Are you sure ?"

"As far as I know."

"What kind of man is this Captain Sataniello. as they call him ?"

"A bloodthirsty villain."

"Is that really the case ?"

"As true as I am standing here.'

"Did they take all your money ?"

"Robbed me of every penny I possessed.

"Was it much ?"

"About twenty pounds."

"What is your calling?"

This was a question which Paublas was far from expecting, and in the first onslaught he was rather taken aback.

"I am a commercial traveller," he replied, after awhile.

The countryman looked at the speaker.

He did not appear at all like a commercial traveller.

"And what were you doing in these parts ?"

"Travelling from Viterbo to Naples."

"Were you on foot ?"

"No, on horseback."

"What became of the horse"

"The brigands stuck to it."

"You do not mean to say so."

"I do."

"Have they got any cattle at all"

"Yes, the Captain, as they call him, always keeps a charger."

"What for ?"

"So as to be expeditious."

"Do they sally forth often ?"

"Frequently."

"Would you know Sataniello again ?,

"That I should."

"What height is he ?"

"About five feet eight."

"Is he good-looking ?"

"Some people would call him handsome.

"Did you see him ?"

"Yes."

"What colour is his hair ,

"Black."

"Is he cruel ?"

"My treatment could only come from a cruel man."

"I suppose you would like to see him taken as a prisoner ?"

"Nothing would afford me greater pleasure."

"Do you think he would be condemned to death ?"

"If all his crimes are brought to light he would.'

"Are all his followers as bad as the captain ?"

"Six of one and half-a-dozen of the other."

"Really !"

"Yes."

"There is ransom offered for his apprehension ?"

"I was not aware.   How much is it ?"

"Over two thousand pounds."

"Will the man that gives him up receive it ?"

"If he is not one of his accomplices."

"If it be the latter ?"

"He obtains a free pardon."

"Are you sure ?"

"Positive."

"How did you get all these particulars ,

"It is placarded all over the country.   The Government would give anything to get hold of him."

"But do you believe they will seize hold of him ?"

"They must."

"He is a slippery customer ?"

"Wonderfully so."

As the countrymen spoke, his wife gazed silently upon Paublas; and had she only a shadow of suspicion, she could not but have noticed the sudden whiteness which overspread her guest's countenance when the word accomplice was mentioned.

"Will you come with me now ?" the countryman inquired.

"That I will."

"Do you think you have sufficient strength about you to face the exertion ?"

"I could not walk, I know."

So speaking, Paublas rose from his seat ; but exhausted by what he had undergone, he fell heavily upon his chair.

"We will drive down to the barracks ?"

"That will suit me better."

"I have a little grey mare which will clear the distance in no time."

"All right ! I am ready then."

"Wait a bit until I go and place it in the harness."

"Would you like me to help you ?"

"No, remain here, I will be back in a minute."

To carry out what he said, the countryman took his departure.

He was not long away.

The rattle of a vehicle warned Paublas of the approach of his host.

It was a gig of a very tasty description.

The countryman helped Paublas upon the seat, and in an instant he was by his side.

He took up the reins in his hand, and drove away.

As they rattled along they came to a wayside inn.

"Will you stop and have a drink here ?" the countryman asked.

We need not give here Paublas' reply.

Although he was a brigand, he was like most of us; so, without saying a word, he allowed the countryman to go into the tavern, and he soon returned with a tumbler in his hand.

"Polish that off, it will do you good."

Paublas did not require to be told twice.

"Have another ?"

"No, thank you."

The two individuals soon reached the barracks.

It was a small white house, which would remind any person who may have been in Ireland, as devoted to the use of the constabulary force.

There were not above seven dragoons located within it.

As the countryman entered, he was stopped by a stalwart-looking soldier.

"What's up now ?" he said, puffing a long clay pipe.

"I wish to see the sergeant."

"He is not here at present."

"Where is he ?"

"Gone to Don Saltara Castle.

"Will he be absent long ?"

"I should say not, although his business is rather a peculiar and an important one.   He was sent for by the old Duke.   It appears that his house has been ransacked by Sataniello, the Dark King of the Mountains."

Here the dragoon entered into a long narrative of all the incidents which we have previously related.

"We think," the soldier continued, "that we shall be placed in possession of such information as will enable us to become masters of a man who has been the dread and terror of these mountains for the last eighteen months."

"This is rather odd that your sergeant should be away on a business very similar to the one which brings me hither."

"What do you mean ?" the soldier said, pricking up his ears with the greatest attention.

"I have come here respecting Sataniello."

"You have—what is it ?"

"I have brought a chap with me that came from the brigand's den."

"Is he outside ?"

"Yes."

"What about him ?"

"He has been robbed by Sataniello, and cast into a dungeon, from which he managed, however, to escape. The poor fellow was was very nigh starved to death when he knocked at the door of my house, and I took him in—at least I did not, for I was in the fields when he came—but my wife did."

The soldier went to the window and gazed through it.

"Ugly-looking customer that !" he said ; "hasn't he got a frightful countenance !"

"I did not like his appearance much."

"I can't say that I do either."

"Do you think he is all right ?"

"How—all right ?"

"He may, perhaps, be one of the brigands, and it may be a snare laid by them to get us into a bad scrape ; they have done so before—they are up to everything !"

"By the Holy Virgin !" the countryman whispered, "I never thought of that !"

"And what do you think about it now ?"

"There may be some truth in it."

"I should not be at all astonished."

"Neither should I either."

"But what could be their motives ?"

"How are we to tell ?"

"What is to be done ?"

"Wait until the sergeant comes back.'

"He may be away all day ?"

"No, he will not."

"How do you know ?"

"Because he must be back for dinner."

"That is a settler."

"Would you advise me," the countryman pursued, "to tell my companion to come down ?"

"I would not."

"What then ?"

"Leave him where he is."

"But if he is one of the brigands he may hook it ?"

"He may, it is true. If he has gone so far, he will not retreat."

"Do you know, friend, that I think there is a good deal in what you say ?"

"We will soon see."

"And what occurred at Don Saltara Castle ?"

"Why, Sataniello's troop went and paid a visit there, and it appears that the Boy Brigand went there in the guise of a marquis."

"In the guise of a marquis ?"

"Yes ; the better to carry out the well-concerted plans of plunder arranged by the brigands."

The astonishment which was now depicted upon the countryman's features was so deep and so intense, that the soldier began to relate as much as he knew, not forgetting to colour the matter in his own plain, exaggerating style, so as to render the expedition to the Castle a hundred times more bold and desperate than it really was.

When he had concluded, the countryman breathed like a man who has an immense weight taken off his shoulders.

"And they carried away the whole of the Duke's money ?" he ejaculated.

"Every farthing of it, so he says."

"What have they done with it ?"

"Doubtless it is now in the cavern."

"Is he broken down by it ?"

"I rather think he is."

This concluded the conversation which took place between the countryman and the soldier."

While the former was pondering on what he had heard, and the latter indulging in a little nap, an incident, occurred which it would be as well to relate in our next chapter.

CHAPTER XL.

WHICH TELLS OF PAUBLAS' DOINGS—WHICH BRINGS CAPTAIN WOGAN FACE TO FACE WITH ONE OF THOSE AGAINST WHOSE CAPTAIN HE KNOWS A GOOD DEAL MORE THAN PAUBLAS ANTICIPATED, AND LEADS TO THE BOY BRIGAND'S CAPTURE BEING CONTEMPLATED.

PAUBLAS was sitting upon the gig outside the barracks, and looking towards the high road, when his attention was suddenly arrested by the appearance of two men who were seen advancing towards the direction where his worthy self happened to be.

A feeling of fear creeped over his frame when the features, becoming plainer, enabled him to see two horses, respectively ridden by a gentleman and by a soldier of the Papal dragoons.

It was Captain Wogan and the sergeant whose presence was so anxiously looked forward to by the countryman.

Paublas felt his heart beating high when he saw the soldier approaching him.

The latter never said a word to him.

He looked at him with a sly, steady look.

In one instant the dragoon was off his saddle.

"Halloa, here !" he exclaimed, "turn out !"

No sooner had he spoken than the whole detachment of soldiers appeared upon the threshold of the door of the house to which we have alluded.

They were ten in number altogether.

With their carbines on their shoulders, they stood like so many statues.

"Here, No. 1," said the sergeant, "take hold of my horse's bridle and that of the gentleman, and lead them into the stable. Give them both a feed of oats, and look after all the other mounts ; we may require, ere long, the whole of our cattle."

While the sergeant had been talking, Captain Wogan had alighted, and was upon the ground.

He stretched out his limbs like men generally do after a few miles' ride.

The gig with Paublas was still outside.

He had to range himself on the distant side of the road.

"Look after this covey, in case he takes it into his head to go away," the sergeant whispered into the ear of the senior of his detachment ; " he is rather a suspicious character, to my mind."

While he walked inside, followed by Captain Wogan, the Sergeant was speaking in the following strain.

"Captain, what do you think ?"

"I do not know, Sergeant."

"You saw that individual on the gig outside ?"

"I did. What about him ?"

"It strikes me he is one of the band of that famous brigand Sataniello, whose body we hope to seize before twenty-four hours are over our heads."

"Do you really tell me so ?"

"Yes."

"What induces you to come to that conclusion ?"

"I could not tell you—my anticipations are seldom wrong. Twenty years' service in the dragoons, constantly pursuing poachers, housebreakers, and brigands, ought not to go for nothing."

"You think he is one of the brigands, then ?"

"I do."

"How shall we find out ?"

"Leave that all to me."

The sergeant now went to a desk, and having opened it, brought out of it a printed form.

Two of the soldiers remained without to see that the sergeant's injunction would be carried out in case of need. The remainder were within the house, ready to do whatever they might be called upon to perform.

"It is useless, Captain," the Sergeant said, "that I should make you go through any unnecessary trouble, but we have certain rules and regulations by which we must abide."

"I do not blame you, my friend," Captain Wogan pursued; "fire away, my man, I always like a soldier to do his duty."

"Your name, if you please, Captain?"

The sergeant knew perfectly well Captain Wogan's name, still it was necessary that he should make him repeat it again, as he was about to take his deposition.

"Captain Wogan, your address if you please!";

"Momentarily staying at Don Saltara Castle."

"As a visitor, I suppose?"

"Yes."

"Are you related to the Duke of Don Saltara, Sir? I beg your pardon for asking what you may think to be an impertinent question; but there is a good deal more in this than what you think."

Captain Wogan smiled.

"Yes," he said, "I am related to the Duke of Don Saltara by marriage. He is my father-in-law, and this accounts for my being so particular in hunting down Sataniello, the Dark King of the Mountains."

"By marriage," the Sergeant repeated, writing down the words on paper. "This will do very nicely — and now for the next passage of our business."

When Captain Wogan gave to the Sergeant the information which we saw him give, the latter opened his eyes, like we do sometimes when we are put in possession of a thing which greatly astonishes us.

If some of my friends who take the trouble to peruse me belong to the country—and, I dare say, many do—they will know how very well the lord of the manor's private affairs happened to be familiar to the surrounding peasantry.

They are acquainted with all that takes place at some of those splendid mansions scattered here and there throughout England, Scotland, and Ireland, as well as Italy.

It will not, though, be deemed odd by those who read this and fully concur with us in the observations made, that the Sergeant was very much taken aback when he heard that the Duke of Don Saltara's daughter happened to be married to an Englishman.

There had been no public ceremony to commemorate the event—no rejoicings had taken place—and his brain began to be puzzled at what he had heard.

However, he bowed respectfully to Captain Wogan; and although before he had been very attentive to the Captain, and as far as he could, the latter could not have found fault with his zeal in answering the Captain's request to call at Don Saltara Castle, from which he just came, still, now that he had an occasion to serve one who, through his family connection, might settle down in the country altogether, he was very cautious in attending to him—more so now than he had hitherto been.

"When did Sataniello enter the walls of Don Saltara Castle?" he pursued.

"Two days ago."

"How long did he and his troop remain within it?"

"I cannot tell you exactly."

"Did he leave the castle with his band?"

"No, he remained behind."

"Would you be able to identify him?"

"Most decidedly I should."

"Did you ever see him before?"

"I did on two occasions."

The English officer now began to relate to the sergeant the two meetings which he had had with Sataniello, the Dark King of the Mountains, and he concluded by detailing his adventure with him at the castle, and how the child had been stolen by him and taken away.

Captain Wogan spoke like a gentleman and like a father.

Although there was in his tone of voice nothing which to a casual observer would have betrayed any strange feeling, the Sergeant thought he discerned a slightly perceptible trembling which a father would feel in alluding to such a subject as that of the loss of one's newly-born.

The soldier caused the Captain to answer a few other questions, upon which we do not think it necessary to dwell; and, when he had concluded what he had to ask him, he closed his book and called one of his men.

He was an intelligent-looking dragoon the man whom we are about to introduce to our readers more forcibly than any of the others.

"Go to the back parlour," he said, "and put down everything which the man whom I am about to question may happen to say in answer to my queries."

"I will not fail to act to your satisfaction."

Then speedily the soldier went away.

"I think we will call your friend in here now," the Sergeant pursued, addressing the countryman. "Just go outside and ask him to step in. Do not, however, let him believe for one moment that we have our suspicions, for, if we do, we may lose a good deal of valuable information."

The countryman went out of the house, and, in an instant, he was in the highroad.

Three yards at the utmost brought him to Paublas.

"Well, mate," he said, "come along with me."

Paublas was far from being at all pleased at the request which was just made to him.

He did not by any means relish the idea of being brought face to face with several dragoons.

People that are in the wrong always dread the authorities that be.

He had escaped from Sataniello, and now he was in a worse plight still.

He knew, however, that to refuse to comply would not serve him,

Hence, with a quickness which greatly astonished all the witnesses of the scene which we are describing, he walked into the barracks accompanied by the countryman.

"What is your name?" the Sergeant began, putting to Paublas the same question which he had just made to the Captain.

"Paulo is my name," Paublas replied.

"Thank you, Maestro," the Sergeant replied. "You have just escaped from Sataniello's cavern?"

"That is right so far, Sergeant."

"How long were you confined?"

"Two days."

"What did you do to him?"

"I did nothing beyond being an honest, hardworking chap, travelling along the highroad. I fell into Sataniello's hands. He gave an order to one of his followers—a tall fellow whom they call the Giant—and the latter dragged me to the cavern. When I arrived there they placed me in irons, and it is only through the most miraculous providence that I succeeded in effecting my escape."

"Did he ill-use you?"

"He handled me roughly. I have still the marks of his violence all over my body. Such treatment I shall never forget."

The former lieutenant of Sataniello pronounced these words with so lamentable an intonation that he began to think for a moment that his suspicions were groundless.

"And what do you purpose doing?"

"I want an escort of as many men as you can spare me, and I will lead you to the cavern where he dwells."

"Do you think you could take us to it?"

"I am sure I could."

Captain Wogan, the sergeant, and the country man were all looking earnestly at Paublas.

"Should you claim the reward which is attached to Sataniello's apprehension?"

"I should not."

"Who do you think would be entitled to it?"

"Yourself and your men," Paublas replied, boldly.

"And why do you act as you do?"

Paublas was about to say out of revenge; but he happily refrained from using the words he was about to speak, and he quickly retorted, "I act as I do to serve the ends of justice."

"And to obtain a free pardon for yourself?"

The sergeant spoke as he did to try if he could discountenance Paublas by pleading the wrong to know the right.

In his suppositions, however, he found that he was correct.

The accusation which he had brought against Paublas was upon trust.

The Lieutenant was of a cowardly nature.

He stepped backwards and tried to have recourse to flight.

His countenance became white, and he trembled like the leaf shaken during a winter's night by the cold blasts of the wind.

"It is no use denying the truth any longer," he said. "I am going to turn king's evidence."

"You are one of Sataniello's followers, then?"

"I am."

"I thought so."

"Why have you left him?"

"To revenge myself."

"What did you do to him?"

"I attempted to assume the command of the troop, and I failed, and was condemned to die by starvation."

"Do you think he knows that you are at large?"

"I could not say; but, if he does, it is all one."

"You are not speaking false, are you?"

"I am not."

The Sergeant now turned round to Captain Wogan. "To-morrow morning, Captain," he said, "I will be at your castle-yard with your troop and this man. Shall you be ready to come with us."

"I shall. I am ready now."

"To-morrow will do, Captain."

"Why not now? The prey may escape us."

"No fear of that. If ever we were in the safe way of apprehending Sataniello we are now; but it will not be without some bloodshed."

"Never mind about that."

"Are you still in the same frame of mind, Captain?"

"Yes. I am decided upon forming part of the expedition."

"You may meet your doom."

"I cannot fear that."

"If you take my advice you will remain away, and leave the matter entirely to us."

"No, I will not. I will go in search of my child. God will help me. The justice of my cause is sure to end successfully,"

"May it be so, Captain, Let us hope that the noble motive which prompts you on will meet with its reward.

Thus speaking, the sergeant accompanied Captain Wogan to the door, and, shortly afterwards, having jumped upon his horse's saddle, he trotted away homeward.

When Captain Wogan returned to the Castle he entered the drawing-room, where he happened to find the Duke, who was giving to his daughter a fatherly kiss.

"I hope, father," the Senorita was saying, "my husband will alter his project and not go to seek death. This Sataniello is a frightfully cruel man—and, if he was to be killed, what should I do?"

"Heaven listen to your prayer, my child. God is good."

It was at the time that the old Duke was pronouncing the last words that Captain Wogan made his appearance.

In vain did she endeavour to make her husband promise her that he would not leave her.

Captain Wogan remained unshakable.

He would sally forth with the expedition—nothing would stop him.

Paublas, in the meantime, had been confined in one of the cells which are to be found in all places which are devoted to the police, and anxiously was he awaiting the morrow.

————

CHAPTER XLI.

WHERE A FEW THINGS ARE FULLY RELATED—AND WHERE ONE OF SATANIELLO'S BAND MEETS WITH A FATE WHICH HE WAS FAR FROM EXPECTING.

EARLY in the morning did Paublas hear the preparations which was being made by the sergeant and his troop.

Ere night his mind would be satisfied.

During his confinement the late lieutenant of Sataniello never slept.

He dreamt that he was engaged in a terrible struggle with the Boy Brigand.

Over and over he tried to sleep, but he was not able to enjoy rest.

Nature assumed her sway at about twelve o'clock, but at break of morn Paublas was awoke again.

Then he would pace up and down his cell.

It was a large one, and he had plenty of room to walk about.

There were iron bars in the door, and he could see throug them.

For hours and hours he listened to the steady and monotonous steps of the sentry outside.

At length the full blaze of morn came.

The expedition set off.

Paublas was provided with a horse.

They soon reached the castle yard.

The servant had already called Captain Wogan.

He was ready to receive the troop.

"You are faithful to your word, sergeant," he said, as soon as he saw the soldier, followed by his men, entering the yard.

THE GIPSY BY THE WELL.

"Which way shall we go now ?" Captain Wogan asked Paublas, who was to be the soldiers' guide.

"Follow me and you will be right," was his reply.

Everything being now settled to everyone's satisfaction, the cavalcade galloped onward.

As they crossed the bridge which led into the country, Captain Wogan turned round to see whether he was watched.

He saw a sweet countenance looking from the drawing-room window.

It was his young wife anxiously gazing upon him.

He placed his hand to his lips and wished her farewell.

He seemed to regret having come at that instant.

"Make your mind easy, Captain," the Sergeant said, as he rode side by side with the officer ; "I know that we will succeed in our undertaking."

The Senorita, on her side, quitted the apartment where she was as soon as the force of Captain Wogan had disappeared from her gaze, and with a despondency that almost reached despair, she returned to the room where the scene which we have described between her and Sataniello occurred.

Faithful to his word Paublas led the men on.

"We will have to dismount shortly," Paublas said ; "we will never be able to get our horses where I am about to lead you."

The sergeant looked suspiciously at the speaker.

"You do not think, surely," Paublas replied, "that I am deceiving you—revenge is too sweet to an Italian for him to lose an opportunity of satisfying it."

He pronounced these words like one who meant what he said.

The whole cavalcade now had come to a spot which needs to be described.

It was a solitary place, indeed.

From it one could look down the vast precipices of granite which formed part of the mountain.

16

These precipices were broken into cliffs, which in some places suspended far above their base, and in others rose in nearly perpendicular lines to the place where the soldiers stood.

Paublas with a dreadful pleasure gazed downwards.

What would now be his joy could he have hurled Sataniello to death.

He gazed upon these precipices, rugged as they were, with larch, and frequently darkened by lines of gigantic pines, bending along the rocky ledges till his eyes rested on the thick chestnut wood that extended on their winding base, and softening to the plains, seemed to form a gradation between the variegated cultivation, there and the wildness of the rocks above.

Round the extensive plains were huddled the mountains, of various shape and altitude, which Paublas had admired more than once—some shaded with forests of olive and almond trees, but the greater part abandoned to the flocks which, in summer, fed on the aromatic herbage, and on the approach of winter descended to the sheltered plain close at hand.

On the left there opened a small narrow pass, which Paublas informed the soldiers led to the cavern.

The horses were left to the charge of one of the soldiers.

Although he could ill be spared, it was necessary that some one should be left behind to attend to the cattle.

The men walked on.

They soon reached the outskirts of the cavern.

"We must be very careful now," Paublas whispered; "there is a sentry, who is always on the look-out. Remain here for awhile, I will be back in an instant."

"No, you will not leave my sight," the Sergeant said.

"Come on with me, then."

The whole of the soldiers followed.

Captain Wogan now regretted having come.

Paublas soon came to the place where the sentry ought to have been on the wall.

There was one of the brigands whom he saw.

It was Tattoo.

Providence served the expedition.

He was fast asleep.

Quicker than we could describe it, he was pounced upon by the sergeant, gagged in a minute, and ere he knew where he was, he was held firmly a prisoner by two men of the troop.

Unable to move he was about to speak,

"Ah, traitor!" he said, recognising Paublas, "ah, traitor!"

"I am not starved to death yet, you see," Paublas replied; "you were the cause of my incarceration—die—die—die."

He closed his mouth tightly, and, like a madman, he darted upon Tattoo, who, being unable to defend himself, was soon laid to the ground by a wound he received in the heart.

Paublas had begun his revengeful work.

With his poniard he did fell Tattoo to the earth.

The murder had been too quickly executed for its prevention to be possible.

Tattoo sighed heavily, and ere a minute had elapsed he had been plunged into eternity.

To remove all traces of the deed, the dead man's body was carried by the side of the precipices, to which we have ere now alluded, and it was allowed to fall downwards.

This was the beginning of the expedition.

Thus there was no impediment to the entrance of the soldiers.

They groped their way steadily.

Not a sound did they hear.

"Where is the Captain's place?" Captain Wogan inquired.

"We will soon reach it."

As Paublas spoke he looked before him.

He saw a dark form gliding along in the distance.

He had recognised the Monk.

"I fear," he said, in an under whiper, "that we have been discovered."

"What leads you to think so?"

"I think I have just caught a glimpse of the Monk."

"Who is the Monk?"

"One of Sataniello's followers—he is the lieutenant."

"Are you certain you are not making a mistake?" the Sergeant pursued.

"I apprehend I am not."

"What is to be done?"

"Let us walk on."

"Are we likely soon to reach our destination?" the Sergeant inquired.

"In half a minute."

The whole of the detachment was gliding swiftly along in the path which led to the Boy Brigand's cavern.

They soon came to it.

It was empty.

Sataniello and Joanitta had taken to flight.

"You have betrayed us," the Sergeant said.

"Why speak like that?" Paublas replied; "what could have been my object in doing so?"

"Everything is not lost yet."

Captain Wogan never said a word.

He looked on every object in Sataniello's late abode—over and under the bed, in the hope of finding that which he sought—namely, his child, who had been taken away—but it was useless.

He groaned like one who is driven to despair.

Once more he looked and was doomed to disappointment.

The Sergeant endeavoured to come in contact with any of the brigands, but strange to say they were nowhere to be found.

At that moment they heard the sound of footsteps.

They recognised Sataniello's features.

"You came here to surprise me," he said; "ah! ah! you will not make me your prisoner this day—in five minutes you will all be blown up—I have set fire to the ammunition room, and you are standing close by it."

"Is that right?" the Sergeant inquired.

"Onward, onward, after Sataniello," the soldier replied.

What between the information which the Boy Brigand had just given to his pursuers and the anxiety which they had of becoming masters of his precious person, we need not say that they followed quickly upon his track.

So much exasperated was Captain Wogan by the bold impertinence of the Boy Brigand, that with the swiftness of the doe he pursued him.

"You will not capture me yet, Captain Wogan; once more you and I am destined to meet. I have got your boy—it is a boy, mind you, and you will never see him again."

"Is he dead?" Captain Wogan anxiously asked.

The Boy Brigand made no reply.

It may, perhaps, seem strange to our readers that while the conversation which we have just related had taken place, no attempt had been made on either side to have recourse to a struggle.

Our readers should, however, remember that the events which we have related had occurred too quickly to give to any one an opportunity to fight.

The Sergeant, followed by Captain Wogan and his men, had now reached one of the numerous ways of exit which the Boy Brigand's cavern afforded to those who were familiar with its precincts.

Had he been by himself he would never have found the spot which he reached, and towards which Paublas guided the pursuers.

In no other part of the subterranean strait did the stone assume stranger shapes. Here it was converted into a dome ; there slanting over an abyss it formed two natural pillars, very similar to the arches of a bridge.

It was towards this particular spot that Sataniello, headed by Joanitta, who held the child in her arms, wended his steps.

CHAPTER XLII.

WHICH TELLS OF SATANIELLO'S MIRACULOUS ESCAPE, AND WHICH SHOWS THAT THE MONK CAN PROVE MORE USEFUL TO THE BOY BRIGAND THAN PAUBLAS EVER DID.

ERE now Sataniello had noticed the irregular order in which time had modelled the rock, and from the rough disposal of the stones he had not been slow in perceiving how easy of access the other side could have been made with a few trifling alterations.

What this was we will acquaint our readers with.

They at once suggested themselves to his inventive mind.

Thus he had put his brains together, and he had ingeniously wrought upon one which he but little knew at the time he contemplated it how useful it would prove to him at no distant period.

The chasm was too wide to enable any one to bound over it, however agile that one might have been, for situated as it was at the top of the mountain, no space was at hand to afford an opportunity to take a start, and any bold attempt to clear the dangerous precipice must have resulted to a failure—instantaneously followed by your being dashed against the rough stones which partly hid the surging waters beneath.

To effect a passage to the opposite embankment Sataniello had placed a wooden beam across the two pillars which covered the whole width and extent of the abyss.

In the midst of it was fastened to a strong iron hook a massive cord, by which help you could easily effect a safe landing, provided you gave to your body a slight, steady inclination previous to taking your leap.

This was the last hope of escape which remained to Sataniello.

It was the thread upon which their existences depended.

His own life—that of his dearest Joanitta !

Upon it also depended the fate of the heir to the dukedom of Don Saltara.

His pursuers were now close upon his track.

Long ere now they would have reached him had not an incident stayed their onward course.

To describe this incident we must say a few words.

One man had been soon hurrying on towards the aperture of the cavern, when the sergeant and his escort had just entered the strait.

Who was that man ?

Paublas said he thought it was the Monk.

He had not been mistaken in his apprehension.

The Monk stood in a cavity, wherein he was as safe as could be, as he was surrounded by the rocks on each side.

He could move his arms, see and not be seen.

Watchful sentry, he remained awaiting the arrival of Sataniello's pursuers.

Headlong they rushed on, thinking that there was no impediment in their way.

The sergeant came first.

A hatchet was seen rising in the darkness—a body was heard to fall.

Another soldier followed.

The same fate awaited him.

A voice was heard to cry, ["Are you safe, Captain?"

Sataniello's answer never reached the listeners.

Captain Wogan wondered where these sudden blows came from.

Swiftly he dashed onward, and nearly staggered in forcing his way across the two dead bodies which beset his path.

The hatchet was seen to rise again.

An oath followed, and the steel was smashed against the rocks.

It was evident that this time the Monk had missed his aim.

During the confusion which followed, the remaining number of the soldiers found their way, and being without any weapon the Monk was unable to do any further mischief.

So awe-struck had they been by the sudden death of their companions, that they never looked around, but with the madness of men suddenly seized with a pain, they dashed towards the spot where the light of day was to be seen.

It was at that moment that Sataniello heard Captain Wogan's voice reproaching his followers with their cowardice.

The sounds of their footsteps were gradually becoming plainer.

Sataniello did not now hesitate for himself.

What was life to him without his freedom.

More than one time he had risked it before now.

But he trembled for Joanitta and her precious burthen.

"If that child is in our way," he muttered to the maiden, "dash it into the surging waters beneath."

"I will not hurt a poor innocent like that," was the reply.

Yet Sataniello feared that Joanitta in her fright would make some untoward movement, and that she would be powerless to refrain her beautiful frame from shaking nervouly and inwardly, and by a slight shake of her body disturb the regular swinging of the rope.

In that case their lives were doomed to a heart-rending fate.

"Joanitta," Sataniello began, in a sharp and quick tone, "we must cross this gaping abyss—do you think that you can muster sufficient strength to face so bold a venture ?"

"Yes," the girl replied.

"Are you ready, then ?" anxiously pursued Sataniello.

"Onward and delay not," the courageous maiden quickly retorted ; "death I fear not—what are you waiting for ?"

Joanitta pronounced those words in a passionate and determined manner.

Although her eye earnestly and intently was bent upon the rocky cliff before her—although she contemplated the edge of the abyss with awe and indescribable fear, she exhibited not one of the symptoms of an intimidation, which would be, perhaps, her lover's determination.

But her lips were as white as snow.

She would not have betrayed by the tenour of her speech the feelings of dread which she inwardly experienced.

"Joanitta," the Boy Brigand pursued, in a tone of voice which was hollow and bitter, "your life—your liberty is at stake—for an instant only endeavour to remain as silent as the grave—as motionless, as the rock beneath your feet."

"Onward, and enough," the girl replied impatiently, "I am no frail woman who fear dangers—act at once without delay, and you will soon see whether I am worthy of your companionship."

Meanwhile Sataniello was making his preparations.

"Clasp your right arm around my neck, darling," he ejaculated, in a quick tone of voice, "and be still!"

These words were scarcely pronounced ere Joanitta replied—

"Why, Sataniello, I am no coward. What are you waiting for?"

Now the sounds of footsteps were becoming plainer and plainer.

The pursuers were now close upon the Boy Brigand.

"Here they are! here they are!" shrieked Joanitta, with a piercing scream."

And she saw a hand endeavouring to lay hold of her garment.

But the sounds of her voice died away upon her lips.

The accents, prompted by the girl's fears, had been sufficient to induce Sataniello to act at once.

With the swiftness of the arrow he plunged into the air.

The pursuers happily had been too late.

When they appeared upon the crest of the hill, Sataniello, Joanitta, and the youthful heir to Don Saltara Castle, were on the opposite side.

"Heavens!" a voice exclaimed, "they are free again; but they cannot go far. Here's the rope which has enabled them to escape."

It was Captain Wogan who spoke thus.

He had seen what he believed to be his son, closely fastened around Joanitta's breast.

A father in search of his son, and to find himself frustrated!

No—never!

He had scarcely spoken, when he seized hold of the rope, which by its slow shunting was in a fair way of coming within his reach.

"I, too," he exclaimed, with all the bitterness of disappointment, "I will cross over, and fight, in a single combat, with this terrible brigand!"

And he was about to leap over, when the Boy Brigand gave way to a hollow, mocking, cruel, loud laugh.

With a quick hand he had cut in two the frail timber, and the beam falling with a heavy crash beneath, soon showed to the captain that once more he was baffled.

The only communication between the pursuers and the pursued, thus, for the time, was utterly withdrawn.

Meanwhile Sataniello and Joanitta were climbing up the rough cliffs above them.

"Let them not escape!" Paublas exclaimed, "fire! fire! fire! Let us destroy and hurl to hell these children of Satan!"

The ex-Lieutenant's orders were instantaneously carried out.

The report of four guns followed his words, and the refrain of the surrounding solitude re-echoed the detonations.

"It is my turn now," Sataniello pursued; who, having heard the order just in time to escape being made the target of the soldiers had suddenly concealed himself.

"Load again, and fire!" Captain Wogan exclaimed, as soon as the Boy Brigand's manly form shown forth again.

"Paublas, here is my last message!" Sataniello exclaimed.

He stood upon the top of the rock, and, like the Angel of Death, he pointed his revolver to his ex-lieutenant's body.

He was a good shot—was the Boy Brigand!

His sentence had scarcely been uttered, than Paublas fell into the soldier's arms mortally wounded.

A bullet had stuck into Paublas' forehead.

He staggered and reeled, and fell into the surging water beneath.

"Heavens above!" Captain Wogan exclaimed, "I am baffled for the third time! Shall I never see justice carried out!"

And as he spoke, he glided along a slanting path which led towards the high road, where he hoped to meet the Boy Brigand.

Meanwhile Sataniello was hurrying forward.

How long his heedless course would have lasted we are unable to say, did he not discover that Joanitta, whom he held in his powerful grasp, had at last fallen into a swoon.

He had just reached the water's side.

It was night.

He heard sweet voices.

It was a singing-party composed of vine-dressers.

They were indulging in a song after the labours of the day.

In the distance he saw several boatmen.

They rested upon their oars, while their company listened to voices modulated by sensibility to utter eloquence that it is not in the power of art to display.

Refreshing, sweet change, after the day's excitement.

Sataniello feared to be detected.

Thus he glided along a promontory whose shaggy masses impended far over the sea.

The deep, clear waters reflected every image of the landscape.

The cliffs, branching into wild forms crowned with groves, whose rough foliages often spread down their steeps in picturesque luxuriance—the peasants' cabins hanging on the precipices, and the dancing figures on the strand all touched with the silvery tint and soft shadows of moonlight.

On the other hand, the sea glistened with the long line of radiance, and showing in the clear distance the sails of vessels stealing in every direction along its surface, presented a prospect as grand as the landscape was beautiful.

CHAPTER XLIII.

WHERE THE BOY BRIGAND AND JOANITTA ARE ONCE MORE TOGETHER, AND SALLY ON A JOURNEY TO ROME.

"I WONDER," Sataniello exclaimed, "what became of the Marquis of Piatelli's sister? I wonder where the Monk and all my brave followers are gone to, and what has also become of them? I will not allow them to think that I have deserted them in the hour of need—no, I would rather die!"

Thus soliloquising, Sataniello contemplated Joanitta, and it struck him that he ought to endeavour to procure some water to bathe her temples.

Under the impression of this welcome idea, he directed his steps towards a little valley, surrounded by thick-growing trees, and after a short march halted by the side of a stream of clear, sparkling, fresh water.

"Water is a blessed thing," he thought, as he quenched his thirst, "and this is a sweet place," he muttered; "it is just removed from the contact of all living souls, and its solitude will just suit me until Joanitta recovers."

He then left the place where he was, and soon brought Joanitta with him.

His love gave him strength, and he carried her in his arms as if she was a child.

"Where are we?" the maiden said, as soon as she came back to her consciousness; "Sataniello, where are you?"

He knelt by her side, and kissed her affectionately.

"Look around," he said, "what think you of this spot?"

"I feared you had left me," Joanitta replied, looking on the clear stream running onwards through its winding course over beds of many-coloured sands amidst pebbles of every size and shape.

Here, where the stream was uninterrupted, it seemed to linger peacefully by the roots of the old trees which crowded the banks near the cluster of berries which it reflected, and the primroses which nodded on the grassy slope.

Here, where its course was for a moment interrupted, it seemed to gain new life and strength from the pigmy rock which it encumbered, leaping in transparent beauty towards the moonlight, and murmuring softly as it wandered onwards.

Sataniello was not slow ere he made up his mind as to what he should do.

"Come on with me, Joanitta."

"Where are you going?"

"Let us go to Rome."

"We shall be doubtless surprised by the police?"

"They must find us out first."

"That is true; but they are on the watch now."

"They will never dream of the possibility of our being so foolish as to face the police after what has occurred; and hence we shall be much safer in Rome than we should be remaining here. Besides, Joanitta, I should say that you ought to like to see your mother after your long absence from her. Besides, that child is greatly in our way, and we must get rid of it."

"What, altogether?"

"What is the use of keeping him with you?"

"I begin to like him."

"You feel anything for a strange child?"

"I do."

It is very probable that had Joanitta and Sataniello's position been a less critical one, the Boy Brigand would have told his sweetheart that it would be time enough to love the child, which at some future period she was bound to have, instead of wasting her affections upon a stranger to her.

But Joanitta appeared to him to be still very weak, and he loved her too much to say anything which might be the means of annoying her.

Hence he allowed the subject to drop for a few minutes.

"Yes, my darling, my dearest Joanitta," he said, "we must to Rome."

"I would like doing so, Sataniello," she replied; "but I feel rather tired, and I do not think that I can manage the long journey."

Sataniello mused for a moment,

"What is to be done?" he said, after awhile.

Joanitta made no reply.

The Boy Brigand's gaze now reverted to the child which Joanitta held in her arms, and which she contemplated with a woman's affection.

No one can deny the following statement :—

Whether a woman is the legitimate wife of a prince or the consort of an honest, hard-working man—whether she be the harlot of a nobleman or the mistress of a brigand, she is woman still.

Her heart is still open to feelings of compassion and pity, and Joanitta could not but feel for the fate of the infant she had in her possession.

"Joanitta", the Boy Brigand began, "a great deal depends upon this child whom you have got with you. He is the heir, you know, of one of the first families in the land, and, as long as we hold him safe, we need not fear for our lives. It is a precious burden, and we must lose no opportunity to bestow upon him all the comforts which he needs."

Joanitta gazed again upon the child.

"He is very young," she replied. "It is a wonder to me how he has outlived all the rough treatment which he experienced. When you were away at the Castle of Don Saltara, Paublas came into my abode, and, but for God's help——"

"What occurred?" Sataniello inquired, eagerly.

He thought that his darling girl might have been outraged by Paublas; and, although he might previously have questioned her relating to what had taken place, still there are certain things which a woman does not like to reveal to the man with whom she lives.

"What occurred?" Sataniello inquired again.

"Oh, nothing," the girl replied, fearing that her lover would not credit the words which she was about to speak. "But for God's help I should have fallen a victim to that horrid monster."

"As it is you did not, I hope?"

As Sataniello spoke, his look contained a volume of revengeful feeling, which it would be impossible for us to describe.

Joanitta trembled, and her frame shook violently.

She feared Sataniello, although she had no reason and no cause to do so.

She looked at him with a mild, soft expression of countenance.

"No, she replied. "Dear Sataniello, I am happy to say that the cries of the Marquis of Piatelli drew him away from me, and that you arrived just in time to prevent a dastardly recurrence of his filthy and disgusting attempt.

Sataniello breathed like one who has been rid of a heavy load.

No words in the British language would be adequate to convey to our young friends the delight which Joanitta's reply afforded to his anxious mind.

He found out at last that Paublas had not carried out his purpose. The terrible suspicion which had lacerated his imagination after he had seen Joanitta lying senseless on the floor of the cavern were now set to rights, and he had the satisfaction to hear from the lips of a girl, whose veracity and truthfulness he would have been the last one to doubt, the real state of things.

"Do you find yourself better now, Joanitta?" he asked.

"Yes, dear Sataniello," she muttered.

"You will not undergo again, dearest," he replied, "the terrible sensation which you have experienced to-day. I intend to let you remain with your mother, and to sally forth on my dangerous expeditions by myself for the future."

"Oh, do you mean to tell me that you will leave me, Sataniello?" the maiden inquired. "Life to me would be dreary without you. I am accustomed to your society. I love you so."

There was such an amount of loving truthfulness, such volumes of blissful confession, contained in Joanitta's words, that Sataniello's heart began to beat, and he found his imagination kindling with the feverish desires which make us long for the possession of those we worship.

It is very probable that had the spot where he was been more conducive to the enactment of some of those pastoral scenes upon which the greatest poets that the different ages have produced delighted to dwell, he would have exercised his rights as Joanitta's companion—we cannot say husband, for up to the present they were unmarried.

Whether, at some future period, the Boy Brigand would, as a reward for Joanitta's constant devotion, lead her to the altar, we are not in a position to state.

It would, however, sound ridiculous, nay preposterous, to bind religion with the unusual and guilty feelings which the Boy Brigand possessed, and which had thus rendered him an outlaw—to dream of the possibility of that which we have hinted at ever coming to pass.

But we must remember that repentance may dawn some day upon the most depraved natures, and that at a given period they may discover the paramount guilt of their deeds and reform, and, by a virtuous mode of life, atone for their past sins.

Would that the Boy Brigand's hour for repentance had sounded.

Such, however, was not yet the case.

"Joanitta," he said, "what shall we do now? Do you feel well enough to move about?"

The maiden replied in the affirmative.

"Bring me a drop of that clear, sparkling water," she said. "I know it will comfort me."

Sataniello was about to carry out the girl's wishes, and he was just in the act of wending his steps towards the stream, when the sound of voices—to which we have alluded in the previous chapter—struck his ears, and he stood still.

Eagerly he listened for a few minutes.

"Remain here, Joanitta," he said. "I will go and see from whence the sounds proceed. May be I may meet friends among them, and obtain for you a shelter until you are totally recovered from your indisposition."

The eyes of Joanitta sparkled with hope, and anxiously she followed the steps of the Boy Brigand, who soon disappeared behind the trees and the foliage which surrounded the spot where Joanitta was reclining on a plot of grass.

CHAPTER XLIV.

WHERE SATANIELLO, BENT UPON AN ERRAND OF HIS OWN, LEAVES JOANITTA BY HERSELF FOR AWHILE.

WHEN Sataniello left his dear Joanitta, he wended his steps at once towards the place from whence the sounds of voices had proceeded.

It was not far distant.

He was not going to rush among people whom he might not know, and meet foes instead of friends.

It should be borne in mind that it was owing to that cautiousness and prudence which were two of the finest traits in Sataniello's character, that he had managed up to the time we see him to preserve his freedom.

For how many would have met their doom ere now had they found themselves in the same position as Sataniello?

But he had a certain way of doing things which had, as no one can deny, answered his purpose remarkably well.

If the Boy Brigand had been by himself he might have managed things far better still, for one single man can manage to get out of a scrape much better than an individual upon whose fate that of many others depend.

Besides his band there was Joanitta.

He loved her too much to place her life in jeopardy.

But there are certain times when we are not our own masters.

Suppose Sataniello had been captured by Captain Wogan, as it was possible he might have been, what would have been the result?

Paublas would have assumed the command of the gallant troop, and he would have made Joanitta his mistress.

Doubtless Joanitta would have had recourse to suicide like a brave maiden—like the Roman matron Lucretia did—sooner than yield to the brutal desires of a man she abhorred.

As it was, all things had evidently been for the best.

The proposal that Sataniello had made to Joanitta was wise in the extreme. He suggested to her that she should go and live with her mother, where proper care might be taken of the heir to the vast estates of the Duke of Don Saltara.

Sataniello was fully aware of a father's affection, not to be in a position to know that Captain Wogan would leave no stone unturned to find his son, who had been snatched away from him.

He had noticed the sad, dejected look of Captain Wogan, when he had, though by a miraculous escape, managed to force his way behind the rocks which had sheltered him from the shots that had been sent after him by his pursuers.

When Sataniello had walked for a few minutes, he came unto the neighbourhood of the place where the voices which he had heard, as it appeared to him, were located.

He took his time ere he appeared among the singers.

There was a large oak tree immediately before him.

Behind it he thought it wise to take a momentary stand.

He knew not in what part of the country he was.

From thence he wished to go to Rome; but he might be a great many miles distant from that city for all that.

Without his presence being detected, he advanced a step or two.

It was a thickly growing place where he stood, and his body was hidden by the foliage.

Anxiously did his eye glance before him.

He breathed freely at last.

Among the group before him he saw a friend.

There were at least three individuals before him, besides a boy.

He knew none of the former, but the latter was no stranger to him.

Apparently they were vine-dressers who reposed after the labours of the day on some pleasant promontory under the shade of poplars.

By thinking deeply he recognised the place where he had found his way.

He had come to a spot in the environs of Naples called the Puzzuoli Baiæ.

This knowledge induced him to alter his plans.

He would not go to Rome yet, and only provided he could place Joanitta in a safe place.

He inwardly made up his mind as to the manner in which he should act.

What that manner was will be told in due time.

But, as many things will be related as we proceed, it is necessary that we should begin a new chapter to that effect.

CHAPTER XLV.

WHICH RELATES TO THE READER THE MANNER IN WHICH THE BOY BRIGAND FALLS ACROSS A YOUNG FRIEND, WHOM OUR READERS HAVE ALREADY MET BEFORE.

WHILE Sataniello, bent upon his errand, was sending his steps towards an opposite direction from at where Joanitta was, the girl gave way to those thoughts which such a forlorn position as that which circumstances had made her would suggest.

Truly speaking, her home had been in the mountains.

Although her abode did not partake of that literal meaning which " Home, sweet home " has given to our English households, still, for all that, she could not but lament the sudden loss of it.

Besides, it should not be forgotten that Sataniello had been compelled to leave his cavern so suddenly that he had not been able to carry away with him the numberless treasures which had been got from Don Saltara Castle.

It may be suggested that he had in his own possession the heir of the Duke, and that such a being was a fortune in itself.

We would be the last one in the world to contradict so very accurate a statement, but it must also be appreciated at its real value.

For how could Sataniello obtain money from the Duke unless he acquainted him with his whereabouts, having at present no one to send on his behalf?

Such were the thoughts which entered Sataniello's brain when he appeared among the vine dressers.

By a most extraordinary whirl of circumstances he saw among them the lad to whom he had generously given a few golden coins to indemnify him for the loss of his brother.

The lad rushed towards him, and shook him vehemently by the hand.

" Holloa, mate," one of the men asked, " what is all this about ?"

" I lost my way," Sataniello replied, " and I come to you to ask you to put me in the right direction."

The vine-dressers eyed Sataniello suspiciously.

" You lost your way, eh, did you, comrade ?" one of the party asked, " and you want us to guide you, do you ?"

Sataniello answered in the affirmative.

Although there were many men there, still, had he found himself in a critical position, he would not have feared them; but he wanted their help, and he thought that, if he wished to gain their goodwill, he should be submissive in the extreme at first.

" Why, friend," said Sataniello, " I am here among strangers. I know that; and, with the exception of the boy, no one, I fear, has seen me before."

" Why it is rather odd, I am d——d if it is not," one of the party observed. " I have lived many years in this here country, and I never saw such a lot of chaps that seemed to have lost their wits. Here is this young chap," and he pointed to Pedro's brother (the Post-boy who had been killed in Sataniello's service), " whom we met in the highroad half dead from exhaustion. He told us a cock-and-bull story about some dashing cavalier who had given him a good round sum of money; and here you are, mate, in the same predicament. How is that ?"

The vine-dresser who had just spoken was a stalwart bulky peasant, whose good-nature was plainly and perceptibly imprinted upon his jovial and kind-hearted features.

But he belonged to a class of men which is very numerous in every country, and he wished people to believe him of a cruel bullying disposition.

The Boy Brigand, however, had too great knowledge of mankind—and among his troop he had been called upon to deal with individuals whose characters were in every respect so peculiarly different—that he felt at once in a much more hopeful humour when the last speaker had closed his lips.

" Why, friend," he replied, " what you say to me is perfectly correct. But every day of our lives we witness new scenes, and there is nothing so very extraordinary, in my opinion, in your meeting two individuals who, from a slight knowledge of this part of the country, happen to have lost their way, and who, wishing to get on the right track again, apply for information to the first one into whose company their steps may lead them."

" Well spoken, my friend," a vine dresser said. " Giacomo," such was doubtless the name of the man who had addressed Sataniello, " for once you have got your answer, and a very good one it is, too."

It would be impossible to state to what amount of recrimination this remark would have led to among the group of countrymen in whose company Sataniello had found himself, had not the Boy Brigand turned their attention to another channel by the following speech :—

" You say that the lad's story seemed strange to you when he informed you that he had a good round sum of money given to him ?"

" I did say so," the man replied. " What of that ?"

For an instant or two Sataniello made no reply.

" Do you think, then, that the lad told you a falsehood ?"

" What induces you to imply to me such an idea?" the vine dresser inquired, to all outward appearance considerably annoyed by Sataniello's observation.

The Boy Brigand noticed the ill-humour of the countryman.

"I should be sorry, my friend," he said, in a cool, collected manner, "to offend you. And, albeit you are an acquaintance whom I may in all probability never see again, I would not like to give you any cause to regret having met me."

"Excuse me," the vine dresser replied. "I have made a mistake. I did not judge you like I ought. Now that I hear you speaking frankly your mind, I confess that I have been a little too hasty."

"It is no use standing upon ceremony," the Boy Brigand pursued. "If I spoke as I did I had my reasons for doing so. If you think that I am not worthy your confidence, ask that lad who acted towards him like as no other stranger would have done."

The attention of the group of vine dressers was now at its culminating point.

"Have you seen that lad before?" one of them asked.

To this request Sataniello made no reply, but condescended to shake his head in the affirmative.

The Post-boy's brother now stepped forward, and in an open, innocent manner of speaking, related to the company his meeting with Sataniello—how he awoke him when he was lying by the wooden cross in the country, and how he supplied him with money to take back with him to his afflicted family.

In all countries of the world, the knowledge that a charitable deed has been perpetrated is sure to kindle feelings of enthusiasm among hard-working, laborious, honest people, and it is needless to state that a loud murmur of applause followed the lad's statement.

They were kind-hearted labouring men these vine-dressers, and they all rose like one man and surrounded Sataniello.

"You need not want for a shelter as long as you think it proper to remain with me," the one who first had addressed Sataniello ejaculated. "Come with me at once, and I will take care that you will not want while you are under my roof."

"I could scarcely find words to express my gratitude," Sataniello replied. "I need nothing for myself. Thanks be to heaven, I have arms to work and a strong constitution to help me on; but I have a wife and child, and I should like to meet with some one to take care of them while I am away on a trip which I am bound to make on business of my own."

The Boy Brigand thought that this was the wisest step to take.

He knew very well that the people whom he had just met would have done anything to serve him and one whom they would have believed to be his wife; but he was also conscious of the fact that, had they been made aware of the reckless life which he had been leading, of the numerous murders with which he had been connected, and, finally, had they been made acquainted with the truth—namely, that Joanitta lived with him in a state of sin, and that the child which she held had been snatched from his real parents, he would have had every reason to fear that his interview with the countrymen would end in his capture, and in his being handed over to the agents of the police.

In everything too much prudence cannot be shown, and, when he had shaken hands with the rest of the party, followed by the vine dresser who had volunteered to give his wife and child a temporary home, Sataniello wended his steps to the place where he left Joanitta, who, unable to remain awake, was indulging in a comforting slumber, from which the arrival of the two personages awoke her rather more unexpectedly than she had anticipated

when, half an hour previously, nature had assumed her sway.

CHAPTER XLVI.

WHICH DESCRIBES SATANIELLO, JOANITTA, AND THEIR NEW FRIEND ON THEIR HOMEWARD JOURNEY, AND WHICH SAYS A WORD OR TWO RESPECTING REBECCA, THE GIPSY.

JOANITTA soon rose up from her reclining posture, and it was with feelings of astonishment mixed with fear that her eye rested upon the herculean proportions and coarse appearance of Sataniello's new companion.

The time being in no way suited for any explanation which would have acquainted Joanitta with that which she could not but detect herself in a very brief period, Sataniello introduced the maiden to the vine dresser, who could not but pass a favourable opinion to the Boy Brigand of the maiden's attractions.

With an attentive ear, and with that delight which we all experience when we hear praises bestowed upon those whom we hold dear, Sataniello listened to his new friend's remarks.

Knowing that Pedro's brother was in the hands of men who would not let him go astray, he had not ventured to ask the lad to come with him ; moreover, he felt that to be his own master without any encumbrance was the most desirable object, which he longed to carry out.

He wished sincerely to be once more free and without his movements being hindered by any one, and then he would sally forth to the subterranean cavern, where he had lived for so many months past, in the hope of meeting with the Monk and with his followers, whom he had been compelled to leave to save his own life and that of Joanitta.

He should not, however, be in the least astonished were he to find on his return all his gallant troop assembled together and awaiting his return.

There was another prospective which also offered itself to his mind.

Behind him he had left all the gold which had been plundered from Don Saltara Castle, and it would have been a sad blow to him had it been carried away by the dragoons and by the companions of Captain Wogan.

It is not extraordinary, then, that Sataniello's anxiety was such that he did not wish, if he could help it, to lose more time than he possibly could, and that he was in that frame of mind which showed him the necessity of attending to that which he had in view without a moment's delay.

He had, it is true, suggested to Joanitta the propriety of her going to Rome; but second thoughts are sometimes best, and, after consideration, he had come to the conclusion that if he could see the maiden in the hands of some worthy person, it was the best thing which could be hit upon.

When Joanitta found herself perfectly ready, the party—which was only composed of herself and of the Boy Brigand and the vine dresser—set out on their journey.

After having followed a path of about a hundred yards in length, they glided round a promontory whose shaggy masses impended far over the sea, in the neighbourhood of which they now were.

Such magic scenes unfolded themselves as Joanitta confessed she had never seen before, and, gazing upon that which surrounded her, she walked quickly along, carrying the child in her arms.

REBECCA AND THE BOY BRIGAND.

"Well, mate," the Boy Brigand inquired from his comdanion, "is your place far from here?"

"No; we are just upon it. If you like to hurry on, a minute or two will bring us to it."

Sataniello whispered a few words to Joanitta, and she made an effort or two; and, although she was as exhausted as a woman could be, still she found sufficient strength to reach the journey's end without difficulty.

As they were clearing the ground they came to a road which seemed to be more frequented than the one they had left, and it was with a heart ready to burst that Joanitto walked across it.

In every face she saw she dreaded to gaze upon the features of one who was hostile to her, so deep was the impression—which she had experienced at the late scene we have related — left upon her youthful imagination.

The three beings now arrived at a steep hill, at the top of which stood a peasant's cabin.

"This is my home," the vine dresser said. "Take your wife by the hand and help her to climb this height."

The Boy Brigand acted in accordance with the wholesme advice which had been given to him, and he helped Joanitta to climb the ascent which led to the cottage where she was to remain located until her husband's return—at least Joanitta thought that she was doomed to remain there by herself, notwithstanding that Sataniello had not yet spoken to her on the subject.

At length they reached their journey's end.

From the height where the party stood the sight was beautiful and inviting indeed.

The deep clear waters reflected every feature of the landscape, the cliffs branching into wild forms crowned with groves, whose rough foliage often spread down the steeps in picturesque luxuriance.

Far away Sataniello saw a ruined villa peeping through the trees.

He asked his new host what habitation that was.

In reply to this query, the vine dresser told Sataniello that it was a country residence which had been inhabited by a young married couple years ago. That the husband, in a fit of jealousy, had one dark night murdered his wife, and that he had been executed for it. That since then the habitation had been allowed to go to ruin, and that it was every one's and no one's property. "Aye, sir," the countryman pursued, "some people go so far as to say that it is haunted, and that, when twelve o'clock strikes at the church of Santo Marco, the ghost of the murdered woman appears, attired in a long white shroud all covered with bloody stains.

Sataniello listened attentively to his new friend's story, but he seemed in no way discountenanced by it.

Not so, indeed, with Joanitta. She was superstitious in the extreme, and any story purporting to relate to ghosts or anything of that description caused her to be terribly frightened.

But, knowing how very annoyed Sataniello would have been had she given way to such pusillanimous fears, she refrained from allowing herself to display what she felt.

"And does no one inhabit that villa now?" Sataniello inquired.

"As a rule no one dwells within its broken-down walls," the countryman replied; "but occasionally there is an old gipsy—a half-crazy old woman—who makes a stay there of a fortnight or a month at a time. She travels through the country with a goat, and I am told that she and her goat are known for many miles around."

"What is her name?" Sataniello inquired, inwardly fancying that he knew the woman alluded to.

"Rebecca," the vine dresser replied. "I have never seen her myself, but some of my mates have. I daresay you will fall in her way when you leave this here place, for she happens to be in the neighbourhood now."

"Rebecca," Sataniello mused. "Why, of course," he thought, "I have saved that woman's life ere now."

Sataniello was right, for, if our readers think it worth while to refer back (Chapter II. of this story, page 14), they will find that the Hunchback acquainted Sataniello with a knowledge which he had obtained to the effect that the gipsy had drawn 100*l.* from the Bank of Viterbo, and he had subsequently suggested to him the idea of robbing her of a sum which Sataniello had disdained to plunder from her.

The Boy Brigand also remembered a prediction which the gipsy had made, and which had come to pass.

She had foreseen the death of Paublas, the lieutenant.

She had said that he would die a sudden death, and, by a strange coincidence, her words had, at a given period, found a striking confirmation in the Boy Brigand's revenge.

How strange that these events had occurred—stranger still that Sataniello should have been brought to remember them after having been hunted like a felon from his mountain-home through the treachery of his former lieutenant.

All these things come now before him, and he finally resolved that he would endeavour to see the gipsy ere he returned to the cavern in search of his faithful companions.

He was in this frame of mind, and his eye, bent listlessly downwards, was gazing upon the landscape before him, rendered still more attractive by the silvery tint and soft shadows of the moonlight.

"My friend, it is getting late," the vine dresser said, interrupting what he thought was the silent admiration of his new acquaintance for what he saw. "It is getting late. Let me introduce you to my wife and children. They will all be attentive to your wife while you are away, and, when you return, I feel convinced that you will have no occasion to regret their acquaintance, although we met each other in rather a strange way."

The manner of the vine dresser was so straightforward, and he appeared so frank, that Sataniello renewed again his thanks for the kindness he had shown, and, following his steps, entered the countryman's abode accompanied by Joanitta, who held in her arms the heir of Don Saltara Castle, who was soon placed in among the children belonging to the vine dresser's family.

It would be useless for us were we to describe to our readers the character and the appearance of the new friends of the Boy Brigand. If we were to adhere to details so minutely as not to glance rather quickly on the numerous personages whom it is the fate of all to meet, the number of people who would come before our readers would be too great to enable them to devote all the necessary attention to those who, from their deeds and actions, have been called upon to perform rather prominent parts in the course of this tale. It will, therefore, be sufficient to acquaint those who may peruse us, that the vine dresser's wife was a comely, fat, good woman, of about forty years of age, who had a family of three children, and who lost no opportunity of showing all the attention which it was in her power to do towards Joanitta and the baby whom she believed to be her son.

When the Boy Brigand had satisfied his own mind that Joanitta was fairly in the safeguard of honest, hardworking people, he induced the maiden to partake of a frugal supper which now lay upon the table.

Everything in the abode—which was not very large, being only composed of two rooms—bespoke cleanliness and comfort.

It would have required no great amount of perception, had the inmates been unknown to Sataniello, to guess that they were thriving artisans who looked carefully after their home.

A bed was prepared for Joanitta as soon as the meal was over, and Sataniello remained in a chair, smoking by the fireside.

He did not wish to go to sleep, for fear that the morning should dawn upon him and thereby prevent him carrying out his plans.

During the early part of the night Sataniello reflected deeply.

More than once his gaze reverted upon the lovely features of Joanitta, and, but for the fear which he had of awaking her from her slumbers, he would have imprinted a kiss upon her beautiful forehead.

When the early dawn of the morning began to peep through the open door, the Boy Brigand arose; and, previous to taking his departure, he went to wish good-bye to his host, informing him that, ere a few days would have gone by, he would be safely back within his abode.

He begged him to take the greatest care of her whom he called his wife, and, to ensure at his hands a faithful execution of his request, he presented him with a couple of golden coins, which made the countryman's features beam with such marks of satisfaction as they doubtless had not displayed for a long time.

Thus, when Sataniello found that everything was carried out in accordance with his wishes, and when he felt confident that the good people among whom he left Joanitta would take care of her, he wished them good-bye and traced his way outside the cabin.

At that instant the rising sun was casting its rays over the sea, trembling with a long line of radiancy, and showing in the clear distance the sails of vessels stealing in every direction along its briny and mighty surface.

THE BOY BRIGAND ; OR, THE DARK KING OF THE MOUNTAINS. 133

Standing opposite the cabin, the Boy Brigand would have been a famous target for any one who might have been sent in his pursuit; but he feared not for his life, and he thought that the hour of peril had gone by for him, and that for some time to come, at least, he would not have any occasion to fear the emissaries of the police.

Whether he was justified in doing so we are unable to tell.

Gradually and steadily he directed his steps along a declivity, taking very good care not to lose his footing by placing his boot upon any of the numerous shaky stones which lay scattered here and there.

After a tedious descent, he at length reached the road,

In the distance he saw the villa where the countryman had said that Rebecca the Gipsy was likely to be found.

Towards it he shaped his course.

Although Sataniello was one of those who looked upon prophecies as absurd things only fit to interest children in schoolrooms, still, for all that, he could not but remember how true the gipsy had spoken regarding the fate of Paublas, and he wished to ask her what was to be his end, and whether he was to marry some great princess of the land.

Now, as an explanation of the following query, which Sataniello was bent upon making to the gipsy in the event of finding her, it may be as well to acquaint our readers that this was a rumour which had been freely circulated among the Boy Brigand's troop.

No one had ever heard Rebecca making a statement to that effect ; and, as to the accuracy of it, only one person could be held accountable, and that was the Hunchback.

Too great reliance in it ought not to be placed, and it ought to be looked upon for what it was worth.

We can only suppose like anybody else, and what we think as extremely likely may be related in a very few words.

The Hunchback at all times had hated Paublas, and, if he did not worship the Boy Brigand, he at least feared him, and he would not have liked to incur his wrath.

Is it not very probable, then, that the cripple, out of spite against Paublas, and out of a natural wish to court his captain's favour, might have placed in the gipsy's lips words that she never had uttered.

The case, however, might have been far different.

This was exactly what the Boy Brigand wanted to find out.

Perhaps there was some ground for the reports which had been freely circulated around concerning him.

At all events, one of them had turned out to be true, and he wished to ascertain in person whether the second was likely to end similarly.

CHAPTER XLVII.

WHERE THE BOY BRIGAND GOES IN SEARCH OF REBECCA THE GIPSY—AND WHERE, IN SO DOING, HE MEETS WITH AN ADVENTURE HE DOES NOT EXPECT.

FEELING perfectly satisfied that Joanitta had been left to the care of honest, praiseworthy, well meaning people, Sataniello hurried on without any foreboding to the lonely house where the gipsy was wont occasionally to dwell.

Had he not met with the kind-hearted vine dresser about whom we have already spoken in the previous chapter, it is very probable that he would have been reluctant to sally forth on his journey without his female companion.

Faithful she had remained to him during the time which he had spent with her, and, owing to that constancy which she had displayed, he entertained for the girl those loving feelings that are naturally experienced by those who, from a long acquaintance with a female's worth, are placed in a position to form no hasty judgment of her qualities.

It should also be remembered that the departure which Sataniello had been compelled to effect from the cavern had been so unexpected, that he racked his brain in useless attempts to guess the fate of his brave followers.

He had in his mind a plan which he intended to carry out, and he had also sundry orders which he wished to give to his followers, but to be able to do so, in the first instance, he needed to find them.

The sudden attack which had been made upon the cavern was such as he had no reason to expect ; and, had it not been for the treacherous behaviour of his late lieutenant, Paublas, never would the quietness and security of the subterranean abode have been disturbed by such an intrusion as that which we have related.

As far as we can be certain of things which have been accomplished—as far as we can trust our eyesight for what we see—Sataniello was fully convinced that Paublas was no more.

He had seen him killed by the shot which he fired from his pistol into the dark depths of the abyss across which he had effected his miraculous escape with Joanitta.

Unless he lived in a fairy land, where the most extraordinary wonders are daily wrought, it was no very far-fetched supposition to believe that for many hours past the lieutenant's soul had been launched into eternity.

Now, we have said, a few lines above, that the Boy Brigand had no reason to expect the arrival of the Papal dragoons.

To enlighten our readers, it may be necessary to explain the meaning of our words.

They will doubtless not forget, from our previous description of Sataniello's abode, that it was so wonderfully concealed from man's gaze by those obstructions and impediments which had been wrought in the soil by the hand of time, that to find the entrance was one of those discoveries that no stranger would ever have been sagacious enough to detect, unless led on by such a man as Paublas, who was so intimately acquainted with every nook and corner of that particular spot, that to show a safe manner to enter unnoticed the mysterious precincts was to him no matter of very great difficulty.

Joyfully, indeed, did Sataniello gloat on the opportunity which had been offered to him to take a striking revenge upon his lieutenant; and he inwardly resolved to slay Captain Wogan at the first chance which he could have, as he knew that he would track him whenever he could, and, like the hunter who pursues the tiger in the wild solitude of the forest, leave him no rest until he should effect his capture.

Whether this last step would have been a wise one on the part of Sataniello it is not our purpose here to discuss, suffice it to say that he could not dismiss from his mind the bitter disappointment which he felt at having been obliged to leave his friends to seek safety in a hasty and what he deemed shameful flight.

Up to the present period, however, it cannot be asserted that he had had any cause to complain of the time which he had spent in following his roving life, for he had met with a success unparalleled in a brigand's existence.

Since that evening when he had left Rome everything seemed to have smiled turn by turn before him. Within his roof he had received an English nobleman, from whom he had exacted a handsome ransom. Subsequently he had been entertained by a noble duke at his sumptuous residence; and what now remained for him belonged to a future dispensation, the success of which he would have forfeited a good deal to fathom within the next hour.

It was with this view that he was stepping quickly towards the house where he had been informed by the vine dresser that the gipsy was sometimes to be found.

Rebecca the Gipsy had, from the Hunchback's own account, made a prediction which had come to pass. Would the latter one prove as correct?

That he was to marry a duchess of the land seemed to him so preposterous and so wonderful of execution that he could not look upon it as ever being likely or true.

If he was ever to be so lucky, in a worldly point of view, what was to become of Joanitta, the poor girl who had left her home to share his destinies, and who, by even remaining with him, had to a certain extent rendered herself open to the same punishment as that which would have been inflicted upon Sataniello had he been caught by the soldiers who had been placed upon his track by the treacherous Paublas?

Yes, what would become of Joanitta?

And then a girl's ire and anger are sometimes to be feared, and the Boy Brigand (we call him so still, although he is now a daring, bold youth) could not but persuade himself that, were he to forsake the Italian maiden, she was not one who would have received the blow without deeply resenting it, or without endeavouring to avenge herself.

Moreover, when Sataniello began to ponder on the events which we have related—his stay at Don Saltara Castle and his subsequent departure—he linked all those different occurrences with the gipsy's prediction, and his wayward imagination pictured to himself the future in warm, glowing colours.

It is very true that, when the mind is young, the heart hopeful, youth are also too prone to indulge in castles in the air, which the first strong breeze is likely to dash away for ever.

On the other hand, Sataniello was justified in fancying that there might be some probability in Rebecca's speech; for, if it had not been for the Senorita Bianca being married to his deadly enemy, and had her father remained in the same frame of mind as that in which he was when he first met the Boy Brigand—then the Marquis of Piatelli—the probabilities might have been that, had he managed sufficiently well to keep up his incognito, Rebecca's words would have found their accomplishment in both instances.

It was under this impression that Sataniello proceeded in thoughtful silence towards the villa.

After having walked for a few minutes, he came to what he thought looked like an orangery, which, from its not having been used for years, and from want of care, was in a most dilapidated state.

He still proceeded onward, and came to a small narrow path which led to the entrance.

The door of the villa was wide open.

Evidently, if it was inhabited, the inmate did not fear being disturbed or troubled by the approach or the attack of any brigands.

This thought dawned across Sataniello's mind, and a smile appeared upon his lips.

The villa was only a one-storey house, but its building was tasty in the extreme, and the Boy Brigand thought that it was a great mistake that it should have been deserted from those motives with which he had been acquainted by the vine dresser.

Boldly he advanced towards the villa, and entered a low-roofed lobby or hall—if we can thus call it—at the end of which he saw a narrow staircase, doubtless leading to the apartments above.

The hall divided the villa into two compartments, in which there were four rooms respectively, namely, two rooms on each side.

He looked into each of them, and he saw no one.

"I wonder," he muttered, "why gipsies are such strange creatures, and why they always occupy such solitary spots as these to enjoy being removed from the company of those who do not belong to their tribe? This, indeed, would have been a snug place for me had I known it ere now, and it would have answered my purpose right well when straying in this part of the country. Who, indeed, would ever dream of looking after Sataniello, the Boy Brigand, in a villa surrounded by trees, and of which the existence never would be thought of except by the surrounding neighbours?"

These were the thoughts in which Sataniello was indulging when he entered the villa.

The house being of rather small dimensions, he could easily ascertain that there were only two rooms on each side of the hall in which he was standing.

The first door on his right stood open, and he entered what appeared to have been used at some time or other as a sitting room.

In that room there was no one.

Gradually and successively he looked in every other.

No one was there to meet his gaze.

"If Rebecca lives here," he muttered, "she is evidently not downstairs."

Thus speaking, he ascended the steps which were immediately before him.

He came then to the top of the house.

There was a door open before him.

Had he been actuated by such a thing as fear—had he for one single instant ever dreamt of the possibility of meeting any foes—he would not have walked so boldly; and, instead of inspecting the villa as minutely as he did, he would have taken his precautions and have acted more prudently.

However, as the case was, he never thought of meeting any one besides Rebecca.

To see her he had come, and the thought that he was likely to meet any one besides herself had never entered his mind.

Thus he unhesitatingly stepped forward.

He entered the room, and, when he had done so, he found that it was too late to retreat.

The sounds of his footsteps had attracted the attention of two soldiers who were within it.

As quick as lightning they both rose to lay hold of his person.

Sataniello recognised in one of them one of his pursuers.

That he could not have forgotten his features was at once palpable to him by the countenance of one of the military men.

While so thinking, one sprang towards him to seize him, but Sataniello prevented him from doing so.

With a quick hand he laid hold of his pistol, and threateningly held it towards the soldier.

It was a case of life and death for the latter, so he said nothing.

Although they were two men against one, they attempted not a struggle.

Sataniello would have doubtless discharged his pistol, and, as the muzzle was directly opposite the breast of him who appeared to the sergeant, he showed no signs of hostility.

Soldiers, as such, are brave men; but, when face to face before one who has a decided advantage against them, they are rather reluctant to show fight—and no one could find fault with them, knowing how valuable and how dear man owns his life.

The military were awestruck.

They had been sent in pursuit of Sataniello, and they had thought that, if they could have bribed the gipsy Rebecca to get her to tell them the Boy Brigand's whereabouts, this would be as easy a way as any to obtain the reward promised for his apprehension.

CHAPTER XLVIII.

WHICH DESCRIBES THE FIRST PART OF SATANIELLO'S INTERVIEW WITH REBECCA, AND HOW HIS CONVERSATION WITH HER WAS SUDDENLY INTERRUPTED.

WHEN Sataniello found by the countenances of the two soldiers that he would have nothing to fear from them as long as he kept his weapon in the same position in which he held it, he thought that it would be perhaps as well for him to make the most of the advantage of his situation, and to back out of the room in as quick a time as he could fairly do so.

Thus, still holding his pistol towards the soldiers' breast, he retraced his way backwards, and when he fancied himself fairly out of sight, he cleared the staircase in one bold bound, and once more found himself outside the villa.

But although he knew that there were within two men who would lose no opportunity to seize him if they fairly could, he yet persuaded himself that it would be folly to leave the villa without seeking at least an opportunity of meeting the gipsy, whose interview he so anxiously sought.

At the back of the villa there was a slanting path which led to a well, hiding the front part of which he saw what appeared to him to be an old woman glancing downward.

He had now no doubt it was Rebecca the Gipsy.

With an anxious mind, and with a beating heart, he walked towards her.

A few steps brought him close to her.

The woman was so deeply engaged looking below, that she heeded him not.

At first he feared to disturb her in that which he deemed was perhaps some of her secret musings, but at length he consulted his own interests, and gently laid his hand upon her shoulder.

Rebecca the Gipsy, for it was her, quickly turned round.

"What brings you here, stranger?" she inquired.

"I wish to see Rebecca," Sataniello replied.

"I am the one you seek," the woman pursued; "what do you need at my hands?"

"I am young," Sataniello replied, "and I wish to know my fate."

The gipsy was an old woman of about sixty years.

She was small, and of low height; and although all traces of youth had fled from her countenance, it was no difficult task to guess that in former days Rebecca must have been rather a handsome gitano.

There was something exceedingly clever and deep in the sparkling of her black eye; and her forehead, furrowed by many a wrinkle, was broad and expansive, and betrayed no inferior mind.

She was attired in the garb peculiar to the country to which she belonged; and but for a rather original head-dress, nothing really worth describing formed part of her dress.

Sataniello had never seen Rebecca the Gipsy before, and now that an opportunity offered, he gazed with wonder upon her.

"You want to know your fate, my friend?" the gipsy inquired.

"Yes, Rebecca," Sataniello replied, calling the gipsy by her name, as if he had been acquainted with her for as many years as he had known her minutes.

"What you ask is too much," the gipsy pursued.

"Why so?"

"Because it is not right to foresee man's end."

"But could you do so?"

"I have done so before."

"I know that."

"You do?"

"Yes."

"In what instance, pray?"

"In that of my lieutenant."

"Paublas?"

"Exactly."

"And who are you?"

"Don't you know?"

"No, I have never seen you before. Who was your lieutenant?"

"Paublas, I repeat."

"Are you Sataniello, then?"

"I am," the Boy Brigand replied; and he seemed proud to acknowledge it.

"I thought so; but why are you here now. I thought you had been tracked like a wild beast by a detachment of soldiers?"

"You are not mistaken; I have been compelled to leave my cavern, and am now wandering about the country."

"And what do you purpose to do now?"

"I am uncertain."

"You do not want my advice?"

"If I did not, I would not have come here."

"Why do you think my advice worth seeking?"

"Because what you say comes to pass."

"Not always."

"In many cases it does. Months ago," the Boy Brigand said, "you predicted the death of my lieutenant."

"I remember having done so."

"And I heard it."

"Who told you?"

"The Hunchback."

"What has become of him?"

"I left him behind me."

"You are not aware of his whereabouts?"

"I am not."

"What became of the Monk?"

"I do not know."

"Would you like to hear?"

"Nothing would afford me greater pleasure."

"I will tell you."

"Will you?"

"Yes."

"How am I to reward you?"

"Never mind about that at present."

"Shall I ever be able to do so?"

"Not if you return to the cavern, as you purpose to do."

"But nothing else remains for me?"

"You are too prone to hurry on conclusions."

"I should like you to advise me."

"You would?"

"Yes."

"But if I advise you, will you adhere to what I say?"

"I will."

"Upon your word?"

"Yes."

"But for awhile you must leave Joanitta."

"She will fret after me, maybe grow desolate."

"That is better than to endanger your life and her own too."

"I admit that," Sataniello replied, as if he could not but acknowledge the substantial wisdom of the gipsy's words.

"If you were to return to your home in the mountains, you would certainly be captured within twenty-four hours."

"How is that?"

"The country for you is no longer safe; there are soldiers everywhere watching you, and if you are not careful your doom is sealed."

Sataniello turned pale when he heard the gipsy speak the last words.

"They would condemn me to death if they were to apprehend me, I fear."

"Not a shade of doubt about that."

"But what am I to do without any money?"

"I will lend you some."

"How shall I repay it to you?"

"Because, ere long, you will get plenty."

"Will you place me in the way of achieving so desirable an end?"

"I will."

"Why are you so generous towards me?"

"Because you have acted generously towards the gipsy."

"I do not remember having done so."

"Is your memory so bad as that you do not recollect having prevented your band murdering me for the sake of a paltry hundred pounds?"

"You astonish me."

"Indeed!"

"How did you come to get such a knowledge?"

"I know everything."

"Did you know, then, that I had to have recourse to flight to save my life?"

"I did this morning, not before."

"Through what means?"

"Two soldiers told me."

"I have already seen them," Sataniello replied; and he explained to the gipsy his miraculous escape.

"They offered me a reward if I were to help them to effect your capture."

"What did you say?"

"I declined their offer, as I intimated that I was unable to be of any service to them."

"What did they reply to that?"

"That I must be one of your accomplices."

"Did they ill-treat you?"

"They did not; and what if they had?"

"Why, I would show them that I am not ungrateful."

"But, my friend, I have done nothing yet for you.'

"Not yet, it is true; but still you have taken an interest in me; and one feels that, when, like myself, one is cast alone in the world, obliged to look out for shelter in the most secret spot that he can find, for fear of being recognised and led home to captivity.'

Sataniello was one of those for whom a woman could not but feel a certain regard. He was young, brave, courageous, enterprising; and whether these qualities are directed towards a good channel or a bad one, they are always certain to enlist the sympathies of those who could not but admire so much bold hardihood concentrated in one being.

Rebecca was gazing placidly upon her new friend's features.

There was a good deal of deep, catechising expression in the gipsy's look.

"You are not endeavouring, I hope," Sataniello said, "to fathom my mind, Rebecca? I have told all—I have told who I really am; and if the sake of a handsome reward did tempt you, I am now in your power."

The gipsy rose to her full height like a woman who has been deeply outraged.

With her right hand she pointed to the country.

"Go away from me, Sir," she said, "if such is the opinion which you hold."

The gipsy's ire was evidently kindled by the Boy Brigand's late remark.

She was hurt at the hasty opinion which he formed of her.

"Do not blame me, Rebecca." Sataniello said. "If I have spoken as I have in the hurry of the moment, as my life and my liberty may be said to hang upon a thread, you will not deem my speech an insulting one, and you will, I trust, forgive me for having uttered it."

The gipsy held her hand towards Sataniello.

He eagerly grasped it, and brought it to his lips.

"You are young and hopeful," the gipsy said, "but you should not tempt Providence. What became of the soldiers whom you say you met just now?"

"What became of them?" Sataniello mused; "why I suppose they are still where they were before."

"That is not an answer to give," Rebecca replied harshly. "You come to seek my advice, and yet you will remain here when you know that your movements are closely watched. Do you think that these men, who covet the large ransom which has been offered for your apprehension, have been idle? Through your undaunted coolness once, you have been successful enough to escape from them; but mind my words, my friend, they have sallied forth in search of a few of their comrades, so as to meet you in such numbers as to make sure of capturing you."

"Am I not safe here, then?" Sataniello inquired, gazing downward, and looking from the spot where he stood upon the Bay of Naples, in the immediate vicinity of which he now was.

He skimmed with his glance its splendid surface, which showed distinctly the whole sweep of its rising shores, the stately city of Naples on the strand below, and spreading far among the hills its terraced roofs, which in a few hours would be crowded with spectators, and the Corso, tumultuous with carriages, filled by all the idle and wealthy Italian citizens.

While he surveyed this magnificent scene, he fancied he distinguished near him the sounds of voices as of persons who feared to be heard, and he listened attentively.

"If you were to be seen here by anyone sent after you," the gipsy said, stopping close by the side of Sataniello, and whispering a few words in his ear, "your doom would be sealed, and myself compromised by it."

After a pause of silence, during which the gipsy

was meditating, and Sataniello impatiently watching the different windings of the neighbourhood, which were not hidden from his gaze by the numerous trees which grew in some parts. He said—

"Do you really believe that any effort to detain me would be effectual? As long as I have a pair of loaded pistols by my side, I fear not."

"Speak not thus," Rebecca pursued. "Give not way to such foolishness. What could you do if you were overpowered by numbers?"

"I would fight and die, sooner than surrender alive!"

"Very fine sentiments they are, certainly!" the gipsy replied. "In the meantime, what fate would await Joanitta, the girl who you say you love? The feeling which you entertain for her cannot be a very great one, if you are are so selfish as to look out and think only of yourself!"

This reproach emanating from the gipsy's lips seemed to bring Sataniello to his senses; and in a tone which betrayed the deep anxiety which Rebecca's last words had produced upon him, he asked her, in a quick, hasty, manner, what he was to do?

"Am I to fly from this spot?" he continued, "or am I to confide entirely unto you, Rebecca?"

"If you do, you need not alarm yourself; but something tells me that ere long our meeting will be disturbed. I cannot but think that these two soldiers whom you encountered ere you spoke to me have not been idle, and that they are trying at this very moment to effect your ruin."

"Did you hear a noise just now?" he inquired.

"Yes," Rebecca replied, "it sounded heavily upon my ear at the time. The reason why I fear that something is about to occur, is because it gave place so suddenly to a death-like silence. If you were watched, they would not pounce upon you unexpectedly, they would take very good care to make sure of their prey beforehand."

"But do you really believe that I have been watched already?"

"Not yet," Rebecca replied; "but ere long a detachment of soldiers will be upon us. It is seldom that my forebodings turn out to be groundless. Hark!"

The gipsy listened again, and so did Sataniello.

Without a moment's delay she exclaimed—

"Go that way!"

And as she spoke, she pointed with her finger to her right.

"Beneath those trees yonder, you will see a small stone—lift it up; you will then find yourself in a narrow, subterranean vault, which leads to the back of the villa. Remain quietly there until I apprise you that you are safe. When you have acted as I bid you, do not, however, forget to replace the stone upon the hole, and I will manage in such a way that you will not be molested.

CHAPTER XLIX.

WHERE SATANIELLO AVAILS HIMSELF OF THE GIPSY'S ADVICE, AND WHERE IT SHOWS THAT HE ACTED WISELY IN ABIDING BY IT, CONSIDERING THE ARRIVAL OF A DETACHMENT OF SOLDIERS, WHO TURNED OUT TO BE NO FRIENDS OF HIS.

WITH the swiftness of an arrow Sataniello wished Rebecca a temporary farewell.

He lifted the stone to which she had alluded, and

he saw an aperture which was sufficiently large to enable him to allow his body to fall through it.

Having placed the stone on one side, he allowed his feet to go down foremost, and when he found that his shoes were upon the ground, he looked around him.

He could not see where the subterranean path where he was would conduct him to; but implicitly relying upon Rebecca's words, he endeavoured to pull the stone over his head, so as to hide the hole through which he had effected an entrance.

For five or six seconds he was unable to succeed in his task, but ultimately he was successful in carrying it out.

"Oh, thanks be to heaven!" Rebecca muttered. "Now he is safe. I cannot help loving that young man—that bold Sataniello."

She was thus musing, when she heard a rustle among the trees which surrounded her, and immediately afterwards she distinguished the uniforms of half a dozen soldiers, who were evidently in search of some one.

Rebecca in no way appeared discountenanced by their appearance.

They were close upon her, but not so near as that she could yet hear the sounds of their voices.

So, heeding them not, she looked down the well, and assumed the same meditative, thoughtful, stooping position from which Sataniello had withdrawn her.

While thus engaged, she began to sing a country ballad, which doubtless had been taught to her in the days of her childhood.

Willingly would we reproduce the verses; but, as they were in her mother-tongue—namely, the Italian language—our readers would not understand the meaning of them; and, as anything loses a great deal of its beauty by being subjected to the process of translation, we will content ourselves by saying that the song dwelt upon a very old subject, which, however, is always new—namely, that of a mother who, having lost her child, was in search of it.

She had scarcely concluded the last verse of it in a melancholy tone of voice, when she was accosted by the sergeant of the detachment.

Her fears, we see, concerning Sataniello had proved true.

"My good woman," he said, in a harsh tone of voice, addressing Rebecca, "you are indulging here in a song which is rather appropriate to the motive which brings us here. You are singing about a mother in search of a child. Behold men in search of a murderer—of a bandit—of a miscreant called Sataniello!"

The marks of the utmost astonishment appeared upon Rebecca's features.

"I have heard that name before" she replied, innocently.

"You have? Where?"

"Late in the course of the night I was awoke by two soldiers from my sleep in this deserted—some say haunted—villa, where I have taken up my abode for want of a better spot to lay down my head. They awoke me from my slumber, and asked me whether I knew anything of the Boy Brigand, and, if I did, to tell them at once."

"What did you say to them?"

"What did I say?" Rebecca replied, repeating the sergeant's query, "that I did not know such a man."

"You never heard of such a man, eh?" the sergeant pursued.

"If I were to go such lengths I should be deviating from the truth," the gipsy pursued. "I have been travelling in the country for many years, and, of course, I have become acquainted from time to time with Sataniello doings"

"Did you ever see him?"

"No," Rebecca replied, boldly, "I did not."

"He was in this neighbourhood but an hour ago."

Rebecca appeared to be thunderstruck by the information.

"It is not wise, for one to remain about here," she pursued, slowly.

"Not if you have any treasures about you. He would very soon rid you of them. He is a nasty customer to have to deal with, and it would be a great boon if we could, through heaven's assistance, find his whereabouts."

"But he is generally accompanied by a large band, is he not?" Rebecca continued, playing with her words, as if she wished to impress the sergeant of the detachment with a firm belief that she had never set eyes in her life upon the Boy Brigand, whose life she had saved but an instant previously.

"He was wont to," one of the soldiers pursued; "but they are all scattered about now, and if we could get hold of the chief little doubt would remain about our capturing the others; but, if he is allowed to remain at liberty, ere long he will be up to his old game again."

"Where is the cavern? Perhaps he has returned to it!" the gipsy pursued, wishing to convince still more the armed men who stood before her that she was endeavouring to the utmost to give them such suggestions as might help them to accomplish successfully the important duty which devolved upon them.

"Only one man knew the road to the subterranean vaults where the Boy Brigand had for so long a time past managed to elude the pursuits of the police. That man is no more. He was one of Sataniello's lieutenants, and he turned king's evidence; but he failed in his attempt to take a revenge upon the captain, against whom he had a grudge for some wrongs which he had suffered at his hands. Yes, his lieutenant, Paublas, died from a death-wound inflicted upon him by the Boy Brigand, and the ends of justice have been defeated once more."

The soldier spoke like one who felt the importance of the post which he held, and he pronounced the last words in a steady, bold, and energetic loud voice.

Now, although Rebecca possessed in a very eminent degree that subtle art which very few are endowed with—namely, of restraining within her breast whatever feeling she might entertain—and whose face might be truly said to be a mask to conceal from strange eyes the deep thoughts of her mind, yet she could not prevent a smile from appearing upon her puckered lip when she heard the soldier conclude his speech.

"Nothing, I am sure," one of the soldiers began, "would afford greater pleasure to Ferdinand, our reigning king, than to be apprised of the Boy Brigand's capture, and I feel convinced that he who should be so fortunate as to secure him would be certain to get rapid promotion in the ranks of the corps to which he might belong."

"Well spoken, my boy," the gipsy pursued; "well spoken. I wish, indeed, I could in any way help you. I cannot do so now; but I may hear something in my wanderings across the country—for where brigands would fear to speak before a man or a well-to-do individual, they might act in a more free-and-easy manner towards a woman—an old gipsy like me. Alas! I should be too glad to have reason to apprehend the Boy Brigand's approach. Had I anything to lose—but I have spent many years in begging, and not a scudi have I been able to place by yet. They would not think me a victim worth their trouble. Having nothing to plunder, they would look down upon me. But from humble sources sometimes very important information may spring. If I were ever to fall across Sataniello what would you have me to do, Mr. Sergeant? I have not the strength or the power to capture him, and an attempt of that kind would only be useless, and its folly find its retaliation in a sudden death."

Rebecca uttered these words in a slow, genuine manner, which won for her the sympathies of her listeners.

Even had they had any suspicion relating to what she had said (and such was not the case) they would have been dispelled like a shadow by the lengthy statement that Rebecca made, and by her forlorn position in the world.

When she paused, at the conclusion of her speech, the sergeant was overcome with delight, and unable to resist the temptation which such an opportunity presented for him to express his ideas. He leant upon the gipsy's shoulder, and, in an under-whisper, he told her that if she would give him at any time such information as would lead to the apprehension of Sataniello, he would give her a share in the profit derived from the reward offered.

"That is enough," she replied, and her eyes sparkled with intense delight.

The soldier noticed the marks of satisfaction which appeared upon the gipsy's features, and he mistook it for the pleasure which she experienced at being made acquainted with such a tempting offer as that which he had made to her; while, if we are candid, we must admit that they were provoked entirely by the undivided satisfaction at having been so successful in baffling their researches—in placing them off their guard—thereby rendering her *protége's* freedom more certain.

"It is no use, then," one of the soldiers pursued, "to remain here any longer, sergeant. Let us beat the paths in the neighbourhood which are less frequented. We may full soon be better rewarded for our exertions than we have hitherto been; and if we do not to-day make Sataniello our prisoner, maybe we may capture some of his many followers, who, to obtain a free pardon, may be persuaded to throw more light upon his mysterious whereabouts."

"I would advise you, my friends," Rebecca said, in a humble voice, "to look after the Boy Brigand in the middle of the night. I should say that he fears the light of heaven, and in every countenance that he meets fancies he sees that of an enemy. When the darkness of night surrounds us, that is the time, I would say, that he sallies forth."

"There is a good deal of truth in what you say, my good woman," the sergeant replied, "I am thankful for your advice. I daresay we shall, ere long, cross the same path again. For the present, farewell."

And the soldier shook hands affectionately with the old gipsy.

"Attention!" he said.

The soldiers all ranged themselves on the edge of the path, which was wide and long enough to allow at least a dozen men to stand abreast of each other.

The sergeant, however, had only acted as he did to show off his military power, and to impress Rebecca—with whom he had had rather a lengthy conversation—with the authority which he possessed.

For the detachment could not keep together, and they soon had to walk together anyhow, as they had to sally forth beneath umbrageous pines, or trave

THE BOY BRIGAND AS THE MARQUIS PIATELLI.

regardless of the heat, the base of the rocks that crowned the shore.

Rebecca remained on the spot where the soldiers left her so long as she could gaze upon the uniforms of the soldiers whom she had so cleverly dealt with ; and, when she had satisfied her mind that they were far away, and her movements in no way watched by any living soul, she wended her way towards the stone through which Sataniello had descended.

It would be impossible to convey to our readers the anxiety which filled the breast of the Boy Brigand as he remained in the subterranean vault wherein he had entered.

The expectation of seeing Rebecca, and of having been told by her that he was safe, agitated him with impatient joy and trembling hope, which still increased as the minutes flew by, and as he approached a small stone staircase, which, doubtless, led to some back entrance of the haunted villa.

Had Sataniello been of a superstitious tone of mind he would have been in a very uncomfortable position during the whole time which he had to remain in that vault, surrounded by nothing but the most intense darkness, and he more than once compared his temporary hiding-place to the damp cells where culprits are thrown to await their doom.

Rebecca fell upon her knees, and, having assumed a stooping position, she called out to Sataniello to walk straight before him until he would reach the staircase about which we have already spoken.

———

CHAPTER L.

WHICH DESCRIBES THE SECOND PART OF SATANIELLO'S INTERVIEW WITH THE GIPSY, AND WHERE SATANIELLO PROPOSES AND REBECCA DISPOSES.

FAINTLY did the gipsy's words reach his ears.

However, he caught the meaning of her words, and, having given her a suitable answer to her request, he awaited in deep suspense her arrival.

The minutes appeared hours to him.

At length he heard a noise, which sounded to him very much like a door running upon its hinges; the light of day dawned upon him, and face to face he found himself before the gipsy.

"In that vault where you have been," Rebecca said, "it is rumoured that the late inhabitant of this villa buried his wife. The soldiers sent after you did doubtless forget the occurrence, or they would certainly have inspected it.

"They would, I feel convinced, have met with a fate which they could not have bargained for, and, if one had ventured within it no one would have renewed the attempt. I had thought of that myself, and I was fully prepared to dispatch with my poniard any one who should have been bold enough to undertake the duty. However, it is all for the best; and now, Rebecca, let me thank you for what you have done for me.

Words would fail to convey the gratefulness which Sataniello experienced. For a few instants he was unable to speak, so full was his heart, so deeply did he value the preservation of his freedom.

"It would not be wisdom," the gipsy pursued, "if, after your narrow escape, you were to lay yourself open to your presence being detected here. Were you to be discovered under this roof you may guess the punishment which would await us both. Longer than you can help you must not stay here; and, once you have made your mind up about your future plans, away you are bound to go."

"Do you wish me to go at once?"

"Certainly not."

"When?"

"When it shall be deemed advisable."

"Would you object to my going back to the cavern?"

"Not if you did not remain there long. But I can see no reason for your doing so, as the approaches to the place are sure to be closely watched, although the soldiery have, perhaps, not yet found the way to its entrance."

"But what am I to do, Rebecca, I ask you again?"

As he spoke, the marks of the utmost anxiety appeared upon the bold features of the Boy Brigand.

"I am without any means. All my wealth—at least, the greater part of it—is buried in my mountainous home. It is true that Joanitta's mother has placed in the bank whatever I can call my own; but I should have to go to Rome, and there my features are known. I should incur too great a risk of being recognised to attempt it just now."

"There is the city of Naples which stretches at your feet. Why not strike the iron while it is hot? No one would ever dream that you dared to appear in the city, and, shortly, all suspicion might be removed. Have you ever been there before?"

"I have," Sataniello replied; and, subsequently, he related to the gipsy his interview with the manager of the Royal Neapolitan Bank, his casual meeting with the Marquis of Piatelli. In a few hurried sentences he detailed to her the series of interesting events which we have narrated to our readers in previous chapters.

"Why not assume the name and rank of the Marquis of Piatelli?" the gipsy said. "That nobleman is dead. Who will there be to prove that you are not he?"

"His family. His connexion must be very large, and they would soon find out that I am only an imposter."

Sataniello was now standing in the middle of the room, and, as the gipsy gazed upon his aristocratic gait, his gentlemanly demeanour, and his handsome features, she could not but think that there were many noblemen in the land who would have willingly parted with a few of their broad acres could they by that means obtain the many attractions which made of the Boy Brigand no vulgar-looking being.

"I know a good deal more about the Piatelli family than you will probably give me credit for," Rebecca said. "He has no living relation in this country beyond a sister. But are you sure that the Marquis is dead?"

"This is rather a strange question coming from you, Rebecca," Sataniello replied. "The Marquis of Piatelli is dead. There can be no doubt about that. If he is not, I must confess that it will greatly astonish me, for he was hung, by the order of my lieutenant, Paublas, to a hook in one of the cells of the cavern, and is hanging, very likely, there still. Unless he is some unearthly being, for many days past he has gone to join his ancestors."

"I thought at first," Rebecca said, "that you would have no occasion to return to your old haunts; but I find that you will have to, although it would be folly for you to go just yet."

"The Marchioness of Piatelli is alive, though." Sataniello mused. "What should we do with her?"

"Oh, that is a matter easily arranged."

"You take that very easy."

"Because it is one of those stumbling-blocks easily removed."

"The Marchioness of Piatelli!"

"Yes, the Marchioness of Piatelli," Rebecca replied. "You surely must be very innocent and very green, my boy, if you are up to this period unacquainted with the ways which are resorted to in Italy to get rid of female relatives who obstruct one's way."

"You do not imply to poison her?" Sataniello inquired, anxiously.

"Not exactly."

"I do not see any other loophole open to me by which I can dismiss such a woman from this world."

"Think, will ye," Rebecca pursued.

Sataniello mused for awhile.

"I am at a loss to make out your meaning," he replied, slowly.

"You have deceived me in the opinion which I held of you," the gipsy replied. "I took you to be a quick-minded youth. I suggest one thing, and your mind reverts at once to murder."

"It strikes me that that is the only way by which any one could be placed out of the way."

"Those are foul means, which lead to the gallows," Rebecca continued, sternly. "Young man, you have sinned enough already. Why sin any more."

"I do not wish to do so unless compelled; and if I am to assume the rank and title of the Marquis of Piatelli—if I am to present myself to the court of the reigning king—I must be fully prepared to do so. I must act in such a manner as to remove suspicion of any kind, and to be so thoroughly and so strongly installed in my new guise as to render it impossible for others to give me the lie. If I am to be the Marquis of Piatelli I intend to be no sham nobleman. Whether such a bold step can be carried out with success appears uncertain to me."

"Stranger things than this have been wrought ere now by the hand of an intellectual man," Rebecca pursued. "Sataniello, if I placed in your head such an enterprising plan, it is because you are remarkably well adapted, in more ways than one to carry out a critical part."

"I respect you, Rebecca," Sataniello replied, and I admire, nay, I dread you. What you prophesied ere now found a terrible confirmation in the death of one man. Is your foreboding to prove true also in my case?"

The gipsy took Sataniello's hand in hers.

She seemed to study the vein in the palm of it.

At first she smiled.

"Yes," she muttered, "I see a great deal of wealth awaiting you. But wait," she continued, still deeply engaged in her study, "do not allow your mind to have too sanguine expectations, for sometimes——"

She did not conclude her sentence.

Away from her she flung the hand of the Boy Brigand, who remained motionless, and hurriedly she rose from her seat.

"Ask me not your fate, Sataniello," she muttered, in a half audible voice. "In some instances I am able to discern the future—in others, God's gift to me is of no avail. From the signs which I see in you—this is wealth, happiness; but that's not to last for ever. I see death. I see blood also. What that means I cannot tell. If I could I would not, for I consider that I have no right to mar a few years of future bliss by sad revelations, provided I had any to make."

Attentively and deeply did Sataniello listen to the gipsy's words.

To resume the conversation, he asked, "What induced you to say just now that I was adapted in more ways than one to assume a title to which I have no right?"

"And how do you know that you have no right to it?" the gipsy inquired.

It would be impossible to adequately describe Sataniello's astonishment.

Not only his astonishment, but his delight, at hearing the gipsy utter her last phrase.

That he could be anything but an outcast had never entered his brain.

He had been brought up, as we have already said, by priests, and they had concealed from his ears his real birth.

He only knew what he had been told—namely, that his father had been a murderer, and suffered the last penalty of the law.

Who his mother was he had not any idea.

Hence his anxiety and suspense were kindled in no small way.

That it should have been so is natural enough, for we doubtless all know that the slightest hint given to us in the shape of our being entitled to some dignity or some fortune—to some boon which we do not expect—gratifies our vanity and excites our curiosity.

It is not to be wondered at, then, by our readers, that Sataniello's anxiety was at its culminating point, and that fixedly and steadfastly he kept his piercing glance bent upon the gipsy's features, and was awaiting the instant when she would make to him some revelation which might place him in possession of valuable knowledge.

CHAPTER XLI.

WHERE REBECCA WILL NOT SPEAK SO FAR AS SATANIELLO WOULD WISH HER—AND WHERE THE BOY BRIGAND IS UNCERTAIN AS TO THE LINE OF CONDUCT WHICH HE SHOULD FOLLOW.

PREVIOUS to speaking Rebecca seemed to collect her thoughts.

It was evident that she was pondering upon that which she was about to communicate to Sataniello, who, in a standing attitude, remained before the gipsy as motionless as a statue, and fearing to breathe, in dread that any of his movements might have the effect of staying the motion of Rebecca's speech.

The gipsy wished to consider deeply ere she uttered a single syllable, not caring to commit herself by any untoward revelation, which at some future period she might have to withdraw.

Had any one of our readers been placed in the same position as that of Sataniello what would have been his feelings?

He knew no more than ourselves what was really his parentage.

There, before him, a gipsy, attired in humble garb, was about to acquaint him with some important communication, the gist of which he could not fathom.

The words of Rebecca rang in his ears.

Could he really have any right to the Marquisate of Piatelli?

Had he murdered one man to step into his wealth and his sumptuous position?

Oh, if he could have compelled the gipsy to speak but he dared not.

Once or twice Rebecca opened her lips, and yet she spoke not.

Was she taking an infinite pleasure in prolonging the young man's suspense?

If such was the case, why have given hopes which were not to be realized?

Sataniello waited as long as he possibly could; but at length his feelings gave way.

The gipsy now placed her head within her hands, and appeared to be plunged in deep reflection.

Gently he advanced towards her, and laid his hand upon her shoulder.

"Rebecca," he muttered, in a soft tone of voice, "why do you keep so silent? What you have just said has filled me with the greatest anxiety. The beginning of your words has filled my mind with an indescribable craving to know more. Do speak, I beseech you. I long to become acquainted with the secrets which you have discovered."

The gipsy glanced at the Boy Brigand, and a smile appeared upon her lips.

"Suppose," she said, "that there is a secret attached to your birth which it would be dangerous to reveal. Suppose that one's own life depended upon it."

"Oh! why, if you did not intend to speak, why have you kindled hopes within me?"

"I have not, that I know of," the gipsy replied; "but, if you give to my words a meaning which I did not wish to convey, you are at liberty to form your own conclusions."

"You are not speaking true," the Boy Brigand pursued, quickly, "for you ought not to fear revealing anything to me. Bad, indeed, must be the opinion which you hold of me if you think that I would ever betray you. No, such is not the way of showing my gratitude. I would sacrifice my life for you if you wanted it. Say one word. Command me to sally forth upon any excursion, however dangerous, you will not find me backward in doing so. You secured my freedom to-day. How shall I ever be able to repay such a service I know not; but believe me, Rebecca, you have not obliged one who will turn ungrateful. If an occasion ever comes to pass where my blood is required to be shed for you willingly will I do so."

"Sataniello," the gipsy replied, "I have allowed

you to give full vent to your feelings to hear what you would say. I always try to judge those whom I would serve ere I take too great an interest in them. If I was the means to-day of saving you from the hands of those who were sent in pursuit of you, I did so because you scornfully rejected, months ago, the dastardly proposal made by one of your band to take away the life of a poor harmless woman. One good turn deserves another. You have not found me wanting. But a great deal more than what I have done lies in my power. I possess a knowledge which no one can gainsay, because I have with me the proofs of what I may assert. But, if I do speak, what guarantee have I that you will not, like the remainder of common mortals, forget me—and once that you are, owing to my means, placed in a higher position, how can I answer for your gratitude?"

"Rebecca," the Boy Brigand replied, "'tis enough. I do not think that I am justified in listening to your speech a moment longer. If, notwithstanding the protestation which you have heard me utter, so strong are your doubts about my gratitude that you will persist in talking as you have done, my presence here is not required?"

Thus speaking, Sataniello directed his steps towards the door.

The Boy Brigand was at a loss to make out the gipsy's meaning, and he uselessly endeavoured to account for the sudden change which came over her.

Sataniello was about to leave the room where the gipsy sat.

Ere, however, he did so, he turned around to bid her farewell.

"Truly you are a foolish boy," she said. "Whither are you going?"

"I know not what to do," Sataniello replied, in an under tone of voice. "Your manners are really so strange, the opinion which you hold of me is so very poor, that I wish to leave your sight."

"Are you taking matters so haughtily as all that, Sataniello?" the gipsy pursued. "I fancy that you are getting rather independent all at once, and, from a few words which escaped from my lips, you have suddenly found an audacity which I must confess I do not admire."

Rebecca pronounced these words in a sharp, peremptory tone of voice.

"I am truly sorry," Sataniello replied, "if I have offended you, but I felt hurt by your silence; at first you take an immense interest in me, and subsequently you act towards me as if I were a loathsome stranger to you. What have I done to alter so suddenly the current of your thoughts? Inwardly, something told me, and tells me still, that you possess some secret which you fear to reveal, and that you know more about my birth than myself; for beyond the remembrance of my boyish days, I cannot recall to my mind anything which would warrant me to hope that the son of a man who died upon the gallows for some terrible murder can ever lay claim to the title of a proud marquis. But, Rebecca, throughout this day, and since I set eyes upon you, towards me you have behaved nobly indeed; and if you can place me in a channel to discover that I am not doomed ever to remain a forlorn outcast, tracked from homestead to homestead, from mountain to mountain, oh, do speak!"

Rebecca listened attentively to Sataniello, who uttered his sentences with such deep fervour, with such anxious rapidity, that ere long she replied—

"Do you remember my advice to you?"

"To go to Naples under the assumed name of the Marquis of Piatelli?"

"Yes, that is what I wish to revert to."

"Nothing would afford me more satisfaction, Rebecca," the Boy Brigand replied; "but ere I do so, I must first ascertain what has become of the sister?"

"That is certainly one of the steps which you should take. Doubtless, she has returned to Naples, and if she has already done so, she has certainly acquainted the authorities with her brother's doom; and if, on the other hand, she may have been detained by some of your followers; if she has, your path is clear."

"Clear for awhile," Sataniello replied; "but I could not leave her in the hands of my followers. Although they seldom interfere with a woman's virtue, still for all that the Marchioness is a very handsome senorita, and I would not a man——"

And the Boy Brigand would doubtless, in his anxiety to speak, have forgotten that he was addressing one before whom such a conversation was far from being suitable, when he suddenly stopped short.

Notwithstanding the disparity of age which existed between Sataniello and Rebecca the Gipsy, who was considerably older than him—comparatively speaking, a youth—she could not help giving way to a smile at Sataniello's allusion.

Indelicate conversation should never be indulged by sober, good people; and we do not doubt but what Sataniello would never have hinted what he did, had he not felt convinced that the conclusion which he thought of was very likely to occur were the senorita thrown entirely at the mercy of such men as those who had formed his gallant band.

"You spoke before now," Sataniello said, "of some means by which the senorita might be cast off and disposed of in such a manner as not to be able to interfere with my plans; were she to regret too deeply her brother's death ever to forget that I was the first author of his captivity, and that upon me ought to fall her revenge. As yet you have given me no reply: would you enlighten me upon that point now?"

"There are such places as convents in this country."

"I know that; and among my followers I had a recruit, who escaped from a seminary where he was about being educated for a priest."

"Rather a wide difference between a priest and a brigand," Rebecca ejaculated.

"Yes," the Boy Brigand replied; "and up to the time we were together, it seems extraordinary to say, has preferred the latter calling."

These being matters which were not worthy of the two beings' attention, the merits and demerits of the Monk's inclinations were not further discussed, and the subject was soon set aside by Sataniello, who returned to the project which he was bent upon carrying out, namely, to go to Naples in the guise of a marquis.

He wished, however—and in acting thus he deserved the highest commendation—to shape all his plans in such a manner as to ensure success.

"Ere now, Rebecca," the Boy Brigand went on "you advised me to become the Marquis of Piatelli; there will be numerous obstacles in my way; I know that, yet I am able to face them all."

"I am acquainted with the whole of the Piatelli family," Rebecca pursued; "and I can tell you that which you, perhaps, had no idea of, namely, that the man whom you captured, and was subsequently placed to death by your lieutenant, holds a very important post at the court of the King of Naples."

"All the better for me."

"True."

"But that makes my undertaking still more dangerous."

"I am fully conscious of that, my friend, "but you would not flinch, I hope?"

"I flinch! oh, never!"

And thus speaking, Sataniello rose to his full height; and then, in looking on his proud and noble countenance, one would indeed have been led to believe that there was some patrician blood running within his manly frame.

Whether there was or not, remains to be seen in our next chapter.

CHAPTER LII.

WHICH DESCRIBES A LONGER INTERVIEW THAN THE PREVIOUS ONES BETWEEN REBECCA AND THE BOY BRIGAND, AND WHICH RELATES HOW IT WAS ONCE MORE INTERRUPTED BY A NEW COMER.

"Now that you have waited patiently for my convenience," Rebecca resumed, "I will tell you, Sataniello, why I spoke as I did."

The Boy Brigand was listening attentively.

"I dare say," the gipsy pursued, "that you will be very much astonished at what you are about to hear."

Sataniello did not require to give an answer, for his countenance betrayed his anxiety.

"Do you not," she said, "remember any incidents connected with your early days?"

"Beyond what I have already told you, I am in the greatest ignorance of who I am."

"You know, I suppose, that your father was executed for a foul murder?"

"I also cannot forget that," Sataniello replied, in a most melancholy tone; "too often has it been a reproach to me."

"Well, notwithstanding that cloud on your name, there may yet be happiness in store for you."

Rebecca pronounced these words in a low, subdued tone of voice.

"Happiness!" Sataniello ejaculated, "do you speak true, Rebecca? are you not playing with me like a child with a toy?"

"When matters of importance are at stake, you will not find me guilty of such cruelty."

"Well, well! I am listening."

"'Tis enough. Do not interrupt me now, I will begin."

Sataniello breathed heavily.

He felt that he was about to hear that which he was so anxious to become acquainted with.

"The circumstances connected with your birth are strange indeed," the gipsy said; "and if they were related in a fairy-book they would not be out of place there. Impelled by all the mad and bitter disappointment of despair, hurled to act as he did by hunger, your father murdered a cardinal of the name of Lottaringi. He was famished, and he did so to procure for his emaciated body a morsel of bread which he needed to sustain his existence. The cardinal slain, he attempted to have recourse to a hasty flight, when he was prevented from so doing by the sudden appearance of a Roman mad girl called Leonora."

"That was my mother, I know!" the Boy Brigand ejaculated. "The world, doubtless would be hard and bitter against me were I led to the scaffold for the deeds which I have perpetrated, but I am not so much to blame; I acted as I did through sheer want."

"Never mind about the motives which prompted you," the gipsy pursued; "this is not a fitting occasion to palliate your guilt; you do not stand before a judge; you are before a woman who wishes to do you good, and who is endeavouring to place you in a position to achieve her aim."

Sataniello bounded towards the gipsy, and he clasped her wrinkled hands to his lips.

"'Tis sweet," he muttered, "in this wide, wide world, to meet with one like you! 'Tis sweet to hear a friendly voice when all others are raised to accuse and condemn him! I am a felon, and yet, Rebecca, you do not desert me!"

"Here you interrupt me again," the gipsy pursued; "why do you constantly stay the thread of my narrative; the hours pass by, and the time flies on, and you should not delay my speech. Every minute ought to be an object to you; will you remain silent?"

The Boy Brigand shook his head in the affirmative.

The gipsy then resumed.

"Who was that Leonora, the Roman mad girl, 'the mad, crazy, Leonora,' as she was called by the people that dwelt in the neighbourhood?"

The Boy Brigand doubtless would have here spoken had he not remembered the caution which had been given him but a few minutes ago by the gipsy.

Prudently he kept his lips closed.

"Well, I will tell you who she was; a great deal depends upon this. She was the only daughter of the elder branch of the Piatelli family. In the event of her marrying, her son would have become that nobleman. People said she did not. People said that she had an abhorrence to matrimony, and that her madness consisted more in giving herself away to the handsome peasants whom she met in her wanderings. That was her folly—that was her disease. Leonora had passions—a burning and feverish nature that no indulgence, however freely enjoyed in the pleasures of Cupid, could satiate. Thus she was not known or admitted in the society of her equals. She met your father, the padre, and she lived with him, and they never were married, at least people say so. When your father died, you were not yet born; and when Leonora died, there was one person by the side of her couch, and to that person she revealed a secret upon which a great deal depends. It did not suit that person who assisted to her dying moments to divulge the knowledge which she possessed at the time. She allowed the woman to be buried; she allowed her son to be educated; she allowed him to become a bandit. She permitted all these things to pass; she permitted the late Marquis's of Piatelli's father to assume a title to which he came by his right of heir-at-law. She kept silent all this while, because the time had not yet come. But only fancy this, Sataniello, what would be the result had Leonora been married by a priest who could confirm the truth of that marriage? What would be the result if a certificate of such a marriage could be found? Why, the fate of certain people, it strikes me, would be greatly altered. It would be a fine day for the son of Leonora!"

Here Rebecca indulged in a loud laugh, which went keenly to Sataniello's heart.

"That woman is bitter, indeed," he muttered, "if she speaks false."

"Yes," Rebecca resumed, "what would be the result, I wonder?"

As she uttered these last words she looked towards the Boy Brigand.

"That's impossible. What Rebecca says cannot be true," Sataniello muttered.

The old woman seemed to guess the thoughts which came over the Boy Brigand's mind—and yet she spoke not.

Sataniello felt his heart beating within his breast with quick palpitations. His hand trembled, and a dizzy sensation came over his brain.

If he was proved the legitimate son of Leonora, oh, what would be his joy. Oh, if he could only lay righteous claim to the Marquisate. But no, there are some incidents in men's lives which are too heavenly ever to be indulged in. That he could face the world in another guise than that of a felon and an outcast could never be.

Gently he knelt by the gipsy, and he besought her again to speak.

"The time has not yet come," she said, "to reveal the truth, Sataniello. Remain under what impression you choose. The idea that you may be better than what you are may give you courage and strength; but this day you will hear no more."

For the third time, at least, since Sataniello's interview with Rebecca, he was disappointed.

"Rebecca knows too much of the world," she said, suddenly, "to part with a treasure which she possesses on the strength of some promises. The day that you can bring to the old gipsy five thousand pounds—she asks no more, she will never hint that which might be—then she will speak out, not before. All she has said may only be supposition. She may have indulged in some wayward dream. Sataniello, this is my last advice, go to Naples as the Marquis of Piatelli."

The words which the gipsy had spoken gives renewed strength to the Boy Brigand.

He could easily have been compared to some convict who, lying under the sentence of death, expects every instant to see the executioner coming to conduct him to the scaffold, and who, instead of that doom which he anticipated, is made acquainted with his reprieve.

"Thank heaven, Rebecca," he said, "thanks."

"For what?" the gipsy inquired.

"For the speech which you have uttered."

"But I have told you nothing yet."

She accentuated the word "yet" as if there was a good deal in the word.

"I know that," he replied, suddenly.

"Why thank me, then?"

"Because you have poured balsam upon my breast."

"This knowledge affords me no slight satisfaction," the old woman replied; "but you have heard my conditions?"

"I should not forget them if I lived a hundred years."

"They are not very hard ones."

"I admit that?"

"What are a few thousands?"

"Very little."

"And do you place credence in me?"

"Would not one in my position do so? Ask the shipwrecked mariner who has been saved by some miraculous means—ask him when he has reached the shore in safety whether the word hope ever left his breast? Ask him whether there is not hope in a man's heart as long as life is not extinct? Ask him whether he has not scanned the horizon, if cast upon a lonely spot, scanning the broad expanse, ex-pecting to see in the distance some sail which might come to his rescue. Hope is in my breast still, Rebecca. You are terrible, you are cruel—bitterly so, too. You possess a knowledge—I know you do—and you will not acquaint me with it. But never mind."

Sad and low was the intonation of Sataniello's voice when he concluded his sentence.

The gipsy's lips quivered. It seemed as if she was about to speak.

At that moment sounds of footsteps were heard without.

Gradually they became plainer.

"Fly away," Rebecca said. "Fly away from this spot."

"I will not," he replied. "I scorn your advice, Rebecca. Inwardly I feel that it is not a foe who is coming. For days past I have met enemies—shall I ever see a friend?"

"You are raving."

"I am not."

"Will you persist in remaining here?"

"I will."

"You will not go?"

"No."

"Only think."

"I do not care."

"Will you go?"

"I will not."

"It may be the soldiers who are coming back."

"Never mind."

"You are distracted."

"You have rendered me so."

"Will you fly, I repeat?"

"I say I will not."

"I will divulge the secret."

"I do not wish to know it yet."

"What do you say?"

"You have blighted my hopes."

"And are you ready to be taken a prisoner?"

"I am?"

"Why so?"

"Because you will speak then."

"How do you make that out?"

"If I am the son of the Marquis!"

"Well, what then?"

"You will want your reward."

"But you are a felon now."

"Alas! I know that."

The sounds of footsteps were gradually becoming plainer and plainer, and Sataniello was about to choose the means of escaping. He was quickly endeavouring to do so, when a joyful exclamation escaped his lips.

Rapidly Rebecca looked towards the entrance.

What was her astonishment.

She saw Sataniello clasping his arm round the neck of the new comer.

"Oh! Captain, I am so glad to meet you."

"Where are you coming from like this?"

"I knew I should find you at last."

"Your forebodings have at length come to pass."

"Take a seat, man. You seem to be tired."

"I am. I have been walking for two days."

"Tell us all about what occurred soon after my departure."

"Time enough for that."

"Well, then, come on."

"Where?"

"Close to this good lady."

"Who is she?"

"Do you not remember Rebecca the Gipsy?"

"Oh, of course, I do."

"Well, I will introduce you to her."

And, thus speaking, Sataniello led the Monk, for it was he, by the side of Rebecca, who was too much thunderstruck to say a word in reply.

These were thrown together once more, the Boy Brigand and the Monk, and then, ere he sallied forth on his errand, Sataniello met a companion whom he was far from expecting at so critical a moment.

CHAPTER LIII.

WHICH REPRODUCES, WORD FOR WORD, THE CONVERSATION WHICH THE BOY BRIGAND AND THE MONK HAD TOGETHER.

THE appearance of the Monk at the time when we saw him in the last chapter is one instance of the extraordinary and wayward current of events.

It is useless to say here that the Boy Brigand could not have dreamt of going to Naples by himself, because it is well known by all that a Marquis, whether it be in this country or in any other, never travels without a retinue of servants.

There are exceptional cases, of course; but when one is bent, like Sataniello, upon the bold undertaking which he was, to prevent suspicion it is as well to conform with the existing customs.

Besides, we must remember that the Monk was the Boy Brigand's confident and factotum. Without him he would have been loth, indeed, to venture to Naples; and, had he not made his appearance, it is very probable that, notwithstanding the gipsy's advice, he would have gone in search of him.

There were also several motives which would have induced Sataniello to return for awhile, at least, to his mountainous home, if he did not intend to remain there; and that was the wish which he had of facing once more his brave followers.

That he must have lost some of his *prestige* in their eyes he could not but admit, having had recourse to his hasty flight; and he also could not but persuade himself that his behaviour on that occasion was far from being in accordance with the high opinion by which he was held by all, owing to which he was so respected.

Had it not been for his dearest Joanitta, it is scarcely worth saying what, doubtless, everyone has thought, namely, that he would have held his ground and fought until the last.

This step would have been certainly nobler than the one he took; and had he had only but himself to look after, surely he would have abided by it.

But there was Joanitta and the youthful heir to Don Saltara's dukedom; and he deserves to be highly commended, in our opinion, for having secured so valuable a prize.

When the Monk had appeared, Rebecca had kept silent.

"Can I speak before her?" the Monk asked from the Boy Brigand, in an under whisper.

"You may fairly do so. She will not betray us," Sataniello replied.

And here he related to the Monk the events which had taken place since his departure.

"Captain," the Monk pursued, "I have a great many things to tell you."

"I am aware of that," Sataniello replied. "Go on."

"'Twas a frightful night, was it not, Captain?" the Monk pursued, alluding to that memorable evening on which Sataniello had been attacked.

"Do not talk about it."

"You settled Paublas at last."

"I am heartily glad of it!"

"Some say that he might not be dead yet."

"What do you mean?"

"The Hunchback told us so."

"I would not believe him."

"He escaped before."

"Yes; but I saw him fall into the chasm."

"Did you?"

"It must be all up with him."

"Could he have clung to some of the stones?"

"It is hard to say."

"Did you look downwards?"

"I never did."

"Do you think the others did?"

"I should say not."

"But if he is alive?"

"What then?"

"He may renew his attempt."

"Oh, Captain, I should not fear about that!"

"What would you do?"

"Well, I do not know!"

"I have an idea."

"You have?"

"Yes."

"What is that?"

"Would you come back to the cavern?"

"If you could show me any use for doing so."

"If you fear Paublas being alive still, why not ascertain?"

"How could that be done?"

"Easily enough."

"We might get a long rope."

"Yes."

"And what then?"

"Well, you might lower me down."

"To the bottom of the abyss?"

"Yes."

"And what would be the use of that?"

"I could ascertain whether his body is there."

"If it is?"

"Well, you would be satisfied."

"Of course I should be."

"If it is not?"

"You would know that you have some one to fear."

"This is not a bad plan."

"Will you carry it out?"

"Not just yet."

"Why?"

"Because I think that Paublas received a wound in the forehead from which people do not often recover; and because I think it would not be wise."

"You do not?"

"No.

"Who would prevent us?"

"No one except the soldiers — and they are troublesome sometimes."

"Do you think the outskirts and the cavern are watched?"

"Not a doubt about that."

"Are you positive?"

"As far as my eyesight has trusted me, I am."

"What say you, then?"

"We must dismiss that plan for the present."

"Will you return to it?"

"At some future period."

"If we deem it necessary."

"Is that settled?"

"Perfectly."

"There is a better game than that on the cards, my friend," Sataniello pursued, when he had heard the Monk's suggestion.

"You astonish me."

"Why?"

"Because you are such an extraordinary man, Captain. You are always up to something or another. That visit of ours to Don Saltara's castle was a rare bit of spree."

"You misbehaved yourself there."

"What do you mean, Captain?"

"I mean to say, that Maria will have more occasion then one to repent of your stay there at the castle."

"Captain, you make me blush."

"It would take a good deal to do that."

"I am sure you seduced that poor girl."

A smile appeared upon the Monk's lips.

"Seduced her! when, and where?"

"Shall I tell you the exact time?"

"I should like to know."

"One morning I went downstairs—"

"I did not see you."

"But I did, though."

"Where was it?"

"In one of the great parlours. I opened the door, and I walked in; but you were so agreeably engaged, that I thought it would have been a pity to disturb you. But I cannot blame you; Maria was a deuced handsome maiden!"

"She had something better than her looks."

"What was that?"

"Oh, Captain! you want to know too much."

There are some things which would be spoiled by explanation.

"I am fully aware of that. But now, my friend, listen to me. If I have been wasting all this time upon a servant girl, I have an object in doing so."

"You have?"

"And I will tell it you."

"What is it?"

"Do you think that the girl was in love with you?"

"Maria! Maria, I rather should say so."

"How do you know?"

"Why, she cried all the night before I left."

"She did, eh?"

"I am sure of that."

"Did she tell you?"

"No; I saw her."

"Were you up with her all night?"

"Yes, Captain; and all the other besides."

"Well, then, to resume. Do you think she would meet you?"

"After what has occurred, I fear not."

"Do you mind trying?"

"I will do that."

"Do you know why I wish to do so?"

"I have no idea."

"Look at me."

"Yes, Captain."

"Do you see me?"

"I do."

"Well, do I look like a Marquis?"

"More like a Duke, I should say."

"No joking, sir, I am serious."

"Well, Captain, I tell you what I think. But why ask me?"

"Because for the future I am the Marquis of Piatelli."

"Oh, he is dead, and no mistake. I buried his body myself."

"You did?"

"Yes."

"But do not, I beg," Sataniello said, "tell me about what occurred yet. All in its place."

"Very good, Captain."

"I am going to Naples, I repeat."

"You are?"

"Yes."

"Now?"

"No."

"When?"

"Shortly. And I will go there holding the rank of the man whom the Hunchback caused to be hung."

"Will you take me with you?"

"Most decidedly."

"Do you understand me now!"

In reply to this query of his Captain the Monk gazed in wonder upon Sataniello. He had heard every word which he had uttered, and yet he could not make out how the fall of the chambermaid, Maria, could ever have anything to do with the Boy Brigand's projects; but he was a careful and a wise fellow, the Monk, and he waited patiently for his master's pleasure.

If, however, he were to forget the pretty maiden, he would, he resolved, take very good care to bring her name on the *tapis* again, so as to refresh Sataniello's recollection.

"Ere I do so, however," Sataniello resumed, ', I must see that all is fair and square."

"What shall I be, sir?"

"My aide-de-camp."

"By Santa Maria, that will just suit me, the Monk pursued. "Shall I have a uniform?"

"Oh, yes; something grand."

"And when do we start?"

"You are getting anxious, are you?"

"You may fancy so. Why, Captain, I do not know what would have become of me had I not met you."

Here Rebeccca returned to the room, which she had left when the Boy Brigand had brought the chambermaid's name in question. She held in her hand a jug full of a wine called Lacryma Christa, and sundry other provisions, which she knew would be eagerly partaken of by her two guests.

She was far from being wrong in her supposition, for the two men soon helped themselves to the luxuries which were spread before them on a table which stood in the corner of the room in a manner which told plainly to the gipsy that her kind hospitality was greatly relished by the recipients of it.

———

CHAPTER LIV.

WHICH DESCRIBES SEVERAL THINGS WHICH HAVE NOT BEEN TOLD BEFORE—WHICH SHOWS THAT OLD FRIENDS VERY SELDOM DISAGREE—AND FURTHER TELLS THE MANNER IN WHICH SATANIELLO TOOK LEAVE OF HIS ELDERLY ADVISER.

"I HAVE told what my plans are," Sataniello began, as soon as he had quenched his thirst out of the jug, and rising from the chair in which he had sat, and stretching out his arms like one who is perfectly satisfied with himself.

"And, if I were permitted to give an opinion," the Monk replied, "I should say that they meet entirely with my approval."

"Every man is entitled to put in his spoke," Sataniello pursued; "and if I was really and *bonâ fide* Marquis of Piatelli I would conduct myself in a liberal manner towards all those who might be depending on me. By so doing I should conciliate, not only the good will of my subordinates but win for myself the respect and good opinion of my equals and of my superiors."

THE BOY BRIGAND CAUGHT AT LAST.

"Hear, hear!" exclaimed the Monk, who was getting quite lively on the libation which he had partaken of. "Hear, hear, Captain!"

We are all of us—at least, if not all, the greater part of mankind—are addicted to flattery, and when he heard his companion's ejaculation, Sataniello smiled pleasantly.

"You and I are made to understand each other," the Boy Brigand pursued. "Although our natures are somewhat different, still we will pull together."

"We must do so, Captain, if we want to get on. Union makes strength, and the greater our number the more success will attend our enterprises."

"Wisely said," Sataniello pursued; "but ere I get you to relate to me what occurred after I left the cavern, I must settle every preparation now. You must, by hook or by crook, get Maria to join you in Naples."

"Very good, very good, Captain," the Monk replied. "Rest assured that nothing could afford me more pleasure than such an order on your part, and that I will do my best to carry it out you may safely rely. If the girl loves me I like her too; and, by those womanly attentions which the fair sex possess to such a degree, she was the means of rendering my stay at Don Saltara Castle one of the pleasantest times of my life. There I could not love her at my leisure; but, if she comes to Naples with me there

will be no one to control me, and I will go in for it like a Turk."

The Monk was not one of those stupid buffoons who amuse sometimes a large party at the expense of their own brains, and who are looked upon as crazy idiots; but he had a good deal of *naivete* about him, and is a youth that is not to be found fault with.

Thus he interrupted the most serious occasions in life with lively allusions.

As the Boy Brigand knew that his follower meant no harm, he would have been the last one to blame him, so he generally contented himself by bringing him back to the point from which he had wandered.

"Maria should come with us."

"I wish she may consent."

"I will tell you why."

"I wish you would."

"Because I shall have a large household."

"That of the late Marquis, I suppose?"

"Well, I expect so."

"But you will not keep them all?"

"By Jove, if I did! No, I know better. I will write to Naples, to the head steward, to dismiss them all."

"Will not that seem odd to him?"

"It may, certainly; but I cannot help myself."

"But would you not be recognised?"

"I dare say I should; but I must chance that."

"If you are, what will you do?"

"I shall take very good care not to be."

"If Maria comes she will be of great service?"

"Of course she will."

"She is a stylish girl."

"Just the one we want."

"Well, this is safely concluded."

"But how will you manage?"

"I cannot tell you now, Captain."

"You want to hear my plan first?"

"Just so."

"And act afterwards?"

"That is my intention."

"You speak very wisely, my friend," the Boy Brigand resumed; "but, ere I see what can be done, I would like you to tell me what became of the Marchioness of Piatelli and all my followers?"

"As far as I know I will answer you," replied the Monk. "Any question which you may please to ask of me will be faithfully replied to."

"I do not fear that," the Boy Brigand pursued; "but it is drawing towards night. With the long conversation which we have had we shall find ourselves soon in the dark."

"I would not advise you to remain here longer than you can help," Rebecca said, leaning upon the shoulders of the Boy Brigand. "Although I am not one who would give way to foolish fears, still, for all that, to be prudent is one of the things which you should study most."

"You are right, Rebecca, and your advice is very wholesome."

"You will, I feel convinced, not blame me for speaking as I do. You are welcome to remain beneath this roof as long as you like; but as it is—but after what has occurred this day—to do so would, to my mind, be sheer folly."

"Rebecca," the Boy Brigand pursued, "what would you have me to do? Now I am not a foolish youth, requiring the advice of every one and abiding by none; but I think that what you say is right."

"Go from this place then."

"Where, to Naples, at once?"

"No. You might spoil every fine opportunity through too much recklessness. Ponder well upon that which you intend to do. Consider before you leap, and you will find that all will go well. There is the Monk,—doubtless, you and he have a great many things to say to each other. Go, and remember my words."

"'Tis a very strange farewell on your part, Rebecca. I did not expect so much coolness from you."

"If I dismiss you thus summarily I have my reasons for doing so. Through your procrastination you may be detected. I am sure that I shall see the sergeant of the troop again here before nightfall; and, if one has been successful in eluding his pursuit, two might not be so lucky. But here, take this before you go. Rebecca is a woman of her word, and she keeps it."

"Keep your money, my good lady," the Monk said, on seeing the movement which the gipsy was making in endeavouring to force a big leather purse into Sataniello's hand.

"What right, man, have you to speak?" the gipsy asked, standing upright, and defying with her glances whatever attempt the Monk might make to reply to her.

"If I am bold enough to open my lips when not spoken to," the Monk replied, "I do so from a good motive, Madam. I have in my pockets more bank-notes than you can form any idea of; you must remember that I come from the cavern."

"How much have you got about you?" Sataniello now inquired of his follower.

"I have not reckoned the bank-notes yet, but there is a good many I know."

"That's another thing," the gipsy replied; "I am satisfied, and so, my friends, good-bye."

And thus speaking, the old woman held out her hand to the Boy Brigand.

He clasped it in his—"I am obliged to you, Rebecca; more so than I can express."

"Those are words which I like to hear, but do not forget my speech."

"I never could," Sataniello replied; "I will see you again ere long."

"Do not come here until you are somewhat settled."

"I promise you that, Rebecca; and now, good-bye."

"Good-bye," Rebecca answered.

And as the gipsy replied, she wended her way back to the villa, while the two men emerged into a different direction leading to the high road.

CHAPTER LV.

WHICH DESCRIBES WHAT THE BOY BRIGAND AND THE MONK DID AFTER THEIR DEPARTURE FROM THE GIPSY'S ABODE, AND ENTERS FULLY INTO WHAT HE HEARD FROM THE LIPS OF THE LANDLORD OF THE GREYHOUND, WAYSIDE INN.

"THAT is a good woman, that Rebecca," Sataniello began, as soon as the villa which he had just quitted had disappeared from his gaze.

"She is, but she has got odd ways about her."

"All gipsies have, more or less; but she has behaved well towards me."

"I do not think that I have any reason to complain either."

"Oh, yes, I forgot, by Jove! didn't you pitch into her grub!"

"I was terribly famished; I had not had a morsel for at least ten hours."

"How's was that? you were not in want of money, from your own account?"

"True enough; but as I have got a good deal, I wish to stick to it."

"Who would take it away from you?"

"No one knows; I do not like to go among people when I am so flush as I am now."

"What nonsense!"

"It is no nonsense. I might get tipsy in company, tell them what I am worth, and the next morning find myself pennyless."

"Have you taken to drinking?"

"Lately I have."

"How is that?"

"Why, since you left, we have all become rather addicted to the bottle. When you were with us, there was some one to keep control; and when they found themselves their own masters, they freely helped themselves to what they found in the cellar."

"That is their own look-out, not mine; but it will not do for us to remain here talking in this place. The country is tracked everywhere, and to see two individuals in such a solitary spot as this, if discovered, we should certainly be done for."

"What do you purpose to do, Captain?"

"Spend the night somewhere."

"Do you mean at a wayside inn?"

"I do."

"But we may be found there?"

"No we shall not, if we play our cards well, there is no doubt about that. The cavern is too far distant from here; we must alight somewhere."

"Where shall we go?"

"There is the Greyhound."

"That's a nice place."

"The landlord would not peach upon us?"

"That is to say, provided he knew who we were."

"But if he had his suspicions?"

"What about them; he must prove what he says."

"That's right enough."

"So come on."

The two old friends now walked on together along a narrow path which ran along the high road.

"I say, it would be rather awkward if we were to fall in with a detachment," Sataniello began, in a laughing mood.

"Do not be so pleasant about these serious things."

"There they come, I am sure, the Boy Brigand pursued. And he looked round as if he was afraid of being surprised.

"You blame me sometimes, Captain, for indulging too often in jokes, but I think that you occasionally are as bad as myself."

"There is some truth in what you state," Sataniello resumed, "but I am not so bad as yourself for all that. But let us hurry on."

The Monk hastened his steps.

"It would be as well to reach the Greyhound before it is quite dark; there is something suspicious about men who enter a house of public accommodation at this late hour."

"You have become wise all in a few days."

"I am glad to hear you say so, Captain."

"I always give the devil his due."

While speaking, the two men reached the outside of the Greyhound.

The grounds of it were strewn with men smoking. Some of them who held long whips in their hands, were about to continue their journey; others had just alighted, and were leading their horses to the stables.

There were carts, gigs, and vehicles peculiar to the country standing beneath an archway built for the purpose, and a long trough for horses to drink out of.

The Greyhound evidently did a good trade.

It was a well-known inn by those who travelled along that road.

The drinks were good, and no trouble was spared by the landlord to attend upon those who favoured him with their custom.

To such a public place Sataniello directed his steps.

On his right the Monk walked briskly on.

There was a stone staircase which led to the inside of the inn.

With a quick, light step Sataniello ascended it.

He had just arrived at the top of it, when he met the landlord.

"Good-day to you, Signor, at least, I should say good-evening. Can I do anything for you? I think your features are not unknown to me?"

"You might have seen me before," Sataniello replied. "I am occasionally about here; you are very crowded just now?"

"Yes, Signor," the innkeeper replied; "to-morrow is market-day, and all these people whom you see are going to carry their goods to town."

"Is your house full, then?"

"Oh, it has not come to that yet, but I daresay before evening it will be so. I hope we shall not be able to accommodate anyone after eleven o'clock; for if we are so far empty, we shall be compelled to take in soldiers.

"Take in soldiers; what for?"

Sataniello pronounced these words in so innocent a tone of voice, that the innkeeper explained to him alone the meaning of his words.

"And are you not aware, Sir, of what is taking place?"

"No, I am not."

"Why, King Ferdinand has doubled a reward offered for the apprehension of a bold bandit called Sataniello. Leave has been given to all who may to go in search of him; and, allured by the reward, the country-people are looking after him."

"Indeed!"

"And to give you an idea, Signor, within the last ten days no less than ten men have been arrested on suspicion, and conveyed to the prison at Naples. They have been subsequently released, and this is a regular house for spies. I am sorry to be compelled to admit that to you, Signor, but you are a gentleman, I can perceive that at a glance, and that is why I am so communicative."

"I am very much obliged for your information, I am sure," Sataniello replied, "but I do not think so much about brigands as other people do. I have travelled throughout Italy, and not once have I ever been attacked."

"You ought indeed to bless your stars, Signor; you were lucky indeed!"

"Do you know, my friend, that if they did not speak so openly about Sataniello, they would have a much better chance of capturing him. It is not likely that he would come to a public place like this. Methinks he would seek the solitude of the forest, and keep aloof."

"Some say he would, others say he would not. Now they related to me the other evening a thing which he did."

Here the landlord of the Greyhound related all the adventures which had befallen Sataniello at Don Saltara Castle.

While he was speaking, the Monk joined them.

When the landlord had concluded his narrative, to which Sataniello paid the greatest attention, he shook negatively his head.

"I do not believe a word about it, do you?"

"I did doubt for a long time; but when the thing is shown to you as clear as the sun at noonday, one must give in."

"And was it shown to you as plain as that?"

"Very nearly."

"In what way?"

"Simply enough; the whole details were given to me from the very lips of one of those who had seen Sataniello."

"Seen him!" the Boy Brigand ejaculated.

Now although Sataniello could be said to be endowed with a coolness which was really supernatural, the exclamation which he gave vent to would have been sufficient to kindle the suspicions of anyone who might have had the slightest doubts about his respectability.

But happily for himself, the innkeeper did not notice it.

"I am not telling you any very wonderful story. What I heard concerning Saraniello, or Sataniello, some name of that kind, you may reply upon. That party, who gave me all the information is the right party too! He is a gentleman of the name of Wogan, and if you wait here a day or two, you are as likely as not to see him. He is not a bad sort; he is an Englishman; but if he is so bitter against the Boy Brigand, he has his reasons for being so. It appears he snatched his child away from him, and has taken him God knows where; some say he smothered the poor creature."

It may easily be imagined by our readers how these words were received by the Boy Brigand and the Monk, and how anxious the former must have been to see Captain Wogan as soon as he should arrive!

"Captain Wogan is one of my best customers; he comes in here two or three times a week, and never goes away without uncorking at least three or four bottles of my best wine. He is the right sort of man for me."

Having concluded his sentence, the innkeeper rubbed his hands together; and having done so, clapped them one against the other, which was a sure sign with him that he had no more to say.

"And now, gentlemen, if you please, what can I do for you?"

A bow such as innkeepers indulge in followed this remark.

"I want two beds for the night, and a sitting room."

"Private, of course?"

The Boy Brigand nodded his head in the affirmative.

"If you like to follow me, Signor, I will conduct you at once to your new apartments."

As he uttered these words, the innkeeper ascended a staircase which led to the second storey of the house. When he came upon the landing, followed by our two friends, he walked towards what might be deemed the left wing of the house.

After having gone a few steps, he halted.

From his girdle he took up a key, with which he opened a door which gave admittance to a very sumptuous and more tastefully-furnished apartment than one could have expected to find in an Italian wayside inn.

"Anything more, Signor?"

In reply to the innkeeper, who could not be said to be wanting in civility or officiousness, Sataniello gave him an order for a couple of bottles of wine and two glasses.

The innkeeper and the wine soon appeared, and, having uncorked a bottle and poured its contents into the glasses of the brigands, the worthy individual withdrew, leaving the two friends alone.

CHAPTER LVI.

WHICH RELATES TO THE BOY BRIGAND AND THE MONK—AND WHERE THE LATTER MAKES ONE OR TWO DISCLOSURES WHICH GREATLY ASTONISH SATANIELLO.

As soon as the footsteps of the innkeeper were heard dying in the distance, the Monk rose from his seat.

With a quick step he walked towards the door.

"Nothing like being careful, Captain," he said. "It is no use to let the door be half open."

"Right you are."

"Don't you see, Captain," the Monk pursued, "we had better be on the safe side. We know not who may be in this house."

The Boy Brigand nodded his head approvingly.

"The walls sometimes have ears, and we cannot be too wide-awake," Sataniello subsequently pur-

sued, echoing, by the above sentence, the idea expressed by his companion.

It was a large room that in which the two brigands were, and, although there was not what one might denominate an over-abundance of furniture, yet the whole appearance of the apartment presented an appearance of comfort refreshing to the eye.

The two chairs in which the brigands were sitting had large broad backs to them, and one could recline the whole of his length when inside them, so large and so comfortable were they.

Sataniello was not long ere he took out from his undergarment a splendid meerschaum pipe, which he ever carried, and he began to puff and puff away in that style which men will adopt when enjoying at length a gratification which they have been prevented from indulging in for a few hours past.

The Monk followed his master's example.

When the two men had evidently made themselves as snug and as comfortable as could be expected under the circumstances, Sataniello began in the following strain—

"Here we are at last."

"Here we are, Captain," the Monk repeated.

"Now you must tell me, my friend," the Captain resumed, "all that occurred after my departure from the cavern. Do not omit a single incident."

"Captain, you may rely upon my accuracy."

"Moreover, you must speak low."

"Let me alone for that."

"It is not likely that we are watched."

"I am aware. Still, as I said before——"

And the Monk was about to repeat the phrase which he had uttered before, concerning the wisdom of displaying an opportune carefulness, when Sataniello stopped him by begging of him to proceed without further delay.

The Monk took the pipe out of his mouth, and thus began—

"Poor Tattoo got killed. I suppose you remember that, Captain?"

This being the first intimation that Sataniello got of his late followers death, he having had no means of ascertaining ere now the fate of Tattoo or of any one else, he gave way to a sigh.

"I am grieved to hear that," he muttered. "Tattoo was one of my most faithful men."

But when the Monk subsequently related to Sataniello how it must have occurred, and how, doubtless, he must have been killed by the hand of Paublas, the Boy Brigand became pale, and within his eye appeared a feeling of bitter disappointment.

"Paublas! always Paublas!" he muttered. "That man was my evil genius. Cursed be the day that I left Rome in his company! cursed be the hour that I chose him for my companion! Had I followed Joanitta's dislike never would the sad winding-up which awaited me have occurred."

And Sataniello's voice became low, and his hand trembled nervously.

"It is of no avail thinking about what is now past," the Lieutenant interrupted, wishing to sooth the Boy Brigand's feelings. "Paublas, let us hope, is dead."

"If my eyes did not deceive me," the Boy Brigand replied. "I think, nay, I am sure, that the bullet of my pistol struck him in the head, and one does not easily recover from such blows. But, never mind, pursue the thread of your narrative."

"Well, Captain," the Monk pursued, "if I were to live much longer than doubtless I shall, I could not forget the excitement which filled my heart when, hearing the sounds of strange footsteps enterng the cavern, I guessed at once that at last we were betrayed."

"I remember," Sataniello replied, "the ominous sounds which we heard, and I knew that it was as much as I could do to fly with Joanitta and the young heir to Don Saltara's dukedom. I have often repented at having behaved so cowardly on so critical an occasion—forsaking my men at the eleventh hour—and I must, I should think, have fallen low indeed in their estimation."

"You have not, Captain," the Monk pursued. "They made allowance for your wife and the burden with which she was entrusted, and they agreed with me subsequently that you had acted throughout for the best."

"This affords balm to my mind," the Boy Brigand pursued. "When I see my followers once more I shall not fear to look them in the face, as I should have done had I not been made acquainted with the details which you have just given me."

The Monk gazed upon his master, and, in the look which he cast upon him, it was easy to see that the same respect and affection which he had entertained for him were still as deeply rooted as they formerly were.

Then the Monk took an opportunity of explaining to the Boy Brigand the part which he took when the cavern had been invaded; and when he narrated the success which had attended him in bringing down the heads of the soldiers from his hiding-place, it drew upon Sataniello's countenance a smile which was expressive of the satisfaction which such a knowledge afforded him.

"Oh!" he exclaimed, "you settled a few of them, did you? I am glad of that. Teach them better manners for the future. Teach those confounded soldiers that they should not dislike such gallant men as Sataniello and his brave followers."

"They will not come back again in a hurry, I should say," the Monk muttered. "The best of the joke is this:—They could not see me, owing to the darkness which reigned in the particular spot where I took up my post; and I feel confident that, up to this hour, those who escaped fancy that it was his Satanic Majesty who gave his help to save us from falling into the hands of those merciless soldiers."

"It matters little what they thought," Sataniello quietly retorted. "I would like to know what became of the Giant, the Hunchback, and Breeze, and whether the Marchioness of Piatelli is still within the cavern?"

"What became of the Hunchback?" the Monk inquired.

"Yes, what became of the Hunchback?" the Boy Brigand replied, repeating the words of his lieutenant, as if he wished to impress upon him the anxiety which he felt at knowing the fate of the cripple.

"That is, indeed, a fair query," the Monk replied. "None of us ever knew, for he disappeared the day after the cavern had been invaded by the soldiers."

"He was always a sly dog," the Boy Brigand pursued; "but where can he have gone to?"

He would make it out when no other would, and out of a joke the Giant said one day that it was very likely that he went away with the Marchioness of Piatelli—that he offered her his gratuitous services as the poor senorita was by herself, and knew not the country where she was. There are many things more impossible than that.

"That's true," ejaculated the Boy Brigand. "In the hope of getting a handsome reward, he might have ventured with the Marchioness.

"And do you know what the reward expected by the Hunchback is?" the Monk inquired from the Boy Brigand, whose attention was gradually becoming to get more and more kindled.

"No, that I do not."

"Why, a kiss."

"Nonsense."

"This is a fact, Captain. The Hunchback—that ugly cripple—fell in love with the Marchioness of Piatelli."

"You do not mean to say so?"

"Yes, Captain, I do."

"What reason have you got for making so ridiculous an assertion?"

"His words, his deeds, his acts."

"What were they?"

"Why, he would be constantly talking of the Marchioness of Piatelli; over and over again he deplored her captivity, and one day he was heard to say that he would set her free were he not afraid of the Captain."

"This renders my enterprise still more difficult!" Sataniello muttered to himself. "Then there is going to be more impediments thrown in my way. What next? Here, then, is an ugly Hunchback who goes and takes it into his head to fall in love with a queen of beauty—with a patrician of the land! What next?—what next?"

CHAPTER LVII.

WHICH SHOWS AGAIN TWO OLD FRIENDS TOGETHER, AND WHERE SATANIELLO KEEPS ON CROSS-EXAMINING HIS LIEUTENANT.

IT is impossible to state how long Sataniello's musing would have lasted had he not been disturbed by the voice of the Monk.

"The Marchioness of Piatelli is no longer in the cavern then?" he asked.

"No, Captain."

"When did she leave?"

"We never knew."

"Your watch must have been well kept indeed."

"There was no watch."

"No watch kept?"

"No, Captain."

"How is that?"

"Why, you being away, discipline went any how, and of course my promotion to my present rank of lieutenant being rather a recent one, they would not have obeyed me like they would you, had I tried to make the Giant and the others adhere to the rules and regulations which had been laid down by you."

"Which shows me once more," Sataniello pursued, "that when the master is away from his home the household run a very good chance of going to ruins."

And doubtless it would have done so had the brigands not remained in the cavern; but they were very particular about keeping everything in order, and your room there is as snug as the day on which you left it."

"Is it, indeed?"

"Yes."

"Your information would very nearly induce me to return to the cavern.."

"Now, if you will take my advice, Captain," the Monk said, boldly, "I would not counsel you to do so just now. The roads, I should think, are closely and minutely watched, and to begin our old game upon the high road at present might place us in a pickle out of which we might not extricate ourselves so easily as we have hitherto done."

" And where are the Giant and Breeze now ?"

" I left them behind me."

" At the cavern ?"

" No."

" Where ?"

" At a wayside inn by the roadside which they have taken to patronising lately. Breeze has turned quite a gentleman now. He wears some of the wardrobe of the late Marquis of Piatelli, and he looks right well in it."

" Who gave him leave?"

" I did not."

" I like his impertinence."

" I do not wonder at you."

" And does he pass himself off for the Marquis?"

" Not exactly."

" What for, then ?"

" For a country gentleman living in the neighbourhood."

" There is no work done on the road, then ?"

" Not now."

" The Giant had Pamela, his mistress, in the cavern. She brought a friend from Rome with her for Breeze, and such larks they had together I never saw before ; and, if I tell you the truth, Captain," the Monk pursued, " I wanted a sweetheart, too, and this is about the reason which brought me away from the cavern."

Sataniello thought that the Monk might have kept his confessions to himself; but knowing ere now the fondness which the would-be priest had for petticoats, he listened attentively to his twaddle without reproving him upon its questionable selection.

" They are evidently following the example of that great general of olden time," Sataniello pursued, " and like Hannibal at Capua they are swimming in luxury and idleness after the many months of the dangerous life which they led with me ; but although such behaviour is not conducive to success," Sataniello continued, " I do not see well how I can blame them."

" They know too well, Captain, that you are just and fair, and they now enjoy themselves while they have the chance."

" And do you really tell me that the Marchioness of Piatelli left the cavern?"

" Yes."

" And the Hunchback too."

" Yes, Captain."

" Can you form any idea where they are gone to?"

" That is more than I can say."

" Do you think they are gone to Naples ?"

" It would be most likely."

" I will have to face her then."

" How will you manage about the servants, Captain?"

" I have already written to Piatelli Palace to the butler. Owing to the temper of the Marquis of Piatelli, with which I got thoroughly acquainted while the unfortunate nobleman was my prisoner, I learnt the name of his butler. But I have not acted like a child. I have taken my precautions, and as I knew right well that old Antonio (for such is the butler's name) would discern the difference of writing, I forwarded him a few lines as if they were penned by some of my attendants."

" Captain, it is a bold step that which you are about to take. Sooner or later you must be recognised."

" I do not know that. Rebecca the gipsy told me that I was very much like the late Marquis,

and that a great many people would mistake me for the deceased."

" I noticed that myself, Captain, and so did some of the band ; but then there is Lord Charlestown and Captain Wogan and his wife, who know your features. You are likely to meet them in Naples, and what if you were recognised ? Besides, do you believe that the senorita whose brother met his death beneath yon rocky abode will remain idle. Italian women are revengeful, and if she has not done so before, she will try to obtain your head as a compensation for the Marquis of Piatelli's murder. You are treading upon difficult ground, Captain, and you would be far safer when you return to the cavern."

" I would have done so had I known this morning that I should have met you, and that you would have given me all the details with which you have apprised me. But Rebecca the gipsy bade me to keep clear from it."

" I would not allow my behaviour or my action to be checked by the ravings of an old gipsy," the Monk pursued.

" Neither would I," Sataniello replied. " Was she not a good prophet. Remember what she said —remember that what she has hitherto foretold has come to pass."

CHAPTER LVIII.

WHERE THE TWO BRIGANDS, STILL IN THE INN, DISCUSS THE EVENTS OF THE PAST.

" I WOULD not, however, place too great reliance on an old woman's words," the Monk followed, wishing, if possible, to check the bold resolution which the Boy Brigand was bent upon carrying out. " The chances are that, had she not spoken as she did, the same events would have occurred."

Had Sataniello only been in the company of Rebecca, the gipsy, for an hour or two the probabilities are that he would have acted by the Monk's advice, whose judgment and common sense he could not but acknowledge ; but it must be remembered that his stay with her had lasted far beyond that period.

The greater part of the long dialogue which had been held between these two has ere now been faithfully reproduced by us in its accuracy ; and, if the memories of those who peruse us do not fail them, easily will they recollect that Rebecca had openly spoken her mind to the Boy Brigand.

From her speech Sataniello had gathered (what we have been inclined also to gather)—namely, that she possessed some important secret which she would not reveal until she thought proper to do so, and until the sum which she had named had been paid unto her.

We should be the last in the world to advocate superstition, and we would use our utmost endeavour to check any belief which might creep into the people's minds were such belief founded upon a gipsy's prophecy, and did it tend to make them indulge in hopes which are in many instances doomed never to be realised—still it must be granted that occasionally a word spoken by one of those belonging to that wandering tribe finds its realisation at some period or another of the existence of the being who has sought the knowledge.

But those who are so weak-minded as to seek from a gipsy's lips their good fortune, never consider that the number who consult them is so great that the truth must be told to some.

As a rule they have always the same story on hand. They tell you that you are to marry before a year is over your head—that you will be rich at a certain period of your life—and all such information, which, being gratifying to one's mind, gives him renewed pluck and boldness to carry out whatever duty devolves upon him to discharge—and hence he is only accomplishing by his own acts and deeds the prophecy which had been made to him.

But enough. This story, not being devoted to similar dissertations as that to which we have unwittingly entered into just now, carried on by the flow of our thoughts, we must return to the Boy Brigand and the Monk.

Now Sataniello could find no words to express the astonishment which he experienced when he had been told by his companion of the strange feeling which the cripple was said to possess for the Marchioness of Piatelli.

That the cripple should fall in love with an Italian Senorita was awkward indeed. If there was any truth in the report, the Boy Brigand foresaw that the Hunchback would be the means of thwarting to a great extent all his movements.

The Hunchback could never hope for the possession of the Marchioness, and he would thus be one of those mute worshippers which are more dangerous than an open feeling.

Sataniello's object—his present idea, we repeat—was to go to Naples; and, if he could carry it out, it would satisfy his most sanguine desires.

But, ere he could establish himself in that city, he must make away with the Marchioness.

He would not take away her life, because he knew that there were less bloody and cruel means left to him to get rid of her. To send her to a convent, where she would be kept in strict confinement, was the safest step which he could follow.

To build those plans in his head was anything but a difficult task; but the next thing was to fulfil them without a moment's delay.

Once the Marchioness should be safely entrusted to the care of Nuns—who, for a heavy consideration, could easily be bribed—he doubted not that he should have no difficulty in easily accomplishing the remainder of the programme which he had laid down.

Always to advance and never to retreat was his motto—and, from the determination which he possessed, we are inclined to think that he would, if he could, abide by this bold meaning.

The two men were standing face to face before each other, when the Boy Brigand took hold of the decanter and helped himself to a glass of wine.

"Here is success to our enterprise," he said.

"With all my heart," replied the Monk, who spoke feelingly. He loved, indeed, his master, and he would have felt as keenly as himself any blow which might strike him unexpectedly.

"I suppose, Captain," the Monk continued, "that you have nothing more to ask from me now, and that you are perfectly satisfied with the information which I have thrown upon all things?"

"I am," Sataniello replied. "From your speech I glean that Breeze, and the Giant, and the other members of my band are behind at the cavern enjoying themselves. That the Marchioness of Piatelli, who was our prisoner, has disappeared, and that the Hunchback has gone away also, without acquainting any one with the motive of his journey. Further you inform me that it is the opinion of my men that the cripple is in love with the senorita. Poor Tattoo is dead, and the Marquis of Piatelli no more."

"In a few words, Captain, you have reviewed the whole of my narrative."

"That is the way to do business."

The Monk nodded his head in the affirmative.

"This last part being gone through, we must now attend to matters perhaps as important."

"I comprehend," the Monk echoed, significantly.

"There are things before us, my friend," the Boy Brigand continued. "The Past—the Present—and the Future."

"We have disposed of the past."

"Without the knowledge of which the present would be a dead letter to us, and the future a greater puzzle than it is already."

"Of course, Captain. Of course."

"Now, my companion," the Boy Brigand resumed, "we must see what we can do. It is incumbent upon us that we should take a speedy determination, and to remain here would be folly. Moreover, the innkeeper told us that this was rather an habitual place of call for Captain Wogan—and God preserve us if he comes here."

"Surely you do not fear, Captain?"

"Fear! No. Still, my friend, you should remember that, in the event of anything disagreeable occurring to us, it would not be a single-handed fight we should have. The whole house would be against us, besides all those men whose waggons and carts are outside. The whole country around would soon be apprised of the event, and we should be fairly caught, like mice in a trap, without a chance to escape."

"I am fully conscious of the danger which we run, Captain. Believe not that I am so foolish as not to know what would be awaiting us were we to display a want of prudence, and, had I my own choice, I would not have chosen such a public inn as this—the Greyhound."

"What would you have done?"

"Gone to a more solitary spot."

"Nonsense, they would be more likely to seek us there, while they would never believe that we should be daring enough to place ourselves in the lion's mouth."

This seemed to be a conclusive answer to the Monk's remark, and so he bowed down his head and did not venture to make another reply.

That there was some truth in the remark cannot be doubted; but the police sometimes come to the same conclusion as the one which Sataniello had expressed, and then they find that they had what is called reckoned without their host.

"How far is the cavern from this place?" the Boy Brigand asked. "Have you got any idea? This is a part of the country which is not so familiar as the other. I thought that I knew the whole of Italy well."

"We are now, Captain, in the kingdom of Naples and of the Two Sicilies. Then yonder, as you doubtless know, stretches the Bay of Naples. In the distance there is the Doria Palace, belonging to one of the richest and oldest Napolitan families. And, there, can you distinguish that speck in the distance?"

Thus speaking, the Monk had risen from his seat and approached the window.

The Boy Brigand followed his example, and then, leaning upon his companion's shoulder, he eagerly followed the direction of his finger.

"Do you mean those towers and battlements?"

"Yes."

"What about them?"

"That is the palace of the reigning sovereign, King Ferdinand."

"You seem to know the place well?"

"I do," the Monk replied.

"Have you ever been in Naples?"

"Frequently."

"You will be a valuable companion to me."

"I hope so, Captain. Besides, you promised that I should be your aide-de-camp, and I have not forgotten it."

"I will keep my word, my friend," the Boy Brigand replied.

The Monk thanked him once more.

"Yes, Captain," he said, "I know Naples well. Do you see that huge dark building there?"

"What, at the bottom of that steep hill?"

"The very one. What is that building?"

"The gaol of Civita Vecchio."

Sataniello became red in the face.

His hand shook violently.

"Why do you speak to me of dungeons," he exclaimed, quickly. "Do you think that this is a place to speak of such things. But, never mind, let us return to our subject. How long would you be going to the cavern?"

"To go there only?"

"No; there and back?"

"I could not go to it under an hour, and I should require a swift horse to go the distance in so short a period."

"Could you go to the cavern and back in two hours?"

"It would be difficult to do so; but, if you want me to, Captain, I'll try. I cannot say more, and you know that I will do my best."

"I am aware of that."

"And do you want me to go the cavern?"

"I do."

"Now?"

"Not yet."

"Before we leave this place?"

"Most decidedly."

"And what are your intentions?"

"I will give them to you," the Boy Brigand concluded; "but as I have all my plans settled, I must know everything well beforehand, and when all that I may wish to become acquainted with is familiar to me, then I will begin."

CHAPTER LIX.

WHICH SHOWS THE BOY BRIGAND STILL DISCUSSING THE PRESENT AND THE FUTURE, AND ACQUAINTS THE READER WITH THE STEPS WHICH HE INTENDS TO TAKE TO CARRY OUT HIS DETERMINATION.

THE Monk knew sufficiently of his master's character to be convinced that he meant what he said; and it was, therefore, with an anxious ear that he listened to the words which might flow from Sataniello lips.

He had acted in a way which no one, not even his bitterest enemies, could have condemned. He had acquainted his captain with every incident which had come within his knowledge; and now he only wanted another opportunity to serve him and to show him his affection and respect.

The Monk, however, was far from expecting sundry questions which had been made to him by Sataniello, and he was at a loss to guess with what view Sataniello would send him to the cavern if it were not to rally round him and his followers. If he was going to Naples, what need he have such men with him?

That this was the conclusion which came to the Monk's mind we are bound to admit, and we know not whether any other would not have flashed across his brain had not his attention been attracted by the voice of Sataniello.

"We are fine fellows I am sure," the Boy Brigand exclaimed, leaving the side of the window, and coming nearer to his companion, "to venture in an inn, like the Greyhound, without any luggage. What will they take us for, I wonder."

For wealthy Signori indulged into an afternoon's stroll, and who being tired, and loathe to return to town, had thought it better to remain on the way, and to put up at a tavern whose name for provender and good wine is known all over the country.

"You have always got an answer for everything, my jolly Monk," Sataniello replied; "and what is more it is generally a very appropriate one. But now, *entre nous*, how much money have you got in your purse, for I have not a scudi."

"I am more fortunate that you, Captain," the Monk replied in an undertone. "I have as much gold as I can carry, and in my portfolio there are a few bank notes, which, had I been inclined to jump on board a fisherman's boat at Palermo or Messina, would be sufficient to keep me from starving for the remainder of my life."

"Have you got any idea what the amount might be?" Sataniello inquired in a cool, collected business line of voice.

The Monk mused for awhile ere he spoke.

After a minute or two's reflection he at length replied,

"I cannot say that I have, Captain. Money has been so plentiful with us, or, at least, with me, that I do not condescend to reckon. There is plenty more where that came from, and it is a consolation to know that these stupid soldiers, led on by Captain Wogan, never thought of instituting a watch in the cavern; once outside the subterranean strait, they did not come back, and even if they had," the Monk continued, "there would not have been many left to tell the tale. Hidden in my nook I quietly awaited their returning, and had they been bold enough to dream of ransacking our abode, one by one would have been beheaded by me as they passed by."

"What!" Sataniello exclaimed, "are the treasures of the old Duke of Don Saltara in the same place as when I left them?"

"They must be there if no one has taken them since my departure. Of course a little havoc has been made. When Pamela and her friend came to visit the giant, she took very good care to take her share of the spoil; but notwithstanding that, there is lots of gold still."

Sataniello seemed to be delighted by the revelation which the Monk made to him.

It is true that all along he knew that the large sums of gold which they subtracted from the vaults of Don Saltara's castle (during that memorable night, when the Senorita Bianca was found to be still alive) were safe within his abode, yet he sometimes feared that it might have been taken away by his followers.

His position was rather a critical one; and although he had fixed upon what he should do immediately after the interview he had had with Rebecca, and although he planned some time before executing that which he contemplated, still it cannot be deemed extraordinary that he should not ere now have reverted to the subject of the treasures which he had stolen from the Duke

THE CHURCH OF SANTO ANTONIO.

Besides he held within his power the son of Captain Wogan, and that possession he knew was a fortune to him. As long as he could hold the child between life and death, he fancied, and with some truth, perhaps, that Captain Wogan would not attempt to interfere with him for fear that Sataniello should revenge himself upon a harmless infant.

Upon the head of Captain Wogan's son a good deal depended, and he was resolved to keep Joanitta in a lonely spot near the place where she was until the moment when he could take her to Naples beneath the roof of the palace.

Sataniello fully expected to find the Marchioness of Piatelli within her home. He dreaded the interview; he apprehended screams on the woman's part —and besides, the butler might see that it was not his master who was coming back, and go alone to the military intendant and communicate his suspicions to the authorities.

Out of a hundred thousand men it is no exaggeration, we think, to state that there would not have been found more than a hundred who would have dared to act as the Boy Brigand was about to do.

Whether he was to be successful and what plan he took will be subsequently shown.

" Reckon your money now, my friend," Sataniello

began, addressing the Monk, "and afterwards I will talk to you."

It struck the Monk that the Boy Brigand had been doing so for a considerable time past; but as it was not the moment for indulging in jokes or nonsense which might tarry the course of the important events about to take place, he wisely abstained from making any of the observations which the thought would have suggested at a different time.

In accordance with his Captain's wish, the Monk took his portfolio from out his under garment—a safe place indeed to keep valuables—and he placed it upon the table.

The two brigands now sat around it.

If Sataniello had followed the promptings of his own mind he would have grasped the leather book, which was so stuffed with notes that it seemed ready to burst; but he remained cool and collected, not wishing to alienate from himself the good opinion which the Monk possessed of him.

Moreover, Sataniello knew that it would only be a question of time, and that he had only to ask the Monk to give him whatever sum he required, and that he would be certain not to meet with a refusal.

That the Boy Brigand was perfectly correct in thus thinking is a detail which we do not think necessary to corroborate, as from the relations which existed between the two youths our readers are aware that such intimacy existed and that the Monk would comply with his captain, only too glad to have a fresh opportunity to display the strong affection which, he knew not why, he felt for Sataniello.

The Monk opened carefully the pocket book, and having taken the bank notes out and laid them upon the table around which they were sitting, he very slowly (doubtless for fear of making a mistake) went through the process of counting them.

"I have three thousand pounds' worth of paper, then, Captain," he said. "I dare say," he continued, that I have about one hundred and ninety or two hundred pounds' worth of gold in my pocket also."

"That looks well," Sataniello ejaculated. "A man is not alone when he has cash to back him, but it is a dreary thing in this world to be penniless. It matters not how money is got in Italy; and I should think, from what I have read, that it must be the same in other places; if you have got it, you are thought a good deal of, people bow to you and court your acquaintance, whereas if you are poor they despise you. Poverty is not a crime, but it is a great drawback, and if you have unfortunately to contend with the latter, you are made to answer for it worse than for the former. I know," Sataniello continued, "that I suffered more when I was a penniless orphan, brought up by the charity of the Romans, than I have since. Then I was young and innocent—I had not then sinned ; now that I am a man and that I have robbed and murdered, I am happy and contented indeed. I fear but one thing—that I should lose my head. But there is a proverb which says, ' The good people die, and the bad ones remain,' and on the strength of that I hope. The heart of man is full of cares, but it is not so with me, and now that I see the money before me I am another man. Wait—wait a bit, my friend," Sataniello pursued, "and when you do see me in Naples, I will show you how gold is to be lavished. I love Joanitta, that's true ? but after all, a marquis like I shall be must make love to a duchess or some marchioness of the land. I shall give great balls, when I will invite all the aristocracy of the land ; and while the Marchioness of

Piatelli, my worthy sister, will be gnashing her teeth in a convent, I shall be reigning amidst all the fashion. I will do good. I shall remember that I was once a poor boy, running about the Piazza del Popoli without a shoe to my foot. I will not forget, either, that I have mingled with the lazzaroni in the Trastervero at Rome. The deserving beggar will never ask alms at my hands without receiving a golden coin instead of a copper scudi. I will give a handsome dowry to the poor maidens who from the want of means are compelled to keep single. I will educate the sons of old soldiers and of old sailors who have become needy. I will establish schools for the propagation of the Gospel in Italy and elsewhere. I will crush down the priestcraft. I will abolish the confessional, destroy spiritual flirting, and spend my fortune in such a manner as will compel the Neapolitan to respect me, the widow to love me, and the orphan to bless the name of Piatelli."

The Monk was literally thunderstruck by the overflow of the Boy Brigand's words. When he had concluded his long-winded sentence, a smile appeared upon his lips and he swiftly directed his steps towards the door of the apartment to ascertain whether there was not some one eavesdropping.

Happily everything without was silent, and the passage which led from the place where he stood to the staircase which conducted below was apparently deserted.

The Boy Brigand indeed had spoken so loud, and so vehemently did he express his various opinions, which contained a mixture of dissipation and generosity which we should not set as a pattern to future Boy Brigands, that the Monk was quite alarmed.

The precaution which he had taken was indeed a very good one, for it was impossible to say whether the innkeeper, hearing such a sound emanating from the apartment, might have thought that his new guests were summoning him to them or perhaps quarrelling, which, in his opinion, would have been far worse.

The inn called the "Greyhound" was not a noisy house; disorderly characters, as a rule, never stepped out of it, although people were allowed to get tipsy upon the premises, so charitable was the worthy landlord that he generally managed to send them to recover elsewhere.

We do not know whether these little details are necessary, but we give them entirely out of good will, in the event of some of our readers happening to take a trip to Italy during the summer months. They will, by the information which, out of pure philanthropy we volunteer, easily see what kind of inn the "Greyhound" was ; or, if addicted to the vice which we allude to, keep clear of a place where all due deference to Englishmen would not be given, were they unfortunately to forget themselves, which we grieve to say some of us sometimes do.

CHAPTER LX.

WHICH DESCRIBES A LONG CONVERSATION, WHICH LEADS TO A SEPARATION BETWEEN THE CAPTAIN AND HIS LIEUTENANT.

SATANIELLO never allowed himself to remain without a watch, knowing how very important it was to him to know the different hours of the day and night.

Then, when he had reckoned the Monk's money,

he said, "There is truly three thousand pounds' worth of gold there."

"I believe that I heard you say before that you had no money with you, Captain?" the Monk replied. You know that you are welcome to the half or the whole of it."

Now some wide-awake friends might suggest that much credit could not be given to the Monk for the kind offer which he was making, considering that it was Sataniello's own fortune, and that he was only restoring to him what fairly belonged to him.

In reply, however, to those who might feel inclined to urge such a base insinuation, we will take leave to inform them that "possession is nine points of the law," and that a great many in the Monk's position would have kept the three thousand pounds in his pocket and never have said a word about it.

Sataniello, however, was not the one to take advantage of his faithful friend.

"Thank you for your kind offer—thank you," he said, evidently moved to tears by the Monk's friendship. "I should not think of depriving you of the whole of it. I will take half."

He knew not how he might find himself situated, and to have a good round sum on hand is necessary sometimes.

The Monk did not make any reply to Sataniello, but acted better than he would have done by speaking, for he presented to Sataniello fifteen bank notes. They were drawn upon the National Bank, and were worth a hundred apiece.

When he felt the crisping paper in his hand, a knowing and good-humoured smile appeared upon Sataniello's lips, and lightened his countenance with a beam of joy, denoting renewed satisfaction, which he naturally experienced in pocketing the "needy."

No better word could have been given to the pecuniary help which had come to the Boy Brigand so unexpectedly, for he was actually without any means, and to set off anywhere without sufficient to pay for travelling expenses—if not the latter, then trifling calls upon your purse, which, at the end of a few days, amount to a good sum—would have been foolish if not hazardous in the extreme.

We say hazardous, because by going about without the necessary sum, there were many chances that Sataniello would jeopardise his valuable freedom.

We do not wish once more to revert to an old, very old topic, but will not my readers agree with me in admitting that if one happen to have left his purse at home, or what's unfortunately sometimes the case, if he happens to have none to leave at home, do not those in whose contact you are thrown look upon you with an eye of suspicion unbearable to one's feelings?

When Sataniello had received half of the contents of the Monk's pouch—which sum we need not name, having already been compelled to enter into sundry details which we should give, owing to our wish to be accurate and to adhere to any occurrence however trifling— he looked once more at his watch and exclaimed—

"Dio mi gardo ! (God help me) It is already two o'clock in the morning, and we are still up, talking."

And it was two o'clock in the morning.

The two friends had been so engaged in discussing together, that the hours had flown quicker than they had anticipated.

They had filled and refilled their pipes and drank their wine.

The tobacco was good, the port was not to be despised, and hence they had forgotten that they had many things to attend to beyond drinking and smoking.

The Monk walked towards the window.

It was one of those fair nights which are so frequent in the southern climes. It was nearly as light as in the daytime, and the moon, which fulminated brilliantly in the blue vault of heaven, cast her yellow brightness upon the country.

Every one in the inn seemed to be plunged into the deepest slumber.

Sataniello opened the windows and inhaled the fresh air.

He appeared to be musing silently and deeply upon many things.

Sitting quietly in an easy arm chair, his companion remained attentive.

"Here, my friend," the Boy Brigand said, calling the Monk, "Come here."

For fear of awaking the inmates beneath him with the sound of his footsteps, the Monk with a light step headed his way to the side of Sataniello.

"Do you know what I have thought of?" the Boy Brigand asked.

The Monk was about to reply in the negative, but Sataniello did not leave him to do so.

Quickly he resumed in an under whisper, "Will you go to the cave to-morrow morning?"

"What o'clock?"

"In four hours' time."

"Six o'clock?"

"About that time."

"How shall I manage about a horse?"

"The landlord will, I should say, let you have one."

"Does he keep them?"

"I should say he does."

"I am sorry we did not ask him."

"I am glad we did not."

"Why?"

"Because he might have thought it odd that I should require a horse so early in the morning."

"Won't he be much astonished when I go to the stable?"

"No."

"How so?"

"Why, look here," Sataniello replied. "You will get up at six o'clock?"

"That's understood."

"You wend your way to the yard."

"Yes."

"You make it all right with the ostler."

"I see."

"You give five or ten shillings."

"I will not fail, and then—"

"Well, what then, Captain?"

"You will appear quite careless, and ask him in a joke whether he has got any cattle in the stable worth looking at."

"He is sure to say, ' The best in the country.' "

"I know that."

"You will ask him to let you have a look at the horse."

"He might object."

"No, if you tip him as I tell you."

"Oh Captain, you are a knowing shot, I am fiddled if you ain't.

"Never mind, let us attend to business."

"I am listening."

"You are a good judge of a good horse, ain't you?"

"And pride myself that I can tell a bad one when I see him."

"I am certain that you will see both kinds in the stable," the Boy Brigand continued. "But to resume what I was saying—You can pick out a good one when you see him, you say ?"

The Monk shook his head with a knowing wink,

" Once you have made up your mind what horse you will ride, you will just say to the ostler that you should like to take a ride in the morning, before breakfast—that you feel unwell—drank too much wine—could not sleep, and all that kind of thing."

" I will make it out, Captain."

" Perhaps he will say, ' I must see master about it."

" What if he does ?" the Monk asked.

" You put him off one way or the other. Tell him that you have known his master for years—that he is a new hand in the yard—that you knew his predecessor, and his predecessor before that."

" But if he finds me out ?"

" He will hold his tongue. He ain't likely to insult you after having received your silver. He will only think that you are having a little game with him, and you will be a gentleman in his eyes all the same."

" You may be right, Captain. Once on horseback, what am I to do ?"

" Go straight to our home.

" Your late home, Captain," the Monk added.

" You will see the Giant and Breeze—"

" Most likely."

" And the others."

" What am I say to them ?"

" Be patient, will you ?"

The Monk's ardour having thus been checked by Sataniello, he kept listening to Sataniello, determined not to say another word.

" Acquaint them with my plans."

The Monk nodded.

" Ask them whether they will join me."

Another sign of assent on the Monk's part.

" Out of the number there are certainly a few who will come."

" When they shall have agreed to do so, what am I to do ?" the Monk quickly retorted, unable to keep his mouth closed.

" Acquaint them with the conversation which you have had with me ; and if they are willing to share my destiny still, await me by the village of Paluzzi. Be certain to bring the post-chaise which we used on our departure from Rome that remarkable night when we took Lord Charlestown prisoner ; and within it do not omit to place the whole of the Marquis of Piatelli's wardrobe and as much gold as you can conveniently carry with you.

" In the event of your followers not wishing to come, what am I to do under the circumstances, Captain ?"

" We will do without them."

" Do you mean as we did at Don Saltara Castle ?"

The Boy Brigand smiled.

" And I think," he pursued, " that we managed so far pretty well together—that we came out remarkably well."

The Monk was about to rise, when Sataniello called him once more by his side.

" You thoroughly understand my directions ?" he whispered in an under tone.

" I have got them all down in my book, Captain," the Monk replied, and he pointed knowingly to his forehead with his forefinger.

" There was one thing more which I forgot to impress upon your mind, my good friend."

" What might that be ?"

" Look out after Maria, if you can. There is nothing like having the females on our side."

The Monk seemed pleased, and upon his countenance appeared a sudden beam of satisfaction evoked by the maiden's name.

" And now for a bumper ere we part. It is getting late, and ere long it will be time for you to be on the move."

The bottles were now drained by Sataniello, who gave the example, which we need not say was followed by his faithful friend and worthy companion.

Sataniello now walked towards the window and gazed downwards.

If he were to be compelled to have recourse to flight, how could he manage to do so without certain death.

But why fear ? He was doubtless safe enough!

The Monk, meanwhile, was preparing himself to take his departure, when sounds of footsteps and a rough voice were heard in the hall, outside the room where the two friends happened to be sitting.

" Who is there ?" Sataniello inquired.

" Please to open the door, as I wish to speak to you, gentlemen," was the reply.

The Boy Brigand recognised the landlord's voice, and it appeared to him that he could distinguish subdued whispers emanating from different people.

" What's to be done," the Monk inquired, grasping his master's arm, under the impression that they would both have to face one of those critical positions of life in which their roving lives had so often placed them before.

" Keep quiet and resume your seat, my friend," he whispered to the Monk, " we must not show any symptom of fear, or we are lost."

" Lost !" the Monk muttered inwardly.

The voice outside spoke again.

" Well, gentlemen," he said, " will you open the door ?"

" My good fellow," replied Sataniello, " it is all very fine for you to ask me to comply with your request so peremptorily. I wish to know, in the first instance, why you have taken it into your head to come and disturb me at this unreasonable hour."

Thus Sataniello was gaining time.

He had pronounced the above words in so cool and so steady a manner that it would have been difficult indeed to detect in their tenour an intonation, however trifling, which could have betrayed any dread at his having been surprised, as we have seen he had been.

There is no doubt but what the landlord was greatly annoyed at the resistance which his guest offered him, and it was with a louder intonation of voice with which he bid him now to receive him.

" We must not remain too long without abiding his request," Sataniello ejaculated to the Monk.

" In the meantime, you keep the bedroom windows ajar, and if you infer by the landlord's conversation that he is hostile to us, you can take to flight and bring my troop to my rescue ere I am led to prison. They will have to identify me before they can take proceedings against me, and at all events I shall not be removed from here before the end of the day, and with God's help you have plenty of time to go to the cavern and back."

" You may rely upon me, Captain," the Monk said ; " but let us hope that we are mistaken, and that the landlord does not come to us as a foe, but more likely as our friend."

And scarcely had he spoken these words when he went to the bedroom, and with a swiftness and agility which none except the Monk could have possessed, he unfastened the window of the adjoining room.

The prospect, however, was anything but inviting, as the two friends happened to be on the second story, and to jump from the window into the yard would not have been a very enviable feat to perform for one who held his life in so great estimation as our friend did.

But there was a high tree which grew a few yards distance from the window, ahd, if he could only clasp it in his arms, he would be enabled by this means to reach the ground in perfect safety.

With one quick glance the Monk noticed the means of exit left to him.

His heart beat with inward satisfaction.

He was in such a frame of mind when he went and opened the door to the landlord.

"Good morning, gentlemen," he said, "good morning."

He pronounced these words in a good-humoured tone of voice, which at once relieved our two friends minds from the sad forebodings which had hung over them, and they both began to bless their stars for the wonderful escape which they doubtless had met with.

The Monk, on his side, thanked the powers that he believed to be for having come thus unexpectedly to his help, and removing the necessity to which he would have been reduced ef having recourse to the dangerous and critical expedient of jumping from a twostory-high window.

"You may wish to know, signor," the landlord pursued, "the motives which brought me hither so early in the morning."

"I have no anxiety to become acquainted with your motives," Sataniello replied, "still, out of curiosity, may I ask what induced you to do so? I have been travelling for many years, and such an unexpected interruption never once before occurred to me."

"This accounts, doubtless, Signor," the landlord pursued, "for your reluctance to allow me to come in?"

"You may form your own conclusion respecting my procrastination," Sataniello replied, "but I hold rather curious notions, and I think that a man's room is his own castle, so long as he chooses to pay for the same."

The landlord was far from expecting such a peremptory, and as we may say, such a pointed answer as he received, yet he did not forget the object of his errand.

Now, the Boy Brigand was far from being totally reassured concerning the landlord's appearance, as he felt confident that if he had some trifling duty to perform, long ago he would have carried it out.

But something more serious must have brought him in his presence, since he had already been talking with Sataniello for some time past, and the latter, notwithstanding the pains which he took to ascertain the objects of the landlord's intrusion, had not yet been able to satisfy his mind about it.

The conversation which we have related had already lasted some time.

"Your ideas respecting a Signor's rights to remain beneath a man's roof when he pays for the same," the landlord resumed, "is also mine; but you should remember that people are not compelled to take in anybody that may ask them for shelter."

This was a sentence of which the meaning sounded rather ominous to Sataniello, and ere he replied to the landlord, he took thirty or forty seconds to consider as to what answer he should give him.

He should not, he knew, be too hasty in pronouncing one single syllable which might commit himself, for he had seen enough of life to feel convinced that a great many persons would never be suspected of any dark deed which they had committed, were they not themselves to place their pursuers upon the right track by a word said without reflection, or an unguarded speech, which is turned against them when strong proof of their guilt has been obtained.

The landlord of the Greyhound was scrutinising Sataniello's features in a manner which, had he felt more at ease, would have been resented by him as an insult; but situated as he was he appeared not to notice it.

"If you have anything to ask me," the Boy Brigand pursued, "I wish you would do so at once, my friend; I have not gone to sleep yet; your wine is very good, your cigars smokable, and instead of taking some rest I have allowed the best part of the night to go by, while I was indulging in my favourite pleasures—drinking and smoking."

When Sataniello had concluded his eulogium of the landlord's goods, the latter bowed like one who feels rather gratified; yet, nevertheless, he did not allow his satisfaction to interfere with the duties which he was called upon to discharge.

"I have only a few questions to ask you, Signor?" the landlord pursued.

The Monk during all this while had not opened his lips, and to revenge himself against the landlord for the scrutinising glance which he bent upon his companion, by keeping his eyes in exactly a similar manner upon his features.

"I am ready to answer you whatever you may wish to know," Sataniello replied.

"You will excuse the liberty, Signor?"

"Excuse you, certainly, my friend."

Sataniello uttered this sentence in so affectionate a tone of voice that the landlord became quite communicative.

The Boy Brigand and the Monk knew that ere long they would hear the real state of things, and be enlightened upon the singular proceeding of the landlord—a proceeding which neither could thoroughly understand.

"What do you think I received two hours after you had retired to your apartments, Signor?" the landlord asked in a quick tone of voice.

"I hope that you received a hundred-pound note, or some very pleasing information of a similar nature."

"Nothing of that kind, Signor. I assure you it was the visit of a detachment of soldiers."

The features of Sataniello did not betray any outward sign of fear, often he had had to face events of a most critical description, and he was to a certain extent always ready to conceal his feelings; but had anyone placed his hand upon his heart, he would have felt it beating heavily, and had he seized hold of his hand, he would have found that it had become cold and trembled nervously, and he would naturally have thought that the new comer at the Greyhound was taken ill, or what was more probable, dreaded the cross-examination to which he was about to be subjected by his worthy landlord.

CHAPTER LXI.

WHERE THE BOY BRIGAND AND THE MONK MAKE THE MOST OF THEIR CRITICAL POSITION, AND MANAGE TO SEND THE LANDLORD AWAY FOR A FEW MINUTES TO HAVE A TALK BETWEEN THEMSELVES.

THE landlord who, since his entrance into Sataniello's abode, had kept his glance rivetted upon his noble countenance, soon got tired of examining minutely the features of a man who had become quite familiar to him, reverted his attention from Sataniello to his companion the Monk. As soon as he perceived that he was to be the point of target of the Italian hotel-keeper for the time which he should remain with Sataniello, the Monk rose and looking in the landlord's face, said to him in as jovial a tone of voice, as it was possible for a Brigand to possess :—

"Now, my friend, it strikes me that you are going to make a long stay here, I am extremely fond of company, so pray do remain; but I would suggest that ere you begin you would go and get us a couple of your "Lacryma Christi," and then we shall be better able to listen to you."

It would be encroaching upon the interest of the story were we to acquaint our readers now with that which it will be the province of the worthy landlord to reveal.

We must, however, state here, in common fairness to the innkeeper's hospitable and jovial propensities, that he fully agreed with the Monk's suggestion, and that he told them that he should only be too happy to oblige them so far as it lay in his power.

This seemed to give relief to Sataniello and to the Monk; and as soon as he had gone the latter whispered into his Captain's ears the following words, " I think that the landlord could be bought over to us, and I daresay that a few golden coin given *apropos* might have the effect of enlisting him to our cause."

"Methinks the same," the Boy Brigand replied, "but we must be very careful, too, mind you that."

Instinctively the Monk walked towards the entrance of the apartment, and he carefully and swiftly placed his forehead against the seams of the door, which was ajar, and his eye swept the length of the landing upon which he was, and along which were many a suite of rooms besides those occupied by himself and his gallant Captain.

The contemplation, however, did not last long; quickly he withdrew his head backwards, as if he had met with some disagreeable apparition, or had hurt his head against some hidden obstacle. In one instant he retraced his steps, and less than five seconds brought him by Sataniello's side.

"We are watched, Captain."

"What?"

"We are watched, Captain," the Monk repeated.

"By whom?"

"I will show you."

"By the landlord?"

"No."

"By whom, then?" the Boy Brigand repeated, his features expressing the utmost astonishment.

The Monk made no reply; but grasping Sataniello's arms, he led to the entrance.

The Boy Brigand then looked without.

"'Tis but too true," he exclaimed, "we shall have a narrow escape of it this time, at all events."

And he staggered backwards.

The Monk first and then Sataniello perceived, at the end of a landing, the stalwart and corpulent form of a Neapolitan soldier, who was pacing to and fro, like one mounting guard.

"What a sly dog that landlord is, to be sure," the Boy Brigand pursued, "not to have hinted anything to us during the time he was with us. Now, my friend, if we are reduced to extremities, you know what to do."

And he pointed towards the bedroom windows, through which the breeze of the morning sent them

an invigorating coolness, which they inhaled with delight.

The Monk shook significantly his head, as a sign of having fully understood the meaning of his Captain's injunctions.

"Whatever may happen, Captain," he said, "you need not trouble for the future ; I will bring you help."

"But were I to fail at last, my friend," Sataniello replied, "may I reckon on you to do one thing for me?"

"Speak, Captain, the landlord will soon be back I know."

"You are a staunch friend of mine."

"For heaven's sake, Captain, go on."

"Can I rely upon you to —— ?"

The sound of footsteps of the sentry were now heard plainer than before.

Across the room the Monk flew.

Quickly he returned to Sataniello.

"He has altered his beat, Captain," he said ; "he is coming closer ; ere long I should not wonder to see him pacing up and down before the door."

The footsteps of the soldier now ceased.

Perhaps he had heard part of the conversation—perhaps the whole of it !

If so the Brigands were lost !

But it was only their fear that suggested to them the thought which we have written above.

Shortly afterwards the soldier resumed his monotonous tread up and down the landing.

"Captain," the Monk said, "just now you uttered these words, ' Can I rely upon you ?'"

There was a moment of breathless suspense.

"I did," Sataniello replied, "and I will repeat them once more, ' Can I rely upon you to take care of Joanitta ; to see that she never wants, if I fall ?' to you I would willingly entrust her, because I know your character—your feelings well. She can never want, however, her mother, Mrs. Lami, in Rome, has some means of mine. Should you not succeed in delivering me, take care of and protect the girl."

"Is it my Captain who fears this ?" the Monk inquired ; "is it my Captain who fears ? is it my Captain who gives way before a sentry ? Sataniello, if you like, fly now, and I will take your place and await the return of the landlord."

Then was an exchange of those tokens of friendship which the two men had given each other so frequently before.

It was a struggle between the two.

"I always like to be certain of the happiness of those I love, my friend," the Boy Brigand began, in reply to the Monk's works, "only if I see that there is some one upon whom I can depend left behind to watch over Janitta's welfare, I ask no more."

It would be useless to expatiate here upon the very short dialogue which was held between the Monk and his Captain.

It would be out of place, also, were we repeat for the hundreth time, perhaps, that Sataniello loved Joanitta like no man ever loved woman before; and to dismiss the matter as peremptorily as we can, we will be content in saying that the Monk pledged himself never to lose sight of the maiden, and that he got thanked heartily by the Boy Brigand for the profession of friendship which he made him.

At that instant the landlord returned.

"Here we are, my friends," he exclaimed, "here we are ! lots of stuff to make life merry. I say this, my friends, life is short, and we should make the most of it."

"I coincide with you," the Boy Brigand and the Monk replied in one voice.

"I see men," the landlord said, "who go hoarding up treasures like as if they were to live for ever; they struggle hard all the days of their existence to keep together and save a round sum of money, and then, when they expect it the least, comes sickness or death, and their money remains behind them. We cannot carry it away with us, and what's the use of thinking so much about it. Now, I have a family of children, and I am not so fast as I used to be; but there was a time when I thought that a pair of blue eyes was worth a good price; and that price I was never reluctant to give."

It struck Sataniello and his friend that this was a rather curious speech for a man, whom they believed (and perhaps they were not mistaken), to be one who had been sent to watch them, catechise them, and find out from their lips whether they were honest men or those bold Brigands upon whose heads so great a ransom had been placed.

Had Sataniello been less a man of the world than he was, he would, doubtless, have been at a loss to account for the strange and total difference which had taken place in the landlord's behaviour, and he soon saw the cause of it.

The landlord, delighted to have been entrusted with a delicate task, and proud to have been entrusted with a post of importance, had been so elated by the confidence that was placed in him, had in his visit to the cellar, helped himself to a few glasses of a nectar much stronger than the wine which he was bringing to the two friends.

Occasionally people get inebriated—very sad failing with some—which all the teetotal meetings and preachers in the world will not destroy altogether.

Well, it happened to be the landlord's failing.

He sometimes, and when in company, indulged, perhaps, rather too freely in the pleasures of Bacchus; and, as a winder up, was wont to have dreadful rows the next morning with his better half.

As he was at the moment of which we speak, no fault could be found with him.

He was, perhaps, a little "lively," and that's about all.

The Monk and Sataniello noticed the proposition of their host, and they took very good care that they should make the most of the opportunity offered to them to pick out of his muddled brain whatever knowledge they wished to get acquainted with.

The wine was soon placed in the glasses.

Instead of drinking his wine Sataniello poured the contents of his glass upon the floor—for the Boy Brigand knew perfectly well that if he wished to attend to his business he should not forget himself.

The Monk, on the other hand, imbibed freely to give himself sufficient *sang froid* and strength of mind to clear the large gap which separated his bedroom window from the tree.

There are many things which a man driven to his last will not do if he be in the full possession of his mental capacities; but if his brain is slightly overwhelmed by a restoring beverage, daring and fearlessly courageous will he prove himself in the hour of peril.

CHAPTER LXII.

WHERE IT IS SHOWN THAT EVEN AN ITALIAN HOTELKEEPER CAN SOMETIMES IMBIBE MORE THAN IS GOOD FOR HIM.

SUCH was the pitch of excitement to which the Monk thought he would work himself.

We have taken some time to describe the various feelings of the different actors of this scene, but it is incumbent upon us that we should do so.

And now let us return to the worthy landlord.

With that complacency and with that good-will which men generally display when enjoying their friends' glasses—with that rapidity and with that gluttony which drunkards entertain for anything that satisfies the palate—he needed not to be pressed to help himself to the wine which was on the table.

We know exactly how our friends' finances—namely, Sataniello's and the Monk's—stood, having seen the latter dividing his money with the Boy Brigand on their arrival at the Greyhound.

We have here given the English name of the hotel, because we are aware of the limited number of our readers who understand Italian.

Ere now we have made the same remark concerning other matters connected with the story.

"Landlord, landlord!" the Boy Brigand now began, "fill your glass, man. You ain't half a fellow to polish off a miserable bottle of your wine. Go on, and here is to the luck of King Ferdinand!"

The worthy innkeeper gazed in wonder upon the Boy Brigand, and through his muddled brain he endeavoured to speak a few words; but he was fairly done out.

But a reaction took place, and he had in a very short time the power to articulate as well as he did when we last saw him.

"My good fellow," the Monk resumed, "when you came here you were about to talk to us about matters of great import. You had a few questions to ask us. Pray do so now—I am anxious to hear them."

Although the landlord had not yet lost all sense of what was passing around him, still, for all that, he had attained that desirable pitch so longed for by the drunkard—when he does not feel unwell, when he enjoys still his glass, and when he can occasionally talk rationally.

He remembered having heard the Boy Brigand ask him to drink to the health of King Ferdinand, who was then the reigning king of Naples; and, if what he had been told was true, why it was very odd that brigands should drink a toast on behalf of a price greater than any other Neapolitan prince for the capture of those bandits who were to be found raging in the mountains of the Abruzzi.

These thoughts, which had entered the mind of the innkeeper, induced him to look upon the reports which he had heard as fallacious, and he was resolved to let his two guests know how very stupid the Neapolitan authorities were.

"Vino veritas!" the Latin proverb which says "the truth is in the wine," was likely to find its confirmation in the landlord's speech.

It is impossible to say to what wanderings he would have allowed his mind to hurry on had not the Monk thought it right to find out their real position from the lips of one who would not be sufficiently awake at the time to a question to keep back any incidents which were in any way worth knowing.

"You told us," the Monk said, "my friend, when

you came here, that you had a few questions to ask us. We are ready to answer them."

"You further stated," Sataniello continued, "that there was a detachment of soldiers who called upon you a few hours after we arrived here."

The innkeeper now thought that he was about to be punished for his being too candid, too frank, and, with a fear which can be easily understood, he rose up to retreat.

No wonder, either. He had two antagonists who could have settled a far stronger man than he was, and they both now seemed bent on attacking him.

They began with words—the blow might follow.

This was the obtuse reasoning which gradually sdrung into the old man's head.

"With a drunken leer he began.

"Now, I know that I am talking to signors of the highest stamp—still, I must acquaint you with the truth."

"Thank you, my friend," the Monk said, good-humouredly. "I could not think but that you were a regular brick."

Had the landlord been sober, such a sudden mark of friendship would have doubtless struck him as being very odd; but, as he was verging upon a less happy state, he took the hand which the Monk proffered him, and shook it as if he had known him for years.

"Do you know"—the landlord repeated again 'do you know,' and he renewed the interrogative sentence at least a dozen times. "Do you know what I was told last night when I had left you here so comfortable ?"

The Boy Brigand and the Monk would have given anything to coerce their guest to keep on narrating his story without stopping at the conclusion of every sentence.

At that rate they would be in a position to learn a good deal in a short time; but he would not do so.

At the end of every sentence he uttered he ceased speaking, and he gazed upon his histeners, as if to convince himself that whatever he said was eagerly swallowed by the two men whose bright eyes were riveted upon his countenance, and who watched at-ten'ively every one of his movements.

"I wish," the Monk was muttering inwardly, "this fellow would speak and not keep me in such suspense. If there is anything underhand every instant which we remain here will lessen the chances which I have of effecting my escape and bringing reinforcements to my good captain's rescue."

Unable, however, to withstand the procrastination of the landlord, the Monk spoke at last..

"Mr. Landlord," he said, " you are beastly drunk. I will not mince matters with you. You speak about one thing and another, and for the last hour that is all, and you have not yet thrown any light upon the object of your visit here. I wish you to finish up as soon as you can, because we cannot wait here any longer. We have business to attend to, my friend and myself. We are employed in the secret service of his Majesty King Ferdinand, and we cannot afford to continue in this manner, which apparently you think we can."

These words, pronounced in a manly voice, and in a quick, hurried tone, could have but two results.

Either to render the suspicions which the land-land had regarding the calling of his guests still stonger, or to cause him to come back to his own conversation, and to try to soften their annoyance by at once complying with their request and satis-fying the natural curiosity which had sprung into their imaginations after all the preliminary ste which he had had recourse to.

We must admit that, had we been in the sam position as Sataniello and the Monk, we shou have been very much inclined to pitch the landlo out of the window, and to send him to his for fathers, and, by breaking one of his limbs, lea him such a remembrance as would hinder him fo the future from indulging in his most absu twaddle.

However, the words which the Monk had so pe remptorily pronounced had the longed-for result.

It was not the first hypothesis to which we hav referred, but the latter; and, besides, it had th effect of bringing the landlord to a proper sense his position.

"Signor," he said, " the truth is sometimes offen sive for those who may be concerned to hear; bu as I believe in my own heart that it cannot hav anything to do with you, frankly will I confess tha you two gentlemen are at the present moment sus pected of being two famous highwaymen."

"Ah ! ah ! ah !" the Boy Brigand laughed. "Ah ah ! ah ! Good joke, landlord, that. I wish I wa a highwayman. They get the prettiest girls, liv like kings, and have no work to do. Oh, I wish was a highwayman !"

And then he sang out—
  " Oh, I wish I was a brigand bold,
    Caring naught for the law of the land."
But he did not conclude the verses of an old song, thinking that he had played his part sufficiently well.

The landlord, at all events, was fairly puzzled, and whatever doubt he might have had upon his mind vanished like a meteor before the joviality of his young listener.

"When you came in last night there were in the bar several people who were talking about Satani-ello—he whom they call the Dark King of the Mountains."

"Oh, I know. I have heard of him before," the Boy Brigand replied; " but I was under the impres-sion that he had been caught and executed long, long ago."

"The Italians and the Neapolitans wish he had, signor. He is one of those daring bandits who waylays all whom he can. They tell me that he is never satisfied unless he kills at least two women a day with his own hand; but before he murders them he does something more to them."

"The scoundrel!" Sataniello exclaimed. "The low hound! He might do the last thing and not the former, and then I should not blame him. But do you really place any credence in those reports ?"

The landlord looked at Sataniello, and slowly replied.

"I cannot say that I do. I daresay he eases the rich man of his coin when he is in want of it; and I would not blame him were he not, besides, to dabble his hands in blood—a step which, in my opinion, is ever justifiable.

Here again the landlord had strayed from his subject, and but a very dim light had been thrown by him upon the real motives of his visit to the two brigands.

CHAPTER LXIII.

WHERE THE LANDLORD SPEAKS SO OPENLY AT LAST THAT THE MONK DOES NOT REMAIN TO SEE HIS ASTONISHMENT.

THE Boy Brigand did not blame his host for

THE BOY BRIGAND HURRYING ON TO NAPLES.

having, for the fourth time, at least, forgotten the point from which he started, and he knew, from his own experience, that over and over again the same thing had occurred to him.

Without being personal, however, the Boy Brigand hinted that, at the rate at which the conversation was being carried on—considering also the interest which the respective personages took in it—it was more than probable that, were they all to be provided with the fare which stood before them, none of the company would be at a loss for something to say.

The innkeeper was not an ignorant man, and, although he belonged to a class of men who in Italy do not shine for being provided w.. a superfluity of brains, yet he soon saw the propriety and the justice of the Boy Brigand's remarks—and to prevent him from indulging again in a complaint similar to the one he had made, he reverted to his subject.

"But a few days ago, signor," the innkeeper pursued, "prayers, I am told, were said in the church of Santo Antonio for the speedy capture of the Boy Brigand—as he is sometimes called also, from the very fact of his having began his adventurous and wayward career at a much tenderer age than any other Italian criminal on record."

It may be fancied by our readers how very awkward the innkeeper would have felt had he known whom he was addressing; and it is not for us to state that quickly indeed would he have stayed his speech had he known that Sataniello was listening to him.

To imagine adequately, also, the feelings of the Boy Brigand when made acquainted with a knowledge of which he could not foresee the importance, would be impossible for any one, except at some period or another he found himself placed in a position where his freedom—and, consequently, his life—hung upon a thread.

"How do you come to be so well acquainted with all these particulars, landlord?" the Boy Brigand asked. "I know many a reverend abbot and many a sanctified bishop, and I never was told that the citizens had gone so far as to offer prayers for his capture. They must have little, indeed, to do or to think of when religion is thus prostituted to such a bad purpose."

The man who proposed a toast for King Ferdinand—who was intimately acquainted with such high dignitaries as abbots and bishops—must, indeed, be somebody of great importance, and ill-founded, indeed, were any suspicions derogatory to the high name which he doubtless bore.

These were the thoughts which entered the landlord's head as he continued, addressing Sataniello.

"Signor, I must confess it, and you will not blame me for speaking plainly, I hope?"

Here the innkeeper feared to conclude the phrase which he had begun.

"Confess what?" Sataniello inquired.

"I do not know whether I am justified in speaking?"

"What an ass that man is, to be sure," the Boy Brigand muttered to himself.

"You are a puzzle to me, Mr. Landlord," the Monk now put in.

"Well, look, signor," the innkeeper pursued, as if he were forcing the words to escape from his lips, "somebody said downstairs that you and your friend were two brigands."

The Boy Brigand turned pale.

Although he expected something was wrong, still he did not expect such a home-thrust.

On the other hand the Monk rose.

He glanced once more towards the window.

"Yes; they said," the innkeeper pursued, "that you were Sataniello, the Dark King of the Mountains!"

"And did you believe it?" the Boy Brigand inquired.

"I did not," the landlord pursued; "but there were others that did—and one of the company was even so officious as to run down to the neighbouring barracks to get the soldiers to come after you."

"But that is a villany!" Sataniello exclaimed. "It is interfering with the liberty of the subject."

The Monk was beginning to look upon his position as critical and awkward; and, if he had had his own will, he would have gone off at once to the cavern to seek the help of the other followers of Sataniello, who, he knew, would have done anything to save their master and captain.

What was to come out of all this he was at a loss to guess.

How framed with dangers was his life getting.

No sooner did he emerge from one perilous escape than he met with another.

Then the dreams indulged in by the Monk—those wayward, happy dreams, which gratified his youthful fancy—when he looked forward to his dazzling uniform, to his post as a Marquis's aide-de-camp—vanished in an instant like a shadow before the stubborn march and rapid approach of reality.

"I do not wish," the innkeeper now resumed, "respected signor, to palliate the conduct of the man who acted in the way in which I have just told you. He is no friend of mine."

"Why did you not stop him?" Sataniello ejaculated, committing himself for once by his thoughtless exclamation, and displaying a fear which he would never have allowed to be detected had he not forgotten for once to whom he was speaking.

But the landlord was not of that disposition which induces one always to suspect his neighbours, and which renders many men who move in the world more like detectives than respectable members of society owing to that disgusting and vulgar propensity which they possess of prying into other people's business.

"Could I have done so, signor," the landlord pursued, replying thus to the Boy Brigand's last exclamation, "willingly would I have done so." And he ceased speaking for awhile.

"You must understand, signor, that it must do harm to my house to give shelter to such a highwayman as Sataniello is—no recommendation for one who lives by the public—and sooner than be discovered with him in my house, may *Dio mi gardo*, I would really, I believe, give him the means of escape.

A thought—a bright and opportune thought—now flashed over Sataniello's mind.

Did the landlord speak true?"

Was he really in earnest?"

Would he prove their friend?"

Could he be brought to save them from the impending ruin which threatened them?"

Such were the musings which entered the Boy Brigand's and the Monk's respective imaginations when they heard the man whose wine they had been sipping express himself as he did.

But to be candid—to be too open—might have compromised matters.

Italians, as a rule, are a false kind of people.

They praise you to your face, and condemn you behind your back.

We say Italians.

Why so? Are there not many Englishmen in this country similarly contemptible?

The Boy Brigand thought of these things, and hence he hurried not his speech.

"My object in coming here so early," the innkeeper said, "was to look on your papers to see whether they were in order."

It had never struck the Boy Brigand that at the period to which we allude Italy was about to be threatened by an invasion of the French; and there was in the part of the country where he then was a system of passports which rendered the movements of any suspicious person constantly liable to be watched.

"Papers! To look over my papers! What the deuce does he mean?" Sataniello muttered.

The landlord saw the lips of his lodger move perceptibly.

"I do not doubt," he pursued, quickly, "that they are all right; but it is only a matter of form, you are aware, and it must be undergone. Now come, show me your passports, and when the captain of the detachment comes I will answer that I have satisfied my mind as to your respectability."

"You are very kind, very considerate, indeed," Sataniello replied, playing with his words, and wishing to find an excuse to enlist the landlord in his favour.

"Don't you see, signor, I am not particular as to who comes here. If I am paid well, that is all I want."

The Monk now shook his pocket.

The landlord heard the gold jingling.

"We have got sufficient metal in our pockets to buy the Greyhound and the whole of its contents, landlord," the Monk pursued. "I don't know what your bill is yet, but I will give you something on account."

Thus speaking, the Monk, doubtless to bribe the

THE BOY BRIGAND ; OR, THE DARK KING OF THE MOUNTAINS.

landlord in a way which could not turn against him, flung upon the table such an amount in Italian currency as would be equal to a five-pound note in this country.

There is something about money which tells its own tale.

With it we buy, if not command, love.

With it we obtain respect.

With it we rise to consideration.

Then, to conclude, with it the Monk attained his object.

Now the landlord would lie for his guests, whoever they were.

Quickly he pocketed the coin.

In doing so he turned round.

He hoped he had not been watched.

Something told him that that gold had brigands' perfume about it—and he even thought that honest men do not part so easily with their wealth.

"That will do, signor," he said. "I am perfectly satisfied, and I am fully aware that you are two inoffensive travellers.

Scarcely had he concluded these last words than the three personages heard a loud noise on the landing.

The voice of the sentry was plainly perceptible.

"I have not moved from my post," he was saying, "and no one has come out of that room."

"By Santa Maria !" a man replied, "to-day we will lay hold of them like mice in a trap."

"They shall not escape us. It is Sataniello, the Dark King of the Mountains. It must be him from the description."

Such were the sentences which reached Sataniello's ears.

"Landlord ! landlord !" the Boy Brigand now said, "can you save me ?"

The landlord stood aghast.

"I am Sataniello, the Dark King of the Mountains. Will you allow a man to be arrested under your roof ?"

"No, never. That is not my way to display my hospitality."

The seconds appeared so many hours to Sataniello and the Monk,

The conversation was still going on outside.

The landlord had acted well.

The Boy Brigand knew that he would not betray him.

"I will save you," he said ; "but I fear it is too late."

"Too late ?"

"Yes."

"How so ?"

"Are your features known ?"

"By a few only."

"Would it be policy to deny who you are ?"

"I think it would."

"And your friend ?"

"Who ? The Monk ?"

"Is that his name ?"

"It is."

"They know less than me."

"What shall we do with him ?"

"He will not remain with us."

"Where will he go ?"

"He has a commission to execute for me."

"How will he escape ?"

"Through the door."

"'Tis useless," the landlord said ; "the landing is watched, doubtless."

The footsteps of several people were heard coming along the landing.

"Do not delay—hurry away," the Boy Brigand whispered to the Monk. "To the stable and pick out the best horse, and away—away—away !"

The Monk rushed towards his mate.

He took his hand and brought it to his lips.

"Farewell !" the Boy Brigand exclaimed.

"Farewell, Captain. For a short time only—farewell."

Thus speaking, the Monk flew across the room and vaulted from the open window into the open air

The Monk was not long in seeking his safety in a hasty flight.

He knew that two lives depended upon the success which should await his endeavours.

To sally forth to the cavern was his only idea.

To bring help to the Boy Brigand—the only hope, the only thread upon which his gallant chief's liberty depended.

Left alone with the innkeeper, the Boy Brigand asked him what he should do ?

"Await patiently the arrival of the soldiers," the innkeeper said, "and I will do my best to help you out of whatever dilemma you may fall into."

The Boy Brigand pressed the hand of the speaker.

What gratitude he felt for this man, who was but a stranger to him a few minutes ago. "A friend in need is a friend indeed."

He had found one.

He was by his side.

It was the innkeeper.

But was he genuine ?

Would he not betray him ?

Would he not divulge the truth ?

Were not his promises so many idle words upon which one could not fairly reckon.

Time would tell.

The seconds elapsed.

They appeared centuries to Sataniello.

Footsteps were gradually approaching.

"Sit down," the hotelkeeper said, who did not seem concerned.

The Boy Brigand acted as he was bid.

To do otherwise would have been folly.

Yet Sataniello felt his pistols, which were in his girdle.

They were hidden beneath his clothes.

No one knew that he was armed.

He would then have the advantage over the new comers, whoever they might be.

Perhaps, after all, they were friends, and not foes.

Perhaps his premises wore wrong.

Perhaps he would not be captured.

In breathless suspense he stood still.

Why were they not coming on quicker ?

They were preparing themselves ere they came.

They wished to make sure of their prey.

"Yes," Sataniello muttered. "I am all right. I have my weapons about me."

They were loaded to the muzzle.

He remembered having done so.

It is wonderful what strength of mind man possesses when he knows that he has about him the means of defending himself.

Sataniello was resolved to struggle hard.

What would one crime more be ?

It would only be one man's life to be added to those which he had already taken.

If he were captured he should die.

He had made up his mind to that.

He felt certain of that dreary fate.

Yet amidst these gloomy thoughts, the hopeful words rang in his ears :—

Was he the rightful heir to the Marquisate of Piatelli ?

Could Rebecca have spoken true ?

If so, never would he be able to show forth his claim to this proud title.

No, he should be free.

The innkeeper was gazing upon Sataniello.

He admired that bold youth.

The footsteps now were heard outside the door.

Instinctively Sataniello rose.

One man entered.

Behind him were seen many others.

There was apparently an officer.

His uniform was magnificent. His blue coat trimmed with gold facings. His white leather trowsers and his riding boots, to which were attached heavy spurs, proclaimed him to be one accustomed to command.

His features were noble and handsome.

Seeing Sataniello rise to welcome him, he bowed to him as a gentleman.

He was evidently a man of the world.

"Sir," he said, addressing Sataniello, "mine is a painful duty."

Sataniello looked at him in astonishment.

A good-humoured smile appeared upon his lips.

"A painful duty, Lieutenant? I am at a loss to understand the meaning of your words," the Boy Brigand replied. "Officers, as a rule, I thought, had not painful duties to perform."

The military paused in reply.

"Perhaps you will explain yourself," Sataniello resumed. I am really kept in total ignorance as to the meaning of your words."

The soldier reflected deeply.

"Mine is a painful duty, sir," he continued, "because, on the strength of my holding the king's commission, I am compelled by the inmates of this house to make a search in the bedroom of a person whom I know not."

"Am I that person?" Sataniello asked, assuming the most unconcerned appearance. "Speak, sir; I shall not be offended. Of course I am inclined to think you mean me, from the fact of your coming into my apartments uninvited.

The officer replied in the affirmative.

The innkeeper shook nervously.

Once he appeared as if he was about to make some revelation.

Sataniello's heart began to beat.

Such perturbation as he had undergone in that inn for the last hour or two were sensations hitherto unknown to him.

He knew not whether the tavern keeper was about to betray him or not.

"I am most happy, Lieutenant," Sataniello pursued, "that you honour me with your company. I shall be delighted to answer any questions which you may be pleased to put to me."

"What is your name!" the Lieutenant asked.

Meanwhile, the men outside the apartment had made no sign of entering the room.

In answer to the question which had been put to him, the Boy Brigand gave the name with which he had entered the house where he was sojourning.

The officer appeared satisfied.

"I suppose you have your passport about you?"

Sataniello was about to reply.

"I will not detain you long," the officer said, "it is only a matter of form; and as soon as I shall have glanced over them I'll retire.

The question which was put to Sataniello was the identical one which the innkeeper had previously made to him.

"I have no papers, Lieutenant."

"I was taking a stroll in the country, and I [ ] my way and came here.

The soldier shook his head.

He seemed to doubt the Boy Brigand's statement.

"Yet, notwithstanding, he did not wish to [ ] abrupt.

"You lost yourself?"

"Yes."

"Are you a Neapolitan?"

"Yes."

"And where do you live?"

This was rather an abrupt question.

The Boy Brigand did not expect it.

That he might have wandered away in the cou[ ] and lost himself seemed probable enough, and [ ] thought that, by making such a quick reply[ ] should have satisfied the lieutenant's cross-exam[ ]tion.

But there were many others besides him w[ ] minds should be set at rest, and they wished t[ ] perfectly satisfied that they were wrong in the [ ]cipation, ere they would allow the Boy Brigan[ ] sally forth free once more.

During the time which elapsed between the q[ ]tion that was put to Sataniello and the mo[ ] when he should answer it, the Boy Brigand had [ ] time to collect his thoughts and to ponder on [ ] he had to say.

"My residence is well known," he replied, "[ ] if you think it necessary, I will tell you what [ ] mansion is called."

"I have seen this gentleman before," the [ ] keeper said, "and I know that what he says is [ ]fectly true."

The phrase which was pronounced by the [ ] keeper was one of those boons which only occ[ ] the lives of great criminals.

It had the means of diverting the lieuten[ ] attention to other matters, and he said—

"I myself am perfectly satisfied with your s[ ]ments, signor; but there are some people here [ ] swear that you are the famous Sataniello, the [ ] Brigand, he that is called the Dark King o[ ] Mountains."

"Let them swear what they like," Satan[ ] replied; "I trust, sir, that as one gentleman tov[ ] another, you will not press a matter, to invest[ ] which there is not a shadow of suspicion worth[ ]ing upon."

"Willingly, as a gentleman," the officer pur[ ] "would I accede to your request, signor, bu[ ] duty forbids me dismissing thus an inquiry wh[ ] am bound to carry out."

Now it must be said that the Lieutenant di[ ] think that the man before him was Sataniello.

Had he thought so, what would he have don[ ]

He most decidedly would not have waste[ ] time in idle talk.

"But, Lieutenant," the Boy Brigand pur[ ] "if a gentleman and an officer like you are sati[ ] no one else has a right to grumble."

The Boy Brigand uttered these words in a m[ ] and insinuating tone of voice, which had all th[ ] pearance of being genuine, and the Lieutenan[ ] half beginning to think that it was useless to[ ] long a search which might be fruitless.

Then he was about to depart.

He made a step towards the door.

A ray of hope entered Sataniello's mind.

His heart trembled with joy.

His eye grew bright and hopeful.

of the hunter in the forest, who sees the tiger rushing madly towards him ready to tear his face to pieces with its cutting claws—who feels that he has not another instant to live—and who, at the moment that he is about to die, finds his ferocious antagonist dashed to the ground by the glittering poniard of an unexpected saviour.

But he had hoped in vain.

His fate was sealed.

He must be captured.

He saw no way of exit.

He once thought of rushing to the open window through which we had seen the Monk disappear but a few instants previously.

But he would remain.

He would face the impending danger.

He would rely upon his star.

This time he would be no coward.

A man can only die once.

He would fight—struggle to the last—sooner than surrender.

Yes, he would——

The officer now returned.

Once more he stood face to face with Sataniello.

"You have no papers," he said, slowly.

Sataniello mused for awhile.

He was about to speak.

The soldier repeated his question.

"I am astonished," Sataniello resumed, "that you should tread over the same ground again, Lieutenant. I have explained to you how I happened to be situated as I am.

"You had a friend with you just now," the soldier pursued.

Here the Boy Brigand heard voices muttering outside, and he heard some one saying, "What became of the other, I wonder?"

"I had a friend just now, Sir—you are perfectly correct.

"Where is he?"

"My friend ?"

"Yes."

"He is gone."

"Where?"

"I know not."

"Is he not within here ?"

"I think not."

"Which way did he go?"

"Through the proper way."

"What, along the lobby ?"

"I see no other way by which he could have effected his departure," Sataniello pursued, in a cool, collected manner, "unless he went by the window."

And here Sataniello indulged in a merry, loud laugh.

"And it is, I fear, rather high."

"The Lieutenant seemed somewhat puzzled.

"Yes," he muttered, "it is rather high."

Owing to that presence of mind which Sataniello possessed under the most difficult circumstances, he would, no doubt, very soon have got rid of the Lieutenant.

But how was he to do so?"

There was a conspiracy against him.

He could have no doubt of that.

He heard voices outside.

Besides, the Lieutenant had been cross-examining him for at least half an hour.

What was his meaning in doing so?

Did he wish to gain time?

Did he wish to entrap him in a snare ?

If such were not the case, why did he not go away and leave him alone?

Sataniello was every instant getting more anxious

to clear his mind about the doubts which hung upon it.

He resolved to conclude the interview.

His pistols were safe.

He would fight hard for his freedom.

"Sir," he said, addressing the Lieutenant, "I have answered you all questions. I have done so courteously—without a murmur. I have had enough of your cross-examination. I am not the man you take me for, and I wish you not to disturb any longer the privacy of my apartments.

The soldier was one of those men who had been educated for the army because he should have a profession.

He was a gentleman every inch of him, and he thought that the person who spoke could not have been a brigand, because, had he been Sataniello, he would have been more cowed than the Boy Brigand appeared to be.

"I do not wish, Signor," he continued, "to be of more annoyance to you than I possibly can. There is a man in this house who knows the Boy Brigand's features. If he proclaim you not to be he whom we seek, you will be free. If not, you will be led a prisoner hence to await your trial."

"Is that fair, Signor ?"

There was no way left to Sataniello to avert the coming blow.

Would he be recognized?

Who could be the man that knew him?

What awaited him ?

After a moment's interval he replied, "Lieutenant, I know not what the result of all this will be; but I will certainly make those repent who are placing me at all this inconvenience without any cause.

The Lieutenant made no reply.

"I am awaiting your pleasure now," the Boy Brigand resumed. "Let any one who knows Sataniello confront me; and, if he says that I am Sataniello, the Boy Brigand, why I shall be satisfied.

CHAPTER XIV.

THE IDENTIFICATION—THE DOUBLE MURDER—THE DEATH STRUGGLE.

WHEN the Boy Brigand had concluded speaking, the Lieutenant walked out of the room with a firm, steady step.

He regretted in his own heart having listened to the suggestion which had been made to him; and, although at times his mind had been overshadowed by doubt, still he thought that the man whom he had threatened to apprehend was not Sataniello.

The last words of the Boy Brigand were so just in their bearing—he seemed to be so anxious to meet the charges which were preferred against him, that the officer could not believe him to be guilty.

The last sentence which Sataniello had pronounced had impressed the Lieutenant that he had nothing to fear from him; and it was under these ideas that he met in the hall those who had besought him to show his authority.

With that delicacy and that decorum which are so essential to a man of birth and education, the Lieutenant had not tolerated any one in Sataniello's private apartment.

He had gone there himself.

He had spoken and cross-examined him.

He had had a long interview with him.

What had passed between them has already been fully related by us.

And the conclusion to the Lieutenant's cogitations was that the lodger at the Greyhound was not Sataniello, the Boy Brigand.

A second brought the military man outside Sataniello's bedroom.

He went into the lobby.

He was shortly accosted by at least eight people.

Two of them were soldiers—not officers, but privates.

The remaining six were civilians.

"Well, Lieutenant," one of the soldiers said, "what has occurred?"

"That you are all mistaken," the officer replied, in a slow tone.

A universal mark of disapprobation was the exclamation which greeted his words.

"Did he answer your questions, Signor?" one of the company asked.

"To my satisfaction he did," the Lieutenant replied.

"And are you going to let the matter drop."

A man, who appeared to be a country horse-dealer, answered in a quiet tone of voice—

"No, I am not."

"What are you about to do?"

"I will get him identified."

"Hurrah for the Lieutenant."

"Hurrah!" the voices re-echoed.

"But is there any one among you who know the Boy Brigand?"

"I do, sir," one of the soldiers said.

"It is not sufficient to say you do.   But can you be certain of what you assert?"

"Perfectly."

"When did you see him before?"

"I formed part of the detachment led on against him by Captain Wogan."

"You did?"

"Yes."

"And saw his features?"

"Like I do yours."

"Are you speaking truth?"

"I am."

"And in the confusion of the moment they struck you?"

"Yes."

"And you would not forget them?"

"Not until I die."

"I remember the Boy Brigand right well," the soldier pursued. "I could never forget him. He stood upon the rock and fired the pistol into the head of a man of the name of Paublas."

"Who was Paublas?" the Lieutenant inquired.

"One of his followers."

"Where is he?"

"Dead."

"Are you sure?"

"As sure as one can be when he sees a human being with a shot in his head falling down a fathomless abyss mortally wounded."

"That is one out of the way, at all events," the Lieutenant said. "Let us hope that you are not mistaken, and that the Boy Brigand is really the man to whom I was just now speaking."

It must be admitted that Sataniello had been unfortunate indeed since the moment when a sudden attack was upon his mountain home. Yet he did not despair.

He glanced upon the Lieutenant as he was taking his departure; and as soon as he found himself with the innkeeper, and no other witness to listen to him, he began thus—

"Do you think, landlord, that it's all up with me now?"

The landlord replied affirmitavely—

"I would not, however," he continued, "be the means of discouraging you; and I would advise you to pluck up, and to remember this—'as long as there is life there is hope.'"

"What became of the Monk, I should like to know," he replied, in answer to the innkeeper; and, with a quick step, he walked towards the window.

The yard beneath was deserted.

Not a soul to be seen.

Not even the ostler walking about.

The door of the stable was closed.

Could the Monk have been baffled in his attempts?

Could he have failed?

Had ill-success attended him?

But he must have gone.

For if he had not, he would have heard of it.

He now saw one of the stable-boys.

He wished he could speak to him—call out to him—and get from him the information which he needed.

But how could he do so?

Would it not seem strange?

Would it not render the suspicion which they had against him stronger.

He would remain quiet.

He would maintain his composure.

While thus musing, the thought of following the Monk's example entered his excited brain.

He was about to carry it out.

He was about to leap forth.

But a noise attracted his attention.

Swiftly he entered the apartment.

He met the innkeeper coming to meet him.

He bid him to hope still.

"Do not commit yourself," he said—"deny all."

The Boy Brigand acquiesced.

The door of the room opened.

The officer appeared.

It was he who had cross-examined Sataniello.

Two soldiers this time accompanied him.

Their features were unknown to the Boy Brigand; but one of them knew him.

Above we have told our readers when he had seen him.

Gradually the room was filled with a large concourse of people.

All were anxious to see the result; and anxiously they awaited the moment when Sataniello would speak.

He never said a word.

He paused, and silently he listened.

There was a moment of breathless suspense.

Not a syllable was uttered on either side.

The innkeeper gasped for breath.

He wished to make others believe that he was deeply annoyed at the incidents which were taking place beneath his roof.

The time had not yet come.

It would shortly arrive.

Not a sign of fear could be traced on Sataniello's countenance.

At length the Lieutenant spoke.

"Signor," he said, in addressing the Boy Brigand, "I am told that you are Sataniello."

"I deny that," Sataniello replied, in a cool, collected tone of voice.

"The appearances are against you."

"What do you imply," the Boy Brigand quickly retorted.

"I imply, signor, that there must be something wrong in suspicion about a man like you."

The forehead of Sataniello now became furrowed with a deep wrinkling, and his eye lit up with the marks of the latent vengeance, and his whole frame shook violently when he heard the Lieutenant's accusation.

"I imply, signor, that you came to the Greyhound without any luggage and any papers."

And to corroborate his words, he received an assent to them from the innkeeper's lips.

The lieutenant turned round towards him.

The innkeeper had but one course left to him.

He feared also to inculpate himself.

He dreaded the suspicion of the assembled crowd.

"What you state, signor officer," he said, "is perfectly correct. This gentleman came here last night without any luggage or any papers, and ordered four bottles of wine, for which, I am happy to say, he readily paid me."

The last part of the innkeeper's sentence was not needed.

It had been volunteered by him, and it had the effect which he hoped it would.

It caused a little merriment.

When silence had been restored, the officer pursued—

"Further, you were accompanied by a friend, who is not here now. Where is that friend, signor?"

The officer pursued—becoming gradually bold, and exciting himself, like a great many will do when they are performing a part, the importance of which they wish to render greater in the estimation of those who listen to them.

"I am not my friend's keeper," the Boy Brigand replied. "He may have gone to some place where it would be indelicate for me to allude."

This reply of the Boy Brigand was not understood at first by the listeners.

But it was very shortly afterwards, and one of the company was despatched on the very critical errand of ascertaining whether the Boy Brigand's friend was—where he might have been.

Thus the most minute details were carried out by the Lieutenant and his followers.

It having been settled that the Monk had taken to flight, the Lieutenant thus summed up—

"Well, signor, having taken everything into consideration, and the strong evidence which appears to be against you, I consider it my duty to apprehend you on suspicion, and henceforth you are my prisoner."

"Since when?" Sataniello ejaculated; "do you take a gentleman into custody upon the mere grounds that you think him to be a rogue and a vagabond?"

"I do not think so only," the officer replied, placing the same emphasis upon the verb "think" as Sataniello had done. "I would have saved you exposure; but as you need it you shall have it."

It should be noted by our readers that this dialogue had been held solely between the officer and Sataniello.

"Exposure!" he hissed, gnashing his teeth; "have I not had it enough for this last hour. Were I the vilest man on earth I could not have been treated worse."

With a haughty disdain and a firm voice the Lieutenant retraced his steps backwards, and slowly inquired—

"Is there anyone here who can prove that this man is the Boy Brigand, the Dark King of the Mountains?"

Sataniello felt his pistols.

A slight click was heard.

He was cocking his fire-arm.

But in the tumult it was not noticed.

A second only, a second respite followed.

Then it was broken.

One of the soldiers stepped forward. He was a tall, handsome infantry-man.

"I can," he exclaimed.

All eyes were turned towards him.

"By Santa Maria, he pursued, I swear that he who stands before us is Sataniello, the Boy Brigand."

Thus speaking, he held out his forefinger, and with his right hand pointed towards Sataniello.

The Boy Brigand's face became white.

"I know you, my friend—my bold friend," the soldier pursued, "and I cannot forget when, on the crest of the rocky hill, twelve yards from your den of rapine and brigandage, you fired at Paublas—your late lieutenant. I know you," the soldier hissed, "and this day you shall not escape."

"Paublas!" Accursed be the name of that demon of h——. Paublas! may the everlasting fire of the nether world for ever burn his rotten bones. Paublas! why should that name be ever present before my mind?"

And the Boy Brigand foamed with rage as he uttered these words.

"Ah! ah!" the Lieutenant hissed, with all the bitterness of one who finds that he has been deceived by one cleverer than himself. "Ah! ah! you confess it now; you no longer deny your being Sataniello."

"It would be madness to do so now," Sataniello replied. "Yes, I am he."

And he stood erect.

His eye kindled fire.

His body shook nervously.

And threateningly he awaited his pursuers.

"I have done my duty now," the Lieutenant pursued. "Men, forward, and seize hold of the prisoner; follow your chief."

And the officer advanced towards Sataniello.

But the Boy Brigand had foreseen that once he should be discovered, they would attempt to seize him.

In each hand he held a pistol.

He had retreated into one of the corners of the room, and his back was against the wall.

Thus he could not be pounced upon unawares.

The eight men were struck with awe.

Not one dared to approach him.

"I never do things in a hurry," Sataniello exclaimed in a hoarse voice; "but the first one that makes one step towards me is a dead man."

His pistols were cocked, and from the appearance of his features it was easy to perceive that he meant what he said.

"Eight to one," he hissed; reckoning the number of his pursuers—"eight to one—I fear not. If the Boy Brigand dies he will be drowned in a pool of human blood."

Terrible words—ghastly words; rendered still more horrible by the imminent peril in which he stood.

Before such determination even the soldiers were fairly cowed.

The Boy Brigand was indeed a bold boy.

Courageously and fearlessly did he brave death.

His last hour was nigh, and yet he feared not.

There is something so manly in one who faces a superior number, that admiration then enters the mind of man, when it would not at other times on any other occasion.

What is more sublime than the general who in the battle-field leads his men on to the forlorn hope when he is doomed to fall?

What is nobler than the act of that soldier who, in the Chinese War, was the first to go and plant the

English ensign on the enemy's stronghold amidst the bullets of his antagonists?

What is finer than the man who dies without fear?

The feeling which the daring conduct of Sataniello inspired must have been a strong one indeed, for the officer never commanded his men to fire upon Sataniello the muskets which they had in their hands.

It is so cowardly to shoot a man down, that few indeed are vile enough to order such a step.

But everything must have an end.

The officer felt that.

"Sataniello, in the name of His Most Gracious Majesty King Ferdinand, I order you to surrender unto me to await your trial."

The officer spoke like one who did not expect to meet with any resistance.

But he was mistaken.

Terribly so indeed.

He knew not the man he had to deal with.

He was not a common brigand.

He was not an insignificant highwayman.

He would not give himself up so easily.

A loud, sarcastic, mocking laugh was Sataniello's answer.

"Await my trial," he ejaculated; "Never, never! The Boy Brigand will never be cast alive into a felon's cell."

And so sonorous and clearly striking were the exclamations which he gave way to, that it indeed could have been heard a hundred yards away.

But no one was passing along the high road then.

That was all the better for him.

For if there had been they would have halted to hear and investigate the cause of it.

They would have inquired from whence came such a shrieking exclamation.

They would have been told that it was Sataniello, the Boy Brigand.

And in Italy—like everywhere else—honest and hard-working people are always ready to lend a willing hand to apprehend men who live by vice and idleness.

Had the Boy Brigand's death-knell sounded?

Was he doomed to die?

And poor Joanitta?

And the heir of Don Saltara Castle?

Then, in the hour of peril, he thought of that girl who had sinned for him.

For Joanitta had given herself, mind and body, to the Boy Brigand.

It is perhaps wrong for us here to enter into details which we think we are bound to give.

The Boy Brigand feared death—now.

He did not before.

Why should he do so now?

Few minutes he did allow his mind to think.

Now sad musings came over him.

The time which we take to write the few above sentences revolved itself away in Sataniello's imagination quicker than we could entrust them to paper.

The Boy Brigand regretted life, because if he did go to a place of which we hear a good deal in this world—where bad women and bad girls go—where bad men and bad boys are supposed to be sent—he would lose Joanitta.

Frightful and terrible in their conception were the Boy Brigand's thoughts.

He regretted Joanitta.

There he would no longer be able to pass his hands over the glossy waviness of her abundant and luxuriant hair.

There he would not be able to press her rosy, luscious lips upon his own, mingling her soft breath with his amorous whisperings.

There he could no longer encircle the symmetrical and well-shaped waist of her warm and handsomely modelled body within his feverish and loving embrace.

There he would not be able to satiate his fiery and voluptuous glance with the imploring and anxious glance of the loving angel's eye, still longing and thirsty for another cup of Cupid's enervating nectar.

There the enamel of her pearly teeth would no longer meet his, and he would be hurled to death with frightful remembrance, with the ghosts of his victims threatening him in his last hour and agony, showing him what he had lost, and, with a fiendish smile singing into his ears a recital of the excruciating pains which awaited him.

No!—a thousand times no.

A slow death would not be Sataniello's lot.

At least five minutes had passed since Sataniello's exclamation.

The officer was tired of waiting.

After all, he was now a brigand's servant.

"Sataniello," he said, "will you surrender?—yes or no?"

"No," Sataniello replied, and he held his right-hand pistol towards the officer's breast.

"If you advance one step, Lieutenant," he whispered, hoarsely, "this pistol will tell its tale."

"You threaten! you threaten!" the soldier exclaimed. "Help me, my men."

The soldiers were cowed.

They heeded him not.

They answered not his appeal.

"What," he exclaimed, "have I cowards to deal with? Well, let it be so. But it shall not be said that I have not shown you the example."

Thus speaking the officer advanced.

He made two steps forward.

One more pace, and he would stand by the Boy Brigand.

He reflected not that Sataniello had the advantage over him.

The Boy Brigand had a couple of pistols, and he only had his regulation sword.

Yet he walked on boldly and fearlessly.

He was taking his last step, and his hand was lifted to fall heavily on the Boy Brigand's shoulder, when a shot was heard.

The Lieutenant's right hand fell by his side, and he attempted to raise his left arm, but he was powerless so to do.

"I am shot in the heart," he muttered inaudibly, and his eyes closed.

His features became as livid as those of a corpse.

His head fell heavily upon his breast.

A shriek—a terrible shriek—followed.

"Revenge! revenge!" a voice exclaimed.

"Revenge! revenge!" the whole company echoed.

The man who had first spoken was the soldier who, but a few moments ago, had identified Sataniello.

The Boy Brigand remained motionless and still.

He was like those martyrs of old who, aware of the doom which awaited them, walked boldly to face it.

THE WORTHY COUPLE'S ASTONISHMENT.

One man's death he had obtained, would he be compelled to take the lives of others.

If obliged to do so he should not flinch.

Meanwhile the soldier advanced.

His eye kindled with fire.

He felt sure of success.

A worthy and a noble example had been set to him, and he was anxious to follow it.

Yes, he would act as bravely as the officer did were he certain to fall in the attempt.

"Come not near me," Sataniello exclaimed.

The soldier took no heed of the words.

He advanced slowly and steadily.

The Boy Brigand allowed him to do so up to a certain distance only.

Sataniello kept his hold.

He wished to know who would make him loose it.

Was it that soldier?

Would it be any one of the company?

No—not if he knew it.

The soldier, however, approached.

His fate would soon be sealed.

"Beware!" Sataniello hissed, "beware!"

These words seemed to have filled the mind of the soldier with renewed pluck and courage.

Instead of shaking his resolution, it only had the effect of strengthening it.

He was now close upon the Boy Brigand.

He was within arm's length.

He was about to seize him.

But it was not so to be.

Sataniello was not to be captured yet.

The soldier held out his hand.

At that moment Sataniello lifted his pistol.

The soldier moved forward.

The Boy Brigand took his aim.

He did not miss his target.

A detonation followed.

He had been as quick as lightning.

The military man fell.

He had been shot in the head.

His blood flowed copiously from his broad and expansive forehead.

His teeth rattled—he staggered—the heavy sound of his body coming into contact with the floor announced to the bystanders that one more had been launched into eternity.

And who was the culprit but the Boy Brigand?

It would be impossible for us to describe adequately the scene which followed.

Like so many madmen the remaining personages of the assemblage rushed upon the Boy Brigand.

He drew forth from his girdle his poniard.

It was a shining blade of steel.

It was one of those Italian stilettos which, when wielded by an experienced hand—as that of Sataniello's undoubtedly was—are terrible in the execution.

Sataniello awaited calmly the moment when the others would be upon him.

They rushed madly upon him.

We have already said so.

This was the last act of the bloody drama which we have described.

The strength of man is wonderful sometimes.

In the Bible we are told of the wonderful deeds accomplished by Samson.

We read how he was deceived by Delila.

There a woman betrayed him.

This could not be said of the Boy Brigand.

No woman was the cause of his fall.

He had never known but one.

She had been his maiden love.

She was his darling Joanitta.

She would not have betrayed him.

She would have died for him—like he would have died for her.

But there were too many against him.

At first he had to contend against eight.

Now only six antagonists remained.

They took him at a moment—when he expected it, of course—but they were too quick for him.

They encircled him.

They disarmed him.

Hence, without his poniard, what could he do?

He struggled hard.

He displayed superhuman strength.

But all has an end.

He was at last finally cowed.

He had to surrender.

And he did so; but not without having laid prostrate two men who had been bold enough to attempt to capture him.

Now he was satisfied.

He had shed blood freely.

And surrounded by the men who held him captive, he was led to the lower apartments of the Greyhound, to await the moment when he should be taken as a prisoner to Naples, to receive a shameful death, instead of the career which he had anticipated, namely, that of a gallant and wealthy Marquis.

CHAPTER LXV.

WHICH REVERTS TO THE MONK, AND DESCRIBES HOW HE MADE THE ACQUAINTANCE OF THE OSTLER OF THE GREYHOUND.

IT is now incumbent upon us to revert our attention to the Monk.

What had become of him?

Had he succeeded in escaping?

Had he carried out his aim?

Had he been able to reach the cavern in safety?

Of course our readers are anxious to know, and so we are ourselves.

It is therefore necessary that we should revert their attention to the Monk.

When he had been bid by Sataniello to fly away, we have seen that he did so.

But his was no easy task.

He had not to walk along steps.

He had to clear a large distance. which separated the tree which we have alluded to from the room where he stood.

He therefore walked upon the window ledge.

He remained uncertain for a minute.

What if he were to miss his object?

His heart beat.

The sounds of footsteps were coming close to him.

He had no time to lose.

He balanced his body, and when he had satisfied himself that the distance was not too great for a human being to clear, he jumped into the open air.

His feet rested upon one of the branches of the tree.

He was now safe.

But should he now reach the ground.

Tearing his clothes to tatters, he at length succeeded in alighting in the yard.

He met an ostler.

"Halloa, mate," he said, "what ails you?"

The Monk enjoined him to silence.

He took a piece of gold out of his pocket, and presented it to the stable boy.

The lad opened his eyes.

He winked knowingly.

"That man must be some distinguished signor," he muttered.

"I am a highwayman," the Monk said to the lad. "Here is another piece of gold for you; now show me the way to the stables."

Now it is well known that men and boys also have a great respect for highwaymen, and that they admire their bold deeds.

They take an interest in everything connected with brigands.

They are curious to hear all about them.

They are anxious to know who were their wives; and we remember ourselves that when we heard the story of "Handsome Bess," the highwayman's mistress, we took great delight in it.

Thus it cannot be wondered at, the astonishment which the ostler displayed.

The Monk, besides, had a good heart.

We have seen enough of him to know that.

There are some beings in this world who go through it without making a friend, and creating enemies at every step they take.

It is their nature.

It is their way of returning kindness.

The Monk was not one of those.

The ostler liked him at once.

"My master," he exclaimed, "might find fault with me."

"Your master! Why, you are a flat, my boy, and no mistake. How is he to know it!"

"Why, you want to take a horse away."

"Of course I do."

"But I cannot let you."

"You can't?"

"Nonsense, my boy," the Monk pursued. "Do not stand upon trifles. I will be back ere your master knows anything about it.

"You will?"

"Yes."

"But if you are not ?"

"Why you would get in trouble."

"That I should."

"How much is your place worth?"

The ostler told the Monk.

Now we know perfectly well this, that had the lad to whom the Monk was speaking been one of those stupid, foolish, idiotic, absurd, imbecile, and thick-headed good-for-nothing boys, he would not have wasted his time in talking to him to any great length.

But he was a smart youth.

His sparkling blue eye—bright with vivacity—bespoke intelligence, and his countenance proclaimed him to be, indeed, fit for a post superior to that which he held in the worthy landlord's household.

"My situation is worth so much," the lad said.

We would not wish to give here the exact amount in Italian, because our readers would not understand the currency of that value at the time of which we write.

Suffice it to say that it was about ten pounds a year, everything included.

This may seem a trifling remuneration, but when we tell those who peruse us that in England a great many ostlers do not get much more than that, and that there are many ready to take their places—to jump at them—they will doubtless not doubt the accuracy of our statement.

"Lead me to the stable," the Monk said. "and then I will show you that I can sometimes reward a service according to its value."

The ostler had no reason up to the present to regret having made the acquaintance of the Monk.

Although he had begun it in rather a strange manner, still he kept his hand in his pocket and rattled the coin which had been given to him.

CHAPTER LXVI.

WHICH STILL KEEPS OUR READERS IN COMPANY WITH THE MONK, AND SHOWS WHAT HE DOES.

WE would like to know to know why the jingling of gold produces such a strange and magnetic effect upon us ?

This something that charms us we like to hear when it is our own gold, of course—not otherwise.

To this feeling, therefore, must be ascribed the willingness with which the ostler helped the Monk to carry out what he had in his head.

The time passed on quickly.

We have taken up some length of our space to describe the conversation which took place between the Monk and the ostler; but our friends know perfectly well that a dialogue is very quickly uttered.

Thus the ostler led on the Monk.

He saw many horses before him.

Some were cart-horses, some were evidently used for the saddle.

None but a connoisseur could have told the difference.

But the Monk had once been well off.

His family was respectable and wealthy.

He had, then, some knowledge of horseflesh.

He picked out a mount at once.

"Ain't you a great judge," the ostler said to him. "Ain't you a 'cute fellow, signor !"

"What induces you to give way to such exclamations?" the Monk inquired, for he knew not to what reason he should assign the words which the stable-boy had uttered.

The lad smiled complacently.

This was evidently his way of showing that he knew what he was about.

"It is only my thought, signor," he said. "But, by the holy Peter, you have hit upon the best horse in master's stable."

"Have I?"

"Yes, signor."

"How so ?"

"It does not require explanation."

"I wish you would give me one ?"

"With all my heart."

"I am listening."

"He is an Andalusian thoroughbred, and he can clear the distance like a deer."

It is probable that the ostler would have indulged in a longer dissertation.

But the Monk had to study his book.

To waste his useful time in idle talk would not answer his purpose.

He knew that.

The Monk stopped the ostler.

"By-and-bye," he said, "you may talk to me like an Irishman could after eight tumblers of good LL Kinahan whiskey, and I will listen to you with the greatest pleasure. In the meantime, attend to business."

"All right, signor."

"I want a good saddle."

"I will go and get the best one we have."

Thus speaking the ostler walked towards a corner of the stable where the object in question happened to be kept.

He soon returned with it.

The Monk looked after the bridle.

He placed the latter himself on the horse's head.

The saddle was soon fastened.

But the Monk had no spurs.

What would he do without them ?

A horse may be good—nay, may even be a thoroughbred of the highest and best blood—still he may take it into his head to show the cur and display his temper, and where is the rider then ?

A good equestrian should study all these things.

The Monk did.

He had experience.

In all matters that is a great thing.

He asked the ostler for the loan of a pair.

This was immediately granted to him.

He attached them to his boots.

Now for a whip.

He soon got that.

He was now ready for the long journey which he contemplated, and before which many would have flinched.

But the Monk knew that his master's interests were at stake.

That he should hurry away.

Confine himself to the stated time.

"A man of my word you will always find me," the Monk now said; "and, as you are running a certain risk, here is a year's salary for you, my boy."

And he gave the amount which the boy was earning yearly to the ostler.

The horse was brought out of the stable.

He vaulted upon his back.

He dashed his spurs into his flanks, and away, away he went, with a rapidity which was really wonderful, and at a rate which we feel bound to state was never equalled in any country of the world—not even by the swiftest races that ever entered the paddock.

CHAPTER LXVII.

WHICH DESCRIBES WHAT OCCURRED TO SATANIELLO
AFTER THE MONK'S DEPARTURE—HOW HE BORE
HIS CAPTIVITY—AND WHAT HE HAD TO PUT UP
WITH.

THE Boy Brigand was at length captured.

As he heard the door of the cell in which he was confined closed with a thundering clap, he could have no doubt that he was the prisoner of those men who had made so desperate an assault upon him.

He stood aghast for a moment.

The scenes which had occurred presented themselves in rapid succession before his bewildered mind, and he had at least the satisfaction to know that he had fought hard ere he surrendered.

Although we have called the place where the Boy Brigand had been thrown a cell, properly speaking it did not deserve that name.

It was a small, low-roofed parlour, which doubtless had been used some years before, for a storeroom where the provisions and the drinkables which were consumed in the inn were in the habit of being stored.

For a moment Sataniello remained motionless and still.

Immediately afterwards he attempted to open the door and to leave the place.

His consternation may be easily imagined when he found that all his efforts were ineffectual.

The thick wood was inlaid with thick bars of iron, and was of such an unconquerable strength that he felt that, without weapons, he should be doomed to remain there until the moment when he would be taken away to be led to Naples.

Sooner than face the Neapolitan town Sataniello would have recourse to suicide.

He thought a moment of hanging himself.

It would be a fine revenge.

Then would his pursuers plans be baffled.

Around his neck he had a silken handkerchief, which he knew would support the weight of his body until life had fled from his frame.

But to do away with himself at such a moment seemed cowardly to him.

"As long as there is life," he muttered, "there must be hope."

"I will wait," he soliloquised, "until I see how matters turn up; and I can always have recourse to suicide when I find that all hopes of escape are gone."

Sooner than face the disgrace of a public court of justice, Sataniello was bent upon acting in the manner of which he was at present thinking; but he had given his instructions to the Monk, and he wished first to await the result of his endeavours.

Again the Boy Brigand searched for some means of escape.

He examined the walls, but as unsuccessfully as before.

It would be very unfair on our readers' part were they to blame the Boy Brigand for his sudden despondency.

Had they been situated as he was they could not have prevented many an agonising thought from entering their over-excited brains.

The change, indeed, was so great—and all the plans which he had formed were not likely to be realised by him now.

Naturally he felt forlorn and downcast.

He looked about the place for a stool.

He wished to sit down.

But there was not a particle of furniture around him.

Insensibly he allowed himself to fall upon the ground.

There he lay, considering what steps he should take.

But to do so was useless.

Now he had no space to move.

The broad expanse of the country was no longer before him.

The whole of Italy before was a wide arena where he could travel—plot deeds and carry them out—with success sometimes. Now he was in a small vault, from which he could see no way of emerging.

What would Joanitta think of his long absence?

Would she also give way to despondency?

This was a conjecture which tortured his heart.

He started from the ground, and paced his prison with quick and unequal steps.

He was restless.

It was no longer a heavy despondency that oppressed him concerning his own fact; but an acute anxiety that stung him; and, with the tortures of suspense, brought also those of passionate impatience regarding the fate of Joanitta.

The longer he dwelt upon the possibility of her being unhappy and fretful, the more probable it appeared to him.

One cannot easily fancy the gloom which imprisonment will cast upon the whole being of one who has been accustomed to be always free.

For it must be remembered that the Boy Brigand had never yet been captured.

And then, perhaps, he would not have been so sad about what had occurred to him had he known he was so close to the city of Naples.

His last acts were enough to get him to be condemned to death.

They had been perpetrated in the open sun—many had been witnesses to it; and he could not rely upon want of evidence to avert from his head the blow which hung over it.

And the more Sataniello yielded to his feelings the more violent they became.

At length his ungovernable impatience and apprehension arose almost to frenzy.

But Sataniello soon checked the gloomy thoughts which came over him.

He would not fret any longer.

He would face whatever might happen, and trust to his fate.

It is impossible to state how long he would have kept up this praiseworthy resolution had not an incident occurred which changed for a few instants the current of his thoughts.

Sataniello had now been imprisoned for two hours.

He heard the sounds of voices outside.

Who could be the speaker?

What did they want with him?

Sataniello of course always thought that he was the person upon whom the thoughts of the people were constantly bent.

He was not wrong there.

He was no secondary and indifferent character.

He was known by the whole inhabitants of Italy.

His band had committed too many daring deeds, and he was too bold and too gallant a chief not to have attracted universal attention.

Sataniello ardently wished that he could have been able to peep above the door of his cell (for it was indeed one for the time being) to see what was going on outside.

His pistols had been snatched away from him.

He had only his poinard left.

He knew that with the latter he might defend his life—perhaps obtain his freedom—but it would be of little use against many, who were provided with guns, pistols, and several other dangerous weapons.

The voices which had struck Sataniello's ear belonged evidently to those men who had seen him in the inn in the apartment when the bloody struggle which we have described had taken place.

"I think," a voice said, "that we should take him out of his prison, and take him outside."

The Boy Brigand endeavoured, but in vain, to find out who was the last speaker.

"It is a very good idea that," another voice pursued.

"Why?"

"Because Sataniello, the Boy Brigand, is such an extraordinary man that he would find ways to escape where others could not."

Sataniello believed that he recognised in the last speaker's voice the sounds of Breeze's voice; and one can easily fancy the balm which such a thought conferred upon him.

If this could be true!

If he were not the toy of his raving mind, oh! what happiness.

There was nothing extraordinary in supposing that Breeze would be among those who were at the inn.

The Greyhound was a place where everyone who had enough money in his pocket to pay his current expenses had a right to alight.

There had been sufficient time for the Monk to go to the cavern.

Had he already returned?

Had Breeze assumed a new guise to liberate his master?

This was too good to be true.

However, time would show.

Now Sataniello knew that where his liberty was at stake he would have no occasion to find fault with his followers' behaviour.

He knew that they would try everything in their power to liberate him.

To effect such a desirable object a little policy was to be displayed.

The Monk could be relied upon.

In difficult cases he had seldom been at a loss for an expedient.

Being known in the inn he could not come back himself.

Therefore he would send some one in his stead.

We have seen how cleverly he had acted.

How he had bribed the ostler.

How he had obtained a mount, and finally how, with the swiftness of the doe, he had sallied forth in search of Sataniello's men.

Perhaps the thought that entered Sataniello's mind had no foundation, and perhaps he had been mistaken.

We suggest this remark because we have heard of similar instances where men have made blunders of the worst description.

Considering the critical position of Sataniello to infer that he might have been wrong cannot be wondered at.

We do not wish to pass any remarks derogatory to his perception or to his general character.

But when we fancy that all hopes of escape are gone, naturally we are inclined to see imaginary beings coming to our rescue.

For instance, when the sailor is shipwrecked in the midst of the ocean, does not the smallest speck in the horizon convey to him the idea of a ship, on board of which he may be taken, and conveyed safely to the home which otherwise he would never have seen again.

The voices of the men outside had ceased, and Sataniello was now still more puzzled.

"What could have been their object," he muttered. "They are gone away again."

Sataniello could not see.

We have said so before.

Therefore it cannot be wondered at his forming the above opinion.

But we are in a position to contradict it.

The men were not gone.

They were engaged in a slow undertone discussion.

"Yes," a voice exclaimed, breaking the silence which reigned, "let us take him out, in the garden facing the high road."

"Agreed," several other voices replied.

The heart of Sataniello beat.

The marks of the most intense enjoyment appeared upon his features.

They were about to liberate him.

At least, he thought so.

Does not this show how very hopeful his heart and mind were?

The steps approached.

They were at least six individuals.

The key ran in the lock.

The door receded.

And the light of day dawned upon Sataniello.

He threw a quick glance upon the new comers.

His eye kindled with hope.

He had seen Breeze among the men who had come to open the door to him.

He made a sign to his captain.

It was perceived by no one except by he for whom it was meant.

Sataniello had seen it.

Breeze was therefore satisfied.

The Boy Brigand knew that it would be unwise indeed for him were he to attempt to escape now.

Among his foes he had seen a friend.

How different was he now from the morning?

But a few minutes he was forlorn and downcast; now he would have gone through fire and water—fought a whole regiment.

The men, who were apparently countrymen and customers who were staying at the inn, were strong-built Italians, and Sataniello soon perceived that if it came to a contest where bodily strength would carry off the prize, he should have no chance of escaping from their hands.

Thus he thought that he should abide his time.

And then to see Breeze close at hand gave him renewed strength.

Sataniello now looked up.

Boldly he gazed into the features of the new comers.

"My friends," he asked, "what brings you here?"

"Who do you call your friends?" a rough-looking man asked. "Low coward—vile hound—murderer—thief—robber!"

These were insults that Sataniello would have wiped out with the blood of him who had uttered them had he been free.

Such a speech was unprovoked.

It was a cowardly ejaculation.

Breeze felt it as such.

Had the man who spoke them been engaged in a terrible struggle with Sataniello, such words might have been excused.

Emanating as they did from the lips of a cool collected individual, nothing cold palliate them.

Insult a being who can defend himself, but do

not spit in the face of him who is powerless to resent it.

There is something too degrading in the behaviour of the man who kicks his antagonist when he is down for us to expatiate upon it.

The Boy Brigand swore revenge against the speaker.

Breeze, on his side, determined not to forget what he had heard.

"Do not be too hard upon him," one of the countrymen observed. "If he has acted wrongly, he will suffer for it. Oh Sebastian, I am astonished at you."

This was the rebuke which was offered to the speaker by one of the men who had paid the visit—which we have minutely described—to Sataniello.

The countrymen surrounded Sataniello.

"Walk before us, you bold brigand," Breeze pursued, in a voice which he attempted to render as rough as he fairly could.

"What are you going to do with me," Sataniello asked.

"You will soon see," another replied.

As he had spoken, Sataniello had turned his face and remained motionless.

"Go on," another pursued, pushing him before him, "and do not stop discussing here, for we have no time to lose."

The Boy Brigand perceived by the last words that it would be wise for him to act in accordance with the request which was made, and so he stepped forward surrounded by the countrymen who had taken him out of the place of confinement where he had been cast after the struggle with the soldiers, who had been sent to apprehend him.

CHAPTER LXVIII.

WHICH RELATES FULLY THE BOY BRIGAND'S BEHAVIOUR, AND WHICH SHOWS TO SATANIELLO THAT OCCASIONALLY YOU MAY MEET A FRIEND AMONG FOES.

WHEN in the morning Sataniello had allowed his mind to wander from one thing to the other, he was far indeed from anticipating the incident which now occurred to him.

That he fully expected to take his departure from the Greyhound at no remote period, it would be idle for us here to say; but he never dreamt that he should be released from his place of confinement in the manner in which he was.

Although he had not much leisure before him to tax his brain as to the fate which awaited him, yet he could not but think that the way of proceeding adopted by the countrymen was strange in the extreme.

He believed that a messenger had been sent to Naples, to go in search of a strong detachment of soldiers, who would be commanded by some officer, who, provided with a warrant, would arrest in the king's name.

The soldier had not arrived yet.

He hoped that there would be some delay, and that they would come too late to seize his person and make him a prisoner.

From the presence of Breeze, the Boy Brigand opined that the Monk must have reached the cavern, and that his follower, not wishing to lose his captain, had hit upon some plans, the subsequent workings of which remain, doubtless, for him to witness.

What that plan was he could not make out.

It was, however, evident that Breeze was at the Greyhound for some purpose.

He felt happy that Breeze had come to his rescue, for his features, to the best of his belief, were unknown in the neighbourhood.

Would Sataniello be free once more?

Would he see Joanitta again?

Would he be able to go to Naples as the Marquis of Piatelli?

For let it not be thought that the Boy Brigand had given up all hopes of assuming the rank of the man who had been murdered by the orders of Paublas.

There is always something which mars our musings. Sataniello wondered over and over again what had become of the Hunchback. He wondered whether the statements which the Monk had uttered could be true, and whether a cripple like him, a being who was a monster of deformity and ugliness, could really have fallen in love with the Marchioness of Piatelli?

Owing to the privilege which we possess as writers of fathoming the most secret thoughts which crowd the brain of the various actors who have and are still to perform a part in the successive acts of this Italian drama, we may fairly assert that we have lost no opportunity of laying before our readers the strange and wayward ideas which enlisted the Boy Brigand's attention.

We have now, we think, fairly exhausted the topic, and no doubt can remain to our readers regarding Sataniello's character.

There was a bold hardihood in that brigand, who, being still a prisoner, looked forward to days of happiness and of pleasure.

Such were his musings as he stepped along the lobby which led from his place of confinement to the place where his guides were conducting him.

Three men walked before him and three behind him.

Among those who were close to him he recognised the features of Breeze, which now kindled with a radiant glow of hope.

"There must be something in store for me," Sataniello muttered to himself, "otherwise Breeze would not seem so contented in his mind."

What could it be?

Oh, how he wished he could have asked him to give him an explanation!

But to do so would have been imprudent in the extreme.

By too much hastiness he might ruin a bold plot.

He might compromise the success of it.

If he were to do so, his last chance would be snatched away from him.

To be patient was, it appeared to the Boy Brigand, the only course which remained open under the circumstances.

"What are you going to do with me?" Sataniello inquired, wishing to break the monotony of his guide's silence.

"Be quiet, and speak not," was the only answer which greeted his ears.

Thus he walked on.

He had now reached the end of the lobby.

Before him he saw a large garden, and a few yards further off the high road.

"Are they going to take me to Naples?" Sataniello muttered again, and imploringly he looked around him.

No one beyond Breeze had heard his question.

Breeze, however, had.

He watched his opportunity.

He threw a cursory glance around him.

The eyes of the men were directed towards the garden.

But they might turn round.

What if they were to detect him speaking to Sataniello?

His fate and that of the Boy Brigand would be sealed.

Yet he longed to communicate something to the Boy Brigand.

The landlord now appeared.

There was a momentary disturbance.

Breeze made the most of the occasion.

He leaned forward, and as quick as lightning, he spoke to Sataniello.

He had not been long in doing so.

But Sataniello rose to his full height.

What he had heard had given him hope.

What had Breeze said to him?

What could have so changed his countenance?

He could not have said much.

Not above a word or two.

And what were those words?

What was that sentence?

It was this—"We are on the watch."

Aye, "We are on the watch," had been the few words which had been swiftly whispered into the Boy Brigand's ears.

Sataniello mused.

"We" had struck him.

The whole band, therefore, were awake to his peril.

They were endeavouring to save him.

A conversation now ensued between the landlord and the countrymen.

We remember how the innkeeper had acted towards Sataniello.

We remember the tacit understanding which had taken place between the two men.

Nothing would have afforded more pleasure to the landlord than to see the Boy Brigand escape from the vigilance of his keepers.

Sataniello had behaved generously towards him.

He had paid for what he had consumed in his house like a prince.

Although the landlord could have no doubt as to Sataniello being now the bandit upon whose head a reward had been offered, still he felt for him a sympathy which he could not dismiss from his mind.

Inwardly he knew that Sataniello would henceforth be his friend.

In Italy a Brigand's friendship is not to be disdained.

Moreover, in those days when they swayed the land with a power and an ascendancy which the authorities were not always successful in shaking.

He was as astonished as Sataniello himself.

He could not make out the meaning of the countrymen in bringing the Boy Brigand in this garden.

Attentively he looked at them.

This did not seem to hinder their movements.

They led Sataniello in the garden.

They reached the side of a high tree, of which the circumference was large indeed.

One of the men brought a rope with him.

It had been lent to him by one of the innkeeper's servants.

Still more astonished than ever Sataniello gazed upon the rope.

He could not discover their object.

"We are going to lash you to this tree," one of his keepers began; "and we will fasten you tight to it until the soldiers come to fetch you."

Sataniello was about to ask what could have in-

duced them to act as they were doing, when one of the men spoke in a manner which acquainted him with that which he wished to know.

CHAPTER LXIX.

WHERE THE BOY BRIGAND BEGINS TO THINK THAT HE WILL HAVE TO DEAL WITH SEVERAL ITALIANS WHO HAVE RATHER STRANGE NOTIONS IN THEIR HEADS.—AND WHERE HE MEETS AGAIN WITH THE LANDLORD.

"THAT was a very good suggestion of our friend," the countryman began. "I should never have thought of it myself."

"Neither should I."

"But what is the object of fastening this man to this tree?" the innkeeper interrupted, advancing towards the group.

"Don't you see it?"

The landlord shook his head in the negative.

Meanwhile the Boy Brigand had been as quiet as a lamb.

"Not only I do not see it, maestro," the innkeeper pursued, "but I think it a very stupid piece of business."

"How so?" ejaculated the tall Italian who had insulted the Boy Brigand but a few minutes ago, and rising as he spoke to his full height.

"I cannot explain myself," the landlord pursued; "but I can only say this—it would have been much wiser to leave the man alone, and not to render his captivity more irksome by an extra display of cruelty. After all you are not executioners, and this is no part of your work."

"But I maintain it is," Breeze pursued. "We wish to attach the Boy Brigand to this tree. Above his head we will place a big label, upon which will be written, 'Behold Sataniello, the Boy Brigand, the Dark King of the Mountains, a prisoner!'"

"What good is there in that," the landlord inquired.

"Are you so stupid as not to comprehend yet?"

The landlord was about to reply that he was indeed at a loss to discern the wisdom of a similar step; but as he knew that he had to deal with men who were as stubborn as Andalusian donkeys he refrained from speaking.

"I will tell you then," one of the peasants pursued, volunteering an explanation, "there are many people who will pass along the high road."

The landlord nodded in assent.

Sataniello was getting more and more interested.

"And what has that Brigand to do with it?" the landlord inquired.

Breeze was looking towards the mountains.

The time was gradually elapsing.

Since the morning he had seen a good many things—he had plotted a deep plan, the success of which was as yet problematical.

But delay was dangerous.

Shortly the soldiers would come from Naples.

The Boy Brigand was also thinking of this heartrending alternative.

"Well, all the people that are passing by will halt by the roadside; they will gaze upon the features of the Boy Brigand, and carry abroad the news that he has at length met with his masters, and that he is no longer to be dreaded.

"Who gave you this capital plan?" the landlord asked.

The man who had spoken pointed with his finger towards Breeze.

The latter withstood the landlord's look.

Not a wrinkle of annoyance appeared upon his forehead.

He knew not that he was one of the Boy Brigand's friends.

How was he to know that?

Now it may be as well ere we go further to explain how Breeze happened to be at the Greyhound, and how he happened to have been the means of bringing the Boy Brigand out of his place of confinement.

It is necessary for us to be explicit in the extreme, so as to enable our readers clearly to understand the thread of this narrative.

How had Breeze met the Monk?

How had they come across each other?

This requires explanation.

We saw the Monk hurrying away from the inn in search of the Boy Brigand's followers.

We told our readers how he managed to pick out the best horse in the landlord's stable, and how he spurred him on to his destination.

While galloping the road, with a rapidity which was really wonderful, he saw an individual, dressed as an Italian padre, journeying along the pathway.

Sataniello's band was not so numerous as not to enable every one of his followers to recognise each other at a glance.

The Monk thought that he knew the tread of the wayfayer.

Further, it struck him that his features were familiar to him.

He directed his horse's head towards him.

One moment brought the two men together.

The recognition was instantaneous.

No time was to be lost.

The Monk asked Breeze whither he was going?

The latter replied that he had nothing on hand.

Then the Monk related to Breeze the peril in which the Boy Brigand had found himself placed, and besought him to go to his rescue.

The plan which we are endeavouring to describe in its minutest accuracy had been concocted there and then, and Breeze had hurried towards the Greyhound, relying upon the Monk to join him with the remainder of the troop.

This was how Breeze happened to be there at the time.

Providence, then, seemed to favour the Boy Brigand.

Perhaps he was meant for greater and better things than those which he had wrought, or perhaps, also he was doomed to perish.

As we have taken a somewhat deep interest in Sataniello's career we hope sincerely he was meant for the former.

Over and over Sataniello looked abroad.

Listlessly did his eye wander far away.

But he could not see.

His sight was obstructed by the peasants.

At one instant Sataniello thought of drawing his poniard and stabbing the first man who should stop him, and rush away to the open country along the road which stretched away before him and gain the mountains.

But he might fail.

But he would not do so if he could help it.

Why should he sneak away like a cowardly cur?

Would it not be better to retire with his face turned to his enemy.

Anxiously he waited.

A minute seemed an hour to him.

He knew nothing of Breeze's plan.

He had been told that his followers were on the watch.

Where he knew not.

He was, therefore, in a state of bitter suspense.

Strange to state—still, nevertheless true—the countrymen had never thought of binding Sataniello's hands.

After the desperate resistance which he had shown to do so would appear to us to have been the first step which they should have taken.

Breeze's suggestion had been looked upon as a very good one.

Beyond doubt it was, had it been a genuine one.

But it was not.

There was something lurking behind it.

But it mattered not.

The peasants were not aware of it.

Had suspicion entered their minds, what would they have done?

Seize hold of Breeze and make him share his captain's fate.

But for that they would have to deal with men of a different character than those of Sataniello and Breeze.

If, at the eleventh hour, no help came, Breeze had made up his mind to release his master and fight the countrymen.

Success, he doubted not, would attend his attempts.

The battle is half won when our antagonist is pounced upon unawares.

The helmets of the soldiers were not in view yet.

Besides, Breeze knew that the Neapolitan soldiery are not in the habit of hurrying their movements; and, knowing Sataniello safely imprisoned, they would take their leisure ere they came to take him away.

"Let us tie him up now," one of the men suggested.

This remark was unanimously re-echoed by the others.

They were all willing and ready to throw ridicule upon a brigand who, for a few years, had been the scourge of the mountains.

"Where is the inscription?" the landlord inquired.

"It has to be written yet," Breeze pursued.

The innkeeper laughed with a jolly, loud laugh.

"You are fine fellows in your way, to be sure," he exclaimed.

A smile appeared upon the Boy Brigand's lips.

His gaze had met that of Breeze.

"I will have nothing to do with this pantomime of yours," the landlord exclaimed. "I wash my hands out of it."

Thus speaking, the landlord walked back to the tavern.

There was a good deal of wisdom in that man.

He knew that Sataniello would not be always so quiet as he had been for the last hour or two, and, dreading violence, he kept out of it.

If we acted always as prudently as our friend the landlord did, we should, in many instances, spend life much more pleasantly than some of us do, and keep clear of the many scrapes into which our officiousness is sure to lead us.

THE BRIGAND'S STRATAGEM.

CHAPTER LXX.

SATANIELLO IS BOUND TO A TREE.—HIS ESCAPE
THEREFROM.—DESTRUCTION OF THE BAND.—
DEATH OF THE PEASANT.—ESCAPE OF THE BOY
BRIGAND.

AFTER some few minutes Breeze took a long rope,
and, advancing towards the Boy Brigand, threw a
portion of it over his shoulders.

As he did so he took occasion to whisper in his
captain's ear—

"Fear not, captain; the band will soon arrive to
rescue you; and should the military reach the spot
before them, you will yet be able to escape."

How so?" asked Sataniello, his dark eye glowing
distrustfully upon his follower.

"Hist," said Breeze; "permit me to pass this rope
round your body and the tree several times; it will
avert suspicion, and likewise aid your escape should
the soldiers reach the spot before our friends can
arrive."

"How so?" asked Sataniello in a whisper.

"This tree is hollow."

"Well."

"You have but to force your back against the
bark, and it will crumble to powder under the force
applied—at least, the portion against which you are
now placed, and you will find yourself in the hollow
trunk."

"And make for myself a secure prison-house,"
exclaimed the Boy Brigand.

"Not so, captain; I had not placed you here did
I not know that at the bottom of the hollow is a

23

trap leading to an underground passage, which runs some distance into yonder wood."

"Ah, where did you discover this?" said Sataniello, in tones of surprise.

"That little matters now, captain," replied his follower; "and anxious eyes are upon us. They must not see us in conversation, or suspicion may enter their minds. Pretend to be indignant at the treatment now offered you. Struggle to release yourself, but press not your back upon the tree, or you will reveal the secret, and prevent your escape. That must be only done should the soldiers arrive before the band; for, though you could easily escape, I should fall."

"Thanks, my friend," whispered Sataniello, as the other gave the finishing twist to the rope, and turned towards the lookers-on.

"Now," said Breeze, pointing to the bound youth; "all who pass this way may see and revile him. Behold the King of the Mountains, the dreaded Brigand! who has carried desolation into the homes of the Italians—who has defied her laws, and scoffed at her power! See him—mark him well! the fearful Bandit—now powerless to harm you more! Friends, the Brigand is captured at last!"

Amid shouts of derision Breeze returned to the side of the peasants.

At this moment, one of the men looking out into the distance, perceived the helmets of the soldiers as they came on at a quick pace towards the inn.

"The soldiers are coming," shouted the man.

"Ah!" exclaimed Breeze, as he started round with an anxious glance upon his face.

But in a moment he checked himself—his hasty exclamation nearly betrayed him.

"The soldiers are coming," he reiterated, making towards Sataniello. "Ha, ha! Brigand, your hour has come—your game is played out, and Italy is freed of one of her greatest scourges."

The Boy Brigand struggled with his bonds.

"Not yet—not yet," whispered Breeze, "the band may still arrive first. They are some distance hence. Should our band fail us I will give you the signal when to disappear. Take this," he hurriedly exclaimed, as he perceived the eyes of all the others fixed upon the advancing military. "Fear not, captain, I will wave my hand as a signal all in good time."

And thrusting a sheathed poinard into the breast of the bound youth, he withdrew a few paces, lest suspicion should fall upon himself.

With a look of gratitude, and a feeling of the same virtue in his heart, the Boy Brigand awaited the appearance of his band or the signal of his follower.

The soldiers came on at a good pace, their helmets glittering between the trees which skirted the road.

Anxiously Breeze gazed alternately at the military and the opposite direction from which they were approaching.

Every moment brought them nearer and nearer, yet there was no appearance of the Bandits.

He grew nervous, and inwardly cursed the delay of the band.

On, on came the military nearer—nearer to the spot on which the bound Brigand stood, anxiously awaiting the signal of his follower.

They were now within a quarter of a mile of the inn.

Despairingly Breeze looked in the opposite direction.

A cry broke from his lips—he saw the tall sugarloaf hats of Sataniello's band.

But they were yet some distance from the spot.

He was about to hurry forward to meet them, but paused as he recollected his promise to give the signal in time for Sataniello to escape.

The trunk of the tree being a large one, and the Boy Brigand's back to the road by which the soldiers were advancing, he was unable himself to know the distance his foes were from him.

There was no help for it, so Breeze must remain.

But with what anxious eyes did he not the approach of his friends as he perceived ever and anon their forms creeping through the trees by the road side.

Nearer and nearer came the Bandits, and nearer and nearer rode the soldiers.

It was evident they would both arrive by the tree about the same time.

Breeze placed his hand to his mouth, and uttered a cry like a bird.

It was a signal of danger and speed.

The face of the Boy Brigand lighted up with joy. He knew the band were near.

The Bandits had heard it, and they quickened their pace, and in a few moments the whole band had burst out into the road.

But too late—the soldiers were upon the spot also, and their number doubled that of the Brigands.

Drawing a dagger from beneath his garments, Breeze leapt forward towards his captain.

"Fly, captain, fly," he exclaimed, at the same time giving the signal; "we cannot release you ere the soldiers will shoot you down. Fly, fly—the tree—press forward, and you are saved."

"Ah, traitor!" exclaimed one of those who had been instrumental in binding the youth. And he rushed towards the tree to prevent the escape of the Boy Brigand.

He believed that Breeze was about to sever the bonds with his weapon.

But ere he had taken two steps forward, the dagger of Breeze glittered in the air, then descended into the breast of the wretch, who, with a cry of agony, fell to the earth a corpse.

For a moment the others stood irresolute, then simultaneously from each throat burst forth—

"Traitor! he's a Brigand—down with him!"

But, like a tiger at bay, Breeze stood before his captain, who, fixing his feet firmly against the ground, pressed with all his force upon the tree.

The rotten bark gave way, and the Boy Brigand, falling backwards into its centre, the cords dropped loosely around the trunk.

At this moment both soldiers and Brigands arrived on the ground.

"The trap, the trap!" exclaimed Breeze; and as he turned and saw the head of his captain disappear beneath the ground, he fell forward into the opening with a bullet in his brain.

The soldiers and Brigands had seen the state of affairs in an instant, and each prepared for the conflict.

The Bandits had come to rescue their captain, but had met with a force against whom it would be madness to fight.

But they were desperate men—had led desperate lives—and desperate means must be used to escape capture.

Having fired their carbines, they rushed madly upon the soldiers, striking at them with the stocks of their weapons.

But the long sabres and the pistols of the soldiers did fearful execution—added to which the military were mounted, and the Brigands could not so easily escape them as they could do among the rocky defiles of their mountain home.

Valiantly, desperately, frantically they fought—they knew that they did so with a halter around their necks, and that if they were taken they would be executed; so they fought on heedless of the numbers opposed to them—without hope, but resolved to sell their lives as dearly as they could.

One by one they fell, and lay upon the ground, with the blood gushing from their wounds, and saturating the fruitful soil with their criminal gore.

Not a word was spoken—there was no time for that; blows alone engaged their whole thought and attention.

The last Brigand had fallen, refusing to surrender—the crack of pistol and carbine was hushed, and the soldiers who remained out of the company, sent to carry the Boy Brigand away to prison, now rested from their fearful work.

But where was the captain of that lawless gang? where was that terror of the mountains—the Boy Brigand?

He had escaped!

But how?

None had seen him go.

The soldiers approached the tree, and examined it. The way by which he had disappeared then became apparent.

One of them drew a pistol, and fired into the opening at his feet.

Then he listened for any cry which might indicate that the Boy Brigand was there.

But not a sound met his ear.

At this moment one of the men who had seen the captain fastened to the tree looked into its hollow trunk, and perceived the opening.

"He has escaped by that opening," he said.

"But is there a passage from this tree?" asked the soldier who had fired into the space at his feet.

The man shook his head.

"I did not know that it was from this tree; yet I have heard speak of a passage that led from a hollow trunk a long way into the woods."

"Then he has escaped thither," said the soldier. "Mount, comrades, and away in pursuit. Our work is but half done if we capture not the Boy Brigand."

The soldiers who remained uninjured mounted their horses and struck off to the wood. But here they were compelled to dismount and enter the wood on foot.

Taking their pistols, which they had again loaded, from their holsters, they darted among the foliage in search of the dreaded bandit.

The man who had spoken of the passage leading to the wood accompanied them; but they all got parted amid its intricacies, although they kept each other well in sight.

Suddenly the peasant paused, and called out to the soldiers, "Here's the spot at which the passage ends."

But, as the soldiers made towards him, he threw up his arms with a loud cry, and sunk down upon the earth stabbed to the heart.

The poniard of the Boy Brigand had found a sheath in his breast.

For a moment the soldiers stood paralysed by the shock which this event caused them; but it was for a moment only, and he who had fired the pistol down the opening at the base of the hollow trunk exclaimed, "This is his work. He is hereabout. Keep a sharp look out and we shall yet capture him; but take him alive, if possible."

The men now commenced a rigid search through the wood, making their way towards the opposite side to that at which they had entered it, and where they expected the Boy Brigand would make his way to.

But they were unable to discover any trace of him.

Chagrined and disappointed, they were about to return and bear away the body of the peasant who had fallen so suddenly in the wood, when one of the soldiers, casting his eyes in the direction of a line of rocks which evidently bounded the sea, saw the form of the Boy Brigand gliding along at their base.

Instantly he drew the attention of his comrades, and together they started off, resolved to effect his capture.

But Sataniello—for he, indeed, it was—had perceived that he was discovered, and commenced to climb the rocks.

The soldiers hurried on, and reached their base at the very instant that the Boy Brigand had gained their summit, some fifty feet above them.

Here the soldiers paused, and the one who appeared to be the leader said,

"Sataniello, your band are all destroyed—resistance is useless. Surrender, and trust to the mercy of the king."

"Never!" exclaimed the Boy Brigand. "If my band is destroyed I am still free, and ere long you shall find me with a troop at my back who shall carry fear and desolation through these proud domains. Surrender! never! Take me if you can—slay me if you dare."

The soldiers presented their pistols—a dozen bullets flew whizzing through the air—and, when the smoke had cleared away and permitted an uninterrupted view of the summit of the rocks, the Boy Brigand, or the Dark King of the Mountains, was nowhere to be seen.

"He is hit," said the soldier, "and rolled down upon the other side."

"He may only be wounded, and yet escape," said another.

"He must not escape," said the first speaker. "We must ascend the rocks, and, dead or alive, convey him to our destination."

The soldiers commenced ascending the rocks. To them this was no easy task, and it took them a considerable time to reach the summit.

But at length they stood upon the top of the long line of grey rocks.

At their feet lay the sea, and the graceful waves were rolling slowly in upon their jagged sides.

In vain they looked for any trace of the fugitive—any trace of blood upon the stones.

But nothing met their gaze but the long line of grey stone, the silvery waters, and the bright blue sky.

They believed he must have fallen from the rocks into the sea, and, as they could detect no speck upon the waters, they concluded that in that fearful fall he must have struck his head against the jagged sides, and, stunned and unconscious, found a grave in the waters which danced and sported at their base.

But Italy was not yet free of the Boy Brigand, or the Dark King of the Mountains.

END OF BOOK THE FIRST.

BOOK THE SECOND.

CHAPTER I.

THE HOME OF BRIGANDAGE—THE MOUNTAIN PASS—
BRIGANDS ON THE WATCH.

ITALY! beloved land of the poet, the painter, the sculptor, and the historian—region of sunny skies and fertile soil—birthplace of the great, the noble, and the brave—home of the Cæsars and the Antonys whose deeds are recorded in history and whose lives are written in letters of gold, couriers of civilisation, who carved in barbarous lands a path for Christianity and Truth—where mountains raise their proud heads to the clouds, and volcanoes belch their mighty tongues of flame and rivers of lava—where the graceful gondola floats over the clear, smooth waters, to the enchanting strains of the guitar—where the silvery stream reflects the colossal statues, palaces, and gorgeous architecture of thy sunny land—where music found birth and the poet Virgil a tomb—who sent forth armies who laid the world at thy feet—whose legions carried thy name from east to west and north to south, and stamped thy greatness upon the soil of the furthermost parts of the globe! Oh, Italy! proud, beautiful, enchanting Italy! how hast thou fallen since thy banner, waving on every coast, proclaimed thee mistress of the world!

Torn by inward commotions—lacerated by the fangs of thine own sons—tyrannised over by thine own rulers—bowed down by thy ministers—thy greatness has dwindled till, like the ashes of thy volcanoes, thou liest with thy power expended, thy lustre dimmed: with but the memory of the past to uphold thy fame; and, in the very centre of thy country, a merciless band of villains finds a safe retreat from the tarnished and keen-edged sword of justice which Cæsar swayed.

On the long line of Apennine mountains which divide Italy from east to west, and lie between the Mediterranean and the Adriatic seas, the brigands of Italy find a home and carry out a system of warfare with their own countrymen, and all who may be unfortunate enough to cross their path, in spite of all the attempts of the authorities to put them down or root them out of their strongholds.

Frequent are the incursions they make into the towns of St. Marino, Urbino, Forli, and even to the very outskirts of Florence, bearing off those for whom they believe a good ransom will be paid, and leaving behind them the trail of outrage and desolation. In vain are troops despatched to hunt them from their strongholds.

With a knowledge of the various defiles, chasms, precipices, and streams which intersect these monuments of nature, they deal death and destruction upon their foes, and set at defiance all the authorities and laws of the nation.

Among the many rents and chasms they find a refuge, only to steal out with loaded carbine and take fearful and certain aim at the head of the confused soldier, who, wearied by a fruitless chase and benighted among the various windings and hollows of those ranges, falls an easy victim to the bandits.

The crack of the carbine, and the small white cloud of smoke as it curls upwards to the bright blue sky, may betray to his fellows the lurking-place of the assassin; but, ere they reach it, the bandit has escaped to some other fortress, and his pursuers, by shifting their positions, have laid themselves within range of twenty carbines, the muzzles of which alone protrude from behind the edges of the defiles and belch forth death and destruction upon their pursuers.

Such is Italy at the time of which we write. Such is the character of the hordes who infest the mountain passes of that bright and sunny land.

It was night. The refulgent moon rode high in the clear blue canopy, and kissed the earth with its mellow rays, tinting with a bright yet subdued light mountain and river, valley and rivulet, and throwing a gleam of silvery gold on the fertile earth.

It lit up the mountain pass, the deep chasm, the rugged precipice—smiled upon the vegetation which grew so luxuriantly upon the sides of those bulwarks of nature on which man can but gaze with awe and admiration, and, in the inmost recesses of his soul, acknowledge that power which sways the destinies of worlds.

In the presence of these huge works of an Almighty hand man must bend the knee in adoration, so wonderful, fearful, and sublime do they appear, with their heads towering above the clouds, and reading to weak man the truth—that his works are great, but that the works of God are sublime!

What can better lead the thoughts of man to heaven than these wondrous works of nature—surely nothing! Yet within the very fastnesses of those glorious monuments men live, and sin, and die, defying alike human and divine law.

On this very night the robbers who make these mountains their home were on the watch.

With carbine by their sides they lay concealed amid the jagged steeps of the mountain passes which skirt the Apennine hills.

It had become known that a worthy merchant of Ravenna, together with his fair daughter and her affianced lover, attended only by a few servants, was on his way to Florence for the double purpose of witnessing the nuptials of his child and attending to urgent business which called him thither.

The lover of the young bride had before crossed the mountains to fetch away his bride from her father's home; but the business which had summoned the father to Florence would not admit of time for the ceremony to be performed at Ravenna, hence the ceremony was delayed till the youth should return to Florence, where he resided, to be wedded there as soon as Sebastian Sernetti, the worthy merchant, should have cleared up the business which brought him thither.

Of course, to Claudio and Paulina, the young lovers, the delay was anything but pleasant, especially to the former, who had fondly hoped to return to Florence a married man.

But "man proposes and heaven disposes," so there was no help for it; and they started forth on their journey, accompanied by Perditta, a young and pretty girl (who filled the office of lady's maid and companion to the beautiful Paulina), and Lucio and Pedro, servants of the merchant.

It was towards night that the merchant and his friends arrived at the mountains.

His daughter begged of him to delay the further progress of his journey till the morrow, as also did the servants, who, independant of being somewhat fatigued, had to convey the bride's *trosseau*, which, by the way, it took both Lucio and Pedro to carry.

To this request only Claudio appeared averse; and no wonder, poor fellow—he was anxious to be married.

The worthy Sebastian, under ordinary circumstances, would have denied his daughter nothing; but he was bound upon an errand which would admit of no delay.

So they entered the mountainous region as the first ray of the silvery moon penetrated the blue vault of heaven.

The brigands, it would seem, have some first-rate means of gaining information, for they were well acquainted with the fact of the party being on their road and the rank of the merchant and his friends.

Out, then, from their cavernous retreats they issued with loaded carbines and bared daggers, ready for plunder, rapine, or murder.

In one part of the defile, or mountain-pass, through which the travellers must pursue their road, a gang of brigands, attired in the fantastic costume they so love to wear, were drawn up in the shade of the rugged sides of the mountain.

One of them, a tall, well-formed man, who held his carbine as though it were a switch, often bending his head to the ground for some few moments, rose and confronted his followers.

"Not yet," he said; "they are somewhat tardy in their march. He must reach Florence within a given time, yet he lags by the way."

"He is old," said one, "and cannot move so swiftly as you or I, Captain."

"He had better place his feet firmer to the ground and take longer strides, or, by the Holy Virgin, my temper will be sorely tried, and I shall put a bullet through his brain the moment he appears in sight."

"He is weak and feeble, and can ill-defend himself, Captain," said Orsino, the previous speaker; "it would be cowardly to slay him."

The man addressed as Captain turned fiercely round.

"Keep your mouth closed, Orsino, or I may force my dagger into your throat."

Orsino clenched his teeth and grasped his carbine tightly, but remained silent.

The words of the Captain had galled him to the quick; but he recollected the oath he had taken to serve him, and remained silent.

Nor was he the only one to whom the words of the Captain were distasteful.

All present felt annoyed at their utterance, for Orsino was well beloved by his fellows, and the Captain disliked by them.

He was cruel and over-bearing, and they fondly hoped that ere long a dagger in his heart or a bullet in his brain might cancel their allegiance, and give them the power to seek a new leader.

Still the Captain listened intently for any sound of approaching footsteps.

"Antonio," he said, addressing one of the brigands; "go to the top of yonder height and watch. Lay yourself flat, so that the moon's light may not reveal you to the eyes of the travellers."

Antonio saluted his Captain, and made for the spot indicated.

"Angelo," continued the Captain, "take your post on the edge of the chain, and give the signal when the travellers are in sight."

"I shall scarcely get a good view of the pass from there, Captain Marcus," said the man.

Marcus turned fiercely upon him, exclaiming—"Go!"

The man departed; but his hand played with his dagger-hilt as he did so.

However, Angelo took up his position as ordered by the Captain, and laying himself flat along the rough, uneven spot, fixed his eye upon the Captain.

"I should like to blow his brains out," he thought, "but that the others might avenge his death."

Having thus despatched two of his followers to give warning of the approach of the merchant and his fellow-travellers, Captain Marcus leant back against the rough side of the mountain and waited.

The minutes wore away tediously, and his dark brows became blacker and blacker at the delay of the travellers.

But suddenly he started.

A low cry had saluted his ears.

It was the signal that the travellers were in sight.

"Back into the shadow," he said, addressing his men. "They are coming — ah, another signal ! There are but five; you need not fire. Wait till they reach this spot, then surround and bind them. Silence, they come!"

The men drew back into the shadow, as also did the Captain, and his dark eye gleamed as, by the bright moon's rays, he perceived the party of travellers wending their way towards him.

CHAPTER II.

THE TRAVELLERS IN THE MOUNTAINS.—THE SURPRISE.—DEATH OF MARCUS, AND APPEARANCE OF THE BOY BRIGAND.

ALL unconscious of the danger which awaited them—unconscious of the serpent in the path awaiting to coil its folds around them and pierce their hearts with its venomed sting, the travellers kept on their way through the defile.

Claudio, dwelling with rapture upon the honeyed words of his affianced bride, thought of nothing but the beauteous being at his side and the soul-entrancing pleasures which awaited him when the marriage ceremony should have made the lovely woman who smiled so sweetly upon him his own.

Sebastian, whose mind was filled with the business which carried him away from his home in Ravenna, had no thought for anything else; whilst Perditta, the pretty, dark-eyed lady's maid so engaged the attention of Pedro and his fellow-servant, that they could hear nothing but her voice, see nothing but her dark eye and glowing cheek as she flirted first with one and then the other, causing alternate feelings of jealousy and love to take possession of their breasts.

Thus the party kept on their way through the narrow defile, the bright moon playing upon their forms and casting long shadows upon the ground at their feet.

The balmy breeze came invigoratingly to their

senses, and the pure, fresh air of the mountains engendered a feeling of happiness in their hearts.

On towards the narrow portion of the pass they went, never for a moment dreaming of danger.

But, hark!

What cry was that?

It sounded like the shrill cry of a wounded bird. The party listened.

But all was silent; and again they moved forward.

A few paces, and the cry which had before attracted their attention was repeated.

Again they paused, and listened intently.

The cry is repeated, but this time from different directions.

"What can it be?" asked Paulina, her dark eye glancing nervously at her lover's face.

"The cry of a night bird, dear one," replied Claudio.

"But, hark! there it is again, and from yonder height," she said, pointing with her white, taper finger in the direction from which the second sound emanated.

"It is but the answer of its mate, dear one," replied the youth.

But as he spoke, he placed his hand in his breast, and grasped the ivory handle of a stiletto.

The truth had flashed upon his mind, but he would not speak to the beautiful girl by his side.

Still he resolved that, if his fears really were true, to defend her to the last drop of his heart's blood.

Scarce had these thoughts ran through his mind, than a slight rustle among the foliage of the trees which grew beside the defile, caused him to turn hastily, and draw the poignard from his breast.

As the bright gleam of the poignard glittered in the moon-beams, Paulina uttered a cry of terror, and clung to her lover.

She had detected the muzzle of a carbine levelled at his head.

"Fear not, dear one," he exclaimed, hastily. "I will not harm you. I scarcely know what prompted me to draw my poignard from its sheath.

But Paulina paid no heed to his words.

In heart-rending accents she burst forth—

"Oh, my father, my poor old father!"

"What mean you!" gasped the youth, now thoroughly alarmed.

"Look—look! See—see!" she gasped, still clinging to his arm in terror, and pointing in the direction of the carbine which still covered the head of her lover.

"Holy mother!" exclaimed Claudio, "we are surrounded by brigands!"

Paulina clung closer to his heart in fear.

"Sebastion—Pedro—Lucio!" exclaimed the youth, "we are entrapped. Look to your arms! —the brigands!—the brigands!"

At this moment, from between the interstices of the trees, twenty carbines protruded—their muzzles glistening in the moon's rays.

The whole party were brought to a dead halt.

The merchant drew his poignard, and strode to the side of his fair daughter and her lover.

Pedro and Lucio, dropping the luggage which they bore on to the ground at their feet, also drew their weapons, and prepared to defend their own lives and that of their master.

Perditta, the handmaid, only sank down upon the earth, and uttered a series of loud screams.

"Silence!" said the merchant, addressing the girl.

"Oh, oh! I'm a going to be murdered and bigamised by a lot of brigands—oh, dear!"

And leaping up from the earth, she flung her arms around the neck of Pedro, and clung to him as fiercely as she could.

"Peace—peace" exclaimed Claudio.

"I shall be all pieces soon!" exclaimed the girl; "they will cut me and hack me, chop me and lop me, and—and—oh, dear! oh, dear!"

And here she gave vent to a series of groans, and wound up with a low whine of despair on the bosom of Pedro.

Claudio could hardly repress a smile at the antics of Perditta, spite of the position in which they all stood.

He turned and looked behind him anxiously.

The muzzle of a carbine covered him and his friends whichever way he turned.

"We have walked into an ambush," he said, addressing the merchant, "and heaven only knows how we shall get out of it."

The old merchant sighed and shook his head.

"I fear most for my daughter," he said.

"So do I," replied Claudio, "but ere they shall offer outrage to her, this body must cease to have life."

"Nobly spoken, sir," said the merchant, grasping the hand of his intended son-in-law. "Come what may, defend and protect my child."

"With my heart's best blood," replied the youth, "I will die to defend her, though in dying I lose her!"

At this moment the tall figure of Marcus, the captain brigand, stepped out from among the trees into the centre of the pass.

He was a noble-looking man, and as the full moon's rays played upon his picturesque costume, and revealed the outlines of his handsome features, on which a look of firm determination sat, the travellers could not but gaze upon him with admiration, though they shuddered with fear at his presence.

Dropping his carbine till its stock rested upon the ground at his feet, he exclaimed, as he rose his hat from his head, and bent low before the travellers—

"Signors and signoras, I greet you."

The merchant frowned, and Claudio grasped tightly the handle of his poignard, whilst Paulina clung the tighter to the arm of her lover.

"We have long waited for you, signor," said Marcus; "so long, indeed, that the patience of myself and followers were nearly exhausted."

The merchant drew his bent form up to its full height.

"Brigand," he exclaimed, "what would you with us peaceable travellers?"

"Simply, Signor, whatever valuables yourself and friends may have about you."

"Robber!"

"Such, Signor, is my calling," replied Marcus, calmly.

"Stand aside, and allow us to pass," said Claudio.

The brigand cast a disdainful glance upon the young lover.

"Your tones are haughty," he said, sarcastically.

"I command you stand aside," said Claudio.

"And if I refuse?" said the brigand, as calmly as before.

"I will drive my poignard to its hilt in your heart," exclaimed Claudio, advancing threteningly towards the brigand captain.

Marcus drew back a pace, and raised his carbine.

"Boy!" he exclaimed, "with this weapon I can dash out your brains as easily as I now give vent to this whistle.

And the brigand blew a loud, shrill whistle.

Its echoes had scarcely died away, ere twenty

brigands stepped out from the trees at the side of the defile, and gathered around their commander.

The travellers drew back in fear at this.

"You perceive, signors, that resistance is useless. You will please to accompany us."

"Whither?" asked the merchant, turning pale.

"To a place, signor, where you will be held close prisoner, till such time as the ransom I shall demand be paid."

"You dare not offer me this indignity," exclaimed the merchant.

"Signor, you mistake. I dare offer an indignity to the king," exclaimed the Brigand captain.

"And if I submit to this," said the merchant, whose greatest fear was for his daughter, "will the remainder of my friends be allowed to pursue their way in peace, and free from all molestation?"

The Brigand looked surprised at this question.

"Signor," he said, "as far as regards your servants, they are free to pursue their way to Florence—at least, the signorita will not—we may find occupation for her here."

"The signorita," gasped the merchant, as his cheek turned pale.

"Even so. Perditta is her name, I have heard. She is a pretty girl, and will form an excellent companion for my Lieutenant, whom I have long promised a reward for his fidelity to me," said Marcus, a meaning smile gathering on his brow.

At these words the pretty Perditta released her grasp of Pedro, and suddenly recovered all her energies.

As long as she remained under the impression that she might have to find room in her bosom for a bullet or a dagger, she could not muster sufficient strength to stand upright; but now that she found the only harm intended her was to make her the mistress of the Lieutenant of a band of Brigands her courage revived, and she withdrew her arms from the neck of her fellow-servant, whom she no longer required to support her trembling frame.

"If," she thought, the Lieutenant is as handsome as the captain, I don't think I shall ever regret falling into the hands of the Brigands."

During this colloquy between the merchant and the Brigand, Claudio was in agony.

He looked alternately at the pale face of the beautiful girl at his side and the Brigands, who stood silently confronting them.

He believed they would try to tear her from his arms, but he resolved that one at least should find he had a heart, arm, and will to defend her.

He grasped his poignard so tightly that he almost lacerated his hands.

Still he spoke not, neither did Paulina.

Anxiously they awaited the turn of events.

"But my daughter," asked Sebastian, after a pause; "surely you will not prevent her journey to Florence?"

Marcus shook his head meaningly, while a strange smile played around his thickly-bearded mouth.

"Your daughter, signor, shall receive no ill-treatment at the hands of myself or followers," said Marcus.

"Then you will permit her to depart in peace?" said the merchant, with a feeling of joy in his heart.

"Depart she cannot."

"Must she then be ransomed?" said Sebastian despondingly.

"The ransom must be heavy indeed that Marcus, the Brigand captain, will accept for your lovely daughter," replied the chief of the Bandits.

"How so?" asked the old man, a sad foreboding taking possession of his heart.

"Simply, signor, because I have marked her for my own," replied Marcus, in a cold, calm tone.

"Brigand, you dare not' exclaimed Claudio, advancing towards the Captain, and threatingly raising his poignard.

But ere he had taken two steps forward, the carbines of the Brigands were levelled at his head, and a loud scornful laugh broke from the lips of Marcus.

The youth drew back in horror, and Pauline, clinging to his breast, burst into tears.

"Villain," exclaimed the merchant; "you dare not."

"Signor, I have informed you that I dare defy the king. Think you, then, that I shall fear to carry out my will with you?"

"Base-hearted villain!" exclaimed Claudio, "you shall not tear her from my side whilst one drop of blood remain in these veins, or one breath in this body."

And throwing one arm around Paulina, with the other he brandished his poignard.

Pedro and Lucio, who had only gazed on in wonder. now stepped to the side of their young mistress, determined to fight for her whilst life and strength remained.

Marcus eyed them contemptuously and smilingly.

"Signorita," he said, "you will find me a worthy man enough; you have little occasion to tremble, since you will hold a position denied to any other woman in our mountain retreat."

Paulina shuddered, and clung the closer to Claudio.

"Friends," said Claudio, turning to Pedro and his companion, "we are but three, and the Brigands are twenty. Shall we surrender the Signorita Paulina into their murderous hands, or struggle to protect her till the last drop of our blood?"

For a moment there was no reply to this.

But Pedro at length stepped forward.

"Signor," he said, "this heart must cease to beat ere Paulina falls into the hands of these ruthless men."

And the man placed his hand upon his breast.

"Thanks," my friend," replied Claudio; "there are two daggers there to carve a passage for her escape."

"Three, signor, exclaimed Lucio, leaping to his side.

But Marcus looked on in silence.

He saw the row of carbines, and he knew he could count upon them.

A scornful smile curled his lip, and a light shone in his bright black eye.

He cast his eyes around the assembled Brigands.

Then he gave the order for them to fall in.

Slowly and compactly the Brigands closed around the lovers and their friends, till the muzzles of their carbines were within a few feet of their breasts.

"Orlando, said Marcus, "take the reward I promised you."

And the captain pointed to the trembling Perditta.

Orlando stretched forth his hand to press the arm of the maiden, when Claudio, raising his poinard above his head, buried it deeply in the Brigand Lieutenant's heart.

With a loud cry the man fell forward, and as he did so Claudio grasped his carbine, and possessed himself of the weapon.

The brigands raised their weapons to execute summary justice upon the man who had slain their officer, when Morcas exclaimed—

"Hold! not by such honourable means shall he die. Spare him now, that we may torture him hereafter."

The brigands drew back at these words.

Then Marcus advanced, and, looking the youth firmly in the face, he said—

"Claudio, for such I know your name to be, you shall suffer for this work."

"Coward! I defy you," exclaimed the young man.

"Seize that girl," ordered the Brigand captain.

The men advanced to obey his commands.

Claudio grasped the dagger still more firmly in his left hand, and raised the carbine of the Lieutenant Orlando in his right.

"The first that lays hands upon her dies," he exclaimed, in a voice of thunder.

But it was drowned in the loud derisive laugh of the brigands, as, keeping their carbines presented at him, they stepped forward.

The youth raised the weapon, but it was instantly dashed from his hand.

His poignard only remained to him now as before.

He called upon Pedro and Lucio to aid him, and then he struck with all his force at the brigand nearest to him.

But the poignard was shivered to the hilt on the stock of the brigand's carbine.

Pedro and Lucio also strove to keep the bandits off, but in vain. They were felled to the earth, and, bruised and bleeding, lay at the feet of their assailants.

Claudio now began to despair, and he flung himself upon the row of carbines and endeavoured to wrest them from the grasp of their possessors.

But they drove him back, till his foot slipped and he fell heavily to the ground.

Then Marcus seized the arm of the trembling Paulina.

The poor girl shrieked aloud for aid.

"You call in vain," said Marcus, as he pointed derisively at the fallen youth, now bound on the ground, and her father, who was held firm by two of the band. "You call in vain. I had been less merciful to your friends but for your sake. I am enchanted by your beauty, and shall claim you for my own."

Then, turning to his followers, he exclaimed—

"Comrades, whatever spoil you may find share among yourselves. This is my portion, and I am satisfied with it."

"Release me, unmanly ruffian," exclaimed the girl, struggling to free herself from the grasp of the brigand.

"No, no," he replied. "You are my share of this night's work. Nay, it is useless to struggle. You are mine, and none on earth can save you."

"Liar!" exclaimed a loud voice at that moment by his side; and, as Marcus turned in surprise to see from whom the word came, he received a heavy blow in the face from a youth who had unseen stolen upon them.

"Ah!" exclaimed Marcus, drawing his dagger from his belt. But ere he could raise it the arm of the youth descended and he fell to the earth, and in his fall unsheathing a poignard which had been buried in his breast.

"Oh! I am slain, and by a boy," gasped Marcus, raising himself upon his elbow and glaring at the youth before him. "Who—who are you?"

The youth flung his arm round the fainting form of Paulina, as he exclaimed—

"Sataniello, the Boy Brigand; or, the Dark King of the Mountains."

CHAPTER III.

THE BRIGANDS PROCLAIM SATANIELLO CAPTAIN.— THE MURDER OF THE MERCHANT.—THE DAUGHTER'S ANGUISH, AND OATH OF VENGEANCE.

As Marcus fell beneath the blow of the Boy Brigand, his followers simultaneously raised their carbines to avenge him.

But instantly they were lowered.

The name of Sataniello, the Boy Brigand, or the Dark King of the Mountains, struck terror to the hearts of that wild band.

They had heard of the daring deeds of the Boy Brigand, and they were filled with respect and awe at his presence.

Often had many of them wished that he were their captain, for the overbearing Marcus was detested if he was feared by them.

And they drew back as they lowered their carbines, and gazed in respectful silence upon the tall, proud form of that Bandit Boy, who had earned for himself a name of terror, which echoed throughout the length and breadth of Italy.

"Brigands of the Apennines," exclaimed Sataniello, drawing his tall form up to its full height, and gazing calmly round upon the banditti as their Captain fell back dead at his feet, "at my feet lies the Captain of your band: would you avenge one whose overbearing nature denied you even your common rights—would you slay the executioner who has given you justice?—is there one among you who can raise his carbine to the heart of the Boy Brigand, the Dark King of the Mountains?"

And scornfully Sataniello looked around the assembled group of bearded men, whose deeds had rendered each liable to a fearful doom.

For a moment there was no reply to these words.

Each looked towards the other as though he would read his companion's thoughts.

Then, as if some magnetic influence pervaded the whole body, they raised their carbines above their heads, and shouted—

"Long live Sataniello, the Dark King of the Mountains!"

"King of the Mountains!" came back in loud echoes from hill and vale, crag and peak, of that wild retreat of the banditti.

A smile played around the lips of the Boy Brigand, and his dark eye flashed with a sudden fire.

Then he planted his foot upon the neck of the prostrate Marcus, and said—

"Have I or have I not done you service by slaying the tyrant who now lies cold and dead at my feet?"

"You have. Long live Sataniello!" exclaimed the brigands.

"You have long suffered under his command," continued the Boy Brigand, "but your oaths forbade you to rid yourself of one whom you could neither love nor respect. But you are now free to choose another leader."

"Sataniello — Sataniello, the Boy Brigand!" shouted the bandits.

Again the eye of the young brigand beamed brightly.

This was the aim he sought.

He had gained it.

His followers had all been destroyed, and he sought another band.

It was before him.

Men well tried and proved in their avocation.

Still he must not appear too anxious.

SIGNORITA PAULINA, THE BRIGAND'S CAPTIVE.

He must lead them to believe that their welfare, not his own aggrandisement, had prompted him to slay their commander.

"Friends," exclaimed the youth, "think well what you do when you offer me the post of your late captain."

"We have—we have!" exclaimed the bandits.

"You know me not," continued the Boy Brigand.

"We have heard of you," said one of the men, and no one is more fit to command us."

"Sataniello for captain!" exclaimed the brigands in a breath.

"Brigands," said Sataniello, "my band has been destroyed, and I myself have had to fly."

"Command us, and we will obey you," said one.

"Think what you do," said Sataniello.

"We are resolved."

"Then I accept the offer," said Sataniello, with a smile.

"Hail to the Boy Brigand!" exclaimed one.

"Hail to the Boy Brigand, the Dark King of the Mountains!" shouted the bandits.

"My friends, I accept the post," said Sataniello.

"And you will be true to your oath?" said Sataniello.

"We will," resumed the brigands in one second.

"'Tis well," said Sataniello; and I feel proud and happy to command so brave a band."

"A cheer," said one, "for Sataniello, the Boy Brigand, or the Dark King of the Mountains!"

The cheer was given, and Sataniello was installed in office as captain.

He had now another band, and the peaceably disposed would once more feel the weight of his power, and tremble with terror at his name.

Meantime the merchant, his fair daughter, her lover, and the servants, had stood gazing on in wonder and fear at the proceedings.

Each had been seized by the brigands, and rendered powerless to offer any resistance.

Paulina trembled. A glow of pleasure had suffused her cheek when she saw the uncouth Marcus struck to the earth, and felt her slender form encircled by the arm of the handsome youth Sataniello.

But now her heart sank within her as she discovered that he was a brigand, and above all, the dreaded King of the Mountains.

She would have fallen to the earth, but the strong arm of the youth supported her.

The merchant, too, trembled for his daughter.

He had heard of the dreaded brigand—the scourge of Italy, and he feared for the worst.

Claudio was in agony.

He cursed the ill fortune that had deprived him of his poignard.

He would have buried it to the hilt in the breast

of the youth who had struck down the protector of his much-beloved Paulina.

Gratitude he would assuredly have felt towards any being who would protect the maiden; but too well he knew that Sataniello had served but his own ends, and that the beauteous Paulina had more to fear at the hands of the Boy Brigand than she would at the hands of Marcus.

The black deeds of the Dark King of the Mountains had penetrated into the very heart of Florence, and rendered his name a terror.

Turning to the merchant, the Boy Brigand said—"As captain of this band I beg to inform you, signor, that your liberty will be obtained only by the payment of a large ransom; also yours," he added, turning to Claudio; "and as the gentlemen of Florence and the merchants of Rowenna are reputed rich, I doubt not you will see fit to comply with my demands."

"What ransom do you ask?" inquired the merchant for the whole party.

"Two thousand pistoles for yourself," replied the Boy Brigand; "the same for your friend, and half that for your servants."

"And my daughter?" asked the merchant.

"Must ransom herself," replied Sataniello, in a meaning tone.

"How?" asked Sebastian.

"By her favours," coolly replied the Boy Brigand. "How say you, comrades; is it not so?"

"And the maid, too," replied one of the Brigands. "Ladies are a commodity much required in the mountains."

"Wretch!" gasped the merchant.

And his hand played with the handle of a small stiletto which he had concealed in his breast.

"Villain!" exclaimed Claudio, endeavouring to break away from those who held him, and reach the side of the now almost fainting Paulina.

"Be calm, signors—be calm," said the Boy Brigand.

"Calm, villain!" exclaimed Claudio; "would that my poignard were in my grasp, and my hand free."

"Why so?" asked Sataniello.

"I would bury it to its hilt in your black and craven heart," exclaimed the lover of the beautiful girl.

"Shame on you," said the merchant. "I had thought that Brigands could respect their captors."

"We love them," said Sataniello, with a meaning glance—"at least the signoritas."

"Love?" said Claudio.

"Aye, love," replied the Boy Brigand; and his arm tightened around the waist of the terrified girl.

Paulina shrank from him.

But Sataniello drew her form closer to his heart.

She struggled to free herself from his embrace; but the strong arm of the Brigand held her powerless, and she shrieked out—

"Claudio—father—save me!"

Claudio struggled fiercely with his gaolers, and would have broken from them, but Angelo raised his carbine and dealt him a heavy blow on the side of the head.

The youth staggered from its force, and became almost insensible.

"Be quiet, signor," said Angelo, "or the next blow may be harder still."

Claudio saw that further resistance was useless, and a sigh escaped his lips.

Not for himself, but for the pale, trembling girl, who he saw nearly fainting in the arms of the Boy Brigand.

"Coward as well as villain!" exclaimed the merchant, his aged form swayed by the powerful emotions which shook his breast. "Release your hold of my child!"

But the Boy Brigand only laughed scornfully, and pressed the poor girl more firmly to his breast.

"Save me, father, from these vile men," gasped Paulina. Pay them any ransom they may demand; but save me—save me!"

"Brigand, ask your price; and, though it ruin me, I will save my daughter."

The Boy Brigand paused.

A thoughtful expression sat upon his brow.

Thus he continued for some few minutes.

The merchant waited in agony his reply.

And the trembling girl rose her eyes to his dark face.

She would read there his decision.

She would mark in those handsome yet cruel lineaments his resolve.

But his was a face which betrayed not the workings of the heart.

Sataniello could command his countenance.

He would have made a great actor.

So well could he conceal or pourtray his feelings.

But he turned at length to his companions.

Fixing his eyes questioningly upon them he said—"How say you, comrades, shall the girl be ransomed by gold?"

And he paused for a reply.

Angelo stepped forward.

"Captain," he said, "in the name of the band, we present the signorita to you."

A smile broke over the face of the Brigand.

And his arm tightened around the form of the maiden till its pressure became painful.

"And yonder maiden?" said the Boy Brigand, pointing to Perditta.

"We will draw lots for her," answered Angelo.

A small scream—but a very small one indeed—broke from the lips of Perditta.

"You hear, signor," said the Boy Brigand, turning to the merchant; "the lady is mine."

"And the ransom you demand—— ?"

"Her love," said Sataniello.

"Fiend! would you blast the happiness of my child, and bow my grey hairs with sorrow to the grave?"

"But," said Sataniello, "she will not wither under the kindness of the Boy Brigand, and, for yourself, you need not fear."

"Wretch," gasped the father; "once more I bid you release your hold."

"You do not command here, signor," said the Boy Brigand; that is for me. 'Tis for you to obey."

"Will you release my child?" exclaimed the merchant.

And his grasp tightened upon his weapon.

"When the passions are satiated and love grows tired she may join you again," said Sataniello.

"Villian!" never shall she fall a victim to such a fiend. Thus do I save her from destruction!"

And the old man sprang forward.

He had drawn the weapon from his breast.

The bright blade glistened in the moonlight.

The Brigand started back, and released his hold of the fair Paulina.

This movement was fatal to the object of her father.

For, finding herself released from the hold of the Boy Brigand, she flung herself upon the merchant's breast.

And the blade remained in the air, lest he should strike his child.

Had Paulina not flung herself upon him it had been lowered in the heart of the Boy Brigand.

The bandits knew not that he had a weapon, so closely had it been concealed.

But now they saw the danger to which their youthful captain had been opposed.

They sprang forward.

They raised their carbines, and the poignard was struck from his feeble grasp.

With a cry of rage he turned like a tiger at bay.

With a cry of fear Paulina clung the closer to his breast.

In a moment the Boy Brigand recovered the surprise into which this circumstance had thrown him.

He advanced towards the merchant and his daughter.

He threw his arms around her waist, and endeavoured to tear her away from her father's breast.

But, with a cry of horror, she flung her arms around the neck of the worthy Sebastian, and defied the strength of the Boy Brigand to tear her away.

With a howl of rage Sataniello drew his dagger from its belt.

"Let go your hold," he exclaimed to the merchant, whilst his dark cheek paled with rage.

"Never, Brigand," exclaimed the old man, encircling the form of his child with both arms.

"Then die!" exclaimed Sataniello.

And he raised his poignard above his head.

The bright blade gleamed in the moon's rays.

Flashed for a moment above the head of the feeble old man.

Then down it descended with the rapidity of lightning.

Down, down to its hilt it was buried in the neck of the merchant.

A quick gasy—a gurgling sound, emanated from the throat of the old man.

His hands relaxed.

His head fell forward.

And the hot blood spurted from the wound as the Boy Brigand withdrew the hellish steel.

Gushing out upon the arms of the Brigand, and over the face of Paulina.

The old man staggered and fell.

A wild piercing shriek of anguish burst from the lips of Paulina; and with her arms still encircling the neck of her father, she fell with him heavily to the ground.

And the hot blood oozed up over her beautiful face and neck, and bathed their alabaster whiteness in its crimson flood.

The living and the dead were clasped in each other's arms.

The father and daughter lie upon the damp ground bereft of senses.

Heaven had been merciful, and, for a time at least, rendered that fair girl forgetful of her misery.

But for a time only did it throw around her the shield of insensibility.

She must wake again to the horrors of her situation—to the fact that a father's arm could no longer shield and protect her—a father's voice no longer whisper words of counsel in her ears.

Awake to the fact that the spirit had fled from its earthly tenement—that the hand of cruel, remorseless man had severed body and soul, and rendered her fatherless and wretched.

Claudio—whom the blow from the butt-end of the carbine had rendered almost unconscious—was fast recovering its depressing effects, and, with a cry of horror, he shut his eyes to the fearful scene.

His first impulse was to rush forward, and endeavour to avenge the death of the merchant; but the row of carbines held him powerless, and he resolved to await an opportunity to effect his purpose.

Meanwhile, the Boy Brigand coolly wiped his blood-stained weapon—first on the grass at his feet, then upon the sleeve of his coat, and returned it to his breast.

Then he stooped down and lifted the insensible girl from the dead body of her parent.

The moonbeams played upon her face as he raised her up.

A face pale as marble.

For a moment Sataniello fancied that she was dead.

So fearfully pale and pulseless was that slender form.

He placed his hand upon her brow.

It was cold and clammy.

He grasped her wrist.

It was pulseless.

He laid his rude hand upon her beautifully-moulded bust.

Her bosom almost imperceptibly rose and fell beneath his touch.

But he knew she lived, and a smile broke over his features.

A smile of joy—but a demon smile.

His hot blood became fired by that rude touch, and he pressed her powerfully to his heart.

Oh, with what agony of mind did Claudio gaze on the actions of the Boy Brigand.

He foamed at the mouth, and gnashed his teeth in rage.

But he was powerless to move, so firmly was he held by the brigands.

His captors seemed to enjoy his sufferings.

They revelled in the agony he endured.

And they mocked his emotions by scornful laughter.

Suddenly Paulina heaved a deep sigh.

Then her eyes opened, and she gazed around, half fearful, like one in a dream.

Where was she?

The whole truth had not yet flashed upon her brain.

But it would come.

Aye, and with terrible force.

It would fall upon her soul like the overwhelming avalanche, crushing everything in its course.

Gradually the truth dawned upon her.

Her eye lightened upon the prostrate body of her father.

Then it wandered to the face of the Boy Brigand.

It rested thereon a moment.

What a world of meaning did not that glance convey.

But it was for a moment only.

Then it dropped again to the earth.

For a moment she was still.

Then a gasp, which seemed to sever the heart-strings, burst from her lips.

With the fury of a wounded tigress she burst away from the arms which encircled her, and stood foaming before the murderer of her much-loved father.

Her dark, lustrous eyes flashed with an unearthly fire.

Her thin lips were compressed.

Her slender form was drawn up to its full height.

For a moment she thus gazed upon Sataniello.

Then her lips parted, and she hissed rather than spoke the one word—

"Murderer!"

Beneath that haughty glance the eye of the Boy Brigand fell.

Before that proud and scornful attitude Sataniello trembled.

"Murderer!" she again exclaimed.

"Peace," said Sataniello, recovering himself, " or my dagger shall drink your blood, as it has done his who defied me."

And he pointed to the still warm corpse of the aged merchant.

"Assassin!" exclaimed Paulina; "look upon the work of your bloody hands. What have you done?"

"Stopped the croaking of an old dotard," said the Boy Brigand.

"Villain!" shrieked the poor girl; "heaven will avenge this hellish deed. His blood calls aloud for vengeance, and it will be answered. Those grey hairs shall rise in judgment against you, and hurl your soul to perdition. Coward and assassin, there shall yet be life for life—blood for blood!"

"Silence!" exclaimed the Boy Brigand, cowering beneath the haughty glance of the fair yet enraged girl. And again he drew his poignard from his breast, and advanced threateningly towards Paulina.

"Strike, assassin, if you have the courage!" she exclaimed, presenting her breast to his upraised arm. "Strike, and tarnish the bright blade with the blood of the child whose father you have murdered. Coward, you have not the courage to lower your weapon to my heart. Back, accursed brigand, I scorn your threats and laugh at your power. I, the child of him whom your bloody hand has slain, scorn and hate you!—back, thou fulsome disgrace to the name of man. Oh, thou foul, unnatural villain—thou blot upon humanity!—may the curse of an insulted woman rest upon your soul; may the prayer of an orphan call down the curse of heaven upon the murderer of her father; may peace be denied you in life, and rest forbidden to your soul in death! Curse you—curse you now and hereafter!"

And overcome by her feelings, Paulina fell insensible at his feet.

CHAPTER IV.

SATANIELLO IS LED TO THE SECRET RETREAT—ANGELO PROCLAIMED SECOND IN COMMAND—THE BRIGANDS DRAW LOTS — PERDITTA AND HER ADMIRER.

FOR a few moments Sataniello stood gazing upon the prostrate form of the young girl at his feet. Her words had struck terror to his soul. Her fierce look had awed his proud spirit. The curse she had uttered had sunk deep into his heart.

Sataniello was superstitious.

An indefinable feeling of fear had penetrated his breast as she gave utterance to that terrible malediction.

The Boy Brigand trembled.

His face became pale.

And the bright moonlight revealed his livid features to his new comrades.

But this state of things was not destined to last long.

He quickly recovered.

Once more he stood erect.

Once more his eye kindled and his cheek glowed.

The Boy Brigand was himself again.

He spurned the dead body of the merchant with his foot, and stooping down, raised the inanimate form of the maiden in his arms.

For a moment he gazed upon her features in silence.

Then he turned to his followers.

"Lead the way to the cavern," he said; "and bring the captives with you."

"This way, Captain," said Angelo, stepping forward and preceding the others.

The Boy Brigand raised the slender form of the beautiful girl in his arms, and followed him.

Through many a narrow and winding path the young brigand captain bore the insensible form of the poor girl, till at length he arrived at a spot densely covered with luxuriant foliage.

It was a narrow gully between the mountains, and the trees and brushwood which grew on the side of either rise completely hid the passage through which the brigands now made their way from the gaze of anyone who might pass in the vicinity.

Penetrating into the interstices of this wild place, they came to a huge rent in the side of the vast bulk of earth, which rose some hundreds of feet above them.

This place, formed by nature, served as a secret hiding-place for the brigands, who for some time had followed their former leader, Marcus, and defied all the efforts of the government to oust them from the mountains.

It was a large cave, or cavern, having for its sides and roof the huge hill in which it was formed, and capable of containing a thousand men.

On either side and running out of it were several smaller caverns, having no other outlet than the one which served as the rendezvous of the brigands, and which were appropriated to apartments for sleeping, storing away of plunder, &c.

Several rude seats and benches were scattered here and there, over which swung rude lamps that dimly lighted the subterraneous retreat.

Bearing his insensible burden to one of the seats, he allowed her slender form to slide from his arms.

Then Sataniello cast his eyes around the place.

The black earth of which the walls and roof were formed were bathed in gloom, and the shadows of the brigands, thrown by the flickering glare of the lamps thereon, gave to the place and unearthly and spectral appearance.

"This is a capital retreat," said Sataniello.

"It is, Captain," said Angelo; "and one that has defied the numerous bodies of soldiery who have sought to encompass our ruin."

"Doubtless," remarked Sataniello; "its entrance will but allow one to pass at a time, and is well adapted for defence."

"You are right, Captain," said Angelo; "and many a bold man has bitten the dust at the entrance."

"Is there no other outlet?" asked Sataniello, gazing around the place.

"None, Captain, that lead to the open air," replied the brigand; "but many which lead to smaller caverns. Yonder is one, used by our late captain; he will require it no longer. It will now serve for yourself and your captive."

And the man pointed to a small opening in the side of the large cave, which was almost indistinguishable in the gloom.

"I will convey this insensible girl there," he said.

"Do so, Captain," said the man, leaping upon the rude seat and detaching the no less rude lamp from the cord by which it was suspended, and lighting the way of the Boy Brigand and the unconscious girl to the place he had indicated.

It was a small square apartment, furnished with a rough seat and a bed of dried leaves; and upon this Sataniello laid his insensible burden.

"She will lay there comfortable enough, Captain," said the brigand.

"For a time, doubtless," said the Boy Brigand as he turned to depart.

A meaning smile played around the face of Angelo. Too well he knew that the sufferings of that poor weak girl were not ended.

They had only commenced.

Better would it have been had she never awoke again.

For there was that in store for her which is worse than death.

In the hands of the Boy Brigand she would suffer all the indignities to which his hellish mind could prompt him.

Sataniello returned to the large, or centre cavern, where Claudio and the servants were still held by the brigands, who awaited the commands of their new captain.

The Boy Brigand advanced till he stood face to face with the young Florentine.

"Where can he be confined?" he asked of Angelo, "till such time as his ransom is forthcoming."

"In a small cavern yonder," said the brigand, pointing to the opposite side of the cave to which Paulina had been carried.

"Lead him away," said Sataniello, waving his hand.

The captive youth drew himself proudly up.

His eye flashed with a gleam of hatred.

His lip curled with a scornful sneer.

But he uttered no sound.

He spoke only with his eyes.

But they conveyed his thoughts as plainly as his tongue could have done.

Too well the Boy Brigand knew the meaning of that look.

It meant revenge.

An Italian's revenge.

A revenge that never slumbers till it is satiated—washed out in the life blood of his enemy.

And the Boy Brigand saw its meaning in an instant.

There was no mistaking it; it could have no second meaning.

And the eye of the Captain followed his captive thoughtfully as he was led away to his prison-house.

Sataniello watched his tall, proud form, till it was lost to sight.

Still that look was impressed upon his soul.

Then Pedro and Lucio were led away by the brigands to another cavern, and Perditta alone remained.

The waiting maid's cheek was pale, and her form slightly trembled, but otherwise she exhibited no sign of fear or grief.

She guessed the fate intended for her, and resolved to submit to it with a good grace.

She felt it would be useless to struggle against, so resolved to make the best of a position into which fate had thrown her.

She was not naturally prone to lecherousness, but she deemed it better to consent to what she could not refuse; so she prepared herself for the worst.

"After all," she thought, "I may be far better cared for as a brigand's mistress than as a poor man's wife."

So she made herself as comfortable as she could, and awaited the turn of events.

When the captives had been safely secured, and the brigands had assembled in the large cavern, Sataniello rose from the rude bench on which he had thrown himself, and, standing directly under the lamp which swung over the centre table, he exclaimed—

"Comrades!"

In a moment every voice was hushed, and the brigands closed around him.

"Comrades," he continued, "you have chosen me for your captain in the place of your former leader."

"We have," replied the brigands, in a breath.

"I accept the office, and will strive to fulfil its duties to the satisfaction of all. But besides the loss of your captain, the lieutenant has also lost his life. Choose for yourselves who shall be next in command!"

"Angelo," said one.

"Decide for yourselves," said Sataniello, "and he whom you may select shall fill the post."

"Angelo — Angelo for Lieutenant!" said the brigands.

"'Tis well," said Sataniello, and he extended his hand to Angelo, who, stepping forward, and gazing around with a look of pleasure on his face, grasped it fervently.

"Now," said the Boy Brigand, "yonder lovely girl—what do you propose to do with her?"

"Draw lots—draw lots, unless Angelo, as second in command, claim her for himself," said one.

Angelo hesitated for a moment.

He fancied he should like the damsel, but he feared lest his claiming her might bring down upon him the ill-will of some of those who a minute before had raised their voices in his favour.

This he had no wish to do.

He preferred friends to enemies.

And he was wise.

So looking proudly round the assembly, he said—

"Comrades, you have been generous to me, and I will be generous to you. I waive my claim, and will take my chance in the lottery the same as yourselves."

This resolution gave great satisfaction to the brigands, and it was applauded vociferously by them all.

Many a lewd and anxious glance did those wild, dark-browed men cast towards the pretty waiting maid as she stood looking alternately from the band of brigands to the ground, and wondering to whose lot she would fall.

The brigands commenced to draw lots for the possession of the damsel, and not a little excitement reigned during the operation, and not a little surprise was expressed when Angelo turned up the winner, after having given up his right according to their rules to take her for himself.

The face of the brigand was radiant with smiles.

Nor was Perditta displeased with her fortune.

She would be the mistress of the Lieutenant, and a handsome young man to boot.

But she kept her gaze fixed upon the ground.

Angelo advanced towards her, and laid his hand gently upon her arm.

Perditta gave a little scream and pretended to be frightened.

But she did not attempt to fly.

No. She suffered the brigand to encircle her

waist with his arm, and imprint a kiss upon her lips.

Then Perditta closed her eyes, and her head dropped upon the breast of Angelo.

The brigand thought she had fainted, and he bore her gently to a seat.

Not so.

The little waiting maid felt it necessary to appear overcome, and so, indeed, she was to a certain extent.

Overcome by her good fortune in having fallen to the lot of the best-looking brigand in the band.

She slowly opened her eyes.

A very little way, though, but sufficient to enable her to gaze into the face of the man who supported her in his arms.

Then she heaved a deep sigh—so deep, indeed, that it almost became a groan.

Angelo strove to allay her fears.

The brigand knew little of Perditta, or he would have been aware that she needed no soothing words to cheer her.

Poor Perditta !

She was young, vain, giddy, and romantic.

She saw only the prospect of having her every wish supplied—her every extravagant fancy pandered to.

She saw not—felt not—the real and dishonourable position she was destined to fulfil.

Perhaps it was better for her that it was so.

Her heart beat now with hope where it otherwise would have ached with despair.

In her case ignorance was bliss.

She saw only the gilded and romantic side of the life she was about to lead.

The dark cloud had not obscured the tinselled horizon, and she was content, if not happy.

Poor girl ! she deserved pity rather than censure.

Youth has its foibles. Old age, only, thinks before it leaps.

——

CHAPTER V.

THE CAPTIVE IN THE CAVE—PAULINA AWAKES TO THE REALITY OF HER POSITION—THE PERSECUTOR AND HIS VICTIM.

ALL was hushed in the cavernous retreat of the brigands.

The centre cave was deserted.

The brigands had indulged till sleep had stolen over them and steeped their souls in forgetfulness, and they now slumbered heavily in the little caverns which led from the centre one, except those who had been sent out on to the mountains to guard and watch.

Perditta lay beside Angelo on his bed of dried leaves, and had sunk to sleep in the arms of the fortunate brigand.

A sleep which brought with it no remorse—was haunted by no painful dream.

Visions of happiness only floated in the mind of the waiting maid, and she slept in peace.

Poor girl! young and untutored she fell.

But, if all was hushed, all were not at rest.

The Boy Brigand was up and doing.

He had retired to the apartment formerly occupied by Marcus.

The place in which the insensible Paulina had been laid.

Eagerly he listened for the last sound of voices.

Soon all was silent.

Silent as the grave.

The Boy Brigand leant over the rigid form, and gazed intently, yet anxiously, at these still pale features, and a bitter smile of triumph curled his lip.

The hot, passionate blood mounted to his cheeks.

His lustful, loving gaze dwelt upon the swan-like neck, beautifully-rounded shoulders, and exquisitely-modelled bust.

Sleep on, fair Paulina.

Better that thy sleep be death than awake to the fearful reality of thy position.

Better, far better, indeed, had it been for thee had thy beauteous form fallen beneath the daggers of the brigands.

For the serpent has thee in his coils.

His sting is death.

For the space of an hour or more did the poor girl remain in her lethargic stupor.

The Boy Brigand sat, eagerly watching for the first signs of recovery.

At last they came.

A sigh broke from the hitherto silent form.

Her eyes opened.

Her lips moved.

And from between her pouted lips came the words, " Claudio, dear Claudio."

The eyes of the eager watcher glistened.

He bent his head down.

His face almost touched her cheek.

The death-like pallor on the face of Paulina gave place to a hectic flush.

She stared wildly around the rude place for a moment.

Then she started wildly from her couch with a loud shriek.

For a few moments she gazed abstractedly about her.

She placed her hand upon her head bewilderedly.

She staggered.

She would have fallen had not the Boy Brigand caught her in his arms.

With bewildered and half-affrighted looks she gazed upon his features.

She struggled to release herself from the arms which encircled her form.

But in vain.

Then she shrieked aloud, " Where am I? Oh ! where am I?"

The Boy Brigand replied not.

" You are not Claudio. No, no, you are not he," she exclaimed, after a moment's pause. " This place !—oh, Holy Virgin, I remember all now !"

And, in an agony of horror, she buried her face in her hands.

Scalding tears coursed each other rapidly down her cheeks.

If that poor girl's beauty had charmed the heart of the Boy Brigand when her cheeks were pale and her form rigid in insensibility, now that the crimson blood had mounted to her temples, and her bosom rose and fell with the violence of her emotions, that passion was enhanced threefold in his breast.

Impulsively he strained the weeping girl to his heart.

The hot blood coursed like molten lead through his veins.

But grief so violent must have an end.

In a short time the heart-breaking sobs of the poor girl were succeeded by long-drawn sighs.

" Where am I ?" she exclaimed again. " What place is this ?"

" Fear not," exclaimed the young captain ; " you are safe."

As the tones of his voice fell upon her ears a shiver ran through her frame.

Not that the tones were harsh or grating, but an instinctive feeling of dread took possession of her soul.

Involuntarily she endeavoured to free herself from his embrace ; but the arms of the young man grasped her far more tightly, while she could feel his hot breath upon her cheek and hiss heart throb violently against her bosom.

That undefined feeling of dread, for which it is almost impossible to account, seized upon her heart, and, as the deep flush of maiden modesty suffused her neck and shoulders, a tremor of horror ran through her frame, and a cold perspiration broke out upon her temples.

She struggled to free herself from the arms which encircled her; but in vain.

His grasp at each fresh endeavour only became the more tenacious.

Turning her tearful eyes full upon his face, she exclaimed, in imploring accents, "Why have you brought me to this strange place?"

"Because it was the nearest to that where you were captured."

"This wild place frightens me. You have saved me from the daggers of your band but to add to my sufferings. Oh, release me! Let me depart to some more genial place."

"Where would you go?" asked the Boy Brigand.

"I know not," she replied. "Anywhere from here—anywhere to seek for one dearer to me than mine own existence."

A scornful, smile curled the lips of the Boy Brigand.

"He is lost to you for ever," said Sataniello.

"Whom?"

"Him whom you call Claudio," replied the youthful captain.

"Oh, heavens! is he dead?" gasped Paulina.

"To you for ever," answered Sataniello.

"And to the world?" she asked, tremblingly.

"No; he still lives," replied the Boy Brigand.

"Heaven be praised!" exclaimed Paulina, clasping her hands together.

Again that scornful smile played around the mouth of the Boy Brigand.

"Are you pleased that he still lives?" he asked.

"Oh, yes! yes!" she exclaimed, in a fervent tone.

"Is his life, then, dear to you?" asked Sataniello.

"He is my affianced husband," replied the maiden.

"And you love him?" asked the Boy Brigand.

"With my whole soul," answered the young girl.

"And would give much to save him?"

"Anything," she replied, eagerly.

"You can do so."

"How?"

"By submitting to my desires," said Sataniello.

"Your desires?"

"Yes."

"And they are——?"

"Surrender yourself to my caresses," said the Boy Brigand, meaningly.

"Never!" exclaimed Paulina.

"Then he dies."

"Brigand, you dare not slay him," she shrieked.

"Maiden, I dare aught which inclination prompts me to do," answered Sataniello, coldly.

"You cannot be so base," she exclaimed.

"I would save his life," said Sataniello.

"Then do so," she exclaimed.

"On one condition," he replied, fixing his dark eyes upon her.

"And that condition?" she asked.

"Your favours."

"Be plain.'

"I will. Maiden, I love you," said Sataniello.

Paulina averted her gaze.

"I hate you," she exclaimed.

"I would save your lover."

"So would I."

"You can do so."

"But at what price?" she asked.

"Your honour."

"Never!"

"Then he dies," said the Boy Brigand, firmly.

Paulina sighed.

There was a fearful struggle taking place in her breast.

She could save Claudio.

But at what a price.

Should she submit?

If she did he might live—if not, he died.

She loved him fondly, and she would sacrifice much to save him.

But should she sacrifice her honour?

It was a terrible alternative.

She paused thoughtfully for a few moments.

Then she raised her eyes to the captain's face.

"How say you—shall he live or die?" he asked.

"Live," she replied.

"Then you submit," he exclaimed joyfully.

"To what?"

"To my will."

"Never!"

"Then he dies," said the Boy Brigand, in a determined tone.

"Coward as well as assassin, heaven's vengeance will yet overtake you," said Paulina.

The Boy Brigand laughed scornfully.

Paulina shuddered as he did so.

"As I defy man so I defy heaven," said the Rover. "You can save your lover by submitting to my wishes."

"Never," said Paulina.

"Fool," said the Boy Brigand; "still must you fall. I have offered you the chance to spare his life; you prefer to become his murderer. I have marked you for my own, and you must submit."

"Never, wretch, never!" exclaimed the young girl, proudly.

"But you shall. Within this mountain fastness none can hear your cries, or come to your rescue. You are mine—mine—spite of man or heaven!"

"Holy Virgin aid me," gasped Pauline.

"You call in vain," said the rover, pressing her still closer to his breast.

His hot breath played upon her pale cheek.

His fulsome lips met hers.

She struggled to free herself from his embrace, but in vain.

He rained kisses hot and fierce upon her lips, cheeks, and forehead.

She shrieked aloud.

Her voice came back in mocking echoes to her ears.

"Away, away!" she exclaimed; "there is blood upon your hands—upon your soul!"

"It is your father's," tauntingly replied the Boy Brigand.

"Wretch, fiend, devil—away!" shrieked Paulina, struggling to free herself from his hold, and striking him on the cheek.

"Curse you," said the Boy Brigand, his temper fairly aroused by the blow. "I'll——"

Paulina gazed steadfastly in his face—

"Strike, coward!" she exclaimed.

The Boy Brigand raised his arm.

But the indignant glance of the maiden's eye cowed his spirit.

His arm dropped by his side, and his eyes rested upon the ground.

"Shameless coward," exclaimed the insulted girl ; base and degraded reptile, I scorn and loathe you ! Back to your lair, where, serpent-like, you wait to sting the innocent and unwary. Dog—for man you are not—I defy you !"

The Boy Brigand ground his teeth in rage, and clenched his hand, as if about to strike her.

But Paulina stood, proudly erect, before him.

"Strike," she said, "if you dare."

"I will strike," he hissed, foaming with rage, "not at your body, but your honour."

"Liar !" exclaimed Paulina ; "a true woman will battle for her honour whilst she has breath ; and never, while life is left her, will Paulina, the merchant's daughter, fall a victim to the Boy Brigand, the Dark King of the Mountains."

CHAPTER VI.

CLAUDIO ATTEMPTS TO ESCAPE.—THE STRUGGLE.— THE DEATH-BLOW.—THE ESCAPE DISCOVERED.

CLAUDIO, the young Florentine, sat upon the rude bench in the no less rude cavern in which the brigands had placed him in an agony of mind better to be imagined than described.

The long and tedious journey had fatigued him ; and the adventures he had passed through had added to the exhaustion of body under which he suffered.

Still sleep was denied him.

He could not rest.

The form of his beloved Paulina was before his mind's eye, and ever present in his thoughts.

In imagination he saw her undergoing the most fearful of indignities which the mind of man could conjure up.

Every sound which came to his ears sounded like the voice of his beloved one calling upon him for aid.

And he would start from his seat, and rush to his prison doors to find that he was powerless to aid her.

Gradually sleep stole over him.

He sank into an uneasy slumber.

Still the vision of his beloved Paulina was before him.

He saw her battling with the Boy Brigand, and heard her calling upon him to save her.

With fitful starts he awoke.

Thus time wore on, and the first streak of early dawn penetrated an opening in the cave.

But, slight as was the ray of light, it enabled the youth to distinguish the place of his captivity.

He perceived that the door was but a rudely-constructed one, with an opening of more than an inch between the panels, across which ran a bar of stout timber.

This Claudio had no doubt was slipped into a socket on either side.

Could he but succeed in working the bar from its sockets, he might open the door and escape.

He would try.

He listened intently.

All was still.

The Brigands still slumbered off the deep potations in which they had been indulging.

He forced his fingers through the openings between the panels, and endeavoured to shift the bar along.

He could move it, but so slightly that if it ran deep into its socket it would take some time to accomplish his object.

Still it could be moved, and there was hope.

He continued to shift the bar bit by bit.

His fingers were cramped and stiffened, and the skin rubbed off them.

Still he persevered.

Slowly yet gradually it shifted along the rude door.

Claudio felt that it soon would fall.

But then he feared, lest the sound caused thereby should arouse the Brigands.

For a moment he paused.

But for a moment only.

Again he continued his work, waiting anxiously for the fall of the bar.

At length it dropped, with a dull, heavy sound, to the floor of the outer cavern.

Claudio held his breath, and listened earnestly and intently.

But there was no sound to indicate that the falling bar had excited the attention of the Brigands.

Cautiously he pushed against the door.

It yielded.

Claudio stood for a few moments upon the threshold, gazing out into the centre cavern, and listening for the least sound.

From various apertures in the roof the grey morning light streamed down upon the rough seats and tables in the place.

The eye of the young lover searched eagerly around for some weapon.

He was not long in discovering one.

On the centre table, around which the Brigands had been regaling themselves, lay a dagger, and, leaning against the end of a seat, a carbine, which had been left there by its owner.

The eyes of the youth glistened with joy as he stepped towards them.

Thrusting his stiletto, or dagger, into his belt, he snatched up the carbine, and hastily examined it.

The weapon was loaded.

Then he looked around the cave, and out towards the opening which led to the mountains.

"All is silent," he muttered ; "not a sound breaks the fearful stillness. The path to freedom is open ; but shall I fly, and leave Paulina in the hands of these accursed brigands. And yet, singly, how can I hope to save her ? And yet to leave her in this place, and to the mercy of these fiends, the thought is horrible. I dare not imagine the fate to which she is consigned. Holy Virgin, guide me how to act !"

And the youth paused, as though he believed his prayer would be heard and answered.

"I cannot hope to tear her from the power of these ruthless wretches without aid. I might slay one or two of them, but should I not myself be slain, and then the fate of Paulina would be certain. I must endeavour to escape from this hellish place, and return with assistance to rescue the girl I so fondly love. Fools ! they forgot to bind my eyes when they brought me hither, so the paths to this accursed cavern are known to me ; and, should I be fortunate enough to reach Florence in safety, I will soon return, and hunt the tigers from their lair, and rescue the victims of their villany."

Still he paused, loth to leave the spot without the poor girl.

Yet he knew that every moment's delay was fraught with danger.

The Brigands must soon awake, and enter the centre cave.

THE BOY BRIGAND DISGUISES HIMSELF

Or those on the watch might return, and then all hope of escape would be gone.

Should he be discovered the brigands would be careful to give him no chance of escape for the future, and Paulina would assuredly be lost to him for ever.

He fixed his eyes intently upon the entrance to the cavern in which he believed she was a prisoner, and slowly made his way towards the entrance.

This he gained without having attracted the attention of the brigands, or in any way disturbed their slumbers.

The bright, blue canopy of heaven's vault he could now plainly distinguish through the luxuriant foliage which hid the entrance to the cavern.

His heart bounded with joy as the fresh morning air came, pregnant with the fragrance of flowers, to his senses, and cooled the heated brow and fevered cheek, and seemed to breathe in his ears and instil in his breast hope of liberty.

Turning his eyes in every direction, the young Florentine reached the opening.

All was still, save the rustling of the leaves as they swayed in the refreshing breeze, and kissed the cool morning air.

Grasping the carbine firmly in his hand, he parted the dense brushwood, and stepped out into the narrow path.

But here he paused and held his breath.

Directly before sat one of the brigands.

He had fallen asleep at his post, and his carbine lay between his knees.

Claudio stood for a moment irresolute how to act.

The path was so narrow that the young Florentine could not pass by without rousing the man.

Claudio raised the carbine, but then he paused.

It would not be wise, he thought, to fire; for, should he succeed in killing the sentinel, the report of the weapon would bring the whole band upon him.

25

At this moment the sleeping sentry shifted his position.

Claudio was in an agony of suspense.

He silently leant the carbine against the side of the defile, and drew the stilletto from his belt.

He must escape, be the consequences what they were.

For himself he cared not, but for Paulina he must reach Florence.

But the brigand sentry barred his passage.

Stealthily he advanced towards him.

He stood by his side.

At that moment the brigand opened his eyes.

A cry of surprise broke from his lips.

He grasped the carbine which lay across his knees, and leapt to his feet.

But the hand of the Florentine was at his throat, and his carbine was dashed to the earth.

So sudden had been the assault that the surprised Brigand staggered beneath it.

But quickly recovering, he threw his arms around the body of the youth, and strove to bear him to the earth.

But this was no easy task.

Claudio was a well-built, powerfully-knit man, and the Brigand struggled in vain to accomplish his object.

Finding that Claudio was more than a match for him the man called out.

But Claudio struck him on the mouth with the dagger, and drowned the cry which might have brought assistance to the aid of the brigand.

Foaming with rage the man strove to tear the weapon from the youth's grasp.

But he only lacerated his hands in the attempt.

So tenaciously, however, did the brigand cling to the arm of the young Florentine, that Claudio was unable to bury the weapon in his breast or shoulder.

Thus they struggled for some few minutes, the brigand endeavouring to deprive the youth of his weapon, or bear him to the earth, Claudio striving to bury the steel in the bosom of his foe.

Still Claudio spoke not. He feared lest the tones of his voice should bring more of the band to the aid of their comrade.

Panting, and almost breathless, the youth looked around him.

If he did not succeed in overpowering his adversary soon, he felt assured that assistance would arrive from the cavern or the mountains, and his hoped-for escape frustrated.

He summoned up, therefore, all his strength, which had been much weakened by the blow he had received on the head the night before, and bent the body of the brigand back till his head nearly touched the earth.

The man struggled to regain an upright position, but, with the force of desperation, Claudio forced him back, till, losing his balance, and endeavouring to regain it, the brigand relaxed his grasp on the wrist of the youth.

The loss of his hold on the youth's arm was fatal to him.

Claudio clutched the stiletto tightly, and drove it to the hilt in the brigand's heart, who, with a loud groan, rolled over dead at his feet.

Claudio seized the carbine, and leapt forward.

As he did so, a sharp report rang through the defile, and a bullet struck the earth at his feet.

CHAPTER VII.

THE SERENADER ON THE TERRACE—A FALSE STORY —A DECEIVED GIRL.

THE large bright full moon rode high in the pale blue firmament, and threw its refulgent rays upon the smoothly-flowing Toronto.

Lit up the graceful and stately gondolas as they floated over the silver surface of the stream, now as clear as a polished mirror, in whose depths were reflected the graceful outlines of the pretty barks as they were propelled hither and thither by the oars of the gondoliers.

The air was fresh and balmy, laden with the perfume of thousands of flowers, which were borne by the wind with refreshing sweetness to the senses.

The silence was only broken by the plash of the oars, as they dropped at measured intervals into the stream, the song of the gondolier, or the entrancing strains of the guitar, as it floated on the evening breeze.

Here and there, upon its banks, proud mansions reared their lofty heads, and threw their shadows far out into the river, bathing the steps which led down to the stream in a pleasing gloom.

On the steps of one of these mansions which were washed by the waters of the stream, stood a tall, handsome young man; whilst moored to the steps was a small gondola, its graceful form rising and falling upon the undulating waters like a babe upon the breast of a sleeping mother.

His dress was rich in texture and ornament, and in his hand he held a guitar, the strings of which he ever and anon passed his fingers over in a graceful manner, as he looked far out into the stream.

"The bell will soon sound to matins," he muttered, "and then the stream will become clear. There are too many gondolas sporting upon it yet for me to obtain the secrecy so much desired;' and the Signorita Marianna may meet with friends who may undeceive her as to the genuineness of the mission on which I wish her to believe she is bound. Even now the gondolas make for the shore, and we shall have a clear stream."

He turned his eyes up to the windows of the mansion.

"That must be the chamber of the signorita," he muttered, "and I will summon her to the window by the strains of my guitar."

As he spoke the sound of the matin-bell floated on the breeze.

The young man raised his cap and bowed his head, as the sound smote upon his ears.

Not that he was actuated by any sense of reverence; but he was superstitious, and believed that his mission would not prosper did he fail to pay homage to that sound.

Then running his fingers over the strings of his instrument, he sang a short love ditty.

Scarce had the strains of the music died away, than the window at which he had been gazing was thrown open, and the head of a beautiful girl was thrust forth.

Again the youth ran his fingers over the guitar, but this time he sang not.

The maiden still remained gazing upon the youth, whose features were hidden in shadow, till at length a low, soft, silvery voice exclaimed—

"Salernio, I am here!"

"Hist, Signorita!" said the young man, stepping forward until he stood right under the window.

"It is not Salernio, but a messenger from him, who would speak with you."

"Speak it," said the young girl.

"Salernio is ill, Signorita Marianna," said the young man, "and prays that you will see him ere he dies."

"Ah!" exclaimed the young girl, as her beautiful face paled, and her lips trembled, "Salernio ill—dying!"

"'Tis even so, Signorita," answered the man, "but will you not leave your chamber, and meet me on the steps, that I may tell you all?"

"I will attend you, Signor, in a moment," replied the girl.

And the pale face and raven tresses disappeared from the opening.

"'Tis well," muttered the young man. "She loves the youth Salernio, and may be easily led away from her home. Her father is rich, and she will surely be worth a heavy ransom. Holy Virgin, here she comes!"

At that moment a beautiful girl, of some sixteen summers, turned the angle of the house, and walked along the terrace up to which the steps led from the river, and in another moment stood before the musician, her tall and graceful form looking queenly in the bright moonlight.

"Signor," she said, "I cannot greet you with the welcome you deserve, for by your words you are the bearer of ill-tidings; therefore, if I want in courtesy, it is that we meet under no joyous auspices."

The young man lifted his cap, and bowed low before her.

"Signorita, happy had I been could I salute you with cheering words; but though I bear ill news, still, Signor Stephano di Luco, by which name permit me to introduce myself, I trust to merit your confidence."

"The friend of Salernio will ever do so," replied the girl.

"Then, Signorita, it is to do his bidding I came hither. The poor youth has been wounded, and little hopes are entertained of his life!"

"Holy Virgin!" exclaimed Marianna, "when was this?"

"But yesternight, Signorita," replied Stephano.

"How—how did this happen?" she exclaimed.

"A young Venetian gentleman spoke slightingly of you, Signorita," said Stephano; "and Salernio, fired with indignation, struck the man who could speak wrongly of the girl he loved."

"Yes, yes!" she gasped.

"The Venitian, goaded to madness by the blow he so well merited, drew his stiletto, and——"

"Ah!" exclaimed Marianna.

"Buried it in the shoulder of Salernio!"

"Holy Mother!" gasped the girl. "Salernio—poor Salernio!"

"When he recovered consciousness, he bade me seek you at this hour; and so that I might not be refused audience, he commanded me to strike my guitar upon this terrace."

"I believed it was his guitar that smote my ears. But where—where is he?"

"He lies in the house of a friend at Aquila," replied Stephano, "and hither he bids you speed lest death seal his lips ere you arrive."

"I know not how to act," she said. "My father is absent, and I cannot seek his advice."

"Signorita, I implore you go; Salernios' love for you is great!" said the man.

"And mine for him," she replied; "but how can I go to-night?"

"My gondola is moored to the steps," said Stephano, "and I will bear you to Aquila, and your lover."

"I will have my own got ready," she said.

"Pardon me, Signorita," said Stephano. "Whilst you have your own got ready, moments fly, and the breath of your lover shortens. A minute only may be fatal to him—to you. If you love my friend, let me implore you to trust yourself to my protection. The night is fair, and my gondola cuts the water with an ease and swiftness superior to your own."

"Signor, I would not do you wrong," she said, "but to me you are a stranger."

"True, Signorita, but to your lover I am a friend; otherwise this mission had not been entrusted to me."

The young girl hesitated.

She feared to trust herself to the guidance of one whom she had never before seen; yet she feared to refuse his offer, or delay a moment, lest her lover die ere she could reach his side.

For she loved Salernio with a love such as only the woman of Italy feels—a love hot and passionate, as in their hate bitter and revengeful.

Stephano turned his head to hide the look of impatience which overspread his features.

"I know not how to act," she said at length.

"You would not have him die without seeing you?"

"Holy Mother! no."

"Then come!"

"I fear."

"What?"

"Alas! I know not."

"Salernio awaits you."

"Yes—yes."

"Shall he wait in vain?" asked Stephano.

"No."

"Then come!"

Still she hesitated.

"Signorita, time is short," said Stephano; "the tide will turn soon, and you may never more see him in life."

"I will come," she said.

"You do wisely."

"But not alone."

"With whom, then?" asked the man, eargerly.

"Julietta, my maid."

"As you please," said Stephano.

"You have no objection?"

"None."

"I will join you directly," she said, turning from him, and walking swiftly along the terrace.

"I shall await you with impatience," he said.

"I will not detain you long," she said, as she hurried away.

As the Signorita Marianna turned the angles of the wall, and was lost to sight, a smile broke over the handsome features of the young man."

His dark eye lighted up with a gleam of triumph.

"She believes me," he muttered. "Oh, love—love," into what dangers will it not lead us!"

He then threw his guitar carelessly across his shoulder.

"I have done with you at least for a time," he said. "You have served me well, but I prefer a carbine to a guitar."

He descended the steps, and unmoored the gondola.

"Little does she dream to whom she entrusts herself," he muttered. "But there—a woman in love is always a fool!"

And he chuckled inwardly as he muttered his thoughts.

"I feared the trap had been laid in vain," he continued; "but we must not leap to hasty conclusions. What a beautiful creature she is! I do not wonder that Salernio should fall in love with her, but do wonder how a youth can stand twanging a guitar beneath her window night after night. I prefer the ring of a carbine to the twang of a guitar—the chink of gold to a woman's smile. Sataniello will be pleased at my success, for the ranson will be a goodly one."

And flinging the guitar into the bottom of the boat, he drew the gondola close to the steps.

"Aquila the Signorita believes to be her destination. Poor fool! the brigands retreat in the mountain will be her home till her father ransoms her; and that will not be long first, I opine."

At this moment the Signorita Marianna and her maid Julietta were seen coming along the terrace towards him.

So Stephano raised his cap, and waited their approach.

In a moment they were by his side.

"Permit me, Signorita," he said, holding forth his hand.

Marianna allowed him to assist her into the gondola, as did also did her maid; then, leaping in after them, the man seized the oars, and pulled swiftly into the stream.

——

CHAPTER VIII.

THE ENTRAPPED MAIDENS—THE BRIGAND REVEALS
HIS TRUE CHARACTER.

THE bright moonbeams glittered upon the face of Stephano as he rowed out from the shore.

There was a smile upon his features.

His eye kindled till a gleam of triumph lit up the dark orb.

He spoke not a word.

Swiftly he propelled the small gondola over the waves.

Marianna, too, was silent and thoughtful.

She was thinking of her lover.

That lover she believed dying.

But what would have been her thoughts had she known that, seated in a gondola which they passed swiftly by, was Salerno, enjoying the best of health, and eager to gaze upon her beauteous features.

But she knew it not—and silently she sat, picturing to herself her lover, wounded and dying, only a few short miles away.

The river was now clear.

Scarce a boat was to be seen upon its surface.

And all was silent, save the plashing of the oars as they fell into the stream.

On went the gondola for some time.

One by one the lights on the shore on either side died out.

Suddenly Marianna was struck by a suspicion that all was not right.

An indefinable fear took possession of her heart.

Yet for a time she could not find it in her mind to speak.

But it grew upon her till it became unbearable.

She turned to Julietta.

"Julietta," she whispered, "I have misgivings."

"About what, Signorita?" asked the maid.

"Salernio."

"How?"

"I know not; but I think this man has deceived me," she said.

"Why should he do so?" inquired the maid, becoming nervous herself.

"Alas! I know not."

"It is the sad news that has made you nervous," said the maid.

"It may be so; yet I fear——"

"What?"

"That we are entrapped."

"For what purpose?"

"I cannot tell."

"You alarm me, Signorita," exclaimed the maid.

"I am alarmed myself," replied Marianna.

"Yet, why should he deceive you?" asked Julietta.

"I cannot say."

"How could he know the Signor Salernio?"

"I cannot tell."

"We may deceive ourselves. He may be the friend of the Signor, and we may wrong him by suspicion."

"We may. Still, I fear."

"Speak to him."

"I will."

"Do so."

"Signor," said Marianna, in a louder tone, "how much further have we to go.

"But a short distance, Signorita," replied Stephano.

But the tones of his voice now were different to what they were on the terrace.

There was a brusqueness, if not insolence, in them.

Marianna sank back on her seat still less at ease.

She gazed out unto the shore with anything but pleasurable feelings in her head.

Suddenly she started.

She had detected a building well known to her on the banks.

"Signor," she exclaimed, hurriedly, "whither are you bearing us?"

"To Aquila, Signorita," replied the brigand.

"To Aquila?" she terated. "No, no. Aquila is far behind. We are close upon Fermo,"

"Why do you imagine so, Signorita?" asked the man.

"Because I can see places well known to me on shore," replied Marianna, tremulously.

"You must be mistaken."

"Oh, no."

"No," she said, in surprise, "'tis you who are mistaken, Signor, not me. Look! there is the Church of St. Julia.

The brigand ceased rowing, and looked in the direction indicated by the finger of the young girl.

Then, assuming a look of surprise and annoyance, he said—

"You are right, Signorita. By the mass, my anxiety to bear you to your lover has caused me to take the wrong course."

"Holy Virgin!" exclaimed the Signorita, "and he may die ere I see him."

"Even so," said the brigand, turning his head to conceal the smile on his face.

"Oh! turn the gondola round and hurry, Signor, or we may be too late."

"Willingly would I obey you, Signorita," said Stephano; "but I am tired, and could never carry you to Aquila."

"No?" said Marianna.

"No," replied the brigand, "we are many miles away from there."

"Then, for heaven's sake, bear me home again.

"Pardon me, Signorita, my strength is exhausted," said Stephano

"What, is to be done?" asked Marianna, becoming every moment more and more alarmed.

Stephano pretended not to hear the question.

It was repeated.

He pretended to consider.

In an agony of suspense Marianna awaited his reply.

"I do not know," he answered at length.

"We cannot remain here," she exclaimed.

"True, Signorita."

"I am sorry I did not have my own gondola, as I intended," she said, in a tone of vexation.

"Signorita," said Stephano, "I am exhausted; and I must inform you that the gondola has got out of trim by some means. I will take you alongside of yonder vessel, and solicit the aid of the captain to bear you either to Aquila or back to your home."

And, as he spoke, the brigand pointed to a vessel some short distance from them.

"Oh! do so," said Marianna, half doubting now the truth of the man's story, and only too anxious to be rid of him.

"I will, Signorita," said Stephano; "my strength will at least permit me to take you alongside."

Annoyed almost to tears, the Signorita Marianna sat down again beside her maid.

She felt sad and miserable.

If the man's story concerning her lover were true, how unkind, she thought, he would imagine her to be in not flying to him.

If it was false, why had she been deceived ?

She knew not what to think.

She could not escape from the boat.

She was in the power of Stephano either way.

So she waited anxiously the arrival of the boat at the vessel's side.

She had not to wait long.

Stephano's strength seemed to have come back to him, for the boat flew over the water.

They were soon alongside.

Stephano hailed it.

A man on the deck looked over the side into the gondola.

"We have lost our way," said Stephano. "May we crave your aid to convey us to Aquila?"

"Certainly," was the reply.

"When do you start?" asked Stephano.

"Immediately," was the reply; "so come on board.

Feeling satisfied that all was right, Marianna and her maid suffered themselves to be assisted on to the deck of the vessel.

Stephano followed them, and a youth who had been standing on the deck lowered himself into the gondola and pulled rapidly away from the ship.

Marianna expressed her surprise at this, believing that Stephano would himself have taken charge of the gondola, after giving them information where they could find the wounded man.

But the brigand only smiled.

Taking his cap from off his head, he bowed low to Marianna.

"Signorita," he said, "I feel a pleasure in informing you that the Signor Salernio is at the present moment, for aught I know to the contrary, in the enjoyment of the best of health.

Marianna staggered back in surprise.

A look of consternation overspread her features.

She became deathly pale.

So did her maid Julietta, and trembled violently.

"What—what is the meaning of this?" gasped the young girl.

Stephano bowed low.

"Simply, Signorita's," he said, in a bland tone, "that the brigands of the Appenines, hearing about the wealth of the Signor Morteni, your father, formed their plan, and left your servant to execute it, by which they get his daughter into their power and thereby procure a princely ransom for her release."

"Holy mother !" gasped Marianna. "Am I, then, a prisoner ?"

"Even so, Signorita," replied Stephano, calmly.

"Oh, no!" gasped Julietta, bursting into tears.

"Oh, yes," replied the brigand. "And as we have not time to take you either to Aquila or your home, we shall land you safe at Cervia, and thence convey you to the mountains."

"Then you are——"

"Stephano."

"Yes—yes—but——"

"A brigand, Signorita," replied the man, in a courteous tone.

"Then you are no friend of Salernio's," she said.

"I never saw him in my life," replied Stephano.

"Never saw him !"

"Never."

"Then how did you know——?"

"I assure you I do not know him," replied Stephano.

"How did you learn his name?" asked Marianna.

"We have means of learning everything we wish to know, replied the brigand.

"What means ?"

"That I am not at liberty to say," replied the man.

"Then you learnt that he——"

"Twanged his guitar beneath your window at night, and sung songs of love. Ah, yes !" said Stephano.

"And by this knowledge——?"

"We were enabled to lay a trap for thee, beautiful daughter of the rich Signor Morteni."

"A trap into which she has fallen but too deeply," sighed the poor girl, with a shudder of horror.

"You must, at least, admit it was cleverly executed," said Stephane.

"But basely," replied Marianna.

"That is a matter of opinion, Signorita," said the brigand.

"And you, too, Julietta," said her mistress, turning to the trembling maid.

"Pardon me, Senorita," said Stephano; "it was by no act of mine that the maid was made prisoner."

"Not yours ?"

"No. I sought not to bear her away to the mountains. But you would insist upon her accompanying you. Therefore 'tis you who have made her prisoner—not I.

"Have you no fear of the laws ?"

"None."

"You may for a time insult and detain a daughter of one of Italy's influential subjects; but, Signor, you will find ere long that there are hands and hearts willing to chastise the ruffians who can entrap and bear from her home a weak defenceless woman."

"Pardon me, Signorita," said Stephano, "but you are mistaken. In our mountain fastnesses we can defy all the force Italy can bring against us. We laugh to scorn its laws and defy its power. We have done so under the command of Marcus, our late captain, and shall do so again under the command of the Boy Brigand, the Dark King of the Mountains."

"The Boy Brigand !" shrieked Marianna, "then we are lost—lost !"

CHAPTER IX.

THE BOY BRIGAND AND HIS CAPTIVE—A WOMAN'S
DEFIANCE—PLEASING INTELLIGENCE.

PROUDLY erect stood the beautiful Paulina—the merchant's daughter, and the pride of Ravenna.

Her dark eye flashed fire.

Her lips curled scornfully.

Her pale face was suffused with the crimson flush of insulted modesty.

Proudly and queen-like she stood before the Boy Brigand.

And the eye of the bandit dropped to the earth.

Shame for a moment took possession of his soul.

That soul stained with the blood of the innocent and good.

That soul blackened by the hellish crimes his hands had perpetrated.

He was brave if criminal—bold if bad.

Yet he quailed before the imperious glance of the scornful and beautiful Paulina.

Still the bad passions of his nature rankled at his heart.

Still his unholy desires held prominent sway in his breast.

He felt that he must revel in the charms of the fair girl before him.

He felt that he must enjoy the caresses of the merchant's daughter.

Her beauty had charmed him.

Her scorn had fired his soul.

Her defiance had but added to his desires.

A stolen kiss is the sweetest.

And resistance to the passions but adds fuel to the fire burning in the veins.

So it was with Sataniello, the Boy Brigand.

Her sorrowful demeanour charmed him more than could her tears and supplications.

Yet he quailed before that defiant glance—that haughty mien.

He, the Boy Brigand, the Dark King of the Mountains, trembled in the presence of a woman.

And that woman his captive.

One whom he held in his power.

A power from which it was difficult to escape.

But soon he recovered himself.

Soon he threw off the oppression her haughty and defiant manner had encased him.

He advanced towards her, and grasped her wrist.

"Girl!" he hissed, "you know not whom you defy!"

"Liar!" she exclaimed, "I defy you—the base and degraded wretch whose crimes and remorseless deeds have curdled the blood of thousands."

"One more shall yet be added to the number," he exclaimed—"Paulina, the daughter of the merchant of Ravenna!"

"Never!" exclaimed the pale, yet proud girl.

"We shall see."

"Aye, we shall see," she replied. "Brigand! a true woman will protect her honour with her life! Sooner shall your dagger's blade drink the blood of your captive, than her honour shall fall at the shrine of a brigand!"

"Silence! or I may be tempted to stretch you a corpse at my feet!" he exclaimed, passionately.

"Coward! you lack the courage," said Paulina.

"By the Holy Virgin!" he exclaimed, "my steel shall pierce your heart."

"Strike, villain!" said the maiden, advancing a step towards him.

Sataniello drew the dagger from his breast.

He raised the glittering steel above his head.

"Strike, wretch!" exclaimed Paulina again.

But the arm of the Boy Brigand remained raised.

He feared to carry out his threat.

The eye of that girl cowered his revengeful spirit.

Her glance fascinated him.

"No, no!" he said, lowering his arm, and replacing the dagger in his belt.

"Why do you not strike?" she asked, scornfully.

"You are a woman," he replied.

Paulina laughed scornfully.

"You are a coward!" she exclaimed.

The Boy Brigand winced.

"It is false!" he said; "had you been a man, I had struck you dead at my feet."

"Yes," she replied, "had I been a man, and my limbs fettered, you would have done so; but had I been a man, and my limbs free, I would have rid Italy of her greatest scourge—her greatest curse. I would have grappled with the wretch who sets alike the laws of God and man at defiance, and have torn from your guilty breast your black and craven heart."

"Girl, beware!" exclaimed Sataniello, "lest in my anger I forget that you are a woman."

"Ha, ha!" scornfully laughed the girl, "forget—you cannot forget that I am a woman. Had you thought me other than woman, your blood-stained hand would have fell nerveless at your side. 'Tis woman only with whom you war singly. The cruel are always cowards—the generous only are brave. You saw me a weak, defenceless woman, and your craven spirit prompted you to do me wrong; but you find me one who can scorn and defy you—one who will sacrifice life to retain honour—one who laughs to contempt your boasted power, and loathes and despises the reptile whose coward hand can strike only at the weak and defenceless!"

The Boy Brigand ground his teeth in rage.

He strode towards the woman who thus defied him.

His hand played with the hilt of his dagger.

But that cold, contemptuous glance, prevented him from again drawing the weapon from its sheath.

That proudly-erect form fascinated him, and held him powerless.

Never before had he met with one so haughty and defiant.

Never before had his cruel spirit been so humbled.

But, like all base natures, he was revengeful.

He would not forget the taunts of his victim.

Nor would he forgive them.

No—they would rankle in his heart, and goad him on to the consummation of his wishes.

Again he seized her wrist, and hissed, rather than spoke the words—

"You defy me—beware!"

But a haughty curl of the lip was the only response.

"I will tame your proud spirit," he exclaimed.

"Never," she answered.

"I will bow you down with shame and disgrace," he continued.

"Liar!" she replied.

"I will make you a thing for the finger of scorn to point at," he added.

"Wretch!"

"And lay you at my feet, bereft of all that woman holds dear!" he added, fixing his eyes upon Paulina with a look of hatred and revenge.

The girl tore her arm from his grasp and started back.

"Brigand," she exclaimed, "in heaven I place my

trust—in that heaven which never yet turned a deaf ear to the cries of the oppressed."

"Ha, ha!" he laughed scornfully. "Call upon it then to aid you. I laugh at its power as I do at your resistance. Sataniello is not to be turned from his purpose by such nonsense. I have refused to fix the price of your ransom, because I had resolved to revel in your caresses—that resolve is fixed and irremovable. Could my will have been altered before it is impossible now. Your haughty spirit but adds fuel to the fire which burns within my breast, but excites the passion already heated by your beauty. You are mine, girl—mine. You must become the mistress of the Boy Brigand. You must surrender your honour to the keeping of the Dark King of the Mountains. Here, my will is law; here my every command must be obeyed—my every wish gratified. I have resolved to make you my own spite of heaven or hell. You tears and scorn are unabating. I have swore to revel in your charms, least in your caresses, and no power on earth can save you from the doom I have consigned you to!"

And Sataniello rushed upon the fair Paulina as he spoke, and threw his arms around her slender form.

"Back, miscreant!" she exclaimed.

"You have defied my power. Now shall you feel my revenge!" exclaimed Sataniello, pressing her tightly to his breast.

"And I defy it still, brigand and murderer!" gasped Paulina, struggling to free herself from his embrace.

"You struggle in vain," replied the Boy Brigand, leaning her forcibly towards the rude couch. "Not all the forces that man or devil can arraign against me shall save you now!"

"Liar—liar!" exclaimed Paulina, drawing the dagger from the belt of the Boy Brigand and raising it above his head. "A woman's hand shall protect a woman's honour, and a woman's courage preserve a woman's chastity! Back, miscreant—back. Heaven has heard the prayer of the weak and defenceless and placed a weapon in the hands of the orphan to save her from the murderer of her father. Back, coward! I would not have blood, upon my soul, though it be the blood of one stained with a thousand crimes. But I will protect my honour with my last breath and strike at the heart of him who dare assail my virtue. Back, villain and coward, or this weapon shall drink the life's blood of one who disgraces the name of man—one who is but a foul blot upon humanity—the condemned of heaven and the despised of hell!"

And Paulina brandished the weapon above his head. A look of triumph gleamed from her eyes. Her features were set and determined.

Surprised and chagrined the Boy Brigand started back.

Foaming with rage he gazed upon the imperious girl before him.

And bitterly did he curse his stupidity in giving her a chance to possess herself of his weapon. His first impulse was to rush upon her and tear it from her grasp.

But that glearing eye bade him pause.

That towering form and upraised arm told him there was danger to be apprehended. So he paused irresolute.

A scornful smile curled the lips of Paulina. But she dropped not her eyes from his face. Fascinated and spell-bound she held him where he stood.

A low scornful laugh broke from her lips.

Goaded to madness, the Boy Brigand waited for an opportunity to spring upon and wrest the weapon from her.

But Paulina was wary, and whichever way he turned, her eye followed him.

And Sataniello, the Dark King of the Mountains, the terror of Italy, stood cowed and subdued before that pale weak girl.

Strong in virtue and honour the merchant's daughter defied him, at the mention of which strong men paled and women trembled in horror.

"Go," said Paulina, advancing, threateningly towards him, "Go—there is pollution in the air you breathe, contamination in your presence—begone—leave me, lest a woman's hand avenge a father's death, and become the executioner of a wretch whose crimes call aloud for justice."

Slowly the Boy Brigand retreated towards the entrance to the large cavern.

And slowly and firmly followed the indignant girl.

Not for one moment did she lower the weapon. Not for one second did she avert her gaze from his face.

And thus walking backwards before her, Sataniello reached the centre cavern.

Hurriedly he cast his eyes around.

A cry of joy escaped him, and he leapt towards one of the tables.

He stretched forth his hand and grasped a carbine.

A weight seemed removed from his soul.

He turned hurriedly and presented the piece at the head of Paulina.

"Ha, ha!" he laughed, "'tis my turn now."

But the girl quailed not before the weapon.

"Lay down that dagger," he exclaimed.

"Never!" she replied.

"Throw it upon the earth, or I will send a bullet into your heart," he said.

"And as this life blood ebbs from my body I will bury this dagger in your coward heart! slowly and determinedly," exclaimed Paulina.

"I speak not again. Release your hold of the weapon," he said, laying his hand upon the trigger of the carbine.

"It were vain to do so, for I should not obey," said Paulina, firmly.

"I would not take your life," he exclaimed.

"But you would rob me of that far dearer," said Paulina.

"Once more. Will you live or die?" exclaimed the Boy Brigand.

"Live," replied Paulina; "but to bear evidence against a villain and assist to consign him to a murderer's doom!"

"Then die!" roared Sataniello, goaded to fury —"die!"

And the Boy Brigand took aim at the heart of the unflinching girl.

But at that moment the loud report of carbines smote upon their ears.

The Boy Brigand turned hastily round and allowed the end of his piece to fall to the earth.

"What means this," he exclaimed, speaking to himself.

Ere the words had scarcely left his lips one of the brigands, who had been out upon the mountains on the watch, rushed hurriedly into the cover.

"How now—speak. What means that report?" exclaimed Sataniello.

"The Florentine has escaped," exclaimed the man, and Franco, who kept watch at the entrance, has died by his hand.

"Holy Virgin, I thank thee!" exclaimed Paulina.

And sinking upon her knees, she clasped her hands and raised her eyes to heaven.

CHAPTER X.

THE PURSUIT OF THE FLORENTINE—THE OATH OF VENGEANCE—THE SECOND REPORT.

FOR a moment the Boy Brigand stood, as it were, thunderstruck at the intelligence brought to him by the brigand.

His dark features paled, and he ground his teeth in rage.

"Escaped!" he exclaimed at length—"escaped!"

"Yes, Captain," replied the man.

"Then has the watch been ill-kept," said Sataniello.

"No, Captain, all were at their posts," replied the man.

"And yet he has escaped!" said Sataniello.

"Even so. I fired my carbine, but the ball missed its aim," said the man, "and struck the earth close to him."

"We must give chase," said the Boy Brigand.

"We may yet overtake him," said the man.

"Among the defiles, of which he doubtless is unacquainted, he would lose his way, and must soon again fall into our power."

"I hope so," said the man, "but we were guilty, Captain, of great negligence."

"How so?"

"We permitted the Florentine to become acquainted with the path to this cave."

"Explain."

"When we brought him hither," said the man, "we omitted to bind his eyes."

"Ah!" exclaimed the Boy Brigand, "we did so indeed!"

"Hence he knew the path to the mountains."

"Curses on it! But he must not escape. Call up the band; we must scour the mountains, and, dead or alive, get him once more in our power," said Sataniello.

But the report of the carbine had awoken the slumbering brigands, and they commenced pouring into the centre cavern, half dressed, but most of them armed.

They imagined that there was an attack upon their stronghold by the military, and eagerly they inquired the cause of the report they had heard.

"The Florentine has escaped," said the Boy Brigand.

"Escaped!" said the brigands, in surprise.

"Yes, and slain your comrade," said the Boy Brigand.

"Who?" they asked in a breath.

"Franco."

"By what means," said one, "he had no weapon."

"Yes he had," replied the man who had brought the news of the escape to the cave, "a poignard."

"Impossible! we searched him, said one.

"He has killed Franco with a poignard," said the man; "he is stabbed in the shoulder."

"No matter now by what means your comrade died," said Sataniello. "Away to the mountains in pursuit. He must not escape, for he knows the position of this place, and may lead on a band against us with which we may prove unable to cope."

The brigands hurried on their garments, and grasped their carbines.

"Curses on him!" exclaimed the Boy Brigand,

"he has the light of day to aid him in his flight. But he cannot have yet got far from the cavern, and the paths are better known to you than to him."

"He'll lose himself among the defiles," said Angelo, who had been the last to rise from his bed, but had learnt enough to know what the commotion was about.

"Doubtless," said the brigand. "Away then at once. Take him alive, if possible, for the sake of the ransom, but shoot him down rather than let him escape free."

The Signorita Paulina arose from her knees.

Her eye gleamed with a joyous light.

Her bosom heaved with emotions of happiness.

Her lover had escaped from the cavern where he had been confined.

He might succeed in making his way to Florence.

If he did so, there was hope.

Hope for her.

For well she knew he would return with aid, and endeavour to rescue her from the hands of the fearful brigands.

These thoughts endowed her with fresh strength, and she nerved herself to resist any attempt on the part of Sataniello to assail her honour or her life.

She secreted the dagger in her bosom.

That bosom which rose and fell with the tumultuous emotions which reigned within her heart.

The greater portion of the band now started off from the cavern in pursuit of Claudio.

The others left the cave to fetch in the dead body of their comrade.

Sataniello stood thoughtfully gazing after them.

Bitterly did he regret the escape of Claudio.

If he should succeed in eluding his pursuers, there was danger to be apprehended.

Not that the Boy Brigand feared danger.

He was too used to that.

But Claudio knew the position of their stronghold.

Knew the paths which led to their retreat.

He blamed himself for not having seen that the eyes of the young Florentine were bandaged, ere they brought him from the spot on which he was captured.

But it was too late now to regret.

That would be useless.

They must prevent his escaping from the mountains.

The chances against him were many.

To him the mountain passes could scarcely be known.

The rugged steeps, defiles, and precipices, could scarcely be known to him.

But to the brigands every inch of ground was well known—every curve and hollow had been occupied at some time or another by them; and therefore the Florentine would have some difficulty in eluding his foes.

As these thoughts ran through the mind of Sataniello, the frown on his brow relaxed, and he turned to Paulina.

"Your happiness," he said, "will be of short duration. Your lover cannot escape."

"Indeed!" she said, scornfully.

"No. Unused to the mountains he will be lost amid the thousand defiles, and fall easily again into our power."

"Heaven grant he may not," said Paulina.

"He must," said the brigand; "and I will then take good care he has no chance to escape again."

"I trust he may escape," said Paulina, "and re-

SIGNOR MARTINI ON THE TERRACE.

turn with a force which will crush you and your guilty companions."

"Even if he do," said the brigand, "he shall not rescue you pure and stainless. If he comes it will be to find you but a wreck of your former self—a thing unworthy to become his wife—the degraded mistress of the Boy Brigand."

"Never."

"He shall. Never shall he bear you to Florence with honour."

Paulina sighed, but she replied not.

Her hand grasped the handle of the concealed dagger in her bosom.

"This," she thought, "shall prevent it. If Claudio return he shall still find me worthy to become his wife or a corpse."

The brigands returned now to the cave, bearing in with them the still warm body of the man with whom Claudio had struggled at the entrance of the cave.

Tenderly they carried him to the centre table, and gently they laid him thereon.

The Boy Brigand stepped to his side.

He placed his hand upon the heart of the sentry to feel if there still remained any pulsation in it.

But no—that heart would never more beat. Life was gone. The soul of the man who had set all law at defiance had fled to the judgment-seat of his Maker—gone to answer for the crimes which lay heaped upon his head, and from which there was now no escape.

Silently and sadly those rough men gazed upon the pale features of their dead comrade, for he was well beloved by them—and then one of the brigands drew his poignard from his belt, and, laying the cross handle upon his lips, kissed it.

THE BOY BRIGAND; OR, THE DARK KING OF THE MOUNTAINS.

"Fabian," he exclaimed, "never till this steel is buried in the heart of him who slew you shall your death be avenged."

Paulina shuddered as the words of the man fell upon her ears.

Too well she knew the undying hatred of an Italian.

A hatred which would never slumber till satiated by blood.

"Comrades," exclaimed Sataniello, "you shall yet have vengeance for this deed. If the Florentine escape now we will track him till his blood atone for the death of him who lies cold and stiff before us. Revenge shall be yours, deep and bitter. Yon girl shall also atone for this deed. When she has fallen at my feet in shame I will surrender her to you. She shall feel the vengeance of the comrades of the man her lover has slain, and learn how bitter and undying is a brigand's hatred."

Again the loud report of a carbine saluted the ears of those assembled in the cavern.

"Ah, ah!" exclaimed Sataniello, "the Florentine has fallen!"

With a loud shriek Paulina staggered forward then fell to the earth.

CHAPTER XI.

THE FLIGHT OF CLAUDIO—THE ATTEMPTED CAPTURE THWARTED—THE OATH OF VENGEANCE OVER THE BODY OF THE MERCHANT.

THE loud report of the carbine had scarce died away along the mountains ere Claudio, the young Florentine, recovered from the shock it had caused.

Hastily snatching up the carbine of the falling sentry, he darted forward at full speed.

Fortunate, indeed, had it been for him that the brigands had not taken the precaution to bind his eyes.

Had they done so, his flight would not have been so easy.

He had marked well the route the brigands took from the mountain pass where himself and friends had been assailed.

Now he felt he should have little difficulty in retracing his steps.

And so on he went, if not cheerfully, at least with a greater degree of confidence than he otherwise would have done.

Placing the poignard in his belt in such a manner as to be the most convenient for use, and seeing that his carbine was on full cock, he hurried along the narrow path.

"Now for freedom," he muttered. "The chances are heavy against me, for behind every crag or peak a bullet may be waiting to bear its message of death. Holy Virgin, have me in thy keeping, and shield me from these ruthless men."

He gained the end of a long, narrow cutting, and soon found himself in an open space, forming a kind of chasm, with the mountains rising high above him on either side, and from whence he knew that the brigands could pour down upon him a storm of shot from which it would be impossible for him to escape should he be detected there.

Anxiously he cast his eyes upon either side.

He expected to see the muzzle of a carbine cover him at every step.

He hurried forward towards the opening at the further end.

He strained his eyes in each direction.

But nothing that indicated the presence of a foe was to be seen.

Yet his heart beat audibly.

His limbs trembled.

His cheek paled.

Still he strode on with unfaltering steps.

He knew his danger, and he resolved to meet it firmly.

The brigands should never take him alive back to the cave.

He would struggle whilst one drop of blood remained.

He would fight to the last.

And fighting he would die.

Such were his resolves.

Yet he could not but feel anxious.

He could not but glance nervously around him.

Those frowning precipices on either side might contain foes from whom there would be no possible escape.

Foes hidden from his view, but, nevertheless, as much to be dreaded, if not more so, than any who might stand before him to bar his passage to liberty.

It was, therefore, with a sigh of relief that Claudio gained the small outlet into a defile at the further end.

Here the mountains rose but a few feet above him, and their sloping sides would have revealed an enemy at some distance.

A weight seemed now to be removed from his heart.

He bounded on with renewed energy.

Claudio had gone some fifty yards along the defile, when one of the brigands, who had lain concealed in a cleft in the side of the mountain, sprang forward and barred his further passage.

"Surrender!" he exclaimed.

And, as he spoke, he put forth his hand to stay the further progress of the young Florentine.

Claudio leapt back.

He raised the carbine.

There was a quick flash and a loud report, and, as the smoke cleared away, he saw the brigand stagger and fall heavily to the earth.

"Another has gone," muttered Claudio. "In faith, if I even escape not, I shall at least have thinned the band and done Italy good service."

But he recollected that the report of the carbine would reveal his whereabouts, and bring down upon him the whole band.

His first impulse, therefore, was to fly, and look out for an opportunity of striking off from the straight track which lay before him.

With this intention he flung down the carbine that had done him such good service.

But then he paused.

"I have nothing now to defend myself with," he thought, "but my poignard. Surely this brigand was not unarmed?"

Claudio went up to the cleft in which the brigand had lain concealed, and looked therein.

A cry of joy broke from his lips.

He stretched forth his hand and grasped a carbine.

The brigand, believing Claudio to be unarmed, had intended to trust to his superior strength to take him captive, and had, therefore, left his carbine in his hiding-place.

"Now am I armed as before," muttered Claudio. "But I must away; the report of the weapon will bring the band upon me."

It was that report which had been heard in the cavern, and called forth the remark from the Boy Brigand that Claudio had been slain.

On went the young Florentine, as fast as his legs would carry him along the defile.

Eagerly he looked right and left, in the hopes of discovering some opening into which he might rush.

For the road he was pursuing was too much exposed to allow him to escape if any of the brigands were in the vicinity.

The desired object was met with at last.

A rent in the sides of the hills was revealed to his gaze.

A moment only he hesitated.

One anxious glance he cast around him.

Then into the narrow opening he rushed quickly.

Here he paused for breath.

The quick pace at which he had made his way from the cavern had told upon his frame.

And he leaned against the rough side of the passage in which he now found himself, panting and exhausted.

As he did so, he minutely examined the place.

It appeared more like a crack in the huge bulk of earth than aught else, as though some fearful convulsion of nature had rent the large mass in twain.

Its sides were jagged and uneven, as though they had been torn violently asunder, and not hewn by human hands.

So narrow was it, too, that not more than one person could have passed along it at a time.

"Here I will stay for a time," he muttered, "till the brigands, if the report call them to the spot, shall have taken their departure with the dead body of their comrade."

Cautiously he stooped down, and looked out from his hiding-place into the defile he had just left.

As he expected, the report of the carbine had reached the ears of some of the band.

He could see two of the brigands hurriedly approaching the spot where their wounded comrade lay.

Quickly he withdrew his head within the opening again, lest they should cast their eyes in that direction and perceive him.

But his curiosity to discover their actions prompted him again to look forth.

So, lying flat down upon the earth, he looked again.

The brigands had lifted their comrade in their arms and were bearing him away in the direction of the cave.

Eagerly Claudio watched their retreating forms.

"What pleasure it would afford me," he muttered, "to send a bullet after them. But I must not obey my inclination, or it would reveal my hiding-place, as did the report of the last carbine reveal the spot where yon villain fell. No, I must be prudent, for, if by any act I destroy myself, I likewise sacrifice Paulina. I must endeavour to escape to Florence, from whence I will return to hunt the villains from their lair and release the maiden from her captivity. Heaven grant I may succeed ere it is too late. I fear the worst that can befall her. The words of the Boy Brigand have struck more terror to my soul than could twenty carbines levelled at my heart. I fear for her—not for myself—for without her life would be irksome ; and the knowledge that she had fallen a sacrifice to the unholy passion of that youth would drive my brain to madness."

And as the youth spoke, his hand played with the handle of the poignard at his breast.

"O that I had him here singly," he murmured; "I would show him how a Florentine can avenge an insult offered to the woman of his choice, and avenge the death of her father. I would bury my poignard in

his heart, and as his life-blood flowed at my feet I would taunt his departing spirit with the crimes he had committed. But we shall yet meet again; then shall he learn that a Florentine's vengeance never slumbers—never till the life of his enemy has been taken by his hand, and he lies at his feet cold and rigid in death."

And again Claudio looked around to see if he could discover any of the brigands along the line of route he wished to take.

But no sign of a human being met his gaze.

Only the dark sides of the mountains, and here and there a tree which grew upon their slopes.

All, too, was silent,

Silent as death.

Claudio again took the carbine in his grasp, and sallied forth into the defile.

As speedily as he could, he rushed onward towards the road to Florence.

But he had tasted no food since the preceding evening, and began to feel the pangs of thirst and hunger.

But the fear of pursuit and re-capture for a time drowned all other thoughts.

Still the want of drink told sadly upon him.

His form was not so erect as it had hitherto been

His pace was less swift.

His step less firm.

Yet on he went, his hopes of escape rising as he placed distance between himself and the cavern.

He gained the road in which the brigands had appeared before him on the previous evening.

A cry of horror broke from his lips.

A shudder ran through his frame.

He closed his eyes for a moment to shut out the sight that met his gaze.

But opening them again he stooped down over the cold body of the Signor Sebastian.

The worthy merchant lay before him on the spot where he fell—lies there exposed to the birds of prey, without covering save his blood-stained garments.

The youth took the cold, clammy hand of the murdered man within his own, and raised it to his lips.

"Father," he said, "for such I hoped to call thee, thou shalt be terribly avenged. Here, beside thy cold remains, I swear never to rest till I have hunted thy murderer to a fearful doom."

CHAPTER XII.

SATANIELLO AND HIS BAND DISGUISE THEMSELVES, AND START IN PURSUIT OF CLAUDIO THE FLORENTINE.

OVERCOME by the sufferings she had endured, it only needed the words of the Boy Brigand that her lover had been destroyed to utterly prostrate the remaining strength of the Signorita Paulina.

The report of the carbine and the exclamation of the brigand caused reason to totter from her throne, and the poor girl found relief from her sufferings in insensibility.

As she fell to the ground the Boy Brigand rushed forward to raise her.

As he had done before he carried her rigid form into the cavern devoted to himself, and laid her upon the rough pallet.

Then he returned to his companions in the centre cave, and awaited impatiently the arrival of Claudio.

In a short time the two brigands bore into their

retreat the man who had endeavoured to bar the passage of the young Florentine, and who, like his comrade, had paid with his life for the act.

Into the cavern they bore him, and laid him upon the table beside his fellow.

For a moment surprise held the Boy Brigand dumbfounded.

But it was for a moment only.

He cast an inquiring look towards the new-comers.

He bit his lips with rage.

He clenched his hands tightly together.

Then his lips moved.

He uttered one word.

"Another!"

"Yes, captain," said one of the men who had brought in the dead brigand.

"And the Florentine—has he done this?" said Sataniello.

"He has."

"And has he escaped?"

"He has."

"Curse him!" exclaimed Sataniello, grinding his teeth in rage.

"Guided by the report of a carbine, we hurried to the spot, expecting to find the Florentine had been captured," said one of the men; "but we found only our comrade, who had met his death by the hand of the escaped man.

"Where was that?" asked Sataniello.

"In the defile leading to the pass, where we stopped the party last night," replied the man.

The Boy Brigand paused thoughtfully for a few moments.

"It will take him some hours," he said, at length, "to clear the mountains."

"It will."

"He will doubtless endeavour to make his way to Florence?"

"Without doubt he intends that place for his destination," said one.

"Where he will raise a band, and return to rescue his affianced bride," said the Boy Brigand.

"Very likely."

"He must not reach Florence," said Sataniello. "For, knowing the vicinity of this cavern, he will have us at his mercy."

"It was a great oversight—allowing him to become acquainted with the paths to it," said one of brigands.

"It was—that cannot be helped now," said Sataniello. "The evil is done, and all we can do is to remedy it. We will start for Florence, leaving only Angelo and his new wife to guard the Signorita Paulina."

"Start for Florence?" said one.

"Even so. We may overtake him ere he arrives there; but should we not succeed in so doing, to Florence we must go, and seize him ere he can solicit the aid of the authorities to rescue the girl, and drive us from our mountain fastness."

"A journey thither by daylight is fraught with much danger, captain," said one of the men.

"I know it. Are you afraid to accompany me?" asked Sataniello, with a curl of the lip.

"No, captain."

"Then sound the call."

The man went to the entrance to the cavern, and blew a long, loud and shrill whistle, which was echoed back from crag to crag and peak to peak of the long line of hills.

Then he returned to his companions in the cave.

"Now," said the brigand captain, "there is not a moment to lose. You have, of course, plenty of means of disguising yourselves."

"We have," replied one of the men.

"Away, then," said Sataniello, "and attire yourselves in any fashion you please. I see that there is a disguise in my cave; I will put it on, and await you here. Be speedy; every moment places a greater distance between us and the man we seek.

At this moment Angelo entered the cave.

The Boy Brigand turned towards him.

"Angelo," he said, "myself and the band will away to Florence."

"To Florence?" said Angelo.

"Yes."

"But, captain——"

"There is no time for 'buts,'" interrupted Sataniello. "We go to prevent the young Florentine from revealing the secret of our retreat. You will remain here to guard the signorita."

"Can I not accompany you, captain?" asked Angelo.

"You will find more pleasure in the company of your new wife I should imagine," said Sataniello. "As the men arrive bid them disguise themselves as best they can, and be ready to start in a quarter of an hour — each one to arm himself with his poignard."

"Your orders shall be obeyed," said Angelo.

Sataniello now entered his cavern, and, casting a look upon the insensible girl, he raised a small heap of clothing from the ground, and commenced attiring himself in them.

Wonderful indeed was the change in his appearance in a few minutes.

Attired in a long, loose pair of trousers, a large coat lined with fur, a skull-cap, and immense flowing beard of snowy whiteness, the transformation was so great that it would have defied his nearest relative to discover in the Oriental, Jew-looking personage the dreaded Boy Brigand, the Dark King of the Mountains.

Placing a pistol and a poignard in his belt, and throwing the ample folds of the loose outer garment over them, he cast one more look upon the insensible girl, and left the small cave for the outer cavern.

His followers started with surprise at the metamorphosis.

His tall form looked even taller than in his brigand's costume.

"It would be impossible for any one to recognise you, Captain, in that garb," said Angelo, looking admiringly upon his new captain.

"My disguise, then, is complete," said the Boy Brigand.

"It is, Captain."

"Are all ready?"

"All."

"Now, Angelo, to you I entrust the safe keeping of the Signorita Paulina," said the Boy Brigand.

"I will be watchful, Captain," replied the brigand.

"You can suffer your wife to attend to her."

"I will do so."

"She still lies insensible in yonder cavern," said the brigand. "Send Perditta to her. She may become more reconciled to her situation when her maid is by her side."

"Her what, Captain?" said Angelo, with a smile.

"Her maid."

"Oh!" exclaimed Angelo, with a grin on his bronzed face. "They should change places, methinks, since Perditta can no longer claim the title."

"Then her mistress can," said the Boy Brigand,

sullenly. "You have been more successful with the maid than I have with the mistress."

"All in good time, Captain," said Angelo. "Women will be obstinate now and then spite of the devil. A little resistance to our wishes but enhances the pleasures of success."

"Perhaps so," said the Boy Brigand ; "but it is not a little resistance I have met with, but a great deal. But, curse her, she shall not escape me. I will show her yet that Sataniello, the Boy Brigand, is not one to be put from his purpose."

. "Quite right, Captain," said Angelo, who felt a secret pleasure at his own success. It is not every man that can claim the title of lady-killer. Your manner, perhaps, is too rough, and she may require tender words to woo her."

"I will break her heart," said Sataniello, spitefully.

"Nay, Captain, I would learn her to love me—once you succeed in so doing, depend upon it, the Signorita Paulina will offer no more resistance to your will."

"Well, well, enough of that for the present. Time presses, and the Florentine speeds on his way. Be watchful and wary. Now, men, to Florence."

And the Boy Brigand strode towards the entrance to the cave, followed by all of the band, save Angelo, attired as traders, peasants, and guides.

The lieutenant stood gazing after their retreating figures as they made their way along the narrow passage from the mouth of the cave ; and when the last had passed through the bushes which hid the opening, he turned, with a smile upon his lips, into the cavern.

"Ha, ha !" he laughed ; "nothing could have pleased me better than to be left guard here. In faith, I'll have a pleasant time of it till they return. I am not yet tired of my new bride, and the hours will pass in happiness and joy. She has not yet risen from her nuptial couch ; so I may as well go and keep her company for a time longer."

And, after peering into the cavern in which the Signorita Paulina lie, he securely fastened the door to prevent her escape, and entered his own apartment.

CHAPTER XIII.

THE SIGNORITA PAULINA AND HER MAID PERDITTA. THE CONFESSION.

It was midday ere, satiated with Love's revels, the waiting-maid Perditta and her brigand-lover rose from the rude couch assigned to them.

The face of the pretty waiting-maid was paler than usual.

Her eyes were vacant and downcast.

Her manner was nervous.

Her gait unsteady.

Ever and anon a sigh broke from her lips.

And her whole appearance denoted her far from happy.

She was ill at ease.

The morning's light had brought reflection to her mind.

She had been reviewing her past life, and surmising the future.

Besides, she had been told by Angelo at Sataniello's request that she should attend upon Paulina.

Perditta loved her mistress, for to her she was a kind and indulgent one.

But she feared now to meet her.

She felt guilty ; and how could she stand in the presence of one of her own sex, who had not hesitated to protect her honour at any cost.

For she had learned from Angelo that the beauteous maiden had repulsed every overture of the Boy Brigand's.

How, then, could Perditta meet the indignant, flashing eye of virtue?

Fain, then, would she have hidden herself from the gaze of her mistress.

Like all guilty people, she feared her sins might be read on her forehead.

She implored Angelo not to send her to the cavern in which Paulina was confined.

But the brigand only said that he must obey his orders.

So there was no help for it—she must go.

With trembling hands she undid the fastenings of the rude door.

With trembling limbs she stepped across the threshhold.

With trembling lips she muttered the name of the Signorita.

Paulina, who had recovered her consciousness, was sitting weeping on the side of the couch when Perditta entered.

At the sound of her maid's voice the poor girl started to her feet.

A gleam of pleasure shot from her eyes.

A ray of hope lit up her features.

She darted forward and clasped the girl in her arms.

"Perditta!" she exclaimed; "oh, joy—is it you?"

"It is, Signorita," answered the girl in a low tone of voice.

But she hung her head, and averted her gaze from the face of her mistress.

"Oh, my poor Perditta," continued Paulina, "what have we suffered?"

Perditta only sighed.

"To what insults are we subjected in this tearful place," continued Paulina. "You—you, I fear, have not escaped them?"

But Perditta answered not.

She knew not what to say.

She feared to utter the truth.

What would it avail her to lie?

So she stood silent.

It was the best thing she could do, she thought.

It was the wisest plan she could adopt.

"Perditta," said Paulina, "are there no means of escape from this fearful place?"

"Alas ! Signorita, none," replied the young girl.

"Then we are lost," said Paulina, in a sorrowful tone.

To this Perditta made no reply.

Was she not already lost?

Had she not already lost all woman holds dear?

What to her would be the use of escape from the cavern?

Whither could she go?

What could she do?

If she even could succeed in getting away from the strongholds of the brigands of what avail would it be to her?

Could she go forth pure as she came into it ?

No.

Then why need she think of escape?

But her mistress ?

Perditta had been happy could Paulina have gone free.

Yet she feared to say as much.

"Perditta," said Paulina, after a pause, "where is the fearful Boy Brigand ?"

"Gone to Florence."

" To Florence ?"

" Yes."

" Then he is not here ?"

" No."

" Holy Virgin be praised!" exclaimed Paulina, fervently.

" He has gone to Florence in pursuit of the Signor Claudio," said Perditta, " and taken all the band with him save Angelo, the Lieutenant."

" How know you this ?"

" Angelo told me."

" He told you ?"

" Yes."

" Why should he tell you, girl ?" said Paulina.

" I know not."

" I should have thought men who devoted their lives to robbery, rapine, and murder would be secret as to their movements," said Paulina. " You must have excited some interest in the breast of this lieutenant to have induced him to make you his confidant."

A purple flush overspread the features of Perditta.

A blush that was not lost upon Paulina.

A strange feeling took possession of her heart as she observed it.

A feeling of dread.

She took the hand of Perditta in her own.

She felt it tremble in her grasp.

It was cold and clammy.

Perditta became agitated.

Paulina looked sorrowfully in her face.

The waiting maid averted her gaze.

Paulina trembled.

Why this agitation ?

What could she think ?

Alas ! she almost feared to think.

Feared lest her thoughts should lead her to wrong that girl.

This she would not have done for the world.

For she loved and respected Perditta.

Still her mind was ill at ease.

" Perditta," she said at length, " I have been submitted to insults which would make your blood curdle with horror."

" With insults ?" asked Perditta.

" Insults the greatest that can be offered to woman."

" By whom, Signoritta ?"

" The Boy Brigand. He has dared to assail my honour. Oh ! Perditta, have you, too, suffered such indignity ?"

Perditta answered not.

" Speak, girl. Tell me the worst," exclaimed Paulina.

" Alas Signorita."

" Speak—speak !"

Perditta burst into tears.

" You have, my girl, you have !" exclaimed her mistress, throwing her arm around the neck of her waiting maid " Oh, that we could escape from this place, and save ourselves from the awful fate to which these monsters would condemn us."

" Would that you could," said Perditta, with a sigh.

" That I could ?" iterated Paulina.

" Yes, Signorita."

" That we both could," said Paulina. " Heaven knows, I would save your honour as well as my own."

A half-suppressed groan burst from Perditta's breast.

Her cheek, which had flushed, now become deathly pale, and she burst into tears.

For a moment Paulina stood gazing upon her.

Her bosom rose and fell with the varied emotions which shook her frame.

Her lips trembled, and a tear glistened in her dark eye.

She grasped Perditta's wrist, and gazed anxiously in her eyes.

" Perditta," she exclaimed, in a hoarse whisper, " speak—speak ! Have you fallen ?"

For a moment Perditta answered not.

Then she forced her arm from the others' grasp, and, tottering towards the couch, sank down upon her knees beside it.

She buried her face in her hands, and gave vent to heart-breaking sobs.

Paulina leant over her, and placed her arms around the neck of the weeping girl.

" Tell—oh tell me the worst," she exclaimed.

" Lost ! lost !" gasped Perditta. " Touch me not. I am a polluted thing—the mistress of a brigand !"

With a loud cry Paulina sprang backwards as though she had trodden on a scorpion.

" Holy Virgin !" she gasped.

Perditta sprang to her feet.

" Signorita," she exclaimed, " I know—I feel that I am loathsome in your eyes. But what could I do to prevent my fall ? I should have been murdered had I offered resistance. Oh, pity me !—do not blame me !"

" I do pity you !" exclaimed Paulina; " pity you that you had not the moral courage to resist the vile desires of these unholy men. Of what value is life without honour ? Girl, I would die to save myself from such a doom ! Sooner would I lay bare my breast to the poignard's blade, than submit to that which you have done ! Here, upon this spot, did I defy the villain to make me that which my soul abhorred ! Here did I prefer death to dishonour—here did I hurl back scorn for insult ! Perditta, a woman's honour should be protected even with her life ; for once sacrificed, she is ruined for ever. Rather would I lay a cold and stiffened corpse at the feet of the Boy Brigand, than surrender that into his keeping which belongs only to a husband. Perditta, I do pity thee—I do pity thee !"

And Paulina, burying her face in her hands, sank down upon the couch.

" Oh," she sobbed, " welcome death if it come, but dishonour, never ! Holy Virgin, look down upon me ! Shield me from the savage villains into whose hands I have fallen, or launch the thunderbolts of destruction on my head, if Claudio be not destined to embrace a spotless bride !"

CHAPTER XIV.

THE LOVER AND HIS FEARS—THE ABSENCE DISCOVERED—THE PURSUIT OF THE GONDOLA.

SIGNOR SALERNIO DI RICO, the lover of the beauteous Marianna Morteni, ordered the gondola to be rowed close to the steps on which we have seen Stephano assisting the ladies into the bark which they were led to believe was to carry them to Aquila.

Stepping from the gondola on to the terrace, the young Italian ordered the gondolier to return for him in about an hour; and as the gondola floated out again into the stream, Salernio di Rico stepped beneath the window at which he hoped to see the face of his beloved Marianna.

But the casement was closed, and the room in darkness.

"Not there," he muttered to himself. "I must make her acquainted with my presence."

And running his fingers over the guitar he carried in his hand, he sang, in a full, melodious voice, a song in praise of the girl he loved.

But in vain were his eyes fixed upon the casement.

It still remained closed.

Marianna appeared not.

Again he ran his fingers over the instrument.

But no response did he receive.

No intimation that Marianna had heard him, or was aware of his presence.

"Strange," muttered the young man; "ever have I found her waiting at her casement to greet me. What can be the cause of her absence from her usual spot to-night? Holy Virgin! I trust that ill has not befallen her."

And again he struck his guitar.

But this time in a louder strain.

Still Marianna appeared not.

The beautiful raven tresses of the Italian maiden appeared not at the window.

Her silvery voice greeted not her lover.

Her winning smile bade him no welcome.

Anxiously the youth kept his eyes fixed upon the place where the features of Marianna appeared every night.

But all remained dark and silent.

Nervously he turned and paced the terrace.

But the echo of his own footfall alone saluted his ears.

Save now and then the plashing of the oars of the gondolier in the distance, or the splash of the waters as they washed the steps leading to the terrace of the mansion of the Signor di Martini.

The youth momentarily became more anxious, and he paced up and down with uneven steps, gazing up at the window, or down at the moonlit stream which ran beneath the spot on which he stood.

"My heart misgives me," he muttered, "and sad forebodings creep into my heart. I must know the worst, come what may."

And the youth strode along the terrace and turned the angle of the wall.

Here he stood in front of the noble mansion.

He cast his eyes up at the windows.

Lights only were to be seen in the servants' apartments.

All else was in darkness.

Salernio knocked at the entrance devoted to the servants, and impatiently awaited the answer to his summons.

He had not to wait long, but his anxiety and fears caused minutes to seem hours to his impatient mind.

He was about to again announce his presence, when the door opened, and an old and faithful servitor stood before him.

"Signor Salernio di Rico!" exclaimed the man, in surprise.

And as he spoke he darted backwards several paces.

His face became livid as death.

He trembled as though he was afflicted with palsy.

"Yes, Tomaso, it is me—Salernio," answered the young man.

"Sa—sa—ler—nio!" stammered the man, holding up his hands as if to keep off some horrible spectre, and his knees literally knocking together with fear.

"Why, what ails you, Tomaso?" asked the youth, in a tone of surprise, "are you not well?"

"Yes—ye—e—s!" stammered the man, still re-

treating backwards, with his hands held out before him.

Salernio became more and more astonished at Tomaso.

What could be the meaning of the man's conduct?

Had Salernio summoned admittance at a time distateful to Tomaso?

Was the man intoxicated?

Had he been bereft of his senses?

As these thoughts ran through the mind of the youth, he stepped into the marble-tesselated hall.

As he did so, Tomaso devoutly crossed himself.

"Holy Virgin protect us!" he exclaimed, in a feeble voice.

"Your conduct alarms me," said Salernio.

"Your presence alarms me, Signor!" gasped Tomaso.

"Why should it do so?" asked Salernio. "What is the meaning of this strange conduct?"

And Salernio stretched forth his arm to lay his hand upon the man's shoulder, as he asked the question.

But Tomaso sprang backwards as though he had been stung by an adder.

"Avaunt, horrible spectre!" he shrieked. "Go back to the grave. Holy mother! have mercy upon us!"

"You have been drinking," said Salernio, unable in any other way to account for the strange behaviour of the servitor.

"No—no—no!" stammered the man.

"Then you have lost your senses," said the youth.

"I—I—shall, Signor—if you do not go at once!" gasped Tomaso.

"My mission here is not yet ended," said Salernio.

"Your mission!" iterated Tomaso. "Holy Virgin protect us!"

"Well, then, the object of my visit," said Salernio.

"Oh, do go away, Signor—oh, do go away!" exclaimed Tomaso, again crossing himself, as a cold sweat broke out upon his forehead, and he dreaded harm to all in that house.

"Where is the Signorita Marianna?" inquired Salernio, in haughty tones, now satisfied in his own mind that Tomaso had been making too free with the juice of the grape.

"The signorita!" stammered the servant.

"Yes, the signorita," replied Salernio, impatiently.

"G—g—o—ne!" stammered Tomaso.

"Gone?"

"Y—e—s."

"Whither?"

"To Aquila."

"For what purpose?" inquired the youth.

"Don't you know?"

"Certainly not."

"You don't?"

"No."

"To see you."

"To see me?" exclaimed Salernio, in bewilderment.

"Yes, Signor, to see you," replied the man.

"Impossible!"

"She will see your body, Signor," said Tomaso, "if she don't your spirit."

"Begone, Sir!" exclaimed Salernio, enraged at what he considered the drunken nonsense of the man, "and tell Pedro I would see him. He at least can give me the information I seek."

"I will, Signor," exclaimed Tomaso, hurriedly darting away, and crossing himself as he went.

For a few moments Salernio awaited patiently the appearance of Pedro, another servant to the Signor Martini.

But the man came not.

The patience of the young Italian was gradually becoming exhausted; and darting along the hall to the farthest end, he called loudly—

"Pedro! Pedro!"

But no answer came back in reply.

"Pedro! Pedro!" he called again, still more loudly.

He listened for the footsteps of the servant he had summoned, and the tones of his voice saluted his ears.

"Holy Mother protect and save us!" he heard Pedro exclaim. "Oh, Tomaso, go for Father Joseph, and beg of him to lay the spirit ere it destroy us!"

"You go," replied Tomaso, "I cannot encounter it again."

"What does it look like?" asked Pedro.

"A shadow—only a shadow!" replied Tomaso.

"But does it look like what he was in the flesh," asked his companion.

"Yes, only much more awful," said Tomaso; "it is the figure and the face of the Signor Salernio, but only his spirit."

"Go for Father Joseph—or stay, go and tell the ghost that the signorita has gone to see him at Aquila, and perhaps it will go away," said Pedro.

"Ah, no! I fear nothing but the priest can send it off," replied Tomaso. "The spirit is angry with the signorita for not being at his side when he died."

"She could not have been so," replied Pedro. "The Signorita Paulina waited for nothing when she heard Signor Salernio was dying; and if he died ere she arrived at Aquila, it was no fault of hers."

Salernio, who had listened attentively, and heard every word that had passed between Pedro and Tomaso, started and trembled.

He could perceive now that the strange conduct of Tomaso was caused by the belief that he stood in the presence of one he considered to be a being of the other world.

But why should they believe him dead?

What reason had they for thinking so?

Why should Paulina have gone to Aquila?

The words of the servants led to the inference that she had gone thither to seek him.

He must fathom this mystery.

He must discover what it all meant.

He must learn from Tomaso and Pedro the true state of affairs.

But he could see that it was useless to summon them.

Their fears would not permit them to leave the place where they now were.

Fears conjured up by the belief that he was dead, and that it was only his spirit which stood there.

He resolved, therefore, to seek them.

He strode on till he came to the apartment in which the two servants stood, gazing horrified into each other's face.

Standing upon the threshhold of the room, he said—

"Tomaso—Pedro!"

The men, who had not observed him till then, turned quickly round.

A cry of horror broke from their lips.

Their features became blanched with terror.

Their hair seemed to stand on end.

Their knees knocked together, and they shook like aspen leaves.

For one moment they stood gazing upon Salernio as he stood in the doorway, and then they both dropped upon their knees, and crossed themselves in abject terror.

Anxious as Salernio was to know the meaning of all that had taken place, he could not restrain a burst of laughter at the scene before him.

But never did merriment grate so harshly upon the ears of human being as it did on those of Tomaso and Pedro.

It sounded to them like some unearthly yell proceeding from the grave.

And, as fast as the trembling fingers could perform the office, they crossed themselves again and again.

Alternately gazing upon the figure of Salernio in the doorway and then upon each other, they sank lower and lower, till their faces almost touched the floor.

"Let there be an end to this absurd scene," said Salernio after a pause. "You believe me, from some cause or other, to be dead; but, the Holy Virgin be thanked, I am alive and well. Rise and answer me."

But though Tomaso and Pedro looked up at these words they made no attempt, nor indeed showed the least inclination, to rise from their kneeling position.

"Fools!" exclaimed Salernio, "rise at once, or I will pull you up by your ears."

And he strode towards them with the intention of putting his threat into execution.

But the moment he stretched forth his hand Tomaso and Pedro leapt to their feet, and darted to the farthest corner of the apartment, where they each strove to get behind the other to shield themselves from the vengeance of the believed spectre.

"For shame," exclaimed Salernio, indignantly; "are you the men the Signor Martini leave in trust of his house; are you the men to whom he confides the care of his child—you who tremble at your own shadows, and fly in abject terror before your fellowmen. Shame on you, cowards!"

"We ain't cowards before real flesh and blood," gasped Tomaso, with difficulty.

"Flesh and blood!" iterated Salernio; "what, then, am I?"

But he received no reply to this question.

"What, then, am I?" he repeated.

"A—a g—h—o—ost!" exclaimed Pedro.

And feeling that some fearful doom would befal him for his temerity, he swung Tomaso round, and held that individual firmly before himself to shield him from the anger of Salernio.

"A what?" exclaimed Salernio.

"A ghost," stammered Pedro, looking over his companion's shoulder as he spoke, but ducking his head behind Tomaso's back the instant the words had left his lips.

"And what's a ghost?" asked Salernio.

"A spirit," answered Pedro, gaining fresh courage now that he held his companion between himself and Salernio.

"And what's a spirit?" asked Salernio.

"A shadow," replied Pedro.

"And do you take me for a shadow?" asked Salernio.

"Yes," replied Tomaso.

"You do?"

"Yes."

"Then let me disabuse your mind of that impression," said Salernio, stepping quickly towards

the trembling men.   "Fools and cowards! feel the substance."

And seizing Tomaso by the collar of his coat he dealt him so hearty a box of the ear that he roared with the pain; then thrusting him into the middle of the room he seized Pedro and served him in the same way.

"Now," he said, "if a ghost is a spirit, and a spirit a shadow, it is evident that neither ghost, spirit, nor shadow could inflict such a blow as that, and I trust that you have received evidence enough to convince you that Salernio di Rico stands before you in the solid, living flesh."

For several moments Tomaso and Pedro stood gazing first at each other then at Salernio.

The same thought occurred to both at the same time—that no ghost could hit so hard as that.

And gradually the truth dawned upon them that it must be Salernio alive and well who stood before them.

The feeling of terror which had possessed them now gave place to one of shame, and they cast their eyes to the ground, abashed at their conduct.

Salernio now felt satisfied that he had convinced them he was no denizen of another world, so, biting his lip to repress his laughter, he said—

"Tomaso, where is the Signorita Paulina?"

"Gone to Aquila," replied the man.

"When did she go?"

"But a short time ere you arrived," he replied.

"With whom did she go?" asked Salernio.

"With her maid Julietta," said Pedro.

"How did she go?"

"By water."

"In her gondola?"

"No, Signor."

"No?"

"Not in her own gondola, Signor," replied Tomaso.

"In a hired one, then?" said Salernio.

"No, Signor," said Tomaso.

"Are you deceiving me?" said Salernio, advancing angrily towards Tomaso.

"No, Signor, indeed, no," hastily replied the man, retreating backwards lest he received another proof that Salernio was no ghost. "I will explain, Signor. You must know that the Signorita was summoned to the casement by the notes of a guitar, when she perceived a young man, who requested speech with her. This she granted; and from him she learned that you had been stabbed in the back by a Venetian, and was dying at the house of a friend at

Aquila; that you implored her to fly to you ere life had departed. Her love for you, Signor, induced her to accompany the young man in his gondola, which awaited for him at the steps, rather than lose a moment by waiting for her own; and she is now, doubtless, at her destination."

A deathly paleness overspread the features of Salernio as he listened to the words of Tomaso.

"Holy Virgin!" he exclaimed; "she has been entrapped for some horrible purpose. This story was false—all false. What colour was the gondola?"

"White and gold."

"Enough; I saw it leave the steps. It took the opposite direction to Aquila. But I will track the villian who has thus deceived her."

CHAPTER XV.

THE INN—SATANIELLO DRAWS THE CHARGES, AND AWAITS AN OPPORTUNITY TO COMMENCE BUSINESS.

It was towards night that the Boy Brigand and his followers entered Pistoia.

So far their search for the Florentine had been fruitless.

Wearied with their long journey, and feeling that it would be useless to push on to Florence that night, the Boy Brigand resolved to seek shelter in a small inn that laid some distance from the high road.

This inn was kept by one Jacques Roberto, a persevering Italian, who never allowed an opportunity of making a ducat to pass by him unheeded.

He was the proprietor of an extensive vineyard; and although that itself yielded him a good income, he had built an inn beside his grounds for his wife to look after, and thus enable him to bag more ducats.

To this place, then, the Boy Brigand and his followers made their way.

Jacques Roberto stood in the doorway puffing a cigarette at peace with himself and all the world, when the party arrived.

Jacques took the cigarette from his lips, opened his mouth and eyes very wide at the sight of the travellers, then bowed very low.

"Welcome, signors!" he said. "You do me honour by your visit."

It was not often that Jacques had so many customers at a time, and he hurried into the house to inform his wife that a large party of travellers had arrived.

The Boy Brigand and his companions entered, and made their way to the public room, where they had scarcely seated themselves, than Jacques, all smiles and bows, made his appearance.

"What is your pleasure, signors?" he inquired.

"Rest and refreshment," said the Boy Brigand; "and be speedy, for we are hungered and tired."

"Travelled far, Signor?"

"From Ravenna," answered Sataniello.

"Did you cross the mountains?" asked Jacques.

"We did."

"It is a passage fraught with much danger, Signor."

"How so?"

"The brigands."

"Yes," said Sataniello. "It was from fear of them that we all came in company," continued Sataniello, wishing to make Jacques believe that the acquaintance of his guests had only been formed for security, and that otherwise they knew little of each other.

"Not a bad plan, Signor." said Jacques.

"Did persons wishing to cross the mountains, either on business or pleasure, resolve to go at one and the same time, they would often find it to their advantage, and do the state some service, by compelling the brigands to retire from their unholy calling, from giving them no chance of plying their trade. Unity is strength, Signor; and it is not likely, desperate as they are, that the banditti would attempt to molest so numerous a body of honest gentlemen."

"You are right," said Sataniello. "I presume you can give us accommodation for the night?"

"I shall be sadly put to, Signor, to do so," said the host; "my house is small."

"Oh, we can make shift! You see, we are desirous of keeping in company, as, having a good deal of money about us, with which we are going to trade in Florence, we fear a descent from the mountains by the brigands. If we keep together we may succeed in beating them; but if we are scattered we might all lose our wealth."

"Well, Signor, my house has never yet been visited by the bandits, and I trust it never may. Still, if ever they do come, they will find Jacques Roberto well prepared to meet them."

"I am glad to hear you say so," said Sataniello, "as I feel more secure in your house."

"Yes, Signor, I always keep a pair of pistols and a carbine loaded in my bed-room, and within reach of my hand."

"A wise plan, truly. I trust you will endeavour to accommodate us all, as I should be sorry to seek it elsewhere; and we have bound ourselves to keep together till we return to Ravenna."

"Well, Signor," said Jacques, anxious not to lose his customers; "I will do my best to conform to your wishes, though I fear that the accommodation I am enabled to extend to you will but be poor and meagre."

"Oh, we don't mind that, do we?" said Sataniello, turning to his companions.

"No, no!" they answered.

"Then, Signors, I will do my best to render you as comfortable as my means will permit me to do," said Jacques, hurrying from the room to assist his wife in procuring refreshments for what he believed to be peaceful travellers.

When Jacques had left the apartment, Sataniello turned to his companions.

There was a smile on his dark face.

His eyes gleamed meaningly.

"Comrades," he said, in a low tone, "like soldiers on the march in an enemy's country, we provide for our wants without other payment than a few inches of steel. Is it not so?"

"Yes," answered his companions.

"This place bears anything but the appearance of wealth," continued Sataniello. "Yet I doubt not that Signor Jacques holds more sequins in his possession than many a gentleman of Pistoia."

"If so, Captain," said one, "we may reward ourselves for the journey hither."

"Such is my intention," said Sataniello.

In a short time the host returned, bearing with him a well-laden tray of viands and a quantity of wine, which he set before his guests.

The Boy Brigand poured out a cup of the sparkling liquid and drank it off.

"Your wine is good," he said.

"It is of the best vintage, Signor," said Jacques; "made from the berries of my own growing."

"Is the vineyard yours, then ?" asked Sataniello.

"It is," replied the man.

"And a profitable one it is, too, I should say," said Sataniello, carelessly.

"It yields well, Signor," said the man.

"Has it been long in your possession ?" said Sataniello.

"Many years."

"And of late the yield has been great ?"

"Very," said the man, with a look of pride, "for experience has taught me how to train them to the best advantage."

"Now," said Sataniello, in a careless tone, "I should say you are a wealthy man, and should think it would be to your interest to enlarge your house so as to afford greater accommodation to travellers."

Jacques shook his head.

"Well," said Sataniello, "a man knows his own purse better than his neighbour's, and appearances are often against us."

"It is not the want of the money, Signor," said Jacques, "that prevents my enlarging my premises; but from the fact that they are equal to the accommodation required, as few travellers turn from the high road to pay me a visit."

"It matters little, doubtless," said Sataniello, "as you have plenty to do with it."

"Well, Signor, I am happy to say I am not a poor man."

"And I am happy to hear it," remarked Sataniello.

As he spoke he cast a meaning glance at his companions.

A glance which was quickly understood by them.

But Jacques noticed it not.

He believed his guests were what they seemed.

Believed them to be honest traders journeying from Ravenna to Florence.

No suspicion of their real character entered his mind.

Had it done so he had been less loquacious.

He had not confessed to being well to do in the world.

Rather would he have asserted that he was steeped in poverty.

Instead of being willing to find them accommodation he would have endeavoured to get rid of them.

Jacques left the room to procure some articles which Sataniello ordered.

When he had gone Sataniello said—

"Comrades, when he returns keep him in conversation whilst I go to his bedroom."

"For what purpose?"

"To draw the bullets from his pistols and carbine," replied Sataniello.

"Good !" said one.

"Hush—he returns."

Jacques entered with the required articles, and set them down on the table.

"Can I do anything else for you ?" asked the landlord.

"Not for me," said Sataniello; "but perhaps some of these gentlemen may require something."

Jacques turned to the others.

As he did so Sataniello rose and left the room.

The brigands were not slow in finding something to talk upon to keep Jacques in the apartment, and he, unsuspicious of their motive, answered any question put to him.

Meanwhile Sataniello made his way up the staircase.

He had taken the precaution to make sure that there was no one who could observe his movements.

There were only four rooms above, and into each of these Sataniello cast a hurried glance.

As usual, it is ever the last one which is required.

Sataniello had peeped into three out of the four without observing any firearms, but the last room contained the objects of his search.

On a small table beside the bed he perceived the weapons.

Looking down the stairs, he listened.

He could hear the voice of the landlord in the public room, and also the tones of his companions.

Otherwise all was still.

He entered the room.

He stole towards the table on which the weapons lay.

One by one he took them up and drew the charges.

Then he replaced them in exactly the same positions as he had found them.

This accomplished, he strode out of the apartment.

He listened on the staircase.

Still not a sound came to his ears but the voices in the public room.

Cautiously he descended.

Unseen he gained the room in which his companions were seated.

Jacques was still there.

The landlord had been held in conversation with the brigands.

A look passed between Sataniello and his companions.

A look of meaning.

One which the brigands well understood.

They knew that their captain had been successful.

Knew that the charges of the weapons had been drawn.

And a smile of satisfaction stole over their features.

Jacques now left the brigands to themselves.

"You have succeeded, Captain ?" said one.

"Yes," replied Sataniello.

"Then we shall have nothing to fear from a bullet."

"No," replied Sataniello, holding up the bullets he had extracted. "He may blaze away as much as he likes, he can do no harm. When he has retired to rest we will make ourselves more intimately acquainted with the place."

"Would it be advisable to press the necessity of his finding accommodation for all of us?" said one. "May he not suspect?"

"I think not. Besides, have I not told him we wish to keep together for security."

"Right."

"Leave it to me to disarm suspicion should it present itself," said Sataniello, "and depend upon it I shall succeed."

No more was said upon the subject, and the hours passed on, till at length Jacques entered the room and announced that he was about to retire.

"But," he continued, "I am unable to provide all with beds, Signors."

"Oh, no matter," said Sataniello, "we can sleep where we are."

"If you have no objection," began Jacques.

"Not the least," said Sataniello. "So that we are all under one roof we care not."

"Is there anything I can do for you ere I retire ?" asked the host.

"Nothing," said Sataniello.

"Good night."

"Good night."

Jacques departed.

Sataniello's features changed in a moment.

"Comrades," he said, "we must now be silent, and lead this man and his wife to believe that we sleep."

The utmost silence instantly prevailed.

"What is the hour?" said Sataniello, after a pause.

"One hour to midnight."

"Rest, then, for three hours. In that time I will arouse you. Then be prepared to search for what valuables the place may contain. We shall need rest to reach Florence and be able to cope with any danger that may present itself."

"True," said Tranio. "We shall then have plenty of time to fill our pockets and get away ere daylight."

"Even so," said the Boy Brigand, "so sleep while you can."

Acting upon this advice, the brigands laid themselves on the benches and the floor, and were soon sound asleep.

Sataniello followed their example, and, in a few minutes, nothing but the loud breathing of the brigands broke the silence that reigned throughout the inn.

Devoid of all suspicion as to the real character of their guests, Jacques Roberto and his wife had retired to rest, not a little pleased at their good fortune in having so many customers at the inn—a thing so unusual at their establishment.

CHAPTER XVI.

MURDER OF THE INNKEEPER AND HIS WIFE—THE SEARCH FOR PLUNDER—THE DEPARTURE.

At the time named Sataniello, the Boy Brigand, rose from his seat in which he had been sleeping.

He called upon his comrades, in a low tone of voice, to awake.

The words were uttered but in a whisper.

Yet they reached the ears of the brigands.

The men started to their feet.

Their slumbers had been light, for their souls were stained with crime.

'Tis the innocent only who sleep soundly.

The guilty, never.

Sleeping or waking conscience ever haunts them.

The slightest sound will arouse them.

They fear the punishment of their sins, and are alive to the slightest noise.

"The hour has arrived," said Sataniello, "to commence work. Are you all ready?"

"All," was the reply.

"Tranio, Varo, and Julius will accompany me to the chamber of the host. The others will ransack the house, and take every article of value which they can secrete about their persons without inconvenience."

Then, lifting the light which had been left burning upon the table, Sataniello beckoned to those he had named to accompany him, and strode from the room.

Up the stairs they went to the chamber of the innkeeper.

The Boy Brigand tried the door and it yielded.

He pushed it open and entered the room.

His companions followed him closely.

The rays of the lamp lit up the chamber, and fell upon the faces of the innkeeper and his wife.

But scarcely had Sataniello set down his lamp upon the table than Jacques sprang from the bed with a loud cry, and grasped his carbine.

"Brigands!" he exclaimed, fitting the stock of the carbine to his shoulder, and presenting the muzzle of the weapon at the head of Sataniello.

But the Boy Brigand flinched not.

Jacques pulled the trigger.

But there was no flash—no report.

His wife now sprang up in bed, but instantly sank back with a loud cry.

"Silence!" hissed Tranio.

And, as he spoke, the brigand placed his hand over her mouth, and pressed it brutally upon her lips.

Finding the weapon did not go off, Jacques flung it on the floor and seized one of the pistols.

This he found to be of no more value than the carbine.

A scornful laugh broke from the lips of the Boy Brigand.

The features of the innkeeper paled till they were as white as his shirt.

He guessed in a moment that the charge had been drawn.

Quick as the lightning's flash he remembered that he had informed the man before of his having the loaded weapons in his chamber.

Bitterly did he now curse his indiscretion.

He saw only too plainly that his own tongue had deprived him of the means of defence at this trying moment.

He was unarmed.

He felt he was lost.

And he trembled violently.

"You perceive, Signor," said the Boy Brigand, "that resistance is useless. You are powerless, unarmed as you now are, to cope with us."

"What do you want here?" asked Jacques, in a tremulous voice.

"Your money and valuables," replied Sataniello.

"I have none," said Jacques.

"Signor, allow me to tell you that you lie!" exclaimed Sataniello.

"I do not."

"You said to-day that you were not in want of money, and, as we are, it would be better, for your own sake, that you gave it into our keeping."

"Never!" exclaimed Jacques.

Sataniello placed his hand in his breast and drew forth his poignard.

The rays of the lamp played upon the polished blade as he held it in his hand.

"You wont?" said Sataniello.

"No!"

"Then, Signor Roberto, I will find a sheath for my poignard in your heart."

"Still you will not get my money," exclaimed Jacques, scarcely knowing what he said.

"Oh, now you admit you have some, then," said Sataniello, with a cold smile.

"I admit nothing," he answered.

"Be advised, Signor. Obstinacy will not serve you. Give up your gold."

"I have none."

"Then I must have blood first and gold after," exclaimed Sataniello, in a fierce tone of voice.

And he strode towards the trembling innkeeper.

Jacques retreated back till the wall prevented him going any further.

He could perceive, by the look of determination upon the features of Sataniello, that the Boy Brigand meant mischief, and grasping the pistol firmly, he hurled it with all his force at the face of the brigand.

Sataniello bowed his head to avoid the missile.

By this act he succeeded in saving his face from a blow that would have spoiled his beauty for some time.

And fortunate was it for him that he did so.

But he did not altogether escape the good intentions of Jacques.

The weapon struck him on the forehead, and for a moment almost stunned him.

With a howl of rage and pain he raised his arm and struck fiercely at the innkeeper with his poignard.

But Jacques, rendered desperate by his position, seized the descending arm and closed with his assailant.

The Boy Brigand struggled to release himself from the innkeeper's hold.

But this was no easy matter.

With the strength of despair, Jacques clung to his wrist and prevented him using the glittering weapon.

"Let go your hold!" exclaimed Sataniello.

But Jacques only clung the tighter to his arm, and, as they struggled, the innkeeper succeeded in giving the wrist of the Boy Brigand a severe twist, and forcing the hand which held the poignard high up behind his back.

The pain caused by this movement was so great that Sataniello dropped the poignard from his grasp.

Jacques let go his hold and stooped to secure the weapon.

But, as he grasped it, Varo sprang forward and drove his stiletto to the very hilt in the back of the ill-fated Jacques.

The murdered man sprang upwards with a loud, piercing cry of agony, then fell heavily forward on his face at the feet of Sataniello.

The Boy Brigand stooped down and tore the weapon from the grasp of the dying man.

"You have saved my life," said Sataniello, turning to Varo, "and I will not forget it."

The cry of the dying husband endowed the poor woman with fresh strength, and, fastening her teeth in the hand of Tranio, she sprang up in the bed.

"Help, help!" she screamed.

Rendered furious by the pain her teeth had caused him, Tranio struck her in the throat with the point of his dagger, and, ere she could again utter a word, the life-stream poured from the wound on to the white linen of the bed.

A convulsive gasp, and she fell back, bathing the pillow in her blood.

Tranio and Varo, as though the deeds they had committed were unworthy of a second thought, coolly wiped their weapons upon the counterpane and returned them to their breasts.

"Curse their obstinacy," muttered Sataniello, "we shall now have to search for their money. They might have spared us the trouble and saved their lives."

"They might have seen we were not to be played with," said Tranio.

"It is a strange thing," said Varo. "Some people will not be advised for their good, and will rather take a few inches of steel than give up a few pistoles."

"And have to part with them after all," said Tranio.

"Yes," said Sataniello; "but time flies, and we must be some distance on our road to Florence by sunrise, if we would prevent our escaped prisoner communicating with the authorities. So to work. Search every box and drawer, and, doubtless, our labours will be rewarded."

The brigands required no second order, but immediately set about ransacking the room.

The drawers, which stood on one side of the bed,

were drawn out one after the other, and their contents scattered about the room.

But no money could be found.

Sataniello ground his teeth with rage.

He began to think that, after all, Jacques had none in his possession.

"Have you found any pistoles, Captain?" asked Tranio.

"No," replied the Boy Brigand, "not a tarin can I discover.

"Nor I," said Tranio.

"Nor I," added Varo.

Impatiently Sataniello kicked the articles across the room which he had thrown from the drawers.

"I can scarcely think but that the innkeeper had money concealed somewhere," said Sataniello. "Ah!" he added, hastily, "I have forgotten the bed."

And, darting to the bed, he raised the pillow.

An exclamation of pleasure escaped him.

"Have you found it, Captain?" asked Tranio.

"I think so," said Sataniello, lifting a small box in his hand and shaking it.

But it emitted no sound.

The Boy Brigand opened it.

"All right," he said, "it is full."

"Of what, Captain?" asked Varo.

"Double ducats," said Sataniello, "and packed so closely that I cannot draw one out."

"Good," said Tranio.

Sataniello closed the lid and placed the box in his pocket.

"Lift the woman up," he said, addressing Tranio, "and let us see if there is anything beneath her head."

Tranio placed his arm beneath the body of the woman whom he had so foully murdered a few minutes before, and lifted her up in the bed.

Sataniello drew aside the blood-stained pillow.

But there was nothing to be seen.

"There is nothing more," said Sataniello.

"Yes, there is, Captain," said Franco, as he let the inanimate body of the poor woman fall back.

"What?"

"These rings."

As he spoke he held up the dead woman's hand, and revealed to the gaze of Sataniello three rings upon the fingers.

"Draw them off," said Sataniello.

Franco endeavoured to do so, but could not get them over the knuckle.

"They won't come," he said.

"Then sever the fingers from the hand," said Sataniello.

"A good thought," said Franco.

And drawing his stiletto, he cut off the fingers of his murdered victim, and coolly put them into his pockets.

"There is nothing else we can conveniently carry with us," said Sataniello, "so let us return to our comrades."

And kicking the body of Jacques, he moved towards the door, and descended the stairs, followed by his companions.

When they reached the public room, they found the brigands all assembled.

There was a blank look on their faces.

A scowl of disappointment on their brows.

They had found nothing of any value, and their tempers were not a little soured by their fruitless search.

As Sataniello and his companions entered, they turned upon them a questioning glance.

But they spoke not a word.

"What success ?" said Sataniello.

"None," they replied in a breath.

"None !"

"No."

"Have you searched ?"

"Everywhere."

"And found nothing ?"

"Not a thing worth carrying away," said one.

"No matter," said Sataniello.

But the brigands seemed by their looks to think otherwise.

"Have you found anything, Captain," asked one.

"Yes," replied Sataniello.

"What ?" they asked eagerly.

"Blood," replied the brigand.

"Then it was necessary to use the dagger ?"

"Yes," said Sataniello; "and there will be a little surprise in the neighbourhood in a few hours, when the bodies are discovered, no doubt. It will therefore be advisable that we continue our journey at once, and push on to Florence."

"And we shall leave Pistora as poor as we entered it ?"

"No," said Sataniclo; "we have discovered the innkeeper's gold. So now to Florence."

And fastening their garments around them, the brigands left the inn and their victims.

CHAPTER XVII.

CLAUDIO CONTINUES HIS FLIGHT—THE MOUNTAIN STREAM—ON TO FLORENCE.

FOR a few moments the young Florentine remained bending over the form of the murdered Sebastian.

His eye lighted up with a revengeful fire.

His lip quivered with indignation.

But at length he rose.

Much as he felt the wish to bear away the body of him who had fallen by the hand of the Boy Brigand, he could but remember that there would be danger in the act.

Danger in the delay it would cause.

It would impede his flight.

It would enable his pursuers to come up with him.

Would prevent the least chance of his reaching Florence in safety.

Moments even were precious to him now.

A few moments delay might again place him in the power of the Boy Brigand.

Prevent his endeavouring to seek assistance for Paulina.

Prevent her rescue from the cavern.

He felt he must leave the blood-stained corpse to the mercy of the birds of prey, that he might save the daughter.

He rose to his feet.

He cast his eyes around.

Then he once more gazed upon the pale face of him whose child he so fondly loved.

His bosom heaved with the tumultuous emotions which shook his frame.

And his eye grew moist as he gazed upon the pale face of the dead.

A sigh escaped his breast.

With a shudder he averted his gaze, and strode away from the spot.

"Holy Virgin !" he muttered, "give me strength to reach Florence, that I may be enabled to bring down vengeance upon the guilty heads of these cold-blooded villains, and save from a fate worse than death the child of the murdered Sebastian."

And as though his prayer had been heard and granted, the step of the youth became more firm, his form more erect, and kept on his way with rapid strides.

Ever and anon he cast a rapid glance behind him.

But not a figure did his eye enconuter.

Nothing but the long narrow defile, shut in on either side by high hills, met his gaze.

Higher and higher, in the clear blue vault of heaven, rose the bright sun, concentrating its rays, and pouring down a flood of light and heat upon the mountains.

Penetrated almost into the very brain of the youth as he sped upon his course.

On—on he went, but the fearful heat began to have a depressing and oppressive effect ubon him.

The want of water to moisten his parched lips and burning throat was severely felt by him, and again his speed relaxed, and his gait became unsteady.

Still he kept on.

But now he staggered and reeled like a drunken man; the mountain sands seemed to dance before his eyes, and his vision became partially obscured.

He felt that he could go no further, but the thought of Paulina in the Brigand's power urged him forward.

Slower and slower became his pace—weaker and weaker his frame, till at length his limbs seemed to refuse their office, and he staggered against the side of the defile to prevent himself from falling.

"I can go no further," he muttered, in despairing tones. "Here must I lie till overtaken by the brigands, and borne back to their accursed cave. Oh, Paulina, Paulina! I cannot save thee!"

And dropping the carbine to the earth, he laid down beside it.

Suddenly he raised his head, and looked anxiously around him.

"Surely that was the sound of water which smote my ears," he exclaimed, "or was it a delusion of my overwrought brain? No, no, there it is again—it must be, but where—where?"

He struggled to his feet.

He shaded his eyes with his hands from the fierce glare of the sun.

He strained his ears to catch the direction of the sound.

Now he could hear it more plainly.

It sounded more like a small body of water falling from a height than ought else.

He lifted the carbine from the ground, and staggered on.

Louder and louder came the sound.

Nearer and nearer it appeared at every step.

He dragged his weary limbs along for some little distance further.

Then he raised his eyes to heaven.

His lips parted, and he murmured—

"Thank heaven!—saved—saved!"

There, in a small cavity of the hill which rose beside him, a crystal stream of cool water bubbled up from a spring, and fell over the uneven surface of the mountain into a little bed worn by its constant fall.

Never did the eyes of traveller light upon an object so beautiful—never did heart bound with joy as did that of Claudio, as, bending his head down, the water, cold and clear, bubbled up over his parched lips and heated brow.

With what pleasure did he imbibe the cool, refreshing draught.

With what a delightful sensation the liquid trickled down his face and neck.

It moistened his parched lips.

It cooled his heated blood.

It strengthened his weakened frame.

He bathed his hands in the cool stream, and played with the water like a child.

He felt as though he could have caressed it.

He placed his hands together so as to form a vessel for its reception, and dashed it upon his head till his hair was saturated.

Then again he buried his lips within it, and drank till he was compelled to desist for want of breath.

Then he felt strong again.

He believed that he was equal to anything that might come across him, and he swung the carbine around his head, so refreshed and strengthened had he been by that cool, bubbling spring.

The despair of a few minutes before now gave place to hope.

All his youthful energies returned. He was prepared to speed onward again.

Once more he bent his head down.

Another long draught he took of the refreshing liquid.

Yet he could scarcely tear himself away.

The water fascinated him.

But the poor girl in the cavern came to his thoughts, and, with a sigh, he strode on.

Refreshed by the cooling draught, his step once more became elastic.

His eye lost its dull, leaden appearance.

It brightened up with a fiery gleam.

On—on—along the narrow road.

On to Florence.

The shades of night were closing over the earth.

The mountains seemed gradually becoming enshrouded in a mist.

The vegetation on their sides became more and more indistinct.

The youth urged himself forward lest darkness should set in ere he could get clear of the hills.

Suddenly an exclamation of joy escaped him.

He perceived the gleam of a light in the distance.

Then another and another.

He knew that he was nearing Pistoia.

His heart leapt for joy.

There he felt he was safe.

There the fearful brigands would be powerless to harm him.

For there were stout hearts and strong hands to be summoned to his aid.

But in Pistoia he would be unable to procure the services of a band to aid him in the rescue of Paulina.

Should he be assailed, he could depend upon aid.

But he would be unable to procure a force to leave the town.

So on to Florence he must go.

There he could lay his case before the authorities.

But Florence was some distance, and he wished to arrive there ere the next morning.

That he could do so on foot in his present fatigued condition was impossible; but he could procure a conveyance at the town whose lights now met his gaze, and caused his heart to bound with joy.

Nearer and nearer—larger and larger—brighter and brighter—loomed the lights in the town.

Another half hour, and with palpitating heart Claudio the Florentine staggered up the steps of an hotel about half-a-mile distant from that where the Boy Brigand and his ruffianly companions had taken up their position.

The moment he entered, Claudio inquired for the landlord.

In a few moments that worthy appeared before him.

He gazed with surprise upon the jaded form of the youth.

Claudio instantly made him acquainted with his name and position, the adventures through which he had passed, and the object of his anxiety to reach Florence.

The landlord listened eagerly and attentively, and when the youth had concluded, he remarked—

"But it will be impossible for you to reach Florence by daybreak."

"Why so?" asked Claudio.

"You are too much fatigued to attempt the journey."

"Not so."

"You have travelled all day, and are worn out."

"Still I must reach Florence."

"Impossible."

"Not so—unless you decline to provide me with the means of conveyance."

"I would willingly do so," said the landlord; "but remember, Signor, that by overtaxing your strength, you may defeat the dearest wish of your heart."

"How so?"

"By laying yourself up."

"I shall not do that," returned Claudio. "I shall be far more likely to do so by remaining. I cannot rest till I have procured assistance, and am on my way to rescue the Signorita from the power of the Boy Brigand and his ruthless companions."

"Well, Signor, if you are bent on continuing your journey to-night," said the landlord, "I will not stand in your way, though I had rather you rested till morning."

"I cannot rest," said Claudio. "Sleep would be chased from my eyes by visions of the Signorita Paulina."

"Do you, then, fear that she may meet with indignities at the hands of the dreaded brigand?"

"Fear?" exclaimed Claudio.

"Yes."

"Alas! too well I know that she will; the cursed brigand's words were too portentuous not to be well understood," said Claudio.

And a flush of indignation overspread his face.

"Still he may but hold her in his power till she be ransomed," said the landlord.

"He accepts but one ransom for her," said Claudio, bitterly.

"But one ransom?"

"Yes."

"And that?"

"Her honour."

The landlord started back.

"Her honour is the ransom he demands," said Claudio. "Holy Virgin, protect her, and send her succour ere it is too late."

"You shall away to Florence to-night, Signor," said the landlord.

"I must."

"You shall have the swiftest horses in my stables."

"Thanks—thanks."

"Take some refreshment, for you sadly need it," said the landlord; "and I will myself superintend the preparation for the journey."

"I am grateful."

"Yes, yes, you must away to-night, signor;

moments are precious in such a case, and heaven speed you."

And, calling to his servants, he bade them place refreshments before Claudio, whilst he himself made every preparation for the youth's departure.

Claudio sat down to the viands, but his heart was too much troubled to permit him to eat; so, swallowing a glass of wine, he rose, and awaited the announcement that all was ready for his journey.

He had not to wait long.

The landlord himself led two horses, harnessed to a light carriage, to the door.

Claudio leapt down the steps.

"Away, Signor !" said the landlord, "and the Holy Virgin speed you."

"Thanks, thanks," exclaimed Claudio, as he stepped into the vehicle.

The driver smacked his whip, and in another minute the youth was hurrying to Florence.

CHAPTER XVIII.

THE PURSUIT OF THE DECEIVER BY THE LOVER.—THE FATHER LEARNS OF THE ABSENCE OF HIS CHILD.

To gain the terrace, and signal for the approach of his gondola, was to Salerino di Rico the work of a few moments.

The gondolier rapidly pulled the little bark to the foot of the steps, and Salernio, his mind a prey to anxious thoughts, leapt into it.

"To Aquila," he said.

"To Aquila, Signor ?" asked the gondolier, in a tone of surprise.

"Yes—to Aquila."

"To-night ?"

"Yes—to night."

The man seated himself, and took the oars in his hands, still gazing doubtfully at Salernio.

"Haste, haste !" exclaimed the young Italian; the Signorita has been decoyed from her home."

"Decoyed from her home, Signor ?" said the man.

"Yes."

"By whom ?"

"That I must discover. She has been decoyed to Aquila by some fraud. Pull, then, with a will, for I must fathom this mystery."

"How was this ?"

"A few moments ere our arrival, a young Italian gentleman waited upon her, and informed her that I lay dying at Aquila and desired her presence, and she accompanied him in his gondola."

"When was this, Signor ?" asked the man.

"She departed from the steps as we arrived," said Salernio.

"Then went she towards Fermo—not Aquila; such was the direction the gondola took which left the steps a few moments ere we arrived."

"Take, then, the same course," said Salernio.

The man turned the head of the gondola, and bent to the oars with a will.

Eagerly Salernio cast his eyes over the moonlit scene.

Anxious was he to discover the sight of a gondola, besides his own, upon the bosom of the waters.

But none could he see.

The stream was clear.

Only the dancing moonbeams as they played upon the dark surface of the waters, and the shadow of his gondola, reflected in their clear depths, met his gaze.

Salernio sat silent and sad.

He was at a loss to discover any motive for the decoying away of the Signorita Marianna.

But he determined to trace her, and inflict chastisement upon the man who had deceived her.

What motive he could have in doing so he was at a loss to divine.

He knew not that he had made enemies.

He was too honourable—too generous—to do so.

On the contrary, he was beloved by all who knew him.

Respected alike by all classes.

Therefore it could not be from such a cause that Marianna had been deluded away from her home.

There must be some other.

And that other he was at a loss to account for.

He could perceive that it was her love for him which prompted her to accompany the stranger.

Her love that caused her to lend a listening ear to a base falsehood.

Her affection which led her from her parental roof at such a hour.

This was the only solace he could find to his troubled mind.

And that was much.

It assured him that he possessed her love.

That she would sacrifice much for him.

And he resolved to sacrifice all for her.

Speedily as did the gondola cleave the waters of the Tronto, yet it kept not pace with his impatience.

Never did it seem to go so slow.

Never did it appear to drag so heavily its way over the stream.

And he sat gnawing his nether lip, and beating his foot upon the floor of the boat.

His eyes were strained in the hope of discovering the gondola in which Marianna had gone far a-head.

Ever and anon he stood up in the boat, and shaded his eyes with his hands.

But not a speck could be seen on the stream, save the white sails of a fine ship.

But he turned his gaze from that impatiently.

Little did he suspect that Marianna was on board that bark.

Not for one moment did the thought occur to him to seek her there.

She had departed in a gondola, and for a gondola only did he scan the stream.

Thus two hours passed.

The gondolier's strength was fast becoming exhausted.

The man's will was good, but his speed slackened.

Salernio could not but observe that the gondolier was exhausted.

He rose and said—

"Give me the oars."

The man resigned them to him, and the gondolier and his master changed places.

Salernio bent to them, and once more the little craft leapt on with increased speed.

But still no signs of a gondola other than their own met their gaze.

It was not long ere Salernio found himself tired by his exertions, and he leant upon the oars in despair.

"There is nothing to be seen which may lead to discover her," he muttered; "yet I am loth to return without her."

"Signor," said the gondolier, "you but exhaust your strength to no purpose. Would it not be better to return to the shore, and despatch persons in pursuit to all quarters."

Salernio paused ere he replied.

He was conjuring up in his mind the best course to pursue.

There seemed no prospect of being successful in their pursuit of the gondola.

Perhaps the advice of his companion was after all the best.

He would act upon it.

By returning to the shore he could obtain the assistance of several in the search for the Signorita Marianna.

He could despatch persons in all directions to make inquiries respecting her.

"It will perhaps be better to act as you propose," said Salernio.

"Then give me the oars," said the man; I am now rested, and can pull to the shore."

Salernio resigned them to the gondolier, and sitting back in the boat, gave himself up to thought.

Shortly after the departure of the Signor Salernio from the house of the Signor Martini, that worthy gentleman arrived home.

Tomaso and Pedro met him on the threshold.

Their pale faces and still trembling limbs were not lost upon the old Italian gentleman.

For a moment he gazed wonderingly upon them. Then hurriedly inquired the cause of their emotion.

Tomaso was not long in making the Signor Martini acquainted with all that had transpired during his absence; of course, keeping to themselves the abject fear they had felt at the sight of Salernio, whom they were now convinced was a being of the living world.

In fact, there could be no longer any doubt of that, since the young lover of the fair Marianna had given them such strong proof of his being in the flesh, that their bones really ached from the blows he had dealt them.

The Signor Martini listened impatiently, then hurrying to his room he took off his walking apparel, and taking from a cupboard a telescope, he strode down the staircase, out of the house, on to the terrace.

Here, seating himself beside a sculptured eagle, he gazed through the telescope long and anxiously over the waters of the shining Tronto.

But nothing met his sight save a small vessel far out in the distance, and with a sigh he leant back against the wall of his mansion, and became absorbed in thought.

CHAPTER XIX.

IN THE CAVERN—PERDITTA'S NARRATIVE.

For some time the Signorita Paulina and her maid Perditta, sat in the little cavern weeping together.

Poor Perditta, she knew she had done wrong,—knew she had fallen too easy a victim to the sensual passions of Angelo, but she strove all in her power to put as good a face on a bad matter as possible.

"Signorita," she said, in answer to some remark of her companion's, "all brigands are not so bad as you believe them."

Marianna shook her head.

"Are they not men," she said "who set alike the laws of God and man at defiance?"

"Some of them are men driven to the life they lead by oppression or wrong," said Perditta.

"No, no."

"Yes, Signorita."

"What wrongs can induce them to lead such lives?" asked Marianna.

"Many. Blighted affections, oppressive laws," said Perditta.

"No man becomes a brigand unless his mind is naturally evil inclined. Who ever heard of a noble-hearted man, taking to such a life?"

"I have, Signorita."

"You?"

"Yes."

"Where?"

"In Spain."

"But not in Italy."

"There may be men in Italy who have been driven to crime as well as in Spain," said Perditta, only too anxious to find some excuse for her conduct.

"I cannot believe that any but a villain could become an outlaw," said Marianna.

"Signorita, I could disabuse your mind of such a prejudice, did you but listen to a somewhat long story."

"I would listen to anything that would but carry my thoughts from their present channel," said Marianna.

"Then while the brigands are making their way to Florence, and we are alone in the cavern, I will endeavour to lead you to think better of those into whose power you have fallen, by speaking of one of the terrors of Spain, the dreaded brigand Labocher; but in order to show you the nobleness of his character I shall have to draw in several other personages, and commence my narrative with two travellers wending their way through Portugal. Will you listen to my story?"

"Willingly," said Marianna. "For I shall only be too happy to hear of any good traits in the character of one who seeks in the mountains security from the officers of the law, and answers a summons to surrender to the outraged laws of his country by a bullet or a dagger."

"Then I will commence my story with the two travellers," said Perditta, seating herself comfortably down.

*   *   *   *

"The head of yonder range of hills is called Monte Moro," said the Spaniard, addressing the young Englishman, and indicating the locality with his finger.

"Why is it thus designated?" inquired the other.

"Because it was once a fortress of the Moors. You doubtless observe that the summits and sides of the hill are covered with ruined walls and towers?" replied the Spaniard.

"I see one structure which appears to be of more recent origin; what may it be?" continued the Englishman.

"It is a convent."

"There are, perchance, many pretty nuns there?"

"Ciertimente—very; I should like to catch a glimpse of the dark-eyed beauties."

"Are all nuns fair, think you, Senor Montisco?"

"Creo qui si—I suppose so; and it is not right that their pretty faces should be eclipsed by stone walls."

The young Englishman sighed, and made no reply.

"Cabellero, you are still thinking of that fair creature whom we saw at Evora. I admonish you to look well to your heart, or some of the Portuguese beauties will drive you to distraction."

"English blood is not so easily disturbed; it seldom quickens at the approach of beauty."

"Be frank, Senor Degrange; confess that you find it impossible to banish the image of the fair stranger from your mind?"

"I never go to the confessional; but if I should ever change my sentiments, and go thither, be assured that I will confess whatever lies with the greatest weight upon my mind. If no circumstance ever troubles me any more than the memory of the pretty stranger to whom you allude, my sleep will be quite undisturbed, and my dreams placid and hopeful. To what class of society does she belong, think you?"

"Possibly she is a hidalgo's daughter."

"Quite as likely to be a peasant's daughter," rejoined the Englishman, with affected indifference.

"Nonsense! you might as well say she is the child of a gallego or bolieiro!"

"She did not travel in very great state, in a sege, drawn by machos; her whole retinue consisting of a driver, and a personage resembling a priest."

"A very common method of travelling in this country, even among the hidalgos. But come, let us descend into the valley. Look yonder! is not that a romantic spectacle, the mountain covered with cork trees? It is called Monte Almo. You observe that it is the third of the chain of hills, of which Monte Moro is the first. Great numbers of goats are feeding upon its sides, and a noisy brook washes its base. Robberies have been committed upon that spot, I have heard."

"Not much of a recommendation for the place, I should think. I never felt a very strong desire to be robbed, and left half or quite dead, in any one of the dark passes of Portugal. I love adventure, and variety of incident, as well as you do, Senor Montisco; but I like neither adventure nor incident which leaves one in such a woeful plight as the kind which you have been good enough to refer to. But I'm willing to descend into the valley where that lonely road winds along towards Evoro; it will pleasantly beguile the time; afterward, we will ascend Monte Moro, examine the ruined walls, towers, and lastly, the convent perched on the summit."

While the two gentlemen are proceeding toward the spot which has excited their admiration, we will embrace the occasion to make a few explanatory remarks in relation to them.

The Englishman was about twenty-four years of age, educated, moneyed, and agreeable.

A native of London, he was travelling to see the world, and experienced the same emotions that all young travellers feel at beholding the scenery of other countries, and studying the habits of other races and nations.

He was brave, athletic, and ardent in temperament, full of the love of adventure, fearless of reverses, and persevering in the pursuit of a favourable object.

He promised himself much happy excitement in the prosecution of his travels, and expected to find novelty and interest upon every spot of earth which he should visit.

Descended from an ancient family, he felt, perhaps, a little pride in knowing that his blood flowed from an honourable fountain, polluted by no base admixtures.

He bore the name that his father had borne before him, and for that matter, his grandfather also; Arthur Degrange.

The Spaniard, who was his companion, was somewhat his senior, endowed with the characteristic energy, warmth, and restlessness of his nation.

Degrange had become acquainted with Montisco at London, where the latter had spent considerable time.

Mutually pleased with each other, they resolved to continue their travels in company.

Montisco being born at Madrid, and well acquainted with places of interest in Spain, gave promise of being an invaluable companion, when our hero should reach that country, after passing through Portugal.

On the day previous to that on which our story commences, during the short excursion which they had made on foot, they had met near Avora, on the road to Elvas, a *sege* (drawn by machos) in which was the fair traveller alluded to by the light-hearted Spaniard.

The beauty of the maiden had indeed made a deep impression on the mind of Degrange; he found it impossible to forget the classic mould of her features, and the exquisite symmetry of her person.

He could have forgotten, probably, these merely external advantages, had he not imagined that he detected the sure indices of sadness and unhappiness upon her countenance.

He fancied that he perceived evidences of a settled melancholy, coupled with anxiety and uneasiness.

Moreover, upon her cheeks he believed he saw a trace of recent tears.

The observations which he had made in relation to the person under whose charge the young lady appeared to be, were not of a nature calculated to inspire confidence in his integrity.

But the time allowed him for studying character was brief, and of the two objects that excited his attention, he rather preferred to bestow most of it upon the maiden.

Don Montisco had not failed to see how much

the loveliness of the senorita had affected his friend, and had embraced every opportunity to rally him in relation to that subject; and Degrange could not but confess to himself, that he had been strangely attracted and interested by the gentle stranger.

Having given the reader, as we trust, a tolerable idea of the position, character, aim, object, etc., of the two personages whom we have introduced, we will no longer interrupt the thread of the narrative by useless delays, but proceed at once with the incidents which we have to relate.

Degrange and Montisco walked towards the base of Monte Almo; they reached the valley, and the murmurings of the little brook fell upon their ears with a soothing sound.

Each absorbed, apparently, in his own meditations, sauntered onward, and unconsciously the locality for which they had started was passed.

Taking the rough and winding road to Evora, they entered a gloomy wood.

Senor Montisco was the first to awaken from the dreams of revery, and look around to discover where they were.

"Senor Degrange!" he exclaimed, "we have lost Monte Almo. Where is it, I wonder?"

"Better ask where we are," returned his companion.

"It's easy enough to know that," replied the other.

"We are evidently in the woods. I hope you have your pistols with you, for this is a spot infested by banditti."

"Be assured that I did not leave them at the Estalagem; I have them in my pocket, in excellent order; and if any of the disreputable gentry whom you have mentioned, want my purse, I am inclined to think that it will cost them more than it is worth to obtain it; for, as you know, I have the reputation of shooting very well. But I am getting a little weary; let us sit by the roadside and rest."

This proposition meeting the approbation of Montisco, they both seated themselves upon a rock and began to converse about whatever objects arrested their attention.

"Look!" cried Degrange, at length. "Yonder comes a *sege*."

"Nothing very remarkable in that," returned the Spaniard; "but your head is probably full of the Portuguese beauty."

"You would certainly do me a favour, if you would endeavour to forget that circumstance. Your own good sense must tell you that a passing glimpse of an unknown female, however fair, would not be very likely to make a deep impression."

Degrange paused and gazed intently at the approaching sege or cabriolet, which was winding slowly along at the base of the range of hills.

Starting to his feet he exclaimed, in an agitated voice:

"See, Montisco! the vehicle stops. It is surrounded by men; a robbery is being perpetrated—come on—to the rescue. My word for it, the fair traveller of yesterday is yonder!"

Having spoken these words with great rapidity, the Englishman drew his pistols from his pocket, and ran as fast as he was able towards the cabriolet, followed by Montisco.

The robbers, intent on their prey, did not perceive the approach of our two friends, until a sharp report of a pistol warned them of their proximity, and admonished them that there was something else to attend to.

One of the banditti, who was attempting to force open the door of the cabriolet, was wounded at the first fire, and the others, perceiving the approach of two resolute men, well armed, took to flight, discharging their carbines at random as they ran.

The first object which Degrange and his companion saw, was the bolieiro or driver, stretched upon the ground beside the mules, half dead with fright.

Our hero hurried to the sege, opened the door and beheld therein a young female, in a state bordering on unconsciousness.

He was not greatly astonished at seeing her, for he had taken it for granted that she was there, the moment he perceived the onset of the banditti. It was the Portuguese maiden whom he had met on the previous day, and who, since that time, had occupied so many of his thoughts.

"You are safe, senorita—the robbers have fled!" said Degrange.

Although he addressed her in English, not knowing whether she understood that, he had the satisfaction of discovering immediately that his intentions were comprehended.

She raised her eyes timidly to his, and the blood flowed back to her pale cheeks.

That one mute look was eloquent with gratitude.

"Where is your companion and protector?" asked Degrange.

"He is gone; he ran away into the wood, on the first indication of danger, for he was conversing with the bolieiro when the bandits appeared," replied the lady, in very good English.

"A brave protector, truly?" said Don Montisco.

The bolieiro had now recovered both his feet and his tongue, and begged that the two gentlemen would walk beside the vehicle until they were clear of the wood, which they most readily consented to do; for the appealing and modest looks of the young lady had had so sensible an effect upon the English traveller, that he would have considered it no great hardship to follow the sege the whole day.

Degrange, therefore, kept close to the cabriolet, while Montisco questioned the driver, and endeavoured to draw from him something in relation to the history of the maiden, whither she was going, her name, family, and lastly, who the person was under whose protection she journeyed.

In answer to all these queries, the Spaniard received but unsatisfactory answers.

The driver was either ignorant, or had been instructed to be silent on the subject.

Hoping to overcome his taciturnity, Montisco slipped a piece of money into his hand, but soon had the mortification of knowing that he was no nearer his object than before; the bolieiro maintained a stupid or obstinate silence, which vexed the fiery Spanish gentleman so much, that he was more than once tempted to beat him soundly.

Meanwhile, Degrange was walking near the sege, stealing frequent glances at the features of the Portuguese lady, forming all kind of conjectures in regard to her rank, condition and purpose.

Moreover, he ardently longed for an opportunity to chastise the cowardly fellow, whoever he might be, who had ignominiously forsaken his precious charge at the very moment when his assistance was most needed.

He felt a strong inclination to enter into conversation with the senorita; but his habitual self-possession appeared to have left him, and he found it a thing so difficult to think of a subject upon which to speak, that he despaired of success.

He reproached himself mentally for his weakness and schoolboy bashfulness; he endeavoured to make himself comprehend more fully, that if the present opportunity for commencing an acquaintance with the charming young woman was allowed to pass unimproved, another might never occur; and so the favourable occasion be lost for ever.

He made some incoherent remarks respecting the difficulty and danger of travelling in Portugal, on account of the roads being so bad and so much infested by brigands.

To these observations the lady replied, with equal perturbation, and the conversation did not assume a very encouraging aspect.

The moment the cabriolet emerged from the wood, Degrange noticed that the lady threw furtive, anxious glances upon either side of the road, as if expecting, yet dreading the approach of some one.

This did not escape the observation of our traveller, and he summoned resolution enough to say,—

"Senorita, may I be bold enough to ask who the gentleman may be, who thought proper to attend to his own safety before yours?"

How the lady would have answered this straightforward interrogatory, we cannot tell; for, as she was about to speak, a person came running towards them considerably out of breath, who had, obviously, been taking some extraordinary exercise.

Both Montisco and Degrange recognised him as the individual whom they had seen on the previous day in charge of the female.

He approached with a somewhat downcast look, as if conscious that he had not played the part of a gallant and trustworthy protector.

Arthur darted upon him a scornful glance, followed by one equally contemptuous from his friend.

The man cast a quick, inquisitive look at the young lady, which did not at all please our hero, and then said, in a calm, cold voice,—

"Senores, receive my thanks for your timely assistance. We seem to be clear of the wood now, and need not trouble you farther; for it is almost unnecessary to say, that people are seldom robbed in an open country like this."

"I trust, senor," returned the Spaniard, mockingly, "that you escaped from the encounter wholly uninjured?"

"With the exception of being somewhat blown with running, I find myself in very good condition, I thank you," added the person addressed.

"Which can be considered little less than a miracle!" said Degrange, drily.

"If the worthy senor will be good enough to give me his name, I shall have pleasure in recommending him to the distinguished consideration of Don Miguel, the lieutenant governor, or even to Don Pedro, the king!" continued Montisco, sarcastically.

"And this fair lady may be induced to say

something creditable to your valour," added Degrange.

The stranger's eyes shot forth flames of malice, but his voice gave no indication that his choler was moved.

"You do me too much honour, gentlemen! In running away, I followed an unerring instinct, which teaches one to preserve his life, if possible. As it has happened, heaven has ordered all for the best; and as I have said, we will not task your kindness longer."

Degrange was about to give a hasty, ironical rejoinder, when an imploring look from the dark eyes of the lady induced him to forego his purpose.

Bowing very low to her, and lifting their hats gallantly, our two friends suffered the sege to go forward and stood gazing after it until it began to wind up the steep road leading to the summit of Monte Moro.

The curiosity of the English traveller was much excited; he felt a strong desire to penetrate the mystery which enveloped the unknown lady.

That she was labouring under some restraint, and that there was little or no congeniality between her and her ostensible protector, was to him very evident.

He was conscious of an irresistible attraction impelling him towards her, and was equally sensible of being as palpably repulsed from her companion.

So much was he absorbed in this subject, that Don Montisco addressed him several times before he was able to arrest his attention.

"Have you lost your hearing, my friend?" exclaimed Montisco, at length, entirely out of patience.

"To look at you, one would be inclined to think that yonder carriage is bearing away all that you value on earth. Shake off your apathy, and let us return to the Estalagem."

Don Montisco took our hero by the arm, and the two went towards the town of Monte Moro, which was situated at the foot of the hill on the other side, and attainable by a narrow road running along at the base.

They reached the inn after a long and tiresome detour.

The Estalagem was neither elegant nor fashionable, but possessed of the characteristic inconveniences of Portuguese inns, and had, in days past, been called the Estalagem de Ladroes, or hostelry of thieves: an appellation certainly not very flattering to its former or present reputation.

But Jose Bedos, the person who had now the honour of being its proprietor, had endeavoured to retrieve the credit of the establishment, and flattered himself that, all things considered, he kept a very reputable house.

Being desirous of examining the place, on account of its antiquities, our travellers had passed the previous night at the Estalagem of Jose Bedos, with that object in view.

They found their servants awaiting their return with commendable patience, both of them being better pleased to remain at rest, regaling themselves with occasional draughts of the native wine, than to tire their bodies by clambering up hills, for the purpose of gazing at the rubbish of Moorish ruins.

Our hero had an English attendant who had been in his service some time; a faithful fellow in his way, who answered to the familiar name of Jerome.

This individual was much attached to his master, and had as few failings, perhaps, as any of his class.

Don Montisco was served by a native of his own country, who was both shrewd and honest, and willing to incur any reasonable inconvenience and risk, to secure his master's comfort and safety.

Alvarez understood the peculiarities of Don Montisco, and was an invaluable attendant; for having travelled considerably, he was acquainted with the habits of the people with whom travellers are obliged to come in contact, and was always on the alert to prevent his master from being cheated.

Immediately after our hero's return to the Estalagem, he took Jerome aside, and informed him that he wished him to go, without delay, or apprising any one of his intention, to the top of the hill where the convent was situated, and learn, if possible, whether a cabriolet, drawn by two machos, had stopped there.

Enforcing his wishes by the bestowal of a piece of silver, Jerome promised to fulfil his commands to the letter.

He started off with alacrity, and was soon after toiling up the ascent, having first crossed a bridge of stone that spans a deep trench at the base.

Jerome was as wise as most servants, but he puzzled his brains in vain to find out what his master's particular object might be in despatching him on such a singular errand.

He wondered what interest he could feel in a sege and two mules; but being determined to obey implicitly the instructions which he had received, he kept diligently on until he reached the convent, which was a large stone structure, blackened by storms, and rendered venerable by time, though somewhat dilapidated, withal.

It was surrounded by a wall of the same material, and apparently of equal antiquity.

On that side towards the town, an ample gate opened into the court, while in the rear there were two private posterns; probably for the accommodation of the abbess and the confessors.

Glancing through the gate, Jerome perceived near it, in the court, a large and savage mastiff, which, though chained, intimidated him a little.

He queried in what manner he should obtain the information for which he had been sent.

He could see neither vehicle nor beast, and began to think that he should be forced to go back no wiser than he came, when he fortunately, as he believed, discovered the handle of a bell attached to the said gate, and doubtless communicating with the convent.

Without pausing to trouble himself respecting the results of such a step, he rang with much energy; whereupon the dog bayed fiercely, showing his sharp, white teeth, as a kind of premonition that strangers had better mind their own business and keep away.

After waiting some minutes, which time was economically improved by the mastiff to make all the noise he could, an ill-natured looking man appeared, who proved to be the porter.

This personage appeared to be, in good sooth, a fitting companion for the spiteful dog, his face being quite as shaggy and repulsive as that animal's.

Through the lattice work of the gate Jerome watched his approach, and did not augur a very favourable termination to his business; and the sequel will show whether his conclusions were just.

"What do you want?" was the first salutation, pronounced in a gruff and impatient voice.

Jerome was somewhat startled at this rude greeting; but summoned resolution to say, in his most courteous tones,—

"Senor, have you seen, within the last half hour, a sege drawn by two machos?"

"A pretty question, truly! Do you think I have nothing else to do but to watch travellers, and to answer simpletons? Begone!" replied the porter, with increasing warmth.

"I asked but a straightforward question, requiring only a plain yes or no; and if such a vehicle as I have mentioned has stopped here, I should like to know it," continued Jerome, who had resolved not to be easily discouraged.

"Don't trouble yourself about other people, but take care of yourself; for if you do not leave these grounds immediately, I will turn the dog loose upon you, and he will put you in a sorry plight, right speedily," added the surly fellow.

"In my country, no one objects to answering a civil question; and we sometimes teach those who do not keep a civil tongue in their heads a lesson of good manners which they do not soon forget. Now if you were only this side of the gate, instead of upon that, I would give you such discipline that you should remember me as long as you live!" retorted Jerome, getting angry in turn.

"I will learn you what it is to be insolent to your betters!" cried the porter, in a rage, slipping the chain from the dog's neck. "I'll warrant, if you escape with your life this time, you will never be seen again, lurking like a thief around these grounds, asking impertinent questions."

The mastiff, upon being freed, assumed a more savage aspect than ever, and Jerome, seeing that the porter was really about to throw open the gate, thought that it behoved him to take care of himself as well as he was able.

Having no means of defence, it only remained for him to run from the spot as fast as he could.

Accordingly, he started at a rapid rate, and the mastiff followed, with swift bounds and fierce and unremitting bayings.

The slight alarm which Jerome had experienced at first, now changed to absolute fear.

Close behind him he heard the quick steps and angry howlings of the brute, and strained every nerve to evade him.

Terror lent him wings, and he descended the hill with a speed which he would a few moments previously have deemed it impossible for human beings to attain; while, to his unspeakable chagrin, he heard vindictive shouts of laughter mingling with the horrible vociferations of the irritated mastiff.

Feeling fully aware that he could not long maintain the unequal race, he would willingly have given all he possessed in the world for some available weapon of defence.

His blood grew hot with terror and exertion, and he every instant expected to feel the fangs of the mastiff fixed in his flesh.

He gave vent to sweeping invectives against cabriolets, machos, convents, porters, masters, and dogs generally, and was on the point of yielding to his fate without further effort, when, luckily, he discovered a small heap of stones, of convenient size to be employed as missiles.

He hastily snatched one of them from the ground, and hurled it at his adversary, who was now within a few yards of him, with his jaws distended, and his tongue thrust out.

Jerome's aim was so good, that the stone took effect between the animal's eyes with such force that it nearly destroyed his equilibrium, and quite checked his velocity.

He followed up his advantage with commendable zeal, and the second stone made the brute yell with pain as loudly as he had yelled with rage a moment before.

Seeing that the dog was getting the worst of it, the porter ran to his assistance, and Jerome, being a thorough believer in the good old maxim that "what is sauce for the goose, is also sauce for the gander," met his advances with a round stone, weighing about a pound and half, which was so skilfully thrown, that the fellow was reduced to a more pitiful condition than his dog, for he fell stunned and senseless to the earth.

Jerome, seeing that the victory had unexpectedly been decided in his favour, did not deem it prudent to remain long to contemplate the field of battle; but giving both dog and man some friendly and useful advice by which to regulate their future conduct to strangers, he hurried towards the Estalagem de Ladroes, to report in regard to the success of his mission.

Degrange was awaiting his coming somewhat anxiously, for he trusted that he would be able to gather some intelligence relative to the gentle traveller in whom he felt so much interested.

He was vexed and disappointed when he heard the doleful history which Jerome was obliged to rehearse; and he was more fully confirmed in the opinion that the unknown lady was the subject of some restraint, and not altogether free to follow the direction of her own inclinations.

The event which had just transpired, instead of deterring him from making further exertions to unfold the mystery which had so romantically affected him, gave him additional incentives to action; and he determined never to desist, until he had arrived at a true understanding of the affair.

He felt called upon, also, to avenge the indignity which Jerome had suffered; for that unfortunate individual still presented indubitable evidences of the terrors of that scene through which he had just passed.

Degrange hastened to communicate to Don Montisco what had happened, and his own feelings and resolutions respecting the same.

The latter heard what he had to relate with sympathetic indignation, and entered readily and unreservedly into the plans and expectations of his friend.

"It is obvious," said the Spaniard, after a pause, "that you are more interested in the lady than you are willing to own; or, possibly more than you are yourself aware of. It is sometimes the case, that others detect in us what we ourselves have scarcely begun to suspect. But let this be as it may; you desire to prosecute the affair, and being your friend, I feel not only willing, but in some sort bound to assist you in all your undertakings. Moreover, I love adventures; they furnish excitement, and excitement is a part of my existence. This matter promises to be romantic; and being so, must, as a consequence, be dangerous also, and danger pleases me. Consider me, then, as yours, and always and very much at your service in all things that require two heads and two sets of hands, with the skill, ingenuity and daring which ought to accompany them. The lady is fair—that is well; she is mysterious—that is better; her protector is cowardly, selfish, and malicious, and that is as it may be. Your servant has been insulted, and must be avenged; so you perceive that we have all the materials to furnish excitement for some considerable time."

"Don Montisco, your words prove to me that I have not over-estimated your generous qualities. You have anticipated much which I wished to say, but dared not, lest I should excite your ridicule. Be assured that I appreciate your zeal in my behalf, and when a proper opportunity arrives, will endeavour to reciprocate the same, in a suitable manner; and I really hope that in order to prove my gratitude, you may become entangled in some dangerous amour, requiring the aid which every faculty of mine in active exercise, can possibly afford. You are right; we must look into this subject; we must reconnoitre the convent, and discover whether the object of our solicitude is therein. Also, devise means to punish the savage cruelty of the porter, who doubtless had received instructions how to act from those whom he serves."

"It does not seem," resumed Montisco, "that either the mastiff or the man escaped entirely without chastisement. Jerome acquitted himself well, and saved his life, doubtless, by the exercise of some self-possession and more skill."

"I am strongly of opinion," said Degrange, "that the young lady is to be immured, for some purpose best known to those interested, within the gloomy walls of yonder convent, shut out from the pleasant scenes of nature, and denied the blessings of freedom which God has intended alike for all. Probably you will say that I am hasty in my conclusions, and arrive at effects without consulting causes; but if you observed the actions of the maiden herself, and the manner of her cowardly companion, you cannot but acknowledge that my suspicions are not wholly without foundation."

"I was not so blind to those circumstances to which you allude, as you are inclined to imagine. I plied the driver with questions, which could not have failed to elicit some information, from one not thoroughly instructed in regard to his duty. I did not succeed in getting from him a single expression which could throw any light whatever upon the name, character, or destination of the female; and I flatter myself that my want of success was not altogether attributable to my awkwardness. I noticed the subject of my interrogatories also, and being less embarrassed by her beauty than yourself, was able to draw more reliable inference from her conduct. The return of the senor appeared to give her more uneasiness, I fancied, than pleasure; and, to be brief, her whole deportment indicated that she was acting not in accordance with her own wishes; but submitting, with as much patience as she could call to her aid, to the authority and tyranny of another, who had by some means, fair or foul, obtained control over her movements."

"I am glad that you was so critical and so just in your observations," rejoined Degrange; "for after the declaration which you have just made, you cannot well accuse me of a want of discrimination. As a preliminary step towards the prosecution of this matter, I propose that we visit the convent as soon as it becomes sufficiently dark, and examine the premises, having care to be better guarded than Jerome against contingencies."

To this proposal, Don Montisco readily agreed, and the two friends beguiled the time in pleasant conversation, until the hour arrived to put their project into execution.

* * *

At this moment Angelo looked into the cavern to see that Paulina and Perditta were safe, and to bring them refreshment.

This prevented any further continuation of Perditta's narrative for the time, so, whilst they partake of the fare provided by Angelo, we will return to Florence, and follow the Boy Brigand and his companions, ere we take up the thread of Perditta's story.

———

CHAPTER XX.

THE ASSASSINATION OF THE MULETEER—THE ARRIVAL OF THE BRIGANDS IN FLORENCE.

SATANIELLO, the Boy Brigand, and his ruthless followers hurried away from the scene of the outrage, and took their way towards Florence.

Satisfied with their night's work, they journeyed on full of spirits, ever and anon indulging in the ribald jest or rude song.

For some miles they met with no appearance of a human being.

Sataniello was somewhat disappointed at not overtaking Claudio, but still his expectations to do so, had been small; the young Florentine having had at least an hour's start of them.

But then, he had hoped, that, fatigued with the heat of the day, and the want of food, would have compelled him to give up, ere he could reach any spot where he was likely to find assistance.

But not having fallen in with him before now, he gave up all hope of meeting with the youth, till he gained Florence; so he urged his companions onwards.

Day broke, and the sun rose and shed its rays upon the luxuriant vegetation still damp with the dews of night; and the band had placed several miles between the inn at which they had stayed, and Florence, when they were overtaken by a man driving a rude vehicle, which was drawn by four mules.

As he passed, Sataniello, the Boy Brigand, asked him if he had seen any one on the road.

"No," replied the man.

"Not a youth, respectably attired?" asked Sataniello, who thought that perhaps they might have passed Claudio, and he described the young Florentine.

"No," replied the man.

"Which road have you come?" asked Sataniello.

"From Pistoia."

Sataniello started.

"Whence go you?" he asked.

"To Florence."

"For what purpose ?"

"To acquaint the authorities with a foul crime that has been committed during the night," said the man.

"A foul crime ?" said Sataniello, in a tone of surprise.

"A foul crime indeed," replied the man.

"Where ?"

"At an inn, a short distance from the high roads," said the driver.

"Indeed," replied the brigand. "What crime is it ?"

"Murder !"

"Murder ?" said Sataniello.

"Yes, a foul murder ; or rather murders have been committed."

"By whom ?"

"That I know not, would that I did."

"Have you any suspicion of the perpetrators of the crime you speak of?" asked the Boy Brigand, hastily.

"I have," replied the man.

"Ah !" exclaimed Sataniello

And his hand stole beneath the folds of his ample coat.

It rested on the handle of his stiletto.

He half drew the weapon from its sheath.

"I have very strong suspicions of the assasins signor," said the man.

"Whom do you suspect ?" asked the Boy Brigand.

"The brigands," replied the man.

"What brigands !"

"The brigands of the Appenines," answered the muleteer.

"Holy Virgin," said Sataniello, "and are there any brigands in these mountains ?"

"Brigands, signor," said the man, "why the hills are filled with them. No one can dare venture across them for fear of being robbed or murdered."

"Is it possible," said Sataniello' in a quiet tone.

"It is, signor," replied the man, "and though I know not who can have murdered my poor master and mistress, I am sure no one would have done it but brigands."

"It is your master then, that has met with his death," said Sataniello.

"Yes, signor. Finding he had not risen at daybreak, as was his custom, I made my way into the inn and up to his chamber, when—oh, horror !"

And the man placed his hands before his eyes, to hide the sight which in his imagination he saw.

A shudder ran through his frame.

He became pale.

His limbs trembled.

"What did you discover ?" asked Sataniello coolly.

"My poor master lying covered with blood upon the floor, and his wife murdered in her bed," replied the man.

Sataniello was silent.

He thought it better to be so.

"The least said is the sooneset mended," thought Sataniello.

But he still looked inquiringly into the face of the muleteer.

"I flew with horror from the place," said the driver, "and roused my fellow servants. Then I harnessed the mules, and leaving the bodies to the care of the others, resolved to hurry to Florence, and make the authorities acquainted with the fearful deed."

"When will you gain Florence ?" asked Sataniello.

"In a few hours."

"And what assistance do you expect from the authorities ?"

"Every assistance, signor. I doubt not they will send a company of soldiers to the mountains in pursuit of the miscreants immediately. So I must hurry on, signor, for the longer I, delay, the greater chance have the villains of escape,"

And the muleteer cracked his whip.

"Hold a moment," said Sataniello, catching the reins.

"What would you, signor?" asked the driver.

"You say you are going to Florence," said Sataniello.

"I am."

"Will you bear a message to the authorities for me ?"

"Willingly."

"Bend down then, that I may whisper it in your ear."

The muleteer bent down till his face nearly touched that of Sataniello's.

Quick as thought, the Boy Brigand drew his stiletto from beneath his coat.

He raised it above the head of the driver.

One moment it flashed in the sunlight.

Then down it came with fearful force between the shoulders of the driver.

With a loud cry of pain, the man sprang backwards.

He staggered for a moment, then fell forward, over the side of the vehicle into the road, at the brigand's feet.

Sataniello kicked the body as it lay upon the ground, exclaiming,—

"Tell the authorities, that if they seek the brigands in the mountains, they will seek in vain ; and that Sataniello laughs to scorn all the force they can send against him."

Then, stooping down, he coolly wiped his bloody weapon upon the coat of the murdered man, and returned it to its sheath.

"Now, comrades," he said, turning to his companions, "conceal the body among the bushes yonder."

Four of the brigands stepped forward, they raised the still warm corpse of the murdered man, and carried it to the road side, and laid it beneath a sort of hedge which parted a large vineyard from the road.

"Unharness the mules," said Sataniello, "they will be of more service to us. The vehicle can be drawn to the road side, and left for any one who chooses to own it."

This was shortly done.

Four of the brigands mounted the mules.

"On once more," said the Boy Brigand. "It is fortunate that the prattling fool made us acquainted with his errand, as I have thus been enabled to prevent the authorities hearing af our night's work, and despatching troops to the mountains ere we can return."

And the whole band strode on once more.

It was just midday ere they arrived at Florence, where, taking up their position at one of the principal hostelries, much frequented by travellers from Ravennar, Cervia, and other towns.

E. BRETT.

At this place each pretended to be traders in different wares, and joined in conversation freely with the other guests.

The object of the Boy Brigand and his companions was now to learn the place of abode of the young Florentine.

But, although they endeavoured to do so from the guests assembled, by mentioning his name as though inadvertently, they did not manage to succeed.

Sataniello was annoyed at this, but he was too wary to show it.

He felt he must adopt some other means.

Taking advantage therefore of an opportunity of speaking with his comrades, he despatched them in different directions.

Two were sent to watch at the different courts and offices where Claudio might go to solicit the aid of the authorities, and Sataniello, Tranio, and Luco, only remained at the inn.

"I had hoped," said Sataniello, "that I might learn the abode of the Florentine, without appearing to wish to do so."

"And you have not succeeded?"

"No."

"That's awkward," said Tranio, "but have you inquired of the landlord?"

"No," answered Sataniello.

"Then I should do so," said Luco, "for he doubtless would be the most likely to know."

"Do you think so?"

"Yes."

"Why he?"

"The Florentine is evidently of a rich family, and the rich are generally known, where the poor are unheeded."

"That's true."

"Then inquire of the landlord," said Tranio.

"I will do so."

The landlord was summoned.

When he entered, Sataniello said,—

"Signor, I have received a few orders in trade from a Florentine gentleman, named Claudio di Coronzo, but have lost the address, and am unable to tell in what part of Florence to seek him. Know you the residence of such a person?"

The landlord looked thoughtfully for a moment, and two or three times repeated the name.

At length he raised his head with a start.

"Certainly I do, signor," he replied.

A smile of pleasure beamed from the eyes of the Boy Brigand

An exclamation rose to his lips.

An exclamation of pleasure.

But he checked it ere it was uttered.

"Yes," said the landlord, "the Signor Claudio di Coronzo resides on the banks of the Arno."

"On the banks of the Arno," repeated the Boy Brigand. "I thank you."

"Yes, signor; his residence is there, and a splendid one it is to, it joins the Church of St. Juliette."

"I remember," said the Boy Brigand, "that he said so, but I had forgotten it."

And Sataniello cast a leering expression upon his companions.

Tranio and Luco sat silent.

Their features were immoveable.

But the gleam in their eyes seemed to say,— "That's false, but it served your purpose."

The landlord retired.

As the door closed behind him, Tranio stuck his tongue in his cheek, and nodded his head.

"So far so good," said the Boy Brigand. "We must make our way to the Arno, and watch the residence of Signor Claudio. I doubt not we have outstripped him, and it is more than likely he may seek his home ere he asks the authorities for aid to assist him in recovering his affianced bride. Confound our want of precaution in not binding his eyes, were it not for his knowledge of the position of the cavern, I would go no further, but he can lead a body of troops to our retreat, and this we must prevent."

"How?" asked Luco.

"How," said Sataniello.

"Yes."

"By any means in our power," replied Sataniello; "the stilleto is the quietest and the safest."

"True."

"Then we must wait for him, and slay him." said the Boy Brigand. "Dead men tell no tales. With his death the secret of the cavern dies, and the authorities may launch all the forces at their command against us, and we can defy them."

"True," said Tranio.

"Then let us away to the Arno, and seek out the residence of this young man, who, to a certain extent, holds us in his power, and watch for the first opportunity to sheath our weapons in his body. Besides, we have another inducement to remove him from our path, besides the secret he holds. The death of our comrade must be avenged."

"It shall," said Tranio.

"Then again, the girl, when she hears that he is no more, and discovers that no succour arrives, may prove less obstinate."

"That only concerns you, captain," said Luco.

"Not so. It concerns all. For once she has fallen, she becomes the common property of the band."

And so saying Sataniello arose and left the room, followed by his companions.

CHAPTER XXI.

THE PRISONERS—HOPES AND FEARS—THE ATTEMPT TO ESCAPE—DESPAIR AND FRENZY.

THE two servants of the Signor Sebastian Ternotti, Pedro and Lucio, after being conveyed by the brigands to one of their small caverns, had sunk to sleep, worn out with the fatigues of the journey, and the load they had had to bear.

They slept soundly till the report of the carbine, which had been levelled at Claudio as he escaped from the cave, awoke them.

With a start they both opened their eyes and glared into the face of each others, asking by their looks simultaneously, "what's the meaning of that?"

Though neither answered, the same thought flashed across both.

The same hope rose uppermost to their hearts.

Each hoped that it announced succour for the captives.

Still neither spoke.

But both listened eagerly.

They strained their ears to catch the faintest sound.

For a few moments all was silent.

It was for a few moments only.

Then they heard the voice of the brigand who brought the information to Sataniello, that Claudio had killed the sentry and escaped.

The words he uttered came clearly to their ears.

So also did the exclamation of the Boy Brigand at this intelligence.

They rose from their rude bed and placed their ears to the door.

A smile of gratification lit up their features as the brigand spoke of their negligence in not binding the eyes of their captives.

There was hope, at least, in that.

For should Claudio succeed in getting clear off, he could bring them succour.

And they prayed that he might.

Then they heard the second report, and the words of Sataniello, which struck so forcibly upon the young girl's heart, that Claudio was dead.

And the hopes that had risen in their breasts faded.

A sigh escaped them both.

For now they believed themselves lost.

A black cloud had obscured the ray of sunshine in their hearts, and darkness more dense than hitherto, fell upon their souls.

But the cloud was again chased away.

Once more a ray of hope shone forth.

The brigands bore into the cave the second victim of the escaped youth.

They distinctly heard the oath of vengeance uttered by the brigands over the dead body of their comrade; and the determination of the Boy Brigand to start with the band in pursuit.

Still they uttered not a word, but kept their ears glued to the rude door to catch the least sound.

Nor was it till they heard the final orders of Sataniello, and his departure with his followers from the cavern, that they turned and gazed into each other's face.

"The holy virgin be praised," said Pedro.

"Heaven grant he may escape them!" exclaimed Lucio.

Then they both sank into a thoughtful silence for a few moments.

Pedro was the first to speak.

"Lucio," he said, "did you hear?"

"What?" asked the other.

"Perditta!"

Lucio sighed.

"I did," he said.

"And that is the girl I loved," said Pedro, bitterly.

"And the girl I loved!" exclaimed Lucio, "but now I hate her."

"So do I," replied the other.

"Yesterday," said Lucio, "I would have fought for her till I died."

"And so would I," replied his companion, bitterly.

"But now I scorn her."

"I would not give a word for her; she is worthless."

"And we were each jealous of the other."

"We were."

"But that is past. I would not now stretch forth a hand to bear her from this accursed place if I could do so."

"Nor I."

"But the Signorita Paulina."

"I would die for her."

"Oh, that we could force this door. We might bear her away now that the brigands are gone."

"We are too firmly secured."

They sat down on the edge of the rude couch, and again sank into thought.

And the thoughts of each ran in the same channel.

The frailty of the poor waiting-maid.

The girl whom they had both loved, but now hated.

After a time Pedro arose.

He stepped up to the rude door.

He examined it minutely.

He pressed his hands against it with all his force.

But it moved not.

It was firmly and securely fastened.

"Lucio," he said.

Lucio rose and stood by his side.

"Let us try if our united strength can force this door. All seems to be silent in the outer cavern."

Lucio placed his feet firmly against the ground and his back against the door.

His comrade did the same.

"Now," said Pedro.

And together they brought all their force to bear upon it.

But the door moved not.

The thick pannelling stood the pressure without betraying the slightest mark of the strain upon it.

But they tried again and again.

Still the same result.

The perspiration poured off their faces from their exertions; but as well might they have striven to lift the mountain.

They paused at length for breath.

"It is useless," said Pedro, in a tone of disappointmnet.

"Quite," replied his companion.

"And we must remain cooped up in this confounded place," said Pedro, "when if we could

but force the accursed doors we might bear the signorita to liberty."

"Yes; for their is but one to oppose us," said Lucio.

"And he, occupied with his prize, might be taken unawares."

"It is useless to regret," said Lucio. "If we would escape we must devise some other means."

"But what means?"

"Alas! I cannot think."

"Nor I."

And again they sat down.

For some time they remained silent.

Each was endeavouring to devise some means of escape.

But none could they see.

None could they think of.

And despair began to prey upon them.

Hope deserted their hearts.

They sat rocking themselves to and fro on the edge of the rude couch.

Not a sound could they hear.

Not a word did they utter.

And silence reigned throughout the cavern.

The silence of the tomb.

Thus the minutes flew by, till an hour had elapsed.

An hour of agony.

They knew not what fate awaited them.

But they feared the worst.

Should Claudio succeed in reaching Florence, there was hope.

But would he succeed?

Alas! the chances were against him.

He was but one pursued by many.

The brigands might overtake and slay him.

If they did, then all was lost.

For who then would rescue them?

No one.

If Claudio fell, their last and only hope was gone.

Every moment they expected to hear the brigands return, and learn that the Florentine was captured or slain.

They listened eagerly for the slightest sound.

At length they heard the footsteps of Angelo in the outer cavern.

It neared the place of their confinement.

They started to their feet.

A look passed between them.

Their teeth were clutched firmly together.

Their eyes gleamed wildly.

Each read the others thoughts in an instant.

They bent their bodies forward towards the door, and their fingers twitched nervously.

They were preparing for the spring.

CHAPTER XXII.

PERDITTA CONTINUES HER NARRATIVE.

THE brigand retired from the cavern leaving the females to themselves, and after partaking of the refreshments set before them, Perditta continued,—

*   *   *   *   *

The night came on dark and rainy, and everything looked so uninviting without, that our hero thought seriously of abandoning his design; but Montisco assured him that so far as the inclemency of the weather was concerned, all was in their favour, and he did not feel inclined to postpone the excursion.

Arming themselves, they issued from the Estalagem late in the evening.

They had no difficulty in finding the path that led to the convent.

Crossing the bridge of stones, they discovered, at the left, some way beyond it, a small chapel.

"Let us enter here," said the Spaniard. "This structure, looming up in the darkness, has an antique look which pleases me."

The gate of the little court being open, the travellers passed in and stood at the door of the edifice.

"The probability is that the bolts are drawn and we can go no further," observed Degrange. "Besides, what could we hope to see in this pitchy darkness, provided we should gain admission?"

"Gently, my worthy friend; be not too hasty, for it is hard to tell what one may stumble upon in a place like this. I am inclined to go in, and will do so, if possible, even providing I shall not be able to penetrate the deep Egyptian night that perchance may reign within."

Don Montisco thereupon tried the door, and it yielded to his touch.

"I have entered churches more than once in Spain," resumed the Spaniard, "and have seen penitents at the altar at a later hour than this. Tread softly, and keep close to me, while I grope my way through the hall to the body of the house."

Degrange submitted to be directed by his companion, and crossing the hall and opening another door, they reached the middle aisle.

Both glanced towards the altar; a very dim, waxen candle was burning in front of a large image of the virgin.

"You perceive that I was right," whispered Montisco. "The chapel is not yet deserted; it has life in it; move this way, and let us stand in the deepest shadows of yonder columns."

Immediately the two adventurers took the position indicated, and silently awaited the developement of events; and both began to feel impatient before anything transpired.

At lenth a private door was opened behind the altar, and a priest, bearing a taper in his hand, emerged therefrom, followed closely by a man whose figure was somewhat bowed, and whose eyes were bent upon the floor.

Both the priest and his companion paused, and seated themselves on the steps of the altar.

Each of the travellers felt assured that they could not be mistaken in regard to the individual who accompanied the monk.

The protector, guardian, or whatever he might be, of the unknown maiden, was before them.

"It is a delicate matter," said the priest, addressing the latter, "and requires to be managed with much adroitness. Have you considered the subject well?"

"I have studied it in all its bearings; I have counted the costs, and engaged in the affair, fully prepared for all contingencies. I am aware that Angela will resist my authority, and baffle me, if possible. I am prepared for obstinacy and intrigue, and have steeled my heart against those arts which females employ to mould men to their wishes. Should you prove yourself worthy of the confidence which I now repose in you, it seems to me my plans cannot miscarry. The game is dangerous, the stakes are high, and I must inevitably win or lose; if the first, I make my fortune by one bold stroke; if the second, I work out my own ruin. You know all I would do; and I desire you to give me a final answer in regard to the course which you intend to pursue. If you will aid me to the extent of your ability, say so, and you shall be suitably recompensed; but should you see fit to decline the service, after the subject has progressed so far, I fancy there will be no great inducement for you to betray my intentions; for the reason that I have in my keeping some secrets which might not be very flattering to your character, or favourable to your repose in the bosom of the church."

The priest listened to his discourse with a grave, thoughtful, and at times troubled air.

He appeared to be caught in a trap from which he could not extricate himself, even were he disposed not to enter into the schemes of the other; but so far as one could judge by external appearances, the part which had been offered him was not so repugnant as it might have been.

"Senor Mondelli, I shall not, of course, refuse to assist you to the extent of my feeble ability. The fair Donna Angela shall be received at the convent of Santa Clara in the manner which you desire."

"Bear in mind, good padre, that she must be kept entirely from the observation of the world; as much so as if she were sleeping beneath the marble with the dust of her kindred. A slight indiscretion would mar all my plans. Her beauty may have attracted already the attention of persons who would spare no pains to secure so rare a prize; but I have been secret and prudent in my movements; no one, save myself, knows the place of her destination, and few eyes have seen her on the way thither; but for an unlucky accident, her pretty face would not have been seen at all. As I have informed you, we were attacked by robbers, and assisted by two strangers—an English and Spanish gentleman. The former was quite dazzled, and I believe quite ready to lay his heart at her feet. I apprehend that he will make some effort to discover her retreat."

"The saints grant that I may have no trouble of that kind to combat with! Heaven deliver me from mad and reckless lovers! Donna Angela shall be kept as much retired as possible; the sunlight shall visit her only through grated windows. Santa Clara shall keep its secrets so well, that not a living soul outside of its walls shall know that such a being exists within the precincts of Monte Moro. For this I expect to touch your gold; such duties cannot be performed purely from motives of friendship."

"I understand you, padre, and cannot blame you, certainly, for claiming a liberal reward. All men are selfish, myself and you with the rest. You know what impels me to this step, and you shall be benefited by the operation that enriches me. You are at liberty to treat the female committed to your care with as much rigor as you think compatible with the general purposes in view. It will be well to tame, humble and subdue the native pride of her character, and make her so plastic that she can be moulded into any shape that I desire."

"Do not trouble youself to dilate further upon the subject," resumed the padre. "I perceive what is wanted, and words are useless to one whose intuitions are quick. The maiden shall be watched, guarded and disciplined in the most satisfactory manner, and not a whisper, or an indiscreet word, shall betray the secret of her being here. Friends will inquire in vain, and lovers shall grow weary of their efforts, and cease to perplex themselves about her fate. Come, Senor Mondelli, this place is damp and chilly: let us go to the convent. A cheerful fire, delicious wine, and comfortable beds are awaiting us there."

The padre and Mondelli arose, passed through the chancel into the aisle, and finally out of the chapel.

"What do you think of this, my friend?" asked Montisco, as soon as the footsteps of the priest and his associate ceased to be heard.

"My worst fears are confirmed; I am burning with indignation! It is a most infamous plot! Heaven, perhaps, designs us for instruments to baffle a plan so deliberately cruel," returned Degrange with emphasis.

"Senor Mondelli is undoubtedly a great villain, and wishes to obtain the wealth of the Donna Angela, so far as one can judge from the conversation just heard. The padre will prove but too faithful and persevering an ally. I wonder if he locked the door when he went out; if so, we are caged, and must get out the best way we can."

Fortunately for the travellers, the door was left as they had found it, and nothing prevening their egress, they issued from the chapel and followed, at a safe distance, the footsteps of the padre and his comrade, who, having ascended the hill, entered the convent by one of the posterns.

The adventures could, of course, go no further, and it only remained for them to walk around the premises and make such observations as they might.

On account of the darkness and lateness of the hour, they could see but little to reward their exertions.

The grim and dismal walls towered up before them through the Cimmerian gloom, presenting nothing attractive to the eye, or congenial to pleasant thought.

Occasionally the light of a taper flashed across a latticed window, and disappeared as suddenly as it came.

The rain fell faster, and the wind increased in vehemence, whistled shrilly about the fabric, shaking the casements with angry violence.

Our hero and Montisco, though thoroughly wet, were loth to relinquish the ground and retire without making further advances in their undertaking.

"Look!" exclaimed Degrange, eagerly catching his companion by the arm. "There is another gleam of light at one of those upper windows; I see a portion of a female figure, and a part of a face—it is hers!"

"I see nothing," replied the Spaniard, coolly; "your imagination is too active."

"She is gone," added the other; "she vanished like a meteor of the night; your eyes are too slow."

"You saw, perhaps, one of the nuns, old and wrinkled, and your glowing fancy has transformed her ugliness into beauty. Come away; we must not longer continue our vigils; we are drenched to the skin. Let us be gone, if you would escape fever, doctors and drugs."

"No, I will not leave the spot; I will stay to get another glimpse of the most lovely of all faces."

"Absurd! you are becoming an enthusiast. Do you hear that? that savage cur has commenced a fierce serenade; he scents us. It would not be strange if he were at our heels in a moment. Look into the court yonder. I can see his eyes gleaming like balls of fire."

Degrange reluctantly turned his face towards the town, his brain teeming with the vision of loveliness which had flitted before him.

In the pitchy darkness they mistook the road, and in a little time were involved in a labyrinth of ruins.

While they were feeling their way along amid vaults, pit-falls and rubbish, the Spaniard suddenly paused, and assured our hero in whispers that he heard footsteps.

Degrange replied that the sounds were only echoes of their own steps; but this explanation Don Montisco would by no means accept, and they both stood still and listened.

Hearing nothing to excite alarm, they again moved forward.

They had not proceeded far, before they were induced to stop by the repetition of the sounds that the Spaniard had previously heard.

"This time," said the latter, "there can be no mistake; some one is dogging us. It is probably a spy from the convent of Santa Clara. I hear the steps quite distinctly now, and I will fire a pistol in that direction, at venture."

"I don't know about the propriety of that; a shot thus discharged might possibly take effect, and involve us in much difficulty," rejoined the Englishman.

"Take effect, my friend! that is precisely what I desire. I shall do my best to inflict a wound. Ah Dois! I hear the rascal."

At that instant a brilliant flash of lightning illuminated the heavens, and threw a glare of light upon the ruins, revealing most tangibly the figure of a man in the act of stepping, with cat-like stealthiness.

Both the young adventurers recognized the individual, for he was no other than Signor Mondelli.

The Spaniard who had levelled his pistol before the lightning had flashed, taking advantage of the circumstance, instantly fired.

Immediately they heard a cry, like that extorted by a sharp pain, and then sounds like some one running.

"You have undoubtedly wounded him, and to-morrow, if we can be found, we shall be taken before the corregidor. We shall, perhaps, be imprisoned, and fare no better at the hands of justice than did the famed Gil Blas. Not a moment is to be lost; the porter and the savage dog will be upon us; let us hurry to the Estalagem."

"Con muchisimo gusto—with much pleasure. I feel so well satisfied with what I have done, that I can afford to put myself out of breath a little with exertion."

The adventurers now attempted to go forward with considerable speed, but they soon learned, to their cost, that it was quite impracticable while they continued in that direction; and changing their course, were soon in the beaten path leading to the town of Monte Moro.

They reached the Estalagem in a condition far from enviable, and the warm hearth and good wine of Jose Bedos were called into requisition.

It was a late hour on the following day before the travellers left their beds, and thought it best to remain within doors until next morning.

Time hung heavily on their hands, but not knowing how seriously Mondelli might be wounded, they preferred the filthy Estalagem to a filthier prison, where they would most probably be lodged, providing any complaint should be made against them.

Jerome and Alvarez laid many hopeful plans to rataliate upon the porter and the dog, but their masters would not allow them to stir abroad to put them into execution.

On account of having seen an alguazil lurking about the premises, they did not go out during the early part of the ensuing day, although it imposed upon them a restraint far from being agreeable.

The tiresome monotony of the travellers' indoor life was broken by the arrival of a Carmelite monk.

Degrange and Montisco were soon in conversation with Father Rosado; they found him to be a man of considerable information, and not so illiberal in his sentiments as many of his brethren whom they had hitherto met.

The interest of our hero in the Carmelite increased to a great extent, when he discovered that he was on his way to the convent of Santa Clara.

He naturally felt a strong desire to know what his business might be in visiting that spot.

But though he interrogated him with much adroitness, he failed to elicit any information in regard to that subject from him.

"Permit me to ask," added Degrange, "from what portion of the country you may have come?"

"From Lisbon," replied the Carmelite.

"Did you not fear, holy father, to travel through the most dangerous part of the Alemtejo alone?"

"What had I to apprehend?" asked Rosado, quietly.

"Much, everything; for the way is infested by banditti of the most notorious character. Have you not heard the name of Sabocha often mentioned?"

"The name you have pronounced is as familiar to my ears as that of my patron saint; and, in fact, I passed within a short distance of the Vendas Velhas, or old inn, which is said to be the favourite haunt of the famous bandit," returned the Carmelite.

"Is it possible that a person so cruel and blood-thirsty respects the priesthood?" inquired Degrange.

"Ah, Dios! do you not know that my order has little to lose? Why, then, should Sabocha trouble himself to look after one like me? Believe me, Sabocha seeks nobler game. The few feathers which such a bird as I may have, would not pay for the plucking."

"You are doubtless well acquainted at Santa Clara?" continued Degrange, after a pause.

"It has been many years since my feet ascended the sides of Monte Moro, or pressed the threshold of yonder convent. At the present I am a stranger to the abbess, and the father confessor."

"You may well be unknown to the abbess, for I understand she is chosen yearly," said Don Montisco.

"Is it easy to gain admittance to the convent?" asked Degrange.

"It is very difficult, except one is a priest or monk; and if you have any worldly curiosity to see the nuns, I would advise you not to attempt to gratify it. You may, perhaps, desire to know the motives that have induced me to travel such a distance to visit Santa Clara. Suffice it that I have most powerful reasons for what I am doing; but they will have little or no interest for strangers. I am engaged in an enterprise in which all my energies and sympathies are enlisted; and death only can put an end to my efforts. I act from principle, and not from mere impulse."

"Causa admiracion—that is good! It evinces strength of purpose, and the power of manhood. Worthy Rosado, let me hope that you will not object to tasting the juice of the grape. Jose Bedos has excellent vintage."

The Spaniard's proposition did not appear at all repugnant to the Carmelite, and the parties were very soon enjoying the fine wines of Portugal.

Rosado imbibed deeply, but never forgot, for an instant, to keep a strong guard upon his tongue; and even after his potations had been kept up until his physical faculties were nearly paralysed, his habitual cautiousness did not forsake him, and the strange interest which Degrange had begun to feel in the object of his mission whatever that might be, was by no means gratified and enlightened by additional knowledge drawn from the monk while in his cups.

Rosado, overpowered finally by the strength of the vintage, ceased to speak, and fell into a deep and oblivious sleep.

While Jerome and Alvarez were removing him to an adjoining apartment, a letter dropped from his pocket, which Don Montisco immediately picked up.

It was folded carelessly, and had never been sealed.

"This individual," said Don Montisco facetiously, "for aught I know, may be a spy, and highly dangerous to the Portuguese government; consequently, it devolves upon all friendly to this vinous country, to guard it against dangerous plots and treasonable practices; as a deduction from the foregoing."

"I doubt the propriety of it; it will be taking an ungenerous advantage of the monk's situation," rejoined our hero.

"You are too conscientious, my friend. The state may be in peril; besides, this may inform us why he visits Santa Clara; something which you have been trying to find out for the last two hours. See! I open the missive; it is written in the barbarous Portugese language. Being translated, it reads as follows,—

"'FATHER LAFONTA,—

"'Presuming on our former acquaintance, I take the liberty to recommend to your kindly offices the monk Rosado, who proposes to visit the convent of Santa Clara during his travels, for the benefit of the order to which he belongs. Make him acquainted with the abbess, and give him all the opportunity in your power to become familiar with the details of the peculiar system by which the convent is regulated; and you will confer no small favour upon your true friend and well-wisher,

"'OLIVELER OMANZHO.'

"This is the very thing you want!" exclaimed Don Montisco.

"What do you mean?" asked Degrange.

"Simply that you can make it serve as your passport to Santa Clara."

"Ah, yes—very true; I understand you; but remember that the document is not mine."

"You can make it yours; Providence has thrown it in your way. It will be slighting her favours, if you neglect to improve the opportunity. See what I will do; Alvarez, bring writing materials, and copy this paper, letter for letter, and comma for comma. Attend to it, and be quick."

Alvarez hastened to do as he was bidden, and very soon produced a fair transcript of the missive, which his master folded precisely like the original, and then ordered him to place it in Rosado's pocket.

"What?" cried Degrange. "Do you really intend to give him the spurious letter, and retain the original? It may be the means of involving him in difficulty; and, much as I wish to visit Santa Clara, to learn something in relation to Donna Angela, I cannot readily bring my conscience to this act."

"Neither will I ask you to, I will do it myself; I will suffer the penalty of the sin, and to you shall accrue all the benefits, without that item being considered, or marked down to your account. If you neglect this opportunity, I shall improve it myself; and I flatter myself that I shall be able to make a very pleasant impression upon the angelic Angela. You now need a monk's habit. Alvarez, run and tell Jose Bedos to hasten hither."

The Spaniard's plan was so congenial in its object to the feelings of our hero, that he did not resist, very strenuously, the means of its attainment.

The master of the Estalagem speedily made his appearance.

"Jose Bedos, can you procure us the habit of a Carmelite monk?" said Montisco.

"Senor, I can procure you anything which you may be good enough to want, small or great, from a corkscrew to a cannon," was the prompt rejoinder.

"You talk like a general, and come to the point at once, without circumlocution; that's what I like."

"About what sized garments does your excellency wish?" inquired Bedos.

"Those which will best fit my friend," answered Montisco, pointing towards our hero, at the same time dropping a few crusados into the hand of Bedos.

In the course of half an hour the master of the Estalagem returned, bringing the articles required, which were instantly put into requisition.

"Now," resumed Montisco, when Degrange had donned the garments, "you look very well; but there is one thing more to be done, you must have the top of your head shaven."

"You are jesting!"

"I am most seriously in earnest; a priest without a shaven crown would be, at best, but an anomalous biped."

"That's a piece of folly which I will never do."

"Think of the dazzling Angela, and conquer your aversion."

"Never! I will wear a cowl, and say I have a vow that prevents me from taking it off. Or, stay! perhaps you can get me a wig, with a counterfeit crown, which will answer every purpose."

"A good thought," rejoined Montisco, and thereupon Jerome was despatched in quest of the article wanted to complete the monkish toilet of our traveller.

It was not long before he came back successful, and his master was speedily made ready to engage in this new adventure.

"Should you not hear from me by to-morrow noon," said Degrange, as he was about to leave the Estalagem, "conclude that some misfortune has overtaken me, and make such efforts in regard to me as your friendship and better judgment may warrant."

"Do not suppose that having once engaged with you in this enterprise, I shall tamely abandon it when the first wind of adversity blows counter to our wishes. My Spanish ardour is not so easily cooled; when I once fairly and resolutely embark in an adventure, my purpose cannot be readily changed. If at the time specified I do not see your friendly English face, I will take immediate, and I doubt not, effective measures, to discover the reason of your detention. If there be any potency or virtue in address and perseverance, I will cause the grim walls of Santa Clara to speak, and tell their secrets," replied Don Montisco, warmly.

It was considerably past the hour of noon when our hero commenced once more the ascent of Monte Moro.

It is true that he felt some hesitancy about encountering the cold, grey, searching eyes of Mondelli, and the cunning glances of Father Lafonta.

The idea that the former might have been seriously wounded by Don Montisco, produced some uneasiness, and on the whole rendered him more dubious in regard to his present design than he otherwise would have been.

He neared the convent; he saw its dark, discoloured walls once more, and strained his eyes towards the window where he fancied he had seen the object of his solicitude on the night of his former visit.

He felt some misgivings when he put forth his hand to grasp the bell-knob, and the tintinnabula which he caused fell with a strange, dull, boding sound upon his ears.

Degrange remained at the gate about ten minutes, when hearing footsteps in the court, he looked in, and perceived, much to his dissatisfaction, that Mondelli was advancing.

"Father Lafonta has read your letter of introduction, and being indisposed, has bidden me to welcome you to Santa Clara," said the latter, with a very courteous demeanour.

Reassured by his friendly manner, our hero followed him, while thoughts of the bewitching Angela were still dancing through his brain.

"I have recently been injured by a fall," added Mondelli, "and it is with some inconvenience that I move about; so you must pardon me, if I make but an indifferent cicerone.

"Have you sustained internal injury?" asked Degrange, watching, as he spoke, the countenance of his conductor.

A cloud, stormy and dark, passed over his face, and he answered, in a suppressed voice, pressing his right hand to the corresponding side—

"My hurts are by no means dangerous, atlhough they may be said to be both external and internal. A few days of rest will set me right again."

Perceiving that this theme was very ungenial, our hero forbore to press it further; and being already within the convent, he was too much absorbed in scrutinizing the objects around him, to follow up the subject, which was at best a dangerous one.

"As the abbess is at this time engaged, and you cannot see her for an hour or more, I will with pleasure conduct you through the different compartments of the convent; for I have received instructions from Father Lafonta to that effect," said Mondelli.

This proposal was too much in accordance with our hero's feelings to be rejected; it being, in fact, the very thing he desired.

Occasionally they met a nun in her simple habit, gliding along the corridors like a troubled spirit, casting, perchance, a furtive glance at the stranger, or flitting onward without raising her eyes.

Degrange was careful to look at each one who appeared in this manner, hoping that he might be so fortunate as to meet Angela in a similar manner; although sober second thought convinced him that such a circumstance was very unlikely to occur, inasmuch as it was Mondelli's object to keep her hidden, as much as possible, from human observation.

Having examined the more public and interesting portions of the convent in the upper stories, they were turning to descend to the base of the structure, when a door was suddenly opened upon the left, into a corridor, and a female figure appeared in view.

She advanced a few paces, without seeming to perceive that any person was near her.

Our traveller's heart beat with indescribable emotions of pleasure, when in this fair presentment he beheld the object of his thoughts, exertions, and aspirations—Senorita Angela.

Mondelli's apathy appeared to forsake him, and an angry frown contracted upon his brow the moment he perceived her.

The maiden was evidently excited, and acting on the spur of the instant.

When she become conscious (which she did immediately) of the presence of Mondelli and his companion, her former perturbation assumed the form of absolute terror.

The discovery paralysed her limbs, and kept her motionless for a few seconds, during which Mondelli did nor remove his fixed and rebuking gaze.

She then turned, entered the apartment from whence she had issued, and closed the door, leaving Degrange to draw his own inferences in regard to the singular circumstances of her appearance and disappearance.

He was about to ask a question in relation to her, when Mondelli, taking his arm, remarked coldly,—

"Her mind is distempered; she has been brought hither that the gentle and soothing influences of the religion of the true and infallible church may work a salutary change in her deranged faculties. Let us descend, good father, to the lower part of the convent; there are rare relics to be seen, which you will be pleased to examine."

With the spell of Angela's beauty still upon him, he accompanied his mysterious conductor like one in a dream.

It would have been exceedingly difficult for him to have told how many flights of steps he had trodden, but the cold and chilly atmosphere which now surrounded him, admonished him that he was in the lowest portions of the convent.

Mondelli continued to make remarks, to which he was more indifferent than heretofore.

"In this room you will find some of the most remarkable relics that the world can afford. Amuse yourself by looking at them until I return, holy father," said his conductor, pausing before a small stone apartment.

Degrange stepped in, and Mondelli, having thus spoken, closed the door and walked quickly away.

So much was the young man's mind preoccupied, that some minutes elapsed before he realised that his mysterious guide had departed, and he was alone.

A vague and but half-comprehended doubt crept into his brain, and he resolved to leave the spot instantly.

He tried the door whence his conductor had issued.

It did not yield to the pressure of his hand.

It did not so much as shake upon its hinges.

It was fast!

No strength which he could exert would open it, although he threw himself against it with all his force.

Degrange began to think that he had been outwitted.

But he could not yet abandon all hope of Mondelli's return.

Perhaps the door had a spring lock, and fastened of itself, and in due time his guide would appear and release him.

Every moment the conviction of its utter fallaciousness took stronger and deeper hold of his better judgment.

The narrow limits within which he was immured told their own story, and needed but little comment.

Every part spoke as plainly as possible, and said "prison."

What fate was in reserve for him?

How long would his imprisonment continue?

Would personal harm be offered him?

And lastly, but not least, was there any possibility that Don Montisco would be able to discover his situation, and release him from the power of the unknown man into whose hands he had unexpectedly fallen?

To add to the gloominess of his position, the light faded from his cell, leaving him in utter darkness, and he knew that it was night.

"How do you like the relics, good Falher Rosado?" said a mocking voice.

"Who speaks?" cried Degrange, starting from the recumbent position which he had assumed.

"I will show you," replied the speaker.

Our hero looked towards the grated window, and saw revealed by the feeble rays of a lamp

the visage of Mondelli—just the features he expected to behold.

"What means this?" inquired the Englishman sternly.

"Rash meddler! hot-headed adventurer! inefficient schemer! you have begun to experience the reward of your labours."

"I demand to be released. You have no power, divine or human, to incarcerate me in this vile place. I am an Englishman, and a subject of the British crown; an insult to me is an insult to my nation; and I will bring you to an account for these proceedings, either before your own tribunals of justice, or others," added Degrange, with dignity.

Upon hearing these remarks, Mondelli laughed aloud; and it was some time before he could subdue his sardonic mirth.

"If you had the sense of a silly fly, you would realize that you are already inextricably entangled in the spider's web. You speak bombastically of your government; I can afford to laugh at that, and you. Cease, foolish young man, to think of things so absurd; rather address

yourself to heaven, and prepare your soul for that scene of existence which canting priesthood avers succeeds the article of death."

"You are the cool and deliberate villain that I suspected you to be. To accomplish your sordid and avaricious designs, you pause not at the commission of any enormity that can stain the human character. Donna Angela is at this moment the victim of your remorseless cunning and cruelty."

"What fiend whispered that name to you?" thundered Mondelli, passionately.

"You do well to be astonished, Sonor Mondelli, and you might tremble, without shaming your courage, for your plots in ralation to the lady whom I have mentioned, are know to more than one. No matter how the secret transpired, although you would give your right hand to know. Heaven always raises up friends to shield and save the innocent and the helpless."

"Your words strengthen me in my resolves, and if I had any doubt before in relation to the manner in which you should be disposed of, I have none now. You know too much for my safety, you are in my power, and the consequences must come home to you with startling truthfulness," added Mondelli, with increasing energy.

"Is this the way you reward me for the service I rendered you not long since, when you were attacked by banditti?"

"Do not waste your breath in useless reminiscences; prepare yourself for the worst."

"Stay yet a moment! who are you, and who is Angela?"

"You shall know me so well before I have done with you, that you will not need to repeat the inquiry; and in regard to the lady, it will doubtless cause you some disappointment, when you are assured that she will remain to you, as long as you live, the same unknown and mysterious being that she is now."

"Tell me, at least, if she is a relative of yours," resumed Degrango, most earnestly.

"I will not. I would not gratify you so much for a purse of golden pieces. She is in my power, controlled wholly and solely by me. With this information, comfort yourself, and await the development of your fate with all the English philosophy which you can summon to your aid."

Mondelli said no more, and our hero was left to make whatever inferences he pleased in relation to the future; and while he is thus engaged, I will return to the Estalagem.

When Rosado awoke from his slumbers, it was nearly dark, and he concluded to defer his visit to the convent until the following morning; accordingly at that time he ascended the hill, and rang at the gate as Degrange had done.

The summons was answered in like manner, and he lost no time in sending his letter of introduction to Father Lafonta.

It is not easy to conceive of his surprise when, after the lapse of ten minutes, the porter re-appeared, and confidently asserted that said letter was a vile forgery.

Rosado was astounded by what he considered the insolent audacity of the porter, and perseveringly maintained that the paper which he had brought was not a forgery, but a genuine document, received from the veritable Oliveler Omanzho.

And the surly fellow approached the dog.

The monk thought proper to cut short his harangue, and attend to his personal safety by hurrying away from the spot; an idea which he was not long in putting in practice, for the howling of the animal was as terrific to him as it had been to Jerome on another occasion.

The reader will be prepared to know that he reached the Estalagem in the worst possible humour.

His ill-nature did not escape the observation of Don Montisco, who was not greatly surprised at his sudden return.

"What!" he exclaimed. "Back so soon! I had supposed that you were at this moment the focus of more than a score of black eyes, up at Santa Clara."

"I have not seen the inside of the convent, on the contrary," returned the Carmelite.

"And why not?" asked the Spaniard.

"For good reasons of their own, I dare say; my letter of introduction was pronounced a forgery," was the reply.

"But I trust it was not!"

"Of course it was not, senor. I would on no account forge the signature of my friend Omanzho."

"Oliveler Omanzho, of Lisbon?"

"The same."

"Then I should know his autography at a glance."

"To quiet any lurking doubts that you may have, I will show you the missive in question. Here it is; examine it as critically as you please. The signature of Senor Omanzho will always speak for itself."

Don Montisco, although he had never heard of the individual in question, until he had seen his name the day before in the manner already known, opened the letter, and after glancing over the characters, said,—

"The good people of Santa Clara were right. This, indeed, is not the handwriting of Omanzho."

"I assure you that you labour under a mistake, for I saw him write those characters myself, unless I was labouring under some strong delusion."

"I beg your pardon, senor, but I must persist in what I have affirmed. This is not the chirography of the person whose name is attached."

Somewhat disturbed and irritated by the confident assertion of Montisco, the Carmelite put forth his hand and took the letter somewhat unceremoniously; and as he did so, his gaze was suddenly riveted upon the characters thereon placed.

A change overspread his whole countenance; his assured manner departed in a moment, leaving him embarrassed and confused.

With staring eyes and open mouth, he continued to look at the paper.

"By the sacred sides of Mount Carmel!" he exclaimed, at length. "I believe my eyes are enchanted! There is indeed some mistake, and yet how can there be, when I saw Omanzho trace these identical lines?"

"Confess frankly," returned Don Montisco, "that you intend to play a trick upon Father Lafonta."

"That I cannot do, for I assure you that I have acted in perfect good faith. There is some mystery connected with this affair. Ah, I have it! Lafonta retained the real letter, and returned this copy to give plausibility to his assertion that I was an impostor."

"But why should he take so much trouble? Has he any reason to dread a visit from you?"

"If my suspicions are correct, he has," replied Rosado, impressively. "As I have already stated, I am influenced in my movements by motives reasonable and powerful; but I have some secrets which I do not feel disposed to divulge."

"Do not imagine that I am striving to win your confidence; confidence, to be agreeable must be spontaneous, and not drawn out by art or persuasion," replied the Spaniard. "Is it then so difficult a matter to gain access to Santa Clara?" he resumed after a pause.

"It is difficult for me at the present time, because my motives are mistrusted. There are those at the convent whose interest it is to keep away the inquisitive," returned the Carmelite.

"A sure sign that there is something wrong going on," observed Montisco.

"I said not that," replied Rosado, quickly; "and yet, perchance, I should not fear to affirm as much."

"Then speak out boldly, regardless of consequences. It is possible that I may be able to assist you," added the Spaniard.

"By no means; not for the world, or, at least, not until I know you better. I never liked the plan of reposing confidence in strangers, in regard to matters of vital importance. Let others do so, if they will; but myself never !" was the emphatic response.

"As you will," rejoined the Spaniard, somewhat contemptuously. "I threw out the proposition for your benefit, not for mine."

"If the offer was indeed disinterested, your conscience will reward you well, I doubt not, and I need express no thanks," was the not very grateful reply.

At that moment Alvarez rushed into the room, much perturbed and excited.

Approaching Don Montisco, he said, in a low voice,—"There is an officer below, conversing with Jose Bedos; he has come to arrest you."

The fiery Spaniard descended the stairs smoking his cigar, and leisurely entered the tap-room.

"We have come, Senor Bedos," said the officer, "to rid your house of a very dangerous person."

"Of what crime do you accuse him ?"

"Of every and all crimes on the catalogue of human depravity," responded the other.

"Name one of his wicked deeds !"

"The crime of taking human life."

"The charge is without foundation," said Don Montisco, impatiently.

"How dare you cavil, sir, when the accusation has been lodged with the corregidor, with abundant proof !" retorted the official, sternly.

"You intend, doubtless, to conduct me to the carcel ?"

"Yes, to the carcel you shall go; come along."

"Keep off, be careful what you do !" shouted Montisco, as the frade cruzio approached, followed by his coadjutors.

He did not heed the warning of the Spaniard, and a blow from the athletic arm of the latter stretched him upon the floor.

Immediately a general combat commenced, in which both Alvarez and Jerome were not unwilling to bear a prominent part.

The battle would soon have been decided in favour of Montisco, had not the other party, at that juncture, been strongly reinforced by four more of the same stamp.

The fight now became more serious.

Jose Bedos, who occupied neutral ground in this contest, now felt himself in a very awkward and embarrassing position.

He was vainly trying to think of some expedient to mend matters, when the hurried and furious clattering of hoofs reached his ears.

In a moment he heard iron feet thundering up to the threshold of the Estalagem; then the door was thrown open, and a singular-looking personage strode in with a fearless and commanding step.

CHAPTER XXIII.

THE NARRATIVE CONTINUED

THE individual who had intruded himself so unceremoniously upon the contending parties, paused and gazed fiercely about the room.

His figure was large, firmly knit, and well proportioned; his face, which was a marked one, presented a luxuriant hirsute growth, which had obviously been for a long time in open rebellion against razors.

His hair, which was dark and long, curled nearly to his shoulders.

He wore a conical hat surmounted by a feather, which drooped gracefully from the brim.

His eyes were uncommonly large; his person was nearly enveloped in a capacious sort of cloak, of rich though light material.

"What means this horrible din ?" he exclaimed, allowing the butt of a carbine to drop heavily to the floor at his feet; at the same time throwing open with his left hand the garment which had hitherto concealed most part of his figure.

The last movement displayed not only the hilt of a sword, but two pistols and a dagger, thrust beneath a belt that encircled his athletic person.

"I am acting by the orders of the corregidor, and must do my duty," replied the discomfited official, vainly trying to look unconcerned and resolute.

"Begone !" exclaimed the stranger, authoritatively.

"But remember that it is by authority of the corregidor."

"The fiend fly away with corregidor ? What is he to me ? I care not for him. I may, perchance, sometime take his nose between my thumb and finger, just in this way."

And to illustrate his meaning more perfectly, he caught one of the individuals nearest him by the leading feature, and gave it a wrench which made him bellow with pain.

"Out, all of you, minions of the law !" he shouted, giving emphasis to his words by stamping upon the floor until it shook beneath the concussion.

With downcast and alarmed expressions, the whole posse quickly evacuated the Estalagem leaving the stranger in quiet possession, and Montisco full of amazement.

He was trying to guess the secret of the man's power, when Jose Bedos whispered in his ear :—

"It is Sabocha !"

Don Montisco turned to contemplate him with additional interest.

"Whoever you are, or whatever may be your name, senor, I should be among the most ungrateful of men, did I not thank you for this timely aid. Whatever reputation you may bear with the world at large, to me you are a friend; here is my hand," said the Spaniard, in his blandest tones.

With an agreeable smile, Sabocha took the proffered hand and shook it warmly.

"Are you aware, sir, that an outlaw holds you by the hand ?" he asked, in his sonorous tones.

"We will not pause to draw nice distinctions about names, but strive to enjoy the present. I must insist that you dine with me, and try also the quality of our amiable host's vintage."

"Since the invitation is so frankly given, and you really seem to desire it, I accept with pleasure," was the urbane reply of the freebooter.

"But reflect one moment, Senor Sabocha," added Montisco, thoughtfully; are you not in great danger here?"

The bandit's nether lip curled contemptuously, as he replied somewhat impatiently,—

"You have been here several days?" said Sabocha, abruptly, when they were seated alone in Don Montisco's chamber.

"I have," rejoined the latter, looking at his new acquaintance with some astonishment.

"Is it not a little singular, senor, that a couple of young travellers should make so long a stay at so insignificant a place as this Monte Moro?" continued Sabocha.

The Spaniard, although surprised at so unexpected a question, replied with as an indifferent an air as he could assume, that they were stopping for the purpose of examining the Moorish ruins.

"Moorish ruins are not usually so interesting to strangers!"

"They have been peculiarly so to us."

"Is it a habit among the English and Spanish to examine ruins at night?" asked Sabocha, with a meaning smile.

"You have more knowledge of our movements than I had reason to expect."

"I have various ways of gaining intelligence, and you need not be very much surprised if I know more of the history of your doings here than you are disposed to give me credit for. Are you good at pistol shooting?"

"I have sometimes had considerable success in that way."

"Do you think the man died whom you wounded, up yonder, the other night?"

"Perhaps you know more about that than I do! but you certainly fill me with curiosity to learn how you acquired your information respecting myself and my young English friend."

"Do not perplex yourself on that point. It is my opinion that a lady interests you more than the Moorish ruins."

"I begin to imagine that you know more about things that I am interested in, than I do myself; but in consideration of the good turn you have done to me, I will forgive your knowledge, and by whatever means acquired, hope you will not make use of it in any way detrimental to my friend or myself."

"It has been reported in a certain quarter that the individual whom you fired at, is dead; what think you of that? Will it not make abundant trouble for you? Do you not already see before you a vision of prisons and desembargadors?"

"If the rumour be true, such visions have a fair prospect of becoming too real; but I doubt the truth of the report."

"And why should you? Have you not confessed that you are a good shot?"

"Because the night was dark, and I laboured under that disadvantage."

"You forget that there were occasional flashes of lightning, which, if properly taken advantage of, might serve to direct one's fire with tolerable accuracy."

"Senor, I perceive that you are deeply versed in the whole transaction, and it were vain to attempt to equivocate, or pass lightly over the matter. I did use my best endeavours to hit the man, and was directed in my aim by a flash of lightning; there is a lady in the case, in whom my friend is too much interested."

"By the way, where is your friend?"

"Arthur Degrange should have been here just one hour ago."

"Has he been absent all night?"

"He has; and his protracted absence alarms me."

"Were I to affirm that beauty had attracted him to a dangerous place, should I be much out of the way, think you?"

"I should say that you had a very fair chance being right. And now I will ask you a question. Do you know of any means by which I can gain access to the convent of Santa Clara?"

"If your conduct has not given those who have the principal control there great cause to suspect your motives, your admission will be a matter attended with no difficulty, for strangers are often admitted; but if, on the contrary, persons interested have by any means imbibed the idea that you wish to meddle with their secrets, it will be anything but easy to accomplish your object."

"Your last supposition is the true one. Both Degrange and myself are unquestionably suspected of harbouring designs not favourable to that secrecy which they wish to throw around some of their plans."

"Your friend's servant fared but poorly, when he made his first attempt to unravel the mystery of the sege and the fair young stranger," added Sabocha, laughingly. "However," he resumed, "the Englishman must hope for a change of fortune anon. If he were only a monk, he might stand a better chance. Has the idea ever occured to you that some of those deep vaults might possibly have subterranean communication with Santa Clara? I have heard that the convent was built upon such a vault, the original wall and foundation not having been disturbed. It is a fact quite well understood by those acquainted with yonder ruins, that there are secret passages, in many instances connecting one with another."

"The thought is a happy one!" exclaimed Montisco, joyfully, "And gives me new hopes, in regard to this adventure, which so far, has been attended with much misfortune. Degrange is, no doubt, at this moment a prisoner in the vaults of Santa Clara. He gained access to the convent yesterday, disguised as a monk."

"Then you need not expect his return," replied Sabocha. "There are minds at the convent that know how to plot, and to carry out their dark schemes. It is true that you have youth, and hope, and strength; but those against whom you are leagued, have the cunning of incarnate fiends. I understand Mondelli and Lafonta: no matter when I began to comprehend them, or how I gained the opportunity of studying their characters and yours. I shall not interfere to mar your plans, but shall look on with much interest to see this game played to the end. To you, so far, it has obviously been a losing affair, as your schemes have been circumvented with scarcely an effort by the opposite party, and indeed your English friend has seemed to rush into the power of Mondelli like a foolish fly into the web of its mortal enemy. I wonder at his want of foresight, but if he ever escapes from the convent he will indubitably be a wiser man, nor rush headlong into perils without knowing anything of their nature or magnitude."

"By all the saints! you alarm me for the safety of Degrange. Your words make me realize the greatness of my temerity. How shall I set myself to work to undo the mischief that has been done? Degrange must not perish like a dog, up in yonder accursed den! I will move the earth to save him?"

"And invoke the powers of darkness, also?" remarked the bandit sarcastically.

"Now you refer to yourself, unquestionably!" retorted Montisco.

"If you will have it so, senor, that construction will suit me as well as any other. But I advise you not to forget, in making your magnanimous exertions for your friend, that the corregidor and his creatures will not lose sight of you, but the moment they think I am far enough away, will pounce upon you like an army of hungry kites. If Mondelli once gets you into the clutches of the law, your life won't be worth a single *reis*; so be good enough not to lose sight of that important item."

The Spaniard made no reply.

Don Montisco seated himself at the table *cara a cara* with Sabocha; but his appetite for food, if he had had any, was now quite gone, and while pretending to eat, he in reality watched the operations of his new acquaintance, who swallowed his food with an excellent relish; fearless, apparently, of all that the future could or would bring.

"In relation to the subterranean communication alluded to by you," said the Spaniard, "it is not improbable that you may have some knowledge of such a thing; if so, you may not object to give me some clue to the same."

"I know that there is such a communication, but it is long since I have been there. Notwithstanding the character which I bear, I consider it right, and my duty even, to help a person, when I can do so without injury to myself. I believe I may be able to find that part of the ruins where the secret passage exists."

"Senor, I owe you a thousand thanks."

"Most men shrink from contact with me, and I had expected little better than aversion from you; but I have been disappointed, and not disagreeably. The somewhat blind confidence which you are disposed to repose in one dreaded by so many, almost makes me feel that the days of my own ingenious and unstained youth have returned, when there were those who trusted, and perhaps loved me."

"It is never too late to have friends."

"Too late for me—too late for me; for friendship must be founded upon esteem; and who esteems me? What stirling qualities has the terrible Sabocha to bind a single true friend to his side? I know what is uppermost in your mind; and now while my heart feels a little of its former humanity, I promise to accompany you this evening to the ruins of Monte Moro, and to share with you some of the dangers of your romantic and hazardous enterprise."

It is now necessary that I should direct your attention to other characters.

As the soge containing the fair Angela ascended the hill and approached Santa Clara, her emotions were varied.

She saw the darkened walls of the convent towering grimly before her, and felt like one hastening to experience a fate most gloomy and miserable.

She would have besought Mondelli to change the place of her destination, to conduct her to some spot less uninviting, where she could at least occasionally look forth and contemplate the beauties of Nature, as displayed in verdant fields and umbrageous forests; but past experience had taught her the inutility of such appeals.

With his eyes fixed upon the ground, Mondelli walked near the cabriolet.

As much as she disdained to hold any communication with this man, Angela overcame her repugnance enough to address him.

"Yonder convent, I suppose, is the place of my destination?" she said.

"Your conjectures may possibly be correct," answered Mondelli.

"Why do you not tell me your purpose at once, nor practise hypocrisy longer? You know that I more than mistrust your designs, and time must ultimately develop the whole," she added.

"If time will accomplish so much, be content to wait for that development," he replied, sneeringly.

"I am doubtless to be immured in yonder lonely edifice, where my very existence will be kept a secret. Do you not fear that Heaven will awaken to your sin, and punish your wickedness as it deserves?" resumed Angela.

"Such anticipations have never troubled me yet."

"If my wealth is so much temptation to you, take it, and allow me in return only the precious boon of liberty. Remember that there are those who share my blood, and feel a lively interest in my welfare. I shall be missed, and the cause of my sudden disappearance will be investigated. Be assured that your plans will ultimately be detected, and you will be required to give an account of your actions."

"You talk bravely, Angela; but know that the things you have referred to have been weighed and considered, and I am acting from a well arranged and matured plan. You say you will yield your wealth to me, and pass your days in poverty, silence and obscurity. Think you I am such an old dotard as to suppose that such a state of affairs could possibly exist? *You* live in loneliness and obscurity! It is the climax of all absurdities. Your beauty would excite attention and bring around you a host of admirers, of all degrees, from the peasant to the noble. And think you that you would not be missed under such circumstances as much as under the present? Would not your absence in such a case excite just as much inquiry? You talk of being inquired after, and say the subject will be strictly investigated. Hear how it is arranged, and wonder at my ingenuity. Those who know you, have long shunned your society:

I have artfully intimated that your insanity sometimes takes a violent and maniacal character, when it is highly unsafe to be near you."

"My insanity!"

"Yes, senorita, your insanity; for it has for a number of months been perfectly understood among your friends that you are *insane*."

"Scheming, inhuman monster!" cried the young girl, trembling with horror and indignation. "As much as I have feared and detested you since I have reached the years of discretion, I have never yet believed you capable of a wickedness like this which you have confessed."

"Those whom you have called your friends, are much relieved by your absence. Did you never observe with what a timid, hesitating air many persons were in the habit of approaching you? I often did, and thought it possible you might wonder at it."

"Now may kind heaven keep me from going mad in reality!" exclaimed Angela, completely overwhelmed with horror. "Yes, yes! too well I remember the stange, uncertain looks that were cast upon me by all who came near me in my solitary and friendless life at Lisbon! The atrocious wickedness you have already perpetrated, can never be excelled; and the heart that could plan and execute it, can never awaken to thoughts of pity and humanity. You have stopped the voice of my pleadings for ever; henceforth shall my lips be mute, and I will bear in despairing silence the fate you have prepared for me."

"Truly, that is the best; you could not act more wisely. You know I have a son senorita, how would you like to compromise the matter by marrying him?"

"What! unite myself for life to that deformed and unhappy creature? Prepare me for any other wretchedness but that!"

"Come, no more! I will not hear you revile my boy, who is as Nature made him, and whose only folly is that he loves you."

"He is little better than an idiot; death itself is less hideous than the connection you speak of. Thank God! we are at the convent; for even that now looks less terrible since you have mentioned your deformed, imbecile son."

"I will not forget this conversation," said Mondelli, as the cabriolet approached the gate. "You have attacked me in the only place where I am vulnerable; the insult shall react upon you with tenfold violence. Bear in mind that I do not renounce the idea of bringing about the proposed union; not to accomplish any wish of mine, but to gratify my boy, whom your artificial outside beauty has driven almost mad. Ah, if he knew you as I do; if he could hear you speak so cruelly and unfeelingly of his defects, his folly would, methinks, end; and he would have sense enough to learn to despise you more than he loves you now."

"Nothing would please me more; I will pray nightly for such a consumation."

"You put me out of patience with your unceasing volubility.; but what is in rsserve for you, will tame your spirit and put a respectful restraint upon your hitherto uncurbed tongue. Know that you will never leave this convent. Your friends will receive tidings, in due time, that your madness increases, and finally that it has conquered your constitution and that you are no more an inhabitant of earth. Which fate do you prefer, this, or my 'wretched boy,' as you see fit to call him?"

"The first—the first, by all means; it will be paradise to the other," said Angela, as she stepped from the cabriolet.

The porter was already at the gate, and our heroine followed Mondelli into the court.

"It will be long," whispered the latter, "before that gate opens to let you out; it is my opinion that you will never pass through it again; that is," he added, with a malignant sneer, "unless your fiery champion of an Englishman should be romantic enough to attempt and accomplish your deliverance, in which event you would, in gratitude, be obliged to marry him."

"He is, at least, a brave and gallant gentleman," replied Angela.

"Yes, and left you in love, a victim to your accursed beauty! But one thing consoles me, he will never see you again."

"And doubtless never desires to," observed Angela.

"I know he would give half his fortune to converse with you five minutes. You were much interested in the courageous stranger; I am glad, for this new-born passion may give you an idea of the misery of my 'idiot.'"

Mondelli accompanied the last part of the sentence with a menacing look; but before he had time to say more, he was met by Father Lafonta.

"This is the young maiden concerning whom I have written to you," said Mondelli.

Lafonta bowed slightly to Angela, who did not condescend to return it.

"If I am to remain here, I would be conducted to my room, or prison, as soon as convenient," she said, with a degree of calmness which surprised and amazed her guardian.

"This way, then," said the confessor, and led the way up several flights of stairs.

"You will occupy this room for the present," he said, throwing open the door of a small apartment.

"This cell, you mean, good father," observed Angela.

"You will not be disturbed here, senorita. A discreet female will be selected to attend you. Here ample time will be allowed you for devout meditation and prayer."

Father Lafonta closed the door upon his fair prisoner, locked it, and left her.

Angela Benevetta examined carefully the room in which she had reason to supsose she would be immured for a long time.

The windows, notwithstanding their distance from the ground, would have been sufficient to deter most persons from attempting to escape in that direction, were secured by substantial lattice-work.

Angela noticed all the articles it contained at a glance; but perceiving a door at her left hand, she opened it, and discovered that it communicated with a diminutive oratory.

From the window she could not see much of anything, save a range of hills stretching far away, and the same which she had observed during her journey.

The town of Monte Moro lay in another direction, and could not be seen from her chamber window.

"Here, then, Mondelli means I shall be buried for the rest of my life," she said, in a melancholy tone. "But I will not be so imbecile as to make no attempt to baffle his sordid, avaricious and unjust designs," she added, with more spirit. "To be passive under such treatment, is to do wrong, and act counter to my highest convictions of right. I will use the sense and reason which God has given, to circumvent and bring this man to punishment for the frightful abuse of the trust reposed in him by my dying father. Unhappy indeed is she who is confided to the care of an unfaithful guardian. Henceforth, let it be my study to free myself from his power, and publish abroad his infamy."

Having laid off her travelling attire, she endeavoured to calm her thoughts and fix upon some settled plan of operation.

Angela was not long permitted to remain alone.

The "discreet female," referred to by Lafonta, in the course of an hour made her appearance; and if age and ugliness have any power to impart discretion, she was, in our heroine's estimation, all that she was desired to be on the part of her employers.

The name of this venerable piece of antiquity, was Jacintha.

In order to blind the eyes of Sister Jacintha, she resolved to act out any emotions save her real ones; that is, so far as she was able, to restrain and govern the many sensations of grief which so often asked for visible expression.

If she could succeed in completely deceiving the duenna, that would be an important step towards the object in view.

Angela resolved to make the impression upon Jacintha that she was deeply in love with a monastic life, and desired few things so much as to become a nun; as Mondelli had doubtless properly instructed the old woman in relation to her thoughts, desires, and feelings on that subject.

She very prudently determined to suffer herself to be convinced of the truly religious beauty and happiness of life in a convent, secured against all the malice, impiety, and interruption of the sinful world at large.

Disguising her aversion to the wrinkled hag, she began in a very respectful manner to ply her with questions; and these questions were propounded with such an air of simplicity, that a person more profound than Sister Jacintha might have been misled.

Our senorita soon discovered that it was a fixed principle with the old nun never to do what she was desired to do; she pretended to be very timid and afraid to remain for a moment alone, and insisted that Jacintha should not leave her oftener than was absolutely necessary, and always remember to lock the door when she did so.

Nor was this all: she feigned also to feel more strongly attracted towards old people than young; consequently it would follow that the society of Sister Jacintha was really a comfort, solace and blessing to her.

This state of things appeared to surprise the old nun at first, and 'cause her to look very frequently and very sharply at her new charge; but Angela played her part so adroitly, that she had the satisfaction of perceiving that she was succeeding beyond her expectations.

You will remember that Degrange had seen, or fancied he had seen, our heroine at the window on the night of his visit to the convent.

At the period referred to, Angela was standing at the said window, watching the flashes of vivid lightning that occasionally illuminated the heavens.

A flash more brilliant and universal than those which had preceded it, revealed to her vision the figure of Degrange so plainly, that she felt that she could not be mistaken.

It is not easy to describe or imagine the tumult of emotions called up by this unexpected disclosure.

With intense interest, Angela waited for another flash to give her yet another view, brief as it might be, of the stranger whose bold and manly demeanour had made a deeper impression upon her thoughts than her maiden modesty was willing to acknowledge.

It was true that Mondelli's affirmations concerning the enthusiastic and admiring glances he had furtively bestowed upon her, while walking beside the sege, had given her blood a pleasurable glow, but she was not conscious that an abiding interest had been awakened within her soul; but the rush of strange thoughts and emotions which she experienced somewhat astonished even herself, and made her ask, mentally, the cause of such unwonted sensations.

Perhaps this unknown gentleman had made some discoveries respecting Mondelli, and her own unhappiness, and was attempting to snatch her from his power.

The thought gave her a thrill of hope, joy and expectation; and to favour his designs, if he had such intentions, she ran to the table, caught the lamp, and returned with it to the window in order that he might see and recognise her.

How successful the operation was, you already know.

Not many minutes had elapsed after this movement, when the report of some kind of firearm reached her ears, which she took to be the discharge of a carbine, or pistol.

The sound filled her with terrible anxiety; she feared that Mondelli had discovered the proximity of the Englishman, and had fired at him for the purpose of ridding himself of one who might prove a dangerous enemy.

She gazed long and intently out into the dark and stormy night, hoping that a friendly flash might throw some light on the subject.

But she was disappointed; she thought she heard a bell ring, and that was all, and she was forced to retire to her hard couch agitated by many melancholy forebodings and harrowing fears.

"Perhaps," she would say to herself, "my generous deliverer has already ceased to live; he has, perchance, been stricken down by the aim of Mondelli, and perished, too, on account of a generous and chivalrous interest in a friendless and unknown maiden."

Troubled by reflections like these, it was nearly morning before the angel of slumber pressed his soothing fingers upon her wakeful eyelids.

On the ensuing morning, Angela received a visit from the abbess.

She was a woman somewhat past the prime of

life, still retaining vestiges of the beauty of earlier days.

"My dear child," she said, "forgive me for not coming to you before. You look pale and careworn, this morning; I hope your malady has not increased?"

"The fatigues of travelling may have affected me, in some degree, but otherwise I am as well as usual," returned Angela.

"The saints pe praised! I feared the excitement of the journey might have a tendency to increase the pain in your head," rejoined the abbess, in a tone intended to be very kind and sympathizing.

"What, good mother?" inquired our heroine.

"I apprehended," she added, "that leaving Lisbon and your friends might, perchance, disturb the equilibrium of your mind too much, and thus aggravate your unhappy malady."

"You are pleased to be ambiguous, *mater*. Travelling, of all other things, has a most tranquillizing influence upon my thoughts," resumed Angela.

"Ah, you relieve my anxiety, and quite restore me to myself; but these disorders that affect the *mind* are so difficult to manage, that one hardly knows what to expect, from any given course of treatment," returned the abbess, casting upon Angela a pitying glance.

"Fair mother, my mind has hitherto been in a healthy state. It is best that we should understand each other at the outset. You are doubtless resolved to treat me as one mentally diseased, while at the same time you are perfectly aware that I am as sane as yourself. Proceed! Be the tool of Mondelli, and let your every word and act be hypocritical; I shall comprehend all, and so will you."

"Unfortunate young lady! how deeply and truly I sympathise with you!"

The gentle maiden felt the indignant blood mounting to her cheeks, but strove to let the shaft pass as if it had not taken effect upon her sensitive nature.

"By the way, how do you like Sister Jacintha?" continued the abbess.

"I am greatly pleased with her," said Angela, quietly.

"She's an excellent creature! I thought you would appreciate her uncommon qualities," she added, with considerable emphasis.

"I hope you will be good enough to let her remain with me as long as I may stay here," continued our heroine, resolved to act her part as well or even better than the abbess did hers.

"I presume you can be thus favoured, my child; I shall do my best to gratify you, in order to please your worthy guardian, as well as to follow my own charitable instincts," said the abbess, with consummate dissimulation.

"You are too good, gentle mater," replied Angela.

"I had nearly forgotten to tell you of an unhappy occurrence of last night. A forcible and desperate attempt was made to enter the convent. Mondelli fired at the miscreants at random, and nothing more was heard of them; but early this morning the body of an Englishman was found near the gate. The shot which your brave guardian had fired had taken effect but too fatally."

Angela heard this announcement with an outward calmness that astonished even herself;

but within, she experienced a conflict of emotions that nearly deprived her of the power of speech.

"Mondelli has no doubt that the misdirected and unfortunate young man is the same who appeared yesterday as your deliverer when you were attacked by robbers. Was he quite tall and handsome, my dear child?"

"I think he was," said Angela, with forced composure.

"With dark whiskers and lofty brows?" continued her tormentor.

"Yes."

"It is the same, unquestionably; Mondelli is certain of it."

After making a few commonplace remarks, and recommending Angela to the care of the virgin, the abbess left, her eyes sparkling with gratified malice.

"Another enemy!" exclaimed Angela, when she was again alone. "One of my own sex, too; cunning, pitiless and cruel; a fitting companion for Mondelli! Alas, what will be my fate? From what source shall I expect assistance? What friendly hand will be stretched forth to save me?

Before night, our heroine had operated so effectually upon Sister Jacintha by various ingenious devices: and Mondelli's ward found herself alone, with nothing to prevent her from passing into the corridor.

Wishing to gain all the knowledge she possibly could in relation to the convent, she resolved to make a few observations, and hasten back to her prison before her absence should be discovered by her jailoress.

While putting this project in practice, she unfortunately encountered Mondelli as has been described.

Though disappointed and confused by this unexpected meeting, she did not fail to cast a searching glance at the person who accompanied her guardian.

His features did not appear to be unfamiliar; a strange thought obtruded itself upon her mind, and a second and more penetrating look followed, which had the effect to confirm the vague and somewhat singular suspicion that had flashed into her brain.

When she turned to seek her room again, it was with the firm conviction that she had seen the young Englishman, disguised as a monk; and that the story of his death, as related by the abbess, was a fabrication.

New hopes and fears entered her bosom.

Her better judgment assured her that her brave deliverer was in danger, for she was too well acquainted with her guardian to believe that he was or could be deceived by the mere change of garb which had been made.

Naturally suspicious and guarded, he would at once penetrate both his disguise and motives.

What would be the result of such a discovery?

It would certainly be most unfortunate for the stranger Englishman.

At this stage of the affair, it had cost Mondelli too much trouble and danger to recede a single step, or stop at the perpetration of new villanies.

The young man once in his power, knowing as he unquestionably did his purpose, what prospect was there of his escape?

In the vaults of Santa Clara the dagger of

the hired assassin might do its work with impunity; especially upon a foreigner about whom little or nothing was known in that portion of the country.

Angela trembled for the fate of the generous stranger.

Upon the morning following, while the old nun was absent, a folded note was thrust noiselessly under the door.

Angela quickly secured it, and read, in a delicate hand, the following lines,—

"I have caught several imperfect glimpses of your person. I wish to ask if you are happy, and stay here from choice. You can communicate with me by writing, until some better method of communication can be devised. Watching an opportunity when Sister Jacintha is not observing you, or is absent, place what you may write beneath the door,

"KATRINA."

Angela was considerably astonished at the contents of this unexpected paper.

She queried whether it might not be a ruse of the abbess to find out the real state of her feelings; but there was an air of sincerity about the note that finally silenced such suspicions, and she resolved to answer it frankly.

She tore a blank leaf from the prayer book which had been left upon the table for devotional purposes, and wrote the following brief reply,—

"I would simply say that I should not have selected Santa Clara for a resting-place, had my own wishes been consulted by one who sees fit, for purposes of his own, to control my movements. I am not happy; and a life of wretchedness is before me, unless some good providence favours my efforts to baffle the designs of a bad man,

"ANGELA."

This note our heroine placed as directed, and in a few moments it was taken away.

The correspondence thus commenced, was continued with spirit; letters passed back and forth, and certain signals were agreed upon by which to know when it would be safe to communicate.

Angela did not scruple to make known her history, such portions of it as had the greatest bearing upon her present situation.

Katrina in turn was not backward in manifesting equal confidence, and Angela was soon in possession of the cause of her being at the convent.

Between Angela and Katrina there was at once established a strong friendship; their positions were similar and their similarity naturally inspiring such sentiments.

Both these maidens were under the direct attendance of sister Jacintha, and in the stolen correspondence which was being carried on, they proposed various schemes to circumvent the old woman, and elude her vigilance in order to escape from the convent.

Katrina proposed that a powerful opiate should be introduced into the wine which she was in the habit of drinking.

By keeping her asleep two or three hours a day, it would give them an opportunity to meet and perfect their plans of escape; they could certainly make such observation respecting the place as circumstances would admit of, and in some lucky moment, perchance, bid adieu to Santa Clara altogether.

The opiate to be employed was fortunately at hand, our heroine finding, among other things in her possession, a small vial of laudanum, which Mondelli had doubtless caused to be placed there, in hopes, probably, that in some moment of despondency she might be tempted to put an end to an existence too irksome to be longer borne.

Angela knew very well the use of this drug, and resolved to use it.

By another little scrap of writing she announced to Katrina her determination to undertake the affair.

CHAPTER XXIV.

PERDITTA RELATES HOW THE TWO MAIDENS ESCAPED.

WHILE Montisco and Sabocha were engaged in the conversation before related, and while Degrange sat unhappy in the damp vault underneath the convent, Angela was preparing to deepen the slumbers of sister Jacintha to such an extent that no ordinary circumstances would disturb them for some hours.

That worthy nun kept constantly at hand an ample bottle of the juice of the vine most agreeable to her taste.

Having medicated the choice beverage, our young lady awaited the result with much anxiety.

The first draught, instead of having a comatose effect, put the virago in high spirits, and rendered her more loquacious than Angela had ever seen her before.

Incessant talking soon made the nun dry again.

The maiden now watched the operation of the drug with feverish anxiety.

The day was drawing to a close, and she wished the virago to be perfectly oblivious by dark; for Angela had agreed with Katrina that the evening or night would be the time to make observations.

At length sister Jacintha's eyes grew more dull and heavy, her voice became thick, and in due time she slept profoundly, without much prospect of her being speedily awakened.

Angela threw a shawl over her shoulders, and taking a lamp left the apartment, locking the door after her.

She found the key of Katrina's door in the lock upon the outside as Jacintha was in the habit of leaving it; she turned it and softly entered.

The young lady was anxiously awaiting the result of the plan which had been agreed upon.

At the first glance our heroine perceived that her new friend was blessed with an uncommon share of personal beauty.

She glided gently forward, and took one of her small hands in both of hers.

"Like myself, you are unfortunate; and the children of misfortune can best sympathize with each other."

"Perhaps it may be the pleasure of heaven that we be useful to each other," replied Katrina, with equal fervour.

"This is a sad place for one like you; with youth, beauty and fortune," observed Angela.

"I will not be so selfish as to think it worse or any harder for me to bear, than it is for you; and indeed your situation, so far as I have been able to learn by your communications, is more hopeless than mine. But now let us attend to what is before us. It is for the happiness of both to leave this dreadful place as soon as opportunity shall offer. If we stay, misery and dishonour are before us," returned Katrina, speaking earnestly.

"True—too true," responded our heroine.

"Did you leave Jacintha in a state of unconsciousness?" asked Katrina.

"The drug will not relax its power for hours."

"Then let us waste no time. I am impatient to escape from a place where I have been so very wretched, and where nothing but mortification and unhappiness are in reserve for me. I thank the virgin that I have at length found one who can sympathize with me, and co-operate so effectually in my plans of escape."

"My idea was this; to take one of these small lamps, to be governed wholly by circumstances during our explorations, and efforts to escape. If we hear any one approaching, we will extinguish the light and hide ourselves in any way we can; and when danger is passed, go on again as before. If fortune should by any unexpected chance favor us, we will bid adieu to this gloomy prison to-night; but that I do not expect. Yet we may at least make some discoveries that may be of much use to us at some future time."

It was now the hour for action, for the night was advancing.

The maidens hesitated no longer, but cautiously passed out into the corridor, and locking the door, took the key with them.

Concealing their faces as much as possible, they proceeded toward the staircase leading to the lower stories of the convent.

They had descended two flights of steps, and were standing near the head of the third, when the sound of footsteps and the murmur of voices reached their ears.

Nor were they destined to remain long in suspense in relation to the name and character of those who were momentarily coming nearer; the voice of Mondelli was too familiar to the ears of Angela to be mistaken even when its faintest accents were heard.

Katrina and our heroine looked inquiringly at each other.

"Alas! what shall we do? I hear the voice of Lafonta," whispered the former.

"And I hear the voice of one still more to be dreaded. The man whom I fear most of all others, is approaching," answered Angela, whose whole frame was now agitated with terror.

"They advance — they are near — we must evade them, or all hope of escape for the present is gone. The next turn will bring them in sight. These steps lead to the vaults of the convent; prepare to descend; I will extinguish the light," returned Katrina, hurriedly.

The next moment the maidens were in total darkness grasping each other's hands, they groped their way to the base of the building, and soon stood upon a stone floor, inhaling the dark and unhealthy airs characteristic of subterranean places.

The sounds which had alarmed them were still audible; they held their breath, and maintained such a rigid silence that they could hear the beatings of their own hearts.

The footsteps echoed over their heads, and resounded at the top of the stairs which they had just trodden.

Angela pressed the hand of her companion tightly, expressing by that mute action, more eloquently than words could do, the new fears that were crowding upon her; Mondelli and Lafonta were following rapidly in their footsteps, and the lamp which they carried actually threw its rays into the deep darkness before them, falling across the lower steps.

Katrina, with much firmness and presence of mind, drew Angela away from the dangerous spot, trusting to chance, and providence, to guide them to some place of security; fully resolved to escape discovery as long as practicable, and to struggle hopefully to the last for freedom.

The impenetrable gloom of night which pervaded the place, baffled effectually the possibility of discerning a single object; and Katrina was obliged to direct her way by keeping close to the wall, in order to be guided by the sense of touch; a most precarious method, when it is considered that she knew nothing whatever of the intricacies of the vault.

Their progress was necessarily slow.

Casting furtive glances behind them, they perceived that the objects of their terror had reached the bottom of the stairs and were moving after them, apparently unconscious that their movements were observed.

Their lamps shed but a dim and flickering light, being nearly overpowered by the mephitic gases.

Both the maidens were beginning to despair of a hiding-place, when Katrina's hand happily discovered a niche in the wall; and without loss of time she availed herself of the circumstance, and drew her companion after her into the recess, hoping that it might afford them the security which they sought.

Mondelli and the priest approached leisurely, like persons who are conscious that they have time enough for their purpose, and feel in no hurry.

They came near, alarmingly near, and to complete the dismay of the fugitives, seated themselves on a large fragment of rock but a few yards distant.

"It would be well to talk this matter over more fully," said Mondelli.

"That is what I wish; I am anxious to know what you intend to do, and what you expect of me," returned Lafonta, depositing the lamp upon the floor.

"The young Englishman," resumed Mondelli, slowly, "as you perceive, is likely to be troublesome."

"I know it, but what can we do? I have already proceeded as far in this business as I dare. There are some things which I think it would not be safe to do. This Englishman doubtless has friends, and, sooner or later, will be inquired after. You are treading on dangerous ground."

"It is evident enough that if this Englishman lives, and is permitted to have his liberty, our designs respecting my ward can never be accomplished; for he is madly in love with her."

"You are hinting at something dreadful, Senor Mondelli; and you know that I hate any work that savors of death. There is something horrible in the thought of destroying life."

"You are quick to take a hint!" retorted Mondelli, with a grim smile. "I trust your objections are not insuperable?"

"I positively will not stain my hands with this matter!"

"How much shall I say for this job?"

"I will not do it! I don't know as I shall even consent to have it done," rejoined the padre, thoughtfully.

"But you must not forget that you are to be benefited by this operation. The spoils of—of my ward are to be divided, you know."

"Very true; but you have the lion's share. If it was pretty near equal, it might be different."

"And your conscience might be less rebellious," retorted Mondelli. "Well, I am willing to do what is reasonable; but, as I said, Degrange must be put out of the way, or he will thwart all our plans, and bring us into trouble. If he wasn't in love with the girl, we might get along, perhaps without proceeding to extremities; but her dazzling beauty has so bewitched him that he is ready to incur any risk to do her a service."

"The difficulties attending what you have in view, you seem to have entirely overlooked. Degrange has a servant much attached to him, and a friend who will go through fire to render him assistance, and to clear up the mystery of his sudden disappearance. It is quite obvious, from what you have told me, that the Spaniard takes a lively interest in this love affair; and his suspicions will naturally be directed towards Santa Clara. He has a servant, also; have you considered what you can do with him, and the other two? You see there are three in all, who will feel in honour bound to make strict search for the man whom you now keep shut up as a prisoner."

"Believe me, good padre, I have not forgotten the details; I have already engaged an honest fellow to look after them. He has a strong arm, a quick eye, and a sharp dagger."

"Come, let us leave this damp place, and arrange, over some good wine, the details of this complicated business; for really it is an hundred-fold more difficult and dangerous than I had anticipated or bargained for. I only expected to keep a simple little maiden shut up until she was frightened into a marriage with your son, or until she—"

The conclusion of this sentence the young ladies did not hear, the priest having arisen while he was speaking and walked towards the steps, followed by Mondelli.

Angela and Katrina felt indescribable sensations of relief when the two men finally ascended the stairs and disappeared.

Katrina was the first to break the silence.

"This is frightful, past description!" she exclaimed.

"Truly it is," returned Angela. "Yet it concerns me more intimately than you."

"It has shown me what Lafonta is. Now I know him but too well. But we do wrong to despair; let us strike a light, and boldly attempt to carry out our purpose," said Katrina.

"You talk with sense and reason. We must not forget, either, that others are involved in the same ruin that threatens us with destruction. In me, it would be the basest ingratitude to forget the brave young man whose name has been mentioned to-night by Mondelli."

The maidens lighted the lamp without difficulty.

Proceeding towards the spot where they had entered, they took another direction and soon came to what seemed to be a series of cells with heavy iron doors.

"I am sure I heard the sound of a human voice!" said Angela hurriedly.

"I thought I heard something, certainly," replied her companion.

"Look, Katrina! there is a grated window."

Angela approached the aperture, and said in a voice as firm as she could assume:—

"If any unfortunate person is confined within these walls, let him speak!"

"Who addresses me?" said a distinct and manly voice.

"One who would gladly assist you were it in her power!" replied Angela.

"Your voice does not sound wholly unfamiliar. Did you not come hither in a cabriolet, and were you attacked by robbers?"

"I came in a cabriolet, and was attacked by robbers; and you, if I mistake not, are the gallant gentleman who came to my assistance?"

"Yes, senorita, I had the good fortune to do you a service; and I shall always remember the fact with pleasure."

"Why did you come to Santa Clara?" asked Angela, timidly.

"Lady, I confess that I was attracted hither by the spell of your beauty, and the hope of being of use to you. I had good reasons for believing that you were not fairly dealt by," returned Degrange.

"I have a friend with me; can we do aught to assist you," replied Angela, quickly.

"Yes, senor, advise us how to act that we may be of service to you," said Katrina, earnestly.

"I suppose that all your movements are watched?"

"We are ourselves deprived of liberty, but still a chance may offer of being instrumental in saving you from the power of Mondelli. Alas! I fear your life is in danger," added Angela.

"Do you think you can provide me with any implements by which I can free myself from this cell? Once out of this dungeon, I think I could easily make my way from the convent."

"We will do all in our power; but this may be our last visit; we have not the least security that we shall ever again be able to exchange a word with you," said Katrina.

"I comprehend; you have outwitted your keepers; can you not do more, and leave this infamous place to-night?"

"I fear not," rejoined our heroine.

"I have a friend at Monte Moro, who, could he learn my situation, would make every effort to aid me. Should you be so fortunate as to escape, be kind enough to let him know what my condition is. His name is Montisco, and I left him at the Estalagem at the foot of the hill."

This commission Angela readily promised to execute, although she had but little hope of having an opportunity to perform it.

"Now," said Katrina, "let us look about and see if we cannot find something which will enable him to get from this damp and dreary place."

For some time the young ladies searched in vain for some effective implement. At length they found upon the stone floor an iron bar of considerable length and thickness, which had once served as a fastening to one of the doors. This heavy missive they raised, and passed it through the grated aperture to our hero, who hoped to make good use of it.

Katrina and Angela now left the vault; the former leading the way.

When they had reached the head of the stairs, Katrina again extinguished the lamp.

"I am somewhat acquainted with this portion of the building," she said, "and think I may be able to grope my way along without difficulty."

They now passed through what appeared to Angela a hall of considerable extent.

"We are near the door that opens into the court; there is a bare possibility that it may not be locked; I will try it."

With but little hope of success, the maiden hastily put her resolve into execution; and to the joy of both the door yielded to her strength, and turned slowly upon its hinges.

Trembling with excitement they hurried into the court; but another apparently insurmountable difficulty was before them; the savage dog was always on the alert.

Nor was this all; the gate was invariably kept locked.

What could they do now?

How could they overcome obstacles like these before them?

With their minds perplexed with ideas of this

nature, they stood irresolute and undecided, momentarily expecting to hear the hoarse bayings of the dog; when they would be discovered and dragged back again to their prisons.

But the animal remained quiet, and instead of the outcry they had anticipated, they heard the tinkling of the porter's bell, which was rung with much energy.

Angela now gave up all for lost, knowing that the summons would immediately be answered; moreover, the mastiff began to bark, which circumstance would serve to accelerate the catastrophe.

"Be firm!" said Katrina. "This way—this way—we may perhaps secrete ourselves!"

The young ladies hurried from the door to the left side of the court.

"Thank fortune, here is a cabriolet!" whispered Katrina; "let us into it; it will screen us from observation. What could be more providential!"

"Ah, I remember this vehicle well. I performed in it a weary and painful journey; but it may now compensate me for some of the wretched hours which I have experienced within it."

The maidens had scarcely time to seat themselves in the cabriolet, before the porter made his appearance, with a light, and they saw him moving sulkily towards the gate; for he evidently did not like being disturbed after his usual time to rest.

"What's wanted?" demanded the porter, in his gruffest tone.

"Open the gate and we'll tell you," said a voice, which the porter obviously recognised, for he opened the gate without further question.

"Now run and tell the abbess that I have brought some friends with me and shall want refreshments," added the man the moment he entered. The porter gave the speaker the lamp and went to execute his commission, but not with alacrity. Meantime, the person who had issued the order, having seen that the gate was opened to its fullest extent, said "drive in;" then a vehicle appeared drawn by two mules.

"Now," said Katrina, "is our time to escape! Come, follow me, and be strong."

The maidens sprang lightly from the cabriolet, and keeping close under the shadow of the wall, glided outside the precincts of Santa Clara, while choking emotions of gratitude filled their hearts, and tears of joy coursed down their cheeks.

CHAPTER XXV.

THE INTEREST OF THE NARRATIVE INCREASES.

WHEN the specified time came, Montisco armed himself; soon after, Sabocha joined him, and they set off together.

It was not very dark, and when they reached the chapel, they entered it, to wait until the evening should be further advanced.

They did not observe that a sinister-looking man was watching them when they left the inn, or that he dogged their footsteps across the stone bridge, and secreted themselves near the chapel after they had entered; but Jerome, who was on the alert, saw the singular movements of this person, and thought it prudent to follow him, and discover, if possible, what his intentions were.

So the faithful fellow set himself at work with this laudable object in view.

When the unknown stopped near the spot I have mentioned, Jerome laid himself quietly down near the bridge.

In about half an hour Montisco and Sabocha re-appeared, and resumed their walk up the hill.

Before they had proceeded twenty yards, the man left his hiding-place and stealthily pursued them as before; while Jerome, adhering to his determination, arose and advanced with an equal degree of caution.

In this order the parties ascended towards the summit of Monte Moro.

Montisco and Sabocha now paused among the ruins and the man who had been dogging them crouched behind a crumbling wall, and rested his carbine upon the top.

Jerome had strong inclination to lay his hand upon the rascal; but he thought he would wait a moment longer, to see if he really meant to aim at either of the parties.

The fellow laid his face upon the breech of the carbine and levelled it at Montisco.

Jerome, leaped from the covert, seized him by the collar and stretched him sprawling upon his back.

This sudden movement caused the carbine to go off, sending its unfriendly contents whistling close to Montisco's ear.

Of course the noise of the discharge, and the struggle which was now going on upon the ground, induced Montisco and his new friend to run quickly to the spot.

"What does all this mean?" cried the Spaniard.

"He was going to shoot you. I pounced upon him as he was in the act of firing."

"Who hired you to assassinate me?" inquired Montisco.

"I don't know his name, but can describe him to you."

"Bah! that's merely an evasion!" cried Jerome.

"He wouldn't tell me his name, but he showed me his gold, which was better."

"Come this way, that I may see your face and know what you are like," added the Spaniard.

The parties moved forward from the shadow of the ruined wall, and stood upon the small eminence beside a vault containing water, and where the moonlight fell more brightly. Jerome kept beside the prisoner, fearing that he might give them all the slip.

While the Spaniard was looking at his features with evident interest, unsuspicious of such a bold movement, he struck him a smart blow with his left hand, and gave Jerome a perfect stunner with the right; and both being thrown from their equilibrium, tumbled headlong into the vault, while the knave took to his heels and gave them a fine specimen of running, and the bandit stood shaking with laughter.

Jerome instantly scrambled out of the mud and water, and without stopping to lend a helping hand to Montisco, pursued the rascal with all his strength, giving utterance to terrible invectives at every step.

Sabocha assisted the Spaniard to a firm footing, and then both of them watched the race until the parties could no longer be seen.

The cause of all this mischief did not take the road leading to the town, but bounded off in another direction towards the forest, leaving Monto Almo a little to the right.

"I recognised the knave; he is the one who drove the mules for Mondelli. It was well for him that he got away," said Sabocha.

The parties reached the bottom of the hill; the pursued being considerably in advance of the pursuer.

The former, taking a footpath, entered the forest, and the latter did not hesitate to follow him; thus they kept on for some time, maintaining the same relative distance between them.

But the whole affair suddenly took a new aspect.

Mondelli's man suddenly put his hand to his mouth and perpetrated a shrill cry; half scream, half whistle, which had the extraordinary effect to bring some half dozen graceless fellows to his assistance.

The tables were now turned, and Jerome ran from it.

He was soon overtaken, and confronting his enemies, fought with true English courage.

"Kill him, boys! make an end of him!" he heard the mule driver vociferate.

Things now looked as bad as they possibly could, and poor Jerome began to despair.

His pursuers crowded hotly upon him, muttering all kinds of outlandish oaths.

He was conscious of giving and receiving blows; finally his eyes failed, his sight grew dim, he saw an infinite number of diminutive stars, and then he knew no more for a long time.

It was past midnight when he began to have some faint perceptions of being in existence.

He had been stripped of most of his clothing, and left for dead; and when he was at length able to drag himself from the spot where he had been concealed, he was in a woful plight.

Fortunately, near by he found some worthless and ragged garments, which the rascals had cast away to don his better ones.

These he contrived to put on, in order to make himself fit to be seen, and supporting himself by a stout stick, he hobbled away from a spot were he had been so hardly dealt by.

He had gone about a mile, when he perceived several fires built in the open air, and quite a number of strange-looking men, women and children, huddled around and near them.

They appeared to be unusually elated about something, and, to his surprise, he discovered that the principal cause of their clamour and curiosity was two well-dressed maidens, who were evidently terrified and agitated.

Angela and Katrina had unluckily fallen among thieves.

Having watched Jerome as long as he could be seen, Montisco and Sabocha turned their attention to the object in view.

That portion of the ruin where the latter expected to find the secret passage was soon discovered.

"Hush," said the Spaniard. "Hush."

Both paused, but could hear nothing but the bats.

"This is the way we are to go, I believe."

The Spaniard kept close at the heels of his guide, treading with cautiousness on the mouldering floors that separated them from the deep vaults below.

Sabocha was on the point of trying the ricketty staircase to see if it would support his weight, when several fierce-looking beings sprang up from the dark corners of the area, and presented pistols and carbines at their heads.

This movement, being wholly unexpected, took the parties by surprise, and gave them rather a poor chance for defence.

"Rendete, Picaro! Rendete, Picaro!" (surrender, scoundrels, surrender.)

"I think you should know me, scoundrels; my name is Sabocha!" shouted the bandit chief, in his deepest tones.

Slowly the muzzles of the weapons were drawn up; the men looked at each other, and then, at a signal from their leader, huddled together at a little distance, and conversed together in hurried whispers.

"Prepare to defend yourself," said Sabocha. "I see mischief in these beasts."

"You are really Sabocha," whose name has made such a stir in this part of Portugal?" said the leader of the knaves, advancing a few steps.

"Yes, villain."

"How much will you give us to let you off?"

"Not a single reis."

"There is a reward offered for your head."

"Are you itching to get it?"

"Money is what we want, captain."

"I thought there was honour among thieves, but I perceive there is not; it's a silly fable; you disgrace the calling."

"We feel that it is our duty to take you before the corregidor."

"You will never do it."

"And why not?"

"You will not live to. Stand back, all of you!" said Sabocha, levelling a pistol, while Montisco followed his example.

The moment Sabocha had ceased speaking, he extinguished the lantern, discharged his pistol at the nearest, and dashed towards the open air.

The Spaniard fired, and pressed after him.

There was a brief struggle in the darkness, in which the athletic arms of Sabocha played well their part, and those of the Spaniard were not idle; then there was a burst of fire-arms, and the rapid and exciting scene was ended.

Balls whistled after them as they leaped the rotten threshold.

"Are you wounded?" asked the outlaw, as they ran from the spot.

"Only a few scratches—how is it with you?"

"A ball has torn the skin from one of my arms a little; otherwise, I am as sound as an hour ago."

"It is strange to me that you have no influence over those fellows," remarked Montisco.

"Ah, you do not understand it! They were some of your Spanish gipseys; gipseys are without honour; one can influence the foul fiend as easily. They are treacherous cut-throats and knaves wherever found."

"We have had rather a narrow escape; let us take breath."

"I am used to all kind of adventures, and such affairs don't move me as they did formerly, when life was new and experience young. My arm pains me somewhat now."

"Alas! I have done nothing for my friend, and that pains me more than anything else. If I had some half-dozen stout-hearted men to back me, I would carry the convent by storm, and hang Mondelli and Lafonta upon the walls."

"Do not be impatient; I dare say you will have it in your power to do them all the mischief you desire, at some future time."

When the two men reached the Estalagem, Montisco learned that Jerome had not yet returned, which circumstance gave him considerable uneasiness, as he had not expected that he would follow the mule driver any further than the base of the hill.

Without communicating his purpose to Sabocha, whom he left making himself comfortable over some wine, he took Alvarez and set off in pursuit of his friend's valet.

By a circuitous route, he reached that vicinity where he had last seen Jerome.

The night was now pretty well advanced, and the forest before him, through which wound the road to Evora, looked threateningly dark and gloomy.

He doubted whether Jerome had mustered courage enough to follow the knavish mule driver any further than the margin of the wood; but inasmuch as he had not returned to the inn, and could not be seen anywhere, he thought it incumbent upon him to keep on.

Feeling disposed to make the task which he had undertaken as easy as possible, he took the road referred to, and with Alvarez at his heels, walked smartly forward.

"I see a peasant's hut through the trees; we will go in and rest us, and inquire if they have seen or heard anything of Jerome," said Montisco.

The Spaniard knocked, and his summons was answered by a person whose countenance could not by any possibility be mistaken for an amiable one.

He was both ragged and dirty, and was smoking the last half of a cigarro.

He regarded the intruders with surly curiosity, and demanded to know what was wanted at such a late hour.

Montisco respectfully informed him that being weary of walking, and seeing a light in his dwelling, they had made bold to knock for the purpose of asking the privilege of resting themselves for a few moments; moreover, to crave a glass of vinho, if it could be obtained for love or money.

The occupant of the hut hesitated at first, and then rather reluctantly, as Montisco thought, bade them enter.

The interior of the dwelling was no more inviting than the exterior, and small as it was, was divided into two or three compartments.

A fire was burning feebly upon the hearth, and a few blocks and benches comprised the furniture.

"You can sit down, if you think you can rest yourself any better here than in the open air," said the man, somewhat impatiently, addressing Montisco.

"Come, my good fellow, do not be ill-natured! Here are some reals for you, which I hope your conscience will allow you to take."

The man frowned and pocketed the money.

"I don't keep an inn," he remarked, "but perhaps I can give you a bottle of very good grape juice."

With these words, he opened a door communicating with the next room and disappeared; and a moment after, the Spaniard heard him conversing, with his voice pitched to a very low key.

But the individual with whom he was talking spoke in a louder tone, and Montisco began to ask himself where he had heard it before.

Wishing to solve the doubt which now arose in his mind, and observing the light streaming through a crack, he arose, stepped softly to the thin wall and looked in.

To his surprise, he beheld Rosado seated at a small wooden table, while opposite to him sat the mule driver.

This was indeed a singular discovery; for what bond of unity could possibly subsist between the monk and the tool of Mondelli?

"It is a mystery," thought the Spaniard, "which may be worth solving."

Upon glancing again at Rosado, he saw that he was approaching a state of inebriation, for his eyes were already vacant and glassy.

The individual who had admitted Montisco, and played so unwillingly the host, was directing his conversation toward the mule driver with his back partially turned to the monk, whose senses appeared too much overcome to feel any interest in what might be said in his presence; and, in fact, he did not trouble himself to notice them in the least.

The Spaniard watched the expression and movements of the parties with acute and eager interest; their faces did not please him, and of one—the mule driver—he already knew enough to condemn him, and stamp him a villain and an assassin.

While thus scanning them, and listening to catch now and then a word, Mondelli's man drew something from his pocket which glistened and reflected the rays of the lamp; it proved to be a small vial half full of a dark coloured fluid. The person to whose eyes he made this exhibition, nodded, smiled and seemed well satisfied. The assassin did not return the vial immediately to the place whence he had taken it, but already emptied a portion of its contents into Rosado's glass.

"So providence has sent me hither to prevent, or be the witness of a murder," thought Montisco, laying his hand on the pistols concealed beneath his light Spanish cloak.

The conversation now took a different turn, for by certain words which he heard, he knew that himself and servant were subjects of discussion.

"The chance is too good to be lost; we'll make a night's work of it!" exclaimed the mule driver "Mondelli pays; he comes out with his gold! The Spaniard and his servant want wine—give it to them, in the name of all the saints!"

The Spaniard looked on as calmly as he could, and saw the fellow drug the wine. He then returned to the seat where his host had left him.

"Don't drink the wine, it is poisoned!" he

whispered to Alvarez. "Feign to drink, but pour it upon the ground, or into your bosom, as opportunity may offer, and be ready to follow my example when the proper moment comes to act.

Their host returned and placed the wine before them.

"My good fellow," said the Spaniard, pouring a glass of the sparkling juice and presenting it to him, "it is fitting that we should drink together."

"Your worship is very good, but I'm not thirsty," he stammered.

"Drink or you die on the instant!" said Montisco sternly.

The sturdy ruffian grew suddenly pale and his grey eyes appeared to dilate with horror. His under jaw fell, and he gazed at the Spaniard with an expression of stupid terror.

"Swallow, scoundrel—swallow, or I'll send you by a shorter cut!"

The fear stricken wretch raised the glass to his white lips.

He paused an instant with the glass at his mouth, glanced into the muzzle of the pistols and then drank off the drugged juice.

"Sit down!" said Montisco.

He was instantly obeyed, for the fellow's limb could scarcely support him.

"Now, Alvarez, keep guard over this rascal, while I visit the amiable mule driver. If he stirs, shoot him through the head!" he continued, addressing his valet.

Alvarez was a bold and resolute fellow, and his master felt but little fear that he would not carry out his instructions.

With a cocked pistol in his hand, the Spaniard threw open the door communicating with the next room.

The mule driver was sitting face to face with his victim, presenting him at the instant with another glass of the poisoned beverage.

Rosado appeared to be already quite stupefied, and could with difficulty maintain his seat.

"Ah, Dios! I have caught you at last, scoundrel!" cried Montisco.

Quick as thought the man snatched a pistol from his pocket, and was in the act of snapping it, when the Spaniard fired and he fell from his seat at Rosado's feet.

The report of another pistol immediately followed.

Glancing into the room he had just left, Montisco perceived that Alvarez had also discharged his weapon, and the individual whom he had been placed to guard, was lying upon the ground motionless.

"He wouldn't keep quiet," said the valet, in extenuation of the act.

"He seems to be perfectly quiet now, at any rate," replied the Spaniard.

Montisco's next care was to look after Rosado.

He found him in a critical situation, and in much need of medical assistance.

The drug was acting powerfully upon his system, and prompt and energetic remedies were needed to arrest its progress.

"What shall we do?" asked Montisco.

"We must by some means get him to the inn," replied the valet. "It is not safe to stay here, for these villains may have friends that it would not be safe to see. Look! here is Jerome's watch," he added, bending over the mule driver.

"Poor Jerome! we shall never see him again," said Montisco.

"You may be sure that we shan't," responded the valet. "This fellow has murdered him. Ah, here is another discovery. He has got on some of Jerome's clothes."

Montisco and his valet raised Rosado, and bore him into the open air.

"We will carry him some distance into the forest, and I will remain with him while you go after a cabriolet to take him to the inn, where he can have proper medical attention," said Montisco.

The proposal was instantly put into operation. The monk was carried from the hut into the forest, and Alvarez was despatched for some means of conveyance.

While passing to and fro in a fever of suspense, he happened to turn his eyes towards a small level at the foot of Monte Almo, and saw smoke arising from among the trees.

Thinking it possible that he might procure relief in that direction, he left the monk and proceeded towards the spot.

At first he walked rapidly, but upon hearing voices as he neared the place, he abated his speed and went on with more caution.

It was well he did so, for in a few minutes he was able to recognise the harsh dialect of the gitanos, and felt by no means inclined to thrust himself in their power.

Montisco's attention was at that moment called to other objects.

Another small party entered the precincts of the encampment, dragging along two females, who manifested the greatest repugnance and terror.

They came near and passed close to the spot where he was concealed.

Of the features of one he was able to obtain a very good view, for the light of one of the fires happened to fall full upon her face.

She was very pale, but her countenance was classically regular and beautiful.

Her companion's face he could not see, for her person was mostly concealed by the former, and those who were hurrying them forward.

The Spaniard's warm blood began to boil with indignation.

He was half inclined to leap from his hiding-place and attack the ruffians single-handed; but a moment's reflection convinced him of the folly of such a step, for in so doing he would only sacrifice his own life, without assisting the fair captives.

He wished to see no more, lest he should commit some act of indiscretion fatal to himself and them.

With great effort he ceased to follow, with his eyes, the movements of the beautiful female whose face he had seen.

Turning from the encampment, he noiselessly left the spot, resolved to turn again and set the unfortunates at liberty.

When Montisco reached the place where he had left Rosado, he was not there.

This surprised him somewhat, but after looking about awhile, he concluded that Alvarez had returned during his absence, and the monk doubtless was then on his way to the inn.

Having settled this matter in his mind to his satisfaction, he proceeded in that direction himself.

He had travelled perhaps a third of the distance when he was met by a party of men on horseback, who drew up the instant they came near him.

"This is the fellow," said one of them; "I remember his countenance well. I watched him while he was at the inn."

"Yes," said another voice, which made Montisco start, "this is the assassin who raised his hand against those that gave him refreshment and shelter—the murderer of Matteo Sterek."

Perceiving that resistance was out of the question, the Spaniard mounted the empty saddle and moved along, surrounded by officers of justice, so called.

His arrest, under such circumstances, he could not consider as a light and trifling matter.

It had a serious aspect, and evidently put his life in jeopardy.

Nor was this the most annoying phase of the subject; his incarceration would frustrate his intentions in regard to Degrange and the beautiful unknown whom he had seen that night, and whose unfortunate condition had made so deep an impression upon him.

He rode on, sometimes chafing with anger, then yielding to feelings of despondency, until they reached the town of Monte Moro, when turning into a dark and dirty street, the grim and frowning walls of the carcel became visible.

———

CHAPTER XXVI.

IN WHICH ARTHUR DEGRANGE EXERTS HIMSELF TO SOME PURPOSE.

HE did not immediately put his plan into operation, but waited until it should be a late hour of the night.

He then placed the iron bar between the grates, and using it as a lever, succeeded in loosening two of them from their fastenings, which made an aperture sufficiently large.

The night was so far advanced that he supposed all the inmates of Santa Clara were in their beds; so taking the bar as a weapon of defence, he groped his way to the stairs and ascended the hall, determined to force his way out, at all hazards.

The danger had to be faced before he had anticipated it; he had scarcely passed the hall when a side door opened, and Mondelli and Lafonta made their appearance, the latter bearing a lamp.

The priest and his associate in crime stood as if petrified with wonder.

Mondelli was the first to recover his self-possession; he thrust his hand into his pocket, drew out a pistol and snapped it.

It missed fire; and then Degrange, with a single sweep of his missile, stretched him bruised and senseless upon the floor.

The blow was not partial or light, but fell upon him with pitiless and crushing power.

"And here is your reward for your share in this diabolical scheme!" cried Degrange, aiming another stunning blow at Lafonta, which he had not the ability to evade; he dropped as suddenly as if he had been shot through the brain.

Degrange did not pause, but opening the door hurried into the court, where there were two obstacles to overcome.

He was met by the surly porter who had on this night been kept up to an unusually late hour.

"Judas," who had been lying quietly in his kennel, sprang out, shook his chain, and growled menacingly. The porter naturally ran towards him for the purpose of letting him loose.

"Stop!" cried the Englishman, in a voice stern and significant. "Stop, or by all the saints that hover about Santa Clara, I will make an end of both you and your mastiff!"

Whether the porter was conversant with English or not, it was obvious that he knew enough of it to understand that Degrange was not in a playful humour; but having no other mode of defence, he persisted in his design, slipped the chain from the dog's neck, and encouraged him to the attack.

The savage cur, intent on mischief, yelled terrifically, and bounding forward sprang at our hero's throat.

The gate was unbolted without further question.

Degrange was not unprepared for this onset, and leaping aside, gave "Judas" a punisher upon the head that effectually tamed his courage, and sent him away yelping out piteous tones of pain.

"Unlock that gate!" said the victor, authoritatively, turning to the porter.

Degrange took the first path that he found, which he supposed to be the most direct one towards the town, and he had got nearly to the bottom of the hill, before he perceived that he was going in the wrong direction; but rather than return he kept on into the road that wound along its base, as it would make no great difference.

He had just reached the road when he heard sounds of distress near him.

He stopped, listened, and heard the same sounds repeated.

He approached the spot, not doubting but some unfortunate person needed his aid.

He discovered a singular looking object stretched upon the ground—the figure of a stout man, covered with a few wretched rags, and presenting a most melancholy appearance.

"Bless me, Jerome! can this be you! How came you in such a miserable plight—what has happened?"

"Slowly, master mine, slowly! Let me ask a few questions; how did you escape, and how came you here?"

Mutual explanation passed between master and man; and the latter was so much strengthened by the sight of the former, that he was able to get upon his feet, and with some assistance to walk toward the inn, which they reached safely in a short time.

The first inquiry which Degrange made was for Montisco; but the worthy host could give but an imperfect account of that personage.

While Joseph was making these statements, they heard the sound of wheels at the door, and upon going out found Alvarez there with a sege and macho.

"What have you got there?" asked Degrange.

The valet partook so much of the general surprise at seeing our hero, that it was some minutes before he could tell coherently the story of his adventures, and of Rosado's situation.

He proceeded to relate circumstantially all that had transpired, relating to Montisco and himself, after they had left the inn together in search of Jerome.

Degrange was ill at ease on account of Montisco; he felt very well assured that he would not have left Rosado without some good cause, and that something unusual had happened to detain him.

He desired to go immediately forth in search of him, but he was in no condition to do so; he needed a few hours sound sleep to restore him to his normal condition.

———

CHAPTER XXVII.

IN WHICH MONDELLI TAKES AN IMPORTANT STEP.

THE mule driver, having escaped the pistol shot of the Spaniard, contrived to have him arrested and lodged in the carcel.

Well knowing where to find his employers, the mule driver entered the convent and passing through the hall, knocked at a side door.

"Who's there?" asked Mondelli.

"Pasquet," was the reply.

The door was speedily opened and Pasquet went in.

His master and Lafonta presented two forbidding looking countenances.

The punishment which the Englishman had inflicted, had produced considerable swelling of the head, discoloring the brows, and making a dark circle under the eyes.

Besides, the anger and mortification of the parties tended to give additional ugliness to their countenances.

"Well, rascal, what do you want?" growled Mondelli.

"I suppose all goes on to your wishes?" said Pasquet, glancing slily at Mondelli's swollen eyes.

"No; all goes wrong: my plans are ruined; we shall have the corregidor upon us, and all his minions. The Englishman has escaped!" returned Mondelli, angrily.

"I suppose your young lady is safe enough?" he added.

"She is in her chamber," said Lafonta.

"But one thing remains for me to do; I must take my ward and set out for Evora with all speed," returned Mondelli, thoughtfully.

"Come, Pasquet, stir yourself; see that the mules are immediately attached to the cabriolet. I will go up and see that my ward gets ready without loss of time."

Without waiting for an answer, Mondelli took a lamp and hastened to Angela's chamber.

He listened at the door; all was silent within.

He knocked, but there was no answer.

He repeated the summons more peremptorily, with the same result.

A few more experiments of the kind put him in a still worse temper.

With an impatient imprecation, he placed his shoulder to the door, and threw his weight against it with such force that the lock yielded, and he was precipitated with more haste than he anticipated into the room.

This sudden movement and consequent fall caused him to drop the light, which was extinguished by the concussion, leaving him in total darkness.

He arose and called Angela; there was no vocal response, but instead thereof, a movement like some one arising from a chair.

Mondelli walked forward, and placed his hand upon some one whom he doubted not was his ward, for he recognised, by the touch, the shawl she was in the habit of wearing.

Wishing to save all explanations and scenes, as well as to save time, Mondelli caught the female in his arms, and being familiar with the way, bore her down stairs without accident, notwithstanding the darkness.

She made little or no resistance, and he wondered at her passiveness.

Pasquet and the porter had drawn the cabriolet to the door, and were attaching the mules, when he reached the hall, and without pausing, at once transferred his burden to the vehicle, congratulating himself that a hard job was accomplished so easily.

"I thought I heard people crossing the stone bridge down by the chapel, when I went after the mules," said Pasquet.

"A posse of officers, no doubt, whom the Englishman has turned loose upon us. Let us be off! Drive towards Evora as fast as you can, we are not safe an instant here," replied Mondelli, hurriedly.

"All right inside, I suppose?" returned the driver.

"Yes, rascal! Go on, if you would escape a prison!"

Instantly the cabriolet rolled away.

When once clear of the court, Pasquet gave the machos the lash, and they proceeded down the hill towards the Evora road at a speed truly frightful.

"If you were not such an obstinate hussy! if you would only marry my son!" said Mondelli, addressing himself, rather than her.

To his astonishment, he was answered by a gentle pressure of the hand.

He at once put what he had just said in the form of an interrogatory, and wonderful to relate, the soft pressure was again given.

Mondelli was quite bewildered, and had Pasquet only abated his Jehu-like speed, he would have felt something akin to happiness in the success of his plans.

He inwardly prayed that Pasquet would soon moderate his speed, that he might think more calmly on this sudden yielding of his fair and hitherto self-willed ward.

His wishes were destined to be gratified in a way not so agreeable as he could have chosen.

A similar vehicle coming from the opposite direction, by an abrupt turn was brought into view, and came in contact with the cabriolet, overturning it at once, giving the parties within a severe shock and sundry contusions, eliciting various exclamations of pain and alarm.

Nor did the other carriage escape without disaster; it met with a parallel fate.

None of the parties were seriously hurt, as it happened; but Mondelli made a mark—mentally—against the mule driver.

"Perhaps it will turn out that in this instance it has brought good luck, for look—there is your fair son!" replied the driver, laying peculiar stress on the last adjective.

Mondelli instantly turned towards the little bundle of cloth, or something else, which the other bolieiro had just succeeded in getting from the sege, and beheld in that presentation the object indicated by Pasquet.

In a moment he was ready to forget all recent terror, for the very opportunity for which he was longing at the instant of the collision, was now offered.

He would carry out his great project immediately, and, to employ the common adage, "strike while the iron was hot."

The course to pursue was most obvious.

His ward had consented to his wishes, and now was the time to make all sure, and end the whole matter.

Chance had singularly enough favoured his intentions, by bringing his son to him in the very crisis when he was wanted.

He would send Pasquet immediately for Father Lafonta, and have the youthful pair united.

This plan was too hopeful and too much to the point, to be neglected.

"Mount one of the mules and go back to Santa Clara as fast as you came away, and tell Father Lafonta to hasten hither," he said, placing money in Pasquet's hand.

The driver promised to do his best, and freeing the mules from the sege, leaped upon the fleetest.

Pasquet rode off, singing a snatch of a robber song.

Mondelli looked after him as long as he could be seen.

Meanwhile the female whom he had brought from Santa Clara sat quietly in the sege, which had been raised to its proper position, while the deformed youth stood staring at his father, wondering what next would happen.

Mondelli did not deign to hold any conversation with the parties during the time his servant was absent, but paced impatiently up and down the road, casting anxious glances towards Monte Moro.

Soon Lafonta appeared.

Briefly Mondelli related what had passed between himself and his ward, and his intentions to have her promise carried into legal effect on the spot, without delay; a step to which the priest willingly assented.

It was now the hour of deep darkness which immediately precedes the dawning of day.

"I bless the friendly darkness," said Mondelli; "it will prevent Angela from seeing the face and figure of my happy boy. The sight of him, even now, might shake all her firmness."

"Let her remain sitting in the cabriolet," whispered Lafonta. "I will manage it all. Young man, approach; senorita, give me your hand."

The female in the carriage, after a little hesitation, languidly raised her arm and put her hand out of the window, much in the same way that a somnambulist might have done.

The deformed advanced, and the padre laid the half lifeless hand into his, and it rested there mechanically.

The bridegroom trembled so much, that his father was obliged to support his puny figure, to keep him from sinking to the ground, for he was literally in a delirium of joy which almost stopped his heart from beating.

He had never expected to realize such bliss; he had not dreamed but Angela would always refuse him, as she had hitherto done; and even his father had never bidden him hope for such an event.

Neither the bride nor the bridegroom made any responses, and the latter heard scarcely a word of the hurried ceremony, his brain was in such a mad whirl of delight.

CHAPTER XXVIII.

AN UNEXPECTED DENOUEMENT.

AFTER escaping from the convent, Angela and Katrina fled, with one idea of placing as great a ditsance as possible between Santa Clara and themselves.

They descended the hill and took the Evora road; not by design, but purely by accident.

They felt no weariness; their minds were too active to permit their bodies to complain.

They were not far beyond the cottage of Matteo Sterek, when human voices reached them, and caused them to hesitate.

No time was allowed them for concealment, for the persons who had excited their alarm appeared suddenly before them, while a light from some unknown quarter suddenly lit up the scene.

Donna Katrina, being more experienced in these matters than Angela, at once recognised the tawny and wild-looking men as Spanish gipseys.

"Where are you going?" asked one of them, first in Portuguese, and then in Spanish.

"To Monte Moro, but we have lost our way," returned Katrina quickly.

"We will show you the way!" retorted the gitano, roughly.

"No, pray leave us, and let us go on as we please!" exclaimed Angela, very much terrified.

"This is a late hour for such bonny birds to be on the wing. Come, this way, we will be your company," added one of the gipseys, with a significant grimace.

"What wild looking beings!" whispered our heroine. "What will be our fate?"

"They are gitanos. It will be useless to resist, we must follow them; I do not think they will harm us," returned Katrina, endeavouring to put a good face on the matter, and exhibit as much firmness as possible.

One of the men turned from the carriage road into a small footpath, motioning the maidens to follow; while the other paused a moment, and then walked behind them to prevent them from escaping.

The hearts of the maidens were now filled with the most distracting apprehensions.

In a short time they came in sight of the encampment before mentioned as having been seen by Montisco and Jerome.

The captain came forward, and having surveyed them a moment, conducted them to a tent, where he assured them they should not be disturbed, but might pass the remainder of the night in security.

Both were truly thankful for this unexpected change in the aspect of affairs, but were too anxious to think of obtaining any rest.

A conversation which they heard outside the tent, did not serve to reassure them in any degree.

The words which Angela and Katrina heard, shocked them beyond measure; and they were well nigh inclined to believe that Heaven had abandoned them to be the sport of fortune.

"A new danger threatens—what shall we do?"

"I know not; we must again set our wits at work. Having circumvented Mondelli and Lafonta, I think we may flatter ourselves that we shall be able to baffle these gitanos."

"Your courage revives mine. What hinders us from making one more effort to regain our freedom? The encampment is getting quiet; no one appears to be stirring, but those to whose conversation we have been listening."

"Very true; they are now lying near the door of the tent. If there was some mode of egress in this direction, we might bid them good night while they are laying plans to make us gipsey wives. Imagine their mortification in the morning to find that the birds have flown!"

"Their disappointment would only be equal to that of Mondelli and Lafonta. The fabric that shelters us is made of canvas, but it is firm and fastened well at the bottom."

"So I perceive. And look! by the faint light of the fire, I see a knife in yonder corner. What is easier than to make an ample opening

in this tent, and leave our vagabond enter-
tainers?"

Katrina then made a large incision in the
canvas, paused a moment, and then stepped out,
followed by Angela.

Their hearts beat with expectation; they
moved forward a few paces, and listened intently.

All remained quiet; not a sound came to
their ears; the gitaneria was hushed in sleep.

With gentle footsteps, the maidens stole from
the spot, and were soon in the sombre forest.

"We will now make such good use of our
limbs, that they shall find it difficult to overtake
us," said Katrina.

Our heroine responded cordially to this proposition; not a moment was wasted, nor a
single effort spared.

It was just the hour of dawn, when they came
in sight of a small hut.

Being thirsty and weary, they resolved to
approach it, and did so with the exercise of
caution.

When they were quite near the dwelling, they
heard the sound of wheels, and immediately
concealed themselves among the trees.

They had been hidden but a short time, when
two persons appeared in view, in close conversation.

Just behind them was a cabriolet drawn by
mules, according to the custom of the country.

"The two persons in advance are Mondelli
and Lafonta," whispered Angela.

"Yes, I recognise them; they are doubtless
in pursuit of us."

They are conversing. Let us listen; perhaps
we can hear what they say."

Both now remained so still, that they could
hear the excited pulsation of their own hearts.

Mondelli and Lafonta drew nearer, and were
apparently in excellent spirits.

"I am greatly astonished, good padre. I
never expected that she would consent to marry
the poor lad."

"What do they mean" said our heroine.

But instead of making any reply, Katrina
placed her hand gently over her mouth.

The first rays of the sun came shining brightly
down through the trees, as the vehicle reached
the cottage.

Pasquet stopped the machos and, with a
curious leer, stood watching the progress of
events.

"Where is my son?" asked Mondelli.

"Close at hand—here he comes," replied
Pasquet, pointing towards the object referred to,
who had been walking behind the carriage.

"Come, my brave lad—assist your bride from
the cabriolet," said Mondelli, with a smile.

The deformed approached the door of the
sege, and Pasquet opened it.

With half-averted eyes, he proffered his hand,
and was conscious that it was clasped by
another; he ventured to look up, and the sun-
beams shining into the carriage, revealed to him
a face wrinkled and old, horrible and haggish,
more disgusting than his own miserable deformity.

He recoiled, pressed his hand spasmodically
to his head, uttered a sharp, heart-broken cry,
and fell to the ground.

Mondelli and Lafonta hastened to learn the
cause of this strange exhibition, and met the
blear eyes and the skinny features of Sister
Jacintha.

Startled at this announcement, the latter
turned towards the deformed; he lay upon the
earth without pulse or motion.

"He has broken a blood-vessel, he has gone!
Mondelli, the God of heaven has put forth his
hand to punish you, and to admonish me to become a better man!" exclaimed Lafonta.

With a deep groan of disappointment and
grief, Mondelli threw himself upon the body of
his son.

"There is indeed a providence in this matter,"
said Angela, seriously.

"Yes, our Father is just; he makes the wrath
of man to praise him. Our escape has not been
discovered. Sister Jacintha has been mistaken
in the darkness for you, and she was too much
stupefied by the drug to explain the mistake,"
responded Katrina.

"I have seen enough, I feel faint and sick;
let us go."

"But where shall we go?"

"We will conceal ourselves in the ruins of
Monte Moro."

The first thing which Arthur Degrange did in
the morning upon waking from his refreshing
slumber, was to inquire if Don Montisco had returned to the inn.

His fears were much excited when he learned
that nothing had been heard in relation to
him.

After dressing himself and partaking of refreshment, he was informed by Alvarez that a
gentleman desired to see him; and soon the
commanding figure of Sabocha was admitted to
his room.

"You are anxious about the safety of your
friend, Senor?" he said politely.

"I am, very much so," replied Arthur, somewhat surprised.

"He is probably, by this time, safely lodged
in the carcel."

"Why do you think so? On what do you
found your opinion?"

"On various data. I know what took place at
the cottage of Matteo Sterek, and that the mule
driver is an arrant rascal. Mondelli I have also
knowledge of, and bribes from him had, before
this, reached the pockets of the corregidor. I
am acquainted with what took place at the
ruins, when your friend fired at the man I have
named; and if there were no other pretext for
arresting both him and you, that would be sufficient. To keep you no longer in suspense, my
name is Sabocha, a cognomen that is not
associated with all that is good, I dare say."

"Alvarez has spoken of you; he has told me
that you saved Montisco from arrest in this very
inn, and were otherwise friendly to him. I am
just as grateful to you for those favours, as
though they had been performed by the best man
in Portugal. And indeed I ought to show some
gratitude, for I am the sole cause of all the
difficulties that now surround him."

"Ah, a pretty maiden, senor, will turn the
heads of the wisest and most discreet among
us!"

"Right well spoken, sir! You must have
been a lover in your time?"

"Now you have touched a sensitive chord.
Yes, I have loved—faithfully and ardently; but

I was betrayed by a villain," said Sabocha, earnestly.

"You had the satisfaction of punishing him, probably?"

"No—that pleasure is still in reserve for me. But the account will be squared soon; the momemt of revenge approaches," returned the bandit, in a tone of deep import. "But I must go and look after your friend; if he is in prison, I will release him," he added, in a calmer voice.

"Does your power extend so far?" asked Degrange, incredulously.

"Further."

"Can you not assist me to see the inside of Santa Clara?"

"I can."

With these words, spoken in a hurried yet expressive voice, Sabocha left the apartment.

.   .   .   .   .

The corregidor was alone, pondering on the late arrest of the Spaniard.

The door of his office was abruptly thrown open, and a large man in a cloak entered.

The magistrate looked up, with a frown, annoyed at the unceremonious entrance of the visitor.

"Who are you?" cried the magistrate, trembling with rage.

"I am Sabocha, do you know me?"

While the brigand spoke, he threw back his cloak, and revealed his side-arms and his stalwart person.

The corregidor gasped spasmodically, and sank back into his seat, whiter than the unwritten paper before him.

"Ha! What, mute? Not an order to give, no irons for my limbs, no prison to hurl me into?"

The bandit threw upon the table a purse, and the avaricious eyes of the magistrate glanced at it with satisfaction. He clutched it, and thrust it into his bosom.

"I am aware, your worship, that there is a bounty offered on my own head; but I will make it worth more to you to try to keep my head on my shoulders, than to take it off, and it would be well for you to understand that. You must release that young Spaniard."

"Ah, senor, I think the young Spaniard is innocent, and therefore it is my duty to comply with your reasonable request. I shall order him to be set at liberty immediately. But allow me to ask why you interest yourself in this person, or in the Englishman, his friend!"

"Because it happens to suit my present temper to do so. I have done mischief enough in my time, and why should I not occasionally perform a generous action! Moreover, those two young men please me; and Angela Benevetta is a divine creature. She reminds me of one who was as dear to me as my own life-blood, a pure and beautiful woman who is now no more. Corregidor, I was an honest man then, for woman's love restrained the bad portion of my nature. When I was robbed of her by a designing knave, I grew sick of the world and of men, and became what I now am, an outlaw determined to wreak my vengeance upon the whole world, for the wrong doing of a single individual. Yes, Angela has the face and form that made my Beatrice an angel; therefore I am interested in her. If you have other questions to ask, say on."

"I would like to know how you discovered all the matters relating to these parties, which have so recently transpired, both at Santa Clara and at other places!"

"My band is large, and my means of watching and knowing whom I will, ample; beside, the rascal Pasquet has for some time been familiar with my gold. Adios, senor." So the bandit took his leave.

Before he reached the inn, he was joined by Don Montisco, which circumstance was the best possible commentary on the promptness and alacrity of the corregidor.

Arthur Degrange, Don Montisco and Sabocha were together, talking of the past and laying plans for the future.

"We are about to visit Santa Clara," said Montisco.

"I trust you will permit me to go with you. I have the best of reasons for making this request; I would defend and protect the innocent and unfortunate, and bring the guilty to justice."

When they reached the gate it was locked as usual.

To Sabocha's request for admission Karl unlocked the gate.

"You will find my master within," said Karl, pointing to an apartment a little further on.

The captain made no rejoinder, but advanced and slowly opened the door. Father Lafonta was seated by the table, with his forehead resting upon his hand, apparently lost in unpleasant thought. Near the priest stood Mondelli, with a face darkened by grief and chagrin. It was evident there had been a terrible struggle within his avaricious and flinty soul. Beads of perspiration, icy in its coldness, stood upon his brow, and rendered silent testimony to the agony of his heart.

Sabocha walked in with a heavy step. Stopping in the centre of the room until his three companions had followed, closed, and locked the door, he drew his stalwart figure to its proudest altitude, and fixed his dark, menacing eyes upon Mondelli. His lips at length curled with withering contempt, and he glanced at Lafonta. The effect of this pantomime was instantaneous and marked. Mondelli shrank back aghast, and Lafonta arose to his feet, trembling in every limb.

"Heaven has found you out at last, and justice stands ready to crush you with her thunderbolts!" exclaimed Sabocha, in a voice so deep, solemn and thrilling, that even Degrange felt awed.

"Both of you know me well. Lafonta, you formerly belonged to my band, and you cannot expect that I should forget you. You can hide *your* sins under the broad wing of the holy mother church."

Turning to Mondelli, he added:

"Miscreant! false friend, and false lover; false to woman, and false to God, we have also met; but this will be our last interview on this side of the mysterious future, where both good and bad men go to be rewarded according to their works. You betrayed me! You robbed me of one who was mine, and then broke her gentle heart by cruelty and neglect. I did not punish you while she lived, but waited my time; now she has gone to her rest—a rest she could not find here—and we will balance the long account. This is not all; your villany has been growing riper and riper ever since, and now is the hour when it should be gathered in with the sickle of death, and be harvested in the great store-house of retribution. You have wronged an angel of innocence, and trampled upon her rights with the adamantine heel of avarice. I have kept track, of you, and knew I should stand before you as I now do—an avenger. Look! here is her kinsman, Ambrose Benevetta, who was recently passed by the name of Rosada. He has returned to his native land after a long absence, to see and care for his fair relative, and by my help he has been able to lay hold of this tangled skein of villany and unwind it.

"These two other gentlemen accidentally saw your ward, Angela, by the merest accident, and were interested in her. I discovered how the matter stood in relation to them, and felt glad that it was so, for I perceived that the Englishman was an honourable man. Had it not been for some important business which demanded my immediate attention, the whole affair would have been brought to a conclusion before to-day. Pasquet, who you hired to take the lives of these men, as been bought over by my gold. He has told me of the wedding of last night, and its awful results upon your unhappy son. It is well; I am glad that it is thus; it is better for him, and no worse for you. Sister Jacintha is now your legal daughter-in-law, and all the world cannot help it. Oh, that was a thing. unforseen! I would have given a purse of gold to have witnessed the first bitterness of your disappointment."

Sabocha paused an instant, and Moudelli gnashed his teeth and smote his breast.

"Ah, you are well mated—you and the padre —but the birds have flown, notwithstanding all your cunning. And listen; Pasquet has found them and they are safe."

"Safe?" cried Degrange and Rosado, in a breath.

"Safe, senors."

"Thank God!" was the fervent response of both.

"Now, Mondelli, your hour has come—you must go to a better place or a worse," added Sabocha, laying his hand upon his pistol.

"But not by your hand! not by your hand, robber!" exclaimed Mondelli, and instantly drank off the contents of a small vial which he snatched from his pocket while the latter was speaking. The subtle poison went hissing down his throat; and then with a wild, triumphant laugh which haunted our hero's ears for months after, threw the vial at the feet of Sabocha, staggered a few paces, and fell dead.

He had taken prussic acid. Thus perished the false guardian. Frantic with horror, and blanched with terror, Lafonta leaped from a window, and falling heavily upon his head on the stone pavement, received an injury which in a few days caused his death, having in that time experienced much suffering, both mental and physical.

"The drama is ended," said Sabocha, solemnly. "We have nothing more to do here. I will now tell you a piece of news, which may, perhaps, detract from the gloom of this scene; when you reach the Estalagem, you will find Angela there, and a fair friend of hers who escaped with her. Pasquet discovered them this morning at the ruins yonder, and by my direction, conducted them to the place I have named. And now, my friends, adieu; when you next meet me, I trust I shall be more worthy of your friendship.

"Why do you leave us, and where do you go!" asked Degrange and Montisco, in a breath.

"I leave Portugal for ever, to become a better man. May my name and deeds be forgotten. Adios, senors."

Waving his hand gracefully, and with a smile, friendly but sad, Sabocha turned abruptly from the parties and walked swiftly down the hill in the direction of Evora.

In due time Angela rewarded Arthur Degrange for his gallantry and devotion by the bestowal of her hand and affections; and he never regretted, in after life, his singular adventures at Monte Moro. Donna Katrina became the life partner of Don Montisco, and thus happily escaped the persecutions of her antiquated lover.

* * * *

"All this happiness was brought about by a brigand," said Perditta.

CHAPTER XXIX.

THE BRIGANDS ON THE WATCH—ENTRY INTO THE MANSION OF CLAUDIO—A HIDDEN WITNESS.

THE moon had risen, and threw its beams in refulgent glory over the limped waters of the Arno.

The long shadows of the church of St. Juliette was reflected, as in a looking-glass, in its clear blue depths.

The residence of the Signor Claudio was enshrouded in darkness, save the room in which he usually sat, and from which the glimmer of a lamp shone forth.

Behind the shadow of the walls stood Sataniello and his followers.

Silent as statues they stood.

Their gaze was fixed on the window from which the light could be seen.

And thus they had stood for some time.

As the hour of nine was pealed forth from the sacred edifice, Sataniello stole from the place of his concealment.

He cast an anxious glance around.

He listened intently.

Not a sound met his ears, save the splashing of the waters as they rolled up the lower steps, then rushed back with a gurgling sound, into the bosom of the stream.

Making himself thoroughly sure that there were none to observe or overhear him, he approached a part of the wall of the building, on which the gables threw a dark shade.

"Tranio," he said.

"All's well, captain."

"Have you observed his shadow?" asked Sataniello.

"Not since I informed you, captain," was the reply.

"You are positive that you were not mistaken?"

"In what?"

"In your report."

"Of the shadow."

"No."

"What then?"

"Of his doings at the office of the corregidor."

"I am not."

"You are sure it was Claudio you saw there?"

"I am"

"And of the words he uttered," asked Sataniello.

"Yes."

"That is well."

"Ill, captain, you mean."

"How so?"

"Because he has placed the authorities in a position to do us harm," said Tranio.

"Perhaps not."

"I think otherwise."

"Why should you do so?" asked the captain.

"Becaues at sunrise they will send a body of troops to the mountains," said Tranio.

"And if they do."

"Our haunt will be broken up," was the reply.

"They will never discover it."

"I fear they will."

"It is not an easy place to find," remarked Sataniello.

"Granted."

"Then we have little to fear," said Sataniello.

"We have much, captain."

"Indeed."

"Yes, for the force will be a strong one."

"And were it of double its strength, we can still defy them."

Tranio shook his head.'

"You doubt."

"I do."

"Your reasons for doing so."

"I have many."

"The troops will never discover the cavern."

"By themselves, no."

"Then we are safe."

"But the, Signor Claudio accompanies them," said Tranio.

"And if he does?"

"He knows the path."

"True."

"And will lead them to it."

"He will not."

"He has promised so to do."

"He will not keep his word," said Sataniello.

"Depend upon it, captain, he will."

"I say he will not."

"He is urged on by more than one motive."

"What motives?"

"Revenge."

"Well."

"And the return of Signoretta Paulina," said Tranio.

"Still he will not guide the troops to the mountains," said Sataniello. "He will doubtless come forth and then—"

"What?"

"Our stilettos will prevent him carrying out his designs."

"And if he come not forth?" asked Tranio.

"We must seek him."

"Where?"

"In yon mansion."

"It will be a dangerous proceeding," said Tranio.

"It may be."

"I fear—"

"What!" exclaimed Sataniello.

"I fear—"

"Fear?"

"Yes."

"You?"

"Yes, me"

"And are you Tranio?"

"I am"

"And a brigand."

"Even so."

"And you fear."

"I fear that to seek him in his own house will be a dangerous proceeding," said the brigand.

"I thought you were a stranger to fear?" said Sataniello.

"In ordinary circumstances, I am," was the reply.

"And should bo in this," said Sataniello.

"Captain, I cannot disguise from myself the fact, that the Signor Claudio is a brave and a prudent man. He has obtained the assistance of the military, and to-morrow, will lead them to our rendezvous."

"Well?"

"In the meantime, he is too prudent to leave us any chance to interfere with his plans."

"But he knows not of our being in this vicinity," said Sataniello.

"He may suspect."

"And if he does?"

"He will keep good watch, and not be taken by surprise."

"We shall see,"

Tranio shrugged his shoulders.

"Depend upon it, captain, that any attempt to enter the house will be futile."

"We are strong."

"True."

"The whole band is here, save Angelo, whom we left in the cavern, and Stephano, who craved so hard to be allowed to carry the Signoretta Marianna to our mountainous retreat."

"We are numerous, I know," said Tranio, "but the Florentine has doubtless given strict orders to have the place well secured, and his servants armed, and on the watch."

"Not knowing our presence," said Sataniello, "I doubt if the suspicion ever entered his mind, that we should dare follow him."

"It may be so."

"I believe it is."

"And you intend to try and gain access to the house?"

"I do."

"When?"

"As soon as the moon goes down," said Sataniello.

"That will be soon."

"In a few hours."

"And then?"

"Make our way to his chamber," replied Sataniello.

"And if you succeed in doing so," asked Tranio.

"Can you ask?"

Tranio replied not.

"Our weapons must be sheathed in his heart," said Sataniello, drawing the glittering steel from his breast, and holding it before the eyes of his follower.

"May the Holy Virgin prosper us," said Tranio.

At this moment the bell of the church tolled to matins.

"Hark!" said Sataniello, in a whisper.

Tranio raised his cap from his head and bowed low.

Then he devoutly crossed himself.

Sataniello did the same.

What a mockery.

Yet these two brigands who, a moment before, talked of murder, crossed themselves like pious men at the sound of that bell.

It was not piety that prompted that act.

It was superstition.

The wicked are ever superstitious.

Their hearts are dead to the cries of mercy.

Their souls quake with fear at the voice of conscience.

But if the sound of that bell called forth a thought it was not one of mercy.

It could not turn Sataniello from his purpose.

He had resolved upon the death of Claudio.

His safety depended upon his doom.

The safety of his band.

The safety of their mountain home.

And he must die.

He waited till the bell ceased, ere he spoke again.

The last echo died away at length over the water of the stream.

Then he spoke.

"Tranio," he said.

"Captain."

"Keep your eye fixed upon yonder window."

"I will do so."

"Let it not waver for an instant," said Sataniello.

"I will be watchful."

"And wary."

"I will."

"If you perceive the shadow of the Florentine, give the signal, and I will be at your side," said the captain.

"Your order shall be obeyed," said Tranio.

Sataniello strolled back to his hiding-place.

Tranio watched the casement in which the light burned.

At length the shadow of a man crossed the blind.

Tranio gazed eagerly.

"It is Claudio," he muttered. "I know his form too well to doubt."

And he blew a low whistle.

In an instant Sataniello was by his side.

"Well," he said.

"The Florentine is there."

"I know it."

"You saw the shadow then."

"I did. The moon is fast going down, and in a short time the place will be bathed in darkness."

"It will."

"When you hear my signal, draw nearer to the door."

"I will."

Sataniello once more left him.

He walked cautiously along keeping within the shadow of the house.

At every few paces he stopped.

And as he did so the figure of a brigand started out from the shade.

"Listen for the signal and draw near," he said, in a low tone to each.

"I will," was the only answer he received from the members of the band.

Gradually the moon sank.

The house became bathed in gloom,

33

And the light in the chamber was extinguished.

Then Sataniello gave the signal.

Simultaneously the brigands started out from the shadow of every column and buttress.

All made towards the centre door.

Silent and cautious were their movements.

In another moment all were gathered around Sataniello.

"Are your daggers sharp," he asked," in a low yet distinct tone.

"They are," was the response.

"Enough. Their sheath must be in the heart of the Florentine. His chamber is the one yonder."

Then turning, he approached one of the windows.

He laid his hand upon the sash.

It yielded.

He thrust it up and leapt through into the handsome apartment.

Then he turned and beckoned to his followers.

One by one they silently passed through the window to his side.

Tranio was the last to enter.

"Are all assembled," asked Sataniello.

"All," was the reply.

"Now to destroy the means by which the military may reach the mountain cavern."

So saying he closed the window.

As he did so the tall form of a youth rose from the ground and made off along the terrace at great speed.

CHAPTER XXX.

A SURPRISE—THE FIGHT ON THE STAIRS—THE BRIGANDS ENTRAPPED—THE REFUSAL TO SURRENDER—THE DARING ESCAPE.

PROCURING lights, the brigands, headed by Sataniello, left the apartment into which they entered by the window, and made their way up the marble staircase which led to the spacious suite of rooms on the upper floors of the mansion.

The Boy Brigand had marked well the position of the room in which he had seen the light, and now made his way cautiously towards it.

All was silent.

Not a sound met their ears.

The house seemed deserted.

Arriving at the top of the stairs, Sataniello paused on the landing.

His followers stood silently awaiting his commands.

And in the dim light a more ruthless band of ruffians could not have been imagined.

The lights they carried cast an unearthly glow upon their swarthy features, and the glittering steels, which they held bared in their hands.

"All is quiet," said the Boy Brigand.

"All," said Tranio.

"Some of you stay here to guard the staircase, and give an alarm if necessary. The others follow me."

Three of the brigands remained behind, while Sataniello and the others ascended the second flight of steps.

As he gained the second landing, the door of the room in which the light had appeared suddenly opened, and Claudio, with a pistol in each hand, sprang out upon the landing.

So sudden was his appearance that Sataniello recoiled backwards, till he stood upon the edge of the stairs.

"Caramba!" exclaimed the Boy Brigand.

For a moment the young Florentine stood gazing upon the array of brigands before him.

Then he raised his weapons and pointed them direct at the head of Sataniello.

"Villain," he exclaimed. "You thought to find me unprepared for your visit. But you are mistaken—behold! What ho, there. Come forth."

The last words were spoken in a loud tone of voice.

And ere its echoes had died away, every door in the large suite of rooms flew open, and a soldier, armed with a musket, stood on the threshold.

Had a thunderbolt fallen at the feet of the brigands, they could not have been more surprised.

Their eyes wandered to the face of the Boy Brigand, who alone seemed to possess the least use of his faculties.

After the first exclamation of surprise, he stood gazing defiantly upon Claudio.

He saw not the looks of his companions.

But like a tiger at bay, he boldly faced the Florentine.

In a moment he had realised the danger in which he stood.

So he put a bold face upon the matter.

He had retreated at first.

Now he advanced.

It was but a step.

Yet that step forward had the effect of inducing his followers to rally round him.

"Signor Claudie," he said, in a calm tone of voice. "You doubtless think you have us in your power. You are mistaken; the whole band are at my beck, and if you place your finger on the trigger of either of those weapons, you die."

"By whose orders?" said Claudio, derisively.

"By the orders of Sataniello, the Boy Brigand."

"Fool," said Claudio, "the Dark King of the Mountains may threaten in its fastnesses, or on the range of hills where he plies his unholy calling, but here his words excite our laughter, not our fears. Sataniello, your time has come."

"Liar!" exclaimed the Boy Brigand, raising his poignard, and advancing another step nearer to the Florentine.

But he paused.

The soldiers brought their muskets to their breasts with a sharp clang.

The muzzles were pointed at his head.

"Ha! ha!" laughed Claudio. "Why do you not give the order for our execution?"

Sataniello was silent.

"Brigand, your time has come. You must die," said Claudio.

"Not by your hand," shouted Sataniello. "Brigands, stand firm and down with them."

"You rush upon your doom," exclaimed Claudio. Soldiers do your duty. Thus do I set you the example, and avenge the death of the Senor Sebastian."

And he placed his fingers on the trigger of the weapons he held pointed towards Sataniello.

Loud indeed was the report, as Claudio and the military discharged their pieces, and for a moment the place was enveloped in smoke.

But as it cleared away, he perceived that the Boy Brigand was unharmed.

He had been borne backwards by his followers as, panic struck, they strove to escape down the wide staircase, on which the bullets found a home in the hearts of three of them.

In a moment he had sprang to his feet. All his evil passions were loosened.

With dilated nostrils and flashing eyes he sprang forward to where Claudio had stood, his stilletto grasped tightly in his hand.

Fortunate was it for Claudio that he perceived his approach.

He sprang on one side.

Sataniello, blinded with rage, struck at space, and so furious was his onslaught, that he staggered and fell.

"Secure him!" exclaimed the Florentine.

And he pointed to the prostrate youth.

A soldier sprang forward.

He stretched forth his arm and grasped Sataniello by the collar.

A smile passed over his face as he did so.

It was something to be the one who secured the furious brigand.

So the man thought.

But Sataniello leapt to his feet.

With one bound, he released himself from the soldier's hold.

The man sprang after him.

He stretched forth his hand again, to secure him.

It touched his collar.

But ere he had obtained a firm grasp, he uttered a loud cry.

His arm dropped to his side.

A spasm passed over his face.

He staggered back, and fell heavily, drawing out the stilletto of Sataniello as he did so from the sheath it had found in his heart.

Two of the soldiers rushed forward to avenge their comrade's death.

But Sataniello sprang past them, on to the stairs.

"Brigands!" he shouted, "to the rescue."

But a panic had seized upon the band, and they showed more inclination to fly than to fight.

"Cowards!" he yelled, "shall I command in vain!"

The soldiers now rushed forward boldly, with the butt-ends of their weapons raised in the air.

Finding he could not bring the men to his side, Sataniello retreated down the stairs, hoping to rally his panic-stricken band on the next landing.

But the soldiers did not follow them.

They remained behind to reload their weapons.

Sataniello saw this, and in a moment he called forth—

"What, shall a few men, not half our number, drive us from our purpose. Shall the brigands of the Appenines fly like curs before a few soldiers. Shame on you Sataniello blushes to feel that he has accepted the post of captain to a band of cowards."

This had the effect of staying the flight of the brigands, and they paused on the landing below that on which the surprise had taken place.

"Will you fly!" exclaimed the Boy Brigand, "and not revenge your comrades."

And he pointed to the three bodies on the stairs, over which himself and followers had leapt.

"Captain," said Tranio, hurriedly, "here we wage unequal warfare."

"We do." said Sataniello. "We are many, they are few."

"True; but they are armed with fire-arms, and hold a position which must tell fearfully against us. If we retreat to the basement, we may yet teach them that, the brigands of the Appenines know no fear."

"Quick, then," said Sataniello, who, looking up, saw that the soldiers were again prepared to pour a volley upon them, from above.

The brigands required no second order.

They flew down the stairs.

Slowly the soldiers, headed by Claudio, followed them.

"This way," said the Boy Brigand, making his way into the apartment which they had entered by the window.

The others followed as quickly as possible.

Then a cry of surprise broke from all.

The room, which was in darkness when they entered the house, was now lighted up.

They cast a hurried look around them.

Which ever way they turned, their eyes encountered the barrel of a musket.

They were caught in a trap.

The room was filled with soldiers.

Ere they could recover from the surprise into which this fresh circumstance had thrown them, the body, headed by Claudio, entered the room.

Sataniello cast one more look around.

This time it was the faces of his own men he gazed upon.

He saw their features were blanched with fear.

He perceived the muscles of their lips were convulsed, and that their limbs trembled.

And more than this.

He saw that which caused his own heart to sink within him.

He saw that it was useless to call upon them to fight.

They were paralysed.

Their brutal natures were cowered.

They felt their career was ended, and that it was useless to struggle further.

In a moment Sataniello perceived all this.

Yet he resolved not to be taken prisoner if he could prevent his capture by any means.

Anxiously he looked around for any means by which he might escape.

His eye rested on the door.

But the soldiers stood upon its threshold.

That hope was gone.

He cast his eyes to the window.

It was open.

He looked out beyond.

The terrace and the river lay before him.

Again his heart beat with hope.

He moved a step forward.

But the soldiers, who had been standing round by the walls of the apartment, moved forward also, towards the centre of the room.

And the barrels of their muskets were levelled at his breast.

Still he seemed not to despair.

He drew himself up to his full height.

He looked proudly and defiantly around him.

He saw his chance of escape was hopeless, but he thought if he could but bury his stiletto in the heart of the Florentine he could resign himself to his fate.

He clutched the weapon nervously.

He fixed his eye upon Claudio.

And the blood rushed to his temples, and swelled the veins upon his forehead, as he encountered the scornful and triumphant glance of the Florentine's eye.

"Surrender," said Claudio.

"Never," he replied.

"Surrender, and trust to the mercy of the king," said Antonio Lorenzi, the commander of the military.

"I have defied him and his legions," said Sataniello, "and I do so now."

"Be wise," said the captain. "Surrender your weapons, and trust to his clemency."

"I will not; as I have lived, so will I die; defiant to the last!" exclaimed Sataniello.

"I would not have your blood," said the captain, "but if you refuse to surrender, I must do my duty."

"And that duty—"

"Is to take you, dead or alive; to rid Italy of the scourge—the Boy Brigand."

"Do then your duty," said Sataniello.

And he gazed contemptuously around at the shining barrels.

"Sataniello," said Claudio. "In the name of his majesty the king of Naples, I call upon you to surrender to the laws you have so wantonly outraged."

"Florentine. I own no laws but those which I make myself, and to those only will I bow."

"Then do your duty," said Claudio, speaking to the captain of the soldiers.

The captain waved his hand, and the soldiers moved from behind Sataniello.

Those in front of him, brought their weapons to bear full upon his breast.

"Once more," said the captain, "I call upon you to surrender."

"And once more I refuse!" exclaimed Sataniello, boldly. "Sataniello, the Boy Brigand, the Dark King of the Mountains, will never surrender to the myrmidoms of a tyrant. I despise your threats, and laugh to scorn your power. You would bear me in triumph to Naples, but the hour has not yet come. Claudio, we shall meet again. Sataniello defies you. Take me, if you can; follow me, if you dare."

"Fire!" exclaimed Lorenzi.

The soldiers placed their fingers on the triggers of their pieces.

With a loud and defiant laugh, Sataniello bounded forward, and leaping into the air, sprang over the barrels of the muskets, as they belched forth their fire and smoke, and leaping through the window to the terrace, he sprang into the flowing river, and struck out boldly for the middle of the stream, as the report of the firearms awoke the echoes around.

CHAPTER XXXI.

ON TO THE MOUNTAINS—THE MURDER ON THE ROAD—THE RECOGNITION—THE FLIGHT AND PURSUIT.

WORN out with fatigue and anxiety, Salernio de Roco, instead of returning to the mansion of de Martini, ordered the gondolier to pull for the shore at the nearest spot.

This he did, and Salernio, having engaged a horse, proceeded to the house of his friend Claudio.

He arrived there at the very moment that the vehicle, provided by the innkeeper for him, stopped before his residence.

Salernio now came to the conclusion, that the Signoritta Marianna had fallen into the hands of the brigands, and he consented to join Claudio in the expedition he intended to lead to the mountains, the instant he could get the permission of the authorities, and the use of the military.

During the day this was arranged, much to the satisfaction of the friends, and Claudio had resolved to start that very night for the stronghold of the brigands.

But a circumstance occurred which prevented this intention.

The boy, who had rowed away from the ship with the gondolier, having overheard a few words which Stephano had uttered to the captain, leaped to the conclusion in an instant, that he might earn a good reward by making the Florentine acquainted with the fact, that Sataniello and his band were on their way to his mansion, with the intention of seeking his life, and destroying the only man who was acquainted with the road to their secret retreat.

When Claudio learnt this, he resolved not to start for the mountains till the following day; and kept a strict watch for the appearance of the brigands, at the same time domiciling in his house several of the soldiers, whose services had been granted him, and leaving the remainder under Antonio Lorenzi, and Salernio, in the church of St. Juliette.

Thus it was that the Boy Brigand found himself entrapped, at the very moment that he believed success attended him.

The suddenness and boldness of the leap which he took over the muskets of the soldiers, for a moment so surprised Claudio and his friends, that they stood irresolute how to act.

Had the brigands have been as quick witted as their leader, they might have succeeded in escaping whilst the consternation of their enemies held them powerless.

But they were equally as surprised as the soldiers, who recovered from their astonishment just in time to secure their prisoners.

When this was done, they prepared to start in pursuit of Sataniello.

With strong and rapid strokes, Sataniello, the Boy Brigand breasted the stream.

He could hear the shouts of the enemy on the terrace, and he gave vent to a loud peal of derisive laughter.

Yet, still he could not but acknowledge to himself that he was in great danger.

Still, his devil-may-care spirit would rise uppermost, and could not repress the longing to show his foes he was not yet in their power.

He was almost exhausted when he gained the opposite bank.

But still he knew that it would be dangerous, perhaps fatal to him, to delay.

So, without pausing for breath, he dashed on towards Pistoia.

The darkness was favourable to him.

He had kept possession of his stiletto, and he resolved to use it, should circumstances occur to necessitate it.

As he scrambled up the bank, he observed, by the hurried glance he cast behind him, a gondola shoot out into the stream.

He had no doubt that this was the vessel of Claudio, and that it was filled with soldiers sent in pursuit.

So on he kept, never for a moment slackening his speed.

He knew that his circumstances were desperate, but he resolved to brave them out boldly.

He felt, too, that his followers were made prisoners, and that he must depend upon himself alone.

And he resolved to sell his life dearly.

But first he would endeavour to return to the mountains, and bear away from the secret cave the Signoritta Paulina.

He was determined that nothing but death should prevent him being revenged upon Claudio, and what more bitter vengeance could he have than the destruction of the girl so fondly loved by the young Florentine.

Her ruin should mark the bitterness of his hatred to Claudio, and his revenge for the destruction of his band.

Suddenly he was aroused from the train of thought, into which he had wandered, by the sound of horse's feet behind him.

He listened intently.

At first he imagined that it was those who were in pursuit of him.

But as he bent his ear to the ground, he discovered that the sounds emanated only from the hoofs of one quadruped.

A gleam of joy lit up his face.

He drew his stiletto from his belt.

He cast a hurried glance right and left.

As far as his eye could penetrate the darkness, his vision encountered no living object.

"I must have that at least," he muttered, "to bear me to the mountains, and by my faith it is no slow runner by the sound of its hoofs."

Thus soliloquising, he stepped out into the centre of the road.

Louder and louder sounded the horse's hoofs on the hard road, and nearer and nearer every moment it came towards the spot on which Sataniello stood.

Grasping the weapon firmly in his hand, the Boy Brigand awaited the approach of the rider.

He had not to wait long.

He could see the animal, now it was within a hundred yards of him, but he also discovered, at the same moment that its rider was a woman.

He thought that circumstance somewhat strange at so unusual an hour, but still he had no time for conjectures.

He knew his foes would press on after him as quickly as possible, and that delay was capture or death.

He must have that horse, though to obtain it he had to bury his steel in the heart of a woman.

On came the horse and rider, till within a few

yards of him, when the woman on its back suddenly pulled up with a cry of fear.

She had just observed the figure of a man in the road, and only pulled the reins in time, to prevent riding over him.

This was what Sataniello desired more than all.

Before the animal could be brought to a halt, he sprang forward and grasped the bridal.

The horse reared, and the woman, uttering a cry of terror or surprise, Sataniello drove his stiletto into her breast.

With a loud shriek, her hold on the reins relaxed, and fell from the horse's back, to the feet of her murderer.

Without a word, Sataniello sprang upon the animal's back.

At that moment, another sound smote his ears.

He paused to listen, and in a few seconds he could plainly hear the sound of several horses feet behind him, in the distance.

"Curse them!" he muttered, "the dogs are in full cry, but the boar will show his tusks, ere they run him down."

And grasping the reins fiercely in his hand, and pressing his knees tightly into the animal's flanks, he was ready for the chase.

The horse, finding that he had a stranger on his back reared and played for several moments, and Sataniello found it was no easy task to prevent being thrown. Whilst endeavouring to urge the animal forward, the moon burst from behind the dark clouds, and threw a flood of silvery light down upon the pale face of her, who lie so cold in death beneath the hoofs of the animal her murderer bestrode.

With a bitter curse at the antics of the horse, the Boy Brigand cast his eyes down upon the upturned face of his victim, so pale, so cold, so still in that mellow light.

A cry broke from his lips; a cry so loud, so piercing, that it startled the animal with fright, and it bounded forward at a fearful speed as the loud shouts of the pursuers rang in the ears of the fugitive.

One look only Sataniello cast behind him.

But oh, what a look of agony and despair.

Then a sob burst from his breast, and he shrieked, rather than spoke the name,—

"Joanitta!"

Then his head sank upon his breast, and he seemed lost to all that was going on.

Like a statue he sat so pale, so immoveable, as the horse tore along towards Pistoia at a fearful pace.

And behind him rung the clatter of the hoofs of his pursuer's steeds.

But he heard them not; heeded not the fearful speed at which trees, and vineyards, seemed to fly past him.

He saw nothing, heard nothing but the pale face and death-cry of her, whom his bloody hand had laid so low in the road behind him.

On, on, mile after mile, towards the mountains. On with the cry of the murdered woman ringing in his ears. On with that pale cold face still before him. On with bloodshot eyes and trembling lips. On to his doom!

CHAPTER XXXII.

DOOM OF THE BOY BRIGAND—CONCLUSION.

PEDRO and LUCIO awaited in breathless anxiety the appearance of their gaoler.

They heard Angelo place his hand upon the bar which secured the door of their prison-house, and panted for the moment when he should shoot it from its socket; but as he was about to do so, a long whistle echoed through the cavern, and they heard his retreating footsteps as he hurried away from the door.

With a look of disappointment they listened anxiously for the cause of his retreat.

They were not kept long in suspense, for in a few moments they discovered from the words which came to their ears, that there were fresh arrivals in the outer cavern.

It was Stephano's signal.

He had brought with him his prisoners, the Signoritta Paulina, and her maid.

This circumstance caused Angelo to forget all about the men who a few minutes before he was about to supply with food; for having seen the two captives secured in one of the caverns, he sat down with Stephano over some wine, and drank till he was intoxicated.

In this, Stephano was no better than himself, for excited by his success, and the prospect of a good ransom for the entrapped maidens, he drank till he could see two Angelo's, who only vanished from his gaze as his head dropped heavily on to the table, from which he found himself unable to raise it, till the first ray of sunshine penetrated through the openings of the mountains.

Then he looked round for Angelo, whom he discovered at length, lying beneath the table.

He stooped to arouse him, and as he laid his hand upon the shoulder of his comrade, the loud report of several muskets rang through the mountains.

In an instant both the brigands sprang to their feet and drew their stilettos.

A look passed between them, and they sprang towards the outer cavern.

But ere they had reached it, a cry of surprise broke from them both, as Sataniello leapt through the opening before them.

"The soldiers are upon us!" he cried, "led on by the accursed Florentine! There is not a moment to lose! The band are all taken but myself! Away to the mountains, and seek safety in flight."

"And you?" exclaimed Angelo and Stephano, in a breath.

"Will die as I have lived, defiant to the last; away, or you will fall into their hands. I have but one more act to perform, an act of vengeance, and then Sataniello's course is run."

"You may yet escape, captain," said Angelo.

"No," exclaimed Sataniello, "my time has come, for she has gone!"

"Who?"

"Joanitta, my wife; gone, murdered and by me—me who loved her so fondly! oh, the sight of that face in the pale moonlight. I see it now; the lips move and tell me that my hour has come. Go, friends and comrades, go, fly! Sataniello is no longer fit to command you. The Boy Brigand would but lead you into fresh dangers now. Paulina, the Florentine loves her, but she must die! Die that I may be revenged on him who has been the cause of what I now suffer; but for him, Joanitta had lived, but for him, Sataniello had still been a bold and fearless youth. She must die, and her death shriek shall strike upon his soul!"

The voices of the soldiers now came plainly to the ears of those in the cavern.

"Another moment and it will be too late!" said Sataniello.

Angelo and Stephano sprang towards the entrance, and Sataniello, rushing into the cavern where Paulina and Perditta were, seized the former roughly by the arm, and drew her into the centre cave.

"Captain, farewell!" exclaimed Angelo.

"Farewell!" said Sataniello, "now fly."

The brigands sprang out of the cave into the passage, but ere they could force their way through the bushes which concealed the entrance, a volley of musketry echoed through the mountains, mingled with their dying groans.

Both had paid the penalties of their crimes, and lay bleeding and dying on the threshold of their lair.

With foaming lips and bloodshot eyes, Sataniello gazed upon the pale face and trembling limbs of Paulina, as with upturned eyes and frightened looks she gazed into his face.

"Girl," he hissed, "your hour has come. Claudio has returned to claim you for his bride, and he shall have you; aye, he shall have you, but no bridal bed shall ever be pressed by you; your time has come, the hour of vengeance has arrived! Claudio seeks his love, but he shall find a corpse!"

And he forced the trembling and horror-struck girl, down upon her knees.

He raised the glittering weapon above her head.

But he did not strike.

Paulina uttered not a word.

The fearful look on the brigand's face held her speechless.

Her eyes were rivetted on his distorted features, but her soul sought heaven for aid.

Sataniello still forbore to strike.

He waited to make his vengeance more fearful.

Claudio must see the blow struck.

Must see the girl he loved stretched lifeless at his feet, at the moment he was about to rescue her, and bear her in triumph to his home.

"He comes," hissed Sataniello; "the bridegroom is hurrying hither to meet his bride, but no smile shall play around her lips, no warm kiss salute his cheeks. No, no, her bridal robe shall turn to a winding-sheet, her nuptial couch her grave. Ha! ha! he is here!"

At this moment Claudio sprang through the opening, into the cave, followed by Salernio and the soldiers.

"Villain!" he shrieked, as his eye fell upon the forms of Sataniello and Paulina.

Grasping his sword tightly, he sprang forward as he spoke, but he recoiled in horror as Sataniello, holding his stiletto over the heart of Paulina, shrieked forth—

"Ha! ha. Florentine, you seek your bride, she is here—here at the feet of him whose destruction you would consummate!"

"Save me, Claudio, save me!" gasped Paulina.

"Hold!" exclaimed Sataniello; "never shall you press her to your heart save as a corpse. Florentine, tremble at the vengeance of Sataniello, the Boy Brigand!"

And bending forward, Sataniello with a fiendish laugh of triumph, swung the weapon above his head, then brought it down with all his force towards the heart of Paulina.

But with a loud, piercing shriek Perditta sprang forward, and flung herself upon the breast of her mistress.

The Boy Brigand saw the movement, but blinded by his rage, and his desire for vengeance, he could not withhold his arm, and the fatal steel sank deep between the shoulders of the maid as she covered her mistress with her body, and the two females fell heavily to the earth.

With a howl of rage and disappointment, Sataniello raised his bloody weapon again to consummate his vengeance, but Claudio and Salernio sprang forward, and ere his arm could descend a second time, they buried their swords in his breast, and as they drew them forth, the soldiers fired, and he fell, riddled with bullets, beside the poor girl who had so nobly sheltered the innocent breast of her mistress, and by her death atoned for her only crime.

Not one cry did Sataniello give utterance to, but as his breath fleeted from his body, he gazed upon those around him with a defiant look.

He died as he had lived, defiant to the last.

And with his death our tale is ended. Still we cannot lay down our pen without acquainting the reader with the fact, that a few months afterwards saw Paulina the happy bride of Claudio, and Marianna was led to the alar upon the same occasion by Salernio. Pedro and Luco, entered the service of the former, and often relate to the children of their indulgent employers, the sufferings they endured in the brigands cave.

But the name of Sataniello still lives, and in many a home in Italy, the mother relates to her offspring, the fearful deeds of Sataniello, the Boy Brigand, the Dark King of the Mountains.

THE END.

The Daily Mail   JANUARY 2, 1931.

GIRL QUEEN OF BANDIT GANG.

HELPS TO KILL EX-LOVER.

"TAKEN FOR A RIDE."

BODY FOUND BY AIRMAIL PILOT.

FROM OUR OWN CORRESPONDENT

NEW YORK, Thursday.

THE amazing story has just come to light of the exploits of a girl, aged 16, who is in custody on a charge of murdering her sweetheart, who was a member of a band of robbers over whom she ruled as queen.

The affair would be regarded as improbable if it formed the subject of a cinema thriller of the underworld.

The girl's name is Margaret Miller, and the slain gangster, who was little older than herself, was Stephen Sweeney.

According to affidavits made by Franco Spiraco, a desperado arrested on a charge of highway robbery, Margaret Miller organised the robber band a few months ago and held autocratic sway over it. The penalty of questioning her authority—acknowledged by a blood-curdling oath taken by each member—was death.

Sweeney was the deputy leader of the band, but the girl, it is asserted, planned and directed the execution of their daring hold-ups and burglaries, exercising her charms to keep away from the scene any policeman who happened to be inconveniently near.

THE RIVAL.

One day a youth named Schoenhart was taken into the organisation, and soon Sweeney found himself playing second fiddle. Schoenhart not only usurped his functions, but also his place in the "queen's" affections.

Sweeney rebelled, and was "taken for a ride" one night by the girl's orders. He did not suspect what was going to happen to him until the motor-car, which the girl herself was driving and in which three "executioners" were also seated, stopped on a lonely road on Long Island. He was told to get out, and seems to have accepted the inevitable calmly.

"I'll take it standing up," Spiraco quoted him as saying.

His bullet-riddled body sprawling in the road was seen by an air-mail pilot flying over the spot at dawn.

Jan. 1931.

In addition to my cutting, pasted over, in 1927, which is of a real BOY BANDIT, again do I demonstrate that "Truth is stranger than fiction" as here we have, four years later, a real GIRL BANDIT. Verily are the old extravagant romances outdone.

BARRY ONO.

POLICEMAN TIED TO TREE.

AMAZING EXPLOITS OF BOY BANDIT.

£2,000 FOR CAPTURE DEAD OR ALIVE.

FROM OUR OWN CORRESPONDENT

NEW YORK, Wednesday.

Matthew Kimes, the boy bandit of Oklahoma, with two murders and a dozen bank robberies to his account has again eluded the police.

For more than a week the State police have been ceaselessly hunting him, but he bears an apparently charmed life.

Less than a year ago he was lodged in gaol after killing a policeman who tried to capture him as he emerged from one of his most spectacular bank robberies. Within a few days he was at large again, thanks to a daring attack on the goal by a band of his boy confederates.

Since then he has roamed the country, robbing bank after bank, until in desperation the Oklahoma Bankers' Association offered a reward of £2,000 for his capture " dead or alive." He was recognised, very much alive, as he parked a motor-car ten days ago in the business district of the town of Pawhuska. Notified of his presence, a group of police rushed to the scene, only to see Kimes drive at high speed out of the town. They pursued him hotly, riddling his car with bullets and puncturing his tyres.

CLINGING TO RANCHER.

The bandit, halting, sprang into a field, ran across it to another road, where he leaped into a motor-car driven by a rancher, to whom he clung so tightly that the police refrained from continuing their fire lest they should kill the rancher.

Kimes later flung the rancher into the road and ultimately abandoned the car, disappearing into the woods.

The next the police heard of him was in connection with a successful robbery four nights ago at two banks and the murder of another policeman. A posse of troopers hunted him last night into the Osage Hills. This morning in a stolen car the bandit speeded through the town of Jennings. A constable brought him to a halt and arrested him, whereupon Kimes tied the constable to a tree and proceeded on his journey.

28, Clifton Street,
Wandsworth Road,
South Lambeth,
London, S.W. 8

June, 21st. 1927

****

Owning as I do, at the time of date above, if not the largest, at least one of the largest collections in the world, of alleged IMPOSSIBLE "Penny Dreadfuls", I have always maintained, that nothing has ever been written in the most extravagant form of fiction, that <u>fact</u> cannot only vie with, but invariably beat. We read the daily paper, and seldom keep these extraordinar happenings, yet it would be interesting to do so, and as the collector has done in this instance, cut it out, and insert it with an extravagant romance on the same subject, to prove the old adage ---
"Truth is stranger than fiction

****

Fredk. V. Harrison,
Known on the Music Hall stage
as

Barry Ono

Barry Ono.

"The Boy Brigand" was published about 1860, as was "The Boy Pirate"

Also, uniform with the above,

THE BOY BRIGAND;

OR,

THE DARK KING OF THE MOUNTAINS.

BY A WILD IRISHMAN.

Comprising the most thrilling adventures, hair-breadth escapes, both by land and by sea, sanguinary encounters, and the endless desperate fights of Italian Brigands.

This tale, written expressly for the Youths of England, will place clearly and prominently before them the roving lives and daring adventures of a troop of the most enterprising bandits that ever dwelt in the rugged paths and wild mountains of the sunny south. It will show the heroic and high-minded behaviour of the Boy Brigand when placed in the most difficult positions of life, and his numberless and ingenious escapes from his pursuers.

THE LIFE AND STORY OF THE "BOY BRIGAND" WILL BE ILLUSTRATED BY THE FIRST ARTISTS OF THE DAY.

The adventures of the Boy Brigand should be read by one and all, and more particularly by the rising generation, who delight in the perusal of exciting, sensational, and thrilling incidents. "The Boy Brigand" may be placed in the hands of everyone, as at the bottom of the tale will be conveyed a sound and substantial moral, which will enable the reader to perceive the right from the wrong, and teach him how to imitate that which is noble and great, as it ever carries its reward with it ; and how to shrink from evil and from those bad deeds which only lead to infamy and dishonour here below—to everlasting punishment in the world above !

LONDON :

J. W. ALLEN AND Co., BLACK HORSE ALLEY, FLEET STREET.

www.ingramcontent.com/pod-product-compliance
Lightning Source LLC
Chambersburg PA
CBHW081323020726

47506CB00005B/1164